SEALED BLOOD
THE COMPLETE SERIES

KIRRO BURROWS

Copyright (C) 2023 Kirro Burrows

Layout design and Copyright (C) 2023 by Next Chapter

Published 2023 by Next Chapter

Cover art by Lordan June Pinote

This book is a work of fiction. Names, characters, places, and incidents are the product of the author's imagination or are used fictitiously. Any resemblance to actual events, locales, or persons, living or dead, is purely coincidental.

All rights reserved. No part of this book may be reproduced or transmitted in any form or by any means, electronic or mechanical, including photocopying, recording, or by any information storage and retrieval system, without the author's permission.

CATCH A RAVEN
SEALED BLOOD BOOK 1

"Don't be," he whispered, his breath hot and heavy as he breathed his words against my skin, allowing his breath to caress me. His hands gripped me tightly through my clothing and I was slightly surprised by his actions. Kisten always maintained an incredibly careful and calm demeanor, always distancing himself from me when he thought he was losing control. He growled softly, his voice sounding animalistic. *"You're all that I want now."*

To Maria Croft
Who never gave up on me.

To Sara Gardiner,
For helping me get here.

To my beautiful daughter,
Who taught me to do what makes me happy.

PROLOGUE

'*You need to go now.*'

"I know," I whispered back quietly, gently leaning on the door as I checked the hallway. No guards, no sign of any of the First. If I was going to make my escape, I knew I had to do it now. I grabbed the wooden trinket as it hung against my exposed bosom, taking a deep breath as I prepared myself for what I was about to do. There would be no turning back once I left the room, no chance to return.

'*Now!*' As my sister's voice ran through my mind, I darted into darkness, quickly making my way down the Hallway. I ran straight to the crossing I had been escorted by so many times, doing my best to remember the directions my sister had given me. *Left, Left, Straight, Right, Right, no wait, Left.* I did my best to move as silently as I could, barely daring to breathe as I ran. The castle felt still, silent, as if everyone within was sleeping as Mother slept.

It wasn't often that Mater Vitae slept: she only tended to sleep after expending great amounts of power, and I wasn't sure what she had done to warrant this surprise slumber. All I knew was that it was probably my last chance to flee and if I didn't take it now, I would never get another. Mother knew my secret and it was only a matter of time before she decided I was too dangerous to exist, just as she had done to Them.

"Who goes?!" My heart pounded to life as I heard a voice, and I quickly pressed myself into the shadows of the stone, thankful for my dark skin as I melted into the darkness. I watched slowly as a light approached the crossing, and one of the guards came into view. Their stern face wore an annoyed expression and it was obvious they didn't want to be wandering the corridors of the castle at night. "Who dares slink about while Mother sleeps?"

I did my best to silence my breathing, gripping the wooden cross tightly as it grew warm beneath my hand. *So close;* we were so close to freedom. I could *feel* the fresh air pouring in from the door to my right, fresh air I had not breathed in centuries. Mother rarely let me out of my room and let me outside even less. She always knew that I would run if she did not keep a tight hold on my chain, but now it was fear that forced me to attempt my escape.

"Why cause such a noise at this hour?" I couldn't help the relief that filled me as I heard one of the First approach the guard, drawing the man's attention. I could feel the vampire's aura as they drew closer to me, and I could only hope they would not sense me in the same way. I saw her shadow as she stopped near him, and I couldn't help my slight feeling of sympathy as I heard him stumble over his words.

"M-m-my apologies, I-I thought I heard some—"

"No one would dare disturb Mother's rest so callously," the vampire interrupted, her voice stern and almost melodic as she spoke. I watched as her shadow passed that of the guard, and I saw her piercing blue eyes as she stepped into my view. She glanced around the hallways, and I could have sworn her eyes rested on me for a moment, but her gaze continued as she spoke. "As suspected, none are about. You would do best to keep your voice down, lest Mother take her anger out on you next."

"Y-y-y-yes, Nisaba." The man bowed, taking his light with him as he walked back down the corridor. The First seemed to linger in the growing darkness, her long white hair moving in an unknown wind as she shook her head. When she spoke next, my heart stopped beating.

"Be quick, she will awaken soon." She kept her back to me as she spoke, following after the guard as she whispered her quiet words. I was frozen to the spot, surprised by what I had witnessed. Had... one of the First... just helped me?

'You heard her, let's go! We have to leave before Mater Vitae wakes up.' My sister's voice once again roused me from my stupor, and I released the cross as it grew warm under my hand. A moment later I slipped out the door into the quiet night air, not bothering to close it behind me. I took a moment just to breathe in the fresh night air, my lungs swelling with the sweet sensation. I could feel my sister's annoyance with my pause, but the soft taste of freedom was exhilarating. Releasing the breath, I opened my eyes, staring at the garden before me.

I carefully made my way across the courtyard, praying to the Gods I could outrun the Hunter Mother would send after me. My thoughts returned to the vampire and a soft sound escaped me as I pushed aside a low-hanging branch. She *had* to know Vitae would find out, and Mother's wrath would know no end once she did. Not only had Nisaba known I was there, she purposefully allowed me to escape: there was no gain in it for her, was there? Maybe she planned to pin the blame on the naive guard?

'Stop wondering why and just be happy she did. Who knows why vampires do anything they do.' My sister snapped and I sighed as I carefully climbed the wall, looking down on the forest below. She was right as always, and I had a long night ahead of me if I wanted to see the dawn. As I dropped from the stone and sprinted through the trees, I couldn't help the quiet words as they escaped me.

"Thank you, Nisaba."

I

"Well, enjoy your weekend!"

"Huh? Oh, 'bye." I waved to my co-workers as I slammed the hood of my trunk, pulling myself from the fog my thoughts had slipped into. I slid into my green Lexus and pulled away from the airport, my hands gripping the wheel tightly. It would be a long drive back home, and a thoughtful one; I had arrived back from NeoKansa after investigating another murder in my current case and while I enjoyed the chance to travel the country freely, I enjoyed living in The Capital and being home more.

Besides, my current case was anything but enjoyable: always arriving too late to prevent the crime was frustrating for the whole team, but especially for me. Any crime can be horrifying and difficult to accept, but this was especially true of crimes committed by Supernaturals, since our abilities allowed us to be far more deadly. By the time my team was called in, the case was a mess and that was never a good situation to be in.

And this case was the definition of a bad situation. Bodies piled up in rooms with no signs of entry, and the perpetrator was able to bypass magical barriers. The list of Supernaturals that could do that was small, and every theory seemed to be killed by the next crime. We had no luck in narrowing it down to even that aspect of who our killer was, and I was beginning to get more and more frustrated with the case.

Before I could dwell on it further, my phone began to ring, the sound distracting me from my spiraling thoughts. I knew who it was before I even began to dig around for my earpiece, sighing heavily as I did so. It was only so long until my boss discovered the plans his daughter and I had made for his Sunday, and I doubted he was happy about it.

"What, Brandon?" I answered, not attempting to hide my annoyance. He scowled on the other end, clearly sharing my sentiment. I could hear he was also driving home, although I knew he lived closer to the airport than I did.

"When was I going to learn about this meeting you set up between me and that... that thing?"

"First of all, Arkrian is not a thing: he's your daughter's fiancé and *Shannon* is the one who set everything up. I merely told her when you would be free." I sighed again, knowing this would be an unpleasant conversation. "There are far worse things to be in this world than a shapeshifter, Brandon."

"How dare you say that, after what that *animal* did to my–"

"Stop right there! That has *nothing* to do with Shannon and Arkrian." I hated having the same argument repeatedly, and I'm sure Shannon was too, which is why she asked for my help. "We *both* know that. Your hatred for what Kynagi did is justified, no one is arguing that. But you cannot keep blaming all shifters for what one did."

"I don't want him anywhere near my daughter, much less me. Why Shannon insists on this bullshi–"

"I wasn't finished yet, *Boss*." I growled through gritted teeth to keep certain words from spilling out as I adjusted my grip on the wheel. The fact that he was being unfair and extremely judgmental of Arkrian didn't matter, there are certain things you don't say to your boss. "Secondly, I know Arkrian personally, and he wouldn't do anything he knows you don't approve of. For crying out loud, you haven't even met him! That's why Shannon set up that damn dinner for you guys: so you could try to get to know him because, whether you like him or not, Shannon *will* marry him."

Silence on the other end. Brandon might not have liked it, but he knew I was right. Shannon had strongly voiced that if her father refused to give her away, she would have her brother do it, who was already a part of the Supernatural community thanks to his vampire bride. It was largely Mark's secret marriage to a vampire that had Brandon so upset about Shannon also marrying a Supernatural, and a shifter at that. Although he swore that it wouldn't affect his judgment on the job, it was obvious that he still blamed all shifters and Supernaturals in general for his wife's loss. It must've seemed like a betrayal for both of his children to fall in love with non-humans, but that didn't justify his behavior.

"I'm hanging up on you now, Brandon. All Shannon and I ask is that you give him half a chance, because if you don't, you're going to lose both of your children. I'd rather not see that happen." I hung up as I pulled into the driveway of my home, parking in my garage as the door opened automatically. I dragged myself out of the car, hoping to relax on my couch as I slammed the door, not bothering to retrieve my luggage from the trunk.

My hopes were instantly dashed as I stepped into my home, however, as a tugging began in the back of my mind. The Overseer was calling me toward him, but I did my best to ignore the command as I stepped into the kitchen. Lucius *had* to know I had just gotten back from my case, and the last thing I felt like doing was playing babysitter to the Coven.

Searching my fridge for anything to settle my thoughts and dumping out old food, I decided on a bottle of yogurt, not wanting to put in the effort to cook. Slamming the fridge with my foot and ignoring the bill from the pet sitter, I made my way back to my living room, where Lira and Xris sat waiting for me. I knew I didn't have time for them but couldn't resist the desire to rest for a few moments while I did my best to ignore the Overseer. My two pretties jumped into my lap as soon as I plopped on my couch, both begging for my undivided attention. Petting with one hand and eating with the other, I gave them both attention as best I could, but my mind was elsewhere and the constant tugging wasn't helping, either. Soon, both cats were meowing their disappointment in my performance.

"Well, you didn't have me for long anyway. Lucius is being a dick, and I have to go pick up someone." I scoffed, pushing them both out of my lap as I stood. I wearily walked down the hall to my bedroom, groaning as I pushed the door open. Tossing my clothing on an ever-growing pile of dirty clothes, I searched through my closet, changing into a simple blue shirt and shorts. My cats followed my every move, tangling themselves in my steps as they begged me to stay with their purrs and meows.

Forcing myself outside and climbing wearily back into the car, I pulled away from my empty shell of a home and began cruising back toward Decver. Out of all the cities in The Capital, it was by far the biggest that remained, but more importantly for me, it was the safest. Vitae's Hunters were always searching for me, and it was only by moving whenever they got close that I had managed to avoid them for as long as I had. In a Governance as large as The Capital, I would have plenty of notice before a Hunter could reach me in Decver.

The sound of my phone ringing forced me out of my thoughts, and I huffed once I saw the name. I generally made it a rule not to talk while driving, but I had to make an exception for Lucius' Coven and my boss. Although I had only taken on the role reluctantly, part of my job in the Coven was to be available to Lucius' people in case he couldn't be, which unfortunately included other Coven members.

"Raiven speaking." I tapped my earpiece as I switched lanes, once again not trying to hide my annoyance.

"Hurry, Raiven, it's already past eight." It was Crispin, First in the Coven and a vampire I absolutely could not stand. He had texted me as soon as I landed to come pick him up from his outing, since apparently Lucius wanted him for something. I had absolutely no intention of picking him up, but now that I was also on my way to Lucius, I lacked a good excuse not to. "Where are you?"

"On the bridge." I felt the familiar bump as I got on the bridge, switching lanes to pass the slow driver in front of me. "It does take a while to get there from my house."

"Your house? I thought you were at the airport."

"No." I retorted. "I went home first."

"Thought gas was too expensive for you to waste." He teased, and I groaned as I did my best not to respond to the obvious bait. Technically, my whole make of car was illegal: gas engines had long been replaced with electric cars and being caught driving a guzzler would result in large fines and an impounded car. However, this car had seen me to hell and back: I would not give her up so easily.

"I hadn't planned on wasting it," I finally answered, glancing at the time as I noticed my exit. "I'll be there soon."

"Just hurry." Turning off onto the state road, I began to move my stuff from the passenger seat as I sat at the light. I wasn't used to having other people in my car, so any seat that I wasn't in was fair game for papers, my gun, and a plethora of trash. I did my best to shove it all onto the backseat, pulling into the parking lot where I saw Crispin waiting. Despite the fact the sun had set hours ago, Crispin's golden hair still seemed to glow as he walked up to me.

"Thanks Rai." He collapsed against the seat as I pulled back into traffic. "I owe you."

"Forget it." I brushed him off as I headed toward our Overseer, annoyed by the ever-growing traffic and the tugging in my mind. I knew it was a holiday weekend, and many were eager to head downtown, but it annoyed me all the same. "Lucius was calling me anyway. Otherwise, I'd be home right now."

"Good. I just hope that Eve isn't there." He sighed, closing his eyes as he slumped further in the seat. His simple shirt was unbuttoned at the top and his dark jeans hugged him tightly, but I tried not to notice as I glanced at him. Crispin was being unusually polite for once and besides that, he never shortened my name for any reason.

My eyes continued drifting over him and I noticed something shiny around his wrist.

"That new?" I nodded to the watch, and then grew worried when he didn't answer. Afraid to take my eyes off the road, I reached over to touch it, activating my power slightly. The moment my fingers brushed it, I knew it contained silver and couldn't help my slight scowl. I yanked it off, tossing it out the window and angrily gripping my wheel as it bounced in the road. "For fuck's sake, Mikael, maybe next time ask about the composition before you buy stupid jewelry."

"Sorry, I meant Crispin." I quickly corrected myself, cursing internally as I realized my mistake. I felt it as his power reacted to me using his human name and I could tell he was staring at me even as I avoided meeting his gaze.

"No, what did you call me?" Crispin's voice was suspicious, and he leaned over to touch my arm. I flinched ever so slightly at the touch, but with him so close, there was no way he missed it. His return to normal was unfortunately quick, and I was starting to wish I had left the watch on him. "Did you... just call me Mikael?"

"Sorry," I muttered as we neared The Landing, grateful to be out of the seemingly endless traffic. I kept my eyes on the road and tried to pretend Crispin wasn't there, even as his gaze burned into me. "Sometimes I slip up with the name changes. I'll try not to dead name you again."

"Unlike Lucius, I don't tend to share my human name. How do *you* know that name?" As soon as I parked, he tried to pull me closer, but I pulled away, fighting the urge to slap him. He was right: under normal circumstances, I shouldn't have known his dead name. However, the situation between me and Crispin wasn't normal, and only I knew the reason why. Before I could say anything more, Kisten came into view, saving me from the vampire's interrogation.

"There's Kisten. Let's go before he gets the wrong idea." I quickly climbed out of my car, thankful for his perfect timing. Crispin was about to make it evident that he wasn't done with me when Kisten stopped, staring at us. Kisten's expression was blank as he looked at us, and he seemed a little distracted.

"Does Lucius know you were out, Cris?"

"No," we answered simultaneously, then Crispin continued: "I went out on my own for a bit. Asked for a ride once Lucius called me back."

"Oh," he shrugged, his eyes lingering on me for only a moment before he looked away. A soft look flashed through his chartreuse eyes, but it passed just as quickly as it had appeared. "Well, Evalyn and Lucius are looking for both of you, so I'd hurry. Especially you, Cris."

"Where are you going?" I asked as he continued down the sidewalk, evidently in a hurry to leave. I was surprised when he actually stopped to answer, glancing over his shoulder. His eyes softened again as they met mine and then returned to their sad and gloomy stare.

"Home." He shifted as he took off down the walk, rushing to get away. I watched him disappear into the darkness of the night and turned to catch Crispin walking the way Kisten had come. Silently, I followed in his shadow and chastised myself for my earlier slip-up. Usually, I avoided Crispin like the plague, not only to avoid what had happened earlier, but because I just couldn't stand who he had become.

"Raiven!" Somewhere in my thoughts, I heard Eve's voice and I realized we had reached the back of The Dream. Lucius owned The Landing and many nightclubs in Decver, but The Dream was one of two clubs that allowed humans and Supernaturals to mingle. By default, that also made it one of the more popular night clubs, and considering it was a holiday weekend, tonight seemed to be no exception.

"Raiven, where have you and Crispin been?" She was in her security outfit and, judging by her attitude, was not happy about playing babysitter at the club. Lucius required all his Coven to help with the businesses, and Eve was no exception, as much as she liked to be. Besides that, we were technically coworkers outside of the Coven, and she never got over the fact I was on the Central team while she was stuck on the local. She failed to understand that I had been working with Division 11 since its inception, and merely saw me as a rival in her quest for power.

The ala was glaring at me as if she wanted to eat me alive and I decided I couldn't pass up the chance to make her even more upset. Besides, Crispin had already managed to find his way on my bad side and I was upset that Lucius had even called me here. I grinned as I crossed my arms, ignoring the concerned look on Crispin's face.

"Well, he needed a ride back," I started, and Crispin sighed, relieved that I was telling the truth. I couldn't help my smirk as I continued. "So, I picked him up and brought him here. Then we got freaky in the car and it was *great*. As you can imagine, we didn't want to rush things."

Crispin and Eve glared at me as I smiled and shrugged, but Crispin cut her off before she could say a word. "Leave it, Eve; it's not true. I did need a ride back, but I accidentally called Raiven instead of you. If you don't want me calling her, get your number changed."

At least my lie was fun. I thought, turning away. I guess it helped to cool her down, because she turned from us, her fists curling and uncurling as she sought to control her anger. Eve's cell number was terribly similar to mine, with only the last two numbers being different and she had been encouraged to change her number several times. However, as usual, she saw it as losing to me and refused to concede.

"*Anyway*, both of you need to hurry. Lucius is looking for you." She stomped off into the club, her red hair waving as she left us in the dark parking lot. Crispin and I walked down further, entering a door that would take us beneath The Landing and into the Coven. Climbing down the dimly lit stairs into the earth, Crispin suddenly stopped, and I unerringly ran into him. He whipped around like lightning and pinned me to the wall with his body. Being so close, I knew he felt my heartbeat quicken and I did my best to hide my anger.

"Why is it every time I touch you, your heartbeat quickens? Do I scare you or…" He leaned in close, his breath dancing across my skin.

I had to fight the involuntary shudder it caused and instead, I glared at him. He chuckled at my glare, clearly entertained. "Is it more?"

"Because I want your body. Now put me down," I quipped, and Crispin chuckled again, moving as if to bite me. Instead, he lightly kissed my collarbone, and it only enraged me more. I moved my leg as if to kick him, but he quickly shifted his weight to stop me. His eyes swirled with power when he looked up at me, and I knew he was using his inhuman strength to keep me pinned.

"Stop with the bullshit, Raiven. You've turned me down every time I've offered it to you." Crispin's expression turned serious, and I couldn't help the slight fear that crept into me. If it came down to a fight, I could likely win, but Lucius would be furious with both of us fighting in the Coven. "How do you know my human name?"

"Let me down and maybe I'll consider being honest." I stared into his eyes as he let me down, his blue eyes burning with mischief. I didn't appreciate the whole 'pinning me to the wall' part, or the light teasing he had decided to indulge in. I rolled my shoulders a bit and cracked my neck, knowing I was only annoying him. "I'll tell you later, if I feel like it."

"In my room, then," he agreed and continued down the stairs, leaving me enraged on the steps. I felt less like telling him the truth and more like helping him to stake himself. I knew it wouldn't kill him, but it would at least get him out of my hair for the rest of the night.

"Coming?" I snapped from my thoughts and jogged down the stairs to meet him as he called back to me. We walked down the hallway together, our steps echoing as I matched his stride. I considered smacking him for being an arrogant prick but lost the chance when we reached the living room of the underground space, Crispin opening the heavy doors.

As soon as we stepped into the room, I knew something was off. Lucius usually kept the living room fairly well furnished: a couple of couches, a few armchairs, two TVs on each side and a coffee station so we could gather and talk. However, now most of the furniture had been taken out: only two couches and the coffee spot remained, making the space seem bigger than it ever had appeared before.

"Crispin, Raiven, please sit." Lucius motioned for us to sit on the couch across from him and his guest as soon as he noticed us. Lounging beside him was a caramel-skinned vampire who was all smiles and his eyes followed us as we moved through the room. Justina stood against the far wall next to the coffee, staring off into the distance. I couldn't see her face, but the air in the room was almost suffocating, which meant she was upset about something. Lucius seemed to be ignoring her and continued as we sat, perching on opposite ends of the couch. "I'd like to introduce our guest, LeAlexende, Overseer of the Southern Grove. He will be visiting with us for the Fest of Peace this weekend."

"Welcome to our territory. We look forward to your graces as we bless you with ours." Ignoring the angry sorcerer, I addressed our guest and he nodded, his already wide grin growing wider, emphasizing the oddity of his purple eyes. He tossed his blonde hair as he laughed, clearly pleased with my words.

"The pleasure is indeed mine." LeAlexende's eyes flashed with mirth as he turned to Lucius. "Rare to find someone who knows the traditional greeting. An interesting one indeed, just as you said."

"Yes, indeed," The Overseer agreed, giving LeAlexende a soft smile before addressing us. I glared at him in return, and he shrugged, still smiling. Sometimes Lucius' arrogance to brag about me was as annoying as Crispin thinking he owned every woman in the world. It was no wonder they got along so well. "While Alexende is in our territory, I will allow excursions, but all members of the Coven must remain here, save those who are out of Decver."

I groaned internally at the order but was careful not to show my disappointment on my face as I spoke. "For how long?"

"Until Monday." Three days stuck at the Coven, except for Kisten. According to Eve, he caused too much commotion when he had to stay and was a 'disturbance'. Considering no one had ever seen it and the fact that Kisten was the most mild-mannered person I had ever met, I think she made it up as an excuse to not have him around to influence Lucius. Kisten never wanted to be around anyway, so I guess it was a decision that worked for both of them.

"I'll be here. I have Monday off from the office." I shrugged, doing my best to hide my annoyance. I wasn't close to most of the Coven, and it was always awkward when I was forced to spend time with everyone else. "But I'm on call for an important case, so if it comes, I'm gone."

"You may leave."

I wasn't sure which way he meant it, but I took it for both: I stood up to escape the room. As I walked by, Crispin grabbed my arm, forcing me to pause in my movement. At that moment, Justina glanced up with her green eyes, her deep blue hair rippling. My own power surged through me, and I knew my eyes had grown brighter.

"Strike two, Crispin. Try me for three." I growled, narrowing my eyes at the vampire. I knew it was rude to fight in front of a guest, but Crispin had been working on my nerves ever since I picked him up, making my already bad mood worse. Lucius didn't say a word but the charge in the surrounding air increased, making the already dense air even harder to breathe in. Crispin glanced at Lucius, who maintained his soft smile and polite expression. He slowly released the grip on my arm and turned away from me.

"Crispin, I'd like to speak with you." Lucius' words were still polite as he looked at LeAlexende and Justina. Justina left without so much as a word and LeAlexende nodded as he stood.

"I can take a hint. We can finish catching up later," the tan Overseer walked up to me, opening the door that led to the rest of the Coven. "After you."

"*Gratias*[1]." I passed him and carefully held the door open as he walked through, making sure to close it behind us. It was about time someone talked to Crispin about his manners, or lack thereof.

"By the way, you have an interesting accent, one I have not heard in a long time. I look forward to getting to know you better... Raiven." He flashed another bright smile before walking away, disappearing in the darkness. Steamed by Crispin's actions and Lucius' bragging, I continued to Crispin's room and slammed the door as I entered. On the other side, I heard someone mutter about me being inconsiderate, but I didn't care in the least. I leaned against the door, the weight of my evening trying to drown me. I hated days like this, when it seemed like the Gods were determined to make me as miserable as possible.

Sighing heavily, I forced myself up from the heavy wood and collapsed into his armchair, closing my eyes as I waited.

2

"Raiven, is that you?" I opened my eyes as Crispin's door opened, and Justina walked in. A glance at the clock told me I had only fallen asleep for a short while and I rubbed my eyes as she closed the door. If it had been anyone else, I would've helped them see their way out. However, Justina was higher ranked than me and on top of that, I liked her. "Why are you in Cris' room?"

"He wanted to talk in his room." I sighed, relaxing back into his armchair, still annoyed and upset from earlier. Justina sat on the bed across from me, her expression showing how much she didn't believe me. I shrugged, sinking lower into the chair. "I'm finally going to tell him the truth so he'll leave me the hell alone."

"Which one?" she joked lightly, until she registered the annoyed look in my eye. Her face turned serious, and her voice dropped in volume. "Oh, that one... Are you sure you're ready? That he's ready?"

"Should've done it forever ago. I'm so tired of him and besides... I need to do this for myself," I closed my eyes, unable to help the weight that started to settle on my chest. The sorcerer said nothing, waiting patiently for me to continue. "He'll be fine. He's turned into such a womanizer that I doubt it'll bother him that much. I'm the one who's been carrying this."

"You've carried your guilt long enough. Time for you to let go," Justina assured me, studying me. Then: "I'll never stop being amazed by you. It's not common to see someone with dark skin and bright green eyes and your hair is so beautiful and unique. It's a shame you cut it so short."

"Oh, don't you start it too: everyone has been complaining about that. We both know I was sick of all that hair and besides, your eyes are brighter than mine. My eyes are far more hazel most of the time." I pointed out, rubbing my hand over my short afro and Justina laughed, the sound filling the room. I couldn't help my slight smile at the sound, standing from the chair as she stood. I allowed her to take my hands in her own, looking up to meet her gaze as her laughter faded.

"*Ой бай*[1]. I'm Russian, Rai. Green eyes are a part of who I am," I closed my eyes as she kissed my forehead before kissing me gingerly on the lips. I enjoyed kissing Justina, but for her, it was a gesture of closeness and trust. I had learned long ago to accept them as merely that and to quell any thoughts of it being more. "But you are not and that makes you unique. I know you don't like being stuck here with the rest of us, but if you can swallow that pride, you can stay in my room tonight."

"We'll see," I answered softly, reluctantly letting her hand slip from mine, and I fell back into Crispin's chair as she left. I closed my eyes again as she gently closed the door, my thoughts turning to the years I had with Crispin before he was turned. Then, way back then, he was kind, sweet, and thoughtful, just like...

"Raiven." I barely moved as he walked in and closed the door silently behind him. I ran my hand over my hair again, keeping my gaze on Crispin as he sat on his bed, studying him, reading him. Hating what being turned had done to him as I fought not to glare at the vampire. It wasn't his fault, but despite what people love to say, being turned *does* change a person.

"What did Lucius want?" I asked softly.

Crispin scoffed in response as he leaned back on his bed.

"To 'remind' me that I'm not supposed to make a scene in front of guests," he repeated sarcastically, making air quotes as he spoke. "Honestly, I think you made more of a scene than me."

"You started it and you damn well know it." I could feel the anger boiling in my chest again, but I forced myself to swallow it down. "Do you want to know why I know your name, or not?"

"Well, I'm going to guess someone told you." He looked at me coyly, crossing his legs as he leaned back on his bed. Crispin was still handsome, his golden hair always somehow falling exactly right around his shoulders. I found myself tracing the stark line of his collarbone with my eyes, following the line that ran down the center of his chest. His top buttons were still open, showing the muscle he had never had before being turned. His dark pants did little to hide his physique but despite the changes, I couldn't help but trace with my eyes what I had once touched with my hands.

Crispin cleared his throat to get my attention, causing me to jump slightly and raise my eyes to his. His face held a devilish grin, and he lifted his hand to his chest, enticingly tracing the exposed skin there. He knew I had been staring at him and I snorted, turning away from his display.

"Yeah, someone did. *You*," I said plainly, and Crispin laughed, throwing his head back for gravitas. I waited until he decided to stop being dramatic and to see that I wasn't kidding. He let out a loud breath, leaning forward on his elbows as he spoke.

"One would think I'd remember if I did," Crispin scoffed, his blue eyes looking into mine deeply as he tried to read me. I met his gaze evenly, wishing I could run away to Justina's room already as he continued. "Like I said, a precious few have been trusted with that information and I *don't* recall telling *you*."

"That's because it was before you turned." I closed my eyes, sighing heavily as I tried to decide how honest I wanted to be. "You and I were once close friends, maybe more than that. We had met at a party and I guess we hit it off well. I know your memories of before are spotty at best, but..."

"I can't say my recollection is the best, but I think I'd remember you. You are quite unusual after all, and an exquisite beauty, even now." Crispin smiled, his fangs appearing as he gazed at me. He undressed me with his eyes as I had done him, and I didn't appreciate the look. "You are much, much older than me, so you would've already changed by the time you met me."

"I was, and the memories might start to surface someday, if I stay here." I sighed internally as I mused. "We spent a lot of time together back then, in the comfort of each other's embrace. But..."

"Oh?" The dark hint that entered his expression as he interrupted me was enough to make me stand and move for the door. However, he was faster and managed to pin me to it, preventing me from leaving. Crispin pressed himself into me, placing his hand over mine on the handle as he kept me pinned to his door. He slid his free hand down my back, gingerly lifting the edge of my top and tracing the skin above my shorts, teasingly playing with the small of my back. I had to fight the desire to arch my back towards him and tried to ignore his playful touch as he whispered into my ear, his voice deep and sultry.

"Well, maybe you should use your embrace to remind me. Perhaps I might remember if I had a taste," I closed my eyes, focusing on my anger before whipping around sharply. He must not have expected me to react so violently, because he was easily tossed back by my movement. His eyes showed shock for a moment, before returning to their devilish intent. "It's an honest suggestion, Raiven."

"Back then, my embrace meant something to you. *I* meant something to you," I spat, taken aback by my tone as I spoke. I was angry, but I was also... hurt. Hurt in a way I thought I had long overcome. "Enough that you wanted–"

I stopped myself, covering my face as I kept the words from spilling out. I owed Crispin the truth, I knew that, but I hadn't expected how much I still cared about him. How much I still hated myself for being the reason he was turned. I took a deep breath before dropping my hands, unable to help the anger in my eyes as I looked at him again.

"But now that you've turned, you're no longer that person. You're selfish, arrogant and nothing like the person I knew, a man who would never have used another person for his own lustful gains." I turned away from his unreadable expression, my chest aching. "I *hate* seeing what you've become, knowing that it's my fault. That I didn't protect you when you needed me the most. That's why I avoid you, why I hate being near you, and why I hate *interacting* with you.

"Mikeal is dead, and now we all have Crispin, with no one to blame but me." With that, I left the room, slamming the door again as I stood in the hallway. I thought I heard him softly call my name, but I ignored it, quickly heading for Justina's room. My gait slowed as I realized I was approaching my door and I paused as I reached it. I slowly fingered the raven carved into the wood, my anger beginning to fade now that I was no longer near the vampire.

Slowly, I went inside, pausing in the doorway of my dark room. My eyes drifted through the darkness before resting on my vanity against the far wall, just visible with the light from the hallway. Turning on the light near the door, I slowly made my way to my small makeup desk and sat down, looking at the rings scattered on its top. I reached for an ornate jewelry box, opening it to reveal the various jewels and gems that had been gifted to me over the years. My eyes rested on a single ring, the reason I had entered my room and been drawn to the desk. It was nothing more than a simple gold band, but I lifted it up, unable to help the turmoil it caused in my chest.

'*Are you finally going to move on?*' My sister's consciousness suddenly spoke, making me jump in my seat. I grabbed the wooden locket that housed my sister's soul as it grew warm under my shirt, her voice annoyed. '*You can't keep holding onto the past forever.*'

"I know." I gazed into the shining metal and this time, I could see his face, hear his laugh as if no time had passed at all. I looked up into the mirror, seeing the dark-skinned beauty that stared back at me. I was abnormal, never to be accepted as a human or a Supernatural. A prize to some, a threat to others, but he had treated me like a treasure, even once he knew what I was. And I repaid that by allowing him to be killed, allowing him to be turned. "I know, I just..."

'Miss him? You can miss him until you're dead, but it'll never bring him back the way you remember him.' I could hear my sister's disdain as she lectured me, and I closed my eyes as she continued. *'Accept what happened, accept that he's changed and stop torturing yourself.'*

"Yeah... I know, I know." I carefully put the ring back where it belonged and, choosing a different one, slowly stood up from my desk. "Go back to sleep, you shouldn't waste energy right now. He knows now, so I'll... I'll be fine."

'Fine. Be well, Raiven.' I quietly left my room as her consciousness faded and I continued to Justina's room. The room was already dark when I stepped inside, and I could hear Justina's soft breathing as she slept. Once inside the dark room, the weight of my day pressed on me, and I felt exhausted as I walked to her bed. Collapsing on top of the sheets next to her, I fell asleep quickly, wishing for the day to end.

3

I awoke late the next day with Justina's strong arms around me and her cool breath on my neck. The scent of vanilla wafted up my nostrils and I quickly realized the being beside me wasn't Justina. I quickly sat up and Aurel laughed as he released me, his grin bright on his face.

"Well, good afternoon. I thought you were going to sleep all day." He sat up as well, revealing that he was shirtless from the waist up. I merely grunted as I rubbed the sleep from my eyes, realizing I was still on top of the sheets. I felt Aurel gently touch my hand, and I allowed him to take it as he spoke. "By the way, I like the ring. It's gorgeous on your petite hands. Whoever got it for you picked it exactly right."

Aurel was studying the band intently, and I couldn't help my slight smile at his fascination. One of Aurel's many hobbies was to collect jewelry from the past and he had quite the collection. After all, he had been collecting for the past hundred years and was jealous of every piece I owned. After a while, he spoke again, the awe obvious in his tone. "This is a classic, the setting and cut of the stone is iconic. Renaissance?"

"Yeah, a good friend got it for me for one of my birthdays." I smiled, loving Aurel's expression as he studied the ring. I glanced around the room for its owner but saw no sign of her. "Where's Justina?"

"Dunno." He shrugged, looking up and releasing my hand. "She left and told me to watch you. Made me promise like I'm a fucking gack."

"So, you decided to climb in bed with me?" I joked as he laughed, unable to help the slight smile that came to my face. I considered Aurel another of the few friends I had in the Coven, but lately, things had become strained between us. Any moment when we could enjoy being friends was a nice reminder of what I wanted to preserve. However, as soon as his laughter began to fade, a soft look entered his eyes and my smile immediately faded.

"Raiven." He reached to stroke my cheek and I pulled back, not wanting him to touch me. Aurel's feelings toward me had begun to shift and while he had yet to ask me to join his harem, he made no small secret of how he felt. I didn't feel anything more than friendship for him and I drew in a deep breath, steeling myself for what I knew I needed to say.

"Aurel, you need to stop." I stated plainly, watching as confusion flitted across his face. I was sure if he had been alive, his face would have changed color, but being undead left his face the same pale color. Those gentle sea-green eyes were starting to show hints of Aurel's annoyance, and I swallowed as I waited for him to respond.

"Stop what, *A ghrá*[1]?"

"That, right there. You need to stop," I insisted, finally standing from the bed as he looked after me curiously. My heart pounded as I met his gaze, but I forced myself to meet it evenly. Aurel was playing stupid, but I knew he understood what I meant. Dragging this out wouldn't help either of us, and I couldn't keep my silence. "We're friends, Aurel. I don't want–"

"Want what, Raiven?" Aurel stood, his eyes glowing dangerously as he let his emotions get the better of him. His curly orange hair almost seemed to expand in his annoyance, but I refused to be intimidated, crossing my arms as he stood across from me. I knew Aurel did not take rejection well, but I would not be coerced. "You only spend time with me when you're forced to be here, so why do you put up with me at all? Is there something you're hiding from me?"

"Maybe because I don't want to hurt you, you idiot!" I snorted, moving away from the bed to Justina's armchair. I gripped the back tightly as I scowled at the lich, my own annoyance growing. "Does forcing yourself on me make you any better? Maybe the reason I don't spend time with you is because you always guilt trip me about it. Sometimes you act no better than Mother, wanting to add me to another of your collections."

Surprised flitted across Aurel's face and I immediately regretted my words as I realized what I said. Comparing anyone to Mater Vitae was a great insult, and the words had flown out of my mouth without thought. Upon recognizing the hurt and anger in his eyes, I tried to apologize, releasing the chair as I spoke.

"Aurel, I'm sorry, I didn't—"

"Of course not. You never do." He walked by me without looking up and pushed his way past Crispin and Justina as they walked in the door. I collapsed down into the chair, cradling my face between my hands as I mentally chastised myself for my hasty words. Justina looked after Aurel as he left, turning a quizzical expression to me.

"What did you do?"

"We had a fight, what does it look like?" I replied sarcastically, sighing heavily as I tried to calm myself down. Getting upset with Justina would get me nowhere and I knew it. I looked up from my hands, glancing at the pair as they watched me with concern. "Why did you leave me with him, anyway?"

"I needed to get Crispin up and I was trying to be nice for once. Plus, I thought you... well, obviously I was wrong." Justina shook her head disapprovingly as I tried to change the subject.

"What did you need to get Crispin up for?"

"That's private." She glanced at him and I didn't like the look they shared, frowning as I dropped my hands from my face. It not only confused me, but it was as if they had a whole conversation with that one look. I knew Justina was Second in the Coven, but it wasn't like either of them to keep secrets. Both were honest to a fault, and it caused them both issues with other members of the Coven in their own ways.

"Is there something I should know about?" I didn't do much to hide the suspicion in my voice as I spoke, pulling my legs into the chair. "I'm going to guess it isn't a Coven matter."

"No, nothing like that," Crispin answered, a little too quickly. I decided not to push it as he continued, still giving him an annoyed look. "I know we have permissions for excursions, but we have to be back before LeAlexende and Lucius wake up."

"And? I care because?" I glanced at the clock above her bathroom, which read a little after one. Justina must've used her magic to wake Crispin early and I glanced at her, trying to judge her intention. She was looking away from me, her expression unreadable as she refused to meet my gaze.

"And, I want to show you something." Crispin smiled mysteriously, and Justina looked up to shoot him an angry glance. I didn't even hesitate with my answer.

"No."

"Raiven, please." Crispin looked ready to argue when Justina stopped him and looked at me, a pleading look in her eyes as she spoke first. I turned to face the sorcerer fully, trying to understand her motives. Justina usually tried to stay on an even footing with everyone in the Coven, especially since her anger and her honest mouth often got her in trouble. I couldn't understand why she was supporting whatever Crispin wanted, but since it was her, I decided I was curious enough to find out why.

"Fine. Just leave while I change."

"Sure." Justina cut Crispin off and pushed him out the door, not giving the vampire a chance to annoy me. I grabbed some clothing that I knew I had left in Justina's room, but I decided to dress near the door so I could hear their conversation. Justina's door never closed all the way, due to a fight she got into with a suitor, and Lucius didn't consider it important to repair anymore. She was constantly breaking it for some reason or another, and I couldn't blame him for not wanting to waste the time.

"Don't play with her, Cris. I mean it," Justina warned, her voice low and heavy, almost as if she were preparing to cast. "You'll pay for it. She'll make sure you do and so will I. You just need to tell her the truth."

"I won't play with her." The vampire promised lightly, and it took all I had not to scoff, lest they hear me. Justina sighed heavily and I heard the door groan as she leaned against it slightly.

"You will, I know it," she sounded defeated, and I leaned forward to hear her next words better. "You will never change."

"And you'll never trust me. You know I don't mess around when it's serious... well, not too much." Crispin laughed softly and it sounded like he moved closer to her. "Let me have at least a little fun, Raiven makes it too easy."

Justina never got to reply because I opened the door at that moment and Crispin quickly stepped back. I frowned, still not trying to hide my displeasure and annoyance with having to spend time with the vampire. "I'm as ready as I'll ever be."

"Good." He quickly linked my arm in his and we walked down the dark Coven hallway into the way-too-bright sunshine. At first I thought he might be annoyed by being forced to deal with the sun, but the vampire seemed just fine as he strolled through the parking lot. He was in no danger from it considering his age, but he still preferred to avoid direct sunlight after being out of it for so long. I watched as he produced keys from his pocket, and I looked at the vampire as if he had grown a new head.

"Since when do you drive?"

"Since Justina said I could drive her car and we don't have the time to walk there," Crispin shrugged, unlocking the vehicle to locate where it was in the parking lot. He glanced back to my smug expression, not trying to hide his own annoyance for once. "I know how to drive, Raiven. I just don't see the point in owning a car."

"Yeah, why own a car when you can be undead and responsible and walk?" I muttered sarcastically as I climbed in the car, waiting impatiently as he joined me. Crispin was far from the only undead who preferred to walk most places, but it was easier to be of that opinion when all the trappings of being alive weren't a problem. "Where are we going, anyway?"

"What fun would that be?" He leaned over and kissed my forehead before I could react. After it occurred to me that this was strike three for him, I slapped him, growling slightly. He actually had the audacity to grin at my retaliation, and I realized he'd kissed me to see if he could get a reaction.

"You must have enjoyed it to slap me that hard."

Seething and resisting the desire to slap him again, I turned away from him as we left The Landing. As my anger passed, my mind floated to Aurel and guilt gripped my mind and chest as I remembered my words. It was the worst thing I could've said, considering all the horrible things Mother had done when she controlled Supernaturals and those in her court. Regardless of my lack of romantic feelings and his bad attitude, he hadn't done anything to warrant that kind of comparison.

"Where are we?" I leaned forward as we pulled into what appeared to be a public garden and my confusion continued to grow. Such gardens were common, making it easier for people to plant and care for their own plot of flowers or vegetables, but I couldn't understand why Crispin would take me to one. The vampire merely smiled, getting out and leaning on the car as he waited for me to join him.

"Just set your watch for two-fifteen so we don't end up being late." He still refused to answer my question as he started for the garden's entrance. I set my watch and, leaning against the car, watched him walk away. He managed to get pretty far before he realized I wasn't following, and I couldn't help my smirk as he sighed. "C'mon, Raiven."

"Why?"

"You'll see." He stood there facing me, arms crossed as he turned around. Stubborn, I equally crossed mine and stared at him, refusing to budge. We remained that way for a while and I took a moment to glance at my watch. If I could hold him for a few more minutes, I wouldn't have to worry about whatever it was he wanted to show me. Then suddenly, he tossed his hair, flashing a stream of gold in the sunlight. "Oh well, let's go. I'll just tell Justina that we drove here for nothing."

I was intrigued by his mention of Justina but refused to move for a moment, just to pay him back for earlier. Crispin waited to see if his words had affected me before he started walking towards the car, shaking his head. I waited until he was within arm's length before I walked past him, twisting so he couldn't touch me.

"I knew you'd give in." He grinned behind me as he followed and I shrugged, pretending not to care.

"It's not always about you," I warned, opening the garden's gate. "I only gave in because if I didn't, it would've been a waste for Justina and unlike how I feel about you, I like her."

"True, true." He nodded, only pretending to agree. I turned around and slapped him again – half for the sarcasm I didn't appreciate, half because he was so cocky. He reached to grab my hand but I was quick to snatch it back, hissing as he walked past me. I growled as I began following him, wanting this outing to be over with.

'Raiven.' My sister's voice rose in my mind again as she responded to my annoyance. *'Who are you with?'*

'Say hello to the new improved Mikael, now known as Crispin.' The locket grew warm under my shirt and out of habit, I reached up to grab it. Once I realized Crispin was watching me, however, I stopped. *'Stay low, sis, or you'll be discovered again and this bastard is the last person I want to find out.'*

'If you don't want to be with him anymore, then leave. No need to get so worked up.' I began to refute her statement but she slipped away before I could respond. I looked up as Crispin moved aside a curtain of beads and he motioned me in as I marveled at the beauty of the garden. It was filled with a variety of flowers, all of which were beautifully in bloom. However, it was more than that: it was my garden, a garden I had tended to what seemed like a lifetime ago.

"I knew you'd like it." My awe immediately faded and I turned to glare as Crispin spoke. He raised his hands in defense and he seemed strangely sincere. "Not like that: you used to have a garden like this, I'm pretty sure. It's where I pro... was going to propose. Never mind, that's not what's important."

Crispin came closer to me and I instinctively stepped back, growling softly at him. He sighed heavily, stepping back as he looked away. All of his usual playfulness was gone from his eyes and he gingerly touched one of the petals, looking at it softly before returning his gaze to me. For a brief moment, he was like his old self again, gleaming in the sunlight as he helped care for a garden he thought so dutifully reflected me.

"I planted this a few years before you came. I'm not much for gardens now, and I didn't really know why, but I just felt compelled to. Justina... helps me with it," his newly softened expression looked strange to me, as if it didn't belong to him. The man standing in front of me seemed more like Mikael than Crispin and I couldn't help but step closer to him, my heart filling with an ache I thought I no longer had. "I know you probably don't believe me when I say this, but... I do appreciate you telling me. I don't remember and I probably never will, but–"

Crispin moved quickly and wrapped his arms around me, holding me close. Before I could object or react, he leaned down and kissed me, but this no longer felt like Crispin. I couldn't help myself as I wrapped my arms around him to pull him closer, my heart aching as I did so. I had never forgiven myself for allowing Mikael to be turned and never realized how much I still missed him. His gentle, uncertain kisses, the soft tenderness of being in his arms... and blood. His lips had the tainted taste of blood and now I tasted it faintly through the kiss. My mental cage to keep my thirst at bay started to break down as I kissed him deeply to taste more of that sweet liquid.

"Raiven." His voice was muffled from the force I was now pushing on him, almost forcing him to the ground. He tried his best to shift his arms to push me away, but I tightened my grip to keep him still. I was starting to lose my grasp on where I was and who I was with; all that mattered was the blood in his mouth and getting more of it. I pulled away from his lips and started for his throat, my fangs extending from my mouth.

"Raiven!" Crispin managed to untangle himself from me and pushed me into a bed of flowers, the gentle blooms crushed by my fall. "What in hell is wrong with you?"

I almost sprang back up, wanting more, but his push allowed me to regain enough control to slam the addiction behind its steel doors. I breathed in the scent of the flowers to calm myself as the lusty glow left my eyes and my fangs disappeared back into my mouth.

"Sorry," I muttered, somewhat embarrassed as I stood. "It has been a while since... since I've lost control like that... and it's almost time, so—"

"I know." The cockiness was still gone, replaced by a kind man. At least, he still looked less cocky and more concerned. "We have to stay away from you when we have injuries, but I haven't been hurt. Not recently, anyway."

"The faintest taste was still there." A glow began in my eyes as I thought about the kiss, but I pushed it back. "It's been months since Lucius fed me, and the mere thought of undead blood is enough to set me off. Such a soft, sweet—"

"Look, Raiven. I'm sorry." He breathed and I was so surprised by it that it overcame the addiction that had tried to take over my mind again. Crispin didn't apologize, not even to Lucius and definitely not to a woman. "I didn't bring you out here to play with you, despite what you may think. Honestly, I need..."

Crispin paused, looking away from me, pouting at a bed of white hibiscus flowers. I wasn't sure what to make of what was happening as I looked over the vampire, doing my best to ignore my thirst. Crispin turned back as if he was finally ready to speak when my watch began to scream, startling us both. It started a shriek that would have made a banshee proud as the alarm went off, declaring the time loudly.

Glancing at Crispin, I left the garden and began for the car, nearly running as we went. Crispin was faster and reached it first, quickly sliding into the driver's seat and I didn't argue as I jumped in. Whether I wanted to or not, we had to return to The Dream before Lucius and LeAlexende woke up for the day or the Oath would punish us both. As Crispin sped us back, I couldn't help but wonder what he had wanted to say in the recreated garden.

4

I leaned against my car as Crispin walked into the Coven, disappearing past the barrier into the darkness below. If we walked in together, it would've raised so many unnecessary problems with Eve that I didn't want to deal with. I could be a smartass when I wanted to, but I preferred to just avoid the ala as much as possible.

As I waited, my mind drifted back to the garden and I didn't like the uncomfortable feeling it caused in my chest. He had seemed... too different from what I had come to expect from him and his demeanor left me confused. Sincerity was not in Crispin's vocabulary and I had never seen him be so soft with anyone. A part of me wanted to believe that Mikael was still in him somewhere, but another argued that he was no longer that person. I had always agreed with the latter, but now, I wasn't sure what to think.

A few minutes after Crispin disappeared, Aurel came storming up the stairs, slamming the door into the wall. Barely glancing my way, he smashed his fist into the concrete, cursing in a language I didn't know. He had still failed to put on a shirt apparently, his alabaster skin practically blinding in the afternoon sunlight.

"Aurel!" I tried to get his attention, my pride screaming at me as I did so. If looks could kill, I would've died ten times over from the glare he gave me. I frowned, displeased with his reaction. "What the fuck's your problem?"

"What's my problem?" Suddenly he was in my face and vanilla flooded my mind until I wanted to push him back before the sweet scent suffocated me. "Oh, nothing, just that Eve is being a fucking annoying scanger!"

"Well, sorry, that's not really news around here." I didn't like him taking his anger out on me, especially when I had nothing to do with it. Most of us thought Evalyn abused her position as Lucius' Retainer, but that was hardly my fault. I realized Eve probably had taken a jab at Aurel's harem again, something he was very protective about. "*I was trying to apologize.*"

The angry lines left his face, but he didn't move, his orange curls bouncing. He looked at me with genuine confusion as he spoke, still leaning over me. "Apologize for what?"

"What I said earlier," I muttered, looking away. "I didn't mean to say it like that or to compare you to Mother. I don't really think you're like her. You're... pushy at times, but you do genuinely care about others. Like with your harem, and that's something she could never understand."

He seemed surprised for a moment before smiling at me, putting his hands on my car, and pinning me to the hood with his body. Aurel leaned down as if to kiss me and I turned away from him. He instead placed a light kiss on my cheek, lips barely brushing against my skin. He pulled back slightly, his eyes now looking at me softly.

"Don't worry about it. I'm over it." Aurel grinned at me and I chuckled softly, gently pushing him back. He let me, still standing as close as he could.

"While I'm glad, it doesn't change what I said before that," I insisted, watching as his smile twitched. I sighed, crossing my arms as I met his eyes evenly. "We're just friends, Aurel."

"What can I say? Things change all the time." He grinned, leaning back over me as he moved to hug me. As he brought his hand to caress my face, I could smell the blood on his knuckles and I had to shove him away. After my encounter with Crispin, my addiction was already barely under control and I looked at him with horror. He looked at me surprised, confused by my refusal of him. "What's wrong?"

"You just injured yourself. You need to leave." I turned away from him, trying not to think about the blood now running through his veins. The black, sweet blood that filled his luscious body, waiting for me to indulge. I grabbed my arm as it shot out to grab him, digging my nails into my own skin. "You need to leave now. You know better than to come around me like that."

"Raiven." His voice whined with how much he wanted to stay, but I knew it wasn't safe for either of us. I shook my head, refusing to look at him.

"Leave now, Aurel, or I *will* make you leave. Don't come near me until you've healed." I found it difficult to speak as my fangs tried to reveal themselves and I fought to keep them in my mouth. After a long, silent pause, I heard Aurel walk away and breathed a sigh of relief as the door to the Coven closed. I opened my eyes to the afternoon sun and tried to control my blood lust.

"You okay, Rai?" I looked down to see Kisten step out of his silver Mustang. He was dressed up with a blue silk shirt and black dress pants, and a simple gold chain around his neck. His hair was combed back into a slick-back style, with a few strands refusing to obey and hanging in his face. I dug my nails into the hood of my car, the screeching sound almost enough to distract my mind. Every fiber of my being was insisting I descend into the Coven, chase after Aurel to drink his sweet, undead blood.

"Go away, don't come near me," I growled through semi-closed lips and I closed my eyes. I was close to crying as I heard Kisten walk towards me, struggling to keep my body from chasing the lich. If I lost the battle and Kisten tried to stop me, there was no telling what I would do to him, and the last thing I wanted was to hurt him.

Suddenly, I felt a sharp pain in my hand and I opened my eyes to see Kisten piercing my skin with his sharp claws. Kisten was such an old and experienced shifter that he could shift any part of himself that he wanted to and his hand and forearm bore his beautiful leopard spots. Despite the blood his claws were now drawing from me, I felt an urge to pet the soft fur gracing his skin.

Before I could ask why he had stabbed me, Kisten forced my hand to my mouth, allowing me to taste my own blood. As soon as the taste hit my mouth, all thoughts of wanting blood faded. The cold, metallic taste was nothing like the sweet taste I craved and was familiar with. It was like jumping into a cold shower: I sobered up quickly and the addiction faded to its usual dark pit. I looked at Kisten in surprise as he released me, still holding my hand to my mouth, and letting the blood flow in. He smiled at me softly, shifting his hand back to being human.

"You never thought of that?"

"I..." I wanted to give some sort of excuse, but I couldn't think of anything to say. Kisten's eyes lit up with mirth, and I saw the corners of his mouth twitch up as he worked to hold in his laughter. I took my hand out of my mouth, and tried my hardest to look upset, fighting my own smile. "Well, why in the world would I ever do that to myself?"

"It seemed like a good idea. Would be bad if you wanted to drink your own blood." He shrugged, turning to walk back to his car. "Give me a moment to get my kit and I'll treat you."

I said nothing and merely watched as he dug through his trunk to find his first aid kit. As the Alpha of The Capital, Kisten took taking care of all shapeshifters seriously and it was obvious why he and Lucius were both good friends, as well as connected as Overseer and Alpha. His kit was fitted to treat any kind of shapeshifter and almost any possible wound that could be sustained, whether from each other or other Supernaturals.

He came back with a large roll of gauze as well as a needle and thread and I winced when I noticed. Kisten set down the supplies and reached for my hand, but I instinctively pulled it away, looking at the needle. Kisten followed my gaze and gave me an incredulous look.

"Are you seriously about to tell me you are afraid of needles?"

"I'm not afraid, just..." The words faded and Kisten sighed, taking my uninjured hand in his. He gently stroked the back of my hand before quickly kissing it, the gesture burning my skin.

"Uncomfortable? Because of Mother?" he whispered, and I nodded, wanting to press his hand to my face, wishing I could relax in his arms. He kissed the back of my hand again before releasing it and gently touching my face with his fingertips, the closest he would get to caressing me. "You know I know what I'm doing. It'll be a quick stitch and taken out tomorrow once you've healed."

"I know." I closed my eyes as he got to work, doing my best to ignore the sensations. Kisten was a surgeon and worked at the local hospital, specializing in treatment of Supernaturals. It was kind of unfair to his patients, since technically, he oversaw so many of them, but I think it was how Kisten preferred it. Working at the hospital gave him the authority that he needed to take care of his people, no matter the circumstance.

"There, done." Kisten patted my freshly dressed wound and I opened my eyes. Green met chartreuse as we looked at one another and, unable to resist, I reached out to touch his face with my uninjured hand. His hand caught mine however, and he held it awkwardly for a moment, before picking up my bandaged hand and pressing it to his face instead. He kept his eyes locked on mine and I felt as if my heart would beat right out of my chest.

"This isn't what I want." I sighed, dropping my hand in frustration as I looked away. Kisten dropped his as well, gathering up his materials from the hood of my car. He held out his hand and I accepted it as he helped me down.

"I know, Raiven, but I can't hurt you again." Kisten's expression resumed its gloomy stare and my heart sank. It had been a long time since I had allowed anyone into my heart, but Kisten...he was different. Kisten had been so lonely for so long, it was as if he didn't remember what it felt like to be loved by another person. I never went long without physical comfort, but before me was a man who had not touched another being in more than two centuries. I never questioned him about it, but I wanted to know why he had chosen to be by himself for so long.

"C'mon, Raiven, you need to get ready." Kisten's voice drew me from my thoughts and I watched as he checked his shirt for bloodstains. It dawned on me that he wasn't supposed to be at the Coven while LeAlexende was in town and I gave him a confused look.

"Actually, Kisten, why are you here? I thought yo–" I was interrupted by the door behind me slamming open, and I turned to see LeAlexende and Lucius bursting up the stairs, carrying someone between them. Lucius turned to look at us and relief flooded his eyes when he saw Kisten. It was then that I noticed the dark blue hair and the constant dripping blood from my friend's body.

"Kisten, it's Justina, she–" Lucius didn't get to finish as I scooped up my friend from the Overseers and rushed her into the backseat of Kisten's car, sliding in with her. Kisten quickly got into the driver's seat and gave a quick nod to Lucius, who simply nodded back. The other two moved to Lucius' car as Kisten peeled out of the parking lot and sped down the road. As he flew to make it to the hospital, I held Justina's hand tightly. She was still alive, but barely and I prayed that we would make it in time.

5

I waited impatiently in the waiting room with the two Overseers, unable to help my pacing. As soon as we arrived, the staff backed out of Kisten's way, allowing him to place Justina on an empty gurney. They recognized who Justina was immediately and merely rushed him off to surgery, allowing him to choose the doctor who assisted him.

She was badly torn up, almost as if she had been hacked by several blades or slashed many times by claws. All Lucius and LeAlexende could tell me was that they woke up to her screaming and when they tried to enter her room with Crispin, they found themselves unable to open the door. Finally, Crispin used his power to rip the door off its hinges and they found Justina in that state, barely conscious from blood loss. Lucius then ordered Crispin to remain behind and to check on the other spellcasters in the Coven, as well as enlist the help of his Fourth, Liel.

I called my boss as soon as Kisten took Justina into surgery and asked him to bring one of the agents with him to the hospital. Although not a perfect fit, the MO fit our current case a little too well for me to ignore it. I wanted to ask Justina what happened, but I knew that Brandon also needed to hear whatever she might have to say.

"What's the status, Raiven?" Brandon walked into the waiting room with Chris, one of our better agents, in tow. Lucius and Brandon exchanged a cursory nod before my boss turned back to me, doing his best to ignore the Overseer.

"Jus... The victim is currently in surgery. It's Justina, second to Lucius and a powerful...witch in her own right." I tried my best to remain calm and professional as I recounted what the Overseers had told me and Chris dutifully wrote it all down. Brandon sighed heavily after asking a few more questions of the pair, rubbing his temples as he groaned.

"I'll be honest, this is a breakthrough if it's related and she survives," he muttered, stretching his neck. "We've never had a survivor before, although I find it strange that she was alone. Usually, there are multiple people in a room before our suspect attacks, in order to claim as many victims as possible."

"That would be impossible inside the Coven," Lucius offered, and we turned to face him. "Never more than three to a room for extended periods of time, and larger groups must take place in open areas with no doors."

"Why such a rule?"

"Infighting, for one. That many different species in a small space can fuel some century-old tensions," I answered, crossing my arms across my chest as I spoke for Lucius. "But also because of Mo... Mater Vitae."

"You mean the one who made Supernaturals?" Brandon asked and I looked to Lucius to explain. Lucius gave me an exasperated glance before returning his attention to my boss. "What does she have to do with groups?"

"If too many Supernaturals gather at once, Mater Vitae can... manifest if she wants, due to all of us carrying her blood," Lucius explained cautiously and it was obvious from his tone that he didn't want to talk about it. "She... is not favorable to have around, so most Overseers have similar rules."

"Hmmm, explains why many of the murders included quite a number of humans..." Chris mused, flipping through his notebook. "But what role do Supernaturals play in his choice of victims? He doesn't seem to be going after a certain species, just numbers. But then, why would he go after Justina on her own?"

"Unless..." An idea started into my head and I didn't like where my thoughts were leading me. "They knew what she was and wanted to take her out first."

"What she was? She's a witch, isn't she?" Brandon gave me a strange look and Lucius' eyes lit up with worry. He almost seemed to be panicked, an expression I was not used to seeing on his face. LeAlexende gently touched his back, giving a friendly rub as the vampire spoke.

"No. No one could know that," he stammered and looked between his hands to the floor. It wasn't like Lucius to let his composure fall like that, but I understood his distress well. "We've never told anyone, no one knows except for members of the Coven."

"Know what?" Brandon asked again, clearly confused and getting frustrated as LeAlexende did his best to comfort his friend. I looked to Lucius for confirmation and he met my eyes with worry. I understood his concern, but I needed to explain everything to Brandon.

'*It could help us catch the one who did this.*' I mouthed to him behind my boss, not even trying to hide my anger. Brandon didn't know I was anything more than human, so I couldn't let him know that Lucius was anything more to me than a friend. However, as Justina's power was a Coven secret, I couldn't say it without permission. Lucius' brow furrowed but he nodded, covering his face with his hands again.

"Justina isn't a witch. She's a sorcerer," I started, breathing deeply, and Brandon and Chris looked at me, waiting for me to continue. "She can cast both without a wand and silently."

"Mental casting?" Chris exclaimed, both shocked and excited and a sharp look from me made him lower his voice. "But the implications of that are huge! Magic is shaped by the sound of a spellcasters' voice and focused through a medium. To be able to cast without doing that would change everything we know about them and–"

"Would make them more dangerous." Brandon nodded, deep in thought. "It makes sense that it would be kept a secret. I'd imagine other spellcasters would not welcome someone like that."

"No, sorcerers often hide their abilities," I answered softly. "But for our suspect to know that, means they must've known Justina before she came to The Capital. I've known Justina for a while and she told me and now, everyone in this room knows."

I shot a glare at Chris and the sullen look on his face and his uncomfortable gulp made it clear that my point had gotten across. I might have needed to share the information for the sake of finding her attacker, but I was not willing to put her life in danger if others found out what she was.

"So, if his plan was to take Justina out so she couldn't cast without him knowing," LeAlexende spoke, his voice soft as he contributed to the conversation. "Doesn't that mean that he hasn't actually committed his crime yet?"

"Shit, he's right!" Brandon cursed, starting to pace as I had done earlier. "Which means he is choosing his Supernatural victims to some extent... he has to be if he knows what they're capable of. That supports the elf theory, but god, that's a lot of work for a bugger like that."

"I'll get the rest of the team on conference and we'll go through each of the previous victims again with this new outlook. Maybe we can find something similar with the other killings before he tries to go for his actual kill." Brandon nodded to Chris and the agent turned to leave the waiting room. "You stay here and call me if she wakes up. Keep me updated on her progress. I don't want to press her if she makes it through, but... if she knew someone who could do this, we could finally stop this lunatic."

"I know." I nodded and Brandon rushed to join Chris, the two talking among themselves. Soon after my boss and coworker disappeared, Kisten came in, pushing Justina's bed into the waiting room. Kisten held the door open as they moved her into a proper room and closed the door as the other doctor went inside to finish getting her set up. As soon as we were alone, Lucius leapt to his feet, clearly worried.

"Kis—"

"She's alive." We all sighed with relief at his words and waited for him to continue. Kisten pulled his gloves off his hands, refusing to look at any of us. "But it is bad. We did what we could, gave her a transfusion, but whoever it was, they were clearly attempting to kill her. She's unlikely to wake up for a few days."

"But she's alive, and she'll survive?" Lucius asked cautiously, clearly preparing himself for a harsh response. Kisten sighed, running his hand through his dark hair as he hesitated with his answer. I wanted to hug him, to squeeze his hand and tell him he had done all that he could, but knew how impossible that was. Lucius walked towards the Alpha, his voice soft. "Kisten?"

"It depends on her. She suffered no major organ damage and it seems like she's been casting a healing spell on herself unconsciously, but considering her age..." Kisten admitted, dropping his hand back to his side as he shook his head. "We stitched up her large gashes and set her bones so that they heal properly, so—"

"Wait, she had broken bones?" I interrupted, my tone incredulous, and Kisten nodded, giving me a strange look.

"Yeah, both of her legs were broken as well..." I turned around to call my boss as Kisten watched me, confused. I heard Lucius explaining to him about my case as my phone rang and Brandon could barely squeeze out a hello before I interrupted him.

"Put me on the call," I demanded and resumed as soon as I could hear the background noise of my other co-workers. "She has broken bones. Both legs."

"Broken bones? Well, that kills the elf theory." My female coworker, Julia, sounded disappointed. "I mean, an elf killing a witch is ludicrous to begin with, but a cunning Dokkalfar could've pulled it off."

"Yeah, but neither Ljosalfar or Dokkalfar would have the inhuman strength needed to break a bone that quickly," Chris spoke, and it sounded like he was still writing on his notepad. I motioned for the two Overseers and Kisten to be silent and carefully put my phone on speaker. "Meaning there's really only two species who can both overcome a magic barrier spell and still possess inhuman strength to snap leg bones."

"Harpies and Cyclops, right?" Brandon offered and I noticed Kisten shook his head, holding up his index finger. I spoke quickly, looking at him, confused.

"Actually, there's one more." Kisten scrambled to the waiting room table and began to write something on one of the magazines. I could hear the disbelief of my colleagues as I waited to see what Kisten wanted to tell me.

"What? We ruled gargoyles out a long time ago and elves just got ruled out," another one of my teammates, Justin, spoke up. "If not harpies or cyclops, then what?"

Kisten finally finished his writing and the name caused a chill to run up my spine. I knew what they were, but I was uncomfortable saying the name out loud, and I understood why he didn't want to, either.

"An empousa." I whispered and the background noise grew deadly silent on both ends of the phone, no one daring to breathe after I said the word out loud. I almost expected Mater Vitae to appear right then, but luckily, no such thing happened as we waited. Quietly, Chris started to whisper on his end with Brandon.

"But... aren't they extinct? I thought they were wiped out by Hunters a long time ago."

"Even with the tell of a copper limb, it would be hard to be sure of that," Justin reasoned. "It is completely possible that a few could've survived and are in hiding to avoid Hunters."

"But records of empousa are scarce, we barely know anything about them and even if we knew more, it's not like any would be registered in our system." Brandon sighed heavily, clearly not happy. "Dammit, every clue we get sets us back more. Raiven, ask Lucius if there is anything he could tell us about these empousa, including if he ever knew any. Meanwhile, we'll keep looking into any connections the other victims could have with Justina. Knowing the species is good and all, but does us no good if we can't find the fucker."

"Will do." I agreed and waited until he hung up before turning to Lucius. He had an unreadable expression on his face and was looking away out the window. I moved to speak, but Kisten stopped me, shaking his head. He stared after Lucius with a painful look on his face and LeAlexende was also pensive.

"One of my former Retainers was an Empousa," Lucius breathed and a pit immediately formed in my stomach as I understood the implication. "But she wouldn't have known about Justina. She... was hunted long before I even crossed the sea. I–"

"Lucius." I stopped him, placing my hand on his shoulder. After a moment, he softly touched it, giving me a slight squeeze. "I'm sorry."

"It's alright, it was my own weakness that allowed Plumeria to be taken from me." Lucius' voice darkened as he continued. "We will not lose Justina to anyone."

"No, we won't," I agreed, stepping away as he released me. I turned back to face Kisten, who was still pensive. "I am more than a little concerned about our culprit possibly being an empousa. I won't say he doesn't have reason to want to attack other Supernaturals, but the Hunters wiped them out, not the community."

"Hunters were ordered by Mother to eradicate them, but they certainly had a lot of help from others," Kisten sighed, shaking his head as he took off his coat and I noticed the blood on his shirt. He must've started surgery before donning his coat; it was probably the other doctor who had forced him to wear it. He folded it over his arm as he continued. "Shapeshifters have always been treated poorly among Supernaturals. I'd imagine many of them were given up to the Hunters once Mother decided to eradicate them."

"But none of our victims have been known to work with Hunters, current or former," I remarked, and Kisten raised his eyebrows. I shrugged, folding my arms across my chest. "Just seemingly random, unless he's hunting those who are related to others who ratted out empousa to the Hunters."

"Then he would have no reason to be here," Lucius sneered,

clearly upset. "Most of my current Coven came after I crossed the sea. Beyond a few, none of them would've known about Plumeria."

"It's okay, Lucius. We'll figure this out." I spoke softly as he turned to face me, his expression still blank. "This is what I do. We didn't have a chance to prevent the other killings, but we won't allow him to kill on our own turf. This is as personal to my team as it is to us, trust me on that."

"I do," Lucius stated plainly, and LeAlexende sighed, finally turning our attention to him. He had remained silent during most of our exchange and I had almost forgotten he was with us. Lucius' expression changed, smiling wryly. "I'm sorry, Alex, but I must ask that you shorten your visit."

"Unnecessary, I'm here to help." LeAlexende's tone was strange as he turned to look at me, a soft smile still on his face. "Raiven, can you tell me where and when all the other killings occurred? I have connections to determine if an empousa was present in any of those areas."

"Connections?" I queried and he nodded, refusing to say more. I was suspicious, but Lucius nodded and gave me a silent order. I knew better than to argue and merely turned to Kisten. "Do you have anywhere I can get actual paper?"

"Yeah, follow me." As I followed Kisten out of the waiting room, I could hear the two friends whispering behind us.

6

"What do you make of this, Kisten?" I leaned back in his chair as I finished writing down the list LeAlexende had asked for. Kisten had taken me to his office, which was down the hallway from Justina's room. The office was pristine and immaculate, not a single paper or pen out of place. It reflected the personality that Kisten projected so perfectly: calm, clean and under control.

Kisten remained quiet and seemed to be deep in thought; He had barely moved as I finished writing my list, staring at one of the many charts in his office. I sighed at his lack of a response, allowing myself to spring forward in the office chair.

"That something still isn't right," he spoke, shaking his head and surprising me with his voice. "It's too convenient. Empousas were hunted centuries ago, so if your suspect was an empousa, why risk exposure like this? And why include humans at all, why not just kill individual Supernaturals? Why kill so many if they aren't the target?"

"I know, and you're not wrong. That's been the whole problem with this case." I closed my eyes, thinking of the previous crime scene. A high school gym, the scene of a prom gone horribly wrong. I still remembered walking into the side room where the murders took place and a shiver ran through me. "It would be incredibly risky and stupid, but if they are a new generation who wasn't adequately taught about Mother, they might try something like this because they can."

"It just seems unlikely it would be an empousa."

"I get that, but then who and why?" I leaned forward on his desk, cradling my head. "It's been my biggest headache. There's no obvious motive, nothing that strings all these victims together. Brandon said it best: the more we learn, the less this all makes sense. Every new crime kills any previous theory."

"So, an empousa is your best lead at the moment." Kisten leaned against his desk and I stood, touching his arm. He absently placed his hand on mine, sighing again. "I don't like this. It feels like we're missing the writing on the wall."

"Don't I know it." I stepped closer to him, releasing his arm, and reaching for his face. He instinctively stopped me, grabbing my wrist without even looking up to me. I grunted, annoyed by his reaction.

"You know you can't." He closed his eyes, refusing to look at me. His grip on my hand tightened for a moment before he relaxed his hold. "I can't keep giving in to–"

"Please," I pleaded, and Kisten looked up to see my face. As our eyes met, I could finally see just how hard this was on him and Kisten's worry for both Justina and Lucius was plain on his face. He once told me that Lucius was like a quiet beehive: if you left it alone and didn't try to knock it over, everything was fine. However, the moment a member of the colony was hurt, the whole swarm would never leave you alone until you paid for your crime.

Kisten slowly released my hand, and I softly touched his face, at first only allowing my fingertips to touch his skin. Even with such a soft gesture, Kisten purred slightly and leaned into my hand, clearly showing how much he craved my touch. My chest ached at the sight of my skin against his; the contrast of my dark skin against his tan complexion always made my heart skip a beat.

Taking a deep breath, I placed my whole hand against his cheek and as he sighed his contentment, I hissed with pain. My whole hand felt like it was burning and the longer I held my hand to his face, the more my body screamed with pain. It traveled down my arm and I pulled it away as the heat reached my chest. I held my aching arm and Kisten quickly grabbed my shoulder, causing me to wince. He loosened his grip, lightly stroking my short sleeve.

"Are you alright? It didn't hurt too badly?" I shook my head as I forced a smile, releasing my still aching arm. He looked at me with concern and my heart began pounding in my chest.

"I'm fine, Kisten. I just wanted to give you some comfort." I smiled as I looked into his eyes and I reached up to touch his face again. This time, he grabbed my arm, stopping me long before I could touch his skin.

"Don't tempt me like this, Raiven," he pleaded, his voice high-pitched as he closed his eyes. My heart pounded from his words, but I remained silent. He slowly opened his eyes, turning his gloomy gaze to me. "I don't want to hurt you anymore."

"You're not, the Oath is," I scoffed, pulling my arm away and Kisten looked as if he wanted to reach for me, but he stopped himself. I reached for him instead, hugging him tightly as I kept my arms on his shirt. He grew still under my touch before gently wrapping his arms around me, careful not to touch my bare skin. I dropped my head into his chest, sighing heavily with my frustration. "It isn't your fault and I would never blame you."

"It *is* my fault," Kisten leaned down, careful to lay his head on my shoulder and to avoid touching my neck. This was as intimate as he would allow us to get and the most he had touched me in more than a year. Any more, and the Oath of Loyalty would ensure that I paid the price. "I should've had Lucius release me from the Oath a long time ago."

"Why didn't you?" I asked tentatively, my voice soft and quiet. Kisten grew still again, and I regretted my question as we remained in silence for a long time, holding each other. I tightened my grip around him and after a moment, he sighed, returning my gesture.

"It didn't matter to me at the time," he spoke softly and slowly, his breath warm against my skin. I felt my heart pound, moving into my throat as he leaned into me more, almost standing from his desk. "I... never thought I'd find someone I wanted like this."

"You mean you've never been with anyone?" I pushed him back, looking at him incredulously. He looked away from me, slightly blushing and I couldn't help the accusing smile that started on my face. "Kisten, you're over three hundred years old, and you're telling me you've never been with anyone?"

"It's not like I never wanted to," he retorted, still blushing at my teasing and I let out a small giggle at his reaction. It faded when he turned to face me, his eyes filled with loss. "I just... couldn't ever be with them and I... gave up when they finally died. I felt like *I* had died."

"I-I'm sorry, Kisten." I started to pull away from him, but he kept his arms wrapped around me, still careful not to touch my skin. I could feel his breath against my face and for a moment, I thought he was going to kiss me and despite how painful I knew it would be, my heart pounded at the thought. Instead, I felt him dig his hands into my side, pulling at the fabric of my shirt.

"Don't be," he whispered, his breath hot and heavy as he breathed his words against my skin, allowing his breath to caress me. His hands gripped me tightly through my clothing and I was slightly surprised by his actions. Kisten always maintained an incredibly careful and calm demeanor, always distancing himself from me when he thought he was losing control. He growled softly, his voice sounding animalistic. "You're all that I want now."

A sudden knock at his door made him release me, and we quickly pulled away from each other. Kisten closed his eyes for a moment as I tried to smooth out my shirt. The shifter adjusted himself, settling into a more comfortable position against his desk.

"Come in," he called out and the door opened to LeAlexende, who quietly stepped into the office. The Overseer had a solemn expression, still perturbed by what he had witnessed at the Coven. He closed the door slowly, still lost in thought as he looked at the floor.

"Is your list ready?" LeAlexende slowly looked up, carefully glancing between me and Kisten. It was clear he suspected something from the look he finally gave me and, clearing my throat, I reached to the desk and handed him the paper.

"Yes, it is. All the known killings that have been attributed to our suspect and their locations." I said as he glanced it over, nodding as he folded it. "I hope it's useful."

"Me too. I'll start as soon as I get settled in Justina's room." Kisten nodded solemnly at the Overseer's words. "Lucius has asked that I remain to watch her while I reach out to my contacts. I will give both of you a call if and when her condition changes."

"Thank you, LeAlexende. For everything." Kisten bowed his head to the Overseer, and after a moment, I followed. LeAlexende merely smiled as he waved us off, his expression somewhat like his previous cheery nature.

"You and Lucius are good friends of mine. This is just as personal to me as it is to you," I gave Kisten a questioning look as the Overseer turned to leave, but he either didn't notice or was ignoring me. LeAlexende paused in the doorway, barely glancing over his shoulder to talk to us. "Oh, by the way, Lucius wants all of the Coven in pairs from now on. You two are to stay together at all times, at least until the culprit is caught."

Both Kisten and I stood shocked as LeAlexende made his way out, closing the door behind him. My heart was pounding as I stared at the closed door, my mind still trying to process what I had heard. Slowly, we turned to look at each other before Kisten bolted to his door, walking out of it with me shortly behind. Kisten walked up to Lucius just as Eve walked out of the elevator into the waiting room.

"Lucius," Kisten called his name plainly, and Lucius turned to face us as Eve settled herself in his lap. Eve shot both of us an angry glance before snuggling up to Lucius and, as usual, her display made me want to gag. Kisten ignored Eve entirely as he continued speaking. "Why am I paired with Raiven? Wouldn't it make more sense for me to be with you? Or even Evalyn?"

"Eve will be with me," Lucius stated matter-of-factly, wrapping his arm around his Retainer. It wasn't uncommon for Overseers to be romantically involved with their Retainer or Alpha, or both in some cases. Despite most of the Coven disliking her, we had no choice but to accept Lucius' decision until she died, or he replaced her. "There isn't anyone else I can pair you with, power-wise. Liel and Crispin are paired, I have Aurel with Grace and Yoreile is with Quinn. Everyone else is out of the area and–"

"Problem, Kisten?" Eve asked innocently and both Lucius and Kisten glared at her. Evalyn went out of her way to try and make Kisten miserable, jealous of his long friendship with Lucius. She lacked the understanding that the two weren't involved romantically in any way and continued to perceive him as a rival. Like her jealousy of me, Eve was excellent at overlooking the obvious if she felt someone was standing in her way. "I didn't think you had anything against her."

"I... don't, but..." Kisten stopped himself, holding his head in his hands as I remained silent, since I understood why he didn't want to be paired with me. Kisten had spent the better part of a year keeping me at arm's length, making sure he wouldn't lose his precious control. He took a deep breath as he chose his next words carefully. "I'm not allowed at the Coven. I was only stopping by today because you asked me to prepare dinner. You ordered Raiven to stay."

"Raiven is only as bound as she wants to be." Lucius spoke nonchalantly, Eve leaning her head against his shoulder. "Besides, I'm now ordering her to stay by your side. She'll just have to stay at your house."

My heart was pounding so loud, I could barely feel the order as it passed through me. Stuck at his house, always required to be in the same space as him: it sounded like torture of the cruelest kind! I could barely stand being alone with him for a few hours before I wanted to embrace him, much less days. Kisten certainly knew this, as he continued to argue until Lucius stopped him.

"I've made my decision, Kisten," Lucius narrowed his blue eyes, his hair bristling slightly as he grew annoyed. "Despite my faith in your and Raiven's power, I will not risk having either of you alone.

Now, unless you can give me a *valid* reason as to why you cannot be with Raiven, this conversation is over."

Kisten stopped, seeing he could not talk Lucius out of this without telling the truth. He stood still for a moment, and I held my breath, waiting to see what he would do. Finally, he dropped his shoulders, taking a deep breath before turning to face me.

"I'll be right back, then we can go," he muttered, walking past me back down to his office. I was slightly surprised that he wasn't honest; I'd imagine if Eve hadn't been there, he might have been. I was torn between whether I was supposed to follow him or stay, when Lucius called my name.

"Raiven, please." I turned to face him, his cool eyes on me as he stroked Eve's side, my heart aching as I watched. When he spoke again, I forced myself to look away from his hand and to his face. "Take care of him. He won't admit it, but he's not as happy being alone as he says."

Don't I know it. I merely nodded as Kisten returned and walked past me without saying a word. I gave Lucius one final glance as I hurried after him, barely making it to the elevator before the door closed.

7

I silently stared out the window as we drove out of Decver, watching the sky as the sun set beyond the horizon as I sent my text to my pet sitter, asking her to watch my cats for a few more days. As usual, she was more than willing to watch my babies and I hummed softly as I laid my phone in my lap. Kisten was silent and kept his eyes on the road, refusing to even look at me. I knew he was thinking the same thing as me: how long could we deal with this before we both went insane?

My desire for Kisten had been purely physical when we first met; he simply was attractive to me. Dark hair, mysterious eyes, longevity and a cool demeanor that just begged to be broken down. After he told me that he was still bound to Lucius and Eve via the Oath, I had tried to just be his friend after seeing how miserable he truly was. Kisten always kept to himself unless he was needed and didn't really go anywhere for fun.

The more time we had spent trying to be friends, however, the more I started to fall for him. Underneath all that careful control was a man who wanted to let go and enjoy life and I felt special that he allowed me to be a part of that. However, after realizing how badly the Oath could hurt me, Kisten started avoiding me, only interacting with me when he had to, just like he did with everyone else.

It also made sense why Lucius would pair us: as far as he knew, we were still friends and he had always approved of my friendship with Kisten. It sometimes seemed as if he was trying to push us into a relationship, with the way he set up some of our hangouts. He had been surprised when we suddenly stopped and I merely told him that Kisten wanted some space, leaving it at that.

"I don't have much at home," Kisten suddenly spoke, his hands gripping the wheel tightly as his words pulled me from my thoughts. I only continued to watch him in the window's reflection and didn't turn to look at his face. He glanced at me before returning his attention to the road, his tone tentative. "Raiven?"

"I heard you." I sighed, closing my eyes. "You know I don't care. You never have much at home."

"Okay," he stopped talking and returned his attention to driving with my curt answer. We sat in silence for a moment longer before he spoke again, his voice barely above a whisper. "Are you gonna be okay with this?"

"I'm much more worried about you," I admitted, leaning back in my seat as I laid it all the way back. I opened my eyes to stare at the roof of the car, frowning slightly. "You're the one who started avoiding me, remember?"

"It's not like I wanted to. But the Oath..." His voice trailed off as he considered his next words and I sighed heavily, closing my eyes. When he spoke again, his voice was quiet as he took his exit off the highway, leaning back as he stopped at the light. "It's not like I didn't miss you."

"I missed you too," I admitted, my heart aching as the light changed. I paused, opening my eyes to watch the trees fly by the window as we drove closer to his residence. My voice was barely above a whisper when I spoke again, filled with my longing. "Every time I have to see other people being happy together, I miss you."

"At least I wasn't the only one," he laughed slightly, moving his hand to touch my leg. Halfway through the movement, it was almost as if he realized what he was doing and he stopped himself, his hand hovering awkwardly. I looked down as he pulled his hand back to the wheel, clearing his throat. It was another long moment before he spoke, turning into his neighborhood. "I just don't want to hurt you, Raiven."

"Like I said earlier, you never have. That's all the Oath's doing, and well..." I paused as he pulled into his driveway, backing his car into the garage as it opened. "If you want to be technical, we both know whose fault that is."

"Mater Vitae?"

"Her too." I let my seat up and unbuckled myself as he turned off the car. Deep in my mind, I blamed Mother for everything that happened and most Supernaturals did. She created us, bound us all to her with her blood, and then placed us in a world where, until recently, we were hated, feared, and killed. Now, as far as most of us knew, she was hidden, protected by her loyal Hunters. Fairies were her last creation before most of us denounced her and shortly after, she retreated, although no one knows why or where. I had my own suspicions as to why, but I had no interest in trying to confirm them.

Kisten unlocked his door and bolted inside his house as I took my time noticing the changes he had made to the garage. I hadn't been in his house during the past year and unsurprisingly, there were hardly any changes. Kisten only occasionally updated his home and hadn't moved from this plot of land since he and Lucius arrived back in the 1800s. He had the garage added shortly before I came to Decver, and only did so because of the city complaining about the state of his driveway.

As such, the inside of his house always had an air of nostalgia and I breathed it in as I stepped inside. Kisten was busy closing his curtains and turning on lights, clearly not expecting to have been gone all afternoon. I leaned in the doorway, watching him as he moved about, starting to notice certain changes about him. Kisten's hair was slightly longer than usual, as it was starting to reach his shoulders. He also seemed to have gained a little weight, filling out his shirt a little better than I remembered. While an amazing cook,

Kisten only ate enough to stay alive and rarely ate for pleasure, meaning his weight gain was probably muscle.

"Uh, Raiven?" I shook my head as Kisten moved in front of me, a worried look on his face. I looked up to him, slightly embarrassed.

"Huh?"

"I asked if you were hungry." He leaned down close to me, taking in my scent. His eyes shone when he pulled back to look at me again. "You don't smell like you've eaten today."

"You know I don't like it when you do that," I huffed, walking past him to the couch.

Kisten chuckled as he walked into the kitchen, examining what little food he had. He pulled out some ingredients as I switched on his TV, turning to some cartoons. I was barely paying attention, however, my mind returning to Justina as I removed my shoes. I couldn't shake the thought that I knew for certain what could cause wounds like that and the answer was evading me. I closed my eyes as I lay down, seeing Justina's wounded body as I held her in my lap. Large gashes as if ripped open by claws, but somehow all avoiding vital areas. Was Justina attempting to defend herself and that's why they broke her legs?

"Why not just kill her, though?" I wondered out loud, looking up to the roof. Spellcasters weren't difficult to kill: their lifespans were only slightly longer than humans and, besides their use of magic, anything that could kill a human would kill a spellcaster. "To torture her? But why? No one else was—"

"Food's ready." The delicious smell wafted towards me as I sat up, looking toward Kisten in the kitchen. He was portioning food on a plate as I wandered up to him and sat at his breakfast bar. He slid a plate with the appetizing food in front of me: it was some sort of chicken and pasta and one bite confirmed my suspicions. My hunger consumed me and I wolfed down the food with all the vigor of a starving animal. Kisten laughed as he watched, leaning on the counter.

"There's more if you want." He nodded to the skillet and I paused in my eating, slightly embarrassed by my behavior.

"You aren't going to eat?"

"Not hungry. I hunted yesterday." Kisten tapped his hand on the counter, smiling at me. Kisten's nearest neighbors were miles away and a decent stretch of woods separated them all. Sometimes Kisten would hunt in the woods, helping himself to any prey he could find. He said it helped to keep his animal in check, and he encouraged all the predator shifters to do so, allowing them to come over whenever they wanted to indulge their animal. Sometimes he would go with the newbies to help them, but he often let them figure it out for themselves.

"You're a good Alpha." I commented, smiling as I took my time finishing my food. His smile broadened slightly at that, and he reached for my free hand. I let him take it and winced as he started stroking the back of my hand, feeling the skin burning slightly. Kisten must've noticed as he quickly released me, standing up from the counter.

"I'll be right ba—"

"Don't go," I choked out, trying to swallow my food so I could stop him. He paused in his movement, leaning against the counter on the opposite side of the kitchen. He was looking away from me, not turning to my gaze as I coughed to clear my throat of food. "It didn't hurt that much. Just unexpected. Usually, just touching my hands doesn't hurt."

"Intentions matter." Kisten sighed, running his hand through his hair as he finally turned around. "Whether I want to be intimate matters."

"Want to be..." I let the sentence trail, keeping my eyes on Kisten as I finished eating. He was still refusing to look at me, keeping his eyes to the floor. He had started to unbutton his shirt while cooking and I could see the hair on his chest, lighter in color than the dark brown waves that graced his crown. Kisten looked so majestic in his simple dress clothes, hiding the passion I knew he kept under lock and key. I finished my food, continuing to undress him with my eyes.

"You want to be intimate, huh?" I purred, standing up as I carried my empty plate into the kitchen. I reached around him to drop the dish into the sink, sliding my bandaged hand around his waist.

"Raiven..." Kisten looked at me as if he feared my intentions, and I smiled, wrapping my other arm around him. Kisten seemed torn between returning my gesture and pulling away, before finally settling on lightly touching my shoulders, careful to stay on clothing. I gripped his shirt tighter, pressing myself into him. I earned myself a soft gasp of surprise and I smiled coyly, looking up to his face.

"Yes, Kisten?" I asked, pressing my body more into his as several expressions passed through his beautiful features. As much as I found Kisten's control attractive, I wanted him to let go. I wanted to see the passion he had only let me experience sparingly, just enough to make me want more.

"Raiven don't do this," he pleaded, his hands digging into my shoulders as he fought himself. I smiled, burying my face into his chest. Ignoring his plea. I pressed my leg between his, and I could feel him as he started to become aroused. He was looking for a way to escape me, but his own desire betrayed him as he kept his grip on my shoulders. My own desire began to grow as I slid my hands up his back and dug my fingers into his skin.

He gasped at the movement and without thinking, he grabbed my chin and slid his mouth across mine. My lips and mouth exploded with fire as he kissed me deeply, forcing his tongue into my mouth. Despite the pain, I felt heat growing in another part of my body and I returned the gesture, sliding my tongue against his as the scalding heat consumed my face. It was as if my skin would burst into flames if the kiss continued, but Kisten pulled back, panting heavily. I was also breathing heavily, touching my lips as the heat began to fade.

"Are you alright?"

"Yeah." I smiled, wincing slightly as I dropped my hand back to his waist. Kisten had a dark look on his face, his chartreuse eyes swirling. His devilish expression reminded me more of Crispin, but on him, it only excited me. Kisten moved his hands from my shoulder to my waist, a smirk on his face.

"Good." With this, he kissed me again and I moaned with both pain and desire. It felt as if he were literally setting me on fire with his touch and it excited me as much as it hurt. I could feel his fingers as he fumbled at my shirt and searing pain followed his hand as he touched my back. I merely clung to him as he stroked me, indulging in his own desires.

It was clear his control was fading as Kisten pulled back again, his fangs visible in his mouth as he panted. I took this moment to free myself of him, leaning against the breakfast bar across from him. Kisten made as if he was going to follow me, but gripped the sink behind him, attempting to restrain himself. Both of us were panting as we watched the other, and I smiled, despite the ache left from his touch and his kiss.

"Gods, Kisten, keep this up and you'll make me a masochist." I breathed, my smile broadening. Kisten merely growled in response, and I felt a clench in my lower regions. We had barely been alone together an hour, and this is where we were, panting on opposite sides of his kitchen. Neither of us was sure if the Oath would kill me or just make me wish I were dead, but I had stopped caring about that more than a year ago.

"Raiven, I can smell you." Kisten growled, almost as if he were in pain and I grew worried as I saw fur start to sprout on his arms and quickly recede into his skin. I couldn't fathom that Kisten was losing control of his animal: he was far too experienced to lose control like this. "I can smell how wet you are, and it makes me want you more."

I shifted uncomfortably as he said this, looking away and trying to calm myself down. I hated it when Kisten mentioned my own scents to me: it always made me feel dirty and transparent. Kisten laughed darkly at my attempts to calm down and I turned away from him completely, facing the breakfast bar. This turned out to be a mistake as I soon saw Kisten's hands on the counter next to mine, and he pressed himself into me, now fully aroused and making me aware of it. I didn't try to hide my moan as he ground himself against me, leaning down to breathe in my scent.

"My animal wants you," he growled into my ear, and I couldn't help but shudder against him. He lightly dragged his teeth against my skin, careful to avoid scratching me with his fangs and his spots appeared faintly on his hands, despite the lack of fur. Smelling my desire, my lust for him was finally sending his animal over the edge, and probably for the first time in a long time, he was losing control. "*I* want you."

"Now who's not being fair, Kisten?" I moaned halfheartedly, doing my best not to push myself against him. Kisten, however, did not care for my restraint and grabbed my hips, thrusting me into the counter. I moaned loudly, dragging my nails against the marble as the shifter behind me repeated his action, loosely grabbing my neck and lifting my head up. He slid his other hand down the front of my body, pressing into my stomach.

"I don't care. I haven't cared for a long time," he whispered darkly into my ear, and even through our clothing, I could feel his arousal throbbing, and it caused me to clench in response. His burning grip on my throat tightened for a moment, and Kisten growled into my skin. "I know you don't, either."

He reached under my shirt again, sliding his free hand up to my breasts. Even through the bra, intense heat danced across my skin as he fondled me and he growled again, kissing my neck as he played with me. His nails began growing into claws and I gave into my moans, not even trying to hide my pleasure from him. This is what I had wanted: for Kisten to give in to me, to give into his desires…

I opened my eyes, having a moment of clarity despite the pain and pleasure. This wasn't Kisten giving in to himself. This was him giving in to his animal and I knew that Kisten would regret it if it went much further. I did my best to hold back my moans and fought to find my voice.

"You're right, I don't," I breathed, trying to do everything to not focus on his breath on my neck and his member throbbing against my back. "But I also don't want you to regret loving me tomorrow."

Kisten stiffened for a moment, his hands relaxing their grip before he released me altogether. His hands reappeared on the counter and it was clear he was trying to rein in the beast. His hands slowly shifted back to being human, and his spots faded, but remained slightly visible on his skin. His throbbing member against my back betrayed where his desires lay, but he was at least trying to regain control of his lust.

Hesitantly, I leaned back against him and he did his best to hold me gently this time, wrapping his arms around my middle. He took a deep breath and released it shakily, burying his face into my short afro. I considered pulling away from him completely, but instead, I gently touched his arm, before carefully resting my arms on his, my skin burning where we touched.

"You're right. I would regret it if this..." Kisten spoke, his voice still containing a slight growl. "I... wouldn't want my first time with you to be like this, with my animal controlling me."

"I won't say it's not hot though." I laughed softly and he chuckled, the sound vibrating in his chest behind me. "Something different."

"You don't have to tell me that," he postured, nibbling on my ear and causing a slight burning sensation there. He leaned down again, licking my earlobe before whispering into it. "I can still smell how much you want me."

"Kisten," I whined, closing my eyes in embarrassment. He laughed again, pressing kisses into the back of my neck, each one a burning sensation of pleasure and pain.

"You say you hate it, but I love it. I love knowing exactly how much you want me." He spoke in between his kisses, slowly sliding one of his hands under my shirt again. The pain that seared across my middle section almost outweighed the pleasurable sensation, but just knowing that he was touching me, that it was Kisten's hand on my skin, made me love the feeling. "How much the pain isn't bothering you. Should've told me how much you loved it."

"I think someone is turning into a sadist," I teased, reaching my bandaged hand up to stroke his face, my fingers burning as they touched his skin. He removed his hand from under my shirt and I was both disappointed and relieved. Suddenly, I was lifted into the air and I reached to grab Kisten as he lifted me up and walked towards his couch. He turned off the television and climbed on top of me, settling between my legs. I fully expected him to drop on top of me, but he remained on his knees, keeping my legs spread with his hands. I reached up to him, laying my hands on his. "Where was this lack of control a year ago?"

"This is all your fault. All your teasing touches, always wanting me, despite me doing my best to stay away. It was only a matter of time before you would win." His eyes swirled again, and I could still see his fangs as he smiled a toothy smile. He lifted my leg to his shoulder, kissing my thigh through the pants. "I could smell it every time, Raiven and it always took so much to walk away. Even now, it's taking all my control not to just take you."

"You call this restraint?" I pulled my hands back, placing them under my head as Kisten laughed again. He laid another kiss on my pants, squeezing my thigh tightly. He leaned down, letting my leg rest on his shoulder as he slid his hands toward my waist.

"I call it compromise." With this, Kisten leaned over, carefully reaching to undo my pants and release me from them. I couldn't help but tense up slightly, but Kisten lightly kissed my exposed thigh before removing the offensive clothing entirely. "Don't worry, I won't undress you more than this."

Before I could question him, I found my lower half being lifted up and Kisten had his face buried in between my legs, breathing in my scent as his hands were carefully placed on my underwear. I couldn't help but be embarrassed as he breathed me in, and I covered my face as he sighed happily. A long, wet lick told me of his intentions, and I moaned slightly, peeking through my arms to look up at him. He had his eyes closed, licking me through my underwear and enjoying both my taste and scent. I still could experience small flashes of heat despite the clothing separating his tongue from me but these small flashes only added to my pleasure. I moaned freely as Kisten enjoyed his treat, keeping my underwear between us as he indulged himself as much as he dared.

8

I woke up the next morning not sure where I was as sunlight streamed on my face. Something on the bed shifted and I finally recognized the dark brown hair that graced the pillow next to me. I smiled, passing his hair between my fingers and pressing my face into him, my body still aching from the torture it had been submitted to.

"That tickles, Raiven." Kisten mumbled, shifting on the bed as he tried to pull away. I giggled, releasing him as I realized I was wearing a dark red shirt and underwear, different from the blue I had passed out wearing.

"It's not my fault you have beautiful hair," I sat up, looking around for my clothing and my pants. A frown started on my face as I failed to find them, and I shook Kisten gently. "Kisten, what did you do with my clothes?"

"They're in the hamper," he yawned, stretching out like a cat on the bed and his toes curling as the sheet shifted down. He opened his eyes and pointed to the small hamper that was overflowing with dirty clothes. "I didn't want to leave you in soiled clothing, so I managed to find some clothes you had left here. It's getting cold outside, so I tried to choose something warm."

"Okay, but what about my pants?"

Kisten groaned as he motioned towards a chair in the corner, with my pants laid neatly across it. I fell back down, yawning loudly as I tried to finish waking up. Kisten was shirtless but was still wearing pants as he lay next to me, fighting a yawn of his own. I didn't remember him ever taking off his shirt, but from the lingering sensation on my arms, I had a suspicion that he had fallen asleep holding me.

I kissed his hair again as I stood out of the bed, surprised by how refreshed my body seemed. My body felt looser and more limber, despite the ache from the pain. I stretched toward the roof, curling my fingers in the air.

"Do you have anything to do today?" I turned around on hearing Kisten's voice and he was lying on the pillow, watching me as I stretched. I looked away, considering what my next steps would be. I wanted to search for Justina's assaulter, but I still didn't have much information to go on. There wasn't much I could do without visiting the office, but having to take Kisten with me would cause too many questions that I didn't want to have to answer.

"I haven't decided," I admitted, sitting back down on the bed, and Kisten shifted behind me, his arms appearing around my stomach. I hummed happily, stroking his arm despite the pain to my hand. "I'm tempted to go to the Coven to check out Justina's room and see the scene for myself. But I can't exactly take you to the office with me."

"Well, I'm supposed to go visit one of the newbies who's having trouble shifting and there was a merfolk who is having issues with her pool and wanted help recalibrating it." He sighed, echoing my hum of contentment. "We could swing by the Coven, then you could join me in helping the pup, and I can drop you off at the hospital while I help the other shifter. I need to check in on Justina and remove your stitches. If you need to go to work, I can drop you off after that."

"So eager to have me break Lucius' order, huh?" I laughed and

Kisten chuckled slightly as he squeezed me. "What happened to having to follow orders?"

"You're only as bound as you want to be, remember?" Kisten laughed, echoing the Overseer's words. "But if that sounds good to you, we should leave soon."

"Sounds good." A faint kiss on my back and I felt the bed move as Kisten stood up and moved to his closet to dress. He peeled off his dress pants and changed into a pair of jeans and a plain green t-shirt. I was surprised Kisten owned such clothing as I had never seen him wear anything so normal before. I slowly stood up and slipped on my own pants as Kisten slid on a simple pair of boots. I glanced around for my shoes, remembering I had taken them off next to the couch.

I started out of Kisten's room when a strong hand grabbed my arm and pulled me against him. He was standing in front of his mirror and looking at us together, holding me tightly against him. Kisten's eyes were looking at me lovingly, and he gently buried his face in my neck, sighing happily. I couldn't help but smile at his immature gesture, and I sighed as well, loving the feel of his arms around me. My thoughts turned to the previous night, and I couldn't help the clench in my middle as I remember the torture Kisten had subjected me to. The man in question looked up, his eyes darkening as he caught the change in my scent.

"Here I am being sweet and *someone* is thinking dirty thoughts," he whispered darkly, his eyes still locked with mine through the glass as he grinned. I cleared my throat as my face flushed and freed myself from his embrace. He allowed me to go, his hands lingering as I slid from him.

"Maybe we should leave before we're stuck in this house all day." I mumbled, escaping down the stairs and could hear Kisten's laugh behind me as he followed, his feet heavy on each step. Somehow, hearing his slow steps down the stairs only served to arouse me more and I almost ran into the living room to try to escape my own thoughts.

"You make it sound like you don't want that," his deepening voice followed me down the stairs as I sat on his couch to slide on my boots. Kisten walked into the kitchen, retrieving his keys from the counter as he chuckled to himself over my embarrassment. I stood up to find Kisten standing over me, and he stole a kiss, burning my lips with his indulgence. "Your body says otherwise."

"Don't we have somewhere to be?" I tried to escape him, walking around the couch away from him, but Kisten stopped me, pinning me against the back of the couch. I leaned back as he leaned into me, chuckling. "Kisten, c'mon."

"What? Aren't you the one who started this last night?" He laughed, leaning down and breathing against my neck. There was no sign of his spots or fangs, so this was him acting without the influence of his animal. Kisten's eyes burned and I had to fight the smile that wanted to creep on my face. "Not up for finishing what you started?"

"I thought you did that." I pouted, closing my eyes as he licked my neck. The trail of fire left by his tongue was starting to excite me and I did my best to ignore the heat growing elsewhere in my body.

"I finished what *I* started," he corrected me, taking my hand and pressing it to his groin, allowing me to feel his throbbing member beneath the fabric. I inhaled sharply and I couldn't help but stroke him and earn myself a soft moan. My whole body ached with the thought and desire to have him love me, but I knew the Oath made such a thing impossible. There was a chance we could find a way around it, just as Kisten had the night before, but we also had more important tasks than finding a way around his Oath.

"Let's continue this tonight," I breathed, trying to be a voice of reason in the madness of our passion as I pulled away. Kisten growled in response, and I stroked his cheek, my wrists growing weak from the pain. "Work first, play later. Trust me, I've been wanting this from you for over a year, and I don't want to risk you changing your mind."

Kisten considered my words, closing his eyes and standing away from me. By the time he reopened his eyes, they were back to normal and he smiled softly at me. His grin still held darker things as he turned away from me, jingling his keys in his hand. I followed the

Alpha into the garage as he unlocked the doors and I slid quietly into the passenger seat. Kisten also climbed in without making a sound and started up his car, the electric engine practically silent compared to my noisy guzzler.

I watched the scenery fly past us as he drove us back into the city, my thoughts heavy with a new fear as he drove. I had already seen the true extent of Justina's injuries, and I was worried what the scene would look like for her to be injured so badly. My thoughts were in such turmoil that I barely noticed as Kisten pulled into the parking lot behind The Dream and was only brought to the present when the shifter lightly touched my shoulder.

"We're here." He offered and I slowly climbed out of the car, my hand lingering on the door as I looked toward the Coven's entrance. I closed the car door and began to walk to the simple entrance, each footstep heavy as I forced myself forward. I threw the door open, the sound of it banging the wall reminding me of Aurel's anger the day before. I looked past the barrier into the encroaching darkness and I paused, unsure in my movements. Justina was usually the one who maintained the barrier protecting the Coven, so I could only imagine Yoreile was doing it in her place.

"Are you okay, Raiven?" Once again, Kisten's voice drew me from my thoughts and I glanced back towards him. He was leaning against his car, a worried expression on his face and he pushed himself away from the vehicle as he walked towards me. I took a deep breath, turning to face the dark Coven stairs once again.

"I'm fine," I insisted, passing through the barrier and climbing down the dark stairwell as my eyes slowly adjusted. The hallway grew darker as Kisten closed the door behind us and I reached the last step, bypassing the living room on my way to Justina's room. I could see the outlines of Quinn and Yoreile as they stood guard over the scene, both quietly talking amongst themselves. Lucius always took protecting crime scenes very seriously, and I wasn't surprised that he was treating this case no differently.

"It's just me," I announced my presence as I saw Quinn tense, the wraith's red eyes glowing as he summoned his power. Upon recognizing me, he released it, giving me a tired smile. Yoreile remained silent, not turning as Kisten and I approached. "I'm just here to see the scene as an agent, not as a Coven member."

"Go ahead," Yoreile whispered, still barely paying any attention to me as I stood in front of him. I slowly pushed the door open and had to immediately cover my mouth from the display and smell. Her room was barely recognizable: it was as if a hurricane had rampaged through the space and the amount of damage seemed unnecessary to kill a single person. There were various scratches and marks in the walls and overturned furniture, along with several dried splashes of blood and the obvious puddle from where the Overseers had found her sitting.

"If I wasn't sure before, I am now." I muttered, forcing myself to enter her room and examined the damage more closely. Kisten remained in the doorway behind me, keeping his distance as I squatted next to the dried puddle of blood. "This is the same killer."

"What gives it away?"

"The spread of the damage. The blood. It looks just like all the other scenes." I motioned to the destroyed room as I stood. "If anyone else had been in here, they would've been killed. Honestly, from this amount of damage to the room, it's miraculous that Justina survived at all. This attack was violent and fast, and it must've taken all her strength to avoid getting killed..."

My voice faded as I considered what I had said, my eyes looking to the overturned bed where it now sat against the far wall. There was no way a random supernatural did this: it had to be someone who knew who and what Justina was, and had every intention of killing her for it. Justina had a temper and it often came back to bite her, but she never picked undeserved fights or ones she couldn't win.

"Are... are you done, or..." Kisten's voice trailed off as he looked away from the scene, it obviously being too much for him to continue looking at. I looked around the room one more time, taking a couple of photos with my phone and scanning the room to capture the scene.

"Yeah. I'll send the scene recreation to Chris for analysis later." I said, walking back to him in the entryway and resisting the desire to press myself into him.

Yoreile quietly closed the door behind me and I nodded to the warlock. He merely looked away, not saying a word to me but I caught the worried expression on his face. Yoreile was often mistaken for a sorcerer due to the powers he inherited from his ala father, so he understood Justina's struggles well. He wasn't very vocal, but I couldn't help worrying as I stared at his fire red hair. Quinn seemed to sense my thoughts and he was quick to smile at me.

"Don't worry, I won't let anyone get close enough to hurt El here," he quipped, his grey hair falling over his shoulder. He was clearly trying to lighten the mood and I couldn't help my slight smile. "I'm keeping an eye in the darkness, so you two just worry about saving Justina and catching the one who did this."

"I plan to," I agreed, without trying to hide the anger in my voice. Yoreile finally glanced at me, his brown eyes meeting mine before he nodded, turning his gaze back to the wall.

"Let's go. *Der Welpe*[1] is probably suffering." Kisten began walking back towards the surface and I followed him, collapsing into the passenger seat as he started up the car. Kisten placed his hand on my leg this time, carefully backing out and on the road. As we sped away from the Landing, I couldn't help but fall asleep to the steady vibration of the engine.

9

I was running through tall grass, the sounds of screams and vicious growling echoing behind me. My sister's body hung limply against me, unresponsive as I dragged her away from the chaos and carnage behind us. I could hear our fellow tribe members being slaughtered, but I closed my eyes to their plight. All that mattered, all that I cared about, was getting away with my sister. As long as I still had her, everything would be okay.

"Don't worry," I breathed, my panic growing as her blood continued to drip down her body, drenching my simple coverings. I fought my own fear and continued to drag her, refusing to stop. Stopping meant death and I couldn't, wouldn't, let her die. Tears started to stream down my face as I passed through the grass, doing my best to keep moving. "I'll be brave this time, no more running. I won't fail you this time."

I glanced down and the body was no longer my sister's, but Justina's, her dark blue hair matted with fresh blood. I looked back up and found myself in an endless void of darkness, the grasslands disappearing as I paused with Justina's body. The sounds of my tribe dying still echoed in the blackness around me and I glanced around, confused at the sudden darkness.

"Why…" I looked back down as Justina spoke, but it was my sister's voice instead of the sorcerer's. She suddenly jerked her head up, the creature's face a grotesque mismatch of the two women, murderous intent in their eyes. It leapt at me, pinning me down as it tried to strangle me, and I thrashed beneath the creature. My wrist started to burn as I tried to push them off, but they only pushed down on me with more force. The eyes of both my sister and Justina glared at me, burning with hate as they pushed their hands more into my throat. "It should've been YOU!"

"NO!" I screamed, waking from my dream drenched in sweat, Kisten holding my wrist. The wooden locket was also warm against my chest, and I could feel my sister's presence, although she didn't speak.

"Are you alright?" Kisten never took his eyes off the road as he released me, the burning sensation fading. I breathed in deeply, blowing the air out through my mouth as I tried to calm myself. The lingering dreads of the dream still echoed in the back of my mind, and I absently grabbed my sister's locket.

"I'm fine, just… a bad dream," I whispered, stroking the wood that kept my sister with me. Taking her locket and placing her soul inside was the last act I had done for her, and it was a decision that I could never escape from. Assured that I would be fine, I felt her presence leave me and I dropped my hand, sighing heavily.

"It's okay." Kisten reached back over, this time placing his hand on my legs. I gingerly placed my hand on his and he smiled, never taking his eyes off the road as I weaved my fingers with his. A tingling of pain spread across my skin as I held his hand, but I ignored it, allowing the soft touch and pain to help pull me away from the terrible nightmare.

"We're here." Kisten pulled into a gated community and after giving the name of the resident, drove in. The houses were nice enough, but were much too close together for my liking. I liked to have space in-between me and my neighbors and considering his home, I knew Kisten felt the same way.

After turning down a side street, Kisten pulled into the driveway of one of the many houses, and a middle-aged man ran outside to greet us.

"Thank goodness, Kisten! I'm not sure what happened, but he tried doing it on his own again." The father sounded panicked, and Kisten quickly embraced him, patting his back. The man returned the gesture, the panic and fear plain in his body. Kisten remained calm, pulling away to meet the man's gaze as he spoke.

"It'll be alright, where is he?"

"The backyard." The man huffed and the Alpha quickly nodded. Kisten walked around the outside of the house to a side fence, the father and me following behind. The young boy was in a corner of the yard, trapped in between being human and being a wolf. His legs almost looked broken as they were trying to change into hind legs and his face had already elongated into a snout. His whimpering broke my heart as his fur started to break through his skin and Kisten slowly walked up to him, talking softly.

"It's okay, you can do this. You don't have to be afraid," he soothed, half-shifting himself to match the boy. He dropped to all fours, crawling next to the frightened teenager. The boy whimpered again, shuffling further into the corner, fur receding back into his body as he tried to turn back to being human.

"I... No! I don't want to hurt anyone!" he cried and I could see the tears pouring from his canine eyes.

I glanced back toward the house and saw a woman and a young girl watching from a porch door. The girl was looking at her brother with concern and even at this distance, I could see the painful look on the mother's face. I looked back to the father and saw tears in his eyes as well.

"Are you..." I asked softly, and the man turned to look at me, at first with confusion but then shaking his head. He looked to the house, locking eyes with his wife for a moment before his expression turned painful.

"No, she's the shifter. I'm human," he tried to smile at her, but it failed to reach his eyes and I looked back to the house, my heart breaking for her. It must've been difficult to watch her son struggle like this, knowing it was her fault her son was suffering, and she could do nothing to help him. The man took a deep breath, trying to steady his voice before continuing. "She's tried to help him, but he gets too scared of the animal taking over. She's never able to get through to him, and it takes all her effort to get him to shift back. We figured with his experience, Kisten could succeed where she failed."

I returned my gaze to Kisten, who was still whispering to the boy, sitting on his hind legs beside him. The teen looked at Kisten, seeing that he was half-shifted as well and Kisten smiled at him. The boy's face filled with concern and he leaned into Kisten, sniffing the air between them. He kept rubbing the boy's back with his furry hand, doing his best to soothe him. "The wolf is a part of you, he won't do anything you don't want. You have complete control."

"It... doesn't hurt?"

"No, if you don't fight it, it doesn't hurt," Kisten soothed, licking the boy's face with his sandpaper tongue. "Your wolf just wants to share your world. He wants you to let him in. Your mother's wolf wants to see her son."

"Her son?" The boy glanced at the house to his mother, who raised her hand to the glass, tears rolling down her cheeks. Kisten nodded, following his gaze.

"Yes, Travis. Just as you have two mothers, she has two sons. A human son, and a wolf son." Kisten hummed. "She wants to share both worlds with you, just like your wolf."

"Mom's... Mom's wolf is hurting too?" Travis looked back to Kisten and it seemed as if the Alpha's words were getting through to him. "But, my wolf doesn't feel like hers."

"Because your wolf is you, and you are your wolf. He's not going to feel like your mother's, but he still won't do anything you wouldn't do yourself." Kisten backed away, getting onto all fours again. "You just have to stop fighting. It'll be okay – I'll be right here beside you."

It was clear his words were reaching the boy and Travis started to calm down. Slowly, the teen got on all fours, matching Kisten, closing his eyes as he lay on the grass. Kisten licked his face again, comforting him and encouraging him to let the transition happen. The boy's hind legs finished shifting, fur beginning to sprout through his clothing as the fabric ripped due to his changing form. Kisten's clothing was made of an expensive material that allowed him to shift without ripping, and he continued whispering and encouraging the young boy, shifting back to being human as the boy's change was complete. The large wolf that replaced him panted, licking Kisten's face while wagging his tail.

"Travis!" The porch door flung open, and the boy's mother ran out of the house, shifting to join her son. The two wolves playfully circled one another, yapping and pawing at each other. The man wiped away his tears and picked up his young daughter as she came over to him, dragging two robes on the ground behind her. The girl looked to where Kisten stood with the wolves, lovingly scratching their ears.

"Is broder okay now?" she asked, looking up to her father as he took the clothing from her. "No more hurt now?"

"Yes, sweet pea." Her father hugged her tightly, his relief obvious in his motions. "I think he's going to be fine now."

Kisten walked over, flanked by his two charges and the mother licked her daughter's face as the father placed the young girl back down. The girl turned to her brother and he backed away for a moment before lowering his head to the ground. She walked up to her brother and patted his head before wrapping her small arms around his neck, hugging him tightly.

"Wolf Broder!" she exclaimed, and he whined happily, his tail thumping the ground behind him. Kisten stood next to me as the whole family embraced, the mother and son shifting back to human. The father quickly draped the robes over his wife and son and they all turned to face us, bowing their heads to Kisten.

"Thank you so much, Kisten," the woman said, her eyes still shiny with tears as she held her robe tightly. "Thank you for helping my son."

"My pleasure, Rachel." Kisten brushed her off, grasping her

shoulders before hugging her tightly. "It's my responsibility as an Alpha and a friend to be there for my pack, no matter how young."

He patted the head of the young boy, who leaned into the touch before leaning against his mother. Kisten's smile was soft and fatherly as he pulled his hand away, meeting the young boy's gaze. "You're not afraid anymore, right?"

"It was... weird. Nothing like I thought it would be," Travis admitted, glancing away as he spoke. Rachel seemed concerned for a moment, but Travis lifted his head as he continued. "But you were right, I was still me. My body was different, but I was me."

"Of course you were," his mother cooed, kissing his forehead as she pulled him against her. "And I'll always be with you, helping you control your wolf."

"Good," Kisten nodded, stepping back to my side as I stood in the yard awkwardly, feeling out of place with the proceedings. I had seen plenty of new animal shifters who had been afraid to shift, but not being one myself, I had never been able to help them. Kisten had probably seen much more of it than me and the expert way he calmed Travis showed his patience and skill. Kisten wrapped his arm around me, nodding to the boy's parents as he pulled me closer. "Well, I have another member of the pack to check on, so we have to excuse ourselves, unfortunately."

Rachel raised her eyebrows at the sight of Kisten's arm around my waist and looked up to my face, sniffing the air in my direction. I cleared my throat, uncomfortable with her scrutiny.

"Is she new to the pack?" she asked, and I couldn't help but cough to hide my embarrassment as I turned away. I hadn't met many of Kisten's pack: in an area as large as The Capital, his pack had hundreds of members and I mostly stayed out of shapeshifter affairs. I always tried to distance myself from becoming too close with anyone who wasn't a part of the Coven, because if they ever committed a crime, I would probably have to be the one to put them down.

Kisten tightened his arm around me, and I looked up to see him smiling broadly.

"Not yet." Before I could refute him, he turned me around and started walking away with me. Once we were back in the front yard out of their sight, he released my waist and turned to look at me, noticing the incredulous look on my face. "What?"

"What do you mean, not yet?"

"Exactly what I said. Not yet." Kisten smiled, his eyes swirling once again. I did my best to look away, but he grabbed my chin, forcing me to meet his gaze. I breathed heavily from the burning sensation on my face, but Kisten didn't release me. Last night seemed to have caused Kisten to throw away most of the restraint he had previously shown, and he only loosened his grip on my chin instead of dropping his hand all together.

"But Kisten, I'm not a shapeshifter, I can't join your pa—"

"As my mate, shapeshifter or not, you're a part of my pack. My Beta." At his mention of the word *mate*, my heart leapt into my throat, and I looked away from him again. Kisten pulled me closer and released my face, pressing my head into his chest. I could hear his heartbeat and couldn't help the shudder that ran through me.

"Kisten, I can't be your mate. You're still bound by the Oath." I spoke into the fabric of his shirt, hugging him tightly. My own chest ached with my words; I didn't want to turn him down, but I knew that there was so much more than what we wanted and other factors that made a relationship complicated. I heard his heartbeat quicken at my mention of the Oath and I hurried my next sentence. "My job also requires that I don't get too close to other Supernaturals and I still have the Hunters to worry about on top of that. I... it's too dangerous for you to be with me."

"You can figure it out with your job. I doubt they'll just drop you after all these years," Kisten stated and I looked up to him, my chin still resting against him. He was looking down at me, his expression showing how serious he was. "As far as the Hunters are concerned, having you as my Beta puts me in no more danger than being Lucius' Alpha. And the Oath and Evalyn... I'll deal with that when the time comes."

"But Kis—"

"I have tried to restrain myself for far too long and abide by rules that don't serve me or my desires. I have only cared for two people in my long life, and last night reminded me how lonely I've allowed myself to become. I can't... No. I refuse," Kisten paused, leaning down to kiss me deeply, once again setting my mouth ablaze. He gripped me tightly, his longing and desperation evident in his touch and kiss. I was left panting when he released me, my body growing weak in his arms. His voice was soft as he spoke again, lovingly stroking my face. "*I refuse to lose you.*"

With this, Kisten released me and continued walking to his car, leaving me in a daze behind him. Court me, make me his Beta... he had basically done the human equivalent of asking me to marry him. I wanted nothing more than to say yes to him, but there were so many obstacles to that sort of future that he seemed to be overlooking.

No, not overlooking, I thought to myself as I followed him into the car, unable to help the warmth in my chest from his words. *Just determined to overcome.*

As we pulled out of the neighborhood and began to head to the hospital, I couldn't help but smile at the thought of Kisten belonging to me.

10

Kisten left me in the waiting room as he walked back to his car, telling me he should be back shortly. As soon as he left, I felt the sting from disobeying Lucius' order but I shrugged it off, quickly making my way to the Supernatural wing. I stood outside Justina's door, closing my eyes as I prepared myself to see my friend. My mind kept flashing to my nightmare and my sister's body, but I shook my head to clear it of those images as I stepped inside.

LeAlexende sat on the opposite side of her bed, dead or asleep in the chair. It was a little after two, so I knew he would overpower death's hold on him soon and I stepped up to Justina's bed, closing the door softly. She was still unconscious, but her breathing was steady, as if she were merely sleeping. I noticed the many bandages on her arms and midsection, as well as both of her legs in casts. I noticed her left arm was also in a cast, and I gently touched her right hand. She didn't move in response, and I squeezed her fingers, fighting to hold back my tears.

"Wake up soon, Justina." I whispered, moving some strands of blue hair as I kissed her forehead. "Help me punish the one who did this to you, *cecmpa*[1]."

The door opened behind me and I moved to the opposite side of the bed near LeAlexende, allowing the nurse to enter. They simply went to work, checking her vitals and running simple checks, ignoring my presence. The nurse was a witch, as I recognized him as one Justina sometimes got drinks with when she went out. He seemed distressed at having to see her like this, but he acted with full professionalism as he worked. Soon, the nurse left with the blood samples to take to the lab, and I remained, looking at the sleeping spellcaster.

I sighed heavily, looking to LeAlexende as the Overseer awoke, flooding the room with power as he escaped Death's grasp. It always felt so dramatic when an elder vampire awoke: the room flooded with energy, a wave of power as they pulled themselves back from the grave. He looked first to me, beaming a soft smile before picking up his phone.

"Have you been here long?" he asked and I shook my head as he checked his missed messages, barely acknowledging my answer. "Good, good, I woke up on time."

I remained silent as I leaned against the wall, unsure of what to do or say. After sending a reply to one of his messages, LeAlexende turned to face me, smiling his cheery smile.

"Kisten's not with you?" he inquired, and I shook my head, unable to resist smiling slightly. LeAlexende hummed thoughtfully, looking at his phone as it vibrated in his hand again. "I'm sure he'll be by later to check on her then. He's become a good doctor."

"He has. He really cares for everyone," I breathed, looking towards the door. My thoughts turned to Evalyn and I shook my head, my smile fading. The Overseer gave me a strange look as I frowned, his blond hair shifting slightly. "Almost everyone."

"Ah, you are referring to Luc's new Retainer?" I gave LeAlexende a strange look, as I had never heard anyone dare call Lucius Luc, not even Eve. I guess being an old friend and an Overseer gave him the right, or at least made him feel comfortable enough to do so. The vampire's smile faded slightly as I nodded and he turned his eyes to the floor. "I must admit, I am not very fond of her, either."

"Really no one is." I shrugged, looking away to a corner again. Something about meeting LeAlexende's gaze was uncomfortable to me, but I couldn't seem to place why. "She doesn't do much to try to change that, though."

"Well, she really does seem preoccupied with her own ambitions." I was surprised how well LeAlexende had been able to read Evalyn despite meeting her for the first time a few days ago. "But Lucius has always had varied tastes and she's not his first ala Retainer. She just seems... a bit more ambitious than the ones he has chosen in the past."

"How long have you known Lucius?" I queried, my curiosity getting the better of me. The caramel vampire ignored me at first, still engrossed with his phone screen. LeAlexende's smile widened as he looked back up to me, and he was genuinely amused.

"Since he was turned. Like him, I'm one of the First and a former member of her court." I looked at him with shock and stepped back a little. My reaction only seemed to amuse him more, although I saw a hint of pain at my discomfort. "Unlike Luc, I changed my identity after I left Mater Vitae. I have no desire to be reminded of my past."

"I..."

He interrupted me, not giving me the chance to speak. "I also know you have changed your name since your time with her, leaving your previous past behind. I'm sure you understand not wanting that burden."

His eyes bore into mine despite his warm smile and I could almost feel his pain. I nodded solemnly, grabbing my sister's locket again through my shirt; those who did not have immortality or long lives failed to understand the burden a name could carry. Just that single word could wound you worse than any weapon and bury you in the sins and grief of the past. My sister rose at my touch and LeAlexende's gaze drifted to my hand.

"Ah, so you still wear it." I looked at him surprised, quickly dropping my hand. LeAlexende laughed slightly, checking his phone again. "Lucius is polite enough to pretend he doesn't remember when you were the Immortal and I doubt he's told your true origins to anyone else but me. To be fair, it's not as if we really knew you, anyway, with the distance she kept you from everyone."

"No one was given the chance," I commented, and my sister drifted away again without saying anything. I knew she was probably still watching me, waiting until I was alone to voice her thoughts. "To Mother, I was a precious pet, only to be appreciated for the rarity I was. I am incredibly grateful to Lucius for his protection and the risk he is taking with me."

"Yes, he is taking a great risk, agreeing to have you in his Coven, especially being a First himself," LeAlexende agreed and he checked his phone as it vibrated for what felt like the hundredth time since I entered the room. "But he always was one to do so. Adds thrill to such a long life."

"What about you?" I asked, and the Overseer laughed slightly, answering his message before looking back up to me.

"Oh no, not me. Just like with changing my name, I prefer to live free of regrets or burdens." LeAlexende smiled his relaxing smile and once again, I couldn't help but return it. "I enjoy my simple life as an Overseer, providing protection and safety for my charges as best I can. Hunters aren't much of a problem for me anymore, and my Retainer is very capable."

"Is that why you pretended not to recognize me?" I pushed, and the vampire nodded, looking to the ceiling before closing his eyes. I realized how little I knew about the First Thirteen: all I truly knew about them was their names. I had seen some of them at times, but there was only one I knew by appearance. It was no wonder that I had approached Lucius without realizing who he was and how meeting LeAlexende had not stirred any memories. My voice was soft as I spoke again, my mind drifting to the First who had helped me escape. "Thank you for helping me, LeAlexende."

"Please, call me Alex. Speaking of helping..." He opened his eyes, glancing at his phone before returning his full attention to me. "I can tell you confidently that there were no empousa present at any of your crimes, before or after. All the locations are far from any Overseers protecting one and none were traveling through those areas at the time of the murders."

I frowned at this news, not trying to hide my displeasure. The Overseer seemed to view this as good news, as he beamed at me while I spoke. "So, we are looking for a harpy or cyclops with an unknown motive."

"I don't think that's it, either," LeAlexende added, and I looked at him, confused. The vampire shrugged as he looked back to his phone, scrolling through a gallery. "I had my contacts tell me a little about the crimes and neither harpies nor cyclops can kill that many people that fast, or sneak into sealed locations without being seen, ability to pass barriers aside. I think you're looking for a hybrid, someone who has a parent who can overpower magic, but still be able to kill large groups of people."

I considered LeAlexende's words as he spoke. He was right: the last crime had a body-count of more than fifteen, and that was a lot for either of those species to try to kill in the time-frame. It also would've been impossible for either species to hurt Justina as badly as she had been and whoever did it had managed to sneak into the Coven while Crispin and I were out.

"I'll let my team know. Thank you... Alex."

The Overseer nodded, turning his gaze to the door as Kisten finally entered. Kisten was looking down at his screen, nodding as he swiped the information onto the screen next to Justina's bed.

"Blood work looks normal. It seems she's healing herself well, which was my biggest concern, considering how old Justina is." Kisten sighed, the relief obvious on his face and I couldn't help my own relief. Justina was only in her thirties, but sorcerers rarely lived to fifty, due to their magic eating away at their life. Other spellcasters said it was the price they paid for breaking the laws of magic and so far, no way had been discovered to help them. "I should be able to remove her casts tomorrow and depending on how things go tonight, she may wake up tomorrow."

"Good. I want to catch the one who did this before then, but..."

My mind turned to what Alex had said, and I couldn't help my frown. "Honestly, I don't think we will without her help."

"I know. Before we go, I was asked to help with another patient before we leave, so I'll be a moment longer." Kisten smiled at me, a gesture I returned as I turned to him. It wasn't surprising that Kisten had been asked to help, as he often got called in on his days off due to his age and expertise. "But first, come here."

Kisten motioned me to his side and I walked around the bed to meet him. He placed down his tablet before gently taking my bandaged hand and began to remove the gauze he had wrapped it with the day before. My hand was already mostly healed from the wound he had given me and he nodded, pleased with the results. He leaned to retrieve a small pair of scissors and cut the stitches, kissing my hand before releasing me.

"You're good. Go help them," I whispered, waving him away. "I'm fine here."

"Okay." His gaze lingered on me as he turned to walk away, and I was once again left alone with the Overseer. LeAlexende chuckled to himself, placing his phone back down as soon as the shifter left.

"Looking to finally settle down?" he asked innocently, and my face grew warm with a blush as I stammered to answer. He stopped me with a wave of his hand, laughing at my embarrassment. "Kisten just didn't seem the type. He always seemed to be inside his own thoughts."

"We're not together," I managed, my heart pounding in my throat. LeAlexende gave me a look that clearly said he didn't believe me and I hurried my next statement. "He's still bound to Lucius and Evalyn by the Oath and—"

"Ah, he should fix that soon," was all the Overseer offered, picking up his phone again to scroll through something, clearly not bothered by this information. "I would hate to see you two kept from each other over something so trivial."

"If only it was that easy. Eve absolutely hates both of us and she would never agree to release Kisten, to spite us." At this, LeAlexende sighed, setting his phone on his lap. I looked away, wondering if I had said too much but I realized that it felt amazing to get this off my chest. "There are... other factors too. We had been keeping our distance to limit the temptation, but being forced to be together is..."

"Guess all that control isn't for show," LeAlexende giggled and once again, my face flushed with embarrassment. His purple eyes turned serious and I cleared my throat under his scrutiny, once again unable to look at him. His voice was soft and serious as he continued. "The Oath will do its best to kill you if you take it too far."

"Yeah." I nodded, clearly remembering the pain from the night before. LeAlexende looked curiously at my face before returning to being absorbed in his phone. When he spoke again, it made me jump and I barely noticed as Kisten returned.

"I would still say something to Luc. He has known Kisten for a long time and could easily force Eve to release her part. Both of you could use a little happiness in your lives." He offered nonchalantly and Kisten smiled, walking over to me.

"I will, but not yet," he pulled me close again, laying my head on his chest. I couldn't see his or LeAlexende's face as he spoke, and I instead breathed him in. "There are other things that need to be taken care of before I go to Lucius about the Oath."

"A stickler for tradition, I see. Just don't leave any marks on her," Kisten's chest vibrated as he laughed at the Overseer's words and the shifter hugged me tighter. "I'd hate to see you scar such a beauty."

"No promises on that, but I'll take good care of her."

"See that you do." LeAlexende smiled at both of us brightly and settled into his chair. With this, Kisten released me and, still holding my hand, led me out of the room. He didn't say a word as we walked through the waiting room, but I recognized something in his gait was off.

I opened my mouth to ask him as we stepped on the elevator, but Kisten swung me into the wall, quickly pressing the button for the lobby before pressing his body into me. The burning sensation on my wrists as he pinned me to the wall told me clearly where his intentions were and I struggled to free myself. Kisten put a stop to this by kissing me, burning my lips and tongue once more. There was no sandpaper texture to his tongue, so just like this morning, his animal was not behind this assault.

"Can you even begin to understand," he released me from the kiss, interrogating me as he nibbled on my neck. I tried to strain away from him, but he held me firmly in place, the pain radiating from my wrists to my hands and arms. He growled against my skin, the sound beginning to excite me. He noticed the change, as he shoved his knee between my legs, kissing me deeply again. I closed my eyes as I melted under his torture. "How much I missed you? Barely an hour apart, and I felt like I was losing my mind."

"I can tell." I moaned, the intense pain overwhelming my senses. Kisten released me just as we reached the lobby and I nearly collapsed to the floor as the elevator stopped. He stood me up as the doors opened and he led me through the lobby, holding my hand tightly. I knew he wasn't done with me when we reached his car and instead of releasing me, he opened the door to the back and tossed me onto the seat. Kisten climbed on top of me and closed the door, pinning me again.

"What have you done to me, Raiven?" He growled again, and I saw that his fangs had yet to appear. There was no sign of Kisten's animal and knowing this was all him was just as exciting as it was terrifying. He kissed me deeply again, undoing the front of my pants as best as he could in the tight space. I moaned loudly into his kiss as he slid his hand to touch me, the heat almost too much to bear. The underwear Kisten had found for me was much thinner than the pair I had originally been wearing, and I could feel the more intense heat that the previous pair had protected me from. "I've never felt like this. I feel..."

"Unhinged? Free?"

"*Insane.*" He pulled up from me and grinned, licking my face and dragging his tongue down to my neck. The searing fire that followed his tongue caused me to moan again and he pressed his hand into me more, forcing me to try to squirm away from him and his painful touch. However, Kisten already had me pinned to the door and I had nowhere to go as he pushed my underwear to the side, and easily slid his fingers inside me.

I cried out at the first wave of pain as it washed over me, and Kisten silenced me with a kiss, drinking in my pain as he moved his fingers inside me. The pain was overwhelming, and I felt as if I would pass out, but I also couldn't deny the pleasure of having him touch me. Feeling him flex and move his fingers deep inside me made me whimper at the intense pain and pleasure, and I couldn't help it as I squirmed beneath him.

After what seemed like eternity, he finally released me, sliding his fingers from me and pulling back from his kiss. I gasped for precious air as the pain stopped and I ached from the echoes of the heat. Kisten raised his hand to his face, playing with my juices on his fingers before placing them in his mouth, closing his eyes as he indulged in my taste. I felt a clench inside my midsection and, despite the pain it had caused, I couldn't help but want his fingers back inside me.

"You are really enjoying this." He laughed darkly, gazing deep into my eyes as he removed his fingers from his mouth and I merely panted in response, still unable to speak. His gaze softened for a moment and he carefully leaned over me, sniffing my skin. "How hurt are you?"

"I'll live," I murmured, getting my breath under control as I smiled. "I'd love a warm bath to get rid of this ache, though."

"I'll start one as soon as we get home." Kisten smiled at me and I laughed, reaching to touch his face.

"It is interesting to see a different side of you. A passionate side." I admitted and he chuckled, leaning away from me. He almost seemed worried as he gazed at the foggy window, and I didn't like the look that entered his expression.

"You're seeing a repressed side." He sighed, running his clean hand through his hair. "Something about yesterday really did something to me. Whenever I'm around you, I feel like I'm losing all the careful control that I've built up over the centuries."

"It's good to just let go every once in a while." I smiled, settling into a more comfortable position on the seat. Kisten leaned over me, sliding his hand up my shirt as he kissed my neck, once again setting my body on fire with pain. I was beginning to grow used to the heat and it was starting to be less painful and more pleasurable each time I was subjected to it.

He really is making me a masochist, I thought to myself as I strained my neck to give him better access. He used his free hand to slide my hand down to his erection and I squeezed him through the fabric of his jeans. He moaned into my skin, and my body grew more excited with his sounds.

"Even if all I want to do is bury myself inside you, consequences be damned?" He moaned, his voice strained as he spoke. I carefully undid his jeans and slid my hand inside, stroking him through the fabric as I had earlier. His underwear was already wet from his excitement and I gulped, holding in my own desire as I stroked him, teasing him with my fingertips.

"I won't tell you no." I moaned, not even attempting to hide my desire for him. Every part of my body wanted him and my heart ached to have him as he lay on top of me, engrossed in my skin as I played with him. Kisten purred low in his throat and for a moment, I wondered if he really was going to take me in the back of his car. Granted, I'd had sex in worse places.

"Just makes me want you more," he finally whispered, moving from on top of me as he shifted my legs until they lay across his lap. He took a deep breath and let it out shakily, clearly trying to calm himself down. He patted my legs as he closed his eyes, focusing on steadying his breathing. "Let me get us home so we can clean up and I can get you that bath before we do something I'll regret."

"Sounds great." I closed my eyes as he redid his jeans and climbed out of the car. I settled in the back seat as he re-entered on the driver's side and started it up, driving us back home.

II

I lounged in the warm water, gently blowing on the bubbles that surrounded me. As soon as we had gotten home, Kisten had drawn my bath, taking a moment to use his shower while the tub filled up. I had fallen asleep on the drive back to his house and awoke as he finished undressing me. Kisten said nothing, merely picking me up to place me in the warm water and kissing me before leaving again.

Kisten was taking a moment to go by my house while I bathed, breaking Lucius' order yet again, but I merely shrugged off the annoying sting. Anyone else in the Coven would have been incapacitated by disobeying an order from Lucius, but at worst for me, the stinging would intensify to a mild burning sensation. I was only bound to his orders if I wanted to be, despite taking the Oath of the Coven like everyone else.

Beyond that, I wasn't worried about Kisten: the culprit really had only been interested in Justina. Otherwise, there would've been plenty of other opportunities to attack any of us and if he really was going after sorcerers, Yoreile would be his next choice. A frown started on my face as my thoughts changed to the case and I shifted in the bath.

"Sis." I felt her consciousness rise as I called out to her and I settled further down into my bubbles. She sat quietly as she had done all day, still not speaking to me and I blew into the bubbles again. "What's on your mind?"

'... *About what?*'

"Anything. Everything. The case." I closed my eyes, sighing as I thought of the man who had been by my side for the greater part of the day. "Kisten."

'*Hmph,*' she grunted, and I could hear a lecture in her voice. I winced involuntarily: lectures from my sister had never been pleasant, even when she was alive. When I had been alone at Mater Vitae's court, all she ever did was lecture me. About how I should've been using my power to escape, how I shouldn't have bound her to a locket, how much she... hated me for being chosen to live. My guilt began to rise again as flashes of my nightmare flicked through my mind, and I knew she felt it, as her voice was soft when she spoke again.

'*Well, this whole Beta thing sounds like your problem. I have no say in that, although we both know what you want.*' She sighed, and I could envision her leaning back in a chair, crossing her legs. I smiled slightly and I could hear the smile in her voice as she continued. '*Kisten is probably one of my favorites. You two are nice compliments to one another; he keeps you grounded while you allow him to let go sometimes.*'

"I thought you liked Rurubelle." I giggled, remembering a previous girlfriend of mine. I could almost feel my sister's embarrassment as she grunted. "You said she was good for me and I was a fool to give her up."

'*Well, I wouldn't have.*' She pouted, and I laughed out loud, lifting some more bubbles in my hand to blow on. '*But, again, I'm stuck in a locket. I can't have anyone.*'

"I'm sorry." I dropped my head again, the nightmare ever-present in my mind. My guilt over my sister's death was one I could never escape from, as a constant reminder hung around my neck; that, for some reason, I had been chosen to live, while she had died. "I want to fix it, but we already—"

'*Stop it, Raiven. I've told you before, I have already moved past this. Your guilt will eat you alive if you let it.*' She sighed, clearly upset over my reaction to her joke. I stayed silent, fighting tears that wanted to flow as she continued, '*You did what you could at the time. I may have hated you for it originally, but I have had more than enough time to get over it.*'

"I couldn't be without you. I just—"

'*I know, but at some point, you're going to have to let me go. I know you have always been... more dependent than me, but I won't last forever.*' She stated, and I knew she was right. Despite still being alive in some capacity, I knew she was fading. She slept more often than ever before, and now neither of us could remember what her name was. Little by little, her soul was slipping away and even if I could find a way to give her a body again, she probably didn't have enough of her soul left to keep it alive. I could give her peace by returning her to where she was buried, but I wasn't ready to give her up.

From what I remembered of my human life, my sister was always the more independent and braver one. We had lost our parents young, although neither of us remembered how or why, and the other tribe members had accepted us, but never raised us. It always felt that they knew we were different somehow, even if they didn't know or understand why. It was almost a revered fear that made them keep us around, and less that they wanted anything to do with us. My sister raised me, tried to help me be brave, but my fear of dying and danger always made me run. Even when I was trying to save her life, all I could do was run.

'*As far as your case is concerned,*' my sister spoke again, dragging me from my memories with her voice; she seemed to understand that I was sinking into the past and was trying to bring me back to the present. '*You're still making it too complicated.*'

"Too complicated?"

'*Yes.*' She groaned, frustrated with me for not seeing it from her perspective. '*You're so sure there's a glorified reason your culprit is killing and you're trying to tie the victims together in a way they don't belong. Since we know it's not an empousa, the motive becomes obvious if you look at it from the mind of a simpleton. Justina's attack proves that.*'

"Why else would you..." My voice trailed off as I realized what she was saying. "No unified reason, but simple, individual ones? Simple, petty..."

'*Not everyone will overlook a slight.*' She reminded me and I jumped out of the tub, wrapping the towel around me as I hurried into the bedroom. I snatched my phone off the bed, quickly plugging in Liel's number and waited impatiently for her to answer. My sister remained for a moment, but then faded back to sleep, humming her delight at my understanding. I finally heard Liel's soft, raspy voice on the other end, and she sounded distracted.

"What is it, Raiven? Do you need Crispin?" She sounded as if she was having difficulty keeping her voice down and I wondered if it was time for her to scream again. Banshees had to scream every once in a while to keep their power under control, just like animal shifters shifted to keep their animal in check.

"No, Liel. I just need to know if you and Justina have gone to The Dream within the last week or so." I impatiently tapped my fingers on the sheets as Kisten walked into the room and I saw his confusion. I motioned for him to sit as Liel hummed with thought and he sat on the bed next to me, waiting patiently for me to finish.

"No, I haven't gone with her lately. Haven't really been in the mood." I heard a male voice in the background and assumed it was Crispin as they spoke. He almost sounded out of breath, as if he had come back from exercising. "Actually, Cris says he and her go every Thursday. That's rude. Invite me sometime."

Crispin must've said something else rude because I heard Liel hit him. He laughed in his usual annoying way and I merely sighed on my end.

"Did they meet anyone, anyone Justina could've upset or made angry?" I waited as Liel repeated my question and my anxiety grew as I heard nothing on the other end. I could hear slight whispering before Liel addressed my question.

"Cris says no, but he wasn't there the whole time. She got upset with him over something and he left early. He said she stayed at least another hour by herself before she left."

Without saying more, I thanked Liel and hung up, immediately dialing Lucius. Kisten opened his mouth to speak but I stopped him with a hand wave, returning my attention to my phone.

"Hello?"

"Lucius." I spoke quickly, determined to follow the path of logic my sister had put me on. "I need the surveillance of The Dream from Thursday night into Friday."

"Done." Lucius said and I think he could tell from my tone that it was related to Justina. I could hear him standing up from his seat, and quickly walking down a hallway. "I'll go get the tapes now, Crispin and Liel will bring them."

"Thank you." I hung up again and this time Kisten spoke before I could stop him. He had moved closer to me on the bed and seemed as if he had something to say.

"Raiven, wait a mome–"

"Not yet." I hand-waved him again as I dialed my boss's number and waited impatiently for it to ring. When he answered, I heard the busy sounds of a restaurant in the background and remembered it was Sunday. Brandon must've taken my warning seriously and went to dinner with Arkrian.

"What's up, Raiven? What can I do you for?" He sounded pleased and I smiled slightly, glad that he had finally taken the initiative. His love for his children was real and I was happy he had put his prejudices aside, at least for one evening.

"I hate to interrupt you when you sound like you're having a good time, but–"

"You were right, this lad isn't half bad." Brandon interrupted me and I huffed, upset that he didn't let me speak. "Did you know that he has a background in football? Even played in college. I thought animal shifters avoided spo–"

"Yes, I am aware." I snapped exasperatedly, my annoyance growing. "But I didn't call to talk about Arkrian. I have a new idea about the case."

"What is it?" All the joy in his voice faded, replaced with the seriousness I was used to. I spoke quickly, standing up from the bed and pacing.

"I think we're looking at the case all wrong. The killings aren't connected in the way we were thinking," I stressed, motioning to Kisten, who handed me the fresh clothes he had bought me from my house, his annoyance on his face. I entreated him with my expression as I continued speaking to my boss. "Can you have Julia and Chris gather all the surveillance they can from any night clubs, bars or similar locations any of our victims may have visited?"

"What are you thinking?" He was intrigued by my suggestion and I paused as I began to dress, carefully placing my phone on the bed as I switched to speaker mode. "We've already pored over hundreds of hours of footage and found nothing."

"That he's a revenge killer." Kisten's expression changed as I said this, and I saw something dark flash across his face. "I think he's killing people who have slighted him or offended him in some way. He's going after a specific person and everyone else is collateral damage. He knows he can kill them, so he just does. It's not about numbers, or killing certain species or anything. Just that person, and anyone else unfortunate enough to be there."

"Fuck, you're on to something." I heard Brandon as he waved down their server and asked for the check. I heard as he apologized to Arkrian before giving me his full attention. "That makes so much sense, it's stupid. It explains the randomness of the killings, why they're so spread out. Why the number of deaths have been on a steady increase and why Justina was targeted alone. Dammit, that's so fucking simple."

"Yeah, he was careful about where he killed before because he didn't know how many he could get away with. Now he doesn't care, being so bold as to even attack Justina at the Coven. He kills the person who slighted him and then," I paused a moment as I pulled the sweater Kisten had bought me over my head. "He leaves to avoid getting caught."

"I'll call Julia and head to the office with her. I'll get Chris to start reaching out to the other Overseers to get us the additional footage." I heard the rush of wind as he stepped out into the evening and hailed the valet. "See if you can find out where Justina has been in the past week. She's our best chance of getting a description of who we're looking for."

"Already working on it." I heard the knock on Kisten's front door downstairs, and he looked at me as I motioned for him to go answer it. His eyes narrowed as he walked away, and I couldn't help but be confused by his reaction as I returned my attention to my phone. "I need to go so I can check the tape. I'll be to the office as soon as I can."

"Keep me updated."

A click on his end and I slid the phone into my pocket, walking downstairs to find Kisten, Crispin and Liel all in the kitchen. As I came down, Crispin held up the flash drive containing the surveillance and I hurried down the last few steps.

"Lucius said this might be related to your case and what happened to Justina," Liel whispered, keeping her voice low. The banshee was wearing her usual garb – a long, black cloak that hid her form and her white dreads flowing from underneath the hood. Her dark gray eyes matched perfectly with her nearly black skin, and she tugged on her hood nervously. She looked to the flash drive and then back to me, her expression gloomy.

Crispin handed the drive to Kisten, giving him a nod as he did so. Kisten took the drive and walked back up the stairs, speaking quietly.

"Laptop's in the office." I watched him leave and then returned my attention to Crispin, taking in the vampire. With him here, I couldn't help but still wonder what he had wanted to say to me in the garden before we were interrupted. He was looking at Liel, but on noticing me looking, turned to face me. His expression was serious, none of his cockiness or playboy attitude.

"How is she?" He whispered, and I realized that he probably

hadn't seen her since Lucius and LeAlexende had carried her away. Liel also looked worried about Justina's state, so it was obvious Lucius hadn't told anyone about her progress. I took a deep breath, meeting their gaze.

"She's hurt, but alright. Kisten says she's healing herself subconsciously and he'll be able to remove her casts tomorrow." Both were relieved at my words, and I heard Kisten coming back down the stairs as I continued. "Hopefully, she'll wake up soon but I'm hoping the footage will help us find the one who did this before that."

Kisten set the laptop on the counter and we all hovered around him as he plugged in the drive and opened the file. The footage began at midnight Thursday morning and Kisten began to scroll through the video.

"We arrived around ten," Crispin offered, watching the time stamp in the corner. "I don't know what time it was when I left, but probably after midnight."

"Stop it when they get there." I insisted, and Kisten obliged, stopping the video after Justina and Crispin walked into frame. They sat at the bar together and ordered their drinks, with Crispin immediately turning to flirt with a girl next to him. Liel and I rolled our eyes at the same time, both turning to look at Crispin in unison. The vampire in question merely shrugged, not bothered by our looks.

"Double the speed," I ordered and once again Kisten obeyed, and we watched with anticipation. The night was normal enough; the dance floor was packed, and people came and went from the bar. Justina remained at the bar all night, drinking her drinks as Crispin flitted back and forth. Then Crispin approached Justina, laying a hand on her shoulder, which she angrily shoved off. "There, slow it down,"

We all watched in silence as Justina angrily gestured at Crispin, clearly done with his constant back and forth. Crispin appeared to be trying to defend himself, but Justina sat back down, ignoring him as she ordered another drink. He tried to talk to her for a little longer before he gave up and left, heading back for the Coven. Shortly after her blowout with Crispin, Justina finished her drink and stood to leave as well, but was stopped by someone.

It looked to be a woman and Justina was clearly excited to see her, embracing her guest tightly and giving her a kiss. The woman was tall, with skin slightly lighter than mine and she was attractive, showing off her toned legs with her short dress and heels. They sat down at the bar together and I reached around Kisten to pause it.

"Do any of you know her?" All three of my companions shook their heads as I took a screenshot and resumed the video.

Shortly after the women sat down, they were approached by another party, a man who was wearing dark clothing. He had his back to the camera, so we couldn't see his face as he talked to the women. Everything was fine at first, with him even buying the girls more drinks. However, he must've said something Justina didn't like because she seemed to excuse herself from the situation. The man was trying to stop her, but Justina was making it clear she was no longer interested in being around him. Her friend was also trying to convince Justina to stay, motioning for her to sit back down, but Justina was having none of it. She brushed her way past the man, and he reached to grab her. Crispin hissed as we watched, all of us knowing what was going to happen.

The man was immediately blown back into the bar, finding himself in Justina's previous seat as she turned to glare at him. The man was still facing away from the camera and moved to turn around. I held my breath, my hand hovering to pause the video as we waited to see his face. The bartender stopped him, however, making it evident that it would be a very bad idea to pursue Justina, who was now leaving the bar using the front door. Her friend was trying to get the man's attention, but he stomped off, leaving the same way Justina had. She sighed, finishing her drink and paying before walking out. As she turned, I paused the video again, got the best angle of her face that I could, and took another screenshot.

"Send those to me," I demanded, leaning away from the laptop and Kisten obeyed, sending the files to my phone. I accepted the images, nodding to myself. "If we can find that man, we find the one who hurt Justina. That woman and the bartender were the only ones besides Justina who saw his face."

"The bartender's Josh," Crispin added, looking at Liel, but the banshee shot him an angry glance. It was clear she blamed him for leaving Justina by herself, but for once, I found myself on Crispin's side. Justina was nothing if not stubborn and she had decided she was done with him for the night. If he hadn't left of his own accord, she would've made him. "But he went out of town Friday to see his mother for the holiday."

"Well, his trip will have to be interrupted for a bit," I spoke bluntly, turning to look back to Kisten's computer. "I'll have him brought into the Local division closest to him so they can question him.

"Meanwhile, I need to get these stills and this video to my team." I ejected the flash drive from Kisten's laptop and started to walk around the breakfast bar when Crispin caught my arm. I whipped around to glare at him, almost instantly summoning my power. "Let me go."

"Wait a moment. I–"

"No." I stopped him, pulling my arm from his grip. Kisten also turned to face Crispin, his face dark. Crispin ignored this and shared another glance with Liel, who turned away, not offering him any assistance. I narrowed my eyes at the pair; this was too similar to how Justina had been with Crispin. "What is it?"

"I have to... tell you something. Just you." His demeanor from the garden returned and my suspicion and confusion increased. I crossed my arms across my chest and interrupted Kisten, who started to stand.

"And it has to be now? I want to find who did this to Justina." I argued and Crispin looked away again, this time looking to the floor. "The longer I hold off on this, the greater the chance that this guy moves again and we lose him."

"I know, and I want to catch him too." Crispin curled his hands into fists and then released them, visibly trying to calm himself down. "I want to do more than catch him. But I have to tell you before she wakes up."

I eyed Crispin, trying to guess his motives. It didn't seem like this was something he wanted to do. Unlike the previous day, where he had played his games before attempting to tell me, he now seemed as if he was being forced. I glanced at Liel, who only met my gaze for a moment before looking away again. She clearly was in on what this was all about, and why Crispin had to tell me before Justina woke up, but the banshee was keeping her distance. I returned my gaze to Crispin, who shuffled uncomfortably.

"And it has to be now?"

"Yes. Please." He replied curtly.

I placed the flash drive back on the counter and motioned Crispin to follow me. Kisten and Liel watched our moves, both of their expressions unreadable as I walked out into Kisten's backyard. It was starting to get late in the day and the sun was already low behind the trees. As soon as I closed the door, I rounded on the vampire.

"Now, tell me what the hell this is about, because if it's just to tell me you're sleeping with her or something, I swear to the Gods I'll end you." I hissed and Crispin looked away from me, not meeting my gaze anymore. He was smiling wryly and honestly looked like he'd rather be anywhere but in the backyard with me. We remained this way for a moment, and my frustration only grew as the silence dragged on.

"She made me swear to tell you before she saw me again. Cast a spell and everything," he whispered and I had to lean in to hear him. His voice held echoes of different emotions, but mostly anger. "That's why I wasn't with her when I should've been, or none of this would've happened. I should have just told you in the garden, but I–"

"Tell me what?"

"That she's pregnant," he breathed, and I froze to the ground I was standing on. I waited for him to say he was joking and laugh his cocky laugh, but he remained silent. When Crispin finally looked up to me, his expression was unreadable. "And yes, I'm... I'm the father."

"So, all that in the garden was..." I let my sentence trail, clearly not seeing the connection. He ran his hand through his golden hair, closing his eyes for a moment. "Was to tell me that?"

"She knew you hadn't forgiven yourself over me turning and she didn't know how to tell you herself, lest it felt like she was betraying you. It was her idea for me to tell you in the garden that I planted, once she and I... started getting serious. She wanted you to see that Mikael was still a part of me, even if I don't remember that life."

Crispin frowned and then chuckled. "She never told me anything about us before you did, even though I suspected there was more to her wanting to keep our relationship a secret. All she would say is that it felt wrong for her to be happy with me the way I was. Well, mostly happy."

I stood awestruck, taking in what Crispin was saying. It was like Justina to think that way, especially since I didn't know she had any sort of relationship with Crispin, much less romantic. I'd told her all my regret and guilt concerning Crispin and it would only make sense that she would feel guilty for actually preferring him the way he was now. I dropped my head into my hand, still trying to make sense of it.

"So, explain to me why you acted the way you did in the garden." I insisted, gesturing with my free hand. Crispin stiffened, clearing his throat. "I know children are a big deal to vampires, and then there's the whole issue with Justina being a sorcerer, but that doesn't explain why you didn't just tell me. Why kiss me?"

"That was, uh... mostly just me being me." He flinched as I lifted my head, my eyes glowing with power. "Mostly, Raiven. Justina wanted you to see that I wasn't just an asshole, but I... I guess some part of me wanted that too.

"I know you don't like me, and I'm not asking you to. Lucius wants us to be civil and I accept that's why he didn't want you to tell me at first. I'm not Mikael: I'm not the guy you fell for." He sounded sincere, and his voice almost sounded like he was pleading with me. I released my power as he continued. "I like my freedom, to flirt around as much as I want, to have whomever I want. But I also really do care for Justina and she gets me, accepts me in a way most people don't. I hate... I... I wish I had met her sooner."

I remained silent at this, unsure of what to say as Crispin's eyes shone with his tears. The vampire took my silence as a hopeful sign, stepping closer to me and gently touching my arm. I didn't pull back, and so he pulled me into a full hug, holding me close. After a moment, I returned his hug, and his body relaxed. He breathed deep into my hair before speaking again.

"You don't have to feel guilty anymore, Raiven. You didn't ruin me." He whispered and it wasn't until I realized his shirt was growing wet that I recognized that I was crying. I thought I had gotten over losing Mikael, that I had forgiven myself for not being there the night he was turned, but when I was forced to face who he had become, I realized how much I was still holding on to the past. I vented to Justina frequently about my frustration, my disappointment, and my guilt over Crispin, and despite that, Justina never said a word to him about his past. She waited for me to do it, waited until I was ready to try to move past it and then wanted me to see that I was wrong.

"I'm sorry, Crispin." I spoke against his chest, not ready to release him. "I...I don't think I'll ever like who you've become."

"You don't have to."

"But," I continued, pulling back slightly to look up at him, "I think I can accept it and move past it."

Crispin smiled down at me and leaned down as if to kiss me. I let him, and he placed a soft kiss on my forehead, lips barely brushing my skin. When he pulled back up, he had a gentle smile on his face and his eyes were shining with tears of relief.

"I'm guessing she can't be far along," I said, releasing him completely and wiping the tears from my eyes. Crispin stepped back from me as well, his smile evolving into a full grin, full of happiness. This only lasted a moment before his smile faded and he looked away, gripping his arm tightly.

"She's not, but do you think I..." His voice trailed off and I nodded, understanding what he wanted me to ask. Crispin had fulfilled the conditions of Justina's spell, meaning he could finally go see her for himself. The spell was probably also the reason Alex had to help Lucius carry Justina to the surface: once he had removed the door, it would have kept him from being able to approach her since he hadn't told me. I doubted that Justina's pregnancy was surprising to Kisten, and he had refrained from saying anything to respect her privacy.

"Let's go back inside. I still want to drop the evidence off at the office and Kisten can take you guys to the hospital." I insisted and saw Crispin raised his eyebrow at my suggestion, confusion on his face.

"You know you're supposed to stay together?"

"It's fine." I waved him off, turning to walk inside and after a moment, I heard him follow me. "We know this is a revenge thing, and he's not targeting us in the Coven or anything. It'll be fine."

Kisten and Liel were still in the kitchen, watching us as we returned. Liel looked to Crispin, who merely nodded at her. The dark-skinned banshee sighed, smiling as she leaned into the counter, her eyes drifting to me.

"Should've told her yesterday." She jabbed and Crispin winced, but he was smiling as he moved to hug her.

"And forgo all the dramatic tension?" He laughed as she tried to evade his arms and I couldn't help but smile as I stood next to where Kisten sat. While Crispin tried to plant a kiss on Liel, who was actively pushing him away, I laid my hand on Kisten's shoulder and ignored the pain as he touched my hand. I looked down to find him watching me, his eyes calm. I started to remember that he had wanted to say something earlier and had just opened my mouth to ask when I was interrupted by Crispin whistling.

"Looks like Justina and I weren't the only ones hiding our relationship." He finally released Liel, who scratched him as he let her go. He hissed at her, but she merely shrugged, turning away from him. I immediately released Kisten and cleared my throat as I looked away. Crispin then turned his attention to the Alpha, leaning across the counter to be eye level with him. "Finally found a Beta? I thought you enjoyed being by yourself."

"Not all of us like to lick every cupcake first." Kisten replied smartly and Liel had to cover her mouth to hide a giggle. Crispin laughed openly, standing back up with his usual gravitas.

"What can I say? I'm a man who likes his dessert." At this Kisten stood, and it looked like he had something to say, but the two men merely locked hands. Crispin seemed genuinely happy for Kisten as he spoke. "Glad you found someone who can deal with you."

"Same to you." Kisten chuckled, releasing his hand and, heading back to the stairs, paused to kiss me. I touched my burning lips as he walked up to the bedroom to retrieve his keys, unable to help my embarrassment. Crispin laughed out loud at this, throwing his head back as he howled. Both Liel and I looked at the vampire in question, who was wiping away tears.

"God, who knew that man could be jealous?" he squeaked out through tears, wiping away the pink fluid. Upon noticing my confused expression, he did his best to quell his laughter. "I came to Lucius shortly after he became an Overseer. Kisten had been here the whole time and never once have I seen that man be with anyone, much less jealous. I thought maybe he wasn't into people, or whatever you guys call it nowadays."

"Asexual." Liel and I spoke at the same time and Crispin nodded, getting his laughter under control. He moved to turn on the kitchen light as it grew darker outside, bathing us all in light once again. Liel giggled slightly in her corner, meeting my gaze as I looked at her.

"I'll admit it, I thought that too." She shrugged, gesturing toward Crispin. "I think most people have that opinion of Kisten. He almost never talks to anyone. In the past fifty years I've been here, you're only like the second person I've ever seen Kisten hang out with."

"Who was the first?" I jumped at the question and both Crispin and Liel gave me a confused look, as if I should've known. Liel opened her mouth to answer when Kisten's arms wrapped around my middle, startling me. He cleared his throat, interrupting the banshee.

"We should get going." Kisten kissed the back of my neck before letting go, walking toward the front door. Liel looked as if she was still going to answer my question before deciding against it, following him out. As Crispin and I trailed behind them, I couldn't help but wonder what the banshee had been going to tell me.

12

"Hey Raiven."

I looked up from my desk as Julia leaned over me, watching me scroll through the video on my computer. As soon as Kisten dropped me off, I passed off the screenshots and video of Justina's night at The Dream to Chris and began working on other surveillance videos that he had managed to get access to. All of the Overseers were more than willing to work with us, providing everything we needed as quickly as they could: they wanted this solved just as much as we did. I paused the video I was working on and looked over my shoulder at her.

"What's up?"

"We got in contact with Josh, that bartender from The Dream." She smiled as she spoke, and I turned around in my chair, waiting for her to continue. She leaned against the wall opposite me, a bright smile on her face. "The local division is questioning him now and Justin and Brandon are joining remotely. Hopefully, he can confirm your theory and get us that visual."

"The footage already does that, at least the theory part." I turned back to my computer, zooming in on the frame that I had paused. It was clearly the same man that Justina had met in The Dream and

Julia gasped as she recognized the form of the man. "This is the third time I've found this man talking to a victim. He is most certainly our killer, but I can't see his face clearly in any of these videos."

"He must be doing that on purpose. He probably looks for the cameras to avoid them." Julia concluded and I nodded, letting out a frustrated sigh. Technology had advanced so much since I had started doing this and still we couldn't identify a killer from a video. Julia shook her head, clearly sharing my sentiment. "We would need video of the first victim, before he would have thought to hide his face."

"Yeah, but we don't have a connection for that first crime." I sighed, leaning back in my chair again as I recited the details. "That was the one that took place in a coffee shop in broad daylight. Eight people died, including the cashiers. The only survivor was the manager, who was in his office with the door closed. Guess he didn't think to check there. Or didn't care."

"Yeah, and as far as we've been able to discover, not one of those victims had visited a bar, club or similar environment leading up to the massacre. Even the café's surveillance doesn't show this guy arriving before the killing, so he must've met his target somewhere else," Julia continued and I nodded. She frowned, clearly trying to piece the puzzle together in her mind. "But if they met on the street or something, we'd have no way to tell who the target was. And now that I think about it, why don't we have a video of the killings?"

"The camera was destroyed during the attack, remember?" I reminded her and she closed her eyes in thought. The local division had been so upset about it that they almost didn't want to tell us. We still hadn't been able to determine if the camera being destroyed was premeditated, or simply a consequence of the violent attack.

"So, we really have nothing about the first one, not even the gender of his target."

"Nope, because he seems to go after men too." I stood, turning to face her, walking away from my desk to find Chris. Julia followed behind me as I continued my train of thought. "We also need to determine why his switch was suddenly flipped. Why did he suddenly decide to start killing? The way this guy gets turned down, insulted or humiliated, there's no way the café was the first time that ever happened."

"Because he got away with the first one?" Julia offered and I shrugged, not slowing my stride.

"Possibly. We weren't called on until the third killing and now, with Justina's attack, we're up to six. The time between killings has been on a steady decline and the number of victims on a steady incline, so he's definitely been getting more confident. We're really on a tight schedule to find him before he leaves again." I shook my head as I knocked before opening the door, letting Julia walk in before me. Chris was still running the woman's face through our database and smiled at us as we walked in.

"Still searching," he glanced at his computer, watching the images fly by. "I've checked if she was human as well as all of our suspected races. I didn't get a match, so we can rule out her being the killer."

"Not yet," I interrupted him, remembering what LeAlexende had told me at the hospital. "It's possible our killer could be a hybrid and we can't rule out that this woman and the guy may be a pair."

"But she hasn't shown up in any other locations, has she? Just the male, from what I've noticed."

"Can't rule out that she's a shapeshifter species," I insisted and Chris nodded, seeing my line of thinking. "It is safe to assume that this would be her actual appearance, as Justina recognized her when she arrived. She was too friendly with the man at The Dream for that to be the first time they met."

"Alright, I'll shift my focus to shapeshifting species." Chris paused his current search and started to change the parameters in the search bar. I nodded as he started the new search, more pictures flashing next to our sample image. He turned to Julia and me, waving us out of his office. "There's no need to stand around, I'll call a meeting as soon as I get a match. Although if she is a shapeshifter, I'll also need to…"

Julia and I had to hide our laughter as we left, closing the door behind us. Chris was by far the most excited when it came to Supernaturals and was our team's current specialist on current affairs. If he had known how old I was, I'm sure he would've loved to sit me down and bleed me dry of my knowledge. However, only the Director knew the truth, and as far as my team was concerned, I was human like the rest of them. My official role was as a history specialist; since so many Supernaturals outlived humans, it was considered important to understand their hidden history and it helped to hide why I knew as much as I did about them.

"Hey..." Julia stopped walking, her expression lost in thought behind me. "Just a thought, but wouldn't he stay until he could kill Justina?"

"What do you mean?" I asked, and she gestured in the empty air between us.

"I mean, wouldn't he be upset about not getting to finish her off?" she reasoned, and I crossed my arms, turning to face her. "I mean, he's always successfully killed his target since he started. That's why he's kept doing it: he's had a taste of retribution and he loved it."

"Except Justina, who somehow survived." I added and she nodded, still lost in her own thoughts.

"Right. I don't think he'll leave town until he gets her. It's almost a matter of pride at this point. He managed to kill more than fifteen people last time, but this time he couldn't even kill a single witch?" Julia had a point and I hummed as I thought of a response.

"That is possible, but..."

"Um, Raiven?" Julia and I were interrupted as the receptionist called out to me, and she was a bit frazzled as she stepped back into the office. I gave her a concerned look and she tried to pull herself together, her voice still shaking. "Um, the Alpha is here to see you. He says it's important."

I groaned out loud, rolling my eyes. I had told Kisten to call me before he came back to pick me up, but it was obvious that my preferences weren't on the table. Julia continued back to her desk as I walked up front with the receptionist, seeing Kisten in the lobby by himself. Both Crispin and Liel had been impatient to see Justina and I would imagine that, now that they had delivered the video, the pair was no longer interested in being with me or Kisten.

"Raiven." Kisten didn't give me a moment to say a word, immediately grabbing me. His tone was worried and his eyes were swirling with power. "We need to get back to the Coven *now*."

"Shh, Kisten, not so loud," I dropped my voice and, giving the receptionist a smile, moved Kisten to the opposite side of the lobby. He looked over to her and back to me, confused by my reaction. I leaned him down, speaking to him in a hushed tone. "No one here knows that I'm more than human, that's part of my agreement."

"The woman is at the Coven. The one from the video," Kisten whispered and I raised my eyebrows in surprise. "She was asking Lucius for protection. Says she knows who did this to Justina."

"Then I need to get Brandon and bring her in."

"Lucius has her locked up in the Basement." Kisten said urgently and I suddenly understood his impatience and concern. The Basement was only meant to hold those Lucius had deemed a danger to others and having her down there meant he would not give her up so easily. I sighed, frustrated by this news.

"Why?"

"He doesn't want to risk that she's the one who did this. He says he'll only give her up to you guys once you have the man in custody as well." Kisten glanced toward the receptionist before looking at me again. "She's a lamia, originally from the west coast, but she never checked in with me when she arrived."

"How do you know she's there then?" From the way he was speaking, it clearly wasn't Lucius who told him, and Eve never would've offered that up for free, especially if it would help me. Kisten groaned, clearly not seeing how it mattered.

"Aurel called me." His tone was annoyed and worried and he gestured toward the door. "We need to go, before Lucius does something to her and you lose the only lead you have. He's beyond pissed."

"Okay, okay," I sighed, and Kisten fidgeted, clearly in a hurry to leave. I gave him a curt nod as I walked back toward the office. "Give me a second to update Brandon and I'll come with you. I'll only be a moment."

"Hurry." Kisten called after me as I walked back through the security door, clearly antsy in the chair as he sat. I made directly for the interrogation room, where Brandon and Justin were still questioning Josh. The poor boy looked terrified on the hologram and was fidgeting as he spoke. I couldn't blame him for his fear; it was likely that Lucius could blame him for what happened to Justina, even though he had no part other than being present. However, he was a shapeshifter and therefore a part of Kisten's pack, so there was no way Kisten would allow any harm to come to him, regardless of Lucius' anger.

I knocked on the door, getting Brandon's attention. He glanced back at the glass and, despite not being able to see me, I knocked against it. He excused himself from the projection and quietly slid out the door to see who it was. He clearly was not expecting it to be me, as his tone was surprised as he spoke.

"Raiven? I'm in the middle of–"

"Lucius has the woman," I said, making it evident that there was no time to waste. Brandon cursed under his breath and he stepped out into the hallway as I continued. "She's a lamia who's not from this area, so he refuses to release her until we have the guy in custody."

"But we don't know if she's involved beyond Justina." he reasoned, echoing what Chris had said earlier and I sighed, slightly frustrated at their naivete. Must be nice.

"I know, but Lucius is not going to risk it. Lamias are shapeshifters who can look like anyone, so it would be hard to be sure. Besides, I don't think Lucius cares if she's involved beyond Justina: she's involved *with* Justina." I countered and he cursed again, clearly frustrated. "I just came to let you know the state of things. I'm heading there now to see if I can convince him to at least let me talk to her."

"Go. The kid's agreed to give us access to his memories and we're just waiting on the tech. Hopefully, we can get the visual of him soon and find the bastard." Brandon agreed and I turned and left, almost jogging through the office as I made it back to Kisten. Julia called my name as I ran past, but I ignored her as I stepped back into the lobby. Without a word, Kisten stood and opened the door for me, and I instantly shivered as the cold air hit me, not expecting it as I looked around for his car.

"Where..." I didn't get to finish speaking as Kisten padded up next to me, fully shifted into his leopard form. He rubbed his head against my hand and lay down, clearly waiting for me to get on. Kisten must've been truly worried about what Lucius would do, as it was dangerous for him to roam the city in animal form. He was one of the few shifters who could probably do so without being spotted, but it was still only something he did when he was in a hurry. I hopped onto the giant cat, grabbing hold of his fur tightly and pressing myself against him. He stood and took off into the night, heading for the Landing.

As the wind rushed past us in the cold night air, I couldn't help but hope we could reach Lucius before the worst happened.

13

I leapt off Kisten's back as we arrived at the Coven and he shifted back to human as I started down the stairs. I wasn't surprised when Aurel and Grace met us in the hallway, hurrying along behind us as we rushed past them.

"Lucius and Evalyn are currently out, they just left Nirvana." Aurel sounded out of breath as we reached the second set of stairs, Kisten and me not pausing as we continued down. Nirvana was one of Lucius' clubs on the other side of town and it would take him a good while to get back to the Coven. "I don't know how long it'll be before they get here. Lucius is absolutely furious–"

"I'm not waiting, he can punish me later," I interrupted, letting Kisten pass me so he could open the door to the Basement. Only one of the Three, or someone with Lucius' permission, could open the door, so I was truly lucky to have Kisten on my side. "There was no telling what Lucius will do to her once he comes back, and I'm not willing to risk losing my only lead to catching the one who hurt Justina."

"Alpha..." Grace's voice trailed off as she fidgeted behind Aurel, and Kisten turned to face her as he finished opening the door. His expression softened and he nodded curtly as he swung the door open. Grace sighed with relief, clutching her shirt as she quickly ascended the stairs. I was confused by their interaction but turned to enter the dungeon.

When we arrived in the Basement, it was as if I had stepped into a different era. The walls were lit with torches and before me was a hallway lined with stone cells, iron bars holding in the inhabitants. I had never been in the Basement and even now, I wanted nothing more than to run back up to the safety of the surface as Grace had done. The medieval atmosphere of the dungeon only brought back horrible memories of my first few years away from Mother and fleeing her Hunters.

Steeling myself, I quietly walked past the cells, only glancing into each in the hope of seeing the woman. I knew most of these people deserved to be down here: to be in the Basement was considered a fate worse than death. Anyone down here had either hurt someone else in the area, or betrayed Lucius' trust. They would be down here until the day they died, or until the day Lucius finally decided to kill them.

"There," Aurel pointed to a cell in front of me and I could hear a woman crying as we got closer. "That's where she is."

"Kisten, go back up. See if you can talk some sense into Lucius once he arrives." Kisten obeyed, nodding as he went back, disappearing into darkness as he ascended the stairs. I stopped in front of the cell Aurel had pointed out, with the lich hovering close behind me. It was indeed the woman from the video, but her lower half was no longer human. She leaned against the wall, tears evident on her face as she sat coiled on her beautiful brown tail. Her scales flexed as she looked at me, a sad expression on her face.

"Are you here to punish me?" she asked softly, barely lifting her head from the stone. She leaned against it again after I shook my head. "You should be. I don't deserve kindness."

"What's your name?" I dropped my voice, doing my best to sound professional and polite. She dragged herself from the wall, slithering across the floor to meet me at the bars. She raised herself to my height and we looked deeply into one another's eyes. She must've trusted what she saw there, because she dropped herself back down, sitting on her coils again before she spoke.

"Irida."

"Why are you in Decver?"

"I'm here with my boyfri–" She stopped herself, sighing as she began to cry softly. I grabbed the bars that separated us, pulling myself closer to the barrier.

"Is he the one who hurt Justina?" She visibly flinched as I said this, and her next response was low and full of her tears.

"Yes... no... yes," She looked up at me again, tears flowing freely down her face. Her top was soaked, indicating that she had been crying for a while, probably since Aurel had brought her down here. "I... you have to help me. Please."

"Why do you need help?" I asked softly, dropping to my knees to meet her gaze. She looked away, as if she couldn't bear to look at me. She started to openly sob again, the sounds echoing through the stone hallways. I pushed my hand through the bars and she took it, squeezing it tightly as she tried to calm herself down. "Has he threatened to hurt you? To kill you, too?"

"No... yes," she stammered. "Not outright, just... I swear, I didn't know what he was doing at the time, it wasn't until Justina that I realized–"

She stopped as the door to the Basement flew open and, from the electricity in the air, I knew Lucius had arrived. I released her hand as I stood, and she slithered back into her corner, terrified of the Overseer. I readied myself as Lucius came into view, both Evalyn and Kisten trailing behind him. His blue eyes were practically glowing, and his calm face did little to hide his obvious anger.

"Raiven," he stated my name and I fought the urge to kneel, ignoring his silent command. Eve looked at me shocked, her gaze turning to Lucius as I disobeyed him. The Overseer continued up to me, standing over me as I remained on my feet, refusing to back down from his gaze. Kisten and Eve stopped a distance away from us, standing side by side. "You cannot take her."

"I am not trying to," I fought my legs as they tried to buckle, and I stomped my foot, planting my legs apart. Lucius' expression did not change, but the electricity in the air changed as he shifted the charge. "I am questioning her."

"There is nothing to question," he stated, and the lamia whimpered in her cell, understanding that he would not help her. I glared back at Lucius as I summoned my own power, my green eyes starting to swirl as the stone around us began to shake. Lucius raised his eyebrow at my obvious threat. "Are you challenging me, Raiven?"

"I am." I growled, the air growing heavy as I summoned my power to challenge his. It was starting to get difficult to breathe between the electricity and dense air, but I would not back down to Lucius. My own behavior was slightly surprising to me, but I pushed these thoughts away as I spoke. "I *will not* allow you to hurt her."

"*You will obey me.*" Lucius' face changed, visibly showing the anger he had kept hidden behind his facade and all of our hair stood on end as the charge in the air increased. I raised more of my own power, the stone beneath our feet shifting and changing as I glared. Lucius scowled at me and even Eve backed away from him, almost cowering behind Kisten as she started to lose her grip on her human form. Her horns started to peek out from her hair as she whimpered, but Kisten ignored her, keeping his eyes on me. I could tell from his expression that he was clearly worried, but I was unwavering in my conviction.

"*I will not.*" I insisted, refusing to look away from Lucius and the glow in his eyes grew brighter with his anger. "And you cannot make me. I *will* question her and I *will* get the information I need."

Lucius seemed ready to raise his hand against me and I readied myself to retaliate. I heard Aurel behind me step back, clearly wanting to get away from the struggle between me and Lucius. Eve shared his sentiments, grabbing Kisten for protection as her tail appeared behind her.

"**Rai–**"

"Lucius!" Kisten interrupted him and Lucius paused, his eyes still locked on mine. Kisten took this as a good sign and took a step closer, forcing Eve to release him. His movements were slow and cautious as he reached out to the Overseer. "This is not how we agreed to do things. Raiven is just trying to do her job."

"Justina—"

"Will be fine." Kisten insisted, still moving closer to his friend. The glow in Lucius' eyes wavered for a moment, but his gaze didn't move from mine. I backed down a bit, recalling my power as Kisten continued. "Blood for Blood, but not this. If you kill or harm this woman, she'll never catch the one who actually attacked Justina. This is not how we wanted to do things; we agreed to never do things Her way."

Lucius closed his eyes at the mention of Mater Vitae and he seemed as if he were taking Kisten's words to heart. His eyes still glowed when he opened them again, but the charge in the air had lessened. I still met his eyes evenly, waiting to see what he would do. He glanced at Irida, who cowered under his gaze and she shifted further into the corner, as if trying to escape him. His eyes softened for a moment, and I ventured a chance to speak.

"By all means, keep her. She wanted your protection, anyway," I suggested, and Lucius returned his attention to me as his eyes narrowed. I fought the urge to cower and took a deep breath. "I just want to question her and get whatever I can from her."

"Then question her." Lucius relented, standing against the wall across from her cell and motioning Evalyn and Kisten to his side. Kisten immediately moved to his friend's side and Eve reluctantly obeyed, leaning against him as he wrapped his arm around her. Taking a deep breath, I turned to face Irida again, dropping to my knees.

"Irida." She jumped as if struck when I called her name, and I spoke more softly. "Please, Irida, I need you to tell me what you can."

"I... I can't," she whined, hiding deeper in her corner as she started to sob again. "He has a spell on me, I can't act against him. I can't even say his name anymore."

"He's a spellcaster?" I coaxed and she nodded, turning her teary eyes to me. She seemed to have some determination despite her fear, and she was trying to figure out what she could say. "A witch, or a warlock?"

"I swear I didn't know. I thought he was a normal human," she moaned, trying her best to speak between sobs as she chose her words carefully. "I didn't know he was using me to do... to do... those things..."

"Wait," Kisten interrupted me, and she jumped at the sound of his voice, turning away again. "He controlled you?"

"Yes." she wailed, the answer sending her into another crying fit. The air charged around us again and I turned anxiously to Lucius. His grip on Eve had tightened and he was looking at Irida darkly as she cried. I was stunned into silence as she wailed, her tears having long since dried from the lack of water. I glanced at Kisten and I knew we were having the same thoughts: only witches had the ability to control other beings against their will. It was rare for one to be able to control humans, and even worse if they could do it to other Supernaturals.

"I didn't know what he was doing, I didn't know he was using me for my mother's ability." Irida suddenly flung herself into the wall, the sound of her body colliding with the stone causing a cracking sound that made my stomach turn. Kisten didn't hesitate as he threw open the bars and rushed in to check on her. Her arm was bleeding, and Kisten reached for the sheet that lay on the simple bed, tearing it to make a bandage. Irida was covering her mouth as she tried to calm herself down, and she looked at me, begging me with her expression. It was clear that it was the spell that had caused her to hurt herself and she was frantic to find the right words. "He said we were going on a road trip and I didn't think anything of it. Ju... Here... I... I realized when I saw Justina..."

"You stopped yourself," I finished and she nodded, covering her mouth again. Her beautiful brown eyes were red from her tears and she pulled in a shaky breath. She was truly trying her best to help me, despite the obvious danger to herself. I curled my fingers in anger as Kisten checked her arm to make sure nothing was broken. I had to close my eyes and take a deep breath before I could speak again.

"That's why Justina survived, why no major organs were damaged. You were able to overpower him once you realized."

"To overcome means to be aware. I was never aware of what was happening. I think he always waited until... I only realized he had taken precautions when I tried to tell Justina," she lamented, slithering away from Kisten and back up to me, taking my hands again. Her grip was desperate and my fingers ached from how tightly she squeezed them together. "She... tried to help me. That's how she got hurt. She was trying to... stop me while he was trying to regain control... Eventually, when they came to the door, he gave up and Justina told me to hide."

"Where have you been all this time?" I spoke soothingly, shifting her grip and stroking the back of her hands. Irida hiccupped as she tried to control her emotions, chancing a glance at Lucius. He was merely watching her blankly and she returned her gaze to me. I hushed her, trying to help keep her calm. "It's okay, just tell me."

"I've... I've been here the whole time," she admitted, her body shaking from fear. "I didn't know how to leave. I don't even know where *here* is, so I stayed hidden in Justina's room. I came out when I knew he was trying to control me again. I knew there were people at the door and I needed someone to help me.

"Please, I don't want to hurt anyone, I don't want to kill anyone!" she screamed, grabbing my hands and squeezing them painfully again as she begged, even turning her gaze to Lucius. "Kill me if you have to, but don't let him use me anymore! Please!"

I turned to look at Lucius, who had turned away from her completely. Kisten was watching his friend as he stepped out of the cell, all waiting to see what he would say. I understood that he had to feel torn: as one of the First, he understood what it was like to be forced to do things against your will, including killing those you cared about. However, his own anger toward her for what she had done was fighting his compassion and I wasn't sure which would win out. I wanted to believe Lucius would be reasonable, but emotions weren't always logical.

"She will stay down here, far from where he can reach her," he stated, his voice still full of anger. "If he attempts to control her, I will kill her, as she asked."

"I'll find him before then," I swore, releasing Irida's hands and turning to face the vampire. He met my gaze, clearly still upset with me for my earlier insubordination. "When he is caught, you will release her, and you can take your anger out on him. He is to blame, not her."

"Of course," he agreed and Kisten sighed, moving to comfort the lamia as she started crying again, this time with relief. Eve watched the whole exchange silently, chancing a glance up to Lucius as her horns and tail retreated. The vampire ignored her however, keeping his eyes on me. "Do you have any leads?"

"We know what he looks like, thanks to Josh, and now we know he's a witch." I revealed, glancing back to the sobbing woman. She was limp in Kisten's arms, her shoulders still shaking from her predicament. "He won't leave without her, so we know he has to still be in Decver. She's his only means of killing those who slight him. If he could've done it himself, he would've a long time ago."

Lucius nodded as I continued. "He has to know she's here somewhere. After all, it's easier to control someone if you're near them and he must not realize she's underground. He must've been at the shops earlier, if he tried before she revealed herself."

"Keeping her down here is the safest," Kisten added, releasing her and standing as he closed the cell door. "It's not the most comfortable place, but she'll be far from the surface and we can make sure she's safe. He would have to be inside The Dream to even think about getting close enough."

"Which means we could lure him in." Lucius suggested and I nodded in agreement.

"Yeah, we could easily have someone waiting for him." I glanced behind me at the lamia, who had dragged herself back to her corner, facing away from us. It must've been heartbreaking to have been betrayed in the way he had used her, and I started to grow angrier on her behalf. "He'll probably try to avoid coming in, but eventually he'll give in to what we want. Even if he wants to take a hostage to bargain, he knows he'll have to come here."

"What makes you so sure?" Eve asked, giving me a look of disbelief. I closed my eyes, sighing heavily. "It would be smarter to leave her and find someone else."

"Not many can overcome magical barriers, it's an exceedingly rare ability," I reminded her and she refused to accept my explanation, still shaking her head. "If he had been able to find someone before, he would've probably started killing sooner. His ability to control her is probably the only thing he's good at,"

"Even if we know who she is, there's nothing to keep him from using her abilities for himself as he has been. A lamia is hard to keep track of, and he's been using that to his advantage this whole time. By not having her check in with local Alphas, he's basically been smuggling her across the Governances.

"It's also a matter of pride and revenge against her and Justina," I continued, glancing again at the poor woman. "She finally resisted him and cost him his kill. He will use her to kill Justina, even if he kills her afterwards."

Eve looked as if she was going to continue arguing with me, but Lucius silenced her, squeezing her in his grip. His eyes were on Irida as she sobbed quietly in her corner, trying her best to stay out of our way.

"Our people or yours?" he asked, and I sighed, running my hands over my hair.

"Both would be best. Plant a member of my team and a member of the Coven in the club, working together. He won't be afraid if approached by a human, but having a Supernatural as back-up would be mandatory. This guy is too dangerous and too cunning if he can control other Supernaturals, so only someone of the Coven would be strong enough to resist him."

Lucius nodded and looked to Aurel, who stepped back to join us. He merely bowed his head to Lucius and started towards the stairs that would take him above ground. Lucius released Eve and started after Aurel, but was stopped by Kisten.

"A moment?" he asked and Lucius agreed, motioning for Eve to go up without him. She hesitated as if to argue, but decided against it, merely glaring as Kisten walked further into the Basement with Lucius. She then turned her attention to me and glared.

"I bet you just love this, getting to be the one to solve this case," she hissed and I ignored her, starting toward the stairs. I'd had enough of the dungeon and while I felt bad about leaving Irida alone, I couldn't stand the idea of staying. Eve stomped after me, her anger radiating off her. "It should've been the local team; it should've been *me*."

"There's no glory here, Evalyn." I huffed, climbing the dark stairs. She scoffed behind me, turning me around once we reached the Coven. Her horns had started to appear again and I met her gaze evenly, despite the heat from her touch. However, I knew the heat from her had nothing to do with the Oath and everything to do with her own flames. I glared at her evenly, almost daring her to use her powers on me; all I needed was an excuse. "All that matters is stopping this lunatic so he can't hurt anyone ever again. Doesn't matter who does it."

Eve merely hissed at me and I pulled myself from her grip, climbing all the way up to the surface, checking my phone for a signal. She paused as if she was going to follow me, but decided against it, turning down another hallway as I closed the door. I leaned against the wall as I waited for a signal, my thoughts turning to poor Irida.

I'll get him, for both of you. I swore, calling the office as soon as my service returned. *He's going to regret this dearly.*

14

After putting the finishing touches to my plan with Brandon and the team, I hung up, closing my eyes as I leaned against the building. I glanced at my phone as it reminded me of its low battery, and I peeled myself from the wall. I walked to my car still in the parking lot, exhaustion hitting me as I sat inside.

I started her up and plugged in my phone, closing my eyes again as I waited for Julia to arrive. I had told her what Aurel looked like and to meet him in front of The Dream, but I wasn't sure if he'd be there. She was supposed to call me if she couldn't find him and I lifted my phone to check the time.

The bright screen told me it was 9:45pm, and I knew The Dream had opened a short while ago. I doubted our suspect would come tonight, but we couldn't rule out the possibility of it happening. Thanks to her refusal of him, he had to know that Irida had betrayed him, and depending on how impatient he was, it was possible that he would do whatever it took to find her.

I looked up as the door to the Coven opened and I saw Kisten step out, a soft look on his face. I had been curious as to what he wanted to talk to Lucius about, but it was obvious that it was private, and not something he wanted to share. My thoughts drifted to his annoyed behavior while Crispin and Liel were at his house, and I readied myself to face him as he looked around for me.

"Here," I turned off my car and opened my door, motioning him toward me. Kisten walked toward me and I was slightly worried as he pulled me out of my car and closed the door. He wrapped his arm around my waist, and I glanced around anxiously. "What are you doing? What if someone sees–"

I was interrupted as he leaned down to kiss me, and for the first time, no intense heat and pain followed. Surprised, but not wanting to let the moment pass, I wrapped my arms around him as he pulled me closer. I let my tongue dance across his lips, enticing him to let me in. He did, and I almost moaned at the sensation of our tongues sliding against one another without the usual pain distracting me. He almost seemed to be trying to drink me in and I let him, clinging to him as we kissed.

"Kisten," I gasped, pulling back after what seemed like eternity. "Why didn't the Oath affect me?"

"Till sunrise." He smiled, hugging me close as if I'd disappear if he let me go. His voice caressed my skin as he spoke softly against it. "Until sunrise, you can be mine."

So that's what you asked Lucius. I smiled, hugging him tightly, silently thanking Lucius for this small gift. "How did you talk him into it? How did you talk *Eve* into it?"

"Being honest. I told him I wanted to make you my mate and court you correctly." Kisten shrugged as he pulled me towards the back door of The Dream, and I pulled against him slightly. "Asked for one night free of the Oath to convince you and he agreed. I'd imagine Eve is not happy about it."

"But why are we..." I started, but Kisten pulled me inside and I found myself drowned in bodies and loud music. He pulled me towards the bar and sat me in his lap.

"You are in dire need of a distraction. Let Aurel and your team handle the case for one night." He waved to the bartender, another member of the pack. She bounced toward him and smiled, clearly recognizing her Alpha. "Vodka for the lady and gin for me."

"Of course, Kisten." She winked at him, a gleam in her eye as she looked at me. As she turned to make our drinks, I tried to slide out of his lap but he wrapped his arms around me to keep me still. Kisten then pulled me higher so that I could know how happy he was to have me there. Just feeling how hard he was, that hardness pressing into my thigh, made me catch my breath.

"I like you in my lap." His voice caressed my ear as the bartender set our glasses down. Her expression told me that she understood her Alpha's intentions and she smiled at me brightly.

"First round's on me, as thanks for earlier," The girl giggled and I watched as her brown eyes shone brightly, and I faintly caught the scent of the ocean as she took my hand. "You take good care of him."

"Do you have to make it so obvious?" I sipped on my glass as she released me and he laughed. I hummed as I refused to look at him, the song drifting into another similar sounding tune.

"They'll all know soon enough." He reasoned, kissing my skin and I sighed with relief. I almost missed the pain but couldn't deny the simple pleasure of feeling his lips on my skin without it. It was as if he was trying to drive me crazy, giving me a taste of what it would be like if I were his mate... if I would say yes to him like he knew I wanted to.

Trying to clear my head of those thoughts, I turned my gaze to the sea of movement. If I hadn't known we were in a club, I could've almost sworn this was some type of sex ceremony. I had never been inside a club like this: even when Lucius required me to help, I mostly stayed outside, helping with security. The intense energy and movement was new to me and I wondered what the appeal of the environment was.

Out of the corner of my eye, I saw a young man walking in the front door and I couldn't help but tense up as he glanced around the club. He spotted me and made a beeline for my seat and as he grew closer, I recognized that he looked nothing like our suspect. Once he saw the Alpha holding me in his lap, he tried to mask his actions and sat two seats away, his eyes still on me. I couldn't help but laugh and give him a wink as I took another sip of my drink. I leaned back against Kisten so he could hear me over the noise. "No competition, hmm?"

"I would certainly hope not." He glanced behind us, looking for my pursuer. Upon noticing the man staring at me, he smiled, his fangs visible as his eyes swirled with power. The man quickly left his seat and I glared at Kisten, hitting him playfully.

"You did that on purpose. Poor guy probably wet his pants."

"I'd buy his fucking drinks if he didn't." He laughed darkly, and I gave him a surprised look. I had never heard such vulgar language from Kisten before and it sounded so foreign in his voice. Having finished his own, he took my drink and nearly drained it. He waved for the bartender to refill them, sliding some bills underneath the glasses. "I saw the way you winked at him."

"Whatever." I turned to my re-filled drink, taking a long swig while trying not to ask the burning question in my mind. Curiosity finally won and I dropped my drink into my lap. "Kisten."

"Yes?"

"Were... are you jealous?"

"Of?" He turned me in his lap so he could see my face, but I gazed into my drink as I avoided looking at him. I couldn't help but remember the dark look he had given Crispin and I suspected Liel had filled him in on the truth about my past with the vampire. His behavior afterwards also appeared to show his jealousy, but I wasn't sure.

"Never mind..."

"Not really," he answered, raising my face to his. He searched my eyes with his before pulling me into another blissful kiss. He was smiling softly when he pulled back, eyes still locked with mine. "Crispin isn't Mikael. You don't like it, but it seems you've accepted that the person you loved is dead. There's nothing to be jealous of."

"Oh." I mumbled, finishing down my drink. Of course Kisten would think that way: with Crispin's relationship with Justina, it was clear that we weren't involved in any way. My mind went back to the other person Liel and Crispin said they had seen Kisten be around and I began to wonder if that had been Kisten's first love.

"Kisten, who did you—"

"Time to dance." he interrupted me, downing his second drink and spinning around in his seat. I hummed with annoyance: it was obvious he was trying to avoid my question, just as he had stopped Liel from telling me earlier.

"But..." I started to protest, but he was out of the seat and pulling me to the dance floor. He swung me so I was in front of him and wrapped his arm around my waist while his other hand gripped mine. His front was pressed along the length of my back, hips intimately touching.

"Tonight's about me and you. Let's enjoy it," he leaned forward as he whispered in my ear, his voice full of darker things. "No Eve, no Crispin, no case: *just us.*"

Since I had never danced before, he started out slow and I followed the line of his body. Once I grasped the movements, it felt as if the beat began to move me; soon I was dancing against him on my own. Kisten whipped me around to face him, still gripping my hand as if I'd run away at my first chance. After a while, I wasn't sure why he was so worried: I was strangely enjoying myself with this new way of dancing.

Soon, however, I got bored with his way of movement: he was keeping it simple, swaying, and a little rubbing. However, this simple dance was not what I wanted, and not what I craved. I did a slow twist of my hips that ground my groin against his, humming with my pleasure. His chartreuse eyes lit with fire as I continued my grinding and twisting.

"Be careful, Raiven." I shuddered slightly as he leaned down and his breath caressed my ear. I flicked out my tongue to tease his earlobe and traced it down the side of his face until I found the warm crevice of his mouth.

"You know I like to play with fire." I smiled, twisting myself again and he growled, planting a kiss on my forehead. "You can't expect me to stop now."

"Is that so?" Once again, our mouths joined in the darkness of the club as he grasped my hips, moving me so that I ground myself against him. With him controlling my movements, the feeling became more intense and I moaned into his kiss. His tongue rolled in and out of mine, mimicking what he wanted to do with my body. I barely noticed as he moved us across the dance floor towards the far wall and I connected with it softly. Kisten gently stroked my face before kissing me again, pressing himself into me. His body was crushing me against the wall, but I loved every second of this pain-free contact. I moved to wrap my arms around his neck, but he stopped me, pinning my hands to the wall above me as I moaned into his kiss. He pulled back after a moment, his eyes now swirling with his lust and desire.

"Decide now, Raiven. Do you want this... want me?" he panted, still trying to exercise some of his careful control. "Because I can't take much more before I decide for you."

I couldn't begin to articulate my need for him. I had wanted Kisten from the moment I had met him, and my desire and love had only grown over the past three years I had been in Decver. I knew this was all to tempt me into being his Beta, but we both already knew what my answer would be.

"Kisten," I began, but I froze against him, tension ringing off my body. Kisten lightly shook me but my mind was completely blank with surprise. "Oh, no-no-no."

"What?" Kisten saw the many emotions flash across my face as my eyes rested on the person at the bar. He leaned across it, his eyes searching as my coworker sat next to him, facing the bartender. Julia's hair was beautifully done and her dress was revealing enough to make me blush, but it was the lich next to her that had my attention.

"Aurel." I could see Kisten's confusion as I began to look for a way to escape, to get away from where he could see me. I felt as if Aurel would be able to pick me out of the squirming crowd, despite how unrealistic that was.

"What's wrong? He's supposed to be here, remember?" Kisten's confusion was obvious in his voice and I squirmed to free my hands from his grip. He held me tightly, however, still refusing to let me go.

"I don't want him to see me like this." I begged and Kisten's eyes darkened with jealousy again as he looked down at me. His growl was barely contained when he spoke again, pressing me into the wall more.

"And why is that? Something I should know about you two?"

"No, I don't..." I stumbled over the words as I tried to explain myself, still twisting to get away. I looked away to the floor but Kisten pinned me closer against the wall, making it evident that he would not let me leave. I moaned as he assaulted my neck, playfully biting and licking me. "Please, Kisten, I just don't want him to see us, this isn't how I want to tell him."

Kisten paused for a moment as he considered my words, his hand tightening around my wrists as he hesitated. Without releasing me, we made our way through the moving bodies along the wall and I knew he meant to take the door leading to the Coven. It was as if the crowd was pushing us where we wanted to go: we floated along the wall, effortlessly moving toward the door. Reaching our escape, Kisten silently opened it and we slipped past the barrier and into the dark stairwell.

As soon as we were in the Coven, Kisten slammed me into the door, assaulting me once again with his mouth as he pinned me against it. The sound of me hitting the door was drowned out by the loud music on the other side and I knew that no one inside was any the wiser to my plight. I moaned openly, my hand grasping his hair as he kissed and bit my neck, working his way down to my collarbone.

"Want to tell me what that was?" he growled, never ceasing his assault on me. I struggled to speak in between my own gasps and moans.

"Aurel, he wants me for his harem." I managed and Kisten paused, standing up straight to meet my gaze. His eyes swirled with a mix of desire and anger and this time, I knew his jealousy was real, unlike the mix of emotions he had shown towards Crispin.

"And?" He spat the word out, no longer touching me sensually but keeping me against the door. I had never seen Kisten angry and I was starting to wish I never had; he loomed over me, his presence and anger filling the stairway as he waited for my answer. I felt like prey as he kept me pinned, and I already knew I would not be able to escape him unless I was willing to hurt him.

"Aurel doesn't take rejection well," I whispered, looking away from Kisten's intense gaze. "I told him I didn't want that, but I haven't told him how I feel about you."

"And?" Kisten pressed, leaning down close to my ear again, breathing his words into me as I shuddered. I could still sense the anger in his words, but it had lessened with my admission and his desire was winning him over again. "How *do* you feel about me?"

"I..." I paused, knowing what he wanted to hear. There was so much more than just how I felt, but that was all Kisten seemed to care about. He was willing to risk everything to keep me at his side, and could I claim to care as much as I did if I wouldn't do the same? Things could be worked out with my job and Kisten was right. I doubted the new Director would be willing to let me go so easily, and as far as the Hunters... he was the Alpha to a First and that made him a target regardless. I closed my eyes, moaning softly as I made up my mind.

"*Kisten...*"

"Tell me." he whispered, taking a deep breath as he breathed in the scent of our combined desire. I knew he wanted to hear me say it, to finally hear me admit it to him. I reached up, cradling Kisten's face with my hands and he let me, his eyes still angry as he waited for my answer. I sighed as I enjoyed the feeling of his skin in my hands, and I couldn't help but stroke his cheek with my thumbs.

"I want you." I breathed. His expression softened at my words, and I whispered my next phrase. "I love you."

"Good." I yelped as he scooped me up and started carrying me down the hallway to his room. I had never been to Kisten's room in the Coven before and barely saw the insignia on the door as he opened it and swung us in. He closed the door with his foot and immediately carried me to the bed, barely giving me time to look around. He laid me on it gently, leaning over me as he stroked my face and I wrapped my arms around him, saying the first thing that came to mind.

"Kiss me."

15

I allowed myself to get lost in his kiss, purely concentrating on how wonderful it felt to have him holding me, kissing me, after all the time we had waited. His arm was firm around my waist, one of my hands tangled in his brown waves while he kissed me, our tongues dancing in passion's embrace. Pulling me closer, he rubbed his groin against mine, and a delicious warmth exploded through my body before settling back in my lower region. I let out a gasp and clung to him as he did it again.

"How badly do you want me, Raiven?" Seeing that masculine smirk on his face, hearing the thickness in his voice, only proved to intensify my desire and I felt as if I might die if I didn't have him in me at that moment. Knowing the effect his words had on me, he held me against his body, and rubbed our groins against each other again. He continued using his body to pin me to the bed until I thought I would fall through it.

"How badly do you want me to be inside you?" Kisten whispered against my skin, enjoying his dominance over me. His words danced over me, flowing like water. "Tell me, Raiven, I want to hear you say you want me."

"This much." I pushed him off me and he let me, lying back on his bed. I slid myself on top of him and relieved him of his shirt. I kissed the crook of his neck as his hands fumbled to remove my shirt and bra. Once he had them off, I slid down his body and, with no great ceremony, I pulled down both his pants and underwear before engulfing his bulging member in my mouth. A gasp hissed from him as I took him in, sucking with deep, rough pulls. His hand found its way to my free one, and he thrust ever so slightly toward me, forcing me to take all of him in.

I came back off him and took my time tasting him, licking every inch. He moaned softly with my tender touches and I felt clenches deep within my own body with every sound that escaped his lovely lips. After an eternity, I slid my lips over him again, slowly taking his throbbing member into my mouth. A moan like a sigh flowed from him as I took it all in until my lips met where my fingers still caressed him. I rolled him in my mouth, moaning softly as I did my best to please him.

He soon pushed me off him and, sitting up, kissed me hungrily, seeking the wet warmth from our kisses. His free hand sought my breast and played with the nub, rubbing, squeezing, and pulling. My soft moans made him smile as his lips pulled away from mine and settled on my other nipple. My hands caressed his head as he licked me with his sandpaper tongue and his hand played with its twin. The lack of pain gave me the chance to focus on the pleasure and I moaned loudly, not even trying to soften my voice.

"Kisten..." I managed to squeeze out his name and he paused, looking up to me. He panted loudly, his fangs visible and his eyes swirling with desire. Light spots were visible on his skin and I knew his animal was helping to drive his actions but, unlike last night, he was completely in control. They were on the same page about it this time, and I couldn't help my excitement.

"Yes?"

"Touch me here, please," I begged, moving his hand from my breast to my wet slit. He kissed the crook of my neck as he undid the snap at the front of my pants and slid a finger along my wet crease, rubbing against my swollen opening. I moaned for him again, my back arching as I finally felt him touch me without pain. The fire had distracted me from just how amazing it was to have him touch me and it was driving me insane.

"This is what you could have," Kisten purred, as he slowly slid two fingers inside and flexed them, watching my face as his actions served to increase my want. My whole body began to throb and pulse with my desire to have him inside me, to have him plunge his hardness into the depths that his fingers now searched. "What *we* could have."

He continued to tease me with his hand while kissing me, using both his fingers and tongue to mimic what he knew I wanted him to do with my body. Soon, my whole body was aflame with my desire for him and I tried to arch away from him, to pull away from his teasing hand and kiss. He wrapped his other arm around my middle, however, holding me where I was, forcing me to endure what I deemed torture. I wanted him inside me, and I knew he could tell; there was no way he couldn't smell how much I wanted him, how much I craved him.

Soon, he broke our kiss to steal a glimpse at my face, and I tried my best to glare, but I couldn't hold onto my annoyance. He smiled and nuzzled my chest and I moaned with frustration. Soon enough, he moved his hand away from my wet slit, and without the added distraction, I managed a halfhearted glare.

"You're being mean."

"I'm being dominant. I am still your Alpha, Raiven," Kisten growled, kissing my cheek as I turned away from him. "Don't worry. I'll give it to you soon enough."

I began to speak when he stood, picking me up and depositing me back on the bed. Swiftly, he removed our remaining clothing, leaving us both nude against the dark blue sheets. After undressing, he climbed on top of me and poised himself above my opening. However, instead of entering me as I wanted, he continued to tease me, only sweeping the outside.

"My, my, you are quite wet down here," I could hear the strain in his voice, knowing that he wanted to be inside me as much as I wanted him there, but couldn't resist the temptation to make me beg him. I began to squirm, and he had to hold me down, pinning my wrists to the bed. He grinned and leaned over me for a kiss, still teasing us both. Even as I kissed him back, I couldn't help my snide smile when we separated. "Feisty tonight."

"Well, if you would just fuck me already, I wouldn't have the energy to be feisty."

"True." He propped himself up and I was so wet, he was able to thrust his full length inside me with one stroke. My hands dug into the sheets as my back arched, and I let out a loud moan as he filled me. Completely inside, Kisten took a moment, his entire body shaking as he enjoyed the sensation of finally being inside me. He leaned over me again, kissing my neck before whispering. "You okay?"

"I'm fine," I breathed, smiling up at him, my eyes half open. "How does it feel to finally give in to me?"

"*Amazing.*" Kisten laughed low in his throat again, causing me to clench around him. Raising himself on his arms, he began to move inside me. The flames of passion that had danced in my lower regions now danced throughout my whole body and I couldn't remain still. I began to squirm as my hands searched for something, anything to hold on to, and soon Kisten had to hold me down again, pinning my wrists to the sheets once more.

"If you had wanted it this bad, you should have just told me." He shook his head and smiled, his eyes still swirling and his spots lightly appearing on his face. Somewhere amidst the thoughts that racked my mind and the heat and pleasure that racked my body, I found my voice.

"I believe I did a year ago, and you turned me down." I shot back and Kisten paused in his movements, leaning down to steal another painless kiss from my lips. I returned it as best I could, unable to help my moans as I raised my hips, trying to force the friction my body craved. The shifter's eyes had completely changed when he pulled away, his grin toothy as he smiled at me.

"Let me make up for that then." With that, he began to pound himself into me, and my hands freed themselves and found his shoulders. The pleasure was almost unbearable, and I felt as if I was drowning in it. Nothing else around us existed to me, except Kisten and the feel of him filling me. I was floating on a cloud of euphoria and pleasure, and he was the balloon that kept carrying me higher.

Moans I didn't recognize as my own and sounds I had never made before began to rise from me, faster and louder as he moved inside me. Kisten's growls grew in intensity as he leaned over me, and I could feel the sharp pain as he held my head with his clawed hand. I could feel the heat from his breath as he panted above me, and I moaned loudly as he bit my shoulder, his fangs penetrating deep.

For a moment, I wondered if I should try not to be so loud, lest someone heard us, but that moment passed, and I decided I didn't care if anyone heard me. The only thing that mattered was the heat and pleasure that resulted from having him inside me and my hands clenched the sheets as I orgasmed for what seemed like eternity. He began to pound himself into me harder and came inside me, whining softly as he released his seed. It was as if he wanted to fill me with his liquid heat and he gripped me tightly as he orgasmed.

Calming down, he gently pulled out and laid down beside me as I panted, still shaking from the residual pulses that my orgasms left in their wakes. Kisten was watching me with a smile, his fangs peeking out of his lips.

"Good enough?" Kisten asked between breaths, obviously tired, his form reverting to human. I merely moaned on the bed beside him, my body still shaking from fatigue. Kisten propped himself up, concerned about my lack of an answer. His hand touched my shoulder, and he looked at the blood with horror. "Raiven!"

"Fine," I managed to pant, giving him a quick thumbs-up as I focused on my breathing. Kisten jumped up from the bed, rushing into his bathroom so he could dress my wound. I hissed slightly as he squeezed the bite, trying to ensure that I would get no infection from his saliva. His movements were slow, as if he were worn out as well, but he dressed the bite properly, taping the gauze over the mark.

"Next time, say something, please." he whined, kissing my shoulder as he finished dressing the wound. I laughed slightly, raising my head to look at him. "You know my saliva is infectious."

"And miss out on that? Never." I blew him a kiss as he gave me an exasperated sigh. "Besides, I'll be all healed by morning from something like this."

"I know you'll heal, but it would not have been fun." He consented, placing the kit on his bedside table before laying a kiss on my stomach and resting his head against me. I closed my eyes, sighing happily as he stroked my thigh.

"I love you." His voice was soft when he spoke again and I sat up at this, forcing him to raise his head. My eyes met his and I reached for him, forcing him to slide back up the bed until we were face to face again. His eyes were shining, and he smiled at me softly as my eyes searched his. My heart pounded in my chest as I took in what he said, cradling his face in my hands. I couldn't help it as I laughed softly, gently kissing his sweet lips.

"I know," I smiled, my chest aching with how much I loved the man in my hands. Kisten purred, sliding us more onto the bed and under the sheets. He intertwined his legs with mine, clearly wanting to enjoy holding me for as long as he could. I buried my face into his chest, breathing him in happily as we settled in to sleep together.

16

I awoke alone in the bed and looked around to see Kisten standing in the doorway to his bathroom, his back to me. I watched him silently for a moment, taking in the view. He had evidently been up for a while; the bathroom mirror behind him was still foggy on the edges and his hair showed signs of dampness. He was fully dressed and engaged in the conversation, laughing quietly at something the other party said.

"...know that's not me." I heard him say, another soft laugh escaping him. From his words, I could only guess that the other person was Lucius, and it was likely they were talking about last night. I sat up slowly, stretching loudly as he turned around to look at me. He dropped his phone away from his ear and smiled at me, moving toward the bed. He covered the mouthpiece with his hand, leaning down to bury his face into my neck.

"Feel free to take a shower," he whispered, and the burning pain from the kiss he planted on my forehead reminded me of how much a blessing the previous night had been. I yawned, taking his suggestion as I slid out of the bed. Kisten hummed with contentment as I walked away and I turned around to find him enjoying the view. He had his phone back to his ear and silently blew me a kiss as I shook my head, stepping into the bathroom and closing the door behind me.

I turned on the shower and waited, looking at the bathroom mirror as I removed the bandage from my shoulder. The first thing I noticed was my hair and I frowned as I touched the glass. Using my power to challenge Lucius had caused my hair to grow quite a bit and I hated how my body reacted to my power. I pulled on one of the thick curls, deciding it wasn't worth cutting again yet. As I looked back to the mirror, I could see finger smudges in the glass and my curiosity grew as I looked at them. I breathed against the glass and revealed what was written: "I love you, *Vogel*[1]."

The words brought a wide smile to my face and I sighed happily as I tried to look at my back. The bite Kisten had given me had mostly healed, and I stepped into the shower slowly, waiting to see if the wound would hurt. The lack of pain was encouraging and I stepped fully into the running water.

As I basked under the warm water, letting it wash away my sleep, my thoughts returned to Aurel. I was still worried that he had seen me and Kisten in The Dream the night before, and I sighed heavily at the thought of having him confront me about it. It was all my fault and I accepted that: I should've told him the moment I realized that his feelings toward me had started to change. Kisten had always had my heart, but I knew how poorly Aurel reacted when he was rejected. He had already begun that process with me, and I just did not want to deal with it.

"Look at the mess you've made for yourself." I muttered under my breath, reaching to wash my body. I cleaned myself up and stepped out of the shower, seizing and wrapping a towel around my still dripping body. I walked back out into the bedroom to find it empty, with no sign of Kisten anywhere. A new outfit lay on the bed and I knew Kisten had not gone to my room to get my clothing. The red sundress that lay on the bed for me was nothing that I had ever owned, and I gingerly picked it up, unsure if I wanted to wear it.

"Still having doubts?" I heard Kisten's voice as he stepped back into the room, standing against the doorframe as I held the dress, turning to face him. His expression was hopeful but wary as he slowly stepped into the room, closing the door behind him. "I won't force you if you're not ready."

"What does wearing it mean?" I asked, and he smiled slightly, stepping closer to me. My heart pounded with his slow steps and I watched his every move until he stood directly in front of me.

"That I've chosen you," he stated, wrapping his arms around the towel as he held me close, pressing his face into my hair. He took a deep breath, releasing it shakily. "It tells others that I've decided to pursue you."

"How long have you had this?" I wondered aloud and Kisten chuckled, releasing me and stepping back to allow me to get dressed. I stood a moment longer, curious to hear his answer as I looked at the dress in my hands again. It wasn't common to see sundresses with sleeves and considering it didn't match any of the fall trends this year, I knew he had to have bought it before even asking me.

"Would you believe me if I said since I told you we couldn't keep seeing each other?" It was my turn to chuckle as I carefully laid the dress down and sat on the bed to slip on my underwear. Kisten merely watched me from where he stood, a smile glued to his face.

"So, your immediate reaction was to buy me a courting gift after telling me to go away?"

"Before. I bought it before," he admitted, looking down to the floor. I paused in my movements, surprised by his words. "I bought it on impulse, and that's when... when I knew I was falling too hard for you. That I would only end up hurting you more."

"I wish you had been honest, Kisten." I slipped on the dress, surprised by how well it fit me. I wasn't the type to wear dresses, so it was a little surprising that Kisten had been able to figure out my size. I spoke again as I slipped on the matching sandals he had provided, glancing around for a brush. "Good guess on the size, though. I'm impressed."

"I'm glad." The shifter handed me a hairbrush and I carefully tried to tame my longer curls, managing to brush them all out of my face. I knew they would spring forward again until I could properly style them, but at least they were out of my face for a while. As soon as I was done, Kisten wrapped his arms around me again, as if it pained him to keep his hands off me. I merely smiled up at him as he rocked me in his arms, smiling like an excited child at the sight of me wearing his dress. It warmed my heart to see him so happy and I carefully wrapped my arms around him, avoiding contact with his skin.

"So how exactly is this courting thing supposed to work?" I quizzed again, pulling back from the man holding me. Kisten grinned, holding his hand to his lips.

"Can't spoil all the fun. This is my first and only time doing this," he chirped, clearly pleased and excited. He motioned for me to follow him as he left the room. "Let me enjoy this."

"Fine, fine." I consented, following him and, closing his door quietly behind us, took a moment to look at his insignia. As expected, it had a leopard carved into the wood, with a large 'A' carved underneath. I assumed it stood for Alpha as I traced the shape, admiring the art as usual. I felt something cold and metallic drop around my neck and I looked down as Kisten placed a necklace on me, fastening it slightly above my locket. The necklace was a simple, gold 'R' and I turned to look at Kisten questioningly.

"Another courting thing?"

"Yes," he grinned, and it was clear he was enjoying this. "I was going to present it when I got home yesterday, but lost the chance with all the stuff going on with your case."

"So, this is what you wanted." I lifted it gently before I let it fall back against my skin. "What does this mean?"

"It shows that I've marked you as my future Beta and none of my pack can touch you or pursue you." Kisten beamed and I gave him a confused glance.

"Isn't that what the dress means?"

"In a way," he admitted, walking down the hall. I followed quietly behind him, waiting for him to finish. "The necklace is a specific sign to my pack: as long as you accept my courtship, you have to wear that at all times. The dress is just for today. Vampires also use red to mark pursuit, so everyone will know that you're mine."

Kisten whipped around quickly, wrapping his arms around me again as he pulled me into a deep kiss. I was again reminded of how nice the previous night had been as my lips and tongue ached with pain, but I forced myself to ignore it, doing my best to kiss him back. When he pulled back, his eyes were bright with a fire.

"It also shows that I've finally marked you." He whispered, his voice deep and sultry. I couldn't help but blush as he referenced the night before and he laughed darkly, releasing me. He motioned for me to continue following him and I found myself in the dining room. Sitting on the large table was a breakfast spread for one, and I knew immediately that this was what Kisten had left to prepare while I was showering.

"Is this another courting thing?" I groaned as I sat, Kisten pushing in my chair for me. He shook his head as he sat across from me, smiling brightly again.

"No, just me taking care of you," he chuckled, leaning on his hands to watch me. "I'm allowed to do something nice for you, aren't I?"

I didn't answer, merely blushing and turning my attention to the breakfast before me. Kisten had really gone out of his way, cooking me everything from waffles, to eggs, to bacon and sausage. He had even shaped the fruit to resemble flowers, making me almost not want to touch anything. Eventually, I began to eat and hummed with delight at the delicious food. After a few bites, I looked up to see Kisten still staring at me, his soft smile on his face. I lifted my arm as I coughed to hide my embarrassment, looking away again.

"What is it?"

"Nothing." He shrugged, never taking his eyes off me. I shifted uncomfortably under his gaze and Kisten chuckled softly again. "You are more easily embarrassed than one would think, huh?"

"It's been a while," I argued, taking another bite of food. Kisten leaned back in his chair, crossing his arms as he waited for me to continue. "I've never been courted before, but I haven't had even this kind of attention for a long time."

"Well, I'll make sure you get plenty of it." Kisten looked away as his phone went off again and he stood, excusing himself as he stepped out to take the call. Finally free of his staring, I focused on the delicious food he had prepared for me. I ate as much as I could and leaned back, quite full from the spread.

You seem happy.' I heard my sister's voice rise in my mind and I sighed contently, closing my eyes in my chair.

"I am," I said aloud, glancing down at the remains of my breakfast. The flowered orange still sat untouched on its plate and I touched the fruit gingerly. "Kisten has a way of doing that."

'So, you've decided then? You chose to wear his dress.' I frowned at this, sitting up in my seat slightly. I heard my sister's exasperated sigh at my lack of an answer. *'Deny it all you want, but the fact you put it on shows where your intentions lie.'*

"I know, I just..." My voice trailed off and I didn't finish my sentence, my thoughts turning to my job, Eve and... Aurel. I shook my head, trying to focus on my determination. "I'm not going to run away, I want this too badly. It's just... it's gonna be complicated."

'Guess you'll have to figure it out.' My sister echoed Kisten's words as the man in question came back, hanging up his phone call. I was confused by the many phone calls as Kisten wasn't usually one to be on his phone much. Even if Lucius was the one he had been talking to earlier, the pair usually talked in person rather than making multiple phone calls. He looked at my mostly empty plates and smiled, removing the dishes from in front of me.

"Give me a moment to wash these and I'll get you to work." He promised, disappearing into the kitchen.

I smiled, closing my eyes again as I waited for Kisten to finish. I opened them again as the door opened, but it was not Kisten I found myself staring at. It was Aurel, who was giving my dress a strange look, eyeing me up and down with disbelief. His sea-green eyes were full of confusion and as they slowly drifted up to meet mine, I stood to explain.

"Aurel, I..."

"Who gave you that dress?" His voice sounded pained as he spoke, as if what he was seeing couldn't be real. The words got caught in my throat and I couldn't say anything as he stepped further into the room, causing me to step back from him. Aurel's expression changed from confusion to anger as he repeated his question. "Do you know what wearing a red dress means?"

"Yes, I–"

"She does." Kisten walked up behind me, sliding a white jacket onto my shoulders. I looked up to see his gaze and he was looking at Aurel, a smug smile on his face. I looked back to Aurel, who was waiting for me to deny it. When I said nothing, Aurel returned his eyes to Kisten, returning his dark glare. "I wouldn't have given it to her without explaining what it means."

"When did this happen?" Aurel sneered and the Alpha behind me chuckled, releasing my shoulders as he walked around the table to stand down the lich. I slowly slid on the provided jacket as Kisten smiled at Aurel, clearly enjoying flaunting this in his face. The lich turned his gaze to me, his eyes dark with jealousy. "Is this why you've been pushing me away?"

"Aurel..."

"No. This happened last night," Kisten interrupted me and Aurel kept his gaze on me, waiting for me to deny it. I shrugged, placing my hands on the back of the chair as I met his gaze evenly. Kisten laughed at his reaction, earning himself a hiss from the lich. "She's wearing the dress, isn't she, Aurel? What more proof do you need?"

"You tricked her." Aurel hissed, clearly not wanting to believe what Kisten was saying. I quickly released the chair, shocked by the lich's words. Kisten shrugged, his grin broadening as Aurel continued. "Raiven wouldn't choose you. She wouldn't lock herself to one person."

"If that's what you want to believe." With this, he turned to me, motioning for me to come to him. "C'mon, Raiven, I need to get you to work."

I carefully walked around the table as Kisten held the door for me, and I kept my gaze from meeting Aurel's as I followed him out of the dining room. Once the door had closed behind us, I took a moment to breathe a sigh of relief. I glanced up to see Kisten looking at me, his dark smile still on his face.

"How was that for him finding out?" He asked innocently and I looked away, still torn about the whole confrontation. I realized that Kisten had probably set Aurel up to see me in the dress, especially after finding out he wanted me for his harem. I started walking away, muttering under my breath.

"Probably as bad as if he had seen us in the club last night."

Kisten chuckled at this, wrapping his arm around my waist as he caught up to me. He took a moment to breathe me in before leading me down the hall, heading for the surface.

"Maybe, but I think I like this better." Kisten leaned to plant a kiss in my hair, never pausing in his stride. I was tempted to look over my shoulder, but decided against it, not wanting to see Aurel behind me. Kisten must have noticed, as he glanced back and waved to someone behind us. From his deep chuckle, I could guess who it was as he whispered into my ear. "Hard to think we were once friends."

"Friends?" I repeated, and Kisten nodded, his dark look fading for a moment to a softer expression.

"Aurel... Well, he never seemed to be bothered by my distant behavior. Eventually, he reached out to me, saying it looked like I could use a friend." Kisten's expression returned to its dark glare and his smile was full of anger. "Turns out he just wanted me for his harem and was trying to butter me up first. As you can guess, I didn't take finding out any better than he took my refusal."

"Sounds familiar," I muttered, thinking of Aurel's words in the dining room. I didn't want to believe that the lich had only befriended me to seduce me, but I couldn't deny the possibility, especially with the way he had handled me choosing someone else. Kisten squeezed my waist, encouraging me to continue. "I mean, Aurel was the one who sought me out to be friends."

"Sounds like him. I'm glad you chose me instead." Kisten released me as we climbed up the stairs and I stepped into the afternoon sun.

I saw that his car was now in the parking lot and looked at him questioningly. Kisten shrugged, pulling out his keys from his pocket. "I woke up this morning. You're the one who slept most of the day."

"Gee, I wonder why," I remarked sarcastically and he laughed, kissing my hair as he walked past me. I glanced at my car, still sitting in her parking spot. "You know my car is here, I can drive myself."

"Of course you can." Kisten smiled, leaning over his open door as I went to my car to retrieve my phone. I had no missed messages, meaning last night had gone smoothly without our suspect showing up. "But I enjoy having you in mine and I'm doing you a favor by saving your gas."

I couldn't help but smile as I closed my door and stepped into the passenger side of his car. As we pulled away, I noticed Aurel standing on the sidewalk outside the Coven. Our eyes locked for a moment and my thoughts turned to what Kisten had said about Aurel's intentions. As we drove away, I couldn't help but worry about the mess I had gotten myself into.

17

I leaned against the glass terrarium, sipping my drink and adjusting my dark sunglasses as the groups of people walked by me. As soon as we had reached the office, Brandon had shooed me right back out; he wanted me to take Julia's place at the Landing, watching for our culprit. She had stayed at The Dream all night with Aurel and was asleep at her house to get ready to do it again. We didn't want to risk him at the Landing without us having eyes there, so I was Brandon's next pick.

We were the only two women on the team and he was hoping we could act as bait for our witch, getting him to approach us of his own accord. This unfortunately would've meant I had to work with Aurel, but a quick call on Kisten's part saved me from my fate. I smoothed my dress, finishing off my beverage and tossing it into the trash next to me.

"Ready to move somewhere else?" Kisten came up behind me and I turned to look at him. He was wearing a dark red button-up shirt and khaki pants, as well as matching shades to mine. A fancy watch finished off his look and he easily blended in with the usual high-class shoppers that frequented the Landing. I was still wearing the red sundress and white jacket, with the added trappings of a red purse and some gold bangles around my wrists. I was uncomfortable with so much extra baggage, but both Kisten and Brandon had insisted it would allow me to blend in better. I glanced at my phone, noting the time before shrugging.

"I guess, let's shift a little closer to The Dream." I stood up and started walking off in front of him, pretending to be interested in the various store fronts. Kisten walked behind me, glancing for anyone following us. He moved a little closer to me, leaning down to whisper in my ear.

"Wouldn't you blend in better if you actually looked like you were shopping?" he offered, and I turned to see the devilish grin on his face. Even with the sunglasses hiding his eyes, I knew his intentions were far from just helping me blend in. I shrugged him off as I kept walking.

"Not really the shopping type."

"C'mon, it'll help you blend in." Kisten stopped my stride and turned me towards a lingerie store. My cheeks burned with embarrassment as I pulled away from him and I could hear him chuckling behind me.

"I guess I could try." I stepped into a clothing store near The Dream and pretended to be interested in the various items of women's clothing. I turned around to see Kisten sitting outside, relaxing on the bench across from the store. I rolled my eyes as I returned to my window shopping, lifting a green halter that was much too short for my tastes.

"Do you need some help, ma'am?" I turned to look as one of the shopkeepers approached me, her fake smile beaming as she waited for my answer. I politely smiled back and shook my head, watching as the harpy fluffed her wings.

"No thank you, just looking."

"Well, let me know if you need anything... else..." Her voice trailed off as she looked me up and down, as if finally noticing my dress. Her eyes worked their way up to the necklace and she glanced outside to Kisten, her eyes widening. Her voice was low and shaking when she spoke again. "You're with the Alpha? A-Are you sure you don't need any help? I can help you find whatever you need. We have the latest in holo-rooms, you can try on whatever you would like..."

"I'm fine, sweetie." I tried to smile, starting to wish I hadn't worn the dress. I hadn't expected to run into anyone from the pack and I was still embarrassed by its implied meaning. The girl seemed worried and she glanced back towards Kisten and I followed her gaze. I couldn't tell if he was looking at us or not due to the sunglasses, but just knowing he was there was enough to frazzle the girl, as if we were testing her. I gently laid my hand on her feathers and she jumped under my touch.

"Hey, sweetie," I started, and she looked up at me sheepishly. I forced myself to smile brightly as I lifted my sunglasses, looking at her face-to-face. "No need to get worked up, I'm simply browsing. I'm not really looking to buy anything here. Kisten's not here to judge you or anything."

"Thank goodness." She was relieved as she walked away and I continued my walk through the aisle, not really finding anything that interested me. I eventually found myself in the aisle containing jewelry and I paused for a moment, taking in the latest trends. I was about to walk away when one of the rings caught my eye and I gently lifted it to get a better look.

It was a replica of one of my rings, although clearly costume jewelry and a poor imitation of the real thing. After escaping from Mater Vitae's Hunters, I had lost the ring before recently reclaiming it from a collector. The man had been proud to flaunt it, as virgin rainbow opals were extremely rare and until discovering my ring, most believed that there was only one in the world. Since my ring held the second known stone, the man had been reluctant to part with it before I persuaded him it wasn't worth his life. It didn't surprise me that it would still be in the public consciousness, considering its rarity and recent spotlight.

"*Arcus Pluvius.*" I read the tag aloud, a name the public had given it. My memories drifted back to the one who had given it to me, during a time long forgotten by most. It had been a parting gift, a reminder that they had once existed before Mater Vitae erased them.

They had already known that she would not forgive them for their trespass, no matter how special they were. Mother was always creating new species back then and killed off any if they caused her too much trouble. Mother never had an issue using her Hunters to kill off one of her mistakes, but they had been different, and she did the deed herself.

We were both singular successes that she had not been able to replicate and thus we were kept in the equivalents of birdcages: able to be looked upon and appreciated for the rarities we were, but never free. I was probably one of the few alive who remembered them, and it had been their death that had given me the nerve to try to escape. Shortly after, the First also rebelled, so it was easy to say that it was their execution that had started everything and led to Mater Vitae retreating to wherever she now was.

"Remembering something?" I dropped the ring in surprise and turned to Kisten who was standing behind me. He slowly bent to pick up the ring from the floor, examining it as he stood. I watched him, wondering if he recognized it. After a while he shrugged, looking at me. "Pretty, for a fake."

"I have the real one." I whispered, watching him place it back. Kisten raised his eyebrows as I met his gaze through the sunglasses.

"Wait...isn't that the ring some big shot collector bought at an auction a couple of years ago?" he wondered, and I nodded, beginning to make my way through the store. "I remember Lucius telling me it belonged to a member of Mater Vitae's court before she killed them. No one had known what happened to the ring until it showed up at the auction."

"It was given to me, right before they were killed. I had always managed to hold onto it, but finally lost it when I crossed the sea. I was surprised when it turned up at the auction." I sighed, weaving my way back through the clothing. "And the collector was difficult to convince, but I wasn't leaving without it. It had been a gift, a way to remember them."

"You knew the Seraph?" Kisten asked and I nodded, stepping out of the store back into the bright sunlight. I looked up to the blue sky with its soft clouds and smiled wistfully.

"We were similar in our uniqueness and Mother had our rooms close enough together that we sometimes got the chance to talk." I spoke quietly, watching the fluffy clouds as they rolled by. Kisten stood next to me, also looking up. "They were the closest thing I had to a friend in those times. I think they felt the same way, since they gave me the ring."

"What did they do?" Kisten asked quietly and I shifted my gaze to him, slightly surprised. "To be executed?"

"You don't know?"

"I only know what Lucius told me when we left Europe, which is very little." Kisten shrugged, glancing down at me. "I was only about fifty years old when I agreed to come with him, and he has never really been talkative about his time with Mother. The most he told me was it was the Seraph's death and your escape that convinced him and the others that they needed to leave too."

"He revealed a flaw in her system. We both always knew that her blood didn't bind us the same way, but we had been careful to avoid allowing her to find out," I admitted, looking back up to the sky. "They disobeyed her command, to save someone else from her wrath. Once she realized she couldn't control them, she killed them. I was sure I would be next, so I found the courage to leave."

'*More like I kicked your ass, but whatever.*' My sister rose to make her snide remark, but Kisten interrupted me before I could rebuke her.

"I assume the First rebelled for similar reasons?"

"I'm not sure." I sighed, closing my eyes and turning away from the sky. My thoughts turned to Nisaba, and how she was the one who allowed me to escape that fateful night. "I never really knew any of the First personally, just their names. If I had to guess, I would imagine that they finally had enough of her and, after finding out I had managed to escape, figured they could do the same."

"And that's how she lost control?" He asked quietly and I nodded again.

"Yeah, the First began to offer protection to those who didn't want anything to do with her, creating the Overseer system." I drew a deep breath, remembering the turmoil that had followed. The Dark Ages had been a time of darkness and madness for those of us who lived in the shadow of humans. "She sent her Hunters after all of us, but as members of the First were killed, other Supes realized they could offer the same protection as Overseers. As the idea spread and more and more Overseers appeared, I think she finally accepted she couldn't regain control through force and disappeared. Hunters still chase after me and any First who remain, but this is a far better life than the one I had."

Kisten said nothing to this, following me silently as I weaved through the sea of shoppers and people. I had never dreamed I would have such freedom while I was in Mater Vitae's court and certainly never thought I would've survived as long as I did. Her Hunters were always searching and never seemed far from my trail, no matter how well I tried to hide it. The fact I hadn't encountered any in the past three years was already a blessing, but I had accepted that there would come a day when I lost this millennia-old struggle.

But not today. I thought, turning to Kisten behind me, who paused as I turned to face him. I studied him for a moment before smiling, and he slowly returned my smile. Stepping up to me, he lifted his sunglasses as he leaned down to kiss me and I leaned up to him, despite the searing pain. He smiled softly at me with his chartreuse eyes before dropping the sunglasses back down and walking past me. I couldn't help my stupid grin as I followed, sighing with happiness.

18

I stood amongst the busy people as Kisten stepped into a store, insisting that he would buy me "something appropriate" for blending in with the other shoppers. I started to argue that plenty of people came to the Landing to window shop, but he was having none of it, disappearing into another women's clothing store. I shook my head as I sighed, unable to help my smile. It was nice to spend time with Kisten like this again, and I hummed as I adjusted the bangles on my wrists.

I began to glance around the growing crowd, ever watchful to catch our suspect. However, I was soon distracted by the number of couples walking around together, arm in arm, hanging all over the other. My heart ached slightly, but a smile soon grew on my face despite the discomfort. I no longer had a reason to be envious of others; it was merely a matter of time before Kisten and I could be the same.

"Raiven?" I instantly froze as I heard the voice behind me and I swallowed hard, refusing to turn around. I could hear his footsteps as he drew closer and I knew that he would not be so easy to get rid of. "Raiven, look at me."

"What, Aurel?" I turned to face the lich, crossing my arms as I did so. His orange curls bounced, and his eyes still held hints of his anger and disbelief. I was glad for my sunglasses, hiding the uncertainty in my eyes while I did my best to speak with confidence. "Shouldn't you be resting for tonight with Julia?"

"Why?" he begged, and if not for the anger that was hidden in his expression, I might have believed his distress was real. I shook my head, frustrated with myself: I should have been able to read through his intentions sooner. Aurel placed his hands on my arms, gripping me tightly. "Why him? You... you're not like that."

"Because I love him." I breathed, breaking free of Aurel's grip as I stepped away from him. My actions had caught some attention, but most people kept walking as if they didn't notice. I glanced around quickly before returning my eyes to Aurel. "He's been my choice since I came here, Aurel. Justina was the only other person I wanted and, well... she's taken."

"He's still bound by the Oath of Loyalty. You can't have him either," Aurel pointed out and I shrugged, doing my best to pretend it didn't bother me. "He's just binding you into a one-sided relationship. You know that."

"Lucius gave him a night free of the Oath to pursue me, so honestly, I'm not all that worried that he won't free him entirely. Evalyn may not want to, but she's not the Overseer." My calm tone hid my inner turmoil and for a moment, I was assured in my relationship with Kisten. The confidence was infectious, and I couldn't help my smug smile as I continued. "I didn't have to wear this dress, Aurel, Kisten didn't force me. I *chose* to because I love him."

"He is tricking you." Aurel hissed, still trying to convince me to side with him. I laughed, finally removing my sunglasses from my face as I gave him an incredulous look.

"Tricking me? Kisten has been nothing but honest with me, even when he pushed me away. If he wanted to 'trick' me so badly, then why keep me at arm's length for more than a year?" I glared at Aurel, refusing to look away from his gaze. "I'm not so sure you can say the same. Kisten told me about your pursuit of him, how you pretended to want to be friends in order to lure him into your harem."

"I have never lied to you, Raiven. I did want to be friends with you, and eventually I wanted more than that. I thought you wanted the same." He insisted, stepping closer to me as I stepped back again. My demeanor cracked for a moment with his plea and he immediately moved to take advantage of it. "I admit what I did with Kisten was wrong, but that was long before I met you. Please, Raiven, reconsid–"

"No," I stated plainly, not letting him finish the thought. I wanted to slap myself for being so stupid. I had valued having a friend so much that I had overlooked the obvious. Aurel was obsessed with his collections, be it jewelry or people and while he treated his collections well, he was relentless when he wanted to add to them. Just as he had begged me for my jewelry, he was refusing to let me slip away from him. "I have made my choice. I made it long before I put on this dress."

"Raiven–"

"Something wrong, *mein Liebling*[1]?" Kisten came up behind me, placing his hand on my shoulder as he leaned around to hand me my shopping bag. It felt heavy as I accepted it and I glanced inside to see it full of various outfits. I looked up at Kisten, who shrugged as he shifted his attention to Aurel, his dark smile returning. "Ah, come to beg some more? I think she's given you her answer."

"Fuck off, Kisten." Aurel hissed, dropping his desperate act for pure anger. Kisten chuckled low in his throat, gripping my shoulder tightly. I was worried for a moment that he was losing control as his hands began digging into my shoulder, hints of his claws stabbing my skin. I looked up at his face, but his expression was calm, only his burning eyes revealing his emotions.

"Or what? I'm the Alpha, Aurel. You can't do anything to me *or* her," Kisten gloated, brushing his hand across my hair before planting a soft kiss. Aurel growled and the semi-interested crowd was now extremely interested, many people stopping to watch the display. I began to feel uncomfortable under their gaze, but Kisten shifted his hand from my shoulder to my waist, keeping me pinned to his side. "I think you should just leave us alone before you get in trouble again."

Again?

"You turned me down, Kisten. I don't like it but I can accept that," Aurel said, not trying to appeal to anyone's emotions anymore. He had his eyes locked on me, his pupils boring into me as he spoke. "But you don't have the right to take her from me. She won't be happy trapped in a relationship with you."

"I believe she told you the truth, Aurel. She chose me long before you decided you needed another 'rare beauty' for your harem." Kisten hissed, no longer trying to hide his anger or jealousy, either. It was starting to seem more like a personal vendetta than fighting over me and I squirmed in Kisten's arms. "Maybe you should learn to accept that not everyone wants you."

"Aurel, *please*," I begged, cutting the lich off before he could speak. His eyes continued to stare into my soul and I sighed heavily before continuing. "I should've said something about me and Kisten before now. Blame me for that if you want, but all of this is unnecessary. I told you yesterday; I have never felt more than friendship for you and I never wanted more."

"Hearts can change easily." Aurel spat, looking up to meet Kisten's gaze as he snarled.

The Alpha smiled, releasing me as he walked up to Aurel, once again using his superior height to stare him down. The crowd was now whispering, and I knew there had to be those present who recognized who we were. All Supernaturals in The Capital had a vague idea of who was a part of the Coven, and many of those in Decver were definitely capable of recognizing us on sight. I clutched the shopping bag with both hands as I tried to ignore the burning stares.

"You're right, Aurel." Kisten's voice was dripping with sarcasm and jealousy as he spoke, his dark smile widening. "But I guess you'll just have to wait and see. Because right now..."

Kisten leaned down into the lich's face, almost close enough to kiss him. He whispered quietly into Aurel's ear and even though I couldn't hear what he was saying, I knew the words he was baiting him with.

"She's mine, and I won't give her up easily." With this, Kisten patted Aurel's shoulder and began to walk away. The gawkers began to awkwardly disperse, and Kisten turned to look at me where I stood. I understood his silent question and, glancing back at Aurel one final time, I slid on my sunglasses as I jogged up to him. The lich was standing still, his eyes still locked on Kisten's back.

"Just doesn't know when to quit, huh?" Kisten breathed, reaching to take my hand in his. I was surprised by the lack of pain and I looked down to notice that he had slipped on a leather glove, protecting me from the pain of this simple gesture. I looked back up to see a soft smile on his face and he lifted my hand to kiss it.

"I don't want to hurt you every time." Kisten whispered, dropping our hands as we continued walking. I giggled softly, squeezing his hand in mine as he continued. "Sorry about Aurel, by the way. He's unlikely to give up for a while, given his persistence in the past."

"Because of you?" I offered and then I dropped my voice, uncertainty filling me. "Or because of me?"

"I mean, we both know Aurel has never taken rejection well." Kisten shrugged, glancing at the other stores we walked past. His eyes lingered on The Dream for a moment, but he led us past, not stopping. "But I'm sure he thinks I'm trying to get revenge for what he did by taking you. And he's not completely wrong, just has things in the wrong order."

"You didn't even know about that until last night," I argued and Kisten shrugged again, his face showing his annoyance. It took me a moment to realize what he had fully said and I looked at him with surprise. "Wait. What do you mean by wrong order?"

"Why do you think I took you to The Dream, knowing Aurel would be there?" Kisten chuckled low in his throat, squeezing my hand tightly. "I almost didn't answer his call last night but I had wanted to rub you in his face. Finding out about Irida distracted me, but never changed my intention. Finding out he wanted you, well, that just made it that much better."

"Rub me in his face?" I asked darkly and Kisten looked down at me and, seeing my dark look, kissed my forehead gently. I stopped walking and he turned to face me, his loving smile back on his face. "I thought you didn't know about Aurel and me."

"I didn't, not until you told me. I just wanted to show him *I* had moved on." Kisten sighed happily as he looked at me. My anger started to melt away under his loving gaze and he pulled me close as he finished. "I'll spare you the details, but Aurel insisted no one else would be willing to put up with me. I wanted to rub it in his face that someone would. He would've hated seeing me with anyone, but because of you, someone who also doesn't want him..."

"Well, let's just say he—" Kisten stopped speaking as he looked up, seeing Aurel walking up to us quickly. The lich's feet barely touched the ground and he was half-flying as he moved toward us. Kisten glanced around and his eyes rested on the bathrooms. He gently pushed me in their direction, and I turned to give him a confused look.

"He's not going to give up and I don't want you to be at the center of it again. This is more about us than you at this point." He smiled and I reluctantly went, looking back as Aurel reached Kisten. He looked as if he was going to strike him, but Kisten merely smiled, not remotely intimidated by the lich's aggression. I walked inside, disappearing before Aurel could notice.

I didn't need to use the toilet, so I merely took my sunglasses off and splashed some water on my face at the sink. I closed my eyes, grimacing at the thoughts that were rising up about Aurel and doing my best to push past them. I took a deep breath and let it out shakily as I began to open my eyes.

"This *courting* thing is really becoming a mess," I said out loud, frowning as I looked at my reflection. My thoughts returned to the girl's reaction in the clothing store and I carefully lifted the necklace Kisten had given me. I was still confused by her worry and fear, and wondered if the necklace meant more than just 'marking me'. Kisten wasn't the type to lie outright, but he was the type to omit information at times. I resolved to ask him as I dropped the necklace, turning to retrieve my bag from the floor.

A gloved hand appeared over my mouth and I immediately moved to retaliate until I felt a knife placed against my chest. I turned my eyes to see our suspect behind me, his dark brown eyes twisted with malice and his matted black hair peeking out from underneath his hood. He was still wearing the same outfit from Thursday night and he scowled at me in the mirror.

"Your Overseer has my Irida." He hissed, pressing the knife into my skin. The knife was silver and he was aiming for my heart, so I knew he had taken me to be a shapeshifter. As I was walking around with the Alpha, it was a reasonable assumption for him to make and I remained still, trying to think of my next move. While the silver itself was not a heavy concern, the knife was and I didn't want to risk him getting away if I defended myself, especially not with him so close.

"What do you want?" I breathed, doing my best to sound scared and worried. He pressed the knife deeper into my skin as he spoke again, the tip drawing a thin line of blood.

"I'm going to take you with me," he snarled, pulling us backwards towards a stall. "I've already left your Alpha a little present, letting him know I have his mate. Unless he brings me my Irida, I will kill you."

I gasped as we started to sink into the floor, failing to realize that he had drawn a Circle into the tiles. The door burst open and I saw Kisten and Aurel rush into the bathroom, not worried about what others thought. I reached up to my chest, tearing the locket housing my sister's soul from around my neck. I tossed it to Kisten before I disappeared completely into the bathroom floor and blacked out in the darkness.

19

When I came to, I was in a dark, dirty cage and surrounded by trees. I groaned as I sat up, trying to see if the witch was anywhere nearby. I couldn't see any signs of him in the darkness, so I tested the bars of my cage.

They were silver, as I expected, and a small test with my power proved that I could easily bend them. The culprit was so sure I was a shapeshifter, he didn't even bother to ensure the cage was sturdy, certain the silver would keep me from trying. Not wanting to give up my advantage, I left the bars alone and looked around the small clearing I was being kept in.

It was evident that he had been staying here for a short while, probably since Irida stopped herself from killing Justina. He knew it was a matter of time before we would be looking for him, so he was at least smart enough not to remain in the city. He had a small cooler and chair, with a dirty sleeping bag next to an equally dirty backpack. I couldn't see anything around me but trees, so I had no indication how far we were from the city or what direction the city would be in. There was barely any sunlight left in the sky above me, and from the drop in temperature, I knew it had been at least a few hours since he had taken me from the bathroom.

"You're awake," I turned around as the witch appeared from the darkness of the woods, and he dropped to his haunches near the cage, glaring at me. I glared back, not even pretending to be afraid. He scoffed at this, producing a gun and he showed me the silver bullets in his other hand before loading it. "Behave."

I merely hissed at this as he walked away, watching him as he moved about his camp, retrieving something to drink from his cooler. He plopped down in his chair while downing the beverage, tossing the aluminum can into the trees near my cage. I saw it was alcohol and rolled my eyes, annoyed by this man's arrogance as he drank a second one. He clearly was too full of himself if he thought capturing me would get him what he wanted. Even if I had been Evalyn, no one was going to hand Irida to him: the only thing he was getting from anyone was a decent helping of death.

"Hmmmm," I looked up as the witch hummed and I nearly gagged from the look in his eyes. He was rubbing himself with the gun, and I knew what he was imagining. I growled at him, allowing my eyes to swirl with power before turning away. All I had to do was keep him near me long enough for Kisten and my team to find me, then everything would be over for him. My locket would lead them straight to me, as my sister could only survive if the locket was near my heart and it was designed to find its way back to me.

"You're prettier than that stupid bitch." I glared at him as he mentioned Justina and he smiled at my reaction, grabbing himself with his hand. "She should've just accepted the threesome with me and Irida and she never would've been hurt. Now I have to kill them both: a waste if you ask me, it'll be hard to find someone as easy to control as Irida."

"*You* are fucking disgusting." I spat and he stood up, overturning his chair and dropping the gun in his anger. He stomped towards me and reached through the bars, wrapping his hand around my throat. I instinctively reached to grab his wrist, but I realized there was no power in his grip. I chuckled, giving him a look of pity as I dropped my hand. "You're so fucking weak. Now I understand why Irida thought you were human. You have to control someone else to pull off a kill because there's no way you could ever dream of hurting someone."

"Shut up, bitch!" He snarled, tightening his grip – but for a Supernatural, it was a joke. I easily pushed his hand from around my neck and sat comfortably in my cage. He seemed ready to reach for me again, but instead, he stood and went back to his overturned chair. He retrieved the gun and released the safety, shooting me in the cage. I gasped with pain as the bullet went through my left arm, and I held my hand to the wound as the red began to stain my white jacket. He laughed with triumph as he came back up to the cage and pointed the gun towards my head.

"Now, it is a matter of time before the silver kills you." He laughed, leaning close to my cage. "Hope your boyfriend is quick on his feet, I'd hate to have to try and steal someone else."

"You won't leave this forest alive." I swore and yelped with pain as he shot me again, this time catching my midsection. I was tempted to free myself from the cage and stomp him into the ground, but his shots were purposely missing anywhere vital. He was counting on the silver slowly killing me, which ironically would be his undoing. Despite having the abilities of vampires, I was much easier to kill thanks to still being somewhat human, and major trauma to my heart or brain would easily render me lifeless. The silver would only slow my healing, so as long as he avoided a kill shot, I knew I would recover from these injuries.

I forced myself to act as if my body was racked with pain as he gloated over me, pleased with my reaction. He looked at the gun with a savage grin and for a moment, I thought he was going to shoot me again for fun. It was obvious from his behavior that he had never thought of using one before, which wasn't surprising. Most Supernaturals preferred their own abilities over human weapons and it was seen as a weakness to rely on them. He placed the gun on the ground before he crouched in front of the cage again.

"Maybe I should have my fun with you before you die," he grabbed my chin, pulling my face closer to his. I spat in his face and it was his turn to growl as he backed away from me again. He wiped my saliva from his face, then he grinned at me, clearly liking this new idea. He carefully picked up the gun again and put it in my face. I was forced to comply as he pulled me out of the cage and stepped on my back, the gun still to my head. "Ruin you as a potential mate."

The witch started to slowly lift the back of my jacket and I began to summon my power as he stroked my back with his free hand. He would kill me if he pulled the trigger, but there was no way I was going to let this sleaze have his way with me. The ground around us began to shake and heave as my power grew and he paused, looking at the shifting dirt around us. Not seeing any reason for the tremor, he instantly connected the dots and he pressed the gun harder into my head, forcing my face into the ground.

"Stop it," he hissed, and I flinched as he fired the gun next to my head. He leaned over me, shoving his foot more firmly into my back. The pain in my side increased from the added pressure and the blood began to flow more quickly as he spoke directly into my ear. "I don't care what you are, a silver bullet through your skull and heart will end you."

I hissed, but withdrew my power, the ground becoming still once again. The witch smiled above me, and he once again began to touch me with his free hand, taking his foot off my back. I clenched my teeth in the dirt, wanting nothing more than to throw this sorry excuse for a person off my back. There was a small chance I could move faster than he could pull the trigger, but I knew there was no way I could dodge the bullet entirely.

I reached my boiling over point when the man's hand slid down to my posterior and I growled as he took his time fondling me, gripping and groping me through the dress. When he started to slide his hand between my legs, I decided to make my move, not willing to let this man touch me anymore. I moved my hands underneath my chest and, ignoring the bullet hole in my arm, began to prop myself up. He pushed the gun into my skull more but, upon noticing that he couldn't force me back to the ground, I heard him begin to pull the trigger.

Moving as fast as I could, I bucked my back and rolled away from the witch as my head exploded with pain. I was slower than usual, as my previous wounds were slowing me down and I held my head as I began to bleed from the gunshot wound. The man stood, aiming the gun at me again, but he was distracted by a tremendous noise approaching us. A large blur shot from the trees behind him and pinned him to the ground, my locket in its mouth. The gun went off as it flew from his hand as he was forced into the dirt and Kisten placed his large paw on the witch's head, growling loudly. The rest of my team followed behind him, with Lucius and Aurel also stepping into the space, the Overseer's presence alone intimidating in the growing darkness. As Brandon placed the barrel of his gun on the man's head, Kisten got off him, padding his way to me as he shifted.

"Raiven," his voice was full of relief which then turned to worry as he noticed the blood flowing between my fingers where I held my head. He was still wearing his red shirt and khakis and I smiled slightly at seeing him. Kisten ignored my smile and turned to call over his shoulder. "Justin, over here, now!"

Justin moved from behind Brandon to Kisten's side, revealing the Alpha's trauma kit as he holstered his gun. Kneeling in front of me, Justin removed my jacket and began to address the wound to my arm as Kisten gingerly touched my side, ripping my dress to examine the wound there. He returned his attention to my face after instructing Justin how to temporarily dress the bullet hole and he laid his hand on mine, gently moving it away from my head. I closed my eyes as he examined the damage, the first tingles of lightheadedness hitting me. The bullet had grazed the side of my head, taking off the top of my right ear and Kisten growled as he moved to dress the wound.

"Kis..." I tried to whisper his name, but now that my adrenaline was fading, I suddenly found myself weak and struggling to speak. Kisten quickly hushed me, placing my locket in my hand. I immediately felt my sister's concern and her voice burst into my mind as soon as I closed my fingers over the wood.

'Raiven, you idiot! What were you thinking, allowing yourself to be bait? This bullshit isn't worth your life, dammit!' She screamed, and I

groaned,' as her yelling was making my headache even worse. '*You should've killed that excuse for a witch the minute he touched you!*'

'*Better me than Julia, and if I hadn't allowed him to take me, he would've just run. We might have never caught him,*' I reasoned, closing my eyes as I answered her. Kisten must've worried that I was passing out as he gently shook me. He sighed with relief when I opened my eyes, and I smiled softly at him again. I could still feel my sister's frustration and relief, but she didn't continue, instead fading away. I knew she was saving her words for later, once I was in a safer place.

"Can you stand?" Kisten's voice was soft and tender as he stood me up and I wobbled on my feet, dizzy from the blood loss. I fell into his arms and he scooped me up, careful to avoid putting unnecessary pressure on my wounded side and arm. Kisten adjusted me in his arms and turned as Brandon finished speaking to the witch.

"... sure the other Overseers would love a chance to punish you for your crimes and usually we'd pass you off to the first one you pissed off. But as you're in my jurisdiction now and harmed a member of my team..." Brandon looked up to Lucius and the Overseer nodded. My boss's face turned savage as Julia pulled the man to his knees, keeping their guns pointed at him. The man hissed at Julia touching him, but she merely shoved her gun harder into his back.

Lucius stepped up to the witch, who, despite obviously being overwhelmed, looked into the vampire's eyes defiantly.

"Fuck you!" He spat on the ground in front of Lucius, but the Overseer barely noticed: his eyes were locked on the sorry excuse for a man before him. The witch spat again, clearly aiming for Lucius' clothing. "You all think you're so much better than me just because you have longer fucking lives."

"*No.*" Lucius' voice boomed through the trees, even though it was barely above a whisper. I heard the birds scatter into the night sky and other creatures scattered as well, sensing the killing intent in the air. "The woman you harmed and the woman you used won't even live as long as you. I'm not better than you because I've lived longer."

"Lamias are good for controlling, weak minds and weak hearts," the witch gloated, clearly feeling no remorse for what he had done to Irida. "As for that other bitch, sorcerers are better off dead anyway."

"You are disgusting," Aurel offered, speaking in Lucius' place. The lich walked up to the man and very cleanly sliced off the man's left arm with his newly shifted claws. I narrowed my eyes as the man screamed, gripping his new stump as his blood poured out. Aurel grinned savagely: due to his body-based magic, Lucius often gave Aurel the honor of doling out punishment to those who deserved it. Aurel licked the blood from his hand, his eyes aglow with excitement. "You will suffer for your crimes."

The man didn't respond, staring at his missing arm with horror and anguish. He looked up and with anger in his eyes, spat in Lucius' direction again, finally reaching the vampire's shoes. At this, Lucius reacted, reaching down and lifting the man into the air by his throat, the vampire's feet hovering above the ground. My team and Aurel stepped back as the air was flooded with electricity, small flashes of lightning visible from the sudden change in charge. The man finally seemed to understand his position as he squirmed in the Overseer's grip, trying to free himself from Lucius.

"You, are simply trash." I buried my face in Kisten's chest as I felt the intense electricity in the air, and I knew Lucius had fried the witch as I heard the corpse hit the ground. Lucius was rarely so violent, usually locking up anyone we caught into the Basement or giving the honor of execution to Aurel, but as the witch was a being without remorse, I understood why Lucius had wanted to do it himself. It wasn't as if we could follow Division 11 protocol, either: even without a proper wand, his ability to control others made him too dangerous to attempt transport and it would've been equally dangerous to try to hold him for another Overseer to arrive.

Kisten watched calmly, only looking down to make sure I was still awake. His expression was as stoic as Lucius' had been and I wanted to reach up to touch his face, but lacked the strength to try. I instead closed my eyes, burying my face against him again as he carried me out of the woods, and into the waiting transport. I chanced a glance as we walked by Aurel, but the lich's expression was unreadable as we passed him.

Kisten placed me on the waiting gurney and climbed into the back of the ambulance beside me. He immediately started prepping my IV and I found the strength to move, using my free hand to touch his leg. He paused in his movements, taking a moment to touch me as his expression softened, and after laying a piece of gauze on my forehead, he kissed me.

"It's okay, Rai," he whispered, placing my hand back on the gurney as I saw pain flash through his eyes. I knew he blamed himself for my capture, especially since he had been the one to send me to the bathrooms. Kisten touched the gauze gingerly and I wished he would touch my skin, despite the pain it would cause. "You can sleep now."

His words were almost like a spell as I immediately began to pass out. My eyes closed and I drifted off to darkness as the ambulance drove off into the night.

20

I woke up in my own hospital room and wondered where I was for a moment, my side and head still aching. Crispin, Justina, Kisten and LeAlexende all stood in the room, talking in low voices on the other side of the curtain. At the sound of Justina's voice, I sat up, wincing as my body ached from the movement. I clumsily adjusted the hospital gown that I had been changed into and cleared my throat as I prepared to speak.

"Justina?" My voice was hoarse as I called out and the curtain was quickly pulled aside. My friend's eyes welled with tears as she flung herself around me, crying openly and I grunted from the added pain to my body.

"You're alright!" She sobbed and I hugged her back as best as I could. I closed my eyes as I squeezed her, fighting my own tears as the three men joined us. "Raiven, I was so worried about you."

"That's what I should be saying," I retorted softly, pulling back and laying my hand on her stomach. "And the baby?"

"Just fine." She smiled and Crispin came up behind her, wrapping his arms around her midsection before kissing her neck. She shrugged him off and he backed away, still smiling. "Should've chosen a better father, though."

"You wound me." I couldn't help but laugh at Crispin's theatrics and LeAlexende merely shook his head. I turned to face the Overseer as he lifted his phone, excusing himself out of the room. Then I looked at Kisten, who was still standing silently away from me. I leaned away from Justina and reached my hands out to him, wanting to touch him. Justina looked at me, confused and then slowly turned to Kisten, the look on her face becoming accusatory. He stepped toward me and I pulled him closer, pressing my face into his coat. He stiffened under my touch, and I looked up to his face to see his unreadable expression.

"It's not your fault," I whispered, rubbing my face against him as I held him as close as the bed would allow. He relaxed a little at this, and he carefully placed his hands on my gown to return my gesture. I took it as a good sign, and pressed little kisses into his stomach. "I let him take me, I didn't want to risk losing him."

"He hurt you," Kisten said and I looked up at him again, seeing all the pain and anguish he felt over me being hurt. He gently stroked my bandaged ear and I leaned into his hand, the bandages protecting me from the pain. "I should've been there."

"We would have never caught him if you had been and besides, you were there when it mattered," I whispered, smiling up at him. "You saved me from the mess I put myself in, just as I knew you would."

"A feat I'd rather you not repeat." Lucius walked into the room, followed by Evalyn and LeAlexende. Kisten stepped away from me, and he moved next to Justina and Crispin at my feet as the Overseer walked in. I winced as he stood over me, fully expecting to be punished for my insubordination. "You disobeyed me several times during this case, Raiven. You forget I can tell when you don't listen."

"I didn't forget." I winced, and Eve smiled smugly, clearly enjoying the proceedings. She loved the idea of Lucius punishing me and was practically giddy as she waited to see what he would do. LeAlexende gave her a curious look, but soon looked away, seating himself into the chair behind Lucius. Lucius stood over me for a moment and I slouched into the bed. To my surprise, he placed his hand on my head and I looked up at him, surprised again by his smile.

"And yet, thanks to you, we were able to punish the one who hurt Justina and Irida." He withdrew his hand, releasing me. Eve turned to him, astonished by his words and her disappointment was plain on her face. "I think the injuries you sustained are punishment enough."

"And Irida?" I ventured, my voice soft as I spoke. Lucius smiled again, his eyes gentle. "Is... is she safe?"

"I spoke with Brandon and he gave me leave to release her back to her Overseer and Alpha." I sighed with relief, leaning back into my bed. "Both have also agreed to help her rehabilitate. This experience and the revelation about her partner has left her mind... fragile."

I nodded, closing my eyes as I sank back into the bed. Irida had seemed like a gentle soul and after realizing the crimes he had been using her for, it only made sense that she would have a mental break. Lucius patted the sheets next to me, looking up to my other three companions.

"Since we're all here," he began and I opened my eyes again, wanting to watch the proceedings. "It seems some adjustments need to be made in my Coven."

Justina looked away sheepishly, but Lucius was far from upset. Instead, his eyes were lit up with mirth as he met Crispin's gaze. He glanced toward Justina's midsection, before looking up to her face. "While I am excited for you both, Crispin has seniority here, and considering your age Justina, you will have to relinquish your place as Second."

"That's fine." Justina nodded, and her lover wrapped his arm around her, sneaking a kiss into her hair as Lucius turned his attention to Kisten. Kisten chanced a glance at Eve, before meeting his friend's gaze. Eve looked at him, confused, before turning to look at Lucius' back, her anger starting to grow on her face. She looked like she wanted to say something, but Lucius ignored her as he kept his eyes locked on Kisten's. It was a long time before Lucius sighed and turned to me, smiling as well.

"If you would like, Raiven, you may take her place." Lucius

offered and I looked at him, shocked. I was certain that I would've been relieved of the Coven as well, since Kisten was pursuing me as a mate. I turned to Kisten, who smiled, touching my bed sheets near my hand. Lucius continued as I turned back to him incredulously. "Normally, you would take First, since being the Alpha's mate would give you more power over the pack. But I have a reliable First, despite his skirt-chasing ways."

Eve looked as if she would lose her jaw to the floor and she passed her eyes between Kisten and me. Her surprise slowly turned back to anger, and then to malicious scheming as her eyes rested on me. I knew that she was thinking what I also worried about: being Kisten's mate would cause a conflict of interest with my job and I would have to reveal my true nature as the Immortal. I gave her an equally challenging look, which took her aback for a moment. Eve was also keeping her nature as a Supernatural a secret and if she outed me, I would out her and I was more likely to keep my job, even if I lost my team.

Lucius seemed not to notice the silent fight Eve and I were having with our expressions and continued speaking, laying his hand on my bed again. "You are the next logical choice for Second and a replacement I think Justina would agree with."

"Of course," Justina chimed, leaning forward from Crispin and smiling at Lucius. "Raiven is stronger than me anyway, she could've been Second the moment she came. The only reason she's in this room is because she allowed herself to be."

"Mostly true," I countered, but I said it with a smile as she leaned back, as if resting her case. Lucius turned to me for my answer and I looked down to my feet, flexing my toes under the bedspread. Moving up to Second would pile more responsibility on me, and I worried that it would do more harm than good. Lucius had insisted that I join the Coven thanks to my age and power, but I only agreed to a low spot. It was already dangerous enough that Lucius had agreed to protect me: the closer I was to him, the more likely it was that the Hunters would find him as well.

I felt a hand on my thigh and looked over to Kisten, who was lightly encouraging me. I sighed heavily, already knowing what my answer had to be.

"I accept, Lucius." I spoke calmly and clearly, the air swirling in the room for a moment before settling back down. Lucius smiled broadly, stepping back as I accepted my new position. "I only hope we both don't regret this."

"If Kisten doesn't, I certainly won't." Lucius answered as he watched Kisten's hand on my leg and he turned to look at LeAlexende, who had watched the proceedings with semi interest. Upon noticing his friend's gaze on him, the Overseer shrugged, looking back down to his phone.

"This is your area, Luc. Your risks are your own." LeAlexende shook his head as he spoke, but both vampires were smiling as Lucius turned to walk away. Eve glared at Kisten and me once Lucius had passed her, clearly not happy with this small victory Kisten had won behind her back. She looked ready to mouth something, but didn't, settling for a malicious grin as she followed her lover out of the room.

Once she left, everyone in the room breathed a sigh of relief and I turned to LeAlexende, who was still sitting in his chair.

"How much longer are you going to stay?" I asked, and the vampire shrugged, not looking up to me.

"Until you're released, I guess." He replied dismissively, motioning toward Justina. "After all, I've spent most of this visit supervising sleeping women in hospital beds. Might as well see it through to the end."

Crispin laughed openly at this, while Justina looked away embarrassed, and I turned to Kisten as he chuckled slightly. LeAlexende smiled brightly, clearly pleased while he engrossed himself with his phone. I returned my gaze to Justina, just in time to see her looking at me. She was looking at Kisten's hand where it still sat on my thigh and she gestured toward it when she spoke.

"So, *cecmpa*[1], when was I going to learn about this?" She inquired and Crispin held her close again, kissing her neck. I looked away, not really sure how to answer her as my cheeks grew warm. I had never shared my feelings toward Kisten with anyone, so her surprise was understandable. Considering how much I complained about Crispin, she probably would've thought I was still stuck on Mikael. At my lack of a response, she turned her attention to Kisten, who was still stroking my leg softly. "Well, Alpha? Since when have you decided to pursue my *птица*², hmm?"

"How long have I wanted to, or when did I start?" Kisten asked softly and I turned to look up at him. He was looking at me lovingly and I hummed under his gaze, leaning into him as he pulled me against his coat once more. Justina lightly turned to LeAlexende when he chuckled and then returned her attention to us.

"I can imagine it started once I could no longer interject." She mused, placing her hand on her hips as she sized up Kisten. She then returned her attention to me and I shifted my eyes away again. From the look in her eyes, I knew she wanted to lecture me about keeping Kisten and I a secret. "And this is who you want, Raiven? Whom you've chosen despite everything?"

I nodded my head, looking into her eyes. She must've liked what she saw as she motioned her surrender, moving her hand to her still flat stomach. A small smile started on her face and I felt a soft ache in my chest.

"I guess I'm not one to judge, considering who I chose." Crispin gasped in fake surprise as she jabbed at him, but she didn't turn as she continued speaking. "I know you don't completely approve of him."

"I don't see the appeal," I admitted, and she chuckled at this, reaching up to touch her lover's face. Crispin leaned into her hand happily, nuzzling her palm. I watched their interaction with surprise: I had never seen Crispin act so sincerely towards anyone since my arrival in The Capital. I shrugged, doing my best to smile. "But that's your choice at the end of the day."

"Well, there's some semblance of a good man underneath and all things considered, at least he can still be there once I'm no longer able to." She stroked his chin and the vampire hummed, wrapping both of his arms around her waist. I felt a tinge of pain in my chest at their display of affection, and from Kisten's tightened grip on me, I knew he felt it too. I looked up at him again and he was looking at the couple with an unreadable expression. I pressed a kiss into his coat, and he looked down to me again, a sad look in his eyes. The night we had together was both a blessing and a curse: it had given us a taste of what we could have and it made it harder to be without it.

Kisten released me, mumbling something about finding a nurse for tests as he left the room. He closed the door softly and I looked after him longingly, wishing I had said something before he left. Justina and Crispin soon excused themselves, citing their need to make Justina's next appointment before leaving me alone with LeAlexende. The Overseer was engrossed in his phone, or at least acting like it, so I leaned back into my bed, closing my eyes as I waited for Kisten to return.

21

Kisten soon returned with the nurse and they checked my vitals, changed my bandages, and disappeared again. I reached after Kisten as he turned, but he left without so much as a backwards glance and I sank back into my bed, dejected. LeAlexende remained engrossed in his videos, a chuckle escaping him every now and then.

'*Sis?*' I reached out to her with my thoughts, gently resting my hand on the wood. Since the vampire was ignoring me, I took the chance to speak with her, wanting to check on her after all that had happened. I grew worried at her lack of a response, and I gripped the locket tighter as I reached out again. '*Sis?!*'

'*Hush... I'm still here,*' she reprimanded, and I breathed a heavy sigh of relief as I relaxed my grip. She was struggling to stay awake, and her voice sounded far and distant. '*Good to see... that you're up.*'

'*Are you alright?*' I queried, and she took her time responding, the long silence causing a deep fear to rise in my chest.

'*I'll live... for now. Separating me from you was... reckless... and stupid.*' She berated me and I winced under her harsh words. '*I know... you were thinking on your feet... and at least... you didn't run away...*'

'*I'm sorry.*' I gripped the wood tightly again, my heart beginning to pound as I considered the worst. Without my power to feed on, it only made sense that the locket would have fed on hers. My impromptu plan had cost me valuable time with my sister, time I could never get back.

'*You... don't have much longer... to make your choice, sis.*' Tears welled up in my eyes at her calling me 'sis', the ache in my heart growing. She was rarely so informal with me, usually using my name rather than a term of endearment. Given our history, it was understandable, but I couldn't help enjoying it when she showed how much she still cared. '*I will... rest as much as possible... and only check on you when... I'm needed. Sound... fair?*'

'*Alright,*' I conceded, dropping my hand as I closed my eyes to the bright white lights. '*Goodnight.*'

'*Goodnight, Raiven.*' As my sister faded, I took a deep breath, letting it out shakily as I touched my longer curls. I felt as if my chest would collapse in on itself from the thought of losing my sister; I didn't want to consider the idea of being without her, but I also didn't want her to fade away. If I didn't return her to her body, her essence would simply fade into the ether and it would be as if she never existed. After all we had been through, after all she had done for me, I knew I couldn't allow her to be forgotten, even if I was the only one who remembered.

I was jolted from my thoughts and opened my eyes to see LeAlexende standing, drawing the curtain to hide me from whoever was walking in the door. I froze in the bed, not sure who could have arrived to give LeAlexende such a reaction.

"I do believe you should not be here." The Overseer's tone was calm and he remained standing, his shadow projecting onto the screen that separated us. The other party spoke and my heart froze as soon as I recognized the voice.

"Now I'm not even allowed to visit her?" Aurel insisted, and he was trying to walk past the Overseer but LeAlexende was insistent as well. He blocked Aurel's movements, keeping him away from the bed.

"Even if you were allowed, she is sleeping," The Overseer lied smoothly, and I closed my eyes, trying to steady my heartbeat in case

Aurel managed to move aside the curtain. "But I do believe you are not allowed near her regardless, since Lucius told me you were injured recently."

"That was days ago!" Aurel whined and I rolled my eyes behind their lids. Even though he knew the rules, Aurel was willing to use any excuse to be near me, especially with Kisten away from my side. LeAlexende must've sensed the ulterior motive as well, as he dropped his voice as he spoke.

"She is injured, she is likely to lose control if she senses undead blood. The only one allowed in her room is me." The Overseer purposely avoided saying Lucius and Crispin had been here earlier, and Aurel fell right into the trap, scoffing as he tried to push past again.

"If she can stand you, she can stand me." I heard him walk to my curtain and I held my breath as I waited to see what would happen. The door opened again and from the shifting energies in the air, I knew it was Kisten.

"Aurel." He said his name plainly, walking past him. Kisten gently pulled the curtain back, placing the results of my blood work on my screen. He stepped back to the other side, separating me from their eyes once more and I took the chance to open my eyes slightly. "You're not supposed to be here. If you want to talk to Raiven, wait your full five days or–"

"Shut up!" The lich hissed and the power in the air shifted again as Aurel grew angry. Kisten remained calm, placing his tablet down before crossing his arms where he stood. "You have no say in this."

"Considering I'm her doctor right now, I do." Kisten replied coolly, but I could feel his power beginning to rise as he grew angry. "Right now, I couldn't care less about your issue with me. Raiven is still recovering and the only reason Alex is allowed in her room is because Lucius trusts him to be able to restrain her if it comes to that. So, wait out your last day and then come see her if you want to talk to her that badly."

"You can't order me to do anything. You are not my Overseer." Aurel sounded as if he meant to force his way to me, but Kisten refused to move, blocking the lich's access. LeAlexende sat down in his chair loudly, his power beginning to fill the room, overwhelming both Aurel's and Kisten's.

"I don't know what your problem is, Sixth," the Overseer threatened, using Aurel's rank rather than his name to address him. I heard the two men turn to the vampire and from what I could see of their shadows, LeAlexende was looking at his phone again. "But you will not threaten the safety of my charge. I am responsible for Raiven as long as she remains here.

"So, you can leave," the vampire paused, and I could feel his annoyance in the air, a slight wind blowing through the room despite the window next to me being closed. "And wait until the end of your five days or I will escort you out, and I will make sure Luc knows how willing you are to break his rules."

Aurel seemed to take LeAlexende's threat to heart, as I soon heard him walk out the room, slamming the door behind him. The air returned to normal as LeAlexende relaxed and Kisten sighed heavily, running his hand through his hair.

"Competition?" LeAlexende asked quietly, and Kisten scoffed, dropping his hand. He appeared to glance at the shut door, considering his answer.

"More like an obsession. You know how Aurel can be when he wants something." Kisten sighed again, his voice soft as he spoke. "And how poorly he takes being denied."

"Hmmm, more like he still hasn't gotten over you." The Overseer offered and Kisten remained silent. I saw his hand on the curtain again and closed my eyes as he pulled it back to look at me. I steadied my breathing to mimic sleep, and he moved the curtain back to separate us.

"That too, but to be honest, I haven't gotten over it, either." He admitted, sitting down in the chair across from LeAlexende. He slouched in the chair, clearly worn out from his labor. Even though I was his main concern, Kisten was on shift today, and was only checking on me in between his other patients. He let out a heavy sigh, almost groaning as he continued speaking. "He is *not* going to let me court her without a fight."

"Well, does your courtship have anything to do with him?"

"No," Kisten answered, and then he sat up, holding his hands in front of his lap. The pair remained silent for a moment and then Kisten spoke softly. "I love Raiven. I want her because of that, not to get back at him for what he did. But... I'll admit, I always intended to flaunt it in his face, and that was before I knew he wanted her."

Kisten sighed, leaning back in his chair, slouching as his feet slid across the floor. "I enjoy showing him that I have what he wants. That he was wrong about me, and I beat him. He thought she would be his so easily and I just..."

Kisten made a grabbing motion with his hands, cupping them as if he were holding a delicate flower; his voice was soft and loving and my chest ached with his words, "... snatched her away. And now she's going to be mine."

"So?" The Overseer offered, putting his phone down as he looked up to meet Kisten's gaze. I desperately wished I could see my lover's face, but I remained silent, maintaining my façade as they spoke. "Are you going to stop pursuing her again? Are you going to let Aurel have his way?"

"No. Never." Kisten's response was immediate, and I smiled at his words, my heart pounding. The Alpha sat up again, his posture determined. "I... stopped myself once from pursuing her because I thought it would be better for both of us. I was wrong. If I won't allow my own worries to stop me, I won't allow him to get in my way."

"Good to see you still have some fighting spirit. A part of me worried you had lost it." LeAlexende chuckled, slouching in his seat and looking back to his phone. Kisten chuckled as well, standing from his seat.

"Never, Alex. I'm still here to save you when you need it."

The Overseer laughed as Kisten went out and we were left in silence again. I almost sat up, wanting to ask the Overseer about Kisten's words, but decided against it, lying back on the bed.

"How long are you going to stay quiet?" LeAlexende's voice startled me, and I jumped slightly as he pulled back the curtain, smiling at me knowingly. I shrugged, closing my eyes.

"Well, I figured I shouldn't let Aurel find out you were lying," I retorted and LeAlexende chuckled, leaning against the wall. I chanced a glance at the Overseer, my eyes drifting to the closed door to my room. "And... it didn't feel like I should interrupt your conversation with Kisten."

"Well, do you have anything to add, Raiven?" The Overseer's gaze betrayed his bright smile and I frowned, returning my eyes to the ceiling.

"I don't like being in the middle." I admitted, closing my eyes as I sighed. "I know they have their issues and I'm not saying Kisten's wrong, but I don't like him using me to get back at Aurel. But... Aurel is really the one making it a huge problem, all because he wanted me for his harem."

I sighed, looking over to LeAlexende again. The Overseer hadn't moved and was still watching me with the same expression and my frown deepened. "I should've told him long before now about my feelings for Kisten, but honestly, at this point I don't think it would've made a difference."

"Want an outsider's opinion?" The vampire offered and I nodded, waiting for him to speak. LeAlexende moved next to the bed and took my hand. He squeezed it slightly, stroking my skin before speaking. "Aurel would've made it about him and Kisten even if Kisten had chosen someone else. He may say he accepts Kisten's decision, but he never will, no more than he'll ever accept yours. Would you like to know exactly what Aurel told Kisten when Kisten turned him down?"

I nodded again and the vampire squeezed my hand again, releasing me as he leaned against the bed, facing away from me. His voice was soft when he resumed speaking.

"Kisten left The Capital that night and came to me in the Southern Grove." I couldn't help the shocked look on my face and LeAlexende chuckled, sensing my surprise despite not seeing my face. "I was shocked, too, until he told me what happened. Aurel had told him that Lucius kept him bound via the Oath because no one else would ever risk being with someone like him. That he was a bound animal, only to be used by its master and had no other value than that use."

I was stunned into silence. I had never imagined Aurel could say something like that: he could be harsh with his words when he was upset, but not only had he tried to demean Kisten, he went as far as to accuse Lucius of being like Mater Vitae. My hands curled into fists at my anger and LeAlexende glanced back at me, his expression amused.

"Of course, when I brought Kisten back, I told Lucius what I had been told." The vampire turned away from me again, his voice holding back his obvious anger at the memory. "Aurel was dropped from third to sixth then, but Lucius wouldn't get rid of him thanks to his power. I warned him then that Aurel would only become more of an issue as time went on."

"I'm guessing Lucius said he'll deal with it?" I offered and LeAlexende laughed, turning to face me again.

"You have gotten a good grip on him in your short time here." The Overseer chuckled and I couldn't help but smile back. LeAlexende took my hand again, his eyes boring deep into mine as he spoke. "I'll tell you the same thing I told him: be wary of Aurel. He only does whatever he thinks will get him his way, and I have no doubt there is no limit to how far he'll go."

"I will, Alex. Thank you." With this, he released me and returned to his seat, resuming his video surfing on his phone. I sank against the pillows, reflecting on what LeAlexende had told me.

What would Aurel have said to me to get me to choose him? I wondered silently, and then I gripped the sheets tightly. *What will he say?*

I shook my head to try to free myself of these thoughts. I rolled on my side, wincing from the pain as I closed my eyes, hoping to sleep away my turmoil.

22

I sat on my couch in the warm afternoon, flipping through channels as Lira and Xris lounged around me. The pet sitter was surprised to see me home without notice, but I was happy to finally be allowed to rest. Brandon had visited me while I was in the hospital and insisted that I stay home for a few days. The team was getting ready to fly out on a new case, but he was adamant that they would call me if I was needed.

I accepted his demand easily: I didn't really want to get back to work so soon. It wasn't the first time I had ever been injured on a case, and I never felt like jumping back in afterwards. I almost convinced myself to tell Brandon the truth but stopped myself. I knew I would have to speak with the Director first, and it would ultimately be his decision as to what happened next.

Kisten released me the day after Brandon's visit and took me home, my car having already been driven from The Dream for me. My two cats were excited to see me after the additional week I had been gone and I was equally happy to see them, crouching down immediately to pet them. Kisten had left silently after seeing me inside, not giving me the chance to say goodbye as he closed my front door behind him.

I hadn't heard a word from him in the past day, and a pit began to form in my stomach as I checked my phone for the millionth time. I wasn't surprised he hadn't come by, but I had expected at least a phone call or a message. My thoughts turned to Eve's mischievous smile at the hospital and Aurel's insistent visit shortly after, causing me to groan loudly into the pillow.

"He won't give up," I tried to reason with myself, lying down as I settled on my usual cartoons. I almost expected my sister to respond, but she remained withdrawn. She hadn't spoken to me since the hospital and if it wasn't for her occasional presence to see how I was doing, I would've thought she had already faded completely. As she had pointed out, eventually I would have to make my decision: to allow her soul to fade into obscurity, or to give her peace by returning it to her body.

The pit in my stomach increased with these thoughts and I groaned out loud, causing my cats to stand up and shift their positions, clearly not wanting to deal with my anguish. I tried my best to pay attention to the colorful characters on my screen, but my own thoughts kept me from paying much attention to the lighthearted cartoon.

A sudden knock at the front door made my heart race and I nearly ran to the door, about to throw it open, when I forced myself to pause. Taking a deep breath, I glanced out the peephole, wanting to make sure it was Kisten before I threw myself into the arms of a stranger. I had nearly done it earlier with another delivery man, who was merely dropping off my monthly order of food for my cats. He was clearly taken aback as I flung the door open and I was more than embarrassed as I signed for the box.

It was Aurel, the lich leaning on my porch railing as he waited. My heart sank again, but not only from disappointment. Aurel's insistence that I choose him over Kisten was truly making me despise him and I regretted agreeing to be friends more and more. After LeAlexende's warning at the hospital, I knew that I had to treat Aurel as a serious threat, and my heart began to pound. He knocked on the door again and I merely leaned against it, wishing for him to go away. I noticed his shadow against my curtained window, and I knew he was trying to see if I was in my living room.

I'm sleeping, go away. I don't want to see you. I thought as he knocked a third time, his patience decreasing with his pounding. I considered locking myself up in my room in case he tried to force my door open, but I forced myself to remain still, lest he heard me walk away. I wanted to look out the peephole again but was too afraid I'd see him trying to look in for me.

"I know you're there, Raiven!" He finally growled and I stiffened, too worried to breathe. I felt my sister's presence rise, but she remained silent as we both waited to see what the lich would do. He pounded on the door again and I had to cover my mouth to hide the sound that tried to escape me. "I just want to talk!"

'*I'd hate to see what he'd do... if he wanted to do more than talk.*' My sister sneered and I nodded silently, jumping again as he continued pounding on my door. I slowly began to back away as I saw my door frame move with his pounding. The last thing I wanted was to face Aurel if things got physical, but I knew I would have no choice if he forced my door open.

"Raiven, please." His voice was soft now and I could hear him leaning against the door. I scoffed: now he wanted to plead with me, as if he had not just been pounding against my door like an angry ex? "I just... I just want to talk to you without him around."

After a moment of silence, I heard him place something on the doorstep and walk away. He paused for a moment at the end of the porch, presumably turning back to look at my door, but he soon continued walking and I breathed a sigh of relief as his car started in my driveway. I waited until I could no longer hear his motor as he drove off down the street before I opened the door, seeing a small package on my doormat. There was no note attached and I looked at it cautiously as I picked it up and closed my front door.

I held the package with disgust, angry that Aurel would even consider leaving me a gift after all that he had done. Knowing him, it was probably a piece from his jewelry collection, trying to show me that he really cared about me, but I didn't want it. It was nothing more than a trap and I was determined to throw it away as I walked back into my home. I was in no way prepared for the solid mass I ran into as I stepped into my kitchen, a blast of cold air also greeting me.

"Distracted?" I nearly flung the package from my hands as I threw my arms around Kisten. My side door was open, and my cats pawed at the screen door, wanting the freedom of outside as I embraced my love. Kisten pulled me closer to him, planting soft kisses into my hair. "It almost seems like you missed me."

"Of course I did." I breathed, resting my chin against his chest as I looked up at him. Kisten smiled down at me, and I leaned up for a kiss, him meeting me halfway. I almost moaned at the searing pain of our lips slanting across each other, but I had missed kissing him more than anything. Kisten pulled back before I could deepen the kiss and stepped away, turning around to close my side door. I placed Aurel's package on the counter as I walked up behind him, unable to keep my hands off my Alpha.

"How did you get here?"

"I ran." He said and I turned him around, trying to measure if he was joking. He still had the same smile on his face as he stroked my scarred face down to my injured earlobe. I had insisted he remove the bandage before releasing me and I was shocked by how normal it still looked. The bullet had taken off a decent amount but it was still less than I expected, something Kisten said amounted to the bullet also grazing my face as I had moved, therefore slowing it down ever so slightly. I leaned into his painful touch, pressing his hand against my face and I closed my eyes as he continued. "I was talking with Lucius."

"About?" I asked, my eyes still closed as I took in him being here with me. Kisten chuckled and I lazily opened my eyes to see his grin.

"Us." Kisten stated, pulling me into another embrace. He kissed my ear, and I sighed happily despite the burning pain. "There are more steps to courtship, and I was going through them with Lucius, including when I would be released from the Oath."

"Hmm," I hummed in agreement, burying my head into his chest. His shirt smelled heavily of sweat even though the fabric was dry, so I knew he must have run from the Landing in animal form. He pressed more kisses into my hair, before looking away from me and his grip on me suddenly tightened. I followed his gaze to the package on my counter, still wrapped and unopened.

"Who's that from?" He asked, and I froze, not wanting to tell him Aurel had been here. He looked at me darkly as my heart pounded and I kept my gaze away from him. His voice was dark and full of suspicion as he spoke again, this time speaking directly against my skin. "Raiven, who is that from?"

"It's fro—" I barely got a word out before Kisten pinned me to my counter, pushing his body into mine. I gasped at the sudden movement, wrapping my arms around Kisten's neck as he lifted me on the marble and began to assault my neck, burning my skin with his licking and biting. I moaned openly at his assault, and he wrapped one of his arms around me, sliding my groin into his as he leaned over me, undoing the buttons of my shirt with his free hand. He growled into my skin, and I moaned for him, loving every second of this punishment.

"Don't accept gifts from him," He commanded, sliding his hand up my stomach once the fabric fell open. I clung to him uselessly, only able to nod at his command. He licked up my collarbone, a trail of pain following his sandpaper tongue. "I don't care if they pile up on your doorstep. I don't want you to touch them. Let me take care of them."

"If you punish me like this, why would I listen?" I moaned and Kisten paused in his torture, pulling back slightly to look at my face. My eyes fluttered open as I breathed heavily, my body full of pain and my desire for him. His eyes were swirling, and he growled above me, the sound causing my midsection to clench with promised pleasure and pain. "I won't touch them, Kisten."

"Good." With no small ceremony, Kisten lifted me off the counter and over his shoulder, jolting me from my stupor. I heard him scrape the package into the trash before carrying me out of the kitchen, and

I knew his intentions before we reached my bedroom. He tossed me on the bed, climbing on top of me before I could even finish bouncing from the impact. His mouth was already back on my neck, and I wrapped my legs around his waist, pulling him closer to me. As I surrendered to the painful pleasure of his touch, I knew I had chosen correctly.

23

LeAlexende lounged on the train station bench, placing his phone down next to him. It seemed the Overseer had exhausted everything he could do, and he slouched, running his hand through his blond hair. He pulled a few strands in front of his face, grunting before pushing them back with the rest. His expression was pensive as he glanced up towards the dark night sky, breathing heavily.

"Sorry I'm late." LeAlexende looked down to see Lucius walking towards him alone, finally without Evalyn tailing behind him. He sat next to him on the bench, and for a moment, the two friends took in the empty station, devoid of life. The silence was deafening: no wind to blow around the debris and trash, no insects to sing their nightly song. A perfect setting for two undead beings to speak and LeAlexende gently placed his hand on top of Lucius'. The Overseer immediately weaved their fingers together, closing his eyes.

"Sorry that your visit was disrupted like this. It was... not ideal." Lucius was first to break the silence, slouching to match LeAlexende. He sighed heavily, and LeAlexende snorted, closing his eyes as well.

"This is your territory: I didn't expect a peaceful visit. Even without Raiven's case, you keep too many dangerous people around," LeAlexende straightened himself and sat up properly on the bench as he released Lucius' hand. A train flew by in the quiet night, interrupting the silence with its noise. LeAlexende watched it with semi-interest as it passed, the lights a blur as it flew by. It left as quickly as it came, bringing with it the façade of life as the wind of its passing moved his hair in its wake. LeAlexende lifted his hand to his hair again as he spoke. "It's more than enough that I got to see you."

"What did you come for? You don't usually visit without warning," Lucius asked, chancing a glance at his friend. LeAlexende didn't answer at first, keeping his gaze on the darkness the train had ventured into. "I know the holiday worked as an excuse, but it's not like you to take a risk like this."

"Basina… is dead." LeAlexende closed his eyes, a painful expression on his face. Lucius' eyes widened in surprise, and he stammered to answer.

"But…she—"

"He finally got her. I heard it from her Retainer." LeAlexende continued, ignoring Lucius' surprise. His expression was heavy and it was clear the news was difficult for him as well. "With her gone, we're the last high ranking First left."

"Just less than half of the original Thirteen now." Lucius sighed, and LeAlexende nodded, his blond hair rippling as his fingers passed through. In a moment, his hair turned white as fresh snow and his purple eyes had deepened almost to black. Lucius was unsurprised by this change and merely looked on as LeAlexende stood. His face and form also seemed different somehow, but his voice sounded the same when he spoke.

"Lucius, I'm the only one left who truly remembers and with Basina gone, I'm the last of the Siblings. It's only a matter of time now before he finds out I'm here." LeAlexende's voice was barely above a whisper and Lucius looked as if he was about to argue. He was stopped, however, as LeAlexende raised his hand in front of Lucius. "There needs to be someone else who remembers."

"Alex, please, don't do this. It'll weaken you too much. If he is after you, you need all of your strength." Lucius pleaded, even as he knelt underneath LeAlexende's hand. It was obvious he didn't want to, but it was almost as if he was being forced to comply. "Let me go get a memory device, that should suffice—"

"No, Luc. We need to do this the old way and you're the only person I trust." LeAlexende insisted, and Lucius was crestfallen at his friend's words. "You need to feel my memories. You need to know the Truth."

Lucius nodded through silent tears, and LeAlexende smiled a sad smile as he brought his wrist to his mouth. He pierced his own skin with his fangs and allowed his blood to drip over Lucius' face. His purple eyes began to glow, and the white hair swirled in the wind his power had called forth.

"Enkidu." LeAlexende used Lucius' human name, causing Lucius' power to come forth on its own. Lightning flashed in the sky above the pair, a storm beginning to form over the train station. "Accept the blood of Mortem and allow my memories to be yours."

With this, Lucius opened his mouth, allowing the blood of his friend and fellow Overseer to flow into him. The storm above them grew in turmoil and LeAlexende lifted his eyes up from Lucius. His eyes seemed to meet mine as the lightning flashed and I woke up as the thunder crashed above the pair.

It was dark in my room after the flash, and I could hear Kisten sleeping peacefully next to me. I carefully stood and walked to my window, seeing the brewing storm on the horizon. I could feel my sister's presence and without words, I knew she was thinking the same as me.

"What was that?" I wondered aloud, and a thought flashed through my mind, my sister pushing the concept to me. "Necromancy..."

Despite my own necromancy saving me from being turned into a vampire, it was not an ability I really ever used. I had only used it once in my long life and that was when my sister died, to bind her soul to the locket. Mater Vitae had forbidden me from ever using it and even after I left her, I had never felt the need.

Necromancers were extremely rare among humans, to the point that most never knew they were one unless they accidentally called upon the power. Just as sorcerers were considered dangerous, necromancers were considered a worse threat, given their ability to raise zombies.

"That's impossible, sis. Necromancy doesn't work on the undead." I rebutted and she left, not arguing with me. I continued looking at the still-growing storm, still trying to process what had happened and what I had seen. Another First was dead: that was the real reason LeAlexende had come to visit. If what he said was true, more than half of the First were now gone and that meant the Hunters would soon be closing in on the few who remained. I gripped myself tightly, my room briefly filling with light as the lightning flashed again.

'Don't...' I was surprised by my sister's voice, and I gripped the locket as she came back, her frustration obvious. I glanced to the floor, afraid to see my own reflection in the glass. *'Don't you run this time. Don't you give this... up out of fear.'*

"I..." I started to dispute her assumption but I stopped myself. I always ran when I knew the Hunters were getting close and I felt the familiar urge to flee now. I turned to look at Kisten, who was still sleeping peacefully on my bed. My heart pounded as I looked at him and I gazed back to the storm that was growing ever closer. LeAlexende had been worried enough that he had wanted to share his memories and power with Lucius and my Overseer was known for his habit of taking risks. Staying with him meant putting everyone in The Capital in more danger but... leaving him meant losing Kisten. Losing everything.

I sighed deeply, pulling myself away from the window and back to the bed. Kisten rolled over to me, draping his arm across my waist as I sat down. I couldn't help my smile as I laid back down, gingerly touching his face with my fingertips. Kisten sighed happily in his sleep, leaning into my touch as my fingers ached with pain. I gripped my sister's locket as I closed my eyes, my heart and mind filled with determination.

'*Don't worry,*' I assured her, breathing deeply as she faded away. '*I won't.*'

SPOT A LEOPARD
SEALED BLOOD BOOK 2

The Grimm, creatures that were neither human nor animal, created by Mater Vitae for one purpose – to kill anything that moved. The same creatures that had ripped my tribesmen apart in front of me and were the ones responsible for killing my sister. The man walking with them now was the same one who had commanded them then and my body began to shake with anger and fear. I spoke through clenched teeth, the sand around me starting to shake as I summoned my power.
"Whistleblower."

To Viv Andromeda,
For supporting me through every step.

To my beautiful daughter,
Who teaches me to enjoy the little moments.

I

I leaned against the pier, looking out over the ocean as the sea breeze blew through my hair and shirt. I didn't visit the ocean very often, and as I looked over the blue expanse, I was filled with a longing for a home I barely remembered. Somewhere, across all that water, was my first home and the place where my sister's body was buried. I held her locket in my hand, trying to encourage her to speak, but the wood remained hard and silent.

'...*Sis?*' I tried to reach out to her with my thoughts but there was no response to my query, no subtle indication of my sister's presence. I couldn't help tightening my hold, sighing heavily as I forced myself to loosen my grip. It was my own fault that she didn't have the power to answer me, and my heart twisted in my chest.

I gently let my hand fall from the wood, still watching the expanse of blue as the waves flowed across the sand. Watching the water was calming, and I closed my eyes as the breeze blew the salty particles against my face. My chest ached with emotion as I opened my eyes, and I glanced up as I heard a seagull fly above, screeching as it searched for its next meal. I was unable to help my slight chuckle as the bird dove to disturb some of the beachgoers, the couple upset at having their walk interrupted.

"Are you alright, *Rabe*[1]?" I turned to see Kisten walking up to me, using one of his many pet names. The Alpha was wearing a sheer white shirt, the fabric hanging loosely around him as it blew in the wind. His shorts also flapped in the breeze and I couldn't help my excitement as he grew closer. I turned around completely as he reached me, a bright smile gracing my face.

"I am now," I smiled, leaning up to kiss him as he wrapped his arms around my waist. My mouth exploded with the familiar pain as our lips touched and I ignored it as I stroked his face with my gloved hands. Kisten purred into the kiss, his hands gripping my shirt tightly as the pain fully radiated up my face. He pulled up from me, his eyes bright with his smile as he tightened his hold on me.

"I'm glad," he glanced down to my collarbone, where his necklace sat around my neck. Kisten was pursuing me as his mate, and the necklace was a part of the courtship process, essentially marking me as his. From what I had experienced so far, most of the process included many gifts, including clothing I had to wear at certain times to symbolize his continued pursuit.

It was all building to a declaration, finally asking me to be his mate in public and I was both excited and scared of that moment. Although I had already given my yes at the beginning of the process, it would be then that I would have to reveal my relationship with Kisten to my job. Only the Director knew about me being more than human, and while I was a member of the Overseer's Coven, I had to maintain my distance from the rest of the supernatural community in order to avoid a conflict of interests. Agreeing to be Kisten's mate would no longer allow me to keep that distance, and I still hadn't heard from the Director what would happen next.

I gently pulled away from the Alpha, leaning against the wood of the pier again as I watched the many bodies move back and forth beneath us. The decorations were already being set up behind the hotel and all in preparation for the wedding that would be happening tomorrow night. It was the union of Arkrian and Shannon, a snake shifter from Kisten's pack and my boss Brandon's daughter. I leaned over more as I sighed, allowing my hands to hang over the wide rail of the pier.

"Are you excited for tomorrow?" Kisten enquired, his words pulling me from my thoughts as he leaned next to me.

"As much as I can be," I muttered, closing my eyes as I enjoyed the breeze that started up again. Kisten hummed, placing his arm around my waist and I leaned into him as he stood, the shifter purring as he held me. "My whole team is going to be there unofficially as security and I'm not particularly excited about them hearing your declaration."

"They were going to find out eventually," he shrugged, laying a gentle kiss on my braids. I sighed again; he was right as usual, but it didn't erase the worry in my chest. Kisten pulled away from me and started to lead me down the pier. "C'mon, we need to find the happy couple."

As the Alpha of The Capital, Kisten had a vital role to play in the ceremony. Apparently, it was tradition for him to preside over the event, officially joining the new couple. After learning I was to be Kisten's mate, Shannon offered me a spot as one of the bridesmaids, but I refused, not wanting to intrude on her special day any more than we already were. Both she and Arkrian were honored that Kisten wanted to make his declaration at the reception and eagerly agreed when he asked them.

The ceremony was already something unique in its own right and an upcoming trend in mixed marriages; similar to what her brother had done with his wedding, Shannon was mixing human traditions with shapeshifter ones. Her take on what traditions to use had upset her father somewhat, as Brandon wasn't exactly fond of shifters or Supernaturals, but he conceded in the end. I was happy that my boss had finally started the process of putting aside his prejudice against Supernaturals, and I could only hope that it would soften his reaction to finding out the truth about me.

"Raiven!" Shannon called out to me, a giddy expression on her face as she ran up the pier, distracting me from my thoughts. Kisten released me as we collided, the petite girl nearly knocking me over as I was forced to take a step back. Shannon was a perfect copy of her late mother: long blond hair, bright brown eyes, a petite hourglass figure, and the attitude of someone twice her height. There wasn't much that could deter her from having her way, and that included her future husband.

Her fiancé walked up to us slowly, shaking his head at Shannon's behavior. Arkrian was much more stoic than his bride-to-be: in a lot of ways he reminded me of Kisten. He wore a cool head on his shoulders, polite to a fault, but also a fierce fighter for what he wanted. He was the Omega to Kisten's Alpha and next to take Kisten's place, an honor he had earned on more than one occasion.

"Shannon," Arkrian sighed as he reached us, pausing to greet Kisten. His deep brown waves blew in the wind, and he took a moment to brush them from his face. "Don't jump on Raiven like that."

"Oh hush, Ark. Raiven can easily catch me." As if to prove her point, Shannon jumped up on me again, wrapping her legs around my waist. I moved my arms to hold her, unable to help my laughter at her antics. Being part undead had its advantages, such as having a degree of inhuman strength and I carried Shannon easily. Kisten laughed as Arkrian shook his head and I gently put the girl down on the pier, our laughter subsiding. Arkrian moved as if to apologize, but I stopped him with a smile.

"Don't bother," I beamed, moving next to Kisten as Shannon returned to Arkrian's side. "We both know it won't do any good."

"That's... true," Arkrian conceded, kissing his bride's cheek as he brushed the wild hair from her face. She glowed at the gesture and leaned into him, clearly happy and excited. My chest hurt at their display of affection, but I kept the smile on my face while Arkrian questioned Kisten about the ceremony.

Despite my future at his side, Kisten was still bound to Lucius and Evalyn via the Oath of Loyalty: a promise made with blood that kept others from touching him intimately. Even the slightest display of affection would cause me intense pain, and I rarely got to experience the intimacy others took for granted. Kisten had promised that the Oath would be released at some point during the courtship, as he had to be released from it before I could become his mate. However, he had never told me when, and the longer I had to wait, the more unbearable it became to deal with.

"Well, Shannon wants to double-check the preparations for tomorrow with the hotel, and then we still need to pick up some things," Arkrian went on, and I returned my attention to him as he hugged his bride-to-be tighter. "We'll see you both at dinner tonight?"

"Of course, *der Welpe*[2]." Kisten smiled and we watched as they walked up the pier, both hand in hand. Kisten looked down at me, and I must've shown my longing on my face, as he grabbed my hand and laced our fingers together. The gloves I wore had been a courting gift, and he lifted my hand to his mouth, kissing the fabric.

"Soon enough," he promised as he lifted his gaze to mine, his chartreuse eyes bright with his love for me. Despite the ache in my chest, I smiled back, closing my eyes.

"I know, Kisten," I stroked his face with my free hand, leaning into his embrace again as he buried his face into my body. I held his head against me, loving the feel of him. "I can't wait."

"We could get joined here too," he offered and I chuckled, tapping his head playfully. The shifter responded by burying his face deeper into my chest, causing me to laugh again. "It could be quite the romantic wedding."

"You really want to copy them?" I jested and it was his turn to laugh as Kisten lifted me into the air, setting me on the rail of the pier. He pressed his face into my midsection, taking in the scent of me that he enjoyed so much. I rested my hand on his head, lightly stroking his hair. "Never took you as one to enjoy the beach."

"I can't say I'm completely fond. I grew up far from the ocean and honestly it scared me when I first saw it," he admitted, looking out towards the sea and a sad look crossed his face before disappearing.

"Besides, crossing the Atlantic in the 1800s was not as luxurious as it is now."

"I'd imagine not," I agreed, looking back over the calm ocean. I could see the faint shadow of a ship on the horizon, and I watched as it drifted further along the expanse of blue. I turned back to see Kisten looking up at me, his expression quizzical.

"Now that I think about it," he started, his eyes meeting mine. "You've never told me where you came from. You had to cross the sea at some point."

I shrugged, not answering his question as I looked back over the water, holding my locket through my shirt. Kisten watched my hand, not pressing me for an answer. After agreeing to be his mate, I confided in Kisten, making him the only person alive who knew the truth about my sister and the locket. Most assumed it was a collar from my time with Mater Vitae, not understanding the true value it held to me. Kisten had insisted he would help me if I wanted to give my sister peace, but it still wasn't something I was ready to do.

My phone started to ring inside my pocket and I awkwardly reached for it as I frowned, hopping down back onto the pier. My team and I were still technically on call if any case was passed on to us, but the Director had already said he would do his best to "let Brandon have his day". The number my phone displayed was not one I recognized and my frown grew as I silenced the call.

"Unknown number?" Kisten offered and I nodded, watching as the call ended and saw the flashing light indicating they were leaving a voicemail. I waited until the light stopped, finally unlocking my phone and playing the message.

"Hey Rai–" The moment I heard the voice, I deleted the voicemail, not even trying to hide my annoyance. It was Aurel, another member of the Coven and a lich I was beyond tired of. We had once been friends, but when I told him I didn't want to be more than friends, Aurel took the rejection poorly. He took finding out that Kisten wanted me even worse, and was making it his life's mission to try to separate us.

"I'm getting real sick of this," I muttered, scowling as I blocked the new number, angrily shoving my phone back into my pocket. I heard as Kisten hummed softly, shrugging as he looked down the beach.

"Honestly, I'm surprised he didn't find a way to come along," the Alpha admitted and I rolled my eyes, shaking my head in my frustration. Aurel had done his best to try to get me to stay behind in Decver while Kisten oversaw the wedding, insisting there was no real reason for me to accompany him. It wasn't until I pointed out that I was required to be present with my team that he gave up, and even then, it felt as if he still wanted to argue the point.

'Raiven...' I nearly jumped as I finally heard my sister's voice, soft and barely above a whisper as she responded to my emotions. I was unable to help as my hands instantly flew to the locket and I gripped it tightly as I felt its usual warmth.

"Sis?" I spoke quietly, and Kisten looked up to me, concern flashing across his features. He reached to touch my locket as well, allowing him to hear her voice as she continued, the strain obvious in her tone.

'Just... checking in. Harder to stay awake now.' She sounded far away and my heart ached as she continued to speak. *'Kisten, keep taking care... of her.'*

"Of course," he smiled and I felt the warmth fade as my sister drifted away again, unable to continue holding on. His hand slowly slid away as I released the locket, tears forming in my eyes.

"She's going to fade soon," I lamented, my voice full of the tears I refused to let flow. "I don't have much time left with her."

"What do you want to do?" I met his gaze as he spoke, his voice full of concern. I closed my eyes, pulling him into a tight hug as I held back my tears. I shook my head against him and he tightened his grip on me, pressing comforting kisses into my hair.

"I don't know," I admitted, speaking into his chest. "I... I don't know."

"C'mon," he coaxed, gently pulling away from me. His hand

caressed my face, the gentle act marred by the pain it caused. "We've got some time before the dinner. Let's walk around for a bit."

As Kisten gently led me down the pier, I chanced one last glance at the ocean. It gently lapped in my direction, as if reminding me that I would one day have to cross it again. I forced myself to look away, squeezing my partner's hand tightly.

2

"Thank you so much! We'll see you tomorrow!" I waved as Kisten and I walked out of the restaurant, Arkrian and Shannon seeing us off before turning to attend to their other guests. I stepped into Kisten's Mustang and settled in as he accepted his keys from the valet and began to drive us back to the hotel.

Dinner had been quite the affair, with all of the bridal party, plus family, in attendance. The restaurant was thrown off by having the Alpha present, but Kisten was as humble as ever, doing his best to soothe their worries about him. Being a part of the main Three had its downsides, and Kisten's presence often rattled those around him, especially members of the pack. They often seemed to think he was there to judge or test them, and he always had to reassure them that he would do no such thing. For my part, I felt a little out of place with so many faces I barely knew, but Kisten had navigated the dinner perfectly, greeting the many members of his pack and being particularly charming to Brandon.

Brandon usually kept his distance from Kisten, refusing to interact with him unless we needed his help on a case. Considering the wedding, however, he had done his best to put aside his issue with shapeshifters and enjoy the dinner for his daughter. He even greeted his daughter-in-law for the first time, Shannon's brother Mark having brought his wife with him. As Shannon had wanted to get married at sunset, Mark and Vanessa would unfortunately miss the ceremony, as Mark couldn't wake from death until afterwards. They had insisted they would be at the reception, however, which seemed to be more than enough for Shannon.

"Enjoy yourself?" Kisten reached over to touch my exposed thigh, his gloved hand pushing my dress up further. Kisten was wearing black dress braces, his tie and gloves matching the suspenders. His dark-green shirt matched the color of my halter dress, and I rested my hand on his before taking it into my own. I looked over at him, watching as he kept his eyes on the road. He chanced a glance at me, smiling when he noticed me staring. "Well?"

"It was a bit awkward for me. Doesn't help that I still don't know most faces in the pack," I admitted and the Alpha laughed as he released my hand, squeezing my thigh. "I was pretty sure that poor server was gonna have a heart attack when she saw the necklace."

"Honestly, same. The poor darling almost lost her human form right there," Kisten sighed, shaking his head as he paused at the light. "Good thing Arkrian was able to calm her down. It would have been awkward to try to get her to the beach."

"What will we ever do without him?" I joked, earning myself a side look from Kisten as he rolled his eyes. He turned his gaze back to the road as the light changed, sliding his hand higher into my lap. Most of the servers had been merfolk, who were well known for losing their forms when their emotions were heightened. Kisten and Arkrian both usually walked on eggshells around them to avoid issues, but all of us had forgotten that Kisten's pursuit of me wasn't officially announced to the whole pack yet. Most of the locals in Decver already knew, but it wasn't surprising that news had yet to spread to the coast.

"After tomorrow, everyone will know anyway," Kisten sighed, not trying to hide the excitement in his voice and my heart pounded as I thought of his proposal. "I can't wait to introduce you as my mate."

"I–" I was interrupted by my phone ringing and I immediately sighed, assuming it was Aurel again. A glance at the number made me smile however, and I gave Kisten an apologetic look as I answered. "Hello?"

"Raiiiiveeeen," Justina's voice whined through my phone and I did my best to hide my giggle as I put the phone on speaker. Being ten months pregnant had taken its toll on the sorcerer and, despite her many pleas, Kisten had forbidden her from using magic to deal with the pains and aches, lest they affect the baby. "I can't do this any longer."

"You're almost there, sweetie." I cooed, doing my best to sound sympathetic. I could hear Crispin in the background, doing his best to comfort his lover, but Justina was having none of it. I could hear her push him away before she turned her attention back to the phone.

"Can't I just have the baby now, Kisten? I know you're there," she whined, and Kisten chuckled, leaning over as he drove. "Wrist feedings would be better than this and it's been *ten months*."

"Now, Justina, we talked about this before I left," Kisten answered, and I had to cover my mouth to hide my own giggles as he did his best to sound professional. While the pain she was going through was real, we all found her whining a bit amusing after hearing it for so long. "If you go into labor while I'm gone, Dennis will perform the procedure. But since the child has Nosferatu Syndrome, we want to avoid a premature delivery. She may take a little longer than you would like, but you already know she'll be here soon."

"But Kisten..." Justina sounded desperate for relief and for a moment I sympathized with her. With vampire fathers, Nosferatu syndrome was a common condition: the fetus would drink the mother's blood, requiring regular transfusions in some cases and premature deliveries could often kill the baby. The severity of the condition could be the difference in carrying the pregnancy to term or having to terminate early and, luckily for Justina, her case was slight. Her baby girl barely drank any of her blood but the discomfort from the sparse feedings always made Justina anxious and she constantly begged for an early Cesarean.

"You'll be holding her soon enough, Justina," I offered, doing my best to turn her discomfort to excitement. I heard Crispin echoing my sentiments and it must have worked, as I heard Justina sigh. She always came around in the end, insisting the pain wasn't that bad.

"I know, I know," she conceded and it sounded as if she was shifting her weight on the bed. "I just want her to be here already. It seems the closer I am, the longer this is all taking."

"Well, you know who to blame," I laughed and she laughed with me.

"Да[1], I do, but he is doing his best to take responsibility," her voice was soft as she spoke, and I could only imagine that she was looking at Crispin lovingly. The vampire had severely cut back on chasing other women, making Justina his main concern as the pregnancy progressed. Although I still couldn't bring myself to like him, I did have to give him credit for giving up his own desires to take care of Justina.

"Soon enough," Kisten echoed, stroking my leg again as he spoke. He had an unusual look in his eye as he drove and I wasn't sure what emotion he was feeling. "She'll be just as beautiful as her mother."

"She will," I finally heard Crispin's voice as he kissed Justina, still comforting his lover. "Get some sleep, beautiful."

"Alright, sorry Raiven…" Justina sounded a moment from passing out and I smiled, blowing her a kiss through the phone.

"Don't be. Have a good night," I hung up the phone, leaning back in my seat. Kisten's gloved hand was still on my lap as he turned into the hotel's parking garage and he leaned back as we waited for the elevator to take us to our floor. The words "Ocean City Luxury" flashed by us as Kisten stroked higher into my lap, sneakily trying to get his hand in between my legs. I lightly tapped his hand, laughing as he withdrew.

"We're almost there, you can wait a moment longer," I giggled, pushing my dress back down as he drove off the elevator onto our level. Kisten also chuckled, pulling into the first free space he found before quickly pulling my face to his. The kiss he indulged in burned more than usual, but I leaned into it, the pain only serving to increase my desire. Kisten slid his hand between my legs again, pushing his fingers against my underwear and he did little to hide his growl as he spoke.

"*I can never wait,*" Kisten quickly unbuckled his seat and mine, pushing over his console and practically was on top of me as he kissed me deeply. I lifted my hands to his shoulder, gripping his suspenders as I pulled him onto me more. Kisten stopped the kiss briefly to pull his glove off his hand and watching him peel the leather off with his feline teeth aroused me more than I wanted to admit. The shifter knew it, grinning as he shoved his hand back between my legs and I loved the pain that shot through my body.

"Kisten..." I moaned, pulling the glove from his mouth as I kissed him again, not caring that we were still in the parking garage. Anyone who walked by would see the fogging windows, would hear my loud moans and I didn't care. Kisten pulled back, his eyes already changed to their cat-like appearance and his fangs clearly visible in his mouth.

"Raiven..." he echoed, growling as he pushed aside my underwear and I moaned loudly with the pain as he slid his fingers inside me. Every movement set my insides on fire and I melted into my seat, torn between leaning into his touch and squirming to escape. But the Alpha had me trapped and we both knew it as he buried his face into my neck, pushing his fingers even deeper inside me.

"Kis, I–" My voice failed me as he explored me with his hand, pressing burning kisses into my exposed neck as I moaned. Despite the awkward position, Kisten worked me knowingly, releasing moans of his own as my sounds only served to arouse him more. I shivered in my seat as I saw his spots start to appear on his skin, the dark marks seeming to pulse with his voice. The fire was starting to radiate all through my waist and I squirmed more to escape the pleasurable pain.

"Soon," he growled against my skin, tangling his free hand in my braids. Despite how short they were, I had styled them in an updo for the dinner, but he quickly undid this, the hair cascading to my shoulders as he indulged himself on my scent. "I can't wait to be inside you again."

"Neither can I," I moaned as I clung to him, his fingers still inside me as I gripped his suspenders tightly. Kisten had only fully embraced me once, a wonderful night in which he had been released from the Oath. He had been free to love me without consequence and I couldn't wait to have that level of intimacy again. Kisten grinned knowingly before he removed his hand, letting my underwear cover me once again. He brought his hand to my mouth and I sucked his fingers hungrily, as if I was dying from thirst. Slowly, he pulled away from me completely, leaning back into his seat while adjusting his outfit. I reluctantly let him slide his fingers from my lips, the pain fading with them.

"Let's go," He opened his door, stepping out and, after taking a moment to catch my breath, I followed him. I echoed his steps as we made our way through the brightly lit parking lot, when a car alarm behind us suddenly went off. I whipped around quickly, my eyes glowing as I summoned my power and my heart was pounding loudly in my ears. Kisten turned, holding open the door that would take us inside.

"Raiven?" he called me after as I walked off, heading to the still-echoing alarm. I could barely breathe as I moved, the air damp and heavy as I walked. Ever since LeAlexende's visit, I found myself constantly on edge, ever watchful for any sign of Hunters. I had already resolved myself not to flee, but I had no intention of being caught off guard as I circled around the car slowly, trying to see what had disturbed the silence. The alarm blared as I made my way around, not seeing anything that could have set it off. I considered getting to my knees and checking underneath, but decided against it, forcing myself to release my power. I looked up to see Kisten walking toward me, a worried look on his face.

"What is it, Raiven?"

"It's... nothing." I glanced back at the screaming vehicle before walking away, meeting Kisten as he embraced me. He sniffed the air above me before kissing my hair and grabbing my hand. I squeezed his fingers tightly, trying to ignore the uncomfortable feeling in my chest as the alarm finally stopped.

"There's nothing here," he affirmed, returning my gesture. "Probably someone in the rooms just setting off their alarm by accident."

"Yeah…" I faltered, allowing my voice to fade as Kisten guided me back towards the hotel. I closed my eyes, doing my best not to glance back into the quiet parking garage.

3

"Now where were we?" Kisten rounded on me as soon as we were in the hotel room, quickly pressing me into the door. He removed his other glove as his hands played with my skin, sliding my dress back up my body. Each touch set my skin ablaze and I moaned loudly as he explored me, the shifter not trying to hide his desire. I swiftly pulled his face to mine for another kiss, loving the pressure as he pinned me to the door with his body. He openly growled into the kiss, sending a shiver through me as I pushed him back, unable to help my grin as I met his swirling eyes.

"You are quite the sadist now," I grinned, grabbing his suspenders again, reaching down to unfasten them as he lifted me into the air. I wrapped my legs around him as he carried me to the bed, managing to release the straps as he laid me down on the soft material.

"Well, it's not as if you gave me much of a choice," Kisten smiled, slowly sliding his hands up my thigh. I sighed happily with pleasure and pain as he pressed his face to my skin, breathing in my scent and planting burning kisses as he went. I playfully pushed him up and he let me, his eyes burning with passion. "You certainly haven't let the pain stop you."

"And I believe you are assaulting a federal agent, Kisten," I spat back, pulling off my own gloves before touching his skin, moaning at the pain that gripped my fingers. Kisten smiled at me darkly, pressing a soft kiss into my hand. "That's a serious felony, Sir."

"Oh is it, now?" he breathed, sliding my hand to his shirt, where I eagerly undid the buttons. His spots were already faintly on his skin as I revealed his chest, and I traced one of them lightly. "I hope I get a life sentence."

"Hmmm," I hummed, my mind falling back to Justina as I continued tracing his spots. Kisten watched me curiously as I dropped my hand to my own stomach, rubbing myself as I considered what it would be like. Shifter pregnancies were vastly different from and yet similar to vampire pregnancies: just as with the undead, it was only ever a non-shifter mother who would be in danger. Problems varied from species to species, but all were serious if not caught in time and I sighed as my mind raced. I wasn't even sure if I could get pregnant, as undead women usually couldn't.

"Something on your mind?" Kisten prodded, moving his hand to rest on top of mine. I looked up to his face, and his expression was the same it had been when he spoke to Justina. He looked at me with a longing look, and his spots darkened, spreading further up his chest. I reached up to his face and he leaned into my touch, purring.

"Just thinking." I whispered, smiling softly as he closed his eyes and continued purring into my hand.

"About?"

"Having your child." Kisten chuckled low in his throat, shifting on the bed to kiss my stomach. My sex clenched with his movement, but it felt different from usual. Kisten's spots retreated slightly, and he rested his head against me, holding my hand in his.

"Already thinking so far ahead? And here I was worried you were having second thoughts," I snatched my hand back as he laughed, sliding up my body to my face. I turned away from him, fighting the blush creeping on my skin. Kisten kissed my cheek, still chuckling in my ear. "It makes me happy, Rai."

"I was just wondering if it would be possible." I retorted, still refusing to meet his gaze. Kisten lifted himself up at this and I could hear him undoing his belt buckle. I chanced a glance just as he dropped back on top of me, his erection pulsing between my legs. He pushed himself against my underwear and I moaned openly, slightly spreading my legs for him.

"Don't worry, Rai," he purred against my skin, fighting the urge to thrust himself inside me. I knew he would go no further than this: despite letting loose when it came to his desire for me, Kisten still exercised some of that careful control he was known for. "I'll be sure to take care of you when the time comes."

"Kisten..." I whined, partly from embarrassment and partly from pleasure as he pushed himself against me, teasing my wet slit that wanted nothing more than to have him thrust inside. I wrapped my arms around his neck, tangling my hand in his hair as he moved against me. One of his hands had found its way to the edge of my dress again, pushing the offensive clothing higher as Kisten slid up my body. He carefully thrusted in between my thighs, his member still pressing my underwear into me as he moved.

"*Fuck...I...*" Kisten moaned against me and I answered him softly, unable to deny the pleasure of such a simple movement. The fabric was soaked as he pressed it against me and each thrust set my thighs and opening ablaze with the familiar fire of the Oath punishing me. Kisten's arms shook as he fought to support himself and move his hips, denying his desire to rip the underwear away and slip inside. The spots appeared on his chest again as he panted above me and I started to see the tips of his fangs peeking from between his lips. "*Raiven...*"

I moaned wordlessly in response, unable to find the words as I gripped the sheets tightly, doing my best not to squirm as he moved. I felt as his hands curled into the sheets next to me and despite the distance between us, I could still feel his hot breath as he panted. I closed my eyes, doing my best not to arch my back to meet his careful movements as he shook above me. It was now a delicate balance between our desire and his animal's, even though all three of us wanted the exact same thing.

"*Gods...*" I finally moaned, and I opened my eyes as Kisten pulled away from me and I couldn't help but reach after him as he sat on the edge of the bed. "Kisten?"

"Hmmm," the Alpha groaned, and I could tell he was trying to calm his animal and his lust, lest he lose control of both. I swiftly reached around him, teasing his throbbing member with my hand as I breathed on his neck. Kisten shivered in my arms as I burned my lips kissing his skin, enticing him to play with me. I knew we couldn't go all the way, but I still wanted to feel him and be loved by him regardless.

"Kist–"

"No, Raiven," he interrupted me, still facing away from me as he slowly moved my hand. I watched as his spots slowly began to fade and I knew he was exercising that control he was so good at to calm himself down. I growled behind him, his display of restraint annoying me as I sat away from him. My own body still pulsed with unresolved desire and I pouted on the bed as I stared at his back. "I... can't right now. You know I wan–"

"You always 'want to'," I whined, collapsing back onto the bed as I looked away. I felt a soft piece of cloth fall onto my skin and I looked to see that Kisten had thrown me a robe to change into. The robe had been a previous courting gift Kisten had given me, allowing him to hold me in my sleep without the Oath punishing me. I let it lie across me, refusing to touch it as I stewed in my annoyance. Kisten soon sat back on the bed, and I barely glanced to see that he had completely removed his shirt.

"We both know that my control hasn't been great lately," he countered and I looked away from him, still upset. I knew he was right: it was extremely difficult to be intimate at times, and lately it seemed more difficult for Kisten to control his animal. Even when all the attention was on me, his animal tried to push things further and I often had to be the one to stop him, lest he do what he feared the most. He sighed heavily as I remained silent, his frustration obvious in his tone as he spoke. "It's not a risk worth taking, especially when we're so close."

"Well, not all of us are experts at ignoring our desires." I snatched up my robe, walking toward the washroom and slamming the door behind me. I leaned against it, gingerly touching my still-dripping slit. I knew he was right, and I hated him for it: I hated him for being able to control his lust and just stop, while I was left frustrated and angry.

"Raiven," I heard him call my name softly through the door and I sighed, sliding down the wood to the cold floor. His voice was soft as he spoke and I closed my eyes, wishing I could just ignore him. "Please don't do this again. You know I want you more than anything. Every fiber of my being wants you."

"I know. *Apparently* that's the problem," I mumbled, drawing my knees to my chest as I traced patterns in the cold tiles.

"Raiven, you know that's not fair."

"I don't have the same control as you," I huffed, pulling my hand back to my legs as I sat on the floor. I heard as Kisten sighed on the other side and I hated the way my heart twisted with the sound. "I can't just... stop like you can."

"I know, and I'm sorry," I heard him press his hands into the door and it creaked slightly under his touch. His voice sounded full of tears as he pressed his full weight into the door, the movement pushing against me where I sat. "But... I can't risk it. It's not fair for you to keep stopping me because I can't control myself when we..."

"Stop," I growled softly at this, my anger rising again but I did my best to force it back down. We were just going to keep going in circles like we usually did, and I wasn't in the mood to argue with him. "Just, let me be, Kisten."

"Raiv–"

"Kisten," I interrupted him, opening my eyes to the empty white bathroom. "Just... leave me alone."

I heard him hesitate before he pulled himself away from the door, and the light clicked as he turned it off. I heard the bed creak as he climbed onto it and I dropped my head to my lap, doing my best to hold back my tears. This was almost worse than when we just avoided each other, and I was left pining for him from a distance. Now, here he was, directly in front of me, and I was still being told I couldn't have him.

I knew something was off with Kisten, as this lack of control was very unlike him. It had started slowly at first, with his spots appearing more often and his eyes changing almost every time we were intimate. Over the months, it had escalated to the fact we could barely kiss and touch each other before Kisten's leopard tried to take over. Kisten had explained it was probably due to the fact he had never been with anyone before, so his animal was overreacting to his constant desire for me. I knew the explanation made sense, but something still felt off with his reasoning. I didn't doubt that there was more than what Kisten was telling me, as he often seemed to hide the whole truth from me, but I had no way of finding out for sure.

I soon lost my battle with my tears and they flowed silently, pouring down my face as I dragged myself from the bathroom floor. I peeled myself out of the dress before wrapping my body in the robe as I stood in front of the mirror. My own green eyes were reflected at me, red and puffy as the tears rolled down my dark skin.

"He just wants to protect you. He's doing this because he loves you." I whispered to the reflection, trying to calm myself down and remind myself he was right. It was too dangerous to risk his animal winning the three-way battle between us, especially when it was only a matter of time before he would be released from the Oath. As much as I was annoyed about being left unsatisfied, it was better than risking the alternative and I knew that.

"So do you truly love him," I asked myself softly, raising my hand to my face and stroking my own cheek to wipe away the streaks left by my tears, "if you get mad over something like this? If this is what keeps pushing you away?"

When I finally stepped back into the bedroom, it was silent and, if not for his soft breathing, I would've sworn I was alone. I gently slipped into the bed, turning away from Kisten as I lay down next to him. I partly expected him to roll over and hold me, but it never happened. I sighed heavily, closing my eyes and focusing on my breathing as I drifted off to sleep.

4

My phone's scream woke me up, and I leaned over to stop its ceaseless noise as I groaned. I opened my eyes to a still dim room, not yet filled with the sun's morning light.

"Kisten?" I called out to him as I rubbed the sleep from my eyes, but only silence answered me as I slowly sat up. I looked over my shoulder and saw that the bed beside me was empty, my heart pounding as I noticed. I quickly grabbed my phone and double-checked the time: I hadn't overslept, so Kisten should have still been there. I wasn't much of a morning person, usually sleeping until late in the afternoon, but he had promised to wait for me so we could leave the hotel together. Because of his extra duties, we wouldn't see each other again until the wedding and I had looked forward to the small amount of extra time I could have with him. He was gone though, and a quick check on my phone revealed that no message had been left behind.

I fell back onto the bed, a pit forming in my stomach as I buried my face into the pillow, resisting the urge to scream. My last words to him were to leave me alone, and he had done as I said, not even waking me as he left. My heart felt as if it would stop altogether as I groaned, flipping onto my back as I kept the pillow on my face.

"Great, Raiven, what if he's changed his mind? You'll be lucky if he still asks tonight," I jabbed at myself, sighing heavily into the soft bedding. My phone began to scream at me again as my second alarm went off and I almost threw it into the wall, but I forced myself to rein in my anger. Instead, I clicked on the TV, wishing for anything to distract me from my own spiraling thoughts.

"The quiet beachside neighborhood got quite an alarm this morning as a lamia was spotted roaming the streets in their true form. Many residents are unused to seeing non-humans and several locals called law enforcement to–" I moaned aloud, quickly changing the channel as it showed a scene of the neighborhood. There was nothing I hated more than the news: I had already lived a lifetime of nightmares and I had no desire to listen to more.

"Only humans would be fascinated by bad news," I groaned as I flipped through more channels before finally giving up and turning off the television. Slowly, I dragged myself from the bed, walking back into the washroom.

I paused as I glanced in the mirror, seeing that the edges were still slightly foggy from where Kisten had showered before leaving. Knowing that he had taken his time only increased the pain in my chest, and I searched the glass for a message in vain. Kisten usually took the time to leave me a message on the foggy surface when he showered, as the shifter often got up before I did. The lack of smudges in the glass only made my heart drop more and I frowned as I leaned into the bathroom mirror.

"He *is* mad at me," I groaned, my anguish growing as I realized I had also messed up my braids. Using any degree of my power had the unfortunate side effect of forcing my hair to grow and, despite barely calling it up the night before, it apparently was enough to loosen my braids slightly. I lifted them as I contemplated if I could hide the growth by pulling them into another updo but it did little to lighten my sour mood.

Dragging myself away from the mirror, I showered reluctantly, my movements slow and sluggish as I forced myself to get ready for the day. I had to pick up Shannon and take her to meet the bridesmaids for a pre-wedding brunch, and then I would join them in the bridal suite to help Shannon get ready. I had no desire to go through with my obligations, wanting nothing more than to lie back down and wallow in my self-pity. A knock on the room door made me jump in the shower, and I stopped the running water, waiting to hear it again. It soon came and, wrapping the towel around myself, I stepped out into the main room.

"Occupied!" I called out, and a male voice answered me from the other side as I heard him fumble at the door.

"Delivery for you, Ma'am. I will leave it in the box next to the door. Please collect it soon." I looked at the door, confused as I heard him place the package and walk away, politely knocking on another door. My curiosity got the better of me as I opened the door, peering into the hallway before reaching in the box. The man was further down the hallway now, knocking on someone else's door as he waited patiently. The cart next to him was full of envelopes and packages: he must've delivered mail to everyone on the floor. Inside my mailbox seemed to be a candy box, and I curiously retrieved it and closed the door.

I set the gift on the bed, looking at it curiously as I sat to dry my braids. The box was plain and nondescript, although it was in the shape of a small Valentine's heart box. I picked it up again, turning it over in my hands and noticed it had a to and from section on the back. In the "from" section, in his beautiful handwriting, was Kisten's name.

Seeing this, I immediately opened the candy, my heart pounding. It was a box of raspberry white chocolates, my new favorite after Kisten had given me some as a gift. There was a small, printed card inside, which I read excitedly:

My dearest Vogel[1],

I apologize for leaving you alone this morning. One of the groomsmen was having trouble controlling his form, so Arkrian called me to help. I thought about waking you, but decided you deserved the sleep. I'm not upset about last night, so don't beat yourself up about it. All of this is temporary and we'll be together soon. I can't wait.

Your Dearest Kisten

I hugged the card and candy happily, falling backwards on the bed. I was relieved to learn that he hadn't left me on purpose: I was so worried that our argument would be the final straw and he would give up on me. My happy moment was interrupted as my phone rang and this time, I reached over to answer it eagerly.

"Hello?"

"Hey Rai," Shannon sounded giddy and I echoed her laugh, looking up at my candy. The bride-to-be sounded absolutely ecstatic and, I had to admit, her excitement was infectious. "You gonna get here soon? We can't have the bride be late to her own brunch."

"Alright, alright," I agreed, sitting up on the bed and smiling to myself in the mirror. "I just got out of the shower, so let me finish getting dressed and I'll pick you up soon."

"Sounds good. See ya soon." Shannon blew a kiss over the phone as she hung up, and I placed the phone back on the bed, moving over to my suitcase. I dug through the clothes to find my courtship gift and required piece of clothing for the day: a bright yellow halter top. I was supposed to wear it anytime Kisten had to preside over an event and I couldn't help my quiet groan. Halter tops were not my style: I wasn't truly in shape and didn't feel comfortable exposing my midsection. I had a different dress to wear to the wedding, but Kisten insisted that I wear the top to the brunch.

Sighing heavily, I reluctantly slipped on the top and finished getting dressed as I snatched my keys. I glanced around quickly to make sure I had everything, grabbing my phone and chocolates from the bed before walking out. The hallway was empty and quiet now as I walked past the many rooms, several of the mailboxes filled with letters and packages. I was surprised at first but I realized that I actually didn't know much about hotels. I had rarely stayed in one despite my long life, as it was often an easy way to be tracked by

Mater Vitae's Hunters. I shrugged as I reached the end of the hallway, double-checking my pockets one last time to make sure I had everything.

"Maybe it's common," I whispered to myself as I slowly stepped into the brightly lit garage, trying to see where I had left my car. My eyes passed over Kisten's empty spot and my mind flashed back to our intense kiss the night before. I could feel his burning touch as he ran his hands over my skin and I closed my eyes, sighing shakily. I could still see him, the brightly lit garage behind him in the windshield as he peeled his glove off with his feline teeth...

"Soon," I muttered, glancing at where the car whose alarm had gone off the night before had been parked. My eyes rested on the empty spot, and I detoured towards it, unable to help my suspicion. I readied myself to see nothing as I drew near to the space, carefully leaning to see the spot. In the pavement where the car had been were two deep marks, as if gouged out by powerful claws, causing my heart to stop in my chest. I took a step back, summoning my power as I whipped around, my glowing eyes searching for any other signs of life. The parking level remained empty and eerily quiet, something that always bothered me about modern lots. Devoid of life's noise and hassle and all about efficiency, they felt more like graveyards than a place for the living. I walked back to my car slowly, refusing to release my power until I was safely inside.

I did my best to calm myself down, taking deep breaths as I started my car up, the noise of my revving engine breaking the deafening silence. My mind raced with the possibility of a Hunter having found me, but I shook my head, realizing it was unlikely. For a Hunter to get this close without anyone knowing would be an astounding feat, as none of Mater Vitae's current Hunters were known for their subtlety. They left massive amounts of death in their wake, unafraid of the repercussions of their actions – and with good reason. Only four had ever been successfully killed, and it had taken multiple Supernaturals working together to accomplish those deaths.

"It's probably just someone having too much fun," I reasoned, reminding myself no one had still been there when we approached the car. The alarm had also stopped, meaning the car's owner had known the alarm was going off and didn't bother to come to the garage to see what might have started it. "Or it could be old, maybe no one has cared enough to tell the hotel about it."

Placing my candy in my lap, I helped myself to a chocolate as I drove to the elevator, doing my best to push aside my fear as I left the hotel. The sun rose over the ocean to my left as I drove to the beach, pulling up to the hotel where the wedding was being held. I could see Shannon scanning for me at the lobby's entrance and she eagerly waved me over as she noticed my car.

"I can smell your car a mile away," she teased, sliding into the passenger seat as I rolled my eyes. Everyone made the same joke about my car being a guzzler, always saying the smell of the gasoline was noticeable. "It's a miracle you haven't been caught yet."

"Cops have better things to do than chase down a law-abiding citizen like me," I retorted, unable to help my smile at her laughter as I pulled back on the road.

"I'm sure being in Lucius' coven and Kisten's future mate has absolutely *nothing* to do with it," the bride laughed and I laughed with her as we drove deeper into the city. It was still early enough that very few drivers were out, and we were able to reach our destination with minimal delay.

"Maybe it does," I conceded, turning off the main road as I reached the small diner Shannon had chosen for the brunch. As Shannon bounced out of the car and eagerly ran up to greet her other bridesmaids, I helped myself to another chocolate, humming with delight.

Today will be a good day. I thought to myself, stepping out of my car as Shannon waved for me to hurry. She already looked magical as the other bridesmaids fussed over her and I couldn't help my wide smile as I walked over to join them.

5

The ceremony was beautiful.

Shannon's dress was based on the 1970s style, all lace and sheer with a matching updo. She had wanted her dress to be tied to when Arkrian was born and had spared no expense in making sure the details were perfect. Brandon looked happy as he walked his daughter down the aisle, planting a kiss on her hand as he stood her in front of Kisten. Shannon's bridesmaids trailed behind her in their blue dresses and, once they all stood at the altar, they slowly turned away from us.

Arkrian came in soon after in snake form, flanked by his groomsmen in human form as his tail rattled. He tasted the air behind each of the bridesmaids, looking for which one was Shannon. Traditionally at shifter weddings, the bridesmaids would wear the same dress as the bride, so it would be up to the male to know his mate's scent and prove his loyalty to her and her alone. On this occasion though, they were wearing different dresses, per Shannon's desire to let them choose their own attire.

Arkrian shifted to human form upon confirming Shannon's scent, gently turning her around to face him. Shannon immediately covered her mouth, clearly in awe at Arkrian's suit as he beamed down at her.

She hadn't known that he would match her 70s-style dress and he stood in front of her in his soft blue suit, smiling brightly. He gently took her hands as she passed her bouquet to her maid of honor, and Kisten closed his eyes as he began speaking.

"Love is one of the greatest gifts life has to offer," despite the lack of a microphone, Kisten's voice easily carried across the room, and I could already see tears starting in the eyes of some of the guests. "Love offers hope, joy, comfort, and security, in good times and bad. Love is what spurs our personal growth and allows us to face life and all its challenges, with the unending support of the person we've chosen to commit our lives to."

"Arkrian and Shannon stand before you today, to share the love and happiness in their hearts as they take their relationship to a deeper level of commitment by making a passage into marriage," Kisten continued, closing his eyes as Arkrian lifted Shannon's hands higher, gently laying a kiss on the lace covering her fingers. "They have elected to recite their own vows, words from the heart that represent their unique journey and the commitment they're making today."

I couldn't help but smile as they said their vows, their obvious love for each other causing several guests to finally lose their battle with tears. Arkrian's father openly and loudly cried and even Brandon had a tear roll down his cheek, unable to help his emotion at his daughter's words. My gaze fell upon Kisten as I glanced around, and my heart quickened as I watched him. His eyes met mine while the couple spoke and for a moment, it felt as if I could hear his thoughts.

This will be us. His eyes seemed to make that silent promise, and my heartbeat became deafening at the thought as I struggled to hide my excitement. Despite the many weddings I had attended for both human and supernatural friends, I myself had never been married in my long life. The thought of having Kisten for the rest of his life, of sharing mine with him, made me happier than I wanted to admit. I often heard it said that every girl dreams of her wedding, and I guess that's still true even if you've lived for thousands of years.

Kisten peeled his eyes from me as they finished their vows and happily declared them mates, allowing Arkrian to pick up his new bride and yell his excitement into the darkening sky. The groomsmen and the other shapeshifters present joined him, eagerly standing from their seats as they celebrated his union. Some of the human guests joined in, and I couldn't help but giggle as Chris and Julia excitedly stood and added their own sounds in support. Brandon gave them both concerned looks as Justin shook his head, clearly just as entertained as me.

The reception took place on the beach and the tents and lighting provided made the night air feel almost magical. Many of the wedding staff had been fairies and they had put every touch of their glamor into the atmosphere. Kisten had tried to come to me as soon as he introduced the new couple, but was intercepted by Mark and Vanessa, who had just arrived after waking up for the night. The couple looked beautiful in their matching pink dresses, Mark laughing as Shannon teased him for trying to steal the spotlight.

After a while, the party started to become suffocating to me without Kisten, and I excused myself as I retreated down the sand, taking a seat next to the water. The gentle waves lapped at my bare feet and I gazed out over the water again, my thoughts from the previous day returning. I sighed deeply, holding my sister's locket as I gazed, my chest heavy with my emotions.

"Getting some fresh air?" Kisten squatted behind me, looking out at the water as he spoke.

"Hmm," I hummed softly, nodding my head to his question. I leaned back to look up at him, and he took the chance to sneak in a painful kiss.

"Just needed a moment," I smiled, leaning into him as I looked out over the dark sea. Kisten sighed happily, following my gaze. We existed in silence for a moment, the sounds of the happy reception behind us almost fading away. I closed my eyes, my smile growing larger as only the sounds of the water surrounded us.

"It was beautiful, Kisten," I finally whispered and I heard him purr behind me, pressing his face into my hair. He pressed kisses into my braids, careful this time not to mess up my style. My dress was a soft yellow and I had accented my braids with a flower pin, which Kisten lovingly fixed.

"Ours will be better," he promised, turning my face so I was looking at him. He was wearing a dark blue suit, his boutonnière a similar yellow to my dress. He had removed his shoes to match me, and I flexed my toes as I enjoyed the feel of the soft sand. He pulled me into another burning kiss and I stroked his face, pulling away once the pain became too much. His eyes were bright with his love and the soft look in his expression made my heart pound. "I promise you that."

"Who would preside over ours?" I pulled his face down into my skin as I turned away and he obliged, pressing his burning kisses into the back of my neck. I sighed happily, the pain only adding to my enjoyment of the gesture.

"Lucius, since he's the Overseer and technically the one over both of us," Kisten purred, drifting his kisses further down my exposed back. I couldn't help the shaky sigh as I started to become aroused and Kisten's actions intensified as he caught the change in my scent. His hands slid down the front of my dress, gripping my breasts tenderly through the fabric.

"Maybe we shouldn't do this in the open, Kisten," I teased, lightly pushing his hands away. He chuckled low in his throat, pressing his face into my neck again. His tongue dragged across my skin and I shuddered, almost leaning into his touch and desires.

"No one's watching," he whispered and I forced myself to stand up quickly, lest I found myself pressed into the encroaching waves. Kisten watched me as I brushed the sand from my dress, standing to join me. I wrapped my arms around his neck as he drew me toward him, laying his head back on my shoulder.

"Are you ready?" Kisten whispered and despite his words, I understood his secret question. He knew it wasn't a matter of me being ready: after all this time, he was still afraid I'd say no, that I would run from him. I lifted his head, cradling his face in my hands. He kept his arms loose around my waist and I leaned back against them, letting him fully support my weight as I stroked his cheek. I searched his eyes with mine and saw what I always found: an unbridled passion and love for me. A longing to be with me and to truly be mine.

I lifted myself closer to Kisten, pressing my lips to his. He tightened his grip on me, as if I'd flow away with the waves if he let go. I kept my kiss soft and tender and pulled away before it could deepen into something more, leaning into my Alpha.

"Let's head back," I whispered and he nodded, pressing another kiss into my hair before releasing me. He slid his hands down my arms, slowly taking both of my hands in his despite the pain it caused me. His actions still carried his fear and worry and I squeezed his hands tightly, trying to let him know that I wanted this too. "I'm ready."

This seemed to finally relax him as Kisten stepped back, keeping only one of my hands in his. My heart pounded as I considered what we were about to do and how my team would react to finding out. I could only imagine that Julia would not be surprised, as she seemed to pick up that Kisten and I were more than just friends. However, none of them knew I wasn't human, and my stomach turned as I considered Brandon's reaction.

Then, as Kisten turned to lead me up to the reception, I heard Shannon's and Vanessa's voices pierce the quiet night, their screams echoing across the dark sand.

"Arkrian!" I quickly looked around Kisten to see Arkrian catching a blur and struggling to hold something back. He was partly shifted, the bottom half of his body already sporting his snake scales and tail as he attempted to keep the thrashing creature from attacking Shannon and Vanessa. Vanessa and Mark had already placed themselves in front of Shannon, clearly ready to protect her if the creature got past Arkrian. Even Brandon and Justin had their hands on their guns, ready to react if they needed to and the wedding staff had already begun to move the guests, encouraging everyone back to the hotel.

After another moment of struggle, Arkrian finally managed to throw it back, completing his change into snake form and keeping himself between Shannon and the creature. The creature resembled a giant rat and a human, almost looking like a shifter who was trapped halfway between shifting. It lifted its giant tail in the air and hissed at the snake, who hissed in response as his rattle shook. Kisten and I immediately began to run back up the sand, fear gripping my chest as I saw the creature.

"Who–" A loud whistle interrupted me as I spoke and the rat creature slowly backed off, turning to run up the beach. I paused in my stride as I saw a figure slowly walking up the shoreline, more of the rat-like creatures surrounding him. Kisten quickly stepped in front of me, using his arm to keep me back and I could feel the anger and panic radiating off his body.

"Kisten?" I spoke his name softly, but he made no move to answer, his eyes locked on the being walking up to us. As the shapes grew closer, I covered my mouth, finally recognizing the creatures as ones I had seen before, although it had been more than a millennia since I last saw them.

The Grimm, creatures that were neither human nor animal, created by Mater Vitae for one purpose: to kill anything that moved. The same creatures that had ripped my tribesmen apart in front of me and were the ones responsible for killing my sister. The man walking with them now was the same one who had commanded them then and my body began to shake with anger and fear. I spoke through clenched teeth, the sand around me starting to shake as I summoned my power.

"*Whistleblower.*"

6

"Well, this really is my lucky day," the man spoke, his voice light and jovial as he approached us. Arkrian hissed angrily, wrapping Shannon in his coils as some of the other Supernaturals moved to protect the fleeing human guests. Kisten remained in front of me, seemingly as if he wanted to protect me from the approaching Hunter. "My first day in America, and I already find such a wonderful *geschenk*[1]."

His eyes were locked on Kisten, who hissed, and I noticed his hand had changed, his fingers becoming claws but maintaining human shape. I continued to summon my power and the sand around me shifted more, agitating the water as the ground shifted below the waves. Whistleblower's eyes drifted to me behind the Alpha, and his smile grew brighter as he recognized me.

"You're here too?" he laughed loudly, exaggerating his lean as if to see me behind Kisten. He threw his head back with mirth, finally pausing in his stride as he did so. When he looked back down to us, his smile was more sinister, and he looked ready to eat us both. "Not only can I reclaim my *sohn*[2], I can even capture Mother's favorite little pet."

"Son?" I looked up to Kisten's back, but I saw him tense at

Whistleblower's words. I looked back to the Hunter who was giving me an amused smile, his teeth showing savagely. He held his hand to his mouth, not even trying to cover his widening smile.

"Oh? I guess he doesn't tell people *that*." His eyes fell back to Kisten, who hissed again at the man claiming to be his father. The more I looked at Whistleblower, the more I could see Kisten in him. The similar jawline, their sharp eyebrows and now their shared use of German: the main difference in their appearances were their differing eye colors and skin tone. Whistleblower's pale skin and bright gray-blue eyes were just as I remembered them, and not like Kisten's tan appearance. However, I knew that Kisten, at most, was 300 years old and Whistleblower was one of Mother's first Hunters, making him older than even me. It wasn't *impossible* that he was Kisten's father, but the age difference alone gave me reason to doubt the validity of the Hunter's claim.

Whistleblower had stopped a fair distance from us, crossing his arms as he glanced up to the reception. The shapeshifters had already started helping the more vulnerable humans and fae back toward the hotel and two more animal shifters had joined Arkrian in facing the pack of Grimm, growling and pawing at the sand. Brandon and Mark were trying to move Shannon, who refused to leave Arkrian as she fought both of them to stay by her husband's side. He seemed amused by their efforts, returning his attention to us.

"Let's see what your pack can do, boy," he boasted, releasing another whistle that pierced sharply into the night. The pack of Grimm behind him lunged into action, going straight for Shannon and the reception. Screams rang out as the shapeshifters engaged them, leaving the evacuation to the other Supernaturals present as they moved to protect the bride and groom. Kisten's pack was nothing if not protective of their own, and they would fight to the death before allowing anything to happen to Arkrian or Shannon. Kisten began to run back up the beach to help protect the wedding, but as soon as he stepped away from my side, Whistleblower was in front of him. I hadn't even seen the Hunter move from his former spot, but he blocked Kisten's path, his eyes glowing in the darkness.

"Not this time, boy." His father grinned, lunging at Kisten and quickly pinning him to the ground under his feet. I moved to help him, but two of the Grimm appeared in front of me, keeping me from reaching the Alpha. I growled, lifting my hands as the sand behind me rose into the air.

"Out. Of. My. Way!" I howled, hurling the sand at the two Grimm, the wall parting around me as it lifted the creatures into the air. I twisted my body, flinging the creatures out into the open water, pushing them down into the depths. I turned back to find more Grimm in my way, and I summoned more of my power to deal with them. The entire ground heaved and the Grimm began to whine with panic as they sank into the loose ground, desperate to free themselves from my trap. I glared as they disappeared into the wet sand, their growls muffled as they choked.

"MARK!" I heard Vanessa's voice ring out, and I looked up to see one of the Grimm pinning her husband to the ground as he struggled to keep it off his sister. Shannon ran to help her brother, wielding a metal pole but was stopped by her own Grimm, the creature's jaw dripping with saliva as it lunged at her. Despite the fear visible in her body, Shannon refused to move, adjusting her grip as she swung at the creature. Arkrian quickly intercepted it, however, sinking his venomous fangs deep into its body as he tossed it away from his wife. The shifter quickly freed his brother-in-law as well, Vanessa and Mark once again attempting to remove Shannon from the fight.

I turned my gaze back to Kisten, who was still pinned underneath the Hunter's foot. Whistleblower laughed, leaning down on his knee as he looked at Kisten, who was trying desperately to throw him off. Kisten clawed uselessly at Whistleblower's clothing however, unable to make him budge. My heart pounded as the Alpha whined with pain, Whistleblower digging his boot into Kisten's stomach.

"*Erbärmlich*[3], all this time to get stronger and you're still so *weak*," he gloated, his eyes glowing brighter as he shoved Kisten into the sand more and it almost seemed as if he was trying to bury him. Kisten tried to summon his animal, but it appeared as if he couldn't, his body constantly reverting back to human. Whistleblower shook his head, making a disappointed noise. "You won't change unless I let you, *junge*[4]."

My anger rose again as I growled and I moved to help him, but the Grimm blocked my way as soon as I stepped in the Hunter's direction. The drool poured from their maws and they inched their way closer to me, as if trying to force me into the waves. I raised my hands as the sand obeyed me, but the fear crept into my heart as I worked to bury the Grimm. There were too many for us to deal with, especially with so many humans around, and Whistleblower knew it. We couldn't openly engage him and the Grimm without putting too many human lives at risk, and he was managing to keep Kisten and me out of the fight to protect the wedding altogether.

There has to be a way! I clenched my fists in annoyance, using the sand to knock one of the Grimm into the waves behind me. The creature struggled to swim before sinking into the treacherous waters and I growled as more appeared in front of me. *I can't... I won't let him win this time!*

'*Do... it...*' I heard my sister's voice softly and I knew what she meant without asking. I gripped the locket tightly as I finished dealing with the Grimm in front of me, glancing back into the dark waters. Beneath waited an ally, an ally only I could call up from its depths, but it required a power I had not used in thousands of years.

"But..."

'*Don't argue,*' I could hear the insistence in her softly fading voice. '*If... you don't... at least try, they... will die.*'

I closed my eyes, refusing to look back to the reception, where I could still hear screams and growls ringing out from the Grimm's attacks. I nodded, accepting her words and releasing my vampiric power as I turned from the creatures. The sand came crashing back down as I ran into the ocean, moving farther out into the still turbulent waves. I could hear Whistleblower laughing behind me as I ran, the sound of his voice mocking me.

"Oh, you can't run this time, pet," he taunted, but I ignored him as I shoved my hands into the waist-deep water, summoning a power I hadn't used since my sister's death. Closing my eyes, I focused on pulling the power up, dredging it from the dark depths to where it had sunk. When I reopened my eyes, I could see by my reflection that they had been swallowed by my pupils and were as black as night as I looked into the waves.

"Cursed dead of the sea," my voice bellowed as my power expanded out from me and I heard Whistleblower's laugh cease as he realized what I was doing. I did my best to ignore him as I found their presence: centuries worth of angry dead, cursing their various gods for their watery and undeserved graves. The dark tendrils danced through the sand around me, reforming their bodies as I felt their rage and I encouraged it as they started to pull themselves free. "Come. Destroy the Grimm and find your peace."

The water around me exploded as the dead pulled themselves from below the waves and countless zombies began to march up the beach. I turned around as they quickly overwhelmed the Grimm that had been chasing me, tearing the creatures to shreds with their bare hands. Despite their decaying bodies, zombies were always ridiculously strong and, thanks to already being dead, impossible to kill. They had no intelligence to speak of, driven only by the command I had given them and they continued up the beach, seeking out their target.

A new wave of screams rang out as my zombies reached the wedding, quickly engaging the horde of Grimm. The shapeshifters and fae adapted, refocusing their efforts to finish evacuating all the remaining humans as well as saving any injured members of the pack. Arkrian carefully swooped up Shannon with his powerful tail, carrying her up the beach in her torn dress.

Whistleblower had his eyes locked on me as I returned to shore, the undead still walking with me. He seemed as if he wanted to attack me and his momentary distraction finally gave Kisten the opening he needed. He pushed the man's boot off his stomach, standing quickly and moving away from his father, panting heavily as he regained his composure. Whistleblower merely seemed amused by this and teleported away again, his afterimage fading as he reappeared further down the beach. He whistled to recall his pack, the remaining members that could still move fleeing back to his side. My zombies moved to give chase but were too slow to catch the fleeing Grimm.

"Until next time, Jezebela," I glared at him as he called me by the name Mother had given me and I began to send the zombies after him, not wanting to let him escape. He had already left, however, using his teleportation to move himself and the Grimm from sight. I began to glance around desperately for him, but there was no sign of him or the creatures left on the beach and I stomped the ground with frustration.

"Raiven!" I heard as Kisten said my name, looking up to meet his worried gaze. Without the Grimm in sight, my zombies had started to wander aimlessly, looking for the target I had given them. I closed my eyes, doing my best to calm myself down as I released the zombies under my command. The bodies collapsed on the beach around us, the sand slowly sucking them back in as Kisten ran up to the hotel, eager to check on his pack. I forced myself to follow, cradling my head as I tried to ignore the headache that using my power had caused.

7

It was chaos up at the hotel; countless people flitted about as the onsite medical staff tried to tend to numerous injuries while emergency sirens approached in the distance. Kisten was lost in the sea of movement, so I instead focused on finding Shannon and Brandon, knowing that my boss would be by his daughter's side. The panic was still obvious for most of the guests present, many focused on their family and friends. Some members of the pack looked at me for help, and when I could, I stopped to give advice on how to temporarily dress some of the wounds. Being with Kisten had taught me more than I realized, and I stood from helping the onsite medical team with one of the harpies, the woman clutching her wounded daughter tightly in her feathers.

"Focus on children first," I instructed, glancing away as I continued looking for Shannon or Kisten. The nurse seemed ready to argue with me but I gave her a stern look that made her pause. It had become apparent that the Grimm had a silver coating on their claws and many of the wounded shapeshifters were suffering from silver poisoning. There was no way that a hotel in Ocean City would be prepared with enough of the antidote on hand and I looked at her confidently, despite my worry. "My mate is the Alpha, and I know he has some on hand and can easily request more from Decver. The adults can last longer than the children, so focus your limited supply on any of them that were injured."

"Yes... Ma'am," the nurse consented, and I quickly turned, not wanting her to see the worry in my eyes. I heard the harpy soothing her child against the pain, and my heart clenched in my chest more. It was likely that we would lose more of the pack to silver poisoning, but I knew Kisten would have insisted on the same thing. There was no way we could get enough antidote in time to save everyone, so we had to focus on saving those we could.

Turning my attention back to my search, I finally caught sight of the bride, Arkrian lying in snake form across her lap. Huge gashes dripped blood onto the remains of her dress and he seemed to be in great pain, but he kept his tail wrapped around Shannon, determined to keep her safe.

"Raiven!" Shannon called out as soon as she noticed me and she held Arkrian tighter, clearly worried as I approached. "Kisten went to his car to get more of the antidote. Arkrian-"

"It'll be okay," I assured her, gripping her hand tightly as I knelt next to Arkrian. He hissed, clearly in pain from the poison, but he tightened his coils around Shannon as he opened his eyes to me. I nodded, and he relaxed, closing his eyes once more as he tried to rest. A loud cry made me look up and I saw Brandon nearby, holding a wailing Vanessa. I was surprised to see the two so close, and I began to look around for Mark.

"He's..." Shannon's voice made me look back to her and I knew from her expression that Mark would not be here. Tears were welling in her eyes as Vanessa's cries grew louder and the vampire fought weakly against Brandon, who was doing his best to comfort her and keep her from running away. My boss' face was also wet with tears, and my heart constricted in my chest.

"NO! We... I can't leave him down there... he's my love! He's..." she wailed, my heart breaking as Shannon pressed her face into Arkrian's scales, gripping him more tightly. As Kisten arrived back with more of the antidote and local medical crews finally arrived, I forced myself away and walked back down to the beach. Despite all the blood on the sand, it seemed that most of the wedding guests had escaped with their lives. I could see body parts sticking through the ground and realized that I had unwittingly allowed it to claim the newly dead as well. I gently summoned my vampiric power, the sands shifting around me.

"Release the freshly killed," I commanded and bodies slowly began to rise to the surface as the sand shifted to push them back up. I saw members of Kisten's pack as well as some of the hotel staff's fae, all who had perished attempting to protect the humans. They had succeeded, as not a single human body was to be found among the dead. As I walked through the sands, searching for Mark, my thoughts turned back to the zombies I had raised.

"Sis."

'...*What?*' Her voice sounded stronger somehow, and I gripped the locket tightly as I began moving the bodies. Ocean City wasn't used to shapeshifters and I doubted they had the personnel to deal with all the injured that were coming their way, much less all the dead. It would fall to Kisten to take care of the bodies and return them to their families, and my heart constricted as I considered my partner's duty.

"We both know something was wrong with that," I stated plainly, lifting a table as I spotted a harpy crushed by the object. Closing my eyes, I gently moved his body from underneath, setting the table back down. "Raising that many zombies at once shouldn't have been possible."

'...*I know.*' She sounded deep in thought as she answered, and I waited for her answer as I continued moving across the sand, retrieving as many bodies as I could. Every body I touched filled me with both extreme sadness and a strange feeling of peace as I gathered them, making it easier for the medical crew once they finished on the patio. All of the newly dead should never have died; there was no reason for Whistleblower to attack the wedding, especially before he knew that either Kisten or I were even there. However, as I finally spotted Mark's arm underneath one of the collapsed tents, it felt as if all of them were at peace with their deaths, accepting that their sacrifice had allowed more to live.

Mark almost looked as if he was merely asleep on his stomach and, steeling myself, I reached down to flip him over. One of the Grimm had completely ripped open his chest and taken most of his heart, leaving a large, bleeding cavity behind. Such an injury was dangerous to a vampire of any age, but considering Mark was turned only a few years ago, he was especially susceptible to such damage. I touched his shoulder lightly, cursing Whistleblower under my breath even as I noticed the smile on Mark's face. He must have died protecting either his sister or wife, smiling to try and give them peace about his death. I summoned my power as I gently lifted his body out of the sand, spooning him in my touch.

As soon as I touched Mark's body, an overwhelming feeling of sadness gripped me and I gently fell to my knees, unable to stop the tears as they poured down my face. Mark, just like his sister, had been an exciting and supportive presence from the moment I had met him; while he lacked Shannon's fire, he made up for it with never-ending kindness and patience. Even when his father basically disowned him for marrying Vanessa, Mark remained optimistic, certain his father would eventually come around. That Brandon was at the wedding, that his father had walked his sister down the aisle was proof of Mark's gentle support and all of that had been taken away because one Hunter decided he wanted to destroy the wedding, for no other reason than that it was there.

"You... you didn't deserve this," I whispered quietly, forcing myself to stand back up as I adjusted his body in my arms. I glanced up to the patio as I heard more sirens approach and I took a deep breath as I prepared to ascend back to his waiting wife. "You deserved to live."

His black blood seeped into my dress as I slowly walked past the other medical personnel, the nurses and staff ignoring me as they moved to inspect the bodies I had recovered. I carried Mark's body back up to the hotel's patio, where Arkrian had finally managed to shift back to being human and was being loaded onto a gurney.

Kisten turned to see me first and his eyes lit up with surprise, quickly replaced with sadness as he saw the body I carried. Shannon and Vanessa were clinging to each other, and Kisten gently motioned for Vanessa to look in my direction.

"Mark!" She quickly released her sister-in-law and flew towards me, her feet not touching the ground as she collapsed where I had stopped. I gently handed Mark's body to her and she clung to him, releasing another wail into the night air. The air grew silent as everyone stopped, watching the vampire clutch her love as she cried. Vanessa was close in age to Arkrian and felt that she had lived as long as she had just so she could find and love Mark, with her marriage to him finally giving her century of life meaning.

Vanessa cried with heavy sobs as she rocked her husband's body, not even noticing as Brandon and Kisten came up behind her. The dark blood stained both of their dresses as she cried and I ran my hand over the stain it had left on mine. I held back my own tears at her display, closing my eyes to keep them from spilling out. Anger started to make my body shake, and I curled my hands into fists as I fought to keep from summoning my power.

"Save him. Raiven, please," I opened my eyes to her plea, and saw Vanessa hold his body out towards me, desperation in her eyes. I had to close mine again, not able to meet her gaze as I shook my head.

"I'm sorry, Ness. I can't bring back vampires, not even as zombies," I heard no response and opened my eyes, afraid to see her expression. Vanessa seemed to be accepting my words and was hugging Mark's body closely again, fresh tears pouring down her face. Brandon gingerly touched her shoulder and she slowly released his body, gently laying him on the concrete. She leaned over his body, giving her lover one last kiss before carefully removing his wedding ring and allowing Brandon to lead her away to rejoin Shannon.

Kisten finally stepped over to me and reached to hug me but he paused, withdrawing his arms. I threw myself into him, hugging him tightly as I heard the medical crews lugging the bodies back up the beach. I pressed my face into him, finally allowing myself to cry again as he held me tightly. I felt my sister's presence, but she quickly pulled away again, not wanting to interrupt us. I felt Kisten's hands grip me tighter as all the bodies were walked by us, and I buried my face into him more.

"I'm sorry," I whispered, not trying to hide the anger in my voice. I wasn't even a part of the pack yet, but every death already felt personal. Kisten also shook with anger and distress, but his voice held no sound of it as he finally spoke.

"Let's go, Raiven." He gently pulled away from me and I followed as we slowly made our way through the dissolving chaos, my heart heavy and aching with the aftermath.

8

The hospital lobby was busy and as chaotic as the hotel had been when Kisten and I finally arrived. It was apparent that they weren't used to having so many supernatural patients and they were trying their best to make room for all the incoming injured. Kisten led me through the chaos, expertly weaving through the bodies. He finally stopped and I looked around him to see Shannon, Vanessa, and Brandon. The rest of my team was in the room as well, all of us still in wedding attire.

Shannon and Vanessa were clinging to each other where they sat, still clearly trying to comfort each other. Brandon stood awkwardly off to the side: it was obvious he wanted to help but wasn't sure how. Julia, Chris, and Justin were spread out across the rest of the room, trying to maintain their space from Brandon's family.

"Kisten, Raiven..." Shannon's voice was soft as she looked up at us, her eyes still red from tears. Vanessa kept her head down, holding Mark's ring tightly in her hand as she pressed it into her chest. Brandon looked our way as well, but he quickly turned away again, uncertainty in his eyes. Shannon was the only one who would look at us. "What... happened?"

"Whistleblower..." Kisten started, but then his voice faded, and he looked away, releasing my hand. Shannon then turned her face to me, and I took a deep breath as I prepared to speak.

"Whistleblower is a Hunter," I confessed, meeting her gaze evenly. She squeezed Vanessa's hand tighter as I continued, worry in her eyes. "He answers only to Mater Vitae and has been given the task of finding and killing any of the First who still live. I'm not sure who his target is, but he must have come to America to find them."

"But why attack us? Mark and Vanessa were the only vampires there, and neither are First," Shannon begged and I opened my mouth to speak when I was interrupted.

"Because he could," Kisten growled, his anger coming through clear in his voice this time. I turned to look at him, but he was keeping his gaze to the floor as he avoided looking at any of us. "That man doesn't care. He attacked the wedding because it was there. Finding me and Raiven was just the icing on his cake."

"So, even if you two hadn't been there..." Brandon sighed, running his hand through his hair as Vanessa clutched Mark's ring tighter.

"He would've slaughtered everyone." Shannon finished, sighing deeply and closing her eyes. Everyone remained quiet at this, no one really knowing what to say. A doctor finally came into the room and he seemed concerned by the atmosphere.

"Um, Arkrian..." he started, and all of us turned to him, eager to hear the news. He seemed to shrink under the attention but forced himself to stammer on. "He'll be fine... the silver in his system had been neutralized by the time he arrived and his wounds are not too deep, despite appearances. We'll release him shortly, as soon as the paperwork is all done, to finish healing at home."

"And the others?" Kisten inquired, and the doctor quickly turned to him, a sour expression on his face.

"Most should be fine, but a few are critical. We're doing what we can."

"Thank you," Kisten nodded and the doctor left quickly, obviously wanting to escape the somber tone in the room. As the doctor left to check other patients, the door behind Kisten and me opened, and we turned to see Lucius and the Director walk into the room. Flanking Lucius was Kisca, her bright pink eyes glowing as the air around Lucius shimmered and I knew she had been using her glamor to conceal his appearance. Brandon turned quickly at the sight of the Director, but he stopped when the Director raised his hand, motioning him back.

"Lucius and I have already been briefed on what happened," he turned to Kisten and me, and Kisten walked further away as we stepped aside to let them into the room. The Director sighed deeply, shaking his red hair as he adjusted his glasses. "Another Hunter has finally come over after so long."

"Yes," I breathed, refusing to meet my team's gaze. None of them had been around for the last time we had to deal with a Hunter so, besides their taste tonight, they had no idea how bad this could get. How many people he could kill in a short amount of time. "This time it's Whistleblower."

"Whistleblower?" Lucius repeated, turning to look at Kisten as the Alpha growled again. He refused to meet his Overseer's gaze, keeping his eyes to the floor as he held himself. Lucius sighed, shaking his head with disbelief. "Then he's here for LeAlexende. But he—"

"Wait, Alex?" I gasped, remembering the night before the Overseer had left. LeAlexende had visited us during the witch fiasco and the Overseer had supervised both Justina and my visits in the hospital. Somehow, I had been able to spy on him and Lucius in my sleep and, besides the Overseer, I was the only other person in the Coven who knew the real reason he had visited us. "But Alex was here almost a year ago, why would Whistleblower come to The Capital instead of going further south?"

"Someone must've known," Kisten hissed and Lucius' eyes flashed with anger before calming again.

"It's possible he knew The Capital as LeAlexende's last location," Lucius conceded, covering up his anger better than his Alpha for once. Kisca looked at him with concern but said nothing as the Overseer met my gaze evenly. The pixie wasn't known for speaking much, but her glamor was unparalleled, earning her my former spot as Fifth in the Coven. "However, he would've found a new goal in you and Kisten, one that will distract him from his Hunt."

"Both of us?" I questioned and the Overseer nodded, turning his gaze to Vanessa, who was still leaning into Shannon. He approached her slowly, and Shannon lifted her sister-in-law to see him. Vanessa slowly turned to him, her eyes still red and puffy from all her crying and her lips twitched at seeing Lucius. She was beginning to look blood-deprived due to all her tears, and Lucius knelt in front of her, hugging the vampire tightly before speaking again.

"Kisten... is his son," Lucius whispered and I felt the air change as Kisten's anger grew. We all turned to the Alpha, but he refused to look at anyone, retreating to a corner, as far away as he could get. Lucius didn't react, gently stroking Vanessa's arm as he continued. "Long ago, Kisten defied him, saving me and LeAlexende from what would've been our deaths. That's why I brought him to America with me, to repay the debt that was my life and to protect him from his father."

"Kisten," I looked at my love, who pounded his fist into the wall, leaving a crack in the material. I slowly walked toward him, touching his back gently. He tensed under my touch and I pulled him into a hug, pressing my face into his shirt. He finally relaxed, but still refused to turn around.

"Whistleblower will do whatever it takes to get Kisten back. He wants his successor, and no one else will do for him," Lucius stated, holding his hand out for Mark's ring as I turned back to look at him. Vanessa handed it over, and the Overseer produced a small golden chain from his pocket. He slid the ring on it before draping the chain around Vanessa's neck, formally passing on Mark's memory to her. My eyes welled with tears again as Vanessa nodded, gripping the ring tightly.

"Then..." I heard Julia's voice croak behind me as she spoke, and I released Kisten to turn to face her, my hand still on his back. "What does Raiven have to do with this?"

It was my turn to stiffen and the air grew deadly silent again.

Brandon turned to look at me and the rest of my team shifted their eyes to where I stood. I opened my mouth to speak, but the words wouldn't come, and instead I turned away from their stares. The Director smiled, however, crossing his arms as he adjusted his stance.

"I can answer that. She's not as human as you've been led to believe," he began and they all looked toward him instead. "She's been around for a long time, even though I don't know for certain how old she is. I can tell you she's been in Division 11 since its inception."

"But that was over 140 years ago!" Chris exclaimed, looking at me incredulously. I shrugged as he stared, still unsure of what to say. The Director chuckled at his reaction, turning to Brandon who watched me with disbelief. My boss' expression darkened as he looked at me and I flinched under his gaze as Chris continued: "Just... how old are you?"

"It explains all her knowledge," Justin sighed, crossing his arms as he chimed in. He seemed the least surprised of the group, merely putting the pieces together in his mind. "I mean, her knowledge of their history was always surprising and she always seemed to know things that would be considered Supe secrets."

"*You—*"

"Don't blame her: part of her agreement is to keep it a secret from the human teams. Helps keep other Supernaturals from thinking she's more than human and I always have a trump card to ensure a team's safety, which I would say worked, considering tonight's events." The Director smiled and Brandon looked at him as he was interrupted. My boss conceded as he sighed again, looking at me with less malice. I sheepishly met his gaze and Brandon seemed unsure of what to think of me. When he finally spoke, I flinched at his words.

"What are you then?" His voice was hollow as he spoke, but I could tell that he was still upset. I looked at my free hand as I lifted it and with my eyes glowing, the whole building shook slightly, scaring everyone in the room from the tremor.

"An undead necromancer, or simply an Immortal, I suppose," I spoke softly, turning to face the rest of my team where they stood. Chris looked on with excitement, clearly intrigued while Julia and Justin still seemed to be in disbelief. "Mater Vitae tried to turn me into a vampire, but my necromancy rejected the taint. I am mostly human with some vampire abilities, including their immortality. As far as I know, I'm the only one to exist."

"Dad, let her be," Shannon finally spoke and I looked at her as I released my power, lest I disrupt the medical team trying to save the injured. He glanced down at her and his expression softened for a moment as she continued. "I've known about Raiven for a while now and, if not for her, none of us would've escaped tonight. It's not like she wanted to keep it a secret."

"That's... true," he conceded, finally looking at the Director again. "So what now?"

"Well, all things considered, Raiven was going to have to be taken off your team anyway," he admitted, turning to me and Kisten. Kisten turned around, meeting the Director's gaze as Lucius also stood, finally releasing Vanessa. He had been whispering something to her, and it seemed that whatever he had said stuck, as she seemed a little better. "But losing her as an agent isn't really an option, either."

"We've reached an alternative decision," Lucius announced, and we all turned our attention to him, waiting to see what he would say. "Considering all the deaths tonight were of our people and no humans died, this really isn't a case for Division 11 or the Governor to handle. It's ours and I intend to see it through."

"But we won't allow you guys to deal with this problem on your own, considering the threat Hunters pose in general and especially this Whistleblower," the Director continued, his smile growing wider as he stared at me. "Therefore, Raiven, I hereby relieve you of your position as an agent of the Central team of Division 11, and I promote you to the S-Men."

"The S-Men!" I heard Chris squeak with more excitement, and even Brandon and Justin gasped loudly. I looked at the Director in disbelief, but he maintained his bright smile as he looked at me. I shifted my eyes to Lucius, who watched me with a calm expression.

The S-Men were a team of Supernaturals belonging to Division 11: after dealing with the first Hunter to come to the Americas, the Director at the time saw it fit to recruit Supernaturals to work for us. They dealt with threats that were too dangerous for the human teams, and often worked alone, although I knew they could be put into teams if the target was extremely dangerous.

"As your first assignment," The Director continued, forcing me to look at him again. "You are to work with Lucius to find and eliminate the Hunter Whistleblower."

"Kisten," Lucius spoke, his blue eyes swirling with power. "You will assist Raiven and me on this task. Another will also be joining us, but considering it was your pack he attacked, you have every right to join as well."

"Damn right I do," Kisten growled, his fingers curling into fists as he spoke. I turned to look up at him and his eyes were swirling as he accepted Lucius' command. "This is my fault, and it's high time I fixed it."

I looked back at the members of my old team, trying to judge their reaction to this news. Julia and Justin still looked starstruck, as if they couldn't process what was happening and Chris looked at me hungrily, clearly wanting to ask me a million different questions. Brandon looked at me with a sad look and he finally pushed himself off the wall, walking toward me slowly. Shannon and Vanessa watched him as he brushed past the Director and Lucius, stopping right in front of me. I wasn't sure what to expect so I braced myself, expecting harsh words.

Instead, I felt his arms wrap around me and I was surprised to find my former boss hugging me tightly, pressing my head into him. I gently returned the gesture and I heard Shannon sigh with relief behind him. After a moment, he pulled back, standing a businesslike distance from me.

"I don't like that this was kept from me, but I'm not sure I could've handled knowing either," he admitted, meeting my gaze evenly. I saw a mix of emotions in his eyes, but I saw determination the most. "You saved most of my family tonight, and I am beyond grateful for that. If you want to make up the rest, kill the bastard who took my son from me."

"I will," I promised, my eyes swirling with power again and Brandon nodded, glancing back to Vanessa. She was finally sitting up, her eyes burning as she nodded her head at me as well. I returned her gesture, accepting her silent plea. "For you and Vanessa, I will make sure he pays in full for Mark's death."

Brandon seemed satisfied with my response and walked back to his daughters just as Arkrian stepped into the room. He had a slight limp as he walked and Shannon immediately stood, throwing herself into his arms. The gesture seemed to cause the shifter some pain, but he returned her embrace, clearly happy to see her. His blue wedding suit was just as shredded and bloody as her dress, but they still managed to look magical standing next to one another. He lifted his head to Kisten, and he looked at his Alpha with a sad expression.

"I'm sorry, Kisten. I failed to protect the pack and my own family–" Arkrian was interrupted as Kisten walked over to him and Shannon, embracing them both. He hugged them tightly before stepping back, his hands on each of their shoulders.

"You did everything you could, Arkrian. I nor anyone else blame you." Kisten assured him as Shannon nodded, burying her head into her husband's chest. Arkrian chanced a glance at Brandon and Vanessa and the vampire stood, slowly walking to him with her father-in-law following. Kisten stepped back as they embraced him, the whole family hugging one another. Arkrian seemed ready to cry with his relief and the Director cleared his throat, catching everyone's attention.

"Well, orders have been given, the groom is safe, but I think we're still missing something. Something that still should happen," he smiled, looking at Kisten. Kisten returned his gaze with confusion and then comprehension as he returned to me. I turned to look at the Director, who merely kept smiling as he motioned to Kisten. I turned back to find the Alpha kneeling in front of me and I began to stammer in disbelief.

"What? No. I mean, this is hardly–" I started but Lucius stopped me, a smile starting on his face as well. Kisten slowly took my left hand and slid a small ring on my finger. I looked down at Kisten and his eyes were glistening with tears as he gripped my hand tightly. The ring was simple, a green and black titanium band that slid on my finger perfectly. I looked up to Arkrian and Shannon and they were smiling at us, with even Vanessa managing to look slightly happy. Brandon shared a confused look with the rest of my team, all of them staring at the Alpha.

"Raiven," Kisten began and I returned my gaze to him as he spoke. "This isn't how I wanted to ask, or how I imagined it. I know it's not the best circumstances either but... but with these witnesses present, will..."

The words seemed to get caught in his throat and he looked away from me, gripping my hand tighter. I took my free hand to touch his face, ignoring the burning pain that came with the gesture. He turned back to me, tears now flowing freely down his face. I wasn't sure why he was crying, but I gently wiped them away, smiling down at him softly. He took a deep breath as he tried again.

"With these witnesses present, Raiven, will you be my mate, the Beta to my Alpha? Will you stand by my side and be eternally mine?"

I said the only thing I could and stood my love up to his feet as I spoke, leaning up to kiss him.

"*Yes.*"

9

I shifted uncomfortably on my seat as the train bounced again, groaning softly as I watched the trees fly by the window. Electric trains didn't have the same bumps as traditional trains but bumped and jostled all the same. Lucius had managed to get us all our own cabins, but even with the more comfortable seats, I still couldn't enjoy the ride.

After leaving the hospital, we all agreed that we couldn't stay in Ocean City or Decver: we would just put more people at risk and I didn't want to imagine the carnage of a full-out battle with Whistleblower in a city. Therefore, Lucius suggested we go to the mountains, into what remained of the Appalachians. It was remote enough that any battle would have limited casualties and we would still have the advantage. He also insisted on leaving Eve behind with Crispin to protect Decver, instead choosing Aurel and Kisca to accompany him.

The door to the cabin slid open as Kisten returned, quietly closing the door behind him. He smiled at me wryly as he sat on the bed, sighing heavily.

"It's hard to find Lucius under all that glamor and Aurel is just being..." His voice trailed off and I finished the thought for him.

"Aurel." I rolled my eyes, groaning as Kisten echoed my sound.

Aurel was doing his best to try and stir an issue, despite Lucius' warning about us behaving. While Kisten and I didn't want to play nice with the lich, at least we weren't the one purposefully *trying* to start issues. Ever since we returned to Decver, he had been doing his best to try to get Kisten to remain behind, finally giving up when Lucius pointed out that most of the deaths had been shapeshifters. Even now that we were on the train, it felt as if he had spent most of the past few hours trying to get Kisten to cause a scene.

I suddenly felt my locket grow warm under my shirt and even with her lack of words, I knew what my sister wanted me to do. Despite feeling stronger at the wedding, it seemed she had faded back to being barely able to stay awake, and it denied us the chance to talk about my necromancy. I sighed, plucking at my tights as I drew my legs into the seat, frowning as I stared at the floor.

"Kisten," I spoke his name softly, not sure how to word the question my sister was pushing me to ask. The Alpha looked up to me, his expression quizzical.

"Yes, Rai?"

"Whistleblower," I watched Kisten tense up at me saying his father's name and I hurried to my next sentence. "Can you... tell me more about him? I don't really know much..."

Kisten said nothing at first, lying back on the bed to stare at the ceiling. I fidgeted in my seat, groaning slightly as the train bounced again. I played with the ring on my finger, the band bringing a slight smile to my face. I had taken off the necklace now that I had the ring, and I wore it now as a bracelet around my left wrist. Kisten told me I didn't have to wear it anymore but after wearing it for so long, I wanted to keep it with me.

"He's..." Kisten's voice jolted me from my thoughts and I turned to look at him as he spoke. He had his arm draped across his face and I could tell from his tone this was not something he wanted to talk about. "He's everything I try so hard not to be."

"Impulsive? Out of control?" I offered and Kisten nodded, not moving his arm.

"To control the Grimm, you have to let them into your mind.

They can overwhelm you if you let them, so my father's method of maintaining control is just going along with their desires," Kisten mumbled and I had to lean in to hear him speak. "He lets them attack wildly and freely, as long as it doesn't go against Mater Vitae directly."

"How loyal is he?" I pushed, and Kisten scoffed, still keeping his arm on his face. I could feel his anger and annoyance growing as he continued speaking about his father.

"Loyal? That man is beyond loyal, he is obsessed," he spat, finally removing his arm as he looked up at the ceiling again. "He worships the ground she walks upon and considers her the only person worth his devotion."

"So... your mother—"

"I don't want to talk about this, Raiven." Kisten interrupted me, finally sitting up. He was gripping the sheets tightly and still refusing to look at me. I frowned, looking back at the ring on my finger as I twisted it more. We sat in the awkward silence for a while, the only sound between us being the occasional bumps of the train. After a moment, I saw Kisten's hand appear over mine and I looked up as he gently took it in his. He was looking at the ring with a pained expression and his voice was strained as he continued.

"He killed my mother once he had no more use for her," his whole body shook as he spoke and despite the pain from him already holding my hand, I gripped his hand with both of mine. A sad smile flashed on his face and he looked up to me, tears in his eyes. "I can't lose you too, Raiven."

"Well, he won't kill either of us, so that's a plus," I whispered hopefully, squeezing his hand tighter despite the pain. He laughed slightly, his tears finally flowing as he closed his eyes. I released his hand, reaching to wipe away his tears. "I won't let him separate us, Kisten."

"He's powerful, Raiven," Kisten lamented, almost as if he didn't even hear my words. He leaned into my hand, his tears still flowing freely as my arm began to ache from the pain. "My father is human, but he drinks Mater Vitae's blood directly. That blood also gives him power you can't even imagine."

I didn't answer him, merely climbing into his lap as I released his hands. I must've surprised him, as Kisten looked at me with shock as I slanted my lips painfully across his. He tasted salty from the tears and I smiled as I pulled back, his eyes meeting mine.

"I *won't* let him separate us, Kisten." I repeated my vow, leaning down to kiss him again. This time he met me, wrapping his arms around me as we kissed. He gripped me tightly as I opened my mouth to let him in and I moaned with the familiar pain. His despair began to turn to arousal as I felt him harden and I slid further up in his lap. He slid his hand along my tights, slipping under my shirt to stroke my back.

When Kisten pulled back to look at me, I was slightly taken aback by his eyes. They were no longer their usual chartreuse, but a bright green, with no hints of the usual brown to accompany it. I reached to touch his face, but Kisten caught my hand, turning away from me sharply. I leaned in to kiss his neck instead, and he shuddered as I assaulted his skin there and his fingers dug into my waist. I adjusted the hand he held so our fingers laced together and I squeezed him as I bit him gently, loving his taste.

Kisten's soft moans and breaths excited me more as I unbuttoned the top of his shirt, working my way to his collarbone with my tongue and teeth. The Alpha was helpless underneath me, and when I pushed against him, he let me, falling back onto the bed. I freed my hand from his and slid it to his bulging member, stroking him through the fabric that separated us.

"*Vogel*[1]..." Kisten moaned, his hands gripping my posterior tightly as I freed him from his pants, and I released a shaky sigh as I sat on his member, the tights doing little to protect me from the pain and pleasure of feeling him press against my opening. I slid myself over him, releasing a small moan as I felt him throb against me. Kisten gasped as I did this and he quickly sat up, pushing me off him and holding me at arm's length. I wasn't completely surprised by his actions, but I couldn't help my disappointment as he loosened his grip. His strange green eyes met mine and his voice was hoarse when he spoke, full of different emotions.

"I can't Raiven, I'm... not... I can't..." His words caught in his throat and I sighed, pulling myself out of his lap. He didn't try to stop me, letting my hand slip slowly from his as he dropped his gaze. I could see the restraint in his posture, how much he was fighting himself and his own desire.

"I know, Kisten. It's... okay," I tried to smile, adjusting my tights and shirt as I turned to the door of our cabin to hide my face. I leaned over to pick up my holster, adjusting the bands across my chest as I stepped into my boots. "I'm going to go look for Lucius. I need answers, but... I don't want to keep bringing up painful memories for you."

"*Vogel*... wait..." I heard him whisper, but I stepped outside the cabin, leaning against the door once I had closed it. It took all that I had not to immediately reopen the door and fling myself into Kisten's arms, but I knew I would not be able to show the same restraint he could. He was doing the best he could to control himself, and I needed to respect that decision, as much as I didn't want to.

I walked away from my room, heading through the cars to find Lucius' cabin. I wasn't sure if he would be there or not, but it seemed a good place to start. Lucius wasn't really one to roam, and he was likely to be somewhere he could stay without being bothered. The train didn't have too many options for quiet sitting, but I decided to start with the closest. I sighed heavily as I stepped into the next car and immediately ducked into a side hallway.

Aurel was walking my way, clearly upset over something as he muttered to himself in his native language. I was willing to bet that his earlier interaction with Kisten was not just Kisten asking where Lucius was, the anger obvious in his body as he stomped down the hall. The two had a habit of getting into a fight whenever they were forced to interact and Aurel was always the loser. At the end of the day, Kisten was higher ranked and more powerful and it was the lich who would be in trouble if he seriously hurt Kisten, especially given their history.

I started to think the spellcaster hadn't seen me as he continued stomping through the car but that hope was shattered as he stopped in front of the hallway I stood in. He barely turned to look at me, not trying to mask his anger as he usually did.

"I know you're there, Raiven."

"And you can keep moving right along," I shot back, not moving from the space as he blocked me in. There was only enough room for one person, and while Aurel could try to trap me, I didn't think he would. I had always been higher ranked than him, but it was more dangerous for him to mess with me now that I was Second, and equal in rank to Kisten and Evalyn. "I'm looking for Lucius, not you."

"You're never looking for me anymore," the lich growled and I echoed the noise, not trying to hide my annoyance. "He really has you tricked."

"The only trick going on is you tricking yourself," I jeered, watching as his orange curls expanded in his anger. Aurel's magic was all body-based, and he was capable of shifting any part of himself that he wanted, although his favorite was to shift his fingers into razor-sharp claws. I watched his fingers twitch in his growing annoyance, and I placed my hand on my gun. "Try me, Aurel, and see what happens."

"You wouldn't," he scoffed, and I growled as his hair continued to move, weaving in the air to form a barrier to trap me. I felt my necromancy starting to bubble up in my anger, but I swallowed it back down best I could, glaring at the lich. "Lucius—"

"At this point, fuck what Lucius says," I growled, tightening my grip on the weapon. "You forget, I'm not here as a member of the Coven, but as a member of the S-Men. All I have to do is say you interfered with my mission and Lucius has to accept it."

The lich seemed to be considering my threat seriously, withdrawing his hair as I relaxed my hold. He stomped off into the car I had come from and I knew he was going to take his anger out on

Kisten. I sighed heavily as I stepped out into the main hall again, debating if I wanted to go help the shifter.

"Kisten can handle himself." I decided, continuing farther up the train as I focused on trying to find the Overseer.

10

I was starting to feel Kisten's frustration as I left the dining car, having failed to find Lucius in his room. I knew if he was outside his room, Kisca was probably by his side, and I decided to focus on finding the pixie, since at least I knew what she looked like. I made my way through the quiet car and, not finding Kisca, continued to the lounge car. Finally, in one of the many reading booths, I caught sight of her short blond bob, swaying slightly as she rocked in the seat. A dark-haired woman sat next to her and I was wary as I approached them.

"Kisca?" I spoke softly, doing my best to avoid bringing attention to the pair. Kisca smiled as she looked up at me and her pink eyes glowed for a moment. The woman melted away before my eyes, revealing Lucius, who was smiling at me brightly.

"Hello, Raiven," his voice still sounded feminine and I knew Kisca had lifted the visual glamor only for me. To anyone walking by, Lucius still appeared to be a woman and I sat down across from them, doing my best to seem undisturbed. "What do you need?"

"I... wanted to ask about Whistleblower," Lucius' expression shifted to a somber one and I started to regret coming to him as well. It seemed to be a topic neither Lucius nor Kisten wanted to address, but I knew I had to get answers out of one of them. Despite knowing he had been the one who killed my sister, I had no idea how he fought or how well he controlled the pack.

'That's because you ran away...' my sister berated, rising only to speak her mind before fading away almost immediately. I wanted to argue, but knew it was pointless and sighed heavily. It was something she would never forgive me for and, despite my excuses, I knew I had no solid defense for my actions. If I had stood by her when she tried to fight him, if I had been willing to stay by her side, then both of us might still be alive.

"He... is the Hunter who was tasked with killing LeAlexende," Lucius started, leaning back from the table as his voice pulled me from my own thoughts. Kisca's eyes flashed again, and his voice was back to normal as he continued. "I first met Whistleblower when he attacked me and Alex in Belgium. I suppose it was his first time taking Kisten on a Hunt and we were lucky he chose to save us instead. But Whistleblower's control over the Grimm is... complete. The pack is his true source of power."

"I know Alex is a First, but what rank was he?" I ventured, keeping my voice low. A sad smile crossed my Overseer's face and he looked down at his book on the table. He lifted a page gingerly, letting it gently fall back down as he released it. For a moment, I wasn't sure that Lucius was going to answer me as he gazed out the window, watching the scenery as it flew past.

"Third," he breathed and I looked at him with surprise, my sister's surprise joining mine. LeAlexende was... he couldn't be.

"I thought... wasn't Third a woman?"

"It was." Lucius smiled, looking up to meet my gaze and I hummed as I understood what he was implying. It was no wonder I couldn't recognize LeAlexende as one of the First, because I remembered him as someone else. My heart swelled as I remembered what he had done for me, and my determination grew as I looked back toward my Overseer.

"Then Alex was—"

"Don't say it," Lucius stopped me, looking at me sharply as I swallowed the name. LeAlexende had made it clear that his previous name was a shackle he no longer wanted, and it was wrong of me to refer to him using it. Lucius dropped his eyes, tracing characters into the table as he sighed again. From the movement of his hand, I recognized the characters as cuneiform and I knew he was writing out his thoughts.

With his paler appearance, it was easy for those who didn't realize his age to think he was simply Greek or Roman. But Lucius was from a far older race, a living relic of a people long gone; he was Sumerian, just as many of the First had been. Thousands of years out of the sun had bleached his skin to appear lighter, but the shape of his face and his angled eyes told of a history long lost to the sands of time.

"He is the last of the Siblings, the first three vampires to exist," Lucius continued, finally meeting my gaze. "That night was to be our last visit before I crossed the sea. At the time, Alex wasn't sure if he wanted to come to America."

"And Whistleblower found you?" I asked and the vampire nodded, finally leaning back in his chair.

"He ambushed us, yes. I had given up my place as Overseer in order to come here and take over for a friend, and so there were many who knew I was on the move," Lucius frowned as he remembered, his expression annoyed. "I was not as secretive as I am now, although I suppose I should have been. Alex had arranged the meeting as I was passing through his area, and Whistleblower managed to corner us. If not for Kisten turning against his father, we both would have died."

"Hmmm," I responded, not sure what to do with what I had learned. Knowing that Whistleblower was strong enough to take on two First at the same time and win put his strength far above anything I could imagine. I finally understood why Lucius had chosen so many of us to accompany him, as well as choosing those of us with complementing powers. I may have hated Aurel for his behavior but, given the circumstances, he was the best option to work with me and Lucius.

"So, what will we do once we reach your retreat?" I asked, sighing heavily as I leaned back in the seat. Lucius' weary smile returned and he picked up his book from the table. He flipped to a new page, tracing another line of words there.

"I doubt we'll have to wait that long," his feminine voice returned as someone walked by and Kisca waited until the person was far enough away before releasing the glamor again. "Whistleblower isn't known for his patience, and probably is already following you and Kisten."

"So, we're bait? Lead him away from the city?"

"That is far from the only reason," he smiled and I shifted uncomfortably. Lucius glanced up at me as he continued. "Rather, I don't think we can win without you two. I'm not strong enough to defeat Whistleblower despite my power, and Aurel has no connection to him. You and Kisten, however, have the advantage that he won't kill either of you."

"So, we're going to use his desire to capture us against him," I offered and he nodded, his smile twitching as I considered his idea. Kisca suddenly looked up to the roof, her eyes glowing a darker pink than previously. Lucius followed her gaze, waiting for the pixie to speak and her voice was soft and musical as she whispered.

"I think... something is here."

I quickly stood at this, looking up toward the roof as I heard scurrying across the metal exterior. I glanced back down to Lucius, who nodded and I quickly made my way to the exit. I heard Lucius and Kisca stand behind me as I exited the lounge, stepping outside the train. The frigid air slammed into me as I leaned out, but I forced myself to ignore it as I climbed up to the metal roof.

A Grimm waited for me, saliva dripping from its jaws as it growled and it held its rat-like tail high in the air at the sight of me. I summoned my power in response, ready to quickly get rid of the creature. Only one Grimm meant that Whistleblower wasn't sure we were on board and he would be waiting for it to report back. Killing it would also be an obvious sign, but it would take him longer to find out than if it managed to return.

I lunged at the creature, sliding on the cold metal as it leapt over me. I quickly drew my gun from its holster and fired, using my power to curve the bullet for a hit. I smiled as the creature fell to the metal, my gun vibrating in my hand. Lovingly called The Caw, my gun was designed to soak up my power and I could use the stored energy to control the trajectory of my shots or to increase the impact force. There weren't many who could dodge me if I wanted to hit them, and its design often saved my life.

The creature's body tumbled on the roof, sliding to the edge but failed to fall off. I quickly stood, making my way to shove it off the moving train and I failed to notice as another Grimm lunged at me from behind. I barely dodged in time, firing off another shot, catching this one straight in the face. The creature's skull exploded in bits of blood and gore and its corpse tumbled as it fell from the moving train. I heard a slight scream from inside the train as the body fell past an open window and I quickly stood to take care of the other corpse.

"You've gotten good with human weapons," I felt my blood run cold at Whistleblower's calm voice and I looked around to find him. I found myself still alone on top of the moving box, noticing that the first Grimm's body was gone. I squatted down, taking the chance to reload my gun as I waited. "And there's no chance of you using that evil power of yours on this moving train."

"Show yourself, or are you afraid this time?" I sassed, still keeping my eyes peeled for any sign of movement. I knew he would approach me from the front: there was no way he wouldn't want me to see him coming. My locket grew warm with my sister's presence, but I knew she would only observe. We would talk later, using her perception of the fight to help us figure out a way to win. After talking with Lucius, I knew I couldn't beat him on my own: this would be a warm-up, a way to learn all I had missed the first time we met.

"Gotten quite mouthy, haven't we, Jezebela?" My body began to shake with anger as he called me by that name again and I growled, my hand ready on my gun as I waited for him to reveal himself. Jezebela was the name Mater Vitae had given me, erasing my original identity after she added me to her court. Thanks to her, I no longer remembered my true name any more than I remembered my sister's.

"I *am not* Jezebela. My name is Raiven," I retorted, finally standing as I started to look for him. "Try it all you want, but I have never claimed that name, and I *never* will."

I heard Whistleblower's laugh echo all around me and I finally saw the shape of the man as he walked toward me on the cold roof. He was dressed the same as he had been at the wedding and more of his pack crowded on the roof behind him. Their nails scratched and scraped across the metal, and I growled as I lifted my gaze back to the Hunter.

"Call yourself whatever you like: it doesn't change that you still belong to Mother," he laughed, a sharp whistle bringing the pack to a halt. He continued walking up to me, but I kept my gun by my side. I knew he would merely dodge if I tried to shoot him directly and I wasn't sure how the teleporting he had shown at the wedding worked.

"Oh? Where is that *sohn*[1] of mine?" he finally queried, pausing to look around in a dramatic fashion as we both ducked to avoid a low branch. He turned back to me with his sadistic smile and I knew what his intention was, my eyes widening in horror. "Guess I'll have to find him myself if he won't come out to play."

I moved before the sound even left his mouth, trying to re-enter the train to warn Lucius and Kisca but I found myself pinned to the roof, my face pressed into the cold metal. I felt Whistleblower dig his boot into my back as I heard the Grimm break the windows, flooding into the train to kill anyone they found.

"You're staying right here, Jezebela," I hissed with anger as I tried to stand, but I only managed to lift myself up slightly before I was slammed back into the roof, Whistleblower laughing at my attempt. His strength was unbelievable, on par with the physical prowess of a lamia or cyclops. "Can't have you running off until I find *der junge*[2]."

"You won't have to wait long," I smiled and Whistleblower barely had time to react as he was knocked from my back. I stood immediately, allowing the wind to blow me away from the Hunter. Kisten leapt back to my side, growling in his giant leopard form as his father stopped himself from sliding off the train. The Alpha wrapped his tail around me, placing himself between me and Whistleblower.

Whistleblower stood up calmly, brushing himself off as he faced us. His gray-blue eyes glowed as he looked at Kisten and he smiled savagely, clearly pleased.

"Hello, sweet son of mine."

II

We stood in silence on top of the roof, the only sounds being the growling of the Grimm in the cars beneath us and the freezing wind as it flew past us. Whistleblower's eyes glowed brightly in the darkening sky and I heard Kisten whine with pain. I looked at him as he shifted back to being human, the process clearly painful and forced. I growled as I looked back at Whistleblower, understanding that it was his gaze that was forcing Kisten to shift, and I fired my gun to distract him. I knew the shot wouldn't land but I didn't expect to be immediately shoved back to the cold roof, Kisten leaping at me to push me out of the way. We quickly stood back up as Whistleblower appeared in my previous spot, clearly entertained by Kisten dodging him.

"So, you *do* still remember how to fight," he applauded, taking the moment to clap for Kisten's reaction time. Kisten merely hissed, his change to human complete but his eyes were still glowing, now more brown than yellow or green. Whistleblower was clearly enjoying our struggle, knowing he could take us out at any moment. Kisten had warned me he was powerful, but this display was far beyond anything I had ever expected. "I was worried being with that vampire had weakened you."

"Shut up," Kisten retorted, not offering more of a response. I felt a brief absence of wind as Kisten disappeared from my side, and I saw him lock hands with the Hunter, using the momentum from his leap to force Whistleblower to step back. The two men fought for control for a moment, Whistleblower clearly having the upper hand. I carefully aimed and shot my gun again, curving the bullet to miss Kisten.

Whistleblower dodged at the last moment, throwing his head back as my shot flew between the two men. He tossed Kisten to the side and appeared in front of me, but this time I was ready. I turned from his reach and fired another shot point-blank at the Hunter. I felt the splash of blood on my face as my bullet connected, but my victory was short-lived. I suddenly felt Whistleblower's hand around my throat and I was forced to drop my gun as he lifted me into the air, dangling me over the edge of the train. The gun slid on the roof, stopping just before falling off the edge into the forest below us.

"You *sneaky, little, bitch*," he growled, blood dripping down his face from my shot. He had been able to dodge it partially but the shot still grazed the top of his head, blood pouring down from the wound. He tightened his grip on my neck and I struggled to breathe, trying to pull his hand away. His other hand shot out quickly to stop Kisten, and the Hunter shoved his son's head into the metal, kneeling on the back of his neck. His eyes glowed with his anger as he dropped me lower off the moving train and I knew he wanted nothing more than to kill me for injuring him. However, his loyalty to Mother was stopping him and we both knew she would never forgive him if I died.

"Leave her alone," I heard Kisten growl, pushing up against the knee on his neck but Whistleblower only dug in more, forcing a yelp of pain from the Alpha. My anger grew as I watched helplessly, still trying to remove the Hunter's hand. Whistleblower kept his glowing eyes on me, noticing the cord around my neck. Confused, he reached into my shirt with his free hand, pulling out and revealing my locket. His eyes widened in surprise and I knew he recognized it as my sister's locket.

"This is..." he began, but I immediately moved to take advantage of his distraction. My necromancy exploded forth without my summoning it, the power pushing into my sister's locket. The wood became as hot as fire and he released it in surprise, his grip on my neck relaxing. I wasted no time as I lifted myself up, planting my feet against the side of the train and headbutting the Hunter. The force from my blow forced him to step back and release Kisten as he fell. My lover quickly grabbed me to keep me from falling and I picked up my gun as he swung me back onto the roof. I coughed as my necromancy faded, sitting up to point the barrel back at Whistleblower.

"You fucking–" the Hunter paused in his insults, his eyes locked on Kisten as the Alpha held me. My head ached from the headbutt but I pushed through the pain, refusing to lower my gun. Kisten had his hand around my waist, gripping me tightly as he supported my weight. "No..."

"I won't go easily this time, Whistleblower," I growled through clenched teeth, my sister's presence stronger once again as her anger joined mine. The Hunter barely acknowledged my words, his eyes locked on his son's arm around me, eyeing Kisten's hand suspiciously. His eyes looked between us before finally noticing the green ring on my finger and the golden necklace hanging from my wrist. He rose to his feet, a quick whistle bringing some of the Grimm back on to the roof with us.

"You didn't learn your lesson the first time, Kisten?" his father growled and Kisten gripped me tighter in response, helping to keep me steady as I kept my aim on the Hunter. The Grimm advanced on us but I ignored them, keeping my gaze on Whistleblower. His calm and confident demeanor had completely faded and his crazed and angry expression was terrifying in the darkening night. I fought to maintain my determination and anger, but every fiber of my being was telling me to run from the creature approaching me. "How many women do I have to kill before you learn? Only Mother is worthy of your love. She should be the *only woman* in your life."

"Fuck you," Kisten spat, and I watched as he quickly knocked one of the Grimm off the train as it lunged at us, doing his best not to move me as I kept my gun trained on his father. Whistleblower's anger grew and he began to stomp towards us, the Grimm echoing his anger with their snarls and growls.

"You don't even know what *that thing* is," he spat back, whistling to call more of his pack. I was forced to take a quick shot, curving the bullet to kill another Grimm as it lunged at us, but I kept my eyes on the Hunter. The wound on his head was already starting to heal, the blood drying on the half of his face. I felt Kisten slide his arm under my legs and I knew he meant to try to move me before Whistleblower could get close. "Does she even know what you truly are? Can she look at your face and not see her sister's killer?"

Kisten stiffened at his father's words but I didn't turn to meet his gaze. I fired another shot, but Whistleblower easily dodged, allowing the bullet to hit a member of his pack. The Grimm moved in to surround us as the Hunter drew closer and Kisten scooped me up in his arms quickly as he stood. I was startled as I was suddenly lifted, but I kept my eyes locked on the Hunter, keeping my gun trained on him as he stopped in his approach.

"She's about to find out," Kisten whispered, stepping backwards off the moving train. I instinctively clung to him as we fell, but I soon found my fall slowed and feathers beneath my hand. I looked up to see Kisten shifting, but not into a leopard; he was shifting into a giant eagle, dropping me to his talons as his arms finished changing into wings. He flew us into the trees, clearly trying to get away from his father's line of sight.

I looked back to see Whistleblower about to follow us, but a bright flash of lightning stopped him, and I knew Lucius had finally managed to find a moment to help. The Overseer required that the train was running with the bare minimum of staff and passengers and required that no humans be aboard, ensuring that everyone would be able to at least defend themselves to some extent.

I was brought back to my current situation as branches began to scratch at me as Kisten lost altitude, falling into the tree line. His feathers were retreating back into his skin and it was clear he was losing the animal, and I tightened my hold on my gun. We crashed into the ground as his change was complete, Kisten turning us so that he hit the ground first. Leaves splashed up around us like water as we slid along the ground and we were soon buried underneath the brown and red foliage as it fell back down to the forest floor.

Panting from the pain, I moved to sit up, but Kisten kept me down, covering my mouth as I heard Whistleblower walking in the trees above us. There was no way he could have taken out Lucius that fast, so I knew the Overseer hadn't actually confronted him. The lightning must have been to give us an extra moment to escape and Lucius was still on the train with Aurel and Kisca, keeping any remaining Grimm from killing the passengers.

"You can't hide from me, *Hündin*[1]!" his voice was still full of his unbridled rage and I could hear the Grimm that leapt from branch to branch with him. He landed on the ground near us and Kisten gripped me tighter under our natural cover. I could hear his heart pounding as Whistleblower tried to discern where we had landed, but the leaves had covered our track nicely. He yelled in frustration, kicking more leaves on top of where we lay. "I will find you, Jezebela, and I will make you *wish* I could kill you."

The Hunter whistled for his pack as he leapt back into the trees, the Grimm following behind him as he continued searching for us. Kisten waited until we could no longer hear the growls and snarls of the Grimm before he loosened his grip on me, allowing me to sit up carefully. It was fully dark now and sparse moonlight filtered through the trees above us as I shook the leaves from my braids. I looked back at Kisten to see him holding his shoulder as he sat up, blood seeping through his fingers.

"Kisten!" I yelped despite the danger, standing off him quickly as I turned to examine the damage. The back of his shirt was ripped to shreds, deep scratches bleeding down his back from the various rocks that had cut him as we slid. He winced as he stood, clearly in pain.

"We need to move, Rai," he insisted, whining as he released his shoulder and tried to take my hand. Instead, I quickly holstered my gun and held him up, wrapping his arm around my shoulders as I began to lead him through the woods. Kisten seemed as if he wanted to argue, but he stopped himself, pointing to a slight incline in the rocks ahead of us. "Down there."

I obliged, helping him down as we stepped into the dripping shade of the rocks, the temperature dropping as we descended lower into the crevice. Ripples echoed around us as we continued, dipping underneath the overhang whenever Kisten heard a creature stir above us. It was unlikely to be a Grimm, but it was clear he wanted to take no chances, forcing me against the stone every time. We eventually reached a natural crevice, a small space between two rocks with an opening on the opposite side.

I fell face-first to the ground as we slid into the space, exhausted from the fight and carrying Kisten. Kisten also sat heavily on the stone, keeping his eyes trained on both openings as I lay on the damp ground. My head still pounded from headbutting Whistleblower and I finally took a moment to close my eyes, the pain fading slightly from the reduced input.

"Raiven," I heard Kisten call my name softly and I pushed myself up slowly, turning to look at the Alpha. His breathing was labored, even as he forced himself up and I dragged myself to him, sitting against the stone next to him. He glanced over at me, his expression pained. "You're hurt."

"So are you," I pushed his head down into my lap and he let me, not even fighting me as he collapsed. He closed his eyes instantly, letting out a shaky breath as he lay his hand on my thigh. "Rest, Kisten. I'll be fine."

The Alpha didn't argue with me and I closed my eyes as I stroked Kisten's hair, calling my power. The stone shook around us and the opening to my right began to close as I forced it together, my head pounding even more as I used my power. The opening to my left grew wider, and I stopped once the opening to my right was no longer usable, except to the smallest of creatures. I glanced out of the larger gap to my left and nodded as I noticed the vines above us had fallen, making it difficult to see inside the cave in the darkness of the forest around us.

I sighed heavily, moving my hand to check Kisten's breath. It was labored but slow, and I knew he had passed out from exhaustion. I ran my hand over his back and felt that some of the scratches were starting to heal, the blood crusting on his skin. I leaned down to kiss my lover's head, ignoring the pain it brought my lips. I sat in silence as he slept, my eyes trained on the entrance to our safe little haven.

12

It didn't take long for me to realize I was dreaming: I was back at the beach, the collapsed tents and broken tables littering the sands around me as I slowly stood. The dress I was wearing was different from the one I had worn at the wedding, and I picked at the dark purple fabric with confusion. I had been watching the entrance to the small cave where I and Kisten sat, trying to keep an eye out for danger as the Grimm prowled above us. I suppose it only made sense that eventually exhaustion would overpower me, and I cradled my head as a flash of pain ran through my skull.

"...*Ven.*" I turned as I heard my name, and almost immediately fell back into the sands as I scrambled to run away. It took a moment for me to realize the statue was not alive and I laughed at my own fear as I stood again, taking my time to look at the behemoth. It was definitely a statue of Mater Vitae, but it also... wasn't, somehow. Something about how her hair was carved, the serene expression on her face, it all seemed wrong from how I remembered her.

A glance down the beach revealed more of the towering structures and I slowly began to walk down the sand, wondering what my mind could be trying to show me as I walked. It wasn't often that I dreamed like this, and more often than not I had nightmares.

However, I was filled with a sense of calm, even as I passed the face of my tormentor. Slowly I began to notice that the statues were changing; still Mater Vitae, but her hair and expression continued to change, and her dress began to morph as well as I continued walking.

"My interpretation of her?" I questioned aloud, glancing up to the statue next to me. This one bore an expression that seemed more at home on her face and her hair was much more similar to how I remembered it being all those centuries ago. I gently touched the stone and almost immediately pulled my hand back, surprised by the sudden cold. The sculpture felt as if it were made of ice rather than stone and I glanced back at the annoyed expression showing through her semi-closed eyes.

A sudden sound drew my attention away from the statue and I fought to steady myself as the ground heaved, the sands shifting underneath me. I looked up as I saw one of the statues had fallen into the ground and I quickly made my way to it, wondering what had caused it to fall. As I reached it, however, I realized that it was no longer a statue of Mater Vitae but of someone else, the wings having shattered when the stone collapsed. Looking down the beach, I noticed the rest of the statues were similarly destroyed, with large pieces missing and leaving the original subject unidentifiable.

"Hmmm," I hummed as I stood, looking out to the dark water as I heard a wave loudly crash onto the shore. I sat on the broken statue, my eyes now drawn to the ocean as I waited, although I had no idea what I was waiting for. I sat in the dark silence for what felt like eternity and it was only when I looked up at the sky, I realized it sat empty and devoid of stars. Only a great black expanse spread above me and I hated the emptiness that sat in my chest.

"Time really does funny things to you, doesn't it?" A voice drifted on the wind as it blew past me, but I didn't bother to look for the source. I knew I was alone on the dark beach, surrounded by the statues of my tormentor and the unknown subject.

"More than most realize," I answered, petting the dark purple fabric as the waves drew closer to where I sat on the stone. The voice laughed at my response before shifting to a voice I knew.

"Still, it flows on, and that's a good thing, right?" my sister's voice danced on the playful breeze and I sighed heavily as I grabbed my locket, unable to help the pain in my chest as she continued: "After all, for the Beginning to matter, there must be an End."

"An End so many are denied," The voice shifted to another I didn't recognize and I nodded my agreement with this new thought. I shivered slightly as the icy water splashed up at me, but I remained on the stone, closing my eyes as the water continued to draw closer. "Even you."

"It will come when it's time," I offered, jumping again as the water touched me, the dress beginning to float as the ocean came for me on my perch. I barely reacted as it rose slowly around me, still feeling strangely calm as I sat on the broken statue. The water was cold, but not as cold as the statue of Mater Vitae had been and I relaxed as my body adjusted to the temperature. "Death always eventually finds us, no matter how hard we may run."

"Is that why you run from it?"

"Is that why you avoid it?"

"Is that why you saved me?" My sister's voice returned as the wind asked its many questions and I sighed, opening my eyes as the water reached my waist, finally calming down as it flowed around me. I felt a foreign presence in the waters around me and I carefully cupped the liquid before allowing it to rejoin the rest. Nothing seemed strange or off about the water, but the presence lingered, almost as if it were afraid to move away from me.

"Death should never come before its time," I whispered softly, an ache entering my chest as I remembered my sister's. I faintly heard the sounds of the Grimm but it was quickly replaced by the sound of the moving water. I turned my eyes back to the empty sky, the wind dancing silently through my hair as it waited for me to continue. "Life should always have a chance first."

"Is that why you run from it?"

"Is that why you avoid it?"

"Is that-"

"No. I avoid it because I am afraid," I interrupted the wind as it began to repeat its questions, running my fingers across the surface of the water. The voice stopped as it waited for me to speak and I sighed heavily, wondering what the point of this dream was. "I run because I fear Death, even though I know it is unavoidable. I know I will die, but I do not wish to run into its arms.

"I saved my sister because she deserved to live. He had no right to take her life." I continued, balling my hands into fists as the sand began to shift, lifting the stone I sat on back out of the water. When I looked up, I couldn't help the awe in my expression from what I saw and I scrambled to my feet.

Three beings, impossibly large, stood in front of me, ones I recognized as the Gods of my tribe and I was stunned into silence. They all had their arms crossed against their chests and their eyes closed, towering over me as they rose from the depths of the ocean. The center one, the God of Creation spoke, revealing itself as the voice that had first come to me on the wind:

"For a Beginning to Matter, there must be an End."

"For an End to Matter, there must be a Middle." The God of Life spoke next, the voice more feminine than its appearance suggested and I slowly watched as it morphed into the appearance of Mater Vitae, turning its hands to the sky. Its eyes remained closed as it moved, and my heart leapt into my throat as the stars suddenly reappeared above us, filling the darkness with their sparse light.

"But no End," my sister's voice flowed from the third God, the God of Death, and I turned as it shifted its appearance to match my memory of her, uncrossing its arms to let them face the ground. The being lifted its head to the sky as it finished speaking, the moon appearing above it and shining brightly, "should come before it's Time."

"I..." My voice drifted as I swallowed my words, realizing there was no point arguing with beings who were far above my understanding. Even if they existed only in this realm of dreams, there was clearly a right and wrong way to respond, and arguing would only cause them to repeat what they were saying. I sighed as I sat back down, my dress wet and cold as it folded under me. The dark fabric flapped softly in the winds that rejoined us on the beach and I was unable to help as a shiver finally ran through me.

"What will you do, Raiven?" The God of Creation asked me, its appearance shifting to that of Nisaba, although it kept its arms crossed as it addressed me. I sighed again, closing my eyes to the behemoth standing over me. "Will you run?"

"Will you give in?"

"Will you fight?" I looked up again as the God of Death spoke, and despite the calm in its face and voice, I almost felt as if it were mocking me by wearing my sister's appearance. I felt as anger and determination swirled in my chest and I stood, looking to the Gods evenly as I answered them.

"I will *live*." I declared and I watched as all three began to smile, their appearances shifting once more. I didn't recognize the appearance they all took, but somehow all seemed familiar to me and I watched with confusion as the God of Creation finally opened its eyes, the gold watching me softly as it slowly uncrossed its arms. There was a soft look on their face as they smiled at me, and I couldn't help but relate its expression to that of a parent watching a child finally understand.

"Then *live*."

13

'*Raiven...*' I jolted back to consciousness as my sister spoke, my locket nearly searing my skin with its heat. I quickly wrapped my hand around it and the fire faded, returning to the warmness I was used to. My sister also sounded stronger, as if she was having less trouble reaching out to me, just as she had at the wedding. I glanced out the entrance to our hiding space, seeing it was still dark outside.

"Sorry," I whispered, stroking Kisten as he lay in my lap, still asleep. I adjusted my position against the stone, doing my best not to shift the sleeping Alpha. "I didn't mean to pass out."

'*It's fine,*' she assured me and I was surprised by her kindness, unable to help my quiet hum. She huffed at my reaction, and I smiled slightly as she continued with her usual accusatory tone. '*I was staying aware while you slacked off.*'

"Well," I sighed, moving Kisten's hair from his face as he shifted, turning to press his face into my stomach. The corner of my mouth twitched up slightly at the gesture and I chuckled softly. "What did you notice?"

'*Kisten is smart. Whistleblower has no idea where you are,*' she nodded, clearly proud of his actions. '*I've heard Grimm pass by a couple* of times, but they haven't found your hiding spot. The flowing water in the stone makes it difficult to track your scent.'

"Good," I breathed, closing my eyes. My sister seemed as if she had more to say, but she remained silent as I rested. I opened my eyes again, looking out the entrance to my left to try to gauge the time. There was no hint of sunrise in the darkness outside our hiding space and I began to worry about Lucius and the others. The Oath would allow him to find Kisten no matter where he was, so it was only a matter of time before he was able to find us. However, I worried that Lucius coming for us would do more harm than good and I sighed again, releasing my locket. "Speak sis. What's on your mind?"

'Something is... not right about all this,' she sighed and I couldn't help agreeing with her. It felt as if everything had fallen apart in the past few days, and it wasn't just the sudden arrival of Whistleblower, either. 'His tune about us changed as soon as he saw the locket. But how could he have not known that you still had it?'

"I don't know," I whispered, gently stroking the wood as I spoke. "I never saw him after that night, so maybe he thought Mater Vitae took it from me? I thought she was going to, until I asked to keep it."

'But why does it matter? Either way, he shouldn't see it as anything other than a trinket; it's not like I spoke to anyone while you were captive. And why did he refer to our power as evil?' she pointed out and her concern started to grow, making my chest ache. The lingering memory of the dream passed through my mind and I closed my eyes as she continued. 'Mater Vitae liked necromancers, and tried to bring them all under her control; that's why she kept you.'

"But... what we can do is not necromancy," I reminded her, my thoughts flashing back to the wedding and how I had spied on the Overseers. "Or if it is, it's necromancy on a level that's unprecedented."

'Which makes it extremely dangerous.'

"In every sense," I agreed, understanding my sister's thoughts. My power, whatever it was, was probably the advantage we needed to win against Whistleblower, but neither one of us understood exactly *what* it was and what I could do. It was possible I could just as easily end up hurting my allies as the Hunter and we didn't have time for me to properly experiment. "I'm not sure this is a fight we can delay though. At least not for too long."

'Raiven.'

"That's just the truth. Whistleblower isn't going to give me time to figure this out," I argued, despite the worry sitting heavy in my chest. "Look, I agree with you, but it's not like we just found out he was coming. He's *here*, and actively looking for me and, given his attitude, doesn't want me to figure out my power."

'*Maybe not, but we may not have a choice. There's no point in fighting a losing fight and if our power is the key to it, then we* **have** *to delay him,*' my sister pointed out and I sighed as I lifted my hand from the shapeshifter in my lap. '*Even if it's only a day or two, you need that time for us to figure out this power.*'

"Maybe there is a middle ground," I offered, and I could feel my sister's annoyance increasing. "If it's the ace we need, maybe Lucius can help us find the time."

'You—'

"What is?" I opened my eyes as Kisten stirred, rolling on his back to look up at me. He was still in pain as he winced, but he took my hand softly in his as our eyes met. I smiled down at him, stroking his hair with my free hand.

"Don't worry about it," I tried to be as consoling as possible but it was clear from the look he gave me that he wanted to push the issue. Instead he sighed, squeezing my hand as he stroked the ring on my finger. I watched him curiously, my thoughts drifting to how we had escaped the Hunter.

"Kisten? Can... can I ask you something?"

"Anything."

"Since when did you have more than one animal?" I whispered, not dancing around my question as a creature scurried on the ground above us. Once it passed, the Alpha sighed, sliding his hand from mine as he forced himself to sit up, groaning as he did so. He almost disappeared into the darkness of the cave and I merely stared at the scars on his back, waiting for his answer. I knew in a day they would be gone, as if they never existed, but for now they were still fresh and red, not unlike the one in his heart.

"My mother," he started, his voice low and soft in the darkness. I reached out to him but stopped myself, dropping my hand into my lap as he continued: "had several children before me. All girls, and my father killed every one of them. He wanted a son, said girls would just be driven crazy by the pack."

"She... was terrified of me once I was born and, just like he wanted, I inherited her powers," Kisten's voice cracked as he spoke and I forced myself to touch him this time, careful to avoid the scars. "Even though I looked like her, she was worried I would be just like him. But I wasn't."

"She was an omnishifter?" I asked softly and he nodded, adjusting his legs as he leaned forward against one. We remained in silence for a while as I waited for him to continue. Then he went on:

"My mother... was gifted to my father by Mater Vitae," Kisten whispered and my heart stopped as I heard his words. Mater Vitae often spoiled her Hunters, rewarding them for their loyalty, but I had never heard of her giving them *people*. "My father wanted an animal shifter for a successor so she created and gave my mother to him. Most onmishifters only have two or three animals, but my mother... had eight."

"Eight?" I repeated with surprise, watching as the Alpha nodded again. "So, do you..?"

"No, I only inherited six," Kisten changed position again as his voice lapsed into silence, and I avoided asking the question burning in my mind. We remained in silence for a long time, before his soft voice once again filled the dark space.

"My father refused to allow my mother to shift, always using his gaze to force her animals back. She loved her leopard, so I shifted into mine for her when my father wasn't around. It... always made her smile. When I turned six, my father decided I was getting too close to her and that she had fulfilled her purpose," Kisten's voice was full of tears as he spoke and I rubbed his skin gently, my heart pounding as I realized the truth. "He... he allowed the Grimm to kill her in front of me. I knew then what kind of man my father was. I already knew I wanted to be nothing like him."

"So, did you..." I let my question trail and Kisten sighed, wiping the tears from his face.

"I was never good at controlling the Grimm. I feared allowing them into my mind, afraid it would be too much with all the animals that were already fighting to be let out. My father hated that, called it weakness," Kisten chuckled softly, dropping one of his hands into the dirt. "They'd listen to my commands, but didn't have any loyalty to me because of my refusal of their desires. He... is always their preferred choice."

"Eventually, I met someone. She's the one who taught me how to control my emotions and the various animals, taught me a way to allow the Grimm into my mind without them taking over me. Over time, I..." My hand stopped moving as Kisten's words trailed off and my heart began to pound in my chest. I thought back to what Whistleblower had said when he saw the ring on my finger, and I pulled my hand back from Kisten. He turned around to look at me, his sad expression making my chest ache even more. "Well, my father already told you what he does to women I care about."

"Kisten, I–" I was interrupted as Kisten threw his arms around me, pulling me close to him. I could feel his fear and desperation in his embrace and I returned his gesture gently.

"I can't lose you, Raiven," He moaned, his voice thick and heavy with his despair. "Not to the Oath, not to him. Not to anyone."

"Kisten," I sniffled, doing my best to hold back my own tears as I pushed his head up, lifting his face to mine. He met my gaze, his eyes a deep green again, the same as they had been on the train. "Are your animals the reason..."

"My control has been so poor?" Kisten leaned up to me, pressing a painful kiss against my lips as he hummed. "You could say that."

"Oh?"

"My snake in particular has been the one to cause most of the issues," Kisten admitted and I watched his face curiously as the green in his eyes swirled with brown before turning green again. "He has been *very* impatient to meet you and has been trying to force his way out. My leopard doesn't like to be forced to the side, hence all the problems."

"So besides leopard, eagle and apparently a snake, who else should I be worried about?" I asked softly, pulling the Alpha more into my lap as I dragged another kiss from his lips. Kisten began to purr deeply in his chest with the gesture, and I could tell his restraint was failing as he leaned up to me more.

"A jumping spider, bear and dolphin." Kisten whispered, gently pushing me onto my back against the stone as he leaned over me, his eyes glowing as I smiled at him.

"Surprised your dolphin hasn't been more feisty."

"He knows he'll get his turn," Kisten grinned, flicking his tongue out to let me know that his snake was beginning to manifest. I chuckled at his display, reaching to stroke his face as my fingers ached. "I'm not sure I can keep holding them all back when it comes to you."

"Well, I'm right here," I whispered, settling into the dirt as I pulled Kisten down to me, burying his face in my neck. Kisten purred into my skin, his tongue flicking out to taste my scent as I moaned softly, unable to help how much it tickled. "I think I can handle your snake if he is so insistent."

"*We all are*," Kisten hissed, his voice sliding across my skin as I felt his legs move and I knew he was fighting his snake's desire to shift. I gently pushed against him and he sat up, looking at me curiously. "I want you more than any of us can stand."

"I know," I breathed, pushing Kisten back until he sat up from me and I grinned at him devilishly from where I still lay on the ground. I stretched slightly, enjoying the thought that had come to mind as I watched the shifter. "Do you think you can partly shift?"

"What do you mean?" Kisten gave me a wary look as I sat up to meet his gaze evenly, my smile still bright on my face.

"I mean as in, just shift your lower half to your snake."

"Maybe, but why?"

"Trust me," I grinned, watching as Kisten's lips twitched with my words. He carefully moved away from me sitting on the ground as I moved to my knees. I watched as soft green scales started to grace his skin, and his legs slowly drifted together as they elongated into his beautiful tail. His dark pants were swiftly replaced by the shiny green skin, and his scales barely stopped under the remains of his shirt. Kisten's breath was heavy as he fought to keep the change under control, and his eyes met mine again.

"Best I can do, without him taking over." Kisten panted and I chuckled, slowly climbing back into his lap. I shivered as his fingers glided over my skin, slightly rough from the scales on his hands and arms. He almost looked like a lamia in his half-shifted form, and I cradled his face in my hands, wishing I had worn the gloves before leaving our room on the train.

"Good enough," I whispered, kissing him deeply as I heard his tail move across the dirt and I was genuinely surprised when I felt it wrap around my midsection. The light squeeze made me moan softly and I smiled brightly at Kisten as he finally showed his own. "Somehow, I'm not surprised you're a constrictor."

"Would you have it any other way?" Kisten whispered, squeezing me more in his tail as he leaned into me, flicking out his tongue to indulge in my scent. I shook my head softly, running my fingers through his beautiful brown hair as he began to press burning kisses into my neck, soft moans escaping me. His tail almost seemed to squeeze me rhythmically as he worked his way down my neck, allowing his snake to meet me and taste me.

"Kisten..." I moaned softly, unable to help my sounds as he reached my collar bone, my skin already aflame from his gentle torture. My whole neck ached from the kisses he had given me and my chest was starting to burn from where his tail squeezed my middle. Kisten moaned against my skin as well, but he paused in his attention, placing his head into my chest.

"It's not fair," Kisten groaned, rubbing his head in between my breasts as his tail tightened around me. I gasped as he forced the air from me and I drew in a shaky breath as he relaxed, unable to help how much the action had aroused me. "*I can't lose you.*"

"You won't," I assured him, gently lifting his head as I stole another kiss. Kisten made no move to hide his passion this time, almost immediately sliding his tongue against mine. The heat he had poured into my neck was now burning my face, and despite the pain, I leaned into him more, desperate to feel him. His new snake-like tongue was different from the sandpaper texture I had grown used to, but I moaned regardless, my fingers sliding through his brown waves. I felt as his own hand shifted to my braids and it was now that I noticed my hair had grown significantly, my braids loose and coming undone.

The Alpha barely broke the kiss as he pressed me back into the dirt, his tail shifting around me. Kisten leaned over me as he hissed softly, his eyes almost a mix of various colors. It seemed all his animals were swirling in his eyes, and I moaned softly as I touched his face, loving the beautiful sight. I was slightly startled as I felt the tip of his tail touch my face, and I realized he had slid his tail higher up my body, now able to squeeze my entire torso underneath my shirt.

"*Vogel*[1]," Kisten whispered, leaning down as he kissed my cheek, his tongue flicking against my skin again as I shuddered, gasping as he squeezed me. "I need you."

"Soon," I promised, moaning softly as I closed my eyes, my hands still in his hair as he kissed me. "I'm not going anywhere."

Kisten kissed me deeply again as he squeezed my body in his coils, causing me to moan rhythmically against him. He never squeezed too tightly, but I loved the feeling of his scales against my skin, despite the pain it caused due to the Oath. My whole body felt as if I was on fire, and yet I held him even closer to me, desperate to feel him. Kisten's whole body shook as he fought to stay in control and I felt as his scales started to creep higher up his back.

"Kisten, we–" I tried to pull away from him but Kisten squeezed me tighter, forcing the air out of me before I could speak. I gasped wordlessly as I met his bright green eyes, seeing the crazed, desperate look in his expression and for a moment, I could see Whistleblower in him. He must have caught the scent of my fear, because at that moment he pulled back, releasing his hold as precious air filled my lungs.

"Raiven, I'm sorry. I–"

"It's alright, Kisten," I smiled, sitting up quickly as he moved away from me. His tail left a trail of fire on my skin as he slowly unwrapped me, and I shivered as I closed my eyes, attempting to calm myself down. "I was going to suggest we pause this for now."

"Yeah," Kisten agreed, and I could see the beginning of the dawn through the crack behind him. Slowly, he gave up the animal, his legs reappearing as the green scales faded back into his skin. I took the time to fix my shirt, unable to help my soft moan of pain as I moved. I would probably ache for most of the day, but I always accepted the pain as a part of loving the Alpha.

I felt as Kisten's hand rested on mine and looked up to see his eyes still swam with all his animals. He sighed softly as he pulled my hand to his face, kissing the skin as gently as he could.

"I know I keep saying it, but soon," he whispered, hovering his lips just above my hand to avoid causing me more pain. I leaned into him again, gently kissing his hair as my heart swelled with love for the man in my arms.

"I know," I allowed him to pull me to my feet and we carefully stepped out of the cave, Kisten sniffing the air before pulling aside the vines. I could finally see hints of the sky brightening and I looked up to the rock edge above me to see the hints of blue peeking through the trees above us. The woods almost looked different in the morning light and seemed less haunted than they had the night before as we slid through them. I knew the morning calm was nothing more than a front though; despite appearances, I had no doubt Whistleblower and the Grimm were still tearing up the forest trying to find us.

"If we can find the river," Kisten began and I looked down at him. He was staring down the path in the rocks, frowning as he spoke. "I might be able to figure out where we are. Lucius probably rode the train to the station, but I don't know how far away we are."

"Okay," I sighed, reaching for his hand and lacing our fingers despite the burning sensation it caused. Kisten looked back to me, taking a moment to kiss my forehead gently.

"It'll also give us a chance to wash off. While I'm likely to smell them before they smell us, the blood will leave an obvious trail for them to follow," I merely nodded in agreement as he began to lead us down the rocks, the sky continuing to grow brighter above us.

14

I followed Kisten through the morning light as we continued walking through the rock crevices. I was surprised by how deep some of the paths went, and I looked up at the forest above us as we descended deeper. Despite claiming to not know where we were, Kisten was surprisingly good at navigating the spaces, and we always seemed to avoid any dead ends or caves.

Movement above us caused us both to pause, and Kisten quickly pressed me into the shadow of the rock as some of the leaves cascaded down into the crevice. My eyes widened with horror as I heard laughing voices, and I glanced up to see the shoes of some hikers.

"Man, there seems to be a lot going on today."

"I know, right?" another voice laughed, kicking a rock down into the crevice. I flinched as it bounced on the stone next to me, but I managed to remain quiet as they continued talking. "It's not every day we get asked about the Alpha. Never knew he came this far to hunt."

"Maybe he's got some newbie animal shifters with him?" another companion offered and I heard as the first one scoffed at the idea.

"Yeah, right, as if Kisten would come this far just to train some newbies," they kicked another rock into the ravine and I bit my lip as it hit my already aching skull. Kisten growled softly as he pressed me more into the stone, but we both fought to remain quiet. "Besides, who knows who that old geezer is. I heard rumors that a Hunter is here in the Governance."

"A Hunter? Really?" the second sounded unimpressed as they adjusted their pack on their back and I couldn't help my relief as it sounded like they were getting ready to move on. "Next you'll tell me Mother is here herself."

"Well, I-I–"

"Let's get moving, you idiots. These fish aren't gonna catch themselves and I wanna sleep in my own bed tonight," the third one sighed, and Kisten slowly released me as the trio moved deeper into the woods. He waited until we could no longer hear their steps before he turned to me and I was surprised by his frown. Then I felt the slight trail of blood as it ran down my face, and realized the rock had actually managed to injure me.

"Rai–"

"I'll be okay," I whispered, touching my head and looking at the blood on my fingers. It didn't feel particularly bad, but given my already pounding headache, I was hardly in a state to tell how much damage the rock had done. I did my best to hide this as I smiled at my partner, who was still watching me with concern. "I'm more worried about what they said."

"Someone was asking about me," Kisten mused, looking away from me as I gingerly touched my head again. My braids were mostly loose from all the sudden growth using my powers had caused and I was debating if I should just start undoing them when Kisten spoke again. "Given that they didn't say it was Lucius–"

"Kisca could've used a glamor," I interrupted, quickly dropping my hand as he turned to me. "Lucius doesn't really want anyone to know he's outside of Decver, remember?"

"Yeah... true," Kisten conceded, but I could still see the worry in his stance. It was also possible that Whistleblower was the one who asked about Kisten, but I doubted that the Hunter would have let the fishermen live if he was the one who had met them first. "I am surprised that rumors of a Hunter are already circulating."

"I mean, it has been days since the wedding, and that big of a massacre doesn't go unnoticed," I shrugged, sighing heavily as I closed my eyes. "No matter what excuse Division 11 and Evalyn give, Hunter rumors are bound to spread."

"Sounds like you know from experience," Kisten offered, finally deciding it was safe enough to keep moving as he took my hand. I let him lead me through the path, deep in thought as I took my time answering him.

"I... was there when The Mist came," I whispered, and I felt as Kisten squeezed my hand. I glanced up to see his expression, but he kept his gaze forward as the path began to incline, taking us back up toward the forest. I frowned as I waited for him to speak, watching the patterns in the stone as we continued.

"I stayed behind when she was here, so that must've been..."

"Yeah, I met Lucius for the first time then," I continued, sighing deeply as I remembered. "I mean, it was right after Supes had been revealed, and Hunters were starting to be known about by humans. We did our best to quell rumors, but all things considered..."

"Her power would make that hard, anyway, especially after the damage Exarch caused," Kisten shrugged, releasing my hand as he started to climb up a short ledge. He reached down to help me up and I let him, unable to help my grunt as I struggled to find the footholds. "Hard to explain sudden ghost towns."

"We're lucky that Lucius came to help," I agreed, remembering that final confrontation well as I paused on the ledge. Lucius' electricity was critical for neutralizing her mist, allowing me and the others to get close enough to kill her. We didn't come out without our own losses, but it had changed my opinion of Hunters after finally seeing one die. I had known that Exarch was killed a few years prior, during the start of the third world war, but watching The Mist be killed was a distinct experience. "It... was good I remembered him when I needed his help."

"Help?"

"I didn't come to The Capital because of Hunters, surprisingly enough," I sighed, forcing myself to stand as Kisten waited for me. "I killed another Overseer, and I needed protection from that."

"Who–"

"Marek." I growled, unable to help my anger at the memory. Judging by the look on Kisten's face, he knew exactly who I was talking about and he snorted as he continued walking.

"Wondered who finally put that bastard down."

"Well, you're looking at her. Killed him and most of his Coven after I found out what he had been doing," I admitted, groaning softly as the pounding in my head increased. A fear was beginning to fill my chest, despite the fact that I saw nothing to be afraid of. "Didn't manage to kill his Retainer, so I fled to find protection from another Overseer. Although if I remember-"

"Nikola eventually got it done," Kisten finished and I nodded, pausing as I held my head. My vision was starting to swim and I felt unsteady on my feet, closing my eyes again to try and lessen the pain. "She decided she wouldn't continue to be the Alpha for... Raiven?"

I couldn't answer the shifter as I fell to my knees, the pounding in my head making me groan loudly. I heard as Kisten rushed back to my side but I barely felt his hand on mine as I cradled my aching skull. My sister's voice rushed through my mind, but even she sounded distant.

'Raiven! Wha–'

"Move." I whispered, feeling my necromancy rise on its own and Kisten quickly scrambled away as the dark tendrils shot out across the pale stones. I reached out into the forest, trying to find what was causing my fear and I opened my eyes as my power found the cause of my worry. Two Grimm, quickly making their way back to Whistleblower to report our location and I growled softly. I felt my power quickly incapacitate them, causing the creatures to fall from the trees and confusion ran through me as it began to drag them into the ground. Necromancy should have no effect on the living, but the power coursing through me disagreed as it continued to bury the creatures. Dirt filled their lungs as they struggled to dig their way back to the surface, and I sighed heavily once they stopped moving, pulling back my power to stop it from raising them.

"Raiven?" Kisten ventured cautiously, and I slowly looked up at him, still breathing heavily as my power faded. My headache lingered but was no longer so painful that I couldn't move and I carefully stood.

"Two Grimm had seen us and were on their way back to your father," I managed, barely catching the flash of concern on Kisten's face. "They've... been dealt with."

"Your necromancy?" Kisten sounded just as confused as me and I shrugged, doing my best to shake off the pain. My sister's worry and concern also sat heavy in my mind and I was starting to agree with her about delaying the fight as much as we could.

"I'm... not sure what this power is, Kisten." I admitted, taking his hand as he offered it to me. I started to say more but stopped myself, deciding it wasn't the time to talk about facing his father. "I think for now, we should just focus on figuring out where we are and go from there."

"I suppose we need to be more careful," Kisten agreed, leading the way again as we continued to follow the incline. I was starting to see the roots of the trees from where they had broken the stone, desperate to find the nutrients they needed to live. The sight reminded me of my dream, and the last answer I had given the Gods, causing me to hum softly to myself. When Kisten spoke again, I was surprised and turned to watch his back. "They must be staying in the trees to avoid me tracking their scent."

"Makes sense, but also makes it harder for them to track ours," I agreed, shaking off the worst of my pounding headache as I felt my desire for undead blood start to rise. My sister's worry increased at this and I grabbed the locket, holding it tightly. "Those two must've been following the fishermen and managed to spot us."

"Hmmm," Kisten hummed in agreement, squeezing my hand tighter as he turned down a side path, once again leading us deeper into the ravine. I started to say more but stopped, instead touching the dried blood that ran down my face. I plucked at the flakes, placing them in my mouth to try and settle my bloodlust.

'*You shouldn't be thirsty.*'

'*I know,*' I agreed as my sister finally spoke and I was unable to help as her worry filled me more and more. '*It must be a side effect.*'

'*Also touching the living? You just used necromancy to kill.*'

'*I know,*' I repeated, glancing up as the stone closed over us and we walked in the darkness of the crevice. I trusted that Kisten wouldn't have entered if there wasn't an exit, and the wet dripping from the walls of the cave seemed to echo with the pounding in my head. '*I think at this point, we can agree it's not necromancy.*'

'*Was our power always like this, or did the vampire taint do something to you?*' my sister pondered and I frowned, my thoughts racing with hers. I had never used my power since sealing my sister, and it seemed that whatever I had done at the wedding had unleashed the beast. The power was coming up without my calling on it and seemed to have a mind of its own, reaching out and doing whatever it pleased. '*You can't face Whistleblower like this.*'

'*Sis–*'

'*Don't "sis" me,*' she hissed, and I released the locket as it started to grow warmer. '*If this power can touch the living, you are just as likely to kill everyone as you are to save them.*'

I had no good response so I remained silent and was barely able to help the hiss of pain as the locket began to sear my skin. Kisten looked back with concern, but I shook my head, smiling as best as I could to ease his worry. My sister growled in the back of my mind and I felt her withdraw, the pain fading with her.

"I want to see how close we are to that river," Kisten whispered softly, and I could see the light streaming into the cave as we neared the exit. "Those fishermen spoke as if it was close and the sooner we get there, the sooner we can potentially find Lucius."

"Alright," I agreed, releasing Kisten as we exited the stone, covering my eyes as we stepped back into the sunlight. The Alpha turned to look at me, a worried look on his face as he saw the blood trail on my face and I did my best to smile. "I'll be alright for a moment. I can't climb as well as you."

"It won't take long," Kisten insisted, cradling my face in his hands as he pressed a painful kiss on my forehead. As the shifter quickly climbed up the stone, I sat in the shade of the rocks, closing my eyes to the bright sun.

15

I sat heavily on the ground as I waited for Kisten to return, shifting on the uncomfortable rocks. He had just disappeared into the canopy of leaves above me and I sighed, my thoughts turning back to the Grimm and how I had killed them. I hadn't even noticed them consciously, but I must have sensed them somehow, causing my power to react on its own to protect me. But to touch the living...

"Sis?" I ventured, reaching to my locket, but only receiving searing heat and a wave of annoyance in response. I glanced up the cliff for Kisten and, failing to notice him, I attempted to summon my necromancy, hoping to lessen my sister's anger.

The power refused to rise at first, struggling like an upset pet on a leash. I frowned, closing my eyes as I focused on trying to find the nearest dead body. My power finally responded, allowing me to feel a body that was trapped in the stone underneath me. My frown deepened as I tried to examine the body: I wasn't sure I could pull a body from solid rock and I was surprised I had even been able to find it. Usually the most a necromancer could do was sense the dead's presence nearby, but I was fully able to examine the shape of the remains beneath me. I had no idea what my power was touching, but I knew for certain it wasn't human.

"What the fuck is going on?" I whispered as I knelt down onto the stone, placing my hands against the chilled surface. I sent my power down into the unfeeling earth, reaching out to the strange body below me. Once again, I found my necromancy uncooperative, the tendrils touching the body only to retreat back to me. I pushed harder, forcing the power to envelop the dead trapped under my feet. I once again tried to determine what it was, but failing to identify it, I attempted to raise it. The stone heaved beneath my feet as the body began to reform itself and as the ground began to shake violently, I quickly withdrew my power. The ground grew still as death reclaimed the body and my breath was heavy as I looked at the stone with fear. I wasn't sure what would've happened if I hadn't stopped, but my instincts were telling me it would have been disastrous.

"Raiven?" Kisten's voice came from above me and I looked up to see the Alpha standing on the edge of the cliff. He expertly climbed down the steep rock face to rejoin me, the concern obvious in the way he moved down the stone. I stood up, my head aching as he landed. "Are you alright? I thought I felt a tremor."

"I'm fine," I forced myself to smile as I spoke, my heart pounding as he glanced back up to the forest above. The tremor hadn't felt so severe that Kisten should have been able to feel it, but now I was more nervous about what my power had touched. My sister's fear joined my own and I spoke quickly, eager to change the subject. "Well, what did you find?"

"We're heading in the right direction. If we keep following the cavern, we'll reach the river," he sighed, reaching for my hand with his. I took it and he began to lead us once again, my thoughts in turmoil behind him.

"Could... could you see the station?"

"No: we're a lot farther away than I thought," he admitted, releasing me as he hopped down a ledge. He reached up to catch me and I hopped down into his arms. He snuck a kiss on my bloody forehead as he set me down, once again leading the way. "Even with

Lucius looking for us, it could be days before he could pinpoint where I am."

"Hmm." I hummed, thinking of my sister's suggestion. If we avoided Lucius, it could give me the time I needed to experiment with my power, but part of me needed to find the vampire. My thirst was starting to feel more insistent as I thought about the Overseer, and I coughed slightly to hide my bloodlust.

"Also," his voice sounded caught in his throat and he gripped my hand tighter as we continued down the path. I lightly returned his squeeze and he continued, his voice soft. "The Grimm are still looking for us."

I stopped walking, his hand pulling from mine as he continued. He stopped a little way in front of me, turning back to see the expression on my face. My thoughts raced as I considered our options, my heart pounding as I looked at the ground. We needed to delay Whistleblower finding us, either before or after we reunited with Lucius, and I was unsure which the best option would be. If my thirst overtook me before we found the vampire, I would likely reveal our location in my blind desperation for undead blood, which made reuniting with Lucius a priority. However, once we were all in the same location, we would have no choice but to face Whistleblower once he found us. Unless...

"What's on your mind, *Rabe*[1]?" Kisten's voice interrupted my thoughts and I shook my head as I walked toward him, frowning as I considered what I wanted to do. I gasped aloud as my locket seared my skin, my sister making her displeasure at my thoughts known. Kisten glanced back as I lifted the cord, pulling the burning wood away from my skin. He looked at the trinket with a hint of sadness in his eyes, and he turned away again.

"You never told me it was Whistleblower," he whispered and I released the locket, letting it fall back against my skin. I said nothing and Kisten sighed heavily, pausing in his stride. I stopped as well, gripping my own arm as I looked to the sky above us.

"I didn't think it mattered." I sighed, rubbing my forearm gingerly. Kisten didn't respond and I released another heavy sigh before continuing. "I don't see him in you, so why would I bring it up?"

"Do you now?" He offered, still refusing to look at me. I walked up to him, placing my hand on his bare back. His wounds from the night before were all but healed, and I rubbed the light scars that had yet to fade.

"I can see him in you, yes, but I don't think you're like him in any way," I admitted, tracing one of the larger marks across his shoulder. Kisten remained silent and I continued, following the wounds with my hand. "It doesn't bother me that you're his son. You didn't kill my sister."

I did. I thought to myself, retracting my hand and letting it fall uselessly to my side. Kisten finally turned around, but now I was the one refusing to meet his gaze, looking at the mix of autumn leaves around us. My sister's presence still hovered in my mind, but her frustration had given way to a mix of sadness and annoyance at my thoughts.

"Look, Kisten, I think–" I paused, my thoughts still in turmoil as I considered what I wanted to say. The shifter turned fully to face me, waiting to hear what I wanted to suggest. "I think... we should try to delay confronting Whistleblower."

"Why?" Kisten's confusion was plain on his face and I gripped my locket tightly as I sighed. I noticed that his stance had changed, showing tension in his shoulders and hands as he waited for my response.

"Because of my power. What I thought was necromancy... clearly isn't," I admitted, looking up to meet his gaze again. "He seems to know more than even I do, and I need more time to figure out exactly what it is I can do before I can possibly use it in a fight."

"Raiven–"

"I know it's risky, but confronting him blindly isn't the way to do things," I insisted, looking away again as I squeezed the wood in my hand. I began to rub it gingerly as my heart pounded with fear and worry. "I didn't think he would be as strong as he is, and with my power being an unknown, I don't want to risk him taking advantage of my ignorance."

"So your promise to Vanessa meant nothing?" I looked up confused as I heard Kisten hiss and I was surprised by the anger I saw on his face. He looked almost ready to attack me and I scoffed, unable to understand what he was thinking. "You're willing to just let more innocents die for you?"

"What? That has nothing to do with what I just said."

"You want to run away," Kisten insisted and I couldn't help as my own anger rose. I glared at the Alpha as he looked down at me, clearly misunderstanding what I had said. "You would rather hide than face him."

"That's not even what I fucking said. Stop putting words in my mouth," I shot back, resisting the desire to raise my power against Kisten. "It's true in the past I tended to run rather than face a Hunter alone, but I am *not* alone, and I have no intention of running from this fight. All I suggested was–"

"Delaying the fight? How exactly would we do that, Raiven? *He's here, now, in these woods with us,*" Kisten growled and I shook my head as I tried to control my own emotions. "He's not gonna patiently sit and wait while you play around. He *will* do everything to draw us out if he can't find us."

"*I know that Kisten,* and I know trying to delay the fight is a risky option. But–"

"But what?" he demanded. I met his gaze evenly as he placed his hands on my shoulders, still glaring at me with his beautiful eyes.

"I *need* to understand my own power before I can use it against him. I just used what I knew as necromancy to kill the living. *The living, Kisten!*" I shoved Kisten's hands off me, hating the way he was acting. "We *both* know that shouldn't be possible. Until I understand what I can do, I'm a danger to everyone, including innocents. Including you!

"Besides, why are you acting like this?" I shot back, shaking my head as I jabbed my finger into his chest. "If anything, I would think you would be okay with delaying things for a moment."

"What is *that* supposed to mean?"

"I mean, you sure have had no problem delaying the process of you being released from the Oath, waiting until 'the time is right'," I glared at Kisten, who was watching me with a surprised expression. I felt my face flush with my anger at his surprise and I stomped my feet in frustration. Kisten took a step back as I leaned up into his face more. "If you're so scared of the Oath killing me, why are you not just as worried about losing to your father if I can't control myself?"

"That—"

"Oh please, explain to me how it's different," I spat, stepping back from him as I crossed my arms. I could feel my sister's concern starting to override her annoyance, but I ignored it as I stared at my partner. "If you're suddenly so willing to just rush in without thinking, then why not just love me, consequences be damned? Why wait at all?"

"I *am thinking*, Raiven. It's why I'm concerned with the lives of the people here, why we can't afford to avoid him!" Kisten insisted and I threw my hands up in frustration. "And this has *nothing* to do with me still being bound by the Oath. I won't risk it killing you before I'm released—"

"Oh, then why are you still bound by it?" I hissed, my blood pounding in my veins as I glared at my lover. "You've been courting me for almost a year now, so why have you delayed it for so long? Do you enjoy watching me suffer, causing me pain while all you receive in return is pleasure?"

"What? No, and you *know* that," Kisten gasped, his confusion and annoyance only bothering me more. My head started to ache as I grew upset and my sister's concern in the back of my mind wasn't helping my mood. "I just wanted to do things the right way and—"

"Then you *agree* that I need time to learn my powers!" I argued, hating the look on his face as he stared at me. "Because if I don't and we rush into this fight blindly, people will *die* and you *will* lose me."

Kisten didn't respond as I continued glaring at him, refusing to back down. I could see he was annoyed about me bringing the Oath into the argument, but I couldn't understand why he was so against avoiding the fight. We both *knew* it was going to happen, and I understood that it was likely Whistleblower would try to draw us out by attacking others, putting more lives at risk. But those same lives were still at risk if I lost control of my power, especially since I barely understood what I could do.

"Look, let's... let's just find Lucius," Kisten huffed, turning away from me as he continued walking through the crevice we were in. "This is all a moot point until we find the others and know where we are."

He didn't wait to see if I would follow and for a moment I wasn't sure if he really wanted me to. I slowly began after him, keeping my distance as he made his way through the crevice, no longer offering to help me climb up and down the small ledges. My chest ached with uncertainty but I remained silent, not wanting to continue the argument pointlessly. I had to at least agree that we needed to find Lucius, but I couldn't understand why he wanted to rush blindly into fighting his father.

'*Maybe there is something he's not telling us,*' my sister ventured, and I gripped the locket tightly as she finally spoke. Her voice was starting to sound weak again, and I was tempted to try and raise my power to restore hers, but I resisted. It was too dangerous considering my loose control of it and I squeezed the locket more. '*I understand his concern but—*'

'*I do too, I'm just as worried as he is,*' I interrupted, humming with my annoyance as I struggled to pull myself up a ledge. I heard as Kisten paused for a moment, and I looked up to see him debating if I needed help. I grunted as I pulled myself up, taking a moment to rest on the ledge as Kisten turned away. I growled softly as I stood, my anger returning. '*But honestly, if I have to choose between Whistleblower killing a few to try and draw us out and me killing everyone because I can't control my power, the math writes itself.*'

'*You... don't need to convince me...*' I could feel the strain in my sister's voice as she tried to continue talking with me and I sighed heavily, stroking the wood.

'*Rest, sis. There's no need to keep forcing yourself to talk with me.*' I sighed, looking to the back of my partner. The scars on his back were barely visible and I couldn't help my angry grunt at being reminded how he had protected me after we escaped the train. I felt my sister's presence fade away as I walked through the forest behind Kisten, my emotions in turmoil.

16

I squatted next to the rocks, sitting in the simple bubbling stream as my clothing dried on the stones next to me. Kisten had drifted into the woods to hunt, hoping to calm the animals stirred up inside of him by our argument. Rocks and trees loomed all around and above me and it was tempting to relax my guard and just enjoy the scenery. I was still filled with my anger however, and I found it hard to relax.

"Stupid hypocrite," I whispered under my breath, splashing the water as it flowed around me. "Says he want to do things 'the right way' when it comes to courting me, but unwilling to even consider being patient when it comes to our fucking lives? Who's the impatient one now?"

I stood angrily, causing a twig to snap behind me and I whipped around, summoning my power as the mud moved toward the sound. The frightened raccoon quickly ran off, and I laughed nervously, allowing the dirt to fall back into the stream. I reached to check my clothes and, deciding they were dry enough, stepped out of the water to dress.

My mind drifted to the train and I began to worry for the remainder of our group as I fastened my holster. Aurel and Lucius could take care of themselves, that I knew; their power and prowess would easily allow them to eliminate the Grimm that had infested the train. Kisca however, like most pixies, wasn't really suited for combat, although she could use her glamor to camouflage and hide herself. I whispered a prayer under my breath for their safety and I slid my boots on my feet just as I heard another animal approach from the trees in front of me.

I looked up to be greeted by yellow leopard eyes and Kisten's maw was covered in blood as he stepped out of the trees. I moved to let him reach the river and he dropped down, taking a drink as he shifted back to being human. He released a long sigh, looking satisfied as he turned to me.

"They're good, for now," he breathed and I gave him a curt nod in return. Kisten's expression shifted and he looked away from me, neither of us ready to talk about what had happened earlier. The moment was interrupted as my own stomach grumbled and I held my midsection in embarrassment. Kisten chuckled, standing from the water and his expression had softened as he looked at me. Despite my anger and annoyance, I couldn't help the slight smile that started on my face.

"Want me... to catch you something? Won't be as luxurious as at home but..."

"No need," I shook my head, releasing my still rumbling stomach. Kisten gave me a confused look as I continued. "I can wait until we're in a safer place. Besides, my thirst is what's really bothering me, so we need to find Lucius as soon as possible before the worst happens."

"That's... unusual. It's not even time," Kisten admitted and I chuckled, giving him a hesitant smile.

"As I said earlier, there seems to be a lot about my power I don't understand," I offered and I turned to look across to the other side of the river. Kisten was giving me a quizzical look when I turned back to him, a tired expression on my face. "Do we have some time before we move on?"

"I guess. Why?"

"I want... to try something," I admitted, shuffling my feet among the rocks, giving one of the larger rocks a slight kick before glancing up to see Kisten nod and step back from me. I steadied my stance and knelt down on the rock bank, pressing my hands to the ground. Unlike earlier, my necromancy responded immediately, but the power felt raw. It was wilder and more unhinged than before and I closed my eyes, focusing on pushing through my intent. The tendrils quickly spread through the ground around me, first touching Kisten but I forced them to pull away from him, growling slightly. They continued to snake through the woods around us, finally finding a body on the other side of the river.

"Find something?" Kisten's voice seemed to echo in the air behind me, and I barely heard him as I tried to determine what my power was touching. I fought to keep it from raising the body, instead tracing its shape and determining that this time, it was indeed a human body. As I touched it however, I began to feel something familiar about the energy the body gave off and I did my best to examine it carefully.

"Kisten," my eyes snapped open and I released my necromancy, standing up quickly as I recognized what my power had found. Kisten looked at me curiously, his voice wary.

"What is it?"

"We need to get across, now!" I insisted, hopping down into the moving water without the courtesy of explaining. I gave no thought to my clothing as I quickly swam across and Kisten met me on the other side, once again in leopard form. I leapt on his back as he ran through the trees, pointing him in the correct direction. Soon we came to a small alcove, the jagged points of the rocks pointing in all directions. Sitting underneath one of them, with two Grimm closing in, was LeAlexende, and the Overseer's eyes widened as he noticed me, blood streaming down his face as he tried to stand.

"...Raiven?" His voice was hoarse as he called out my name and his hair was white as snow, similar to how it had been the night he left. I leapt from Kisten's back and quickly fired my gun, killing the two Grimm before they could react. Kisten scooped up LeAlexende in his mouth, leaping down into a crevice between the rocks. I leapt down after him, shivering as I felt the cold water splash with my landing. I quickly pressed myself against the stone as I heard more Grimm arrive above us, the sound of my shots drawing them to us. I could hear their snorts and growls as they examined the dead body of their kin and their angry hisses as they tried to determine which way we had gone. Soon, they began to move around the alcove and I moved into the shade of the rock as they passed above us. I held my breath as one of the Grimm attempted to look down into our crevice, but the entrance was too narrow and the space dark enough that the creature failed to see us. The flowing water would have made our scent near impossible for them to notice and I looked down towards the men to see that Kisten had shifted back to human and was holding LeAlexende in his arms.

"So, it was you who touched me," the vampire sighed quietly, coughing up more blood as he tried to speak. Kisten hushed him, adjusting the Overseer in his arms as the vampire struggled to control his breathing. LeAlexende smiled, wiping away the lingering droplets from his lips. My thirst flared at the sight of his blood and I hummed painfully as I fought the desire to taste it. LeAlexende looked at me curiously and I turned away, refusing to look at him as I spoke.

"What are you doing here, Alex?" I pressed, keeping my voice soft as we squatted in the cold stream. I knew Kisten wanted to move, lest the Grimm summoned his father, but it was dangerous to try to shift while the Grimm still prowled above us. The only path out of the crevice was back up the way we entered and so we were forced to wait until the Grimm moved on. The smell of undead blood in the small space made my stomach growl more, but I did my best to ignore it as Alex spoke.

"I heard about Whistleblower," the Overseer wheezed, doing his best to keep his voice low as he answered me. "I... had to help."

"Idiot," Kisten finally reprimanded, adjusting the vampire in his arms, doing his best to keep the Overseer out of the chilly water. "We were doing this to keep you safe, not to have you run into his arms."

"You need more saving than me, Kisten," LeAlexende countered, and Kisten growled softly. "If I'm caught, I'll just be killed. You both have a fate worse than death if we fail to erase him."

"At least someone understands," Kisten muttered, shooting an accusatory glance at me and I glared at him in response. I opened my mouth to retaliate when a voice rang out above us.

"HOW COULD YOU LOSE HER!" We were all stunned into silence as Whistleblower arrived, his voice booming above us. I could hear the Grimm whimper as he approached the pack, the few with him rejoining the rest. "I gave you a simple order! Kill the Overseer if you found her and not only did you fail such a simple task, you've lost track of her! HOW?"

I gave Kisten a concerned look but he motioned me to remain silent, placing his hand over LeAlexende's mouth. I saw the red liquid drip from the shifter's palm and I knew he was feeding the vampire in order to help him heal. There was a chance Whistleblower could find us where his Grimm had failed, and we were in a worse position now than we had been on the train.

"FIND NISABA NOW!" The Hunter bellowed, and I watched as LeAlexende doubled over in pain from the use of his dead name. I worried for a moment that Whistleblower would sense us, but the angry Hunter merely stomped the ground. Whistleblower whistled angrily, instantly sending the pack fleeing into the trees as he remained. I heard him move toward the bodies I had killed and his growl sent another shiver through my body. There was no way he didn't recognize the shots from my gun and I heard as he threw the body back to the ground.

"Seems my son and his new *Hündin*[1] are responsible, but that doesn't excuse the uselessness of these fucking creatures. They managed to kill that other one so easily, why are they struggling with the weakest one?" He complained, smacking his hand against one of the rocks, causing the stone to shift and the ground to shake. More leaves cascaded down onto us in our hiding spot but the Hunter seemed too preoccupied with his anger to look. "I'll have to ask Mother to make the next pack slightly more intelligent. I thought less would be better after what Kisten did, but this is infuriating."

Whistleblower finally stomped off, whistling to call some of the pack back to his side as he rejoined them in their search. We remained in our space a moment longer, waiting until the woods above us were truly silent. Kisten peeked his head out first, looking around before climbing up, helping LeAlexende and me out of the hole.

"Well, that was close," the Overseer sighed, brushing the leaves and dirt from his clothing. He turned to look at me, a slight smile to his face. "I'm lucky you were able to feel me."

"Yeah, you were," I agreed, reflecting on how it had felt when my power touched him. I drifted into my own thoughts as Kisten interrogated the Overseer, trying to learn exactly why he was here. I knew my power could interact with the living to some extent, but the idea I could have any effect on the undead was baffling to me. Not only had I been able to feel LeAlexende as a dead body, I felt as if I could have raised him and my heart pounded as I considered what that could mean.

But how do you raise a dead body that's already alive? I wondered silently, watching the Overseer with interest as he answered Kisten's questions. Feeling my eyes on him, he turned to me again, smiling knowingly as he tapped his temple. Seeing his blood again made my thirst flare and I swiftly turned away, covering my mouth as I fought to control myself.

"For now, Kisten," the vampire finally spoke, interrupting the Alpha's next question. "All that matters is reuniting you two with Lucius. Luckily, I have a surprisingly good idea of where we are and where we need to go."

"You do?" I pressed, and the Overseer smiled, pointing in the direction we had come from.

"Yes. That river runs right next to Lucius's retreat, although we're quite a bit downstream," LeAlexende revealed, casting a soft look to Kisten. "I'm sure Kisten realized that too, but what he didn't know is Lucius is already there, waiting for you to get close enough for him to feel you. I went downstream, and he sent Aurel and Kisca upstream."

"Lucius knows you're here?" I gasped and LeAlexende's smile widened with mirth. "Are you trying to get yourself killed?"

"While I am indifferent about it, not particularly. Lucius was about as upset as Kisten here and I imagine he'll be even more upset once we find him," he shrugged and Kisten sighed heavily behind him. "But the fact is I'm here now, so I might as well make myself useful. After all, I'm the only one who can match Whistleblower's power if fought head on."

"Then let's get going." Kisten nodded, heading back towards the riverbed we had come from. I allowed the Overseer to walk in front of me before I followed behind, trying to maintain my awareness as we walked. We quickly made our way back to the river and Alex took a moment to wash the blood from his face. I sighed with relief as the scent faded, and we began heading upstream, Kisten forcing us to pause and hide whenever he suspected the presence of the Grimm.

As I walked, I couldn't help the provocative questions in my mind as I stared at LeAlexende's back. He seemed very unimpressed by my ability to feel him and instead had spoken about it as if he expected it from me. Whistleblower also seemed to know my power was more than what I had understood it to be and I began to wonder if Lucius knew anything as well. After all, the First were slightly below the Hunters when we all belonged to Mother's court, so I wouldn't have been surprised if all the higher ranked First knew the truth about me.

Because I certainly don't. I thought to myself, balling my hands into fists as we continued walking along the river. After walking for what felt like eternity and the sky growing dark above us, I saw a pair of bright pink eyes appear in the foliage ahead of us and the pixie's voice was soft as she exclaimed.

"Here!" Kisca quickly called out to her companions before running up to us, the air around her shimmering as she approached. Her relief was plain on her face as she reached us and she smiled softly as Lucius and Aurel quickly moved to join her.

"Kisten, Raiven..." Lucius' voice was full of relief as he embraced us both and we awkwardly hugged him back. It was obvious that Aurel was not happy to see us, and he kept his distance from us as the

Overseer embraced us. Lucius soon pulled back, giving an annoyed look to LeAlexende. "I told you to wait with me at the retreat. Coming out here—"

"Made more sense. By splitting up, we cover more ground and Kisca can't be sent on her own," LeAlexende smiled, earning himself another exasperated sigh from Kisten. "Besides, I found them and was able to lead them close enough for you to feel us. All is well."

"It isn't, but we can talk about that later," Lucius conceded, clearly still worried and annoyed about LeAlexende's behavior. Despite saying he wanted to live, Alex was being very callous with how he treated his life and our clear worry about him. "We need to get back to the retreat, the Grimm are still roaming these woods in full force. We can talk more there."

"Let's go," Kisten agreed and Kisca smiled, showering the six of us in her glamor. I could no longer see Kisten as it took effect, but I felt him reach for my hand. I was tempted to let him take it, but instead crossed my arms across my chest, denying him the chance. I heard Kisten sigh next to me and my heart sank as we walked in silence. I knew we needed to talk about our argument from earlier, but I had no intention of doing so without telling Lucius what was going on with my power. If the Alpha was unwilling to listen to reason, maybe the Overseer would.

We arrived at the lodge shortly after sunset and I couldn't help the wave of fatigue that washed over me. Using my power had seemed to exhaust me more than usual and I swayed on my feet as Kisca released the glamor. Kisten seemed to notice my fatigue, and the Alpha caught me as I started to fall.

"Raiven! Are you alright?"

"No," I grunted, pushing myself from his arms as I stood, sighing with the pain in my head. I turned over to look at Lucius, who was also watching me with concern. "My thirst has accelerated, my head is pounding and I feel like I'm going to pass out. Whatever this power is doing to me is beyond my understanding."

"Power..?" Lucius seemed confused at my words, but I noticed LeAlexende was deep in thought.

"Perhaps it would be best to let Raiven rest," Alex suggested, earning himself looks from both Lucius and Kisten. The Overseer shrugged, his eyes still locked on me as he continued. "She clearly is in no condition to discuss any sort of plan, and thanks to the glamor on this place, it's not as if Whistleblower can find us unless someone leads him here."

"That's... true," Lucius conceded, running his hand through his hair as he turned back to me. "It would be a poor idea to push ourselves to our limits, especially when I doubt you've had any decent rest in the past day."

"I haven't." I admitted, and the vampire nodded, making up his mind as he dropped his hand.

"Then let's get inside, so I can allow you to drink and rest. Once you wake up, we can discuss what we want to do moving forward," Lucius decided, climbing up the stairs that would take us inside. Aurel followed quickly after him, brushing his way past Kisten as the Alpha growled. LeAlexende motioned for me to go ahead of him and, barely glancing at Kisten, I headed into the retreat, eager to rest and recover.

17

When I finally woke up, it was still dark outside and I groaned as I sat up from the sheets. It was pitch black in the room I sat in and I gently touched my lips, the thought of blood no longer making me thirsty. Lucius had fed me after allowing me to finally change clothes, and I had passed out shortly after drinking his blood, my fatigue taking over me once my thirst was satiated.

"What the fuck..." I sighed aloud, dropping my hand back to the bed as I felt my holster on the sheets next to me. I usually went months in between feedings from Lucius, only typically needing to drink undead blood twice a year. But it had been barely two months since Lucius had last fed me, and the only reason I could give for the sudden desire was the use of my unknown power.

I lay back down as I considered the past few days, still feeling tired as I stared at the ceiling. Arkrian and Shannon's wedding already felt as if it was a lifetime ago and I couldn't help but worry about all the ones we had left behind in Decver and Ocean City. I knew they were safe, at least for now; after all, Whistleblower was out here with us. But I knew Kisten was right about how his father would react to not finding us and I frowned as I was once again torn on what the best course of action was.

"I won't figure it out up here," I sighed, standing up from the bed and slowly making my way downstairs. Kisca sat in the armchair, tightly wrapped in her blanket, and I noticed the fireplace was lit to drive out the frigid air. She had her feet drawn into the chair, and her usually bright pink eyes were dull and lackluster as she stared at the flames. Using her glamor so much had left her drained and even her blond hair was starting to look more like straw than hair. She felt my gaze as I stared at her and I coughed to cover up my embarrassment as her eyes drifted to me.

"I'm fine," she whispered, her voice surprising me as she spoke. It no longer was the soft and musical tone I was used to, but sounded much deeper and huskier. I watched her expression change at my confusion and then she chuckled softly. "Oh, I forgot you didn't know. I'm a bit too worn out right now to mask my voice."

"Ah no, it's fine. Just slightly surprising," I murmured, but the pixie shook her head, never looking away from the crackling flame.

"It's alright, sorry for surprising you," she smiled and hummed softly to herself, closing her eyes as she rested her head on her knees. "They are waiting in the dining room, if you want to go join them."

"I will. Don't strain yourself." I smiled, and the pixie nodded slightly as I walked past her. I approached the door she indicated and taking a deep breath, pushed it open. Lucius, LeAlexende and Kisten were all seated at the table, talking quietly while Aurel stood off to the side. As soon as I walked in, the conversation stopped and I couldn't help wondering what they had been talking about as I sat in one of the empty chairs.

"Sorry for the delay," I began, lounging as I put my feet on the table. I could feel my sister's presence as she rose, although it was still weak and I knew she was putting all she had into staying awake. "But I'm here now, so let's get started, I guess."

"As we should," Lucius agreed, sitting back in his chair as he glanced at Aurel. The lich shrugged but remained standing, and the

Overseer sighed. "But first, I would prefer if you would tell me more about what's going on with your power."

"To be honest, Lucius, I don't really know," I admitted, glancing at LeAlexende as he met my gaze. He was still smiling nonchalantly and I shrugged as I continued. "I always assumed I was born a necromancer and that's why Mother had an interest in me, but clearly what I can do is not necromancy anymore."

"Wait, you used your necromancy?" Lucius sounded genuinely surprised and I gave him a confused look until I remembered he wasn't at the wedding. It hadn't seemed important at the time to tell him exactly *how* we all escaped with our lives and therefore it wasn't surprising he didn't know.

"I used it at Arkrian's wedding to drive off the Grimm: that's why so many of us survived," I sighed, finally taking my feet off the table as I sat properly. I closed my eyes as I remembered the wedding, taking a deep breath. "Except I raised a whole horde of zombies, not just five."

"A horde..." Alex repeated thoughtfully and we all turned to look at him. Lucius gave Alex a worried look, but his fellow vampire merely shrugged, still smiling as he relaxed. "It's... interesting, to be sure."

LeAlexende wasn't even trying to hide that he knew more than he was saying and, from the look Lucius was giving him, it was clear my Overseer expected Alex to explain further. But the vampire remained silent, and Lucius sighed heavily as he turned back to me.

"Do you think you could do it again?"

"Maybe? Like you saw earlier, my body has been reacting strangely, making me extremely tired and causing my thirst to increase. I also seem to be able to touch the living with my power," I frowned, looking toward Kisten as he avoided my gaze. The Alpha was folded up in his chair and barely seemed interested in the conversation. I felt my annoyance growing, but I did my best to swallow it down. "I probably could, but I would need more time to understand it and exactly what I can do and know that I'm not accidentally going to turn everyone into a zombie."

"I agree," Lucius sighed, leaning in his chair as Kisten looked up sharply. I couldn't help my expression as the Overseer agreed with me, tapping his fingers on the table. "I know Mother always forbade you from using it in her court, and I suppose I always assumed you had already experimented with it after leaving. But if this is the first time it is truly awakening, it's too dangerous without understanding."

"We can only delay so long," Alex added and his fellow vampire nodded, still tapping the table as he closed his eyes. "Whistleblower knows we haven't left and eventually Raiven using her power will draw his attention."

"Could always give him Kisten," Aurel suggested and I immediately stood, my anger exploding through me as the lich spoke. "Would give her more time."

"*Fucking excuse me?*"

"Let him take Kisten. He's obsessed with finding him, right?" Aurel continued, looking at me calmly as I balled my fists in my rage, fighting to keep my power from spilling forth. "He still won't leave without killing LeAlexende or capturing you, but it would provide enough of a dis–"

"*No,*" I interrupted Lucius before the vampire could even speak, and I stomped my way around the table, glaring at the lich as he met my gaze. His eyes were cold and even, and it was clear he had no fear of me as I glared at him. "I've about had enough of you, Aurel."

"Raive–" Lucius started to stop us but the lich interrupted the Overseer.

"And *I've* had enough of this stupid game Kisten wants to play. I suggested it because it makes sense but I won't deny I like the idea of removing Kisten from being glued to your side," Aurel admitted, not even trying to hide his true intentions as he watched me calmly. "Maybe then you could see things clearly."

"I can see just *fucking fine*, Aurel," I hissed, my sister's anger joining mine as I lost the battle to withhold my power. I could see the reflection of my black eyes in Aurel's sea green as my power slithered through the room, touching all of the room's occupants. Only LeAlexende didn't flinch as my power wrapped around him, but I fought to keep it from doing anything to them. "And I *know* I'm fucking tired of your bullshit."

"He clearly has—"

"Shut, the *FUCK UP!*" I yelled, focusing all my power on the lich as it released the others, causing Lucius and Kisten to sigh with relief. Aurel stiffened even more as my power enveloped him and I could see dark tendrils appearing on his alabaster skin. I wasn't sure what would happen if I didn't withdraw it from his body, but I was starting to not care as I glared at the undead spellcaster. "You *will* leave me and Kisten alone, or I swear, I *will* kill you, Lucius be damned."

"Raiven, please," I flinched as I heard the pleading tone in LeAlexende's voice and I glanced over at him to see him watching me with concern. I hummed angrily as I released my power, Aurel gasping with relief as the dark marks left him. I still gave the lich a cold glare as he coughed, trying to recover what little breath he had.

"Kisten belongs to *me*. No one will take him away," I insisted, walking back to my chair as I sat down angrily. Aurel looked at me with surprise, as if after all this time, what I was saying was still unbelievable. I loudly put my feet back on the table, my eyes still locked with his. "No one will leave these mountains until Whistleblower is dead at my feet."

"Raiven, be reasonab—"

"No, Aurel," I hissed, turning away from him and I looked back to Lucius and Kisten. The Alpha was giving me a concerned look to match Lucius' but I merely met it with my annoyed expression. "If you have nothing useful to add, then you can fucking leave."

"Raiven," Lucius' voice was calm and smooth despite the look he gave me and I scoffed as I crossed my arms.

"Yes, Overseer?" My voice dripped with sarcasm as I spoke, and even I was slightly taken aback by my tone. Lucius raised his eyebrow in surprise as I cleared my throat, doing my best to swallow my anger. "I'm sorry, Lucius. I-"

"It's... fine." He interrupted me, a worried smile flashing across his face as he watched me. "There may be another way, even if you are unable to control your power."

"Try me."

"Kisten can call the Grimm to him," LeAlexende offered and I looked to Kisten with surprise, but the Alpha refused to meet my gaze. He was back to looking away from me as he sat next to Lucius and Alex cleared his throat to return my attention to him, his expression wistful. "It's actually what allowed him to save us the first time, and I'm fairly confident it'll work again, with all of us supporting him."

"We won't do it immediately, as he needs time to mentally prepare," Lucius added, clearly trying to assuage my worry. "But Whistleblower will be significantly weakened without the full force of the Grimm at his side and only Kisten has the ability and the knowledge to take them away from him."

"Will they still listen to Kisten?" I asked, and Kisten nodded, finally taking a glance at me. He quickly turned away, trying to hide his expression from me as I frowned. "I thought they preferred Whistleblower."

"He only ever has part of the pack at a time under his direct control, about forty or so. The full pack has more than a hundred members, that's why his numbers at the wedding seemed endless," Kisten revealed, his voice soft as he finally spoke. "When not actively by his side, the rest of the pack is usually nearby but basically on standby. I can still reach out to those Grimm, and they'll follow me instead of him, at least at first."

"At first?" I pressed and he nodded.

"I will still have to fight my father for complete control, which is where you and Lucius would come in," Kisten shot a dirty look to Aurel, who scowled in response. "Aurel is refusing to be cooperative and Kisca will have to mask LeAlexende, so Whistleblower can't find him."

"You and I can face Whistleblower together." Lucius continued, meeting my gaze evenly as he spoke. "While your natural power may be a mystery, I'm confident that between your control of the ground and my electricity, we can distract Whistleblower from focusing on Kisten."

I nodded at the vampire's words, seeing the value in the idea even as my heart pounded in my chest. "We'd force him to fight a battle on two fronts. One for mental control of the Grimm and a physical battle with Lucius and me."

"Exactly," Kisten nodded, but his expression was still sour. "But that still doesn't mean it'll be easy. The fact that Mater Vitae's blood flows through him does still make him a force to be reckoned with, physically and mentally."

"Still, our odds are better if he can't focus on one battle at a time and since we can't rely on Raiven to deal with the Grimm, it's the best alternative," Lucius interjected, tapping his hands on the table again. "You are always weaker the more you spread yourself out and more likely to make mistakes."

"I... don't like it, but it is a good idea," I agreed and I heard Aurel stomp behind me, throwing open the door and slamming it as he left the room. Lucius chanced a glance after the lich but returned his attention to me as I continued: "So what do we want to do? Give me a chance to learn my power or just depend on Kisten to fight a mental battle for the Grimm?"

"Regardless, the very real truth is we can't afford to give either of you the time you need or deserve," LeAlexende finally sighed, his smile fading. "Ideally, both of you would have days to prepare, but I honestly think we'd be lucky to put this off for more than one day before Whistleblower would start devastating the whole forest."

"True," Lucius agreed, closing his eyes for a moment before looking between Kisten and me. "I'll give you both tomorrow to prepare yourselves however you wish, and tomorrow night, we'll make our decision."

'I doubt one day will be enough time for us,' My sister whispered and I sighed, shrugging my shoulders slightly as I closed my eyes. I brought my hand to the wooden cross, rubbing it slightly as I hummed to myself.

'I agree, but they are right; we honestly can only barely afford one.'

'Still, both plans—'

"Is something the matter, Raiven?" I dropped my hand as Lucius spoke again, looking at me with concern as I opened my eyes. The Overseer was staring at my locket curiously and I sighed, considering that I would eventually need to tell him the truth about my sister.

"No, Overseer," I insisted, glancing over at Kisten as I considered what my sister had been about to say. The Alpha was still avoiding my gaze but I knew he felt it as he shifted uncomfortably in his chair. Frustrated, I stood, grabbing Kisten and dragging him outside the room. Kisca looked up as I continued past the fireplace, not stopping until we stood outside. The Alpha looked at me in confusion as I slammed the door to the lodge, turning to glare at him.

"Raiven, wha—"

"Why didn't you tell me you could still reach out to the Grimm?" I shouted, not even trying to keep my voice down. My voice echoed through the woods around us and Kisten looked around us worried.

"Raiven, please keep your voice down," he reached for me, but I backed away, not wanting him to touch me.

"Why didn't you tell me?" I repeated and Kisten frowned, looking away from me.

"Because I don't want to do it. I didn't want to present it as an option," he muttered and I felt as if my head would explode from my anger. I curled my hands into fists, resisting the urge to punch Kisten. "But you said you need to delay the fight so you can have time to control your powers. We can't afford the delay so this is the only other option we have."

"So, instead of risking innocent lives, I'm supposed to risk your life? Just let you throw yourself at Whistleblower, and you don't even know if you can win?" I spoke through gritted teeth and Kisten growled as well, turning to face me. "I'm getting a mighty heavy hint that you don't care about my feelings at all."

"I'm doing this for you!" Kisten insisted, stomping his foot as he towered over me. I looked up to him defiantly, stomping my foot as well. "This is the only way we have a chance against Whistleblower.

If I don't try to control the pack, then he'll kill all of them and you and I will be separated forever."

"And if you can't control the Grimm and your animals at the same time?" I countered and I saw Kisten falter. "You already barely have any control over them now because of me and you don't have murderous, bloodthirsty creatures trying to bend you to their will. What good is it if we all live and we lose you anyway?"

"So it's better to just let my father rampage and do whatever he wants for God knows how long while you have a little training session?" Kisten growled and I slammed my fist into the wall next to me, still fighting my desire to hit the shifter.

"Dammit Kisten, neither of us are ready to face him! This isn't just about me!" I argued, glancing back at my angry lover. "If I really wanted to delay Whistleblower, I would give myself to him. That would give you all more than enough time to be ready to face him while he gave me back to Mother and you-"

"Absolutely not!" Kisten insisted, finally reaching for me. I pulled away from him, still glaring at the Alpha. "He cannot have you."

"Oh so now you understand that trading is unacceptable! Glad to know we're finally on the same page!" I shouted, causing birds near us to take flight. The door behind us opened at my shout but I ignored the two Overseers as they stepped out. "And here I thought you were all about trading. Your mind to win, my pain for your pleasure. It seems to me that all that matters to you is what you think is right and damn everyone else!"

"Raiven, you know that's not–"

"Do I, Kisten?" I hissed, leaning up more into his face as he growled at me. "After all, you pushed me away for a whole *year* because it was the 'right way' to do things. You're willing to make me suffer with the Oath because you want to do things the 'right way' and now you want me to just agree to you doing something obviously dangerous because *you* believe it's the 'right way' to do things!

"Well sorry, *Alpha*, but I don't agree!" I slid Kisten's ring off my finger, clutching it in my hand as I raised it high in the air, ready to throw it into the darkness. Kisten's eyes widened in horror as he saw me consider tossing it, my fingers digging into my palm. My body shook as I considered what I was about to do, but I felt my sister push a concerned aura towards me, very clearly warning me. I forced myself to lower my hand, my arm shaking as I opened my fingers to look at the smooth band.

"What does this even mean?" I started, my voice soft and exhausted from my yelling. I closed my eyes, tears starting to pour down my cheeks as I shook my head. "Why ask me to be your mate at all if you are so willing to throw me and everything else away? You always say it's because you don't want to lose me, but then why is it always okay for me to lose you?"

I didn't wait for Kisten to answer, instead turning away from him. I pushed my way past the two Overseers, who allowed me to walk back inside the lodge. I stomped my way back to the bedroom I had awoken in, slamming the door behind me. I collapsed with my back against the door, sobs filling the empty room.

18

I leaned against the railing, sighing heavily in the afternoon sun. Both of the vampires were still asleep for the day and Kisca was also sleeping to recover her powers. Kisten and Aurel were awake, but Kisten was meditating, and I had no idea where Aurel had gotten off too. I had spent the morning practicing with my power, but the pounding in my skull soon forced me to stop and I closed my eyes as I hummed to myself.

Tonight. I thought to myself, gripping my locket tightly. My sister still remained cold and distant, although I knew she could talk to me thanks to practicing with my power. I assumed she was waiting until something important happened, so as to not waste the boost my power gave her. I cast my gaze out into the dense forest of trees and rocks and sighed again, pushing myself up.

"One last time," I promised, leaping off the railing onto the ground below. I only walked a little way from the cabin, squatting in the underbrush behind the building. I summoned my necromancy, the power bursting from me like a tidal wave as my headache also increased. It immediately began touching everything near me, even enveloping the two vampires in the cabin. I fought to pull it back, struggling to keep it from raising any zombies as I growled with frustration.

"No, dammit!" I cursed, finally managing to pull the power back and I breathed heavily as I knelt on the damp leaves. My thoughts flashed back to the wedding and I pounded my fist into the ground, causing a few creatures to scurry away at the sound. "What was different? Why can't I control it now?!"

"Something wrong?" I looked up to see LeAlexende behind me and I scrambled to my feet, surprised to see him up so quickly. The Overseer seemed slightly amused at my surprise and he did little to hide his chuckle. "I felt your power touch me again, although this time it felt a bit more frantic."

"How did you–" I started but he stopped me, raising his hand in defeat. LeAlexende opened his eyes to look at me softly, his smile just as gentle as it had been the day before when we found him.

"I don't actually die at sunrise, I just fall asleep," he admitted, chuckling softly. "Me and my sisters just learned to imitate Lucius and the others to avoid Mater Vitae finding out. We... are a bit different from the other ten."

"I... see," I took in the Overseer as he walked toward me and I couldn't help the mix of emotions as they swam in my chest. "Thank you, by the way."

"For?"

"You... you helped me," I whispered, grabbing my locket as a soft smile graced my face. When I looked back at the vampire, his smile had spread across his face as he realized what I was referring to. "I never would have had the head start I did without you."

"You needed to escape; not only for yourself, but also so I and my sisters could convince the others of it. They were always too frightened to try, and rightfully so, all things considered," LeAlexende spoke quietly, and my heart pounded with his soft expression. "But enough about the past; are you doing alright?"

"I... I'm having trouble controlling it," I admitted, kneeling back into the underbrush. The Overseer knelt beside me, waiting for me to continue as I played with my hair. I had long since taken out the braids, giving up on taming it as it now hung halfway down my back. "It either resists me and doesn't want to raise anything, or it rushes out, trying to turn every dead body it can into a zombie."

"Is it always like that?" The Overseer quizzed and I frowned, looking at the dense vegetation.

"No. When I summoned it at the wedding, it was easy to control. Difficult to pull up, but once I had, it was as natural as breathing," I admitted, brushing the leaves with my hands. "And it's come up on its own a few times, but I could control it."

"And what did those moments have in common?"

"In common?" I echoed, looking up to see the vampire's face. He was looking at the large looming rock in front of us, his expression pensive as he questioned me. He refused to meet my gaze, keeping his eyes on the stone as I pondered his question.

"I was... afraid?" I wondered aloud, and LeAlexende finally turned to look at me. "Every time I could control it, I was either angry or afraid. It's how I saved my sister's soul, and I was scared both at the wedding and on the train. Even..."

My voice faded as I thought how I had used my power to kill the Grimm and I frowned. I had been afraid, but I also wasn't the one who noticed them at all and my power instantly reacted to protect me. It technically still counted as me controlling it since I didn't try to stop it but at the same time, my power felt like it had a mind of its own.

"Last night with Aurel?" he offered and I scoffed.

"No, last night I was angry. I was angry at him for suggesting we use Kisten as a distraction," I rebutted, grabbing one of the plants tightly in my fist. "The power just flowed naturally with my anger."

"Well, are you angry or scared now?" LeAlexende offered, his purple eyes soft as he looked at me. I frowned as I met his gaze, seeing where his questioning was leading.

"No, but it does me no good if I can only control it when I'm angry or scared," I sighed, slamming my palm into the ground again. LeAlexende looked at me strangely but said nothing as I continued. "I mean, it may be okay for dealing with Whistleblower, but I'll never get the hang of it if I can't control it when I'm calm."

"Maybe you have to be scared or angry," the vampire offered and I once again gave him a confused look. He shrugged, returning his gaze to the rock in front of us. "You've never used it except to try to help yourself survive, and so the power has prepared itself for that. Regardless of your intentions, it only has that one goal in mind."

"Keeping me and those I care about alive?" I finished and LeAlexende nodded. We sat in silence as I mulled over his suggestion, my thoughts racing. It did make sense to a certain extent, but it didn't make it any less frustrating. "So, I have to be scared or angry to use it now, since that's all I've ever used it for."

"At least for now," the Overseer acquiesced, shifting his legs so he sat next to me. He tenderly touched one of the leaves, a soft smile coming back to his face. "It's easy to forget that our powers are merely extensions of ourselves and another way to interact with the world around us. With age comes control, but it still requires use and practice, just like any other part of our bodies. That's how Whistleblower almost killed me last time."

"What do you mean?" I queried and LeAlexende's smile faded slightly, although he kept his gaze on the plants.

"You know who I am now, Raiven, so let's not pretend otherwise. I am one of the First, but I am also one of the Siblings," he offered and I nodded, remembering the pain Whistleblower had caused him when using his dead name. I felt a shiver run up my spine as LeAlexende continued: "Despite having my power for centuries, I stopped using it once I left Mater Vitae."

"Stopped?"

"Yes. I... hated what she had used me for, what she had used my sisters for." Anger slightly seeped into LeAlexende's voice and my heart twisted with his words. We sat in silence as he seemed to be lost in his memories for a moment and I jumped slightly as he spoke again.

"That night forced me to realize that it didn't matter how powerful I was on paper: I was weak if I couldn't control it. Fear and a desire to leave my old life behind had caused me to ignore a vital part of myself," the Overseer finally finished, raising his eyes to meet my gaze. His expression was full of many emotions and I felt the ache in my chest increase. "If I had not allowed my power to just sit unused, I might have been able to kill Whistleblower then. I was definitely stronger than him, but I didn't have the control necessary to win. It took all we had just to wound him and escape."

"And now?"

"Well, the advantage is gone now. This new pack is nothing like the old one," LeAlexende admitted, pulling his knees to his chest. "I can maybe help turn the tide if needed, but I no longer hold much of an advantage over Whistleblower."

"Alex..." I let my voice trail off and the Overseer turned to look at me, his expression quizzical. I took a deep breath, forcing myself to look him in the eye. "Why are you really here?"

"I told you—"

"No, really. I know Basina is dead and you're the last Sibling." I stated and LeAlexende's eyes widened in surprise but quickly changed to a knowing smile. He looked away from me again, sighing heavily.

"Then you were watching us that night," he mused and I nodded, watching him intently as I waited for his answer. The Overseer chuckled at my admission, but he hardly seemed surprised. "So you also know I'm weak because I shared my memories with Lucius."

"The Grimm would have never cornered you otherwise," I added and he chuckled again. The vampire didn't even try to argue with me, stretching out in the underbrush. "You seemed stronger at the hospital than you did facing the Grimm."

"I was stronger. Using the old method weakened me more than I realized it would. I knew there was a reason we all avoided it, but I never truly knew the extent of the exchange. Lucius was always strong, considering he was Fourth, but now he probably has enough power to rival me at my prime. He lacks control however, and I doubt he has practiced with my power as much as he should." LeAlexende finally stood, brushing the leaves and dirt from his clothing. I stood with him, waiting for him to answer my question. He turned his purple eyes to me, filled with determination and resolve.

"I am here to make sure none of you die." He announced and I gave him a surprised look. "Like I said yesterday, if I die, I get to see my sisters again. However, you and Lucius *must* live no matter what, and I would hate to see Kisten become a prisoner to that man again."

"But Alex—"

"My Retainer has already taken my place as Overseer. I am no longer in charge of Southern Grove," the vampire smiled wistfully and my shoulders dropped as I clenched my hands. If he had already relinquished his place as Overseer of Southern Grove, then LeAlexende already knew he stood no chance in a fight against Whistleblower. Yet here he was, ready to help in any way he could. "I have accepted whatever may happen here. But I shared my essence with Lucius, and I cannot allow that to die."

"Are the memories you shared that important?" I whispered, looking toward the rock he had been staring at. LeAlexende followed my gaze and nodded, his tone still determined.

"They are, perhaps, more important than anything else in this world," the vampire pulled me into a hug and I returned the gesture, gripping him tightly. Despite not knowing him as well as I would have liked to, LeAlexende had already made quite the impression on me and I felt a pit form in my chest at the thought of losing him. The vampire must have felt my sorrow because he chuckled softly before kissing my hair. "I'm sorry, Raiven, that we didn't get to know each other better."

"It's enough," I answered, pressing my face into his chest and I could feel his happiness as he released me from his hug. His smile was soft, and he gripped my shoulders tightly. I felt my sister rise at his touch and she seemed just as upset as me at his decision.

'*What is it?*' I queried and I could feel her uncertainty as she took her time answering.

'*I... don't know,*' she admitted and I frowned slightly as LeAlexende released me, watching me with a curious expression. My eyes lingered on his face as her sense of loss filled me, and I gripped the necklace tightly. *'I just don't want him... to die.'*

'Me neither.'

'No, I feel...' she paused, clearly confused by the feelings LeAlexende had caused to rise in both of us. *'This is... strange.'*

"Indeed," I breathed, looking up into the cloudless sky. LeAlexende followed my gaze and chuckled, looking up to the loft where Kisten sat meditating.

"Have you spoken to him yet?" the Overseer offered, and I looked back at the ground, not wanting to answer his question. I heard LeAlexende sigh and I glanced up to see him shaking his head. "You should really talk to him before tonight."

"Why?" I spat, surprised by the anger still in my tone. "It's not like he'll listen to me anyway."

"Has Kisten told you his story? About his mother and Hanne?" I looked at LeAlexende confused and he sighed deeply, clearly frustrated with both of us. "Kisten had given up on having anyone in his life after watching those two die at the hands of his father. His suffocating concern for you makes sense considering what he's seen. He doesn't want to risk losing you now that he's finally decided he wants you, hence his reluctance to delay. He blames himself for being too afraid to face his father in the past."

"But what's the point of rushing in if we just lose? Why not wait until we know we can win?" I insisted and the vampire sighed, running his hand through his snow-white hair.

"I know, and I understand your side as well. In the past you have always fled from the Hunters, not willing to risk your life in a battle you knew you would lose. Not that I am judging you for it, I have done the same thing but it's a difference of perspective," LeAlexende continued and I felt my anger start to lessen with his words. "He has lost from being too cautious, and you prefer to only fight battles you can win."

"I'm not asking him to just give up and run away with me," I muttered, turning my gaze to the ground as I held myself. LeAlexende hummed in agreement, waiting for me to continue as I looked up to the treetops again. "I just want to make sure that we'll *both* come out of this. We're too close to being together to lose now."

"He wants the same thing and he's trying to make that happen, in the only way he thinks he can," LeAlexende offered, and I looked back down to see his purple gaze. The Overseer's eyes were soft and he motioned toward the loft again. "That's why you need to talk to him before tonight. You two can't let Whistleblower tear you apart like this. I've said it before: you both deserve a little happiness in your lives."

"Fine," I conceded and the vampire smiled, reaching out for my hand. I allowed him to take it as I followed him back to the cabin, my mind racing with what I would say.

19

I stood at the door to the loft, my hand resting against the wood. LeAlexende had walked away after guiding me to the stairs, excusing himself to somewhere quiet as he waited for Lucius to wake up for the day. I shifted on the stairs, my heart pounding in my chest as I hesitated. Alex had told me more about Kisten's past as he escorted me to the loft and I made sure to wipe away the tear trails his words had brought to my face.

"Now or never," I muttered, gripping the ring where I had placed it back on my hand. It felt heavy as lead as I twisted it on my finger and I forced myself to push open the loft door. I quietly made my way into the room, careful to drop the door gently as I entered. The space was dusty and dirty, filled to the brim with boxes and other junk. Part of me wondered what Lucius could possibly be storing here as I carefully stepped around them, looking for Kisten.

"Kis..." I let my voice drift as I found him sitting on a low table, facing the little window that looked outside. I took a moment just to take him in, unable to help the soft smile that started on my face. He was sitting in a meditation pose and although I couldn't see his face, I imagined his eyes were closed, showing that powerful control

Hanne had taught him. His breathing was steady and methodical and I started to step away, not wanting to disturb him.

"What is it, Raiven?" I was forced to stop as Kisten called out to me, and I turned to see that he hadn't moved from his position, still facing the window away from me. I cleared my throat, fully turning back around to face him.

"I... wanted to talk," I admitted, casting my gaze to the stack of boxes next to me. I gave them a gentle push and the cardboard rocked for a moment before settling back down. "If you don't have time, it's okay. We can talk la–"

"Now is fine," Kisten called, still not turning to face me. I moved closer to him, clutching the ring around my finger. "Talk."

"I was hoping to talk with you, not at you," I fought to keep my anger under control, taking a deep breath as I stood next to the table. I was tempted to reach out to the Alpha but forced myself to keep my hands in front of me. Kisten growled with annoyance, but he slowly shifted on the table, turning to look at me. His eyes were swimming with different colors again, and I laced my fingers together to fight the desire to touch him. "I wanted to talk about tonight."

"What about it?"

"I... accept that it's a good plan, Kisten. Honestly, I don't think there's really any way around it; one of us is just going to have to take a risk to defeat Whistleblower and you dealing with the pack puts less lives at risk than if I can't control my power," I began, closing my eyes as I forced myself to take deep breaths. "But I can't help but worry about you. I... just don't want to lose you, not like I lost Mikael. I don't want to watch you lose everything I love about you."

"And I don't want to lose you the way I lost my mother," Kisten retorted and I took another deep breath, squeezing my fingers together tighter.

"What about Hanne?" I offered and Kisten's eyes widened, looking at me with shock.

"How do you know that name?" he demanded and I refused to answer, looking away from him. I heard Kisten scoff and looked back to see him sitting on the edge of the low table. "Never mind, I know who told you."

"Kisten, look, I just want you to be open with me," I admitted, forcing myself to look into his eyes. He met my gaze evenly, his annoyance still on his face. I did my best to remain calm, not wanting my anger to take me over again. "I've always thought that me becoming your mate was too dangerous for you, I didn't want the Hunters to come after you and Lucius too. But for the first time, I decided it's not enough just to stay alive and keep losing everything I cared about."

"Raiven–"

"I knew the Hunters were coming. I didn't know it would be Whistleblower or that you would have a connection to him, but I did know months ago that *someone* would be coming," I breathed, glancing away from his gaze. The dream I had in the forest passed through my mind and I took a deep breath as I continued. "Trust me, I really wanted to run, to leave before they could find me, but I'm still here now for the same reason I stayed this whole time: I don't want to lose you. I'm *trying* to do the right thing, and still be reasonable, despite my fear."

"And?" he demanded and I forced myself to meet his gaze again. The colors danced in his eyes and I watched as dark black fur sprouted on his arms before receding again.

"And it means I won't stand by while you throw yourself away," I spoke defiantly, and I watched as surprise flitted across his face before disappearing. "I know you blame yourself for being too afraid to act against your father in the past, but I can't, won't support you just rushing in."

"You just said it was the best plan," he retorted and I nodded in agreement. Kisten gave me a confused look and he finally stood from the table.

"It is the best plan," I confirmed, looking up to him as he stood over me. Every fiber of my being wanted to embrace him, but I forced myself to resist. "But it doesn't mean I support it as is. You have no idea what will happen once you let the Grimm in and you have no plan if you lose to your father. That I cannot and will not agree with."

"But I have to try, regardless. You and Lucius won't stand a chance if I don't. I can't let my fear stop me anymore." Kisten insisted and I finally lost my composure, releasing my ring.

"No!" I protested, gripping the shirt Lucius had given him. Kisten placed his hands on my back as if to push me away but I shook my head, fully wrapping my arms around him. I buried my face into his chest, doing my best to fight back tears. "There has to be a safer way for us to do this."

"There isn't, Raiven. We don't have time for you to fully experiment with your powers, and while it has been a while, I *do* remember how to control the pack," Kisten asserted, lifting my chin to look into my eyes. His irises swirled with the many colors and I spent a moment watching the shades shift and move as he studied my gaze. "Blood for Blood. Whistleblower needs to pay for the lives he has taken. My mother and my sisters. Your sister. Mark."

"What about me? You?" I squeezed him tightly, my anger from earlier starting to return. "You keep saying you can't lose me. I can't lose you either Kisten."

"I know, Raiven. I–"

"No Kisten," I insisted, stepping back from him and Kisten released me. My eyes were heavy with tears as I gripped my left hand, the ring feeling heavy on my finger once again. "I have wanted you from the moment I met you, I've loved you since you pushed me away. I refuse to agree to losing you now."

"Raiven, I–"

"All this talk about you can't lose me to the Oath, how you don't want your father to claim anymore lives, and I'm just supposed to say sure, go ahead, allow the Grimm to claim your mind. Your life for mine," I groaned, closing my eyes as tears flowed down my cheeks. "You don't know what will happen once you let the Grimm in, especially with how riled up your animals are. Even if we manage to win, killing Whistleblower means *nothing* to me if the cost is you."

"If we don't try something, then he's going to take you back to

Mater Vitae," Kisten insisted, and I looked up to see tears rolling down his cheeks as well. His eyes were pleading with me as he spoke, and he hiccupped with his tears. "If I don't stop him now, I'm going to have to watch him take you away from me. I can't Raiven, I won't. I need you. I love you."

"I love *you*, you idiot! That's why I don't want to rush this, why I don't want to lose you either! Does my love not matter?" I begged, my tears pouring down my face as I sobbed. I gripped my top tightly, my hand over my aching heart. "What good is stopping him if I have to watch you become him?"

Kisten said nothing to this, instead closing the distance between us and wrapping his arms around me again. I tried to pull away from him but he tightened his grip, dropping us both to our knees. I wailed into his shoulder and Kisten cried with me, dropping his head down to mine. I gripped his shirt tighter, unable to help my outpour of emotions as we cried together on the floor of the loft.

"Your love matters. Your love is why I'm here," Kisten finally breathed through his tears, releasing a choked sound as he spoke. "It's why I'm making you my mate. You never gave up on us, even when I did. Even when I was too afraid to act, you never stopped pushing me."

"I love you too much," I sobbed, attempting a chuckle but failing. "I can't just give up on you."

"Then don't," he whispered, raising his head from my shoulder as he lifted my chin to meet his gaze. His tears still flowed as he looked at me, but his gaze was determined. "If I... if I lose myself, pull me back. Make me come back to you, just like you always have."

I shook my head as I looked deep into his eyes, still unable to help my uncertainty. I wanted nothing more than to keep arguing with him, but I understood we would get nowhere if we kept going back and forth. As Alex had said, it was a matter of perspective, so instead, I grabbed his face in my hands and I kissed him deeply. It wasn't until I felt his tongue slide past mine that I realized there was no pain accompanying the kiss and I forced myself back, gasping for air.

"Kisten," I panted, touching his skin more and I was still met with a lack of pain, unable to help my surprise. "Kisten, it doesn't hurt."

Kisten's expression matched mine for a moment and then a slight smile grew on his face. He chuckled softly as he closed his eyes, his smile only growing wider.

"Lucius was supposed to release me from the Oath after you accepted my proposal, but we decided to keep it in case something happened while we were fighting Whistleblower. I guess he just forced Evalyn to release her part," he revealed, pressing his face into my neck, assaulting the skin there with his teeth and tongue. I released a shaky breath as he marked me, unable to help as my breathing accelerated with his actions. Kisten purred at my reaction, pulling away from my skin. "I'm sorry I didn't tell you or ask you first. Are... are you upset?"

"Actually, I am," I admitted, a frown on my face as I stroked his cheeks. "Can you at least promise to stop hiding things and make decisions *with* me, instead of without me?"

"I'm used to hiding everything about myself, Raiven. What I am, what I'm thinking, how I feel," Kisten sighed, burying his face into my neck again. "I've been afraid and alone for so long, I... no, that's just an excuse."

Kisten pressed a gentle kiss into my neck as he sighed, clearly doing his best to find the words to answer me. "This is why I need you. You force me to be better, to be willing to risk everything instead of hiding. I need to do better, to let you in despite my fear."

"And I want to work with you, not against you and for that, you have to be honest with me," I conceded and ran my fingers through his dark hair as he purred into my skin. "I'm used to being on my own too, but I want to stay by your side, no matter what."

"So do I," Kisten whispered, and I hummed softly as he began to kiss me again. The gesture felt wonderful but I couldn't help my slight disappointment at the lack of pain. I felt as Kisten's smile changed, him giving me a dark look as he leaned up to whisper in my ear.

"I can still make it hurt, if that's what you want," he slid his hands under my shirt and I shivered as I realized he had shifted them into claws, dragging the sharp points along my back. Kisten chuckled again as I moaned, my arousal growing as he lightly scratched at me. He moved to push me back onto the dusty floor and I let him, wrapping my arms around his neck. He moved one of his claws to my front, gripping my breast tightly. "Want to do it now?"

"Here?" I asked, looking around at the dirty, dusty loft. Kisten chuckled, burying his face in my chest to hide his laughter.

"Raiven, I almost made love to you in a cave and now you have an issue with a dirty loft?" he teased and I smiled, lifting his face to mine as I sat up.

"*Make me yours.*"

20

Kisten kissed me again, and this time I openly moaned at this painless embrace. It had been so long since I had last been able to touch my love without the Oath punishing me, and, from this moment on, I could finally touch him as much as I wanted.

"You seem in a daze," his voice snapped my mind back to the present and I took him in, my eyes searching for a reason to believe this wasn't real. I ran my fingers through his hair, careful to be gentle and he closed his eyes for a moment, sighing with contentment. "Change your mind?"

"I... I honestly don't know if this is really happening or if I'm dreaming," I admitted, turning my face away from him. I kept my gaze on a nearby stack of boxes, my thoughts racing. "It seems too much like what we want for it to be real, all things considered."

Kisten said nothing for a moment, and then I found myself pressed into the dirty boards. One of his knees was in between my legs, spreading them slightly. I heard him chuckle above me, and then the lips that were kissing me earlier were now on my neck, assaulting the skin there. I couldn't help myself as a moan escaped my lips and the Alpha drew back at the sound, turning my face so that our eyes met.

"Do you want this, Raiven?" He stole another kiss from my lips and skin and I cradled his head against me, wanting to feel him as much as I could.

"You know that I do."

"Tell me again," he whispered, causing my cheeks to flush and not for the first time, I was thankful for my dark skin. Despite the many times Kisten had loved me, something felt special, different about this time. This was the first time Kisten would embrace me without the threat of the Oath lingering over us and I felt a nervousness I couldn't explain. I murmured my answer under my breath and the Alpha laughed at my embarrassment.

"Sorry, I couldn't hear that," his knee moved between my legs, pressing up against me. I was so aroused it almost hurt, and my eyes fluttered at the slight pressure. Kisten smirked again, repeating the action. "Do you want me, Raiven?"

"Yes," I moaned, my physical wants and desires pushing away my emotional embarrassment. "Yes, please, I want you."

Another kiss, and I parted my lips to let him in, desperate to taste my amazing partner. His sandpaper tongue slid past the moist barrier and found mine, Kisten purring into the kiss. As if lost, I sat up slightly as I draped an arm around Kisten's neck, pulling him down a bit and I parted my lips more, darting out my tongue to meet his. Kisten's mouth was so warm and inviting and soon I was lost in kissing him. I used the shifter to support me as I moved my other hand to work on unbuttoning my top, eager to progress toward what I craved.

Kisten shifted his weight back, and soon I found myself sitting in his lap. I could feel his hardness rubbing against me through my pants and my efforts to remove my shirt quickened. Soon the last button was undone and the top hung open, but I quickly shrugged the clothing off and returned my hands to caress my Alpha's skin. Kisten broke the kiss, leaning back slightly to slide one of his hands between us to grip my chest.

"Beautiful," he murmured more to himself than me, and I smiled, loving his expression as he dragged his claw across my skin. I leaned my head back as I sighed with pleasure and my voice was shaky as I spoke.

"Do you want to play with them?" I moved his hand over my breasts and I dragged his sharp claw across my erect nipples. I gasped slightly at the pain, the pleasure it caused both surprising and intense. "Please, play with them."

Kisten shifted me so I sat a little higher in his lap, and he began to play with my chest, molding and scratching me with his claws. I closed my eyes, concentrating on the feel of his hands when I unexpectedly felt something warm and rough across my nipples. I opened my eyes to see him pulling back slightly before leaning forward again, this time taking the left one into his mouth.

My left hand found its way to the shifter's head and I had to stifle a small moan as he sucked on my sensitive flesh and harassed it with his tongue. Kisten's other hand adjusted to match the rhythm of his mouth, and I felt such a delicious clench in my midsection from the joined sensations. I moaned through my closed lips, my eyes closed and my mind started to swim with pleasure. It was so different to experience this soft pain that Kisten was giving me, rather than the intense fire with which the Oath used to punish me. I knew there would be times when I would desire that level of pain again, but for now, I felt as if I was in heaven, able to just focus on Kisten.

My eyes fluttered open as he pulled off my breasts and I was more than slightly disappointed as I glanced down. Kisten's colorful eyes glanced up to meet mine and he smiled before switching to my right nipple and sucking hard. A sharp intake of breath stole the air from my lungs and his left hand wasted no time in replacing his mouth on its twin.

"Kisten," I finally spoke softly, my voice more of a moan than anything else, and he pulled back to meet my half-closed eyes.

"Yes?"

"Here," I loosened the clasp on my pants and I slid his clawed hand inside, letting him feel how much I enjoyed what he was doing and how much I wanted him. Without much else, Kisten pushed me back and I peeled the clothing off myself. I reached for my underwear and stopped, my embarrassment finding me again but Kisten smiled as he reached down and removed it for me. I looked away from him, my face flushing again as I imagined him looking at me, as the Alpha often loved to do. Kisten loved to indulge in both the sight and scent of me and I often found his attention both gratifying and embarrassing.

Then I felt his finger sliding in between my lips, running along my slick opening and teasing my sweet spot. I felt his weight shift and I could almost feel his face near mine as his breath danced against my cheek. I wanted to open my eyes, but embarrassment kept them closed as I let a sound escape my lips.

"Touch you like this?" He teased my opening, running his claw along the crease, but not pushing in. I shook my head, finally opening my eyes to meet his as I moaned. Kisten's smile was pure bliss as he watched me and I couldn't help matching his expression as I reached to cradle his face.

"No? Like this, then?" He pushed in slightly, and I moaned, loving his smile as he pushed his finger in farther. He curled his finger inside me, his claw lightly scratching my walls and I bit my lip, not wanting to let him know just how I enjoyed what he was doing. The pleasure must have been visible on my face however, because he kissed me before doing it again, and my breath quickened. I kissed him deeply as that lone finger moved inside me, until I almost wished he'd slide in another to join it.

"Raiven," I opened my eyes on hearing my name, and once again met his colorful eyes, filled with his own desire and need. He didn't say anything else, and I took a moment to just look at him, my body shivering on the cold floor. I stroked his cheeks gently with my thumbs and he closed his eyes, leaning into my hand. Pushing against his wrist, I slid his finger out of me, my body aching to have him inside me. I pushed lightly on his shoulder and Kisten laid on his back, looking at me questioningly.

"Take these off," I ordered, motioning to his pants and he sat up to comply, shifting his hand back to human. After the offending clothing was removed, I took a moment to slide my hand under his shirt, enjoying the feel of Kisten's muscles as I laid my face next to his manhood.

"So warm," I murmured, lightly stroking him with my hand. I almost glanced up to see his face, but decided against it as I darted my tongue out to taste him. I took the moistened end into my mouth and sucked lightly as I played with him. I took my time tasting him before pulling back, licking farther down, and making him slicker. I glanced up to Kisten's face to find him watching me, his eyes full of his desire for me and I could see his leopard spots starting to appear on his skin.

Done with my licking, I placed my hand around his base and took him in until my lips reached my fingers. Once there, I began sucking and rolling his member in my warm mouth, making sure to use my tongue to inflict more pleasure. I felt his hand find its way to my hair and at this I pulled back, sliding my body up his.

"We can't have you finish in my mouth, now can we?" I began to stroke him with the hand I left around his base as I stole another kiss from his luscious lips.. "Are you ready to embrace me, to feel me after so long?"

"Are you?" He answered, his eyes looking at me lovingly. I nodded, releasing his throbbing member and I sat back from him as he removed his shirt. I took a moment to take in the view of my lover, sitting naked on the dusty wooden floor, leopard spots visible on his tan skin. Despite the clutter around us, Kisten was still majestic as he watched me and I climbed into his lap, resting my slit against him. The Alpha rested his hands on my waist as he lay down on the dirty boards, his hair resting around him like a halo.

"You never answered me," I said with a smile, leaning over him. "Are you ready to love me?"

"Always, *mein Liebling*[1]," Kisten's voice was soft and tender, his hand moving from my waist to my face. Adjusting myself over him, I slowly slid down and he raised his hips to meet me. After a few thrusts, he was all the way inside me, stretching me deliciously. I paused, closing my eyes to focus on the feel of him inside me. Here it was, the feeling I had craved, the sensation I desired: finally, I could enjoy every inch of him.

"I love you, Raiven. My mate, my Beta," Kisten breathed and I smiled, placing my hands on his chest. The shifter shuddered underneath me, his expression almost pained as he smiled, clearly overtaken with his emotions. I knew my expression matched his own, closing my eyes as I released a shaky breath.

"I love you too, my Alpha," I began rocking my hips back and forth, loving the feel as he moved inside me. I closed my eyes, not wanting to see his face and wanting to concentrate on finding the right angle for better pleasure. His hand found its way back to my hips and he used them to help me move, although Kisten seemed content to let me control things.

I sat up slightly to get a better angle, sliding him almost all the way out. I suppose he thought I was going to slide off, because he pushed me back down using his hands and I had to stifle a moan. Wanting more of that feeling I began to move faster over him, still pushing him as far as I could and reveling in the pleasure. His hands picked up on my pace and soon he was moving up to meet me, and I could no longer hold back my sounds. It felt so wonderful, and I leaned forward to feverishly kiss him. I began to squeeze myself around him as we moved and his breath caught in his throat. Pleased with his reaction, I did it again and he began to move more frantically, stroking for the release he craved.

"Do you like it?" I asked, my voice airy and moaning as he pounded himself into me. "Does it feel good?"

"Yes, Raiven," his voice came out strained, his hands still helping my hips as I met his every thrust, our bodies making a wet slap with every meeting. He began to pound himself into me as fast and hard as he could, and I forced myself to match his pace, my voice alternating between moans and pants. "Yes, you feel amazing."

Feeling my own orgasm approach, I bent my arms until my breasts brushed across his skin, still moving my hips to keep the rhythm. My hands found their way to his shoulders just as it hit me, the pleasure spreading up and out of where our bodies met and I moaned louder, digging my hands into his skin. Feeling my orgasm and my body tightening around him, he thrust into me one last time and I felt it as he erupted inside me.

As our respective orgasms faded, I fully collapsed onto the shifter, both of us panting heavily. I removed my hands from his shoulders and slid my legs down until I was resting on top of him, his member still throbbing inside me.

"Did you enjoy that?" He panted and I chuckled, my face resting against his chest.

"Very much so," I closed my eyes as he wrapped his arms around me, hugging me tightly.

"Will you accept me?" Kisten purred, his fangs peeking through his lips as he lifted my head up, waiting for my answer. Every fiber of my being wanted to say yes, but I instead closed my eyes, focusing on the feel of his member inside me. He growled at my lack of a response, his restraint fading. "I love you. I've always loved you. Do you accept me, Raiven?"

"I love you Kisten," I finally breathed, opening my eyes to meet his again. I dragged my hands from his cheek to his neck and he closed his eyes, purring happily with my touch. "I want you, no matter what."

"Do you accept me?" He repeated and I looked at him strangely, sliding my hands down to his chest as I sat up. He opened his eyes to meet my gaze and I saw a mix of emotions dancing across his face. Longing, love...and fear. He knew our plan was risky, and he knew it could cost him everything he had fought so hard for. This encounter with his father showed the cracks in our relationship and he needed to know that I still would want him, no matter what happened.

I pushed myself off Kisten and he let me, watching as I sat next to him on the floor. I looked at the band on my hand, twisting it on my finger as my thoughts raced. My chest still ached as I thought about the plan and every fiber of my being still insisted there had to be another way. But Kisten had said it best; we simply lacked the time to find an alternative, and the only hope he had of coming back was his love for me.

So fight with him, not against him. I thought to myself, my hands curling into fists against the boards. *If this power, whatever it is, will only listen to me when I'm afraid or angry, then use it. It's not as if Whistleblower doesn't make me both. We **can** win, I know we can.*

"Together," I turned to look at Kisten, my eyes burning with a fire I didn't know I had. Kisten smiled as he saw the look in my eyes change and he reached forward, grabbing my left hand. I laced my fingers with his, my heart pounding in my chest as I spoke. "We'll do this together. I won't let you fight alone."

"Nor I you," Kisten agreed as he leaned over to kiss my forehead, standing me up from the dusty floor before pulling me into a tight embrace. I gripped him tightly, loving the feel of my skin pressed into his. We stood there for what felt like an eternity, both of us scared and determined. We had no idea how the battle would go, but we also knew we had no choice, and as frightening as it was, we had to depend on each other if we were going to stand any chance of winning.

"Let's head downstairs," I gently pulled back, reaching for my clothing and dressing as Kisten did the same. As we returned downstairs to rejoin the vampires and Kisca, I was renewed with my fresh determination.

21

Kisca was the only one inside as Kisten and I stepped into the living space and she was looking much better as she still sat in one of the armchairs, curled up in her blanket. The pixie smiled as we reached the bottom steps, her voice back to being light and musical as she spoke.

"Alex and Lucius are still upstairs," she smiled softly and I returned her gesture as the pixie adjusted in her warmth, snuggling more into the chair. "They should be down soon."

"Do you know where Aurel is?" Kisten asked cautiously and I watched as Kisca's smile faded, and she sighed as she looked back to the empty fireplace.

"He's upstairs too, although I'm not sure what he's doing," the pixie admitted, sighing softly as she snuggled into her blanket more. Kisten released me as he moved to the kitchen to begin preparing food, and I sat in the armchair opposite of Kisca. The pixie glanced over to me as I folded myself into the chair, looking at the empty fireplace as well. "You two seem better."

"We are," I confirmed, leaning my head on my knees as I looked at the pixie. Her pink eyes were glowing and I noticed the pink bracelet around her wrist. "Does that maintain your glamor?"

"What, this?" she hummed, lifting the jewelry for me to see better. I noticed it was a resin bracelet filled with little flower petals, and watched as she carefully removed it. I saw her body shimmer slightly, but frowned as I failed to notice anything different about her. The pixie chuckled at my confusion, sliding the bracelet back on her wrist. "It doesn't maintain anything important, but I do enjoy wearing it sometimes."

"Ah," I nodded, still not understanding what had changed when she removed the bracelet as Kisca laughed at my confusion.

"You remind me of my parents. My father was a pixie, my mother a fairy," she giggled, looking back to the dark fireplace. I followed her gaze as I hummed, waiting for her to continue with her story. "They used to have a betting jar, trying to determine which I would be."

"Was your mother upset?"

"Oh, far from it! She was excited to have a pixie daughter," Kisca laughed, the memories bringing a bright smile to her face. This was the most I had ever heard the pixie talk, and I couldn't help but smile at her infectious laughter. "I used to practice my glamor on her all the time, and she's the one who taught me about enchanting objects with a glamor."

"What about your father?" I asked, and watched as her smile twitched slightly.

"Ah, he... he didn't take having a daughter so well," she sighed and my heart ached slightly as she adjusted her position under the blanket. "He's kinda accepted it now, but you know. It's hard for both of us."

"Yeah..." I let my voice trail, trying to think of a way to change the subject. "How do you feel about being Fifth?"

"Hm? Oh! I feel honored," Kisca chuckled, giving me a bashful smile before glancing back at Kisten. Whatever he was cooking was starting to smell up the lodge, and my stomach growled at the thought of eating actual food for the first time in two days. "I never thought Lucius would regard my glamor so highly."

"Considering what I've seen of it, he's right," I turned back to look at the pixie and she was beaming with my praise. "It took three days before you even started to show signs of exhaustion. Most would have turned into a shade trying to replicate that."

"It's nice to feel useful," Kisca hummed, her bright eyes shining as she met my gaze. "I know pixies and fairies aren't regarded very highly because glamors are often considered weak and I was honored to make the Coven at all. I was surprised when Lucius asked me if I wanted your former spot.

"I'm not much good in a fight, but if my power can keep others safe, then I want to do all I can," her voice trailed off as she shifted her gaze to the floor and my heart swelled with worry for her and LeAlexende again. They would be the most helpless during all the fighting and while I had no doubt that Kisca could keep them hidden, if anything went wrong...

I was snapped from my thoughts as I heard the doors upstairs open and the undead members of our little group came downstairs to join us. Aurel trailed behind the two Overseers, a sour expression still on his face as they approached me and Kisca. Kisten remained in the kitchen, still working on dinner as Lucius stopped behind my chair.

"Have we reached an idea?" He asked softly, and I looked up to see his expression. Blue met green as I tried to gauge his thoughts, but his emotions were carefully hidden behind his calm exterior. I glanced over to LeAlexende as he stood behind Kisca, but he shrugged at me, his usual smile on his face.

"I suppose," I sighed, glancing toward the kitchen as I saw Kisten putting the finishing touches on whatever he had cooked. It smelled heavily of pork and my stomach growled again as I looked back at the vampire. "Kisten will attempt to control the Grimm while you and I fight Whistleblower."

"Hmm."

"But I won't promise that I won't use my necromancy, or whatever it is," I continued, catching the worry that passed across Lucius's face. I took a deep breath, grabbing my locket as my sister rose to catch our conversation. "My control isn't that great, but I won't fight it if it comes up on its own."

"But—"

"It's a risk, I know, but this whole idea is," I interrupted, squeezing the wood tighter as my sister's determination joined my own. I glanced at LeAlexende and he only gave me a slight nod as I turned back to my Overseer. "I have been able to control it in the past when I let it come up on its own. It's only when I try to force it that it just does what it wants."

"I'll trust your judgment then," Lucius conceded, looking over toward LeAlexende and Kisca. The pixie simply nodded, accepting the silent order our Overseer was giving her. I hummed as I considered the danger to both of them and carefully glanced at Aurel, who was still ignoring us all as best as he could.

"One more thing."

"Yes?" Lucius looked back down at me as I fully turned in my seat, glaring slightly at the lich. Aurel darted his eyes to look at me and I caught the slight fear in his sea-green eyes before he turned away, his curls bouncing.

"Have Aurel protect Kisca and LeAlexende," I demanded, the lich quickly turning back to look at me and his expression gave away his displeasure with the suggestion. I could almost feel Alex's concern as he gazed at my back, but I ignored it as I turned back to Lucius. "While I trust Kisca's glamor to keep them hidden, they should have someone with them to help in case something happens."

"Hmmm," was Lucius' only reply and I could see that he disagreed with my suggestion as well. I had no doubt that the same worry that was running through LeAlexende was running through Lucius; Aurel had already shown his loyalty only went so far. He hadn't done anything to disobey Lucius directly, but this was hardly the time to test if he would. The lich had made it clear he was not happy about being here and even less pleased with the plan we had to defeat the Hunter.

'*Risky*,' my sister offered and I closed my eyes, not trying to argue with her.

'*I know, but we need someone to be with Kisca and LeAlexende and it's better than leaving him to his own devices. Alex doesn't trust him, and will be ready if he tries something,*' I pointed out and I felt my sister's surrender. I saw the same look in the Overseer's eyes as he sighed, looking over to the pissed off lich.

"Aurel will protect them from the fight," Lucius conceded and Aurel didn't try to hide his displeasure with the order. We all turned as Kisten cleared his throat, gaining everyone's attention as he lifted the pan in his hand.

"Food's ready," he announced, and Kisca and I both stood at the same time as a wistful smile passed across his face. "Probably shouldn't fight on an empty stomach."

"Agreed," LeAlexende beamed, his usual smile returning as he glided over to the breakfast bar, sitting on one of the stools as Kisten turned to begin portioning out the food. Kisca and I soon joined the vampire and I turned to see Lucius still standing next to the armchair. I watched as he motioned to Aurel and he took the lich to the dining room, closing the door behind them. My heart pounded with worry, but I did my best to ignore it as Kisten slid a plate of food in front of me.

It was some sort of pork and rice skillet, and despite my hunger, I did my best to take my time as I ate. Kisca shared none of my restraint, eagerly eating her food as LeAlexende carefully tasted his share. The vampire hummed with delight, a bright smile on his face as he looked at the shifter.

"Just as amazing as I remember. It's a shame I was denied your cooking when I visited last year," Alex acclaimed blissfully, and I couldn't help my chuckle as I saw Kisten's slight blush at the praise. Kisca nodded in agreement, still chewing a mouthful of food as she beamed at the Alpha.

"Better late than never, I guess," Kisten huffed, leaning against the counter as he watched us. I wasn't surprised to see that he wasn't eating, considering he had hunted the day before, but I felt my worry starting to creep back in as my hunger faded. Every rational part of me screamed that we needed more time to come up with a safer plan, but I did my best to push it aside. We had already used up all the time we could spare and I knew waiting for Whistleblower to come to us would only make things worse.

My eyes met Kisten's as I glanced up and he gave me a small smile, pushing himself off the counter as he leaned to kiss my forehead. I let him, humming softly as no pain came with the gentle gesture of affection. His smile had grown as he pulled away, and I gently took his hand in mine, giving it a strong squeeze as I continued eating with the other. I released him as I heard the door behind us open and we all watched silently as Aurel stepped out. He barely looked at any of us as he stomped back upstairs, disappearing back into his room as we shared a look.

Lucius carefully appeared next to Kisca, taking a seat as Kisten slid a plate in front of him. The Overseer almost seemed surprised, looking up to see the Alpha's smile.

"I'd never forget about you, Lucius," Kisten offered, and my heart swelled as a small laugh escaped the vampire. Lucius looked at the food longingly and we all watched as he slowly took a bite. He hummed with delight at the taste, his expression pure bliss as he closed his eyes. After a moment, he must have sensed us all watching him and a slight blush passed through his cheeks as he turned to meet our gaze.

"You don't have to watch," he coughed and both Kisca and I laughed at our Overseer's embarrassment. For LeAlexende's part, he settled for covering his grin, turning away as Lucius' embarrassment grew. Even Kisten let out a soft chuckle and Lucius turned away from all of us as he continued eating. As my laughter died away, I couldn't help the smile on my face as Kisca asked Kisten for seconds and the Alpha happily piled Aurel's portion onto her plate.

'I... *kinda like this*,' I admitted, stroking the wooden cross as LeAlexende continued to tease Lucius, much to the enjoyment of Kisca and Kisten. 'Having... *friends, I guess*.'

'*You don't have to... stay so distant anymore*,' my sister offered, and I made a soft sound of agreement, unable to help my soft laugh as Lucius turned the tables on Alex, forcing the caramel vampire to cover his cheeks as he started to blush. The pixie was utterly entertained as she tried to balance laughing and eating and Kisten did little to hide his laughter as he watched. '*We... are allowed to be happy.*'

'*Yeah, we are,*' I agreed, turning to my food as I began to finish eating, my worry fading into hard determination.

22

I fidgeted as I walked next to Kisten, his hand in mine as we moved through the trees. The forest once again seemed foreboding, filled with unseen enemies, but Kisten walked on undeterred. The Overseers followed behind me, with Aurel and Kisca bringing up the rear. Aurel was reluctant to participate, but thanks to the order from Lucius, the lich had no choice but to go along with our plan.

I sighed deeply, lifting my other hand to my locket and holding it tightly through my shirt. My sister failed to stir but I knew it was due to weakness rather than anything else. Unless I used my power, she was incapable of talking to me anymore, now only able to push concepts and feelings. I longed for any sort of encouragement from her but dropped my hand when I realized none was coming.

"Here," Kisten finally stopped, causing all of us to pause with him. His colorful eyes were glowing in the dark and he turned to look at all of us. "The rest of the pack is nearby."

"Whistleblower?" Lucius ventured and the Alpha shook his head.

"Not here. We'll have a few moments once I start," Kisten answered and we all felt relieved with his words. Kisten took a deep breath, scanning the area. "You and Raiven should stay with me:

LeAlexende, Kisca and Aurel should find a crevice nearby where they can still see us. That way Kisca doesn't have to use her glamor as much."

"Done." Lucius turned his eyes to Aurel, who scowled at the silent order. The lich stomped off, motioning for Kisca and LeAlexende to follow him. The former Overseer exchanged a worried look with Lucius, but my Overseer merely smiled, giving LeAlexende a reassuring hug. I felt a desire to embrace LeAlexende as well, an urge I ignored as I watched him disappear into the brush with Aurel and Kisca. The three of us stood in silence, no one knowing what to say.

"Kisten, are you sure?" Lucius finally broke the silence, his eyes resting on where Kisten held my hand. I chanced a glance at Kisten's face and I could see the fear and worry in his expression,

"Yes. It has to be this way," the shifter squeezed my hand tightly and I lifted his hand to my cheek, pressing it against my face. Kisten pulled me into a tight hug, pressing kisses into my hair and face. When he pulled back, his determination had returned. "It has to end tonight."

"Alright," Lucius conceded and Kisten released me, stepping in between the trees. He sat on the ground, closing his eyes as Lucius and I stood in front of him. I felt the air change as Kisten whistled for the pack and within seconds, we were surrounded, the snarling mouths of the Grimm closing in on us. The growls and dripping mouths sent a shiver through my body but I did my best to ignore it, instead summoning my power as I drew my gun. The ground around us immediately began to shake and heave, causing the Grimm to pause at the power pouring out from me.

It had been a long time since I had pulled out the full extent of my power and I was a little taken aback by how malleable the ground felt. It usually took most of my effort to manipulate its shape, but I couldn't help my slight smile as the Grimm began to sink into the leaves, my power easily allowing me to trap them. Lucius gave me an impressed look and I shrugged, returning my attention to the Grimm. They growled as they fought to keep from sinking into the loosened dirt beneath them, still snarling and snapping in our direction. Kisten cried out behind me and I turned around to look at him.

He was doubled over in pain, cradling his head as he fought to control his animals and the Grimm. Several types of fur spouted through his clothing, only to recede almost as quickly as it appeared. I wanted to reach out to him, but I forced myself to look away: Kisten had warned that it would be too dangerous to touch him while he was attempting to control the pack, as he would be most likely to lash out.

"My my, what is this?" My blood froze as I heard the Hunter's voice and I looked up to see Whistleblower standing in the trees, his loyal Grimm flanking him on either side. His eyes were locked on Kisten and he seemed both furious and pleased. "You're finally opening up to the pack, although it seems you're still doing it for the wrong reasons."

"I'm doing it for the right reasons," Kisten's voice barely sounded human, and he had lifted his head to meet his father's gaze. His hate and anger was etched into his features and the fur receded, the animals finally under his control again. The Grimm surrounding us seemed confused, some of them drifting closer to Kisten and growling in Whistleblower's direction, while the rest shifted with uncertainty. Whistleblower laughed, and I adjusted my grip on my gun.

"Using your hatred to make them align with you, I like it," the Hunter admitted, his grin growing savage again. "You can't use their intelligence this time, so why not drop to their level? You want to take the pack from me, *Bübchen*[1]? I'd like to see you try."

Whistleblower leapt at us, moving faster than my eyes could follow, but this time, I could feel him as he moved. The air was so soaked with my power that I felt him moving through it and I was able to pull both Kisten and Lucius out of the way as the Hunter landed in our former position. He turned his savage expression to me, growling loudly as he began to sink into the loose dirt, just like the Grimm. He forcibly pulled his feet out, leaping up into the trees to avoid my power.

"I've had enough of you, Jezebela," he growled, but before the Hunter could attempt to come after me, he was stopped by a bright flash of lightning. Lucius' electricity immediately caused my hair to stand on end, striking the tree the Hunter stood in. Lucius stood next to me, the air around him buzzing with the charge as Whistleblower leapt to another branch, avoiding the attack.

"So have I, Whistleblower," I fired a shot, Lucius' electricity colliding with the metal of the bullet as it flew through the air. The Hunter attempted to dodge again, but the electrified bullet was faster, catching him in the shoulder as he moved. He held the wound, blood seeping through his fingers as he barely landed in another tree. He glared at me and Lucius, his expression already wild and angry as he called out to the pack.

"Kill them both!" he commanded, whistling his order to the Grimm on the ground. His loyal creatures came at us, but another whistle came from behind and Kisten's Grimm met his father's, stopping them from reaching us. The undecided creatures quickly backed off, whimpering as their confusion increased while watching the pack fight. The two factions engaged fiercely with one another, their snarls and growls echoing in the darkness of the forest. The Hunter quickly turned his attention to the undecided members of the pack, growling as he glared at them. "I gave you an ORDER!"

I heard Kisten whistle again, gaining the attention of a few of the undecided creatures and I quickly fired another shot, giving Kisten an opening to turn more to his side. The Hunter easily dodged my shot, turning his attention back to Lucius and me. My eyes glowed in the darkness and the tree he stood in began to shake as I forced its roots from the ground. Whistleblower barely managed to dodge another bolt of lightning as Lucius attacked and I couldn't help smiling as more of the Grimm sided with Kisten.

"JEZEBELA!" Whistleblower roared my former name as he clung to the tree, and I fired another shot at him as Lucius charged the bullet, almost missing as one of the Grimm leapt at me. I quickly raised my hand to knock away the creature, only to watch as it froze in mid-air, the confusion in its eyes echoed in my own. I felt as the humidity in the air increased, and the creature slammed into the ground, disappearing into the thick mud. I looked at my hand curiously, flexing my fingers as the humidity responded, and soon I held a small ball of water in my hand.

"Raiven..?" I heard Lucius' voice behind me, but I had no more time to examine what was happening as I felt Whistleblower leap at me, attempting to take advantage of my distraction. I quickly flung the water at the Hunter, sliding on the mud as I called out to the Overseer.

"Now, Lucius!" I watched as the water collided with the Hunter and a bolt of lightning quickly followed. It almost seemed as if it ran from droplet to droplet through the air and I could feel as my hair expanded even more with the increased discharge. Whistleblower barely managed to avoid the bolt, the attack instead scorching through some of the Grimm. Lucius' attack definitely affected the morale of the creatures, encouraging some of them to join Whistleblower's side, while others shifted to Kisten.

For his part, Kisten was still seated on the ground and I could see the concentration etched into his features. It was clear it was taking all of his focus to maintain his connection to the pack and I frowned as I turned to the enraged Hunter. While he hadn't managed to touch me or Lucius yet, it was clear that we also hadn't done much to lessen Whistleblower's concentration and I gritted my teeth as I felt Lucius move next to me.

"We need to help Kisten," I muttered, feeling the electricity as it radiated from the vampire. Lucius made a noise of agreement, and I quickly holstered my gun, closing my eyes as I focused. I was tempted for a moment to call up my necromancy but resisted, instead focusing on my vampiric power. The ground heaved more as I changed the shape of our battlefield and the Grimm whined in confusion as stone began to shoot through the dirt, impaling some of the creatures. Whistleblower snapped at me as he abandoned the tree he was in, barely dodging the slab of rock as it split the tree in half.

The humidity began to soak my clothing as I did my best to trap

Whistleblower, the rocks and trees following him as he moved through them. Some of his loyal Grimm attempted to attack me, but Lucius was able to quickly put an end to them, leaving more scorched marks in the earth as he did so. I was distracted momentarily as I heard Kisten whine with pain, and I saw he had finally moved, throwing one of his father's Grimm off him. His creatures quickly moved to protect the Alpha, snarling and growling at their former brethren.

"Kisten!" I was unable to help my concern as I called out to him, but my distraction proved to be the opening Whistleblower needed.

"YOU WILL NOT TAKE HIM!" the Hunter bellowed, his voice vibrating through the air as he rushed toward me and Lucius. My Overseer attempted to strike him with lightning but Whistleblower avoided him, quickly knocking Lucius into one of the stones next to us. The stone cracked as Lucius collided with it and I soon found myself pinned to the ground, the Hunter's boot on my neck. He looked at me with murder in his eyes, pushing down as he attempted to crush my throat. "You will not take what belongs to *me*, whore."

My vision started to go dark on the edges as I struggled to breathe and I raised my hand at the Hunter, the ground heaving next to me as a stone flew at him. Whistleblower barely reacted, leaning back as he avoided the attack but refusing to move off of me. I heard as one of Kisten's Grimm leapt at the Hunter but was intercepted by another, whining with pain as it was knocked away. The man over me chuckled as I desperately tried to throw him off, barely able to focus on my power from the lack of air.

"You first, since Mother has decided she no longer needs you alive," Whistleblower revealed, leaning onto my throat with more weight and I felt as if my larynx would snap under the force. I knew he was doing it on purpose to draw out the pain, his eyes glowing with his glee and sadism. "Then I'll deal with Nisaba and her little pets. They've played with my son for long enough, and it's high time I teach him to respect his father."

"No!" My fear and anger erupted in that moment as my necromancy finally responded, the dark tendrils exploding from me as they reached deep into the wet mud. Whistleblower seemed to sense the change and quickly leapt back from me as a hand reached for him out of the dirt.

I quickly sat up, coughing and breathing in precious air as my zombies clawed their way from the dirt, all making their way towards the Hunter. My throat ached with pain, but it seemed that he had failed to do any permanent damage as I slowly stood. Whistleblower quickly set his Grimm upon the undead, taking the chance to kick the skull of a zombie that had come too close to him. My power continued spreading out from me, touching Lucius where he had fallen and enveloping him.

My power swirled around his body, attempting to raise him and I paused, still uncertain of what would happen if I tried. Turning to face the Overseer, I didn't pull it back, instead allowing my power to focus on him. I saw Lucius looking at me with fear, attempting to fight me as I poured my power into him, the other zombies crumbling back into the dirt as the dark tendrils reached his face. I watched as his blue eyes were enveloped by black and I heard Whistleblower growl behind me.

"So you finally show your true colors, *Ungeheuer*[2]," he spat, quickly setting the pack on me as I finished forcing my power on the vampire. I whipped around quickly and the Grimm were easily blown back from me by the sudden blast of wind. The Hunter's eyes grew wider as my Overseer stood in front of me, one of his eyes glowing blue and the other purple. I could still feel Lucius' fear at having his body controlled, but he had surrendered, my power fully taking over. I barely understood what I was doing, but I did my best to focus on my anger, dropping my hand back to my side as Lucius' body mimicked mine.

"Now, Whistleblower, let's finish this," I smiled savagely, Lucius' face echoing my expression. Whistleblower lunged at us, but I easily dodged, Lucius leaping with me as we moved through the heavy air. I quickly waved my hand and sent a blast of air at the Hunter, knocking him back to the ground as he started after us. I narrowed my gaze and he began to sink into the leaves again, channeling my vampiric power through the Overseer. He looked at Lucius with surprise, his eyes soon narrowing with comprehension as he pulled himself up.

"So, you carry Nisaba's essence. That's how you wield her wind," he smiled maliciously, cracking his fingers as he stood. "Guess I have to kill you too, in order to have a successful Hunt."

"Good luck," I answered, Lucius' voice echoing my own. The Hunter didn't answer, instead lunging at me again and this time I didn't try to dodge him, maintaining my stance as he approached. Whistleblower managed to reach Lucius, but instead of backing away, I made Lucius grab the Hunter. Whistleblower's eyes widened with surprise as I leaned back and headbutted him, filling him with Lucius' stored electric charge. I smiled as I heard the Hunter's teeth chatter from the intense shock and I stepped away as Whistleblower fell to the ground.

I heard as the pack reacted and I looked up to see the rest of the undecided members siding with Kisten, circling the Alpha as they protected him from his father's half. Thanks to us finally landing a sizable hit on the Hunter, Kisten was finally winning the mental struggle against his father and I watched as he finally started to shift, black fur sprouting through his skin and clothing.

"You—" Whistleblower shook off the effects of the shock and stood, even though his gait was now wobbly and uncoordinated. He began after me again but his movements were sloppy and the Grimm behind him faltered, clearly confused by losing their connection to him. I easily avoided his next lunge and waved Lucius' hand, using another blast of air to blow the Hunter away. Whistleblower's expression was growing increasingly unhinged as he realized we were starting to gain the upper hand and he screamed his frustration into the empty night air.

Then my blood ran cold as I heard Kisca answer with a scream of her own.

23

I turned to where the sound had come from, only to see LeAlexende's surprised eyes meeting mine. Blood dripped from his head and chest from where he had been impaled and he smiled slightly as our eyes met. The silver on the claws glistened as they moved and ripped through him, spraying his black blood onto the nearby plants. Kisca caught his body as it fell backwards, quickly scrambling away from LeAlexende's attacker. My own chest exploded with Lucius' pain and I glared at the one who had done the deed, the lich stepping out of the underbrush proudly. Aurel looked at the bits of LeAlexende's heart with disdain before tossing the pieces to the ground, a smirk on his face.

"*Aurel,*" I growled, Lucius matching my sound as I completely turned my back on the Hunter, unable to help my growing rage. My sister's anger rose in tandem with mine, and I felt as if my body would combust into flames from the combined heat of our emotions. Aurel met my eyes evenly, his sea-green eyes glowing as he approached me, licking the Overseer's blood from his hands as they changed back to normal.

"I tried to save you from this, Raiven," he finally spoke, stopping a distance away from me. Whistleblower lunged at me again, but I knocked him away with a blast of wind, barely paying any attention to the enraged Hunter. My eyes were locked with Aurel's, Lucius' anguish beginning to fill me and fuel my rage even more as the lich spoke. "Just like I warned you about going to the wedding, all you two had to do was be mine."

"*You.*" I whispered, Lucius's voice echoing mine as I realized what Aurel was admitting. *The wedding... Mark... all those deaths.* My body began to shake and I could barely hold myself back as I spoke, the sky above me growing turbulent as the winds picked up around me. "Do you even *realize* how many people died at that wedding? And for what? So you could have me?"

"Why would I care about them? I am only loyal to myself and Lucius knew that when he accepted me into his Coven," Aurel shrugged, clearly unaffected by my words. "And I didn't have to break his orders. He told me to leave Kisten alone no matter what, and to protect LeAlexende and Kisca. He never said *I* couldn't kill them and then take you."

"Whistleblower has no intention of letting you have me, you *IDIOT!*" I screamed, unable to help as the wind picked up again, the force striking Aurel in his shoulder as it ripped his arm away. The lich groaned with pain, but his expression was merely annoyed as his remaining hand began to glow. He used his magic to quickly regenerate his arm and my eyes flashed with my annoyance as he flexed his new fingers.

"Just means I have to deal with him too," Aurel sneered, readying himself to face me as his hands glowed a bright orange before shifting into claws again. He dragged his claws against the stone, shifting his gaze to Lucius, and I could feel Lucius' rage increase as their eyes met. Thanks to my power, I could feel his emotions as if they were my own, and I was surprised to feel that a majority of his anger was directed at himself. *If only he had listened to Alex, if he hadn't kept Aurel out of pity...* "I think I've made it clear that I have no issues betraying others when it suits me."

"*I'm going to end you,*" I whispered and Aurel barely had time to react as lightning quickly struck where he stood. He looked at me shocked as I moved my arm and he was quickly struck by a gust of air, catapulting him into the trees. I watched as his curls expanded to catch the branches, rubber banding the lich as he launched himself toward me. I narrowed my eyes as I moved, the mud splashing up as he landed on the ground. I watched the air glimmer behind him as Kisca hid herself again, and I closed my eyes as my heart constricted in my chest.

'*He might make it,*' my sister reasoned, and I growled angrily as I turned, avoiding the Grimm that leapt at my back. Lucius grabbed the creature, and the smell of burnt skin and fur filled my nostrils as he electrocuted it, dropping its body back to the ground. '*Even with the silver, you stopped Aurel from removing his heart.*'

'*It shouldn't be up to chance,*' I spat back, barely moving as Aurel attacked Lucius, his claws extending toward the vampire. Stone shot out of the ground to block the lich's attack, scattering into hundreds of pieces as Aurel shattered it. '*I am going to **kill** him.*'

"I'm not done with you!" I barely turned in time to catch Whistleblower as he charged at me, our hands locking as I kept him from attacking me. My control of Lucius faltered as I struggled against the Hunter and I heard as Aurel lunged at the Overseer again. I withdrew my power from the vampire as I pulled the tendrils back to my body, watching as they swirled up my arm and began to push onto the Hunter. Whistleblower immediately withdrew as it touched him, shaking his hand in disgust. "How dare you–"

Kisten quickly appeared in front of me, fully in his bear form as my power returned to me, the dark marks swimming on my skin. He roared into the night air, the sound carried by the growing storm above us and the Alpha pawed the ground, growling as he stood between me and the Hunter. I could hear Lucius combating Aurel behind me and my anger grew as I considered the spellcaster.

"Kisten," my voice carried all of my rage as the shifter glanced back at me, his eyes still swimming with colors even in his bear form. "Can you deal with Whistleblower while we kill Aurel?"

The Alpha growled in response, pawing the ground as more of the Grimm loyal to him moved to his side, and I saw that Kisten only had a slight advantage over his father. Most of the Grimm were dead and the remaining were split evenly between the pair. Whistleblower's Grimm returned to his side, growling and snarling as Kisten roared, his creatures racing forward to engage the pack.

"You–" the Hunter was interrupted as Kisten lunged at him, not giving his father the chance to force him back to human form as he launched mud at his face. Whistleblower was forced to turn away as Kisten slammed the ground in front of him, quickly swiping his paws to knock away a member of his father's pack. The Hunter turned to face his son again, but Kisten had already moved, getting behind his father as he slammed Whistleblower into the ground. He lifted his eyes again to meet mine, lowering his head to encourage me.

"Alright," I whispered as I turned away from the fight to face Aurel, reaching out with my power to raise Lucius. This time the Overseer let my power fill him willingly, no longer afraid of what I could do as we faced the lich. Aurel was regenerating one of his arms again, and I winced from the slight pain of Lucius' injuries. It seemed the undead spellcaster had managed to land a hit or two while I was distracted, but they were superficial, even with the silver, and I shook off the pain.

"How long do you want to play this game, Aurel?" I hissed, my hair beginning to blow around me as I summoned the wind again, ripping a tree from the ground as I launched it at the lich. He was barely able to lacerate it with his regenerated claws, the pieces crashing into the woods around us. I began walking toward him, Lucius matching my steps as the humidity in the air began to increase again. "Your magic won't last all night."

"You may have better control over LeAlexende's powers than Lucius, but you don't have the experience to beat me," he gloated, clearly still thinking he could win and I smiled at his ignorance. I ducked under a branch he launched at the Overseer, hearing the yelp as it struck one of the Grimm instead. "Once I kill Lucius, everything else will be easy."

"Kill a First, especially one that now carries the power of a Sibling?" I laughed, the electricity leaping through the air again as I struck the ground in front of the lich. Aurel quickly moved, barely dodging the stone that rose to impale him as he stumbled back into the brush. I gave the lich a pitiful look as I followed him, my eyes focused on where I wanted him to go. "You really are too good at deceiving yourself, aren't you?"

I didn't give the lich a chance to answer as I arched another bolt at him, the ground heaving as Aurel sank into it. He was unable to dodge as the full force of the attack caught him, burning his body almost black from the intensity. The undead spellcaster managed to free himself before I could attack him again, but I could already tell his magic was starting to run out. He was wasting too much healing himself and I grinned savagely as I forced the lich to move further into the forest.

"He had no *right* to refuse me. *You–*" Aurel finally spat out, his words interrupted as he coughed up blood from my constant barrage. I ignored his cry, striking him again with another gust of wind and the lich was thrown back into the air, crashing into more of the trees. I chased after Aurel as Lucius and I leapt into the air, still pelting him with gusts of wind and lightning. His desperate cry only enraged me more and I couldn't help my rising disgust.

"*You* had no right to kill all those people!" I screamed as another slab of rock rose from the ground and Aurel collided with it, sinking deep in the stone. He started to pull himself free but I quickly waved Lucius' hand, the ground sealing his hands and feet into the surface. The lich looked at me with fear as I struck him with lightning again, finally finding what I was looking for as the current coursed through his body. "You had *no right* to touch Alex!"

"You were supposed to be mine!"

"I was *never* going to be yours," I whispered, the sounds of the other fight fading behind me as I looked down at Aurel. His orange curls were matted with blood and the glow faded from his once beautiful eyes as he exhausted all of his magic. In front of me was a man I had once called a friend, a creature Lucius once felt pity for and my hands shook in my fury. I closed my eyes as I saw Mark's broken body in his pink dress and I glared at the lich as I continued. "All you had to do was accept that, Aurel. That's *all* you had to do."

"I need to have you both, why did you refuse me?" He screamed, ignoring my words as he still pulled against the stone. He attempted to summon his power again but I growled softly, watching as his hands sank further into the smooth surface. He was trapped up to his elbows before he stopped, a crazed and desperate look in his eyes. "Why am I not good enough for you two? What do I have to do to make you mine?"

"If you still have to ask," I reached down and Lucius echoed me, reaching into Aurel's pocket as he grabbed the phylactery. I watched as the lich's eyes widened in terror, finally realizing what I was going to do. He struggled against his prison as I pulled the flask back, forcing Lucius to hand it to me as we stepped away. I watched the white liquid as it swirled, able to feel the pulse of life as I held the lich's soul in my hand. I released Lucius from my control as I focused my power on the flask, watching as the black began to invade the milky fluid and Aurel cried out in pain. He thrashed and struggled as I slowly destroyed his soul, the expression of horror locked on his face as the flask fully turned black. "Then you'll never understand."

I dropped the glass to the ground, barely stepping back as it shattered, the black liquid disappearing as soon as it came in contact with the air. I recalled my power as it started to touch Aurel's body, refusing to connect myself to the lich in that way. I shared a glance with Lucius as the vampire nodded and we turned away from Aurel's corpse, working our way back to Kisten's fight with Whistleblower.

24

The Grimm surrounded the pair as Lucius and I returned, all the remaining creatures completely under Kisten's control. The ground was littered with dead Grimm as I made my way back to him, carefully stepping around the bodies and I continued towards the Alpha, counting only maybe a dozen or so Grimm that had survived. My power still sat on the edge of my fingers and I fought to keep it from reaching out to raise the creatures.

"So, you've finally awoken to your potential," Whistleblower sighed, a strange mix of pride and anger once again in his voice. Kisten growled, the entire pack mimicking the sound and the Hunter laughed, lazily looking at me and Lucius as we approached. "And all for *her. Der Monströse*[1]."

"Stop referring to my mate that way," Kisten demanded, the Grimm moving closer to their former master. Whistleblower looked at the creatures with disgust, spitting onto the ground in front of them. The Grimm merely snarled, their rat-like tails high in the air as they waited to pounce.

"This is what I get for making them stupid," he groaned, looking up to meet his son's eyes. "But you probably would've found a way anyway. You would've made a great Hunter for her."

"I was never going to be her Hunter," Kisten spat, motioning for the pack to pause. The creatures pawed the ground anxiously as I heard thunder crack above us, the storm caused by me and Lucius growing stronger on its own.

"No, instead you became hers," he once again cast his angry eyes to me and I pulled my locket from under my shirt, allowing Whistleblower to see the cross. He narrowed his eyes at the trinket and turned his gaze to his son one last time. "Only time will tell if you will regret it, *lieber Sohn von mir*[2]."

We watched as Kisten whistled, the creatures descending onto Whistleblower as the Hunter laughed. His laughter soon turned into gurgles and then silence as the pack tore him apart, giving him the same death he had given Kisten's mother. Kisten turned his colorful eyes to me, and I held my breath as I saw his expression. His angry face was an exact replica of his father's, and I felt my heart pound as his eyes bore into mine.

"Kisten?" I asked cautiously and for a moment, I saw his expression soften. The moment passed, however and I watched in horror as Kisten lifted his arm, pointing at me. The Grimm stepped away from Whistleblower's remains, growling and snarling in my direction. I attempted to swallow my fear and slowly walked closer to the Alpha. "Kisten, come back to me."

He merely growled in response, the Grimm snapping at me as I approached. I jumped, pausing for a moment, but I took a deep breath and forced myself to continue walking. I could see how much Kisten was fighting the Grimm's will to kill me, but now that his own anger was fading, the creatures were trying to push their desires onto him.

"Raiven, don't," I heard Lucius call out from behind me, but I ignored him as I continued forward. One of the Grimm swiped at my ankle as I passed, but without an order from Kisten, I knew their threats were empty. They could not attack without permission and I had to bring Kisten back before they forced him to give it.

"You are stronger than them," I spoke confidently despite my fear, reaching out to Kisten's face as I looked into his eyes. I could feel as the Grimm snapped at me, but I kept my eyes focused on him. His eyes swam with such hate and anger and I did my best to keep calm, focusing on my love for the man in my hands. I searched his eyes with mine, doing my best to push through to the shifter as I spoke. "I am your Beta and you are my Alpha. They cannot take me away from you."

"No," Kisten finally spoke, whistling his order to the pack. I closed my eyes in fear but instead of attacking, I heard the creatures whine as they backed off, sitting on the ground. I threw myself into my lover's arms, relief over taking me. Kisten returned my embrace, holding me tightly as he pressed kisses into my hair.

"It's over," I breathed and Kisten purred his agreement as he stroked my hair. I heard Lucius sigh with relief as he approached us, placing a hand on Kisten's shoulder. Their eyes met before Kisten released me, moving to hug Lucius instead. Suddenly, the Grimm jumped to their feet, growling in the direction of Whistleblower's body. I watched in horror as the remains began to twitch and jerk, my power instantly reaching out in my fear.

"Don't," my blood became ice in my veins as a female voice rang out, and I watched with fear as Mater Vitae manifested from Whistleblower's remains, her blood flowing up from the corpse to form her appearance. She looked the same way she had a thousand years ago: Blond, flowing hair slightly covering a full, time-worn face. Shining ice-blue eyes, set deep within their sockets, glaring angrily as she stepped out of the corpse's shell. Her blood-red lips twitched in her annoyance and she kept her eyes locked on me as I placed myself between her and Kisten.

Her refined dress flowed from top to bottom and had a scoop neckline, which tastefully revealed the delicate dress worn below it. The smooth, loosely tied fabric of her dress covered her stomach where the continuous flow was broken up by a small ribbon worn quite high around her waist. She looked as if she had stepped straight out of my memories into the present and her many layers blew in the wind as the storm continued to build around us.

"I see you have killed my most loyal Retainer," she spat, her musical voice not matching her savage expression. I resisted the urge to step back, but I could feel the fear radiating off Kisten as he groaned. He had never met Mother before and her presence alone was enough to leave him shivering next to me. I quickly pushed him behind me, moving to protect him from her aura. Her eyes drifted to him and she pointed to the ground. "Kneel, dog."

Kisten immediately dropped to the ground, crying out in pain as he collapsed to his knees. The Grimm mimicked his sound, lying on the ground while whimpering as he was forced to release his connection to them. I heard Lucius move behind me and Mater Vitae quickly lifted her chin, casting her gaze down on her former attendee.

"Kneel–"

"No," I interrupted her, using my power to once again take control of Lucius, allowing him to resist the command. I felt Lucius' relief fill me as Mater Vitae's eyes widened, only to return to slits as she glared.

"So, he was right. You *are* beginning to awaken," she smirked at me, raising her head so that she was looking down on me. Looking down on me as she had my whole life and my sister's anger rose to join my own as I glared. I snarled, stomping my foot on the ground and hands reached from the dirt, grabbing at her dress and sleeves. Mother quickly jumped back, stomping at the hands with her foot as I released them, smirking at her reaction.

"You don't look so dignified when you're dancing, *Mother*," I laughed, and she shot me a look full of malice. I knew it was mostly for show: despite her control of Kisten and Lucius being very real, she wasn't physically present and therefore couldn't use her other powers. Her control over me was never absolute and I watched as she snarled at me yet again. "Perhaps you should return to your hovel before I tarnish your curated appearance."

"I will not allow your... pet to control my Grimm," she retorted and waved her hand over the remaining pack and I watched in horror as they disintegrated before my eyes. The creatures howled in shock and pain as their bodies melted into festering puddles, and Kisten behind me howled with fear as well. I turned to see him holding his head, the death of the Grimm clearly affecting his animals. Feathers and fur began to ripple across his skin and Kisten was trying his best to rein in the frightened animals inside him.

I returned my glare to Mater Vitae, who looked pleased with the steaming piles of goo between us. I could feel Lucius' fear adding to my own, but I forced myself to look at Mother defiantly.

"Didn't want them anyway. And he's my equal, not my pet," I spat and a small, malicious smile started on her face. She turned her icy gaze to the Alpha, who remained kneeling as he whimpered in pain. "But you wouldn't understand that concept."

"We'll see, girl. We'll see," Mater Vitae's visage began to fade with her words and I sighed, releasing Lucius from my control. The Overseer collapsed to his knees as I knelt next to Kisten, placing my hand on his back. His spots had appeared on his skin and I knew Kisten was trying to summon his leopard to quiet the others.

"Can you move?" I coaxed and Kisten slowly sat up, his eyes still a mess of colors. He was clutching his head as he nodded, gasping for air as he attempted to move.

"That was–"

"Terrifying," Lucius finished, still shaken up from her sudden appearance. He held himself as he knelt on the ground, visibly shaking on his knees. I reached for him as well, and I felt as the vampire jumped under my touch. "It has been over a thousand years and I still can't face her without–"

"It's okay, Lucius," I called out to him and he looked up at me, the fear plain in his eyes. I smiled at him softly as I began to rub his back, doing my best to reassure him. "She scared me too, and I know she can't make me obey her."

"She spent millennia making us afraid. That won't go away so easily," I quickly looked up to see LeAlexende walking toward us, Kisca doing her best to support the wounded vampire. He had mostly finished regenerating the hole in his chest, and only a slight scar remained to indicate the damage to his head. They collapsed on the ground near us and we quickly moved to embrace him, unable to help our surprise and relief. Lucius clung to his friend, tears streaming down his face.

"Alex..." my voice was full of my questions and LeAlexende smiled a lazy smile at me over Lucius' shoulder.

"Aurel was in too much of a hurry, it would seem," he admitted, gently returning Lucius's embrace despite the pain he was in. "If Kisca hadn't alerted you with her scream, he might have succeeded in killing me and her."

"I wish we could kill him again," Lucius fumed, pulling back from embracing his fellow vampire. LeAlexende chuckled at this, confusing all of us as we waited for his laughter to end.

"I'm sure if you ask nicely, Raiven will let you," he met my eyes with his and I realized he was joking. I couldn't help but shake my head, a smile starting to creep on my face.

"No thanks," my smile quickly faded as I considered how we had won against the Hunter. Kisten was chastising LeAlexende for making light of his own death when I leaned forward, touching Lucius gently. My Overseer finally released his friend as everyone turned to me and I knelt on the ground next to LeAlexende. I took a deep breath, choosing my next words carefully. "Alex, necromancy... can't control vampires and can't kill the living."

"No, it can't," he answered, his expression growing serious and everyone turned their gaze from me to him. LeAlexende held his hand to the shrinking hole in his chest and Kisten and Lucius quickly moved to help him sit up.

"How did I control Lucius?" I asked slowly and LeAlexende met my eyes as Lucius looked between us. We remained in silence before he closed his eyes, shrugging.

"Why do you think I would know?"

"Because you know more than you want to admit," I pointed out, refusing to look away from LeAlexende. "The first time my power touched you, you immediately recognized it as me. That shouldn't be possible; regardless of what my power is, there's no way you would have known without expecting it. You also weren't surprised that I had been able to spy on you and Lucius."

Lucius' eyes widened as he realized what I was referring to and he turned his gaze to his friend, who still had his eyes closed. The night air between us grew stifling as we waited to see what LeAlexende would say, despite the growing storm.

"I think you've already realized it isn't necromancy. As far as what it is, who knows," he finally answered, and I opened my mouth to keep questioning, but I swallowed my words as I felt my sister rise. It was clear she wanted me to ask in private, realizing LeAlexende would not be honest with everyone present. The thunder crackled above me from the growing storm and I sighed, standing quickly and scooping the vampire into my arms. My other companions looked up at me with surprise as I adjusted him in my grip and began to walk off.

"We should head back to the retreat. Alex needs a safe place to heal," I started and I heard as the others quickly scrambled to their feet, following me silently as I made my way back to the cabin.

25

I leaned back in my seat, wincing again as the train jostled. Kisten slept in the bed next to me, his breathing slow and heavy. Brown and white feathers rippled across his arms in his sleep and I knew he was dreaming of flying again. Since he had been disconnected from the Grimm when Mother killed them, Kisten's animals only responded out of fear, but it still left his control fragile. He managed to keep them from overtaking him, but when he slept, they often manifested, causing him to shift in his sleep. The first time it happened had been terrifying, but I knew that I could merely wake Kisten if his animal got out of hand.

I sighed, standing as I made my way to the small window, watching as the scenery flew by. We had stayed at Lucius' retreat for a few days after the fight, hoping to give ourselves enough time to recover before returning to Decver. Lucius had informed Crispin and Eve of Aurel's betrayal and from the tone of the call, it sounded as if Lucius intended to have a meeting with all of us upon our return. It seemed that such a heavy betrayal from Aurel had been a wake-up call to Lucius about his laid-back ways and he was determined not to make the same mistake twice.

"I wonder who Sixth will be now," I pondered aloud, watching as an empty station flew by me in the quiet night. Lucius would have no choice but to reorganize command, as Thirteenth had been empty since Justina was relieved of command and Kisca and I were moved up. However, with two spaces now empty and Mater Vitae focused on us, he had to find replacements in the Coven.

"Vitae..." I whispered, looking back to Kisten's sleeping form. I had known she wouldn't hide forever, but I always hoped I would be long dead before she ever chose to come out. Something about my power had her scared, scared enough that she decided I was no longer worth recapturing. There was no way she wasn't going to try and track down where Lucius and I were, and it would only put the Capital at more risk.

Despite the risk however, staying put was the best decision for all of us. Even if Lucius wanted to leave, we would be putting ourselves at a disadvantage and we both knew it. Supernaturals were no longer secret and Mater Vitae knew she would not get away with a large-scale massacre like the ones she had committed in the past. She would have to be more underhanded, and we could force her to play on our turf, where we held the upper hand.

"Raiven? Are you awake?" LeAlexende's voice was soft and tentative as he called through the door, interrupting my thoughts. I opened the door for him, inviting him into the small space as I forced a smile. The Overseer looked at the sleeping Alpha with a warm gaze, and quickly turned to leave. "I can come back la—"

"Stay," I insisted, sitting down on the bed as I motioned for him to sit across from me. He conceded as my locket grew warm and I pulled it from underneath my shirt. LeAlexende had passed out shortly after we returned to the cabin and I had been so distracted with helping Kisten that I failed to finish my questioning of the Overseer. LeAlexende relaxed in the chair across from me, watching me with a curious expression as I stroked the wood.

"Thank you," he finally said and I met his gaze evenly, merely nodding in response to his words. The vampire chuckled at my reaction, his eyes resting on my cross. "That never was from Vitae, was it?"

"No," I confirmed, feeling my sister's interest as I continued petting the wood. "This... this was my sister's and houses her soul. Although there's not much of her left after so long."

"... I see." LeAlexende nodded, and he seemed to be deep in thought as he continued looking at the locket. I waited patiently as I stared at his white hair, wondering why he had hidden it when I first met him and why he still hid his eyes. Perhaps he had been worried I would notice he used to be Nisaba? Even so, it seemed... odd that he wouldn't *want* me to realize the connection and I hesitated as a million questions danced through my mind. I dropped my gaze as the vampire moved, holding his hand out to me. "May I?"

I looked at his hand and felt my sister as she tried to push a concept to me, but it was too complicated for me to understand. I sighed, taking a deep breath as I pulled up my power to push into the locket. It took all my concentration to keep it from spilling out, but I managed to push enough into the locket in order to hear my sister's voice.

'*Do it,*' she ordered and I carefully lifted the cord from over my head, gently handing the locket to LeAlexende. The vampire took it carefully, cradling it as if it would shatter in his hands. I saw his surprise as my sister began talking to him and watched his expressions as they spoke.

He seemed to be answering her with his thoughts, as the air between us remained silent while he cradled the locket. I glanced toward the sleeping Kisten, whose feathers had faded in favor of snake scales. I gently reached over to stroke him, earning myself a quiet sigh from the shifter. I smiled softly as I remembered how excited his snake had been to meet me, and I couldn't resist petting the green scales that were now covering his exposed skin.

"Here, Raiven. I believe you two have a lot to talk about," I pulled my eyes away from Kisten as LeAlexende spoke and I gingerly accepted my cross back from him. My sister's voice filled my mind as soon as I dropped the cord back around my neck.

'*Give me a moment to process, Raiven. I'll... tell you what I can in a bit,*' my sister's voice held her confusion and worry and I couldn't help as her concern spilled into me. She felt my changing emotions and hurried her next statement to assuage them. *'It's not bad, just... a lot to take in. I'm not sure I understand it myself to be honest, much less how to explain it to you.'*

'Alright,' I conceded, returning my attention to LeAlexende, who was watching Kisten as the Alpha slept. His gaze was warm and loving, as if he were looking at a child. I returned my gaze to my lover as well, laughing softly as Kisten rolled over in his sleep.

"I hope he recovers swiftly," he spoke quietly, never taking his gaze off the sleeping Alpha. I nodded, looking at LeAlexende again and the vampire had a pained expression on his face as he spoke. "Vitae is as cruel as ever. She could have easily killed the pack without that display: she did it to frighten you and Kisten."

"She did," I agreed, my hand curling into fists. "She was probably hoping to break his mind as well. I doubt she knew he was already disconnected from the pack."

"I have no doubt that was her intent as well, and we are lucky she failed," LeAlexende agreed, touching the bed next to Kisten. "This has still hurt him, but I know he'll overcome it."

"What will you do now? Where will you go?" I finally asked, causing the vampire to turn to face me. He glanced away in thought, before finally shrugging, sliding down in his seat.

"I don't know. I was thinking about going home, back across the sea." He glanced at the faraway window, a melancholic expression starting on his face. "As much as I'd like to stay, I'd only be in the way. You all have a lot to prepare for and besides, I..."

The vampire's voice trailed off into silence, his eyes locked on the passing trees outside the dark window. I watched him for a moment longer, unable to help the ache that started in my chest again. Every part of me wanted to ask Alex to stay but I knew he was right. We needed to prepare for war against Vitae and having him stay would only put his life in more danger.

"Miss home?" I finally offered and LeAlexende chuckled, turning to look at me.

"Home has been gone for a long time now, I can't return to those days, even if I wanted to," he admitted, meeting my gaze with a sad look. Something about his soft purple eyes made my heart skip a beat and I felt a deep desire to hug him. "But I want to visit my siblings. Both Alrune and Basina are buried back home and I want to stay there with them."

"I understand," I nodded, grabbing my cross as my sister's regret filled me. I forced myself to smile, clearing my throat as I spoke. "I hope you will come to see Kisten and I when we are married?"

"Of course," he promised with a smile, the expression finally reaching his eyes and LeAlexende grabbed my free hand with both of his. "As long as I still live, I'll be there."

"Thank you," I reluctantly let his hands slip from mine as LeAlexende stood and quietly left, leaving me alone with the sleeping Kisten once again. I sighed deeply, drawing my legs into the chair as I took in the silence. I felt a scaled tail begin to wrap around my ankle and I quickly sat up.

"It's just me," Kisten's voice was soft as he spoke and still full of sleep, and I turned to see his soft eyes looking at me. They were a bright green like his scales, and still held all of the love he felt for me. I couldn't help but smile as I reached for him, and he took my hand in his scaled one.

"How much of you is snake?" I asked jokingly and Kisten chuckled, quickly kissing the back of my hand. The lack of pain was still always surprising to me, and I knew it would be a while before I learned to accept it was gone for good. The Alpha lifted up the cover to reveal his lower half completely changed, once more looking more like a lamia than a shifter.

"Want to cuddle?" Kisten offered, and I laughed quietly as I stood, tucking the wooden cross back into my shirt.

"You won't crush me right?" I asked jokingly, lying down next to Kisten as he wrapped his tail around me, pulling me closer to him as he threw the covers over both of us. He quickly pressed a kiss into my forehead, sighing happily as he draped his arm across me.

"Not unless you want me to," he muttered, clearly only moments from falling back asleep. I gently stroked his cheek, cradling his face in my hands. Kisten purred as I did this, and despite the scales currently on his skin, I watched as his spots began to manifest as well.

"Sleep Kisten, before you turn into a weird half leopard, half snake person," I teased, lightly tapping his face as he closed his eyes, only nodding at my suggestion. I waited until his breathing evened out and his spots disappeared before I settled against my lover, his tail holding me in place. I stared up to the ceiling, kept awake by the jostling of the train.

"Sis?"

'I'm... still here,' her voice still sounded conflicted, and I closed my eyes, humming softly as Kisten's tail tightened around me. *'I'm honestly not sure what to say.'*

"What do you mean?"

'So much of what Alex said doesn't make sense, and he said it wouldn't until we start to remember,' she sighed and I echoed the sound, wrapping my hands around the cross: *'Apparently our power awakening is the beginning of that process, but he didn't say what would happen next. Just that we should return to where Vitae found us.'*

"Back home..." my thoughts trailed off as I opened my eyes, unable to help the sound that escaped me. I always knew it was a journey I would have to make soon anyway for my sister's sake, but now LeAlexende was saying that returning would help me to understand this new power. "Something more must've happened there than what we remember."

'That's my best guess as well,' she agreed and I closed my eyes again as Kisten squeezed me tighter in his tail. *'Our memory of that time is spotty at best, and we both just accepted what Vitae told us.'*

"Guess it's time to find out the truth for ourselves," I decided and I felt my sister's agreement as she finally faded away. I took a deep breath, letting it out shakily as I considered what my power could possibly mean. It made sense that Mother would lie about it, considering how afraid of it she seemed to be, but why? Why had she simply not killed me then, if she was so afraid of what I might become?

"Questions without end," I whispered to myself, snuggling into Kisten more on the bed as I watched the train pass by another station outside the window. I did my best to quell my swirling thoughts, letting the steady breathing of my mate's breath lull me into a gentle sleep.

KILL A DOVE
SEALED BLOOD BOOK 3

"Vogel." I heard Kisten's voice as he shifted behind me, the rest of the pack turning their attention to their leader. I could vaguely hear her snapping at them as they began to inspect the corpses of their dead companions. Their fear of death still seemed to wash over me, but I ignored it as some of them shifted back to their human form. They quickly picked up the bodies and disappeared back into the grass, hoping to escape us in my distraction.
"Who... who is that?"
The being smiled softly as I stopped, searching the eyes of the person in front me as I tried to determine if they were real. When I finally spoke, my voice was barely above a whisper.
"The Seraph."

To my beautiful daughter,
Who gives me the strength to face my fears.
To my partner,
For being my strength.

I

I sighed as I spun on the projector again, doing my best to let Shannon see the dress from behind. She frowned as she leaned back in her seat, balancing the tablet on her knee as she made several different noises. Then finally, she shook her head, blowing a raspberry as I glanced over my shoulder. She was running her hand through her blonde hair, a pouty expression on her face as she glared at the screen.

"It just looks too... princessy," she complained, swiping on the tablet as I turned to face her again. Justina laughed in the chair beside her, adjusting her wrap as she shifted baby Noelle in her arms. "Too much fabric, and it's just way too big."

"Is my *cecmpa*[1] not good enough to be a princess for her own wedding?" the sorcerer joked, and I couldn't help my slight laugh as Shannon rolled her eyes at the two of us. I spread my arms out as she chose another dress and the image around me shimmered before adjusting. This particular dress shop had actually been recommended by Vanessa, but the vampire had declined to accompany us for the fitting, saying it still held too many memories for her.

I sighed as my thoughts drifted, barely hearing what my other bridesmaids were saying as they fussed over the detail of the dress. It hardly seemed like only three months had passed since Shannon's wedding and Mark's death, and I couldn't help as I pushed against the ring on my finger. Vanessa was Mark's surviving wife, and while she agreed to still be a bridesmaid for my union, she excused herself from most of the planning, more than content to leave it to her sister-in-law and Justina.

"Feathers? Just because she's named after a bird doesn't mean she should look like a plucked *курица*[2]."

"With the way you're acting, I would think this was *your* wedding, Bridezilla."

"You are insane if you think I'm going to let you do that to *my* Raiven," Justina spat, and I couldn't help my giggle as the two went back and forth, Justina trying to take the tablet from Shannon. Both were strong-willed and stubborn, neither willing to back down once they had made up their minds about something. Luckily, their partners liked their fire, and I simply found it endearing as Justina finally stopped trying to take the device, settling for reaching over Shannon's arm instead.

I jumped slightly as my phone vibrated and I was careful to pull it from my pocket, not wanting to disrupt the projection. It held a message from Kisten and I couldn't help smiling as I opened the device.

<I swear these two are worse than their wives,> he complained, and I laughed out loud as Justina changed my dress again. Kisten and I were only separated by the wall behind me, Arkrian and Crispin helping the Alpha to choose his suit. The shop specialized in holo-designed wedding attire, and the couples could easily share their designs with each other via the designing tablets. It was exciting to think that we were so close, but would still remain unaware until the day of the wedding, my heart pounding as I considered seeing him in his suit.

"There it is!" I returned my attention to my bridesmaids as Shannon exclaimed, excitedly selecting a new dress. I was unable to help my surprise as the hologram changed, the fabric now dragging from my hand as I lifted my phone. Even Justina seemed interested in the more goddess-like style, humming her agreement as she finished feeding Noelle.

"The style is nice, but white looks absolutely hideous on Raiven," the sorcerer mused, reaching over to tap on the tablet in Shannon's lap. I watched as the material around me flashed through an assortment of colors and shades, the women trying to agree on a color. I carefully slid my phone back into my pocket, looking up to notice baby Noelle watching me curiously. Despite the danger to such a young vampire, Justina took Noelle with her everywhere, wanting to enjoy as much time as she could with her child. Considering it was likely the sorcerer wouldn't even live long enough to see her daughter's tenth birthday, it was a choice that made sense and my chest clenched slightly with the thought.

"Hey." I pushed away my morbid thoughts, waving slightly and the little girl tilted her head more, still watching me as her mother adjusted her again. Noelle had been born right after the incident at Shannon's wedding with Whistleblower, and her bright green eyes were an exact match of her mother's. Justina and Crispin were still betting over whether her hair would be blue or blonde, but I had a feeling they would both be wrong as I made a face at the baby. She looked at me curiously before attempting a smile, and I was unable to help my chuckle as Shannon spoke again.

"C'mon Justina, dark purple with glitter is perfect, look!" Shannon gestured toward me as the hologram shifted again and the dress shimmered as I moved. The purple was a slightly lighter shade at the neckline, but slowly deepened into almost a black color, and the glitter twinkled like stars as I moved. I turned to see myself in the mirror and my heart pounded at the sight. I found myself grinning as I considered Kisten seeing me in a dress like this, and I heard Justina sigh with defeat.

"Well, given that stupid smile on Raiven's face, I'll have to concede," the sorcerer said, giving me a soft smile despite her dismissive tone. I shrugged and smiled back and Justina shook her head as she turned to Shannon. "Looks like you win this round, Дорогой[3]."

"If it makes you feel better, I'll let you have full rein over the bridesmaid dresses," Shannon offered, leaning back in her chair as she smiled at Justina.

"Good to leave that to someone with taste," the sorcerer jabbed and Shannon laughed, motioning the attendant over as she sent the design to her husband. As the hologram faded from my body completely and I gently pulled my sleeves back down, I felt my phone vibrate again and was unable to help my amusement at Kisten's new message.

<I don't know what you guys did, but it set a fire under these two. I'm likely to be here for at least another hour.>

<Wait until you see.>

<Now, Vogel[4], we agreed on no teasing.> I glanced up as I saw Shannon motion for me, and I gingerly stepped off the projector as the attendant turned to face me.

"We should have the dress ready in about five weeks, and we can go ahead and schedule your next fitting to ensure no adjustments are needed!" The siren beamed, taking a moment to adjust her hair as she cradled the tablet. Her hands shone with glitter and from the way her fingers danced around the tablet, it was clear that she was excited by the dress my companions had designed. "Will that do, messere[5]?"

"That should be more than enough time." I nodded and the girl giggled, her chestnut brown hair swaying as she rocked with excitement. Shannon and Justina both stood to walk away with her, eager to see what options they would have for the bridesmaids. I glanced at the phone in my hand to see the time and responded to Kisten's text.

<As much as I would love to wait for you, I need to get to the Coven. Lucius should be awake by now.>

<Go. I'll meet you there later.> I hummed with delight as I exited the dress shop, quickly spotting my car in the parking lot across the street. Traffic was already starting to pick up in the late afternoon and I waited impatiently to cross the road. The light changed soon enough and I walked briskly across, the first hints of thirst starting to rise. As soon as I slid into my car, I felt the need hit me like a train and I gripped the steering wheel tightly, trying to bury it as best I could.

My thirst for undead blood used to barely bother me, but ever since I unlocked my true power, I could barely keep my addiction under control. Where once Lucius only had to share blood twice a year, I could barely go a week before I needed to drink from him again. It used to be intensified by using my power, but it had started to progress on its own, leaving me nearly desperate in my need.

"We don't have much time," I growled as I managed to start my car, and I could feel my sister's faint agreement as I pulled out into the growing traffic. I had already been told that I needed to return to my birthplace and the location where Vitae found me to understand my new power, but between my new placement in Division 11 and planning for the wedding, it was hard to justify the time I needed. I wasn't even exactly sure where I needed to go, as where I grew up was unlikely to be marked on any sort of map. Even after Europeans had started to be interested in Africa, they had not done a decent job of marking locations in those early days and while I could likely get close to my birthplace, much of the search would have to be done manually. Mater Vitae herself was also a concern, since both Lucius and I had no doubt she was trying to locate where we were and I worried she would use my absence as a chance to attack if she learned of it.

I arrived at the Landing, pulling out of the growing traffic and into the back of the Dream. The parking lot was quiet for now, and I knew it would quickly fill up as the day dragged on, as most of the workers would be arriving to start their nights once the sun set. For my part, I started down the sidewalk, quickly making my way to the door that would take me down into the Coven. A few of the workers waved to me as I passed, and I politely returned the gesture, my thirst starting to bother me again.

I quickly reached the door that would take me underground and as I opened it, I pushed against the magic barrier, hating the way this new one required more force to push through. All things considered, I couldn't blame Lucius for being cautious and I shook the threads of magic from my hands. I took my time as I descended down the steps, making my way down the dark hallway into the living room. Liel and

Quinn were relaxing in the redecorated space, both lounging on opposite couches as they talked. The TV was on the wall beyond them, but it seemed the pair was no longer paying much attention to the show.

"Just because it's predictable doesn't mean – oh Raiven, wanna join?" The wraith grinned at me, his red eyes full of mirth as he looked up at me. He was lying over the edge, his dark gray hair almost touching the floor. "We're debating whether or not *Glitch and Force* is a good show or not."

"It's over-the-top and melodramatic," Liel rasped, rolling her eyes as Quinn gasped with fake surprise. The banshee barely shifted on her couch, sipping on her tea as she ignored the wraith. "Besides, the story is contrived and too predictable."

"But the animation!" Quinn argued, finally sitting up as he began to gesture with his hands towards the TV. I looked at the device as the show returned from a commercial break, humming as I recognized the episode. "The animation is beautiful and the jokes are funny without being distasteful. A predictable story doesn't take away from that. C'mon, Raiven, you gotta agree with me."

"Well, sorry Quinn but Liel is right about the story. We both know it's been done a million times," I started, watching the wraith as he lay back down, throwing his hands up in defeat. I chuckled as I continued, looking over the banshee as she gave Quinn a smug grin. "But I agree with you, it is a good show despite that. The way it's presented makes up for the lackluster story, and the animation is a nice departure from most media we see now."

"Ha! See, Raiven agrees with me so I win!" Quinn's sour mood quickly changed to glee and Liel rolled her eyes again as she leaned into her couch. I couldn't help laughing as I continued through the living room, doing my best to ignore the banshee's annoyed glance as I left. I continued down the hall to find Lucius' room, pausing outside as I considered I had failed to tell him I was on my way. I didn't want to deal with Evalyn if she was with him, and I had started to walk away when I heard him call out to me through the door.

"It's alright, Raiven. You can come in." I hummed with embarrassment as I slowly let myself in, and found the Overseer sitting in his armchair, facing away from the door. From the copper smell in the room I knew he had recently fed, and I hesitated near the door, unsure if I had interrupted him. Once again, Lucius seemed to sense my thoughts, chuckling softly as he beckoned me closer. "It's alright, I woke up and was... thinking."

"About?" I asked, taking my time as I approached the vampire, kneeling on the floor next to him as I waited for permission to feed. My thirst was unbearable as I sat and I was unable to help as my body reacted, my stomach rumbling as I tried to swallow it down. The Overseer glanced at me with his blue eyes, black hair cascading over his shoulder. He was wearing one of his more casual outfits, a red button-down shirt with black pants, although it seemed as if he had slept in the clothing. "Something important?"

"Yes, but we can talk about that in a moment," he said softly, motioning me closer as I slid across the carpet, adjusting my hair as I laid my head in his lap. I had cut it to a short afro again, but just as the thirst had accelerated, my hair was growing unnaturally fast whether or not I used my power. It had already grown past my shoulders again, and I did my best to pull it back as I waited for Lucius.

"Alright." I felt the Overseer wrap his arm around me, gently holding me as he placed his wrist in front of me. I could barely resist the desire to immediately bite down and indulge in his sweet blood, but I forced myself to gently cradle his arm, waiting for permission as Lucius hummed again.

"Go ahead, drink your fill, *ama*[6]."

I didn't hesitate as my fangs extended past my lips and I sunk them into his skin, humming with delight as the blood hit my tongue. It was the sweet, filling taste I desired and I closed my eyes as I drank with deep pulls, unwilling to spill even a single drop. Lucius shifted slightly as he leaned into me, and I felt him wrap his arm around me tighter as I lifted his wrist, still drinking from the Overseer. This was always Lucius' preferred way to feed me, as it allowed him to be comfortable while I indulged my thirst and he was easily able to pull his wrist away from me if I started to drink too much. I enjoyed the gesture for the trust he showed me; most others that had been willing to help satisfy my thirst would only present me with blood they drew themselves. I could understand the fear of having their blood drunk, but it always stung slightly that none of them had believed that I could control myself.

"You called, Lucius?" I barely moved as Crispin's voice interrupted the silence and I heard him as he paused in the doorway. "Oh, I can wait if—"

"You can come in. Raiven is almost done," Lucius called out, barely shifting his position as Crispin obeyed, slowly closing and locking the door as he entered. I heard him as he moved behind us, sitting on the Overseer's bed as Lucius gently pulled against me, and I released him, still humming with delight. My thirst had settled into its usual mild annoyance and I sighed as I opened my eyes, lifting my head from the Overseer.

"Thank you," I breathed as I stood, adjusting my hair again as I moved to the bed to join Crispin, the vampire shifting to give me space. I didn't particularly like Crispin, especially since I had known him before he turned and didn't like what becoming a vampire had done to him. However, he was with my best friend, and I was slowly discovering that he still had echoes of who he used to be, even if he wasn't that person anymore.

"So, what did you need us for?" Crispin offered, leaning back on the bed as he waited for Lucius to speak. The vampire playfully tossed his hair as he grinned at me, and I resisted the desire to roll my eyes. Despite giving up his pursuit of me as a lover, Crispin still enjoyed teasing me whenever he could and it always took all my effort not to give him the reaction he was fishing for. However, both Crispin and I quickly turned to look at the Overseer as Lucius spoke and I felt my heart pound with worry.

"We need to talk about Evalyn."

2

Both Crispin and I remained silent after Lucius' quiet statement and the pair of us shared a look as the vampire slowly sat up next to me. As First and Second in the Coven, we were considered of equal rank to the Three, but both of us preferred to not look at our positions that way. Neither of us particularly wanted to become an Overseer and Lucius wanting to talk about Eve without even Kisten present was a bad sign.

"What about her?" I cautioned, watching as Lucius sighed, sinking deeper into his chair. He hesitated to speak and both Crispin and I fidgeted uncomfortably on the bed. "Did she do something that has you worried?"

"She... has been acting differently since the incident with Whistleblower. It used to be impossible to get her to leave me alone, but since returning, she has become distant," the vampire admitted and I barely swallowed my sound. Eve had indeed seemed more independent since our return to Decver, but I assumed it was due to Lucius' change in attitude. "I know she was moved to the S-Men as a result of her true race being revealed, but she seems as if she's gone on her missions far longer than she should be."

The silence between us was deafening as none of us spoke, and I fidgeted on the bed again as my mind raced. Lucius had a point that Eve's sudden shift in behavior was worrisome, as the ala was fairly predictable in how she reacted to things. An ugly thought began to form in my head, and I couldn't help the noise that escaped me as the frown on my face grew.

"You think she had something to do with Aurel?" I offered, ignoring the concerned look Crispin gave me as I spoke. I felt the charge in the air increase as I said the lich's name but Lucius only hummed angrily in response. "We know he tried to betray us to Whistleblower, and you said it started right after that."

"I should hope not," Lucius finally spat and I growled softly, sharing the Overseer's sentiment.

"Unfortunately, I can't say it would surprise me," Crispin finally spoke, rubbing the back of his neck awkwardly. We both turned to look at him, but the vampire was frowning as he avoided our eyes, instead glancing at the bed sheets. "When you called us after killing Whistleblower, Evalyn definitely was not happy with the news. At first, I thought it was because she hated the idea of you making changes to the way you handled the Coven, but–"

"It easily could have been because she was hoping to *not* hear from you," I interrupted, flinching at the slight sting I got from the electrified air. Lucius was doing his best to contain his anger, but, all things considered, he had every right to be upset. Aurel's betrayal had caused many deaths, and almost included Lucius' longtime friend LeAlexende. The idea that Evalyn had been a part of the lich's plot was alarming at best, and I pulled my hair back together as I continued. "After all, it would explain how Aurel knew Whistleblower would want Kisten and that LeAlexende was one of the First."

"To be fair, I didn't even know about Whistleblower and Kisten, and I'm First in the Coven. If anyone should have known about that, it should have been me, not that bastard," Crispin scoffed, tapping his hands on the sheets as he mulled over his thoughts. It was clear that in some part, Crispin also blamed himself for not seeing through Aurel sooner and I watched the vampire angrily brush his blond hair off his shoulder. "He's lucky we didn't have Richie yet."

"True," I sighed, thinking of our two new additions to the Coven as Lucius hummed in his chair. Richie was another lich that had taken Thirteenth, and he specialized in serums and potions while Sixth, Aurel's former spot, had gone to a fairy named Emelia. At first, I worried that Emelia and Kisca wouldn't get along, as fairies and pixies often fought over whose glamor was better, but they were actually very cordial with each other when they had to interact.

"It also would've worked out great in her favor had Aurel succeeded," Crispin continued, the vampire's expression lost in thought as he tried to logic out Eve's plan. "I mean, you left her and me behind, and if Aurel just so *happened* to betray you so he could get Raiven, and you died, she would've become Overseer."

"And she wouldn't have had to worry about Aurel revealing the truth, because Whistleblower would kill him for trying to keep me. Kisten would also be out of the picture, so no one would be left to really voice their opposition to her," I said, mentally cursing the ala as I considered her involvement. It was exactly the type of underhanded trick she would try, especially if she thought the odds were in her favor. "She becomes Overseer through a bad circumstance, and while no one likes her, they'd have no choice but to accept it."

"Exactly; the only person who would have the power to contest it is me, and I'm sure she would have found a way to try and eliminate me from the equation as well," Crispin said angrily, clearly also hating how much it made sense. "She could even keep her tie to Whistleblower, since she'd easily be able to feed him information about the remaining First in exchange for favors."

"So, you believe she may be involved with Vitae?" Lucius finally asked, his voice soft with his hurt and anger. I felt my heart twist as I hesitated to answer, unable to help my pity for the vampire. While it had always been clear to the rest of us that Evalyn was only with Lucius for the power boost he offered, it was also clear that he cared about her. I wasn't sure it could really be called love, but even the idea of her betrayal was obviously enough to make his heart ache.

"I doubt directly: if she was, I would imagine Vitae would have found us by now. She probably passed the info to Aurel to see what the outcome might be, especially since if he failed, we'd kill him and not learn about her involvement," I breathed, choosing my words carefully as I spoke. "It's likely that she has a contact, probably one of Vitae's servants. A Hunter wouldn't hesitate to just kill her or torture her for the information they needed, so she must be working with someone below them."

"Someone who would be willing to work with her in hopes of betraying her later on," Crispin agreed, sighing heavily as he leaned back on the bed again. "I'd bet she's just using them to try and figure out where Mother is herself. After all, Vitae's blood would be the biggest power boost she could ask for at this point, especially if she's decided Lucius is of no more use to her. A Sibling would be another option, but LeAlexende is the only one left and he would never help her."

Silence filled the space again as Lucius took in our words and I shared another glance with Crispin. The question in the air was obvious, but had no good answer: what would we do now? If she *was* working with Mater Vitae, it was too dangerous to simply dismiss her, as nothing would stop her from running to Vitae and making her betrayal obvious. Killing her was the simplest solution but also dangerous, as we had no way of knowing if she had tasted any of Vitae's blood yet. If she had, taking her on would be equivalent to taking on a Hunter and considering her flames, the damage she could cause would be devastating. There was also Division 11 to consider: even if she was dismissed as Retainer, she would still be a member of the S-Men, and therefore still have access to information about Lucius and the Coven. Remembering the agency brought a new idea to my mind and I leaned back on the bed.

"Hmmm... I could try talking to the Director," I offered quietly, and Lucius finally looked up from the floor to meet my gaze. I could see the quiet tears that flowed down his face and I forced myself to keep speaking. "I know that any option is a dangerous one, especially considering how much of a threat Vitae already is. But if I talk to the Director and Evalyn *is* meeting with a servant of Vitae, he could have her detained via our protocol. Any contact with Mater Vitae or one of her vassals is ground for immediate termination and imprisonment, pending review and punishment by the Overseer."

"That would also take the blame off us," Crispin agreed, sighing deeply as he slid his hands along the sheets. "If the agency finds her guilty, then we look like we're merely reacting to what they found, rather than having caught on ourselves. Also gives you time to choose a new Retainer to have ready once the Division imprisons her."

"And you trust them to be able to hold her, if she has been drinking Mother's blood?" Lucius whispered and I nodded my head.

"We've never *really* tested it with a Hunter before, but Valkyrie should be able to negate her powers. It has worked on an Overseer during our live test, and the research team gave it a 75/25 percent chance on a Hunter," I admitted, crossing my arms as I considered the device. Valkyrie was a marvel of science and magic, a device that made holding dangerous Supernaturals possible and could neutralize the powers of most beings. It had only been used twice since its creation, but considering it was only six months old, it was an amazing achievement and the Director already had our research team working on a portable application. He seemed to be hoping we could use it out in the field to put a stop to Hunters and other Supernaturals with the potential for large amounts of destruction.

"Crazy what humans come up with." Crispin sighed and I echoed his sound, giving him an annoyed look.

"Valkyrie was a joint project, not just human. If not for Supernatural input and help, it wouldn't work as well as it does and I doubt it would work at all if not for the Dokkalfar being willing to add their magic," I pointed out and the vampire shrugged, clearly not interested in arguing with me. I shook my head as I looked back to the Overseer, who was still watching me with hurt and concern. "Point stands, it should be able to hold Evalyn, at least until we can deal with her and Valkyrie is stored underground just in case it fails. Her damage would be limited to a small area and that's safer than if she's outed above ground."

"Tell the Director as soon as possible," Lucius finally ordered, and his blue eyes swirled with power as I shivered. "I'll look for a replacement Retainer in the meantime. Once I have one, I'll reach out to the Director myself."

"And while we wait?"

"Until Evalyn is dealt with, this conversation never happened," Lucius commanded and both Crispin and I nodded, understanding the silent order. We weren't allowed to discuss Lucius' doubt about Evalyn with anyone, but he also wanted us to keep an eye on her for any possible admission of guilt. As much as I was certain Lucius wanted to tell Kisten his worries, the Oath of Truth made it impossible; even if the Alpha was good at speaking in half-truths when it suited him, there was no way he could avoid tipping off Eve if she questioned him.

"Well, if we're done with our chat, I'd like to get back to my little family." Crispin stretched and I watched Lucius' lips twitch into a slight smile. The vampire stood with his usual flare, tossing his gold hair as he continued. "Justina will kill me if I keep finding excuses to escape my parental duties."

"By all means, don't let us be the cause of your death," I joked, unable to help my own smile as the vampire strolled out, not trying to hide his laughter. I slowly followed behind him, surprised to see him waiting for me in the hallway. I quietly closed Lucius' door, sealing the Overseer in his room. "What, had a change of heart that quickly?"

"No, I—" Crispin paused, and I felt my heart twist as his expression changed. Since learning about our past together, I became the only person besides Justina that he would let his guard down around. As much as his flirtatious nature was who he had become, he still was the same soft and insecure man he had been when I first knew him. "I wanted to... ask you something."

"Which is?"

"All this with you and Kisten has me wondering... should I... I mean... Justina..." Crispin sighed with frustration and I felt my heart ache for him as I understood what he wanted to ask me. Crispin had already expressed his desire to give the sorcerer anything she wanted, wanting to make the limited time they had count. "I mean, I don't want her to feel worse than she already does, but I–"

"I think you should ask her this, not me," I offered, and Crispin scoffed, crossing his arms as he turned away from me.

"What a shitty way to propose."

"Can't be worse than bleeding to death in a garden after she runs away," I offered and Crispin laughed softly, shaking his head. I hummed softly as I gently laid my hand on his shoulder, turning him to look at me. "You know she would love to."

"She already feels bad for 'trapping me with a kid', even though I agreed when she asked me," Crispin said, placing his hand on mine and stroking it gently. I felt a spark of annoyance as he played with my fingers, but did my best to swallow it down. "And she feels bad that I've been limiting myself more to her, despite the fact we don't have sex. I try to get her to understand it's because I want to, but she just insists I don't need to. We have so little time left, and I..."

I hummed my agreement as his voice trailed again, letting the vampire squeeze my hand. Crispin had all but given up his chasing of other women to focus on Justina and Noelle, and I knew Justina was convinced it was due to her impending death. She didn't want him to feel trapped by her, just as much as he wanted her to understand that it was his choice.

"Still, you should be talking to her about all this, not me," I repeated, slowly pulling my hand away as his blue eyes met mine. "You know better than to coddle her and Justina knows that, it's just... she doesn't want you to change who you are because of it."

"Yeah... I know," Crispin agreed, turning down the hall to head to Justina's room and I watched after him for a moment, my heart aching for him and Justina. Their situation was not unique, and I couldn't prevent my thoughts from turning to me and Kisten. I definitely had a lot longer with the Alpha, but as an Immortal, I would eventually face the same situation as the vampire. Knowing that he was going to die, while I...

"That bad, huh?" I quickly glanced up to see Kisten leaning against the wall further down the hallway, and I accepted his embrace as he pulled me into his arms. I took a moment to bury my face into his chest as he took in my scent, humming softly. "I won't ask; if it were something I could know, Lucius would've called me, too."

"Yea..." I breathed, moaning softly as I held the Alpha tighter in my arms. Kisten reacted immediately, sweeping me off my feet in one fluid motion and the shifter began carrying me down the hall. "Kisten, wha–"

"I have had to spend all day being good and not seeing my mate," he pouted, pushing his door open with his foot as we entered and I couldn't help my chuckle as he set me on the bed. I gently wrapped my arms around him as he buried his face into my neck again, moaning softly. "I'd like to enjoy my treat."

"By all means," I whispered, lifting his head as I gazed into his chartreuse eyes, stroking his face as I did so. His eyes met mine for a moment before drifting down to my lips, and I laughed again as I pulled his face to mine, kissing my Alpha deeply.

3

He purred against me, dragging his kisses from my face down to my neck. I fully surrendered to his gentle love and touch, unable to help how much my chest ached as I moaned softly. My fingers danced through his strands, and I soon dragged his face back to mine, wanting to taste his soft lips again.

Kisten growled softly as he pushed onto me, sliding up my body more until most of his weight rested on top of me. I hummed shakily into the kiss, sliding my hands down to the edge of his shirt as I slipped them underneath. Despite the fact Kisten had been free of the Oath for months now, I still was surprised by the lack of pain, and I slowly broke the kiss, giving the shifter a dazed look.

"You almost look drunk," Kisten laughed and I merely hummed in response, dragging my fingers along his back. "Guessing you missed me too."

"You know I did," I sighed, holding him tighter against me as I breathed him in. I lacked his acute sense of smell, but I enjoyed his natural musk all the same, and found myself giving a happy sigh. I moaned softly as he moved against me and my body reacted, my hips rising to meet his. The shifter slowly sat up from me, adjusting his legs and I frowned as I was forced to release my grip on him. Kisten smiled at me knowingly as he removed the shirt, tossing it to the floor before placing my hand on his chest.

"Thought I'd help you out."

"How considerate," I hummed, loving the feel of his laugh as he leaned over me again, dragging another kiss from my lips. I eagerly leaned into him, wishing I had removed my own shirt so I could feel his skin against mine. His fingers fumbled at my waist and I felt him begin to pull down my pants, causing me to laugh into the kiss slightly.

"Allow me to continue," Kisten chuckled, leaning away from me again as he finished removing the offensive clothing. He tossed it to the floor to join his shirt before lifting my waist, burying his face in between my legs as he enjoyed my scent. I couldn't help both my arousal and my embarrassment as I turned away from the sight and the Alpha laughed at me as he noticed. "I would think you'd be used to this by now."

"Hmmmm," was all I would say, and a loud moan escaped me as I felt his tongue press my underwear into my opening. There was no reason for Kisten to do this anymore, but the shifter apparently loved teasing me this way, soaking my underwear with his saliva as he pressed his tongue into me. Every press, every teasing lick only aroused me more, and soon I was whining with my want, my desire to have him remove the clothing and let me feel him.

"*Delicious,*" Kisten breathed as he paused, and I finally managed to open my eyes to see the Alpha. The look on his face was pure bliss as he held me and he continued his licking as he carefully lay down on the bed and I loosely wrapped my legs around him, unable to help my own sounds. My hand found its way to his hair and I lifted his head slightly, releasing him as our eyes met. The shifter's expression was full of desire. He was chuckling as he licked me again, and the moan that escaped me now was long and desperate as I turned away.

"Kis... please," I begged softly, my hands gripping the bed under my head tightly as I squirmed. I could feel his laugh as he adjusted his position and another loud sound escaped me as I finally felt his sandpaper tongue against my sensitive opening. Without the barrier in the way, Kisten dug into me, as if the underwear had been the only thing restraining him. He purred and growled into me loudly, and I couldn't help it as my orgasm began to build from the pleasure and his sounds.

Every touch and sound seemed to set my body on fire and I instinctively arched into him, desperate to feel him more. Kisten reacted by shoving his face into me, the bed creaking as he adjusted his weight. The shifter was treating me like I was the only source of pure water and he had been dying of thirst his whole life. I tightened my legs around him, unable to control my growing pleasure as he responded to my movement and sounds. I knew he could smell how close I was, and the Alpha was determined to give me my release.

"*Vogel*[1]..." I felt Kisten adjust me again, his claws ripping into the sheets as he moaned and the sound only aroused me more. I wasn't sure which animal was trying to come forward, but just knowing that Kisten was losing control due to his desire for me made me moan louder. The shifter dug his tongue into me even further as my scent changed again and my hands flew to his head, gripping him tightly.

"Kis-Kisten!" I called his name loudly as my orgasm finally hit me, washing through my body like waves on sand. He stopped as I shook around him, waiting until I relaxed my hold to move and I collapsed backwards. I heard him slide up the bed beside me as I closed my eyes, doing my best to focus on controlling my breathing. I took my time reopening my eyes, turning to meet his black gaze. I carefully reached up to touch them, a small smile coming to my lips. "B–"

"Yeah, bear," he confirmed, watching me softly as I did my best to recover from the pleasure he had inflicted on me. His face glistened in the soft light of the room and I gently pulled his face down to mine, eager to taste myself on his skin. The Alpha was unable to hold back his growl as I licked him clean, my tongue eventually seeking the warm crevice of his mouth.

Kisten placed his hand gently on my waist as we kissed, and I could still feel his claws through my shirt as he squeezed me carefully. I broke the kiss to see the black fur that traveled up his arm, humming as I pet the coarse hair.

"Want to meet him?" Kisten asked quietly and I nodded, sitting up as the shifter slid off the bed. I had already met most of his animals, the only exceptions being his dolphin and bear. Whenever Kisten wanted me to meet his bear, usually his snake or leopard would push their way forward instead, and until the saltwater pool at his house was finished, I had no way to meet his dolphin. I watched carefully as Kisten shifted, the room shaking slightly as he fell onto all fours, breathing heavily as his body changed.

"Hello," I spoke softly as I slid to the edge of the bed, reaching my hand out to him as Kisten came closer to me again. I watched as he sniffed my hand, and was unable to help my giggle as he sniffed higher up my arm, his breaths tickling me. He grunted with happiness as he buried his face into my stomach and I laughed as I began to pet the coarse fur again. "You are so childish."

He merely snorted in response as he buried his face into me more and I couldn't help leaning down to hug him, my chest warm with my love. I jumped slightly when he put his paws on the bed, leaning up to lick my face. I shook my head at his silly behavior, wrapping my arms around him again as he began to change back. I felt him shrink in my arms, and began laughing again as Kisten continued licking my face, this time with his human tongue.

"Only one left," he whispered and I nodded, still holding him tight as he wrapped his arms around me.

"Soon enough. Maybe if *someone* hadn't been hiding the fact he was an Omnishifter, you could have had the pool," I teased and despite not seeing his face, I knew Kisten was rolling his eyes at me. "It's not like anyone cared and Lucius already knew."

"Well, it's less of an issue now that my father is gone. I don't have to worry about him finding me anymore," he breathed, and at the mention of his father, I felt my heart drop in my chest again. The shifter smelled the change as he slowly pulled back from me, sitting on the floor as I looked down at him. My hand absently drifted up to my locket and I stroked the wood as my thoughts raced.

"Monster..." I whispered softly, remembering how Whistleblower had insisted on referring to me. At first he had called me Jezebela, hoping to use the name Mother had given me to hurt me, but since I had never claimed it, the name had no power over me. Once he had seen my true power, however, his tune changed, and he insisted on calling me "it" and a "monster". Even Mater Vitae's opinion of me had changed, her goal changing from recapture, to death at all costs and I was constantly worried and on high alert.

"You need to go soon," Kisten whispered, and I forced myself to meet his gaze. He was watching me with worry and concern and I slowly dropped my hand as I sighed. "You are no closer to controlling it. Your thirst is getting worse, and she's almost gone. We can't keep putting this off."

"I know, but there's no time," I complained, my hands shaking in my frustration. "Mater Vitae is hunting for us and I'm sure she knows just as much as Alex and Whistleblower do. I just *know* she's waiting for me to leave and I–"

I paused in my words, my heart twisting as I met his anxious gaze. I reached my hand to stroke his face and he leaned into the touch, closing his eyes as he did so. Kisten pressed a gentle kiss into my hand as he cradled it against his face and I felt my heart twist even more. My thoughts turned to my sister and Justina and I swallowed hard as I began to whisper.

"I can't let her take you too..." My voice was broken with my tears, and I looked away as the Alpha looked back up to me. "I already don't have enough time with you."

"It'll be enough," Kisten purred, leaning up to touch my face as I held his, gently touching our foreheads together. He sighed heavily as he slid his skin against mine, doing his best to comfort me. "I love you."

"I love you, Kisten," I sobbed, unable to hold back the tears that finally rolled down my face as I gripped him tighter. We existed in silence for a moment as I fought to control my emotions, doing my best to calm down and quiet the feeling rising in my chest. I thought of Crispin's uncertainty in the hallway, a soft scoff escaping me. "Crispin's gonna ask you about proposing to Justina."

"Huh?"

"He was asking me if he should propose to Justina," I revealed, leaning away from the shifter as I wiped away my tears. "He's worried she'll take it poorly."

"Of course she will," Kisten agreed and I gave him a tired look. The Alpha rolled his eyes as he watched me, finally rising from the floor to sit next to me on the bed. "Look, I love Justina and all, but she will one hundred percent assume it's because she's dying and he's pandering to her."

"I mean, yeah, but she'll still say yes."

"Are you sure about that?" Kisten pressed, everything in his expression saying he didn't believe me. I sighed, giving him an equally annoyed look. "I highly doubt it. She almost changed her mind about the pregnancy about a million times, and *she* asked *him* for that."

"Yeah, but she never meant it. She'll be a bitch about it, but she'll say yes," I insisted, flicking Kisten's hair out of his face. "Fake flowers she'll say yes."

"*OH,* so that's how it is!" Kisten's eyes lit up with mischief and annoyance and I couldn't help my smug grin. The Alpha was insistent we have real flowers for the wedding and I loathed the idea, wanting to use fake flowers instead. I crossed my arms as I leaned away, knowing the shifter would take my bet if it meant getting what he wanted. "*Fine.* Real flowers that she'll be a bitch about it."

"That's a given."

"Real flowers she'll refuse," he corrected and I grinned more brightly as he leaned into my face, sealing our bet with a kiss. I hummed happily as he pulled away, an equally smug smile on my face, and I knew he had no intention of playing fair. To be honest, neither did I. "What are you thinking? Before or after Christmas?"

"Christmas Eve," I suggested and I loved the way he laughed, tangling his hand in my thick curls. I hummed as he squeezed my hair, pulling it slightly as he moved.

"It's almost like you don't *want* to win." His eyes swirled as he leaned close, kissing my cheek before whispering in my ear. "You could just say yes to the flowers."

"Never in a million lifetimes, my dear," I cooed, running my fingers through his hair as I leaned into his neck, slowly licking his skin before I gently blew against it. I felt the shiver as it ran through him and I chuckled softly as I kissed his neck. "You know I play to win."

"That you do," Kisten agreed, standing from the bed and I released him as he leaned over me, pushing me back onto the bed as he lay down next to me. I immediately turned into him, throwing my leg around his waist as he stroked my face, still looking at me defiantly. "And so do I."

"Winner takes all," I breathed, pulling him close for another kiss as his hand drifted to my hip, pulling me even closer to him. I hummed as our skin pressed together, and I was starting to wish that we had finished undressing before lying back down. Kisten seemed to share my thought as he slid his hand under my shirt, dragging it up as he stroked my back.

"I mean, either way I still get to marry you, so I would say that's a win in itself," he murmured, pressing kisses into my face, and I was forced to turn away as I giggled. "I just know you'd be beautiful surrounded by roses."

"And I'll still be just as beautiful if they're fake," I insisted, still laughing as I leaned back from him, squeezing my leg around him as he pressed his hand into my back more. The shifter shook his head, his eyes starting to turn green as he thought about indulging his snake and my smile grew. "Guess you better hope I'm wrong."

"Guess you better hope you're right," he shot back, finally sitting up as he quickly removed my shirt and I laughed as he lifted me up, setting me in his lap as his eyes fully turned green. Kisten's dark pants were swiftly replaced by his bright green scales and I giggled even more as his tail wrapped around me. The shifter hummed delightedly as he paused the transformation, flicking his tongue against my skin as he indulged in my scent.

As my laughter died down, I smiled softly and rested my hand on his head again as he began to kiss me, his tail constricting around me rhythmically. As he loved and explored me, I did my best to let go of my worries, focusing on the Alpha in my arms.

4

I bounced on the elevator nervously as I waited to reach my floor, the pounding in my chest not helping my worry. As soon as I stepped into the building, the receptionist let me know that the Director wanted me to come to his office. I knew I wasn't in trouble, but it still wasn't a good sign for my day to start like this. Most days, I simply walked into work and found new assignments waiting on my desk, or I worked on filling out paperwork from previous assignments. Due to the wedding, I was mostly given assignments in Decver and luckily, it meant I didn't have much to do. The Local team was more than capable of handling most cases that came to Division 11, so I spent my time just pushing papers or acting as a consultant for them.

The S-Men floor was in the same building as my old team, so I still saw Julia and Brandon from time to time. Brandon sometimes came up to our floor to reach the Director's office, and would talk to me if I wasn't busy. He would always joke about "stealing me back" and, silly as that notion was, it was nice to see he had accepted my non-humanity. He would also check on Vanessa if she was around, but the vampire frequently stayed out on assignments. I only noticed her on the rare occasion she was filling out paperwork, but I didn't have the heart to bother her. She was clearly still grieving, and I wasn't sure if she was ready to have anyone reach out, despite her father-in-law's attempts.

"Well, well, if it isn't the princess herself." I scowled as the elevator door opened to show Evalyn, the ala glaring at me as she waited to step on. Being added to the S-Men only seemed to make her hate me more, even though now we were technically on the same team. After talking with Lucius, Eve's attempts to agitate me worked on my nerves even more than before and I did my best to ignore her as I stepped off. "I thought you were too busy getting married to work."

"At least one of us should experience it," I shot back casually, unable to help my slight smile as another of our co-workers fought to hide her giggle. I refused to look at the ala as I continued to my desk, even though I knew she was glaring at my back the whole time. I felt my tension ease as I finally heard the doors close, and I tossed my bag into my chair as I walked past. The stairs to the Director's office were on the opposite side of the floor and I punched in the code for the door. My thoughts raced as I climbed the stairs, but I did my best to hide my expression as I neared the top of the floor.

"Good morning, Raiven." I heard the Director's voice as I reached the last step, looking up to see him smiling brightly at me. His dull red hair was neatly pulled back and his glasses reflected the light as I sat down in front of his desk. Despite being fully human, the Director's presence alone carried such authority and weight that it often felt as if *he* was the one truly in charge of The Capital rather than the Governor. "How goes the wedding planning?"

"Good." I smiled, doing my best to remain polite. "Kisten is handling most of the details with input from me."

"Sounds like the Alpha, he sure does like his control." The Director laughed and I allowed myself a slight chuckle as he cleaned his glasses. I caught a brief glimpse of his brown eyes before he slid the spectacles back on, his smile now a bit more serious. "But now, on to–"

"One moment."

"Yes?" The Director seemed genuinely surprised that I had interrupted him, and I took a deep breath. I carefully crossed my legs as I leaned back in the chair, trying to swallow the lump in my throat.

"Lucius wanted me to talk to you." I watched as his smile faltered slightly at the edges. He started to frown as he laced his fingers together, studying me intently. "He's... concerned about Evalyn's behavior lately and we believe she may be involved with Mater Vitae."

"Well, I did not expect this conversation so soon," the Director said with a sigh, leaning back in his chair as he tapped his desk. My surprise must have shown on my face, as he chuckled when he looked back at me. "Lucius is far from the only one to notice something is off with Ms. Boone."

"So—"

"Ms. Boone seems to have trouble returning from assignments on time, especially when they take place out of The Capital. I'm sure you've noticed she has been given more local assignments as of late." The Director's smile returned and I hummed in acceptance, my surprise fading as I met his gaze. He was nothing if not attentive and it wasn't that surprising that he would have reached the same conclusion as us. "However, I assume if you are bringing this up with me, Lucius also lacks proof of her involvement?"

"It's merely a concern, given her behavior and the... convenient circumstances," I offered, uncrossing my legs as I sat up straighter. "Lucius is hoping Division 11 will handle the situation."

"Of course, that makes everything less messy and easier to control than if she's dismissed directly from the Coven. Given her attitude and aggressive behavior, I doubt Ms. Boone would take such an action with grace," the Director agreed, immediately coming to the same solution I had offered to the Overseer. "It would be a good test for Valkyrie as well. Testing on someone with Hunter strength would be—"

"Wait, she's already at Hunter strength?" I interrupted, feeling a sudden surge of anxiety. The Director kept his calm smile however, nodding at me slightly.

"As are you, Raiven, although I doubt you see yourself that way. You fail to understand just how strong your natural power is, and I doubt few will be able to stand against you once you can control it." I fidgeted slightly in the seat, unable to help my discomfort. After the Whistleblower incident, I had told the Director about the change to my powers, although I left out about me needing to return to my birthplace to learn how to control it. I simply told him I needed more time and a safe place to practice before I felt comfortable relying on it, and he agreed, saying that he would do his best to have a space prepared for me, or to give me the time to travel elsewhere. Our first attempts for me to train at the Headquarters had been nearly disastrous and despite our researchers' excitement, I refused to train around the living anymore.

"Still, you are more at the upper end of Hunter strength as we understand it and she is on the low end. Hmm..." I looked up, but his expression had not changed as he stared at his desk. "I also can't confirm whether it's because she had any of Vitae's blood, or just a natural increase from being around so many other powerful beings."

"One as likely as the other, but I hope it's the former," I muttered and the Director nodded as I did my best to swallow my fear. "The idea that she is already naturally that strong makes the potential of her getting Vitae's blood practically terrifying."

"If she could control it, indeed," the Director agreed, taking a moment to tap on his tablet and he seemed to be writing something down as I waited in silence. The Director soon finished whatever he was doing, and looked back up to me. "I'll see if I can get her an assignment out of the area. I believe I know the perfect agent to get us the proof we need to move forward."

"Alright," I conceded, leaning back in the chair again as I accepted the decision for Lucius. I didn't like the idea of giving Eve another chance to meet with her contact, but it was the only way for any of us to get the proof we needed. Lucius wanted Division 11 to handle prosecuting her, so I no longer had any say in how the Director went about it. "So, what did you need me for?"

"Of course, let's get to it," the Director stood from his chair, the screen behind him lighting up as the room dimmed. I sat forward in my chair as I watched the images start to pop up on the screen, frowning softly as he continued. "I'm sure you may have heard other S-Men talking about the 'Dusters' they've encountered in their assignments."

"A little bit."

"Really, we don't know what they are, or why they have suddenly started appearing. As far as we can tell, they were normal Supernaturals living unassuming lives," the Director continued, and I groaned softly as crime scenes started flashing on the screen instead. "Then, after withdrawing for a short time, they begin to go on killing sprees, murdering everyone they come in contact with. When apprehended, they apologize for 'failing to find it' and their bodies turn to dust. No way has been found to restore the body once it disintegrates, or to stop the disintegration process."

"Hence 'Dusters'," I agreed, forcing myself to examine the images closely. "Sounds like magic to me."

"Normally I would agree with you, but it seems to not be magic related." The Director sighed wearily, shaking his head as more images flashed on the screen. "We've tested them with a reader before, and no signs of magic or magical control can be found. Even Sherry seems of the opinion that it is more like fanatical belief than magic, although it doesn't explain why their bodies disintegrate."

"True," I agreed, my frown deepening as I considered the possibilities. "Is it limited to the UCA?"

"No, we seem to be encountering them worldwide. Many Overseers have reported the phenomenon happening and are just as concerned as us, despite its rarity. It could possibly be the power of a new Hunter, but at the moment, we have no idea." The Director turned from the screen to face me, looking tiny compared to the monitor behind him. He adjusted his glasses again as he moved back to his desk, sitting down heavily. "I'm hoping that, with your powers, we may be able to capture one alive and learn more about why this is happening."

"Hmm," I agreed, seeing his point as I crossed my legs again.

Even without my unknown birth powers, my control of the ground would, in theory, allow me to keep their bodies from disintegrating immediately. Probably not long enough to allow transport, but at least long enough that I could question one. "Do we know the location of any?"

"In the dark hours this morning, a banshee by the name of Sidon suddenly left his basement after not leaving for a week and killed his neighbors." The Director tapped his tablet and another image appeared on the screen, showing the suspect. "His wife claims all he said to her was 'I must find it' and left. She then heard the scream of her husband at their neighbor's farm and called law enforcement. She claims no one came to visit before it started and her husband has never been religious before."

"Is the wife human or Supe?"

"A banshee as well and, by all accounts, she's telling the truth. She said he had simply been sitting on the porch one day and when he came inside, he went straight to the basement. He seemed to understand that she was not the 'it' he was looking for, so he simply left her alone." A map of The Capital replaced the image and I watched as his path was marked. "The local team and law enforcement have already warned all the other homes along his path not to open their doors to him, as he doesn't seem interested in attacking unless he sees them. So far, we haven't had reports of any other attacks, and the road he seems to be walking down is a back road, so not much car traffic."

"There." I pointed, the map zooming in to where I indicated and the highlighted path continued to the new location. "At the pace he's walking, he should reach that small town by tonight."

"Then it seems you know where you need to be." The Director smiled and I nodded, quickly standing from my chair. I turned to leave and was making my way quickly to the stairs when I heard his voice call after me, "Be careful, Raiven."

I paused in the doorway, slowly looking over my shoulder back to the Director. He was smiling at me pleasantly, but I had known the man long enough to notice the worry in the way his hands sat on the desk. The slight tension in his fingers, the overacting in his face; he was worried about sending me straight into the arms of a potential Hunter and I shook my head. I carefully pulled my hair back, doing my best to tame the curls into a ponytail as I smiled at the Director.

"I always am," I answered, swiftly climbing back down the stairs. I noticed Vanessa at her desk and offered the vampire a quick nod as I swiped my bag from my chair. Rather than wait on the elevator, I headed straight for the stairs, determined to beat Sidon to his destination.

5

I sighed as I pulled into the small parking lot of a diner, exhausted from my long drive. It had been more than seven hours since I left the Director's office and, with the exception of a short stop for gas, I had driven non-stop to reach the town in time. Finally turning off my car, I picked up my phone, checking the predicted path for my target. It showed him about an hour away and I leaned back in my car, closing my eyes for a moment as I considered my options. He would have to walk right by the diner to pass through the town and besides the lit sign flashing 'Silk Morning', the town seemed completely asleep. I felt my phone start to vibrate and without checking the caller, I answered it.

"Hello?"

"Hey." It was Kisten, and I sat up in my seat once I heard his voice. I had sent him a text to let him know where I was going, but I was surprised he was still up so late at night. "You okay?"

"Yeah, just got to the town. Was debating if a coffee was worth it," I said, looking at the inside of the diner as the hostess leaned on her counter, joking with one of the patrons inside. There was also a couple hiding away in the corner, very obviously on a late night date as they laughed and giggled. I couldn't help the slight smile that came to my own face as I spoke. "I've got some time."

"Sounds like it," Kisten said with a laugh as I opened my door, finally stepping out of the car. I glanced at the road again. It seemed to stretch off into the infinite darkness and I forced myself away as I stepped into the diner, switching to my earpiece. The hostess immediately greeted me with a smile as I sat at the counter, motioning she'd be over in a moment. "Think you'll be gone long?"

"Nah," I hummed, marking my order on the paper in front of me and setting the paper on the plate for the girl. When she finally came over, I merely motioned to my earpiece and smiled and her relief was obvious on her face as she turned to make my drink. "I should be back by late morning."

"That's good to hear." Kisten sighed and I echoed his sound, glancing at the young couple in the corner again. They were leaning on each as they talked, barely paying any attention to the drinks that sat in front of them.

"They're here every night." I glanced up as the hostess came over to me, and she was watching them softly as she finished setting down my cup. "Girl's an ala and he's an elf. Girl's parents want her to do better and find someone with a longer life, but she's happy with him. This diner is their little secret to keep her parents from making a fuss."

"A fuss?"

"They don't dislike him. Honestly, he's a good lad." The hostess smiled, keeping her eyes on the young couple as she spoke. "They're a well-off family in town, and they've kept her pretty sheltered. They just don't want her to know that pain."

"How long...?" I started and the hostess sighed, shifting her weight as she leaned against the counter.

"I'd say, about five years now?"

"F-f-five years?"

"Yeah, they're the real deal," the hostess said softly and I turned again as I heard the boy laugh, slowly pushing the girl's hair from her face. Watching the soft, patient look on his face reminded me so much of Kisten that my chest hurt, and I could barely tear my eyes away as the hostess continued. "She's twenty-three, and he turns twenty-one in a few weeks, so he'll officially be free to marry her. Her parents won't like it, but she's already decided she doesn't care if they can't be together her whole life."

"It's enough," I whispered, my heart twisting as I thought of Kisten. I gently touched my warm cup of coffee, knowing the Alpha could hear our conversation. "It's enough to have someone you love."

"Sounds like you understand it perfectly." The hostess smiled as the young couple finally stood and I couldn't help smiling too as I finally took a sip of my coffee. The door jingled as they stepped out into the night and the hostess turned her full attention to me. "If you don't mind me asking, whatcha doing out here? We don't get too many visitors this late at night."

"Here on business, I'm afraid," I admitted, showing my gun tucked under my jacket as I leaned back. The hostess frowned thoughtfully as I released the clothing and took another sip of my drink. I heard Kisten grunt with disapproval in my ear, but I shrugged away his concern. "Merely waiting."

"You're here about Sidon then. Knew him a bit, no idea what's happened to him," the waitress told me, crossing her arms as she gazed out the window again. Her lips twitched as she stared out at the dark road and I caught the hurt expression that flashed across her face. "He and his wife would always stop in on their way to the city. Never seemed the type to do... that."

"To be honest, I still don't think he is," I admitted, hearing another sound from the Alpha in my ear.

"Raiv–"

"Well, I guess that's why you're here? To find out?" the girl asked, and I shrugged, taking another sip of my drink. I could feel her eyes on me as I ignored her question, until she finally gave up expecting a response, uncrossing her arms as she walked away. I slowly lowered the cup, looking back onto the dark road. I could see the young couple still outside, drawing out their separation for as long as they could as they stood on the corner of the lot.

"Raiven," I turned my gaze away as the Alpha spoke again, and I closed my eyes as I leaned on the counter, "you know you should be more careful."

"I've been careful my whole life," I quietly whispered back, playing with the edge of my cup as I glanced at the dark beverage. "I know what I can and cannot say. Remember that whole 'trust me' thing we've talked about?"

"I don't mean it that way, Rai. I'm not worried about you if you end up fighting him," Kisten shot back and I held my breath as I took another sip. "I trust that you know what you're doing, but you know you're most likely gonna kill that guy."

"And?"

"You don't have to make it more difficult for those who know him." Kisten's voice was soft as he continued and I placed my cup back down, glancing outside again. The couple were sharing what seemed to be their final hug and kiss, their hands lingering as they started to walk away. My heart started to pound as I noticed the boy began jogging down the main road, and I glanced at my phone to see the suspect's predicted location. It showed him mere moments away and I quickly stood. "All you had to say–"

"Gotta go." I quickly cut off the shifter as I hung up the call, tossing some bills on the counter as I ran out of the diner, the blood pounding in my ears as I took off after the kid. The girl paused as she saw me run down the street, but I barely paid her any mind as I saw the boy in front of me. I knew I couldn't catch him, but I had to stop him from running into the banshee. "Hey, kid!"

I watched as he paused in his run, turning back to look at me with a confused expression. My worry grew as I saw the dark shape coming towards him and I could barely restrain my power as it burst forth, the black tendrils shooting along the ground. They zigzagged along the pavement, but somehow the banshee was faster, moving with an unnatural speed once he spotted another target to kill.

"Move!" I yelled, watching as the boy finally heard the man coming up behind him. I felt his terror as the banshee stood over him. Sidon was not very tall, but knowing that he had every intention to kill the kid made him seem gigantic as he placed his hand on the boy's hair. The tendrils reached the pair then, and I quickly wrapped them around the kid, flinging him off to the side, away from the banshee.

The banshee watched the boy curiously as I withdrew my power and he started after the kid as I continued running toward him. I felt the heat from flames as they rushed past me, and Sidon was forced to step back as the boy quickly drew a portal in the air to escape. I turned to see the ala panting behind me as her fire died, and it was clear she was new to using her powers as she stumbled. The boy stepped out of his portal beside her, barely catching the girl as she started to fall.

"You." The voice was barely above a whisper as I turned to find the banshee standing over me, and my power quickly adjusted, his skin and clothing soon becoming covered in the dark tendrils as our eyes met. His eyes glowed a sickly gold and I stepped back, struggling to keep my power from killing my captive as he watched me calmly. "You."

"What about you, Sidon?" I asked calmly, keeping my eyes on the banshee as he started to struggle against the hold I had on him. "You were about to kill that kid. Why?"

"Find it. I must... find..." he continued, his expression still blank as he struggled to take a step forward and I frowned, raising my hands as the tendrils tightened their hold on him. He was forced to stop again, his glowing eyes still stuck on mine. "You."

"You had to find *me*?" I repeated, my heart starting to pound as I struggled to maintain my calm. I could hear that the hostess and other patron had made their way to the kids behind me and my frustration grew as the banshee fought against me, taking another step toward them. "Why did you need to find me?"

"Find you. I found..." he repeated and I couldn't help my cry of pain as my hands began to burn, the tendrils on his body starting to glow the same sickly gold as his eyes. I felt as if my soul was on fire and my sister seemed to feel the pain as well, her voice echoing in my mind as I stumbled. I barely had time to react as he stood in front of me, his hand reaching to touch my face. I quickly stepped away, clutching my wrists as my hands pulsed with the pain. "I found you."

"Sure did," I repeated, stomping the ground as he began to sink into it, releasing my natural power for the vampiric power as the burning sensation left my body. I could feel my sister's relief as the pain subsided and I grabbed the cross I wore round my neck out of habit as I looked down to the banshee. He was stuck up to his waist in the pavement and I stopped him from sinking in further. "Why are you looking for me?"

"They needed me to find you. Had to find…" he repeated, his blank expression never leaving my face and I squatted in front of him, my concern growing. This was sounding more and more like a new Hunter, and I didn't like the idea that Vitae could be this close to finding me and Lucius. "Have to…"

"Have to what, Sidon?"

"Tell them," he stated simply and I was blown back as the banshee forced himself from the ground, his whole body now glowing the same sickly color as his eyes. I quickly pulled myself up as he began to run past me and I sprang to my feet, determined to not let him escape. The other group had already retreated back to the diner, and I cursed under my breath as he ran, confusion running through me as my natural power pulled itself up. The tendrils dug into the ground, seeking bodies to raise and the banshee was forced to pause again as his ankle was grabbed, the zombies doing their best to stop him.

'What in the world is happening to him?' My sister's voice flowed through my mind as I watched the glow flicker around him as the zombies grabbed higher and he looked to them with the same blank look. *'I sense no magic but—'*

"Something is clearly wrong with him," I growled, unholstering my gun as I watched the glow return and he started to pull himself free of the zombies. "He's not simply a banshee anymore."

'No…' my sister agreed as I fired, the bullet catching Sidon in his side as he finished breaking free of the zombies that had fully risen out of the ground to stop him. I heard the hostess as she gasped from

the doorway of the diner, but I was focused on the banshee in front of me as he examined his wound. His expression still held no emotion, no pain or confusion as he turned back to look at me, and I readied my aim. The zombies moved slowly toward him, but his sickly gold eyes were locked on me.

"I have to tell them," he repeated and my confusion grew as I watched a Ljosalfar portal appear behind him as he started back towards it. I fired again, catching him in the shoulder as he slowly walked, but again, he seemed unaffected by the wound. I released the zombies as I started after him, my anger starting to make my head pound as I saw him get closer to the portal.

'Raiven!'

'I know!' I screamed back at my sister, reaching into my jacket as I pulled out the tracking device. I hated using them, but I wrapped my fingers around it tightly as I saw his first foot disappear into the portal. I growled with frustration as I flung the small tracker, watching as it barely landed on his leg before he stepped back into the bright reflection. His expression remained unchanged as he disappeared and I was left panting alone on the sidewalk.

I slowly looked down to my hands, still able to feel the residual burning on my skin as the dark tendrils swirled across my palms. My body started to shake with my anger and annoyance as I turned to my car, barely noticing as the hostess recoiled from the door. I slammed my door as I got in, peeling out of the parking lot and starting my drive back to Decver.

6

I slammed the doors open as I walked into the Division 11 Headquarters, barely noticing the receptionist as she jumped in her chair. She seemed like she was about to ask me why, but upon seeing my expression, she recoiled back. I immediately turned into my old office, stomping my way through the desks as I slammed my hands on Justin's. He looked up at me with confusion and fear, but all I did was growl at him.

"Find him. NOW."

"Rai, find who—"

"Tracker. Find him. *Now*," I repeated, slamming my hand on the desk again as Justin turned away from me, quickly typing on his computer. I turned round to see Julia and Chris watching me with concern as they walked into the office, but both looked away upon seeing my expression. I knew Kisten and Lucius were on their way to me, as I had ignored every call from both of them since leaving the small town. My anger from watching the banshee disappear into the portal had yet to die down, and I shrugged off another call from Lucius as the tugging began in my mind.

"Raiven, what are you doing down here?" I glared as I saw Brandon step into the office, and he instantly stopped upon seeing my face. He did his best to maintain his composure but I could see the fear and worry as it radiated off his body. "Do I... do I want to know what happened?"

"I need Justin to find a tracker," I growled, doing my best to restrain my power as the tendrils swam on my skin and I watched Brandon's eyes turn to visible fear as he saw them. He had been one of the few present when I had attempted to control my powers in the training rooms, and unfortunately knew how deadly they were. I turned to Justin as he whimpered, and I closed my eyes, trying to calm myself down. "Once he finds it, I'll be on my way."

"Okay. Are ya... gonna calm down?" he asked cautiously and I glared at him, my anger rising again as the ground started to shake beneath the building. I barely noticed as the lights flickered and Justin cried out in fear behind me as I fully turned to face my old boss.

"I'll calm down," I started, the building continuing to shake as my tendrils expanded from my body, snaking along the walls as I did my best to keep them from touching any of the living occupants. My sister's voice was nowhere in my mind, but I could feel her frustration and anger with my own, and it took all I had to maintain some level of control over myself. "When Justin finds the tracker."

"Rai–"

"*Raiven!*" Brandon was interrupted as Lucius finally stepped into the room and I turned my glare to the vampire. His eyes widened at seeing me but he quickly recovered. Kisten and Evalyn were with him as he walked closer to me. Seeing the ala only made me angrier, and I could barely stop myself as the tendrils curved toward her. "Stop. *Now.*"

"Sorry, Lucius, but *I will not,*" I growled, shifting my gaze to him as the tremors grew stronger and the lights above us started to flicker more. The walls of the room were almost black with my power as I shook my head, still barely managing to control myself. My hair reached most of the way down my back now, still expanding in my anger. "I will *stop* and *leave* once I know where *he* went."

"*Oportet te prohibere*[1]," Lucius insisted and I hummed with annoyance, Justin crying out again behind me as I stomped my foot.

"*Nulla*[2]."

"*Quid*[3]?" Lucius insisted and I shook my head, my anger crackling again with his simple question. Why did I feel so angry? There was no reason to take out my anger on anyone around me and yet the more they insisted I calm down, the angrier I grew. I looked up as Lucius loomed over me, seeing my blacked-out eyes reflected in his. "This is not like you, Raiven."

"Is it?" I offered, the tremor finally stopping as the lights stabilized, and Justin whimpered as he continued typing on his keyboard. I retracted my power back to my body and heard the collective sigh of relief from the other occupants. "Know something I don't?"

A crackling behind us interrupted the Overseer and we both turned as a projector came to life, the lights in the room going out completely as it attempted to project an image on the screen. The figure it showed was not Sidon, but I somehow knew it was exactly who I was looking for. I fully turned as the figure spoke, their voice distorted by static.

"Sorry to have caused such a fuss. I did not think touching you would cause such an imbalance."

"What imbalance?" I growled, walking toward the wall as my power swirled across my skin and I heard the figure sigh.

"My power touching yours seems to have caused an imbalance in your emotions, although your annoyance is understandable, given the circumstances." They seemed to turn away from the image and I growled as I stood in front of them. "You should return to normal soon."

"Why are you looking for me?" I crossed my arms, my sister's intrigue starting to crack through my anger. My power was giving her more strength, but she failed to offer any words as I glared at the projection. It was strange that there was still no magic in the air and my confusion only seemed to anger me more. "What are you doing to the Dusters? How did you make them?"

"I needed to find you and they were necessary to meet that need."

"Well, here I fucking am," I growled through gritted teeth, the ground once again shaking slightly as everyone in the room gasped. The figure on the other side seemed aware of what I was doing, and they sighed heavily before speaking again.

"Not yet. I need you to come to me," they offered and I heard Justin exclaim behind me, and I turned to see him typing more furiously. "Things will begin to make more sense then."

"Like why you've been killing dozens of innocents worldwide?" I turned back to the figure and they seemed to shrug, not concerned by my accusation.

"An unintended consequence of my plan, but again, I need you to find me before anything will make sense."

"So what?" My anger finally started to subside as I managed to withdraw my power and I could hear Lucius sigh with relief behind me. My sister seemed to be the one forcing me to calm down, the heat from her locket becoming more noticeable. "There's supposed to be some grand reason?"

"I don't expect you to understand yet, Raiven, just–" the figure's voice began to break into pure static and I failed to understand what they tried to say, "–see me. I hope you will come."

"Don't worry, I plan to." I turned away as Justin stopped typing and I saw him looking at me with worry and fear as I walked back up to him. I heard the projector turn itself off and I did my best to place my hand gently on Justin's chair as the lights came back on. "Where?"

"Ethiopia," Justin whispered and I nodded, looking up to my Overseer as I leaned away from him. I noticed the Director had entered the room and he was standing near the door, giving me the same concerned look as everyone else. My sister seemed to hum her concern in my mind, but I did my best to push it aside as I met their gaze.

"I'm going."

"Rai–"

"*I'm*," I repeated, interrupting Brandon before he could speak and he visibly recoiled at meeting my gaze; I closed my eyes before I continued, locking my gaze with the Director's, "going. My assignment is not complete yet."

"Yet, I do not think we can let you." The Director smiled, seemingly the only one in the room not afraid of what I had just done. I watched him as he walked closer to me, giving off the same friendly and calm aura he usually did. "I'm even more worried that this 'individual' may be a Hunter sent to lure you into a vulnerable position."

"All the more reason for me to go," I insisted, shifting my gaze to Lucius. "As we clearly all just saw, their power touching me can affect my emotions and they aren't even here. Through me, they could kill everyone in Decver."

"And yet we can't just—"

"What else do you suggest!" I yelled. My power rose once again as I interrupted the Director and the building shook as one of the lights finally crashed from the ceiling. Julia and Chris joined Justin in his cry of fear and I closed my eyes as I struggled to calm myself down again. My sister's voice finally flowed through my mind as I flexed my fingers, her cross buzzing with heat.

'Something is wrong, Raiven.'

'No shit.'

'This is likely a trap, but we still have to go. Ethiopia is close enough to where we were born that we can get answers while you hunt this person,' my sister reasoned and I forced myself to take a deep breath, once again releasing my power as I raised my gaze back to the Director. 'I have a feeling... Hunter or not, this person is related to what is happening to our power.'

"I have to go," I repeated softly, taking another deep breath as I fought to remain calm. "This... *power* is only becoming more and more dangerous and I *need* to understand it. If this Hunter wants to draw me to Africa, so be it."

"Raiven..."

"It's the only place I'll find answers and it's too dangerous for me to stay here if they can affect me like this," I insisted, turning my gaze back to Lucius. He was giving me a concerned look, but there was a hint of sadness to his eyes. I turned my body to fully face him, crossing my arms as I did so. "You know I have to, Lucius."

"Not alone," the Overseer whispered, turning his gaze away from me as I watched him carefully. I knew Lucius carried the memories of LeAlexende, and Alex had already revealed he knew more about my power than even I did. He had given a cryptic message to my sister that he said would only make sense once I returned to my birthplace, so I had no doubt Lucius knew exactly why I wanted to go. "It is no accident that a Hunter is waiting exactly where you need to be."

"Then choose who is going with me, 'cause I'm not going to wait for him to use me," I insisted, and I watched as Kisten stepped forward, meeting my gaze evenly. I started to open my mouth but the Alpha quickly interrupted me.

"Not giving you a choice, Raiven. I promised I would go with you from the beginning, and no Hunter is going to change that," Kisten insisted and I frowned as I met my fiance's chartreuse eyes. I knew there was no arguing with the shifter, but no part of me wanted to take him along. When it had simply been a matter of returning my sister's soul, I welcomed Kisten's company, but I was not as eager to drag him halfway across the world to potentially face another Hunter.

I slowly walked toward the shifter, watching as Lucius backed away from us as I stopped in front of Kisten. The Alpha's face showed no anger or fear, just simple determination as his gaze met mine and I could feel my sister's acceptance for his help. I closed my eyes as I sighed, unable to help the smile that crept on my face.

"I'm leaving tonight."

"Good thing I'm always ready to go," Kisten answered and I shook my head as I looked back up to him. He was smiling down at me now, his concern finally showing through as he watched my expression. "Arkrian is more than capable of handling things while I'm gone. It'll also be good practice to have him work with Lucius."

"Don't do more than is needed, Raiven." I turned as the Director spoke again, his smile still soft and calm as he watched me. I took a deep breath as I faced him, doing my best to squash my guilt over what I had done to the building. "If you need help, let us know and we'll send you the backup you need. Facing a Hunter is no easy task, and I am sending you rather unwillingly, I might add."

"But I have to go," I repeated, my gaze shifting to Brandon where he stood next to Chris and Julia. Their fear and worry was plain on their faces and I was forced to take another deep breath as I closed my eyes. "I can't stay and wait, especially when they know exactly where I am. Better I go and delay them from coming here."

"Indeed, it seems Vitae has forced our hands in this matter," Lucius pointed out and my heart constricted as I considered the Overseer's thoughts. He was sending away both his Alpha and his Second after realizing Vitae probably knew where we were and to top it off, his Retainer had likely already betrayed him to her. I slowly walked over to the vampire, watching as he met my gaze with confusion and worry. I stopped right in front of Lucius, looking into his striking blue eyes as I fought to speak.

"I'll come back," I whispered, refusing to look away as his gaze changed to calm determination. The wind in the room picked up slightly as one of his eyes took on a purplish tint and I smiled softly at the Overseer. "She doesn't get to win this."

"And bring my Alpha back in one piece. I like Arkrian, but I'm not ready to give up Kisten so easily," Lucius stated calmly and I nodded, accepting the order as I stepped away from the vampire. I glanced back over my shoulder to Justin, who still seemed to be trying to calm himself down.

"Sorry Justin."

"Don't worry about it, just make sure you get 'em," he took a deep breath as he spoke, but I could see that his hands were shaking as he tried to put his desk back in order. "Never seen you mad like that before and would rather never see it again."

"Yes, please," Julia echoed, and I turned to see her and Chris also doing their best to calm down from their fear. Brandon seemed to have buried his fear under his work face and I sighed heavily as I faced Kisten. The Alpha was waiting for me patiently and merely motioned towards the door.

"Let's go." Kisten waited for me to walk past him before following me out and I forced myself to ignore Evalyn as I passed by her. Even if we were wrong about her betraying Lucius, she loved any time Kisten and I weren't around and I knew she had to be beyond happy with the circumstances. I took a deep breath as I stepped back outside into the chill morning air, trying to focus on the task ahead as Kisten and I headed back to our cars.

7

The warmth was apparent the moment we stepped off the plane and I adjusted my jacket as we stepped into the airport. It had been a long twenty-four-hour flight, with only a brief stop in Lome and I felt it as I stretched. Kisten seemed even more antsy than me as he paused in the terminal, sighing heavily as he adjusted our carry-on across his shoulder. Even though we had to book the flight last minute, Lucius had pulled strings with the Director to get us on the shortest flight possible and the pair promised they would contact the local Overseer before we landed.

"You okay?" Kisten breathed, pausing as I glanced around the terminal, trying to determine where to wait for the Overseer. Lucius had said they would meet us in the airport, but he had never told me who or what I was looking for and I jumped as the Alpha touched my back. "Rai?"

"I'm fine," I breathed, trying to ignore the fear and excitement in my chest as I started toward the central terminal. Despite the hour, the airport was still busy, with people bustling to reach their terminals in time. Several lounged in the seats as flight attendants and pilots joked and laughed, ready for their homestays in between flights. I stepped onto the moving walkway, leaning against the glass as we moved through the space. "Nervous, I guess."

"That's a given, all things considered," the Alpha sighed, dropping the bag to his feet as he leaned next to me. He wrapped his arm around my shoulder and I leaned into him, closing my eyes as we moved. I had barely slept during the flight and I could feel the exhaustion as I rubbed my head against him. Kisten took a moment to brush my curls from my face, humming quietly as he squeezed me. "I'm right here with you."

"I know," I whispered, opening my eyes suddenly as I felt a new presence. I glanced toward the end of the walkway. I couldn't see anyone waiting for us yet, but I knew the Overseer had arrived as I leaned away from the Alpha. Kisten seemed to understand something had changed as he picked up our bag and we both stepped off the walkway. I saw the crowd begin to part in front of us and a trio appeared from the other end of the terminal, walking quickly to meet us.

"You must be Raiven." The Dokkalfar was smiling politely as they walked up to us and waved their hand as several of the Supernaturals present scrambled to bow to them. They were flanked by two people I assumed to be their Retainer and Alpha, both seemingly more imposing than the short Overseer. I knew, however, that no one rose to the title of Overseer easily, and I bowed my head, waiting for them to continue. "I am Eba, and Lucius has informed me of your purpose here."

"We will do our best not to impose on your good graces for too long," I offered, meeting their soft brown eyes evenly as they nodded. Their dark hair was beautifully done in short braids and their outfit almost seemed as if they had stepped out of either a meeting about fashion or a fashion magazine. The dark color of the suit complimented their dark skin nicely and their smile was small but polite.

"A Hunter is a concern for all of us, whether we are among the First or not," Eba offered and I watched as they motioned for me to follow them. "But tonight it is late, and you must be tired. You may start your search tomorrow, with a clear head and full stomach."

"Thank you," I accepted, taking Kisten's hand as we walked after the Overseer. The Alpha and Retainer fell in behind us and I couldn't help the feeling of being trapped as we walked through the airport. I felt my sister's presence as she nudged me and I carefully summoned my power to push into the cross.

'*What?*'

'*They are afraid of us,*' she pointed out and I looked at Eba as they walked in front of us. Now that she had pointed it out, I noticed the slight shaking in the way they walked, like a prey animal that was uncertain when the starving wolf would strike. I hummed under my breath, trying to keep my emotions under control to avoid tipping off the Alpha as she walked behind us beside the Retainer. I had no idea what her animal was, but I knew that most Alphas were predators, and just as Kisten could often tell the changes in my mood from my scent, I was sure the Alpha would be able to as well. '*Lucius told them what we were.*'

'*Does he know what we are?*'

'*More than we do,*' she offered as we arrived at the luggage claim. Kisten left me with the Overseer as he walked with the Alpha and Retainer to wait for our bags. I fidgeted awkwardly next to the shorter Dokkalfar and I nearly jumped when they spoke again.

"Your necklace." Their voice was still calm and assured, but I noticed they didn't look to meet my gaze as they spoke. "May I?"

"Sure," I agreed, pulling the wooden cross from underneath my shirt. Eba stepped in front of me as they examined the locket closely and I started to feel uncomfortable with the scrutiny. I looked up to see Kisten watching me, and did my best to smile as he waved to me. It seemed he had caught on to the worry and fear surrounding us as he dropped his hand, asking me with his expression if I was alright. I nodded slightly as Eba hummed, and I looked down as they stepped away.

"You'll want to go south of here," Eba said quietly, still looking at the wooden cross around my neck as I nodded, tucking it back in my shirt. They looked up to meet my eyes and I struggled to meet their intense gaze. "Near Yangudi Rassa, we have unearthed many similar to your necklace."

"You... have?" I asked softly, unable to help the hope in my voice. I had yet to check the updated location of the tracker, but I was awed that my sister's intuition had been right. My memory of where I had been taken from was poor, and understandable considering the circumstances, but I couldn't help the hope that my sister had remembered more than me. Eba hummed to themselves again as the luggage train finally began to move and the bags started to tumble onto the moving platform.

"There was a time when they were easy to find. One could hardly dig without finding one," they offered and I clutched my locket tightly as they continued speaking. "However, we stopped looking for them, once we understood what we had done."

"Understood...?" I didn't try to hide the confusion in my voice and saw Eba watching me cautiously as I glanced down at them. Their braids shook as they looked away from me and I followed their gaze as Kisten and the others returned toward us, our bags in tow. "Understood what?"

"You will see," was their only reply, as they finished leading us out of the airport and we stepped up to the waiting cars. I paused as one of the Three opened the door for us to step in, sharing one last glance with Eba as they watched us. "My Alpha and Retainer will meet you in the morning to assist with any needs you may have. As I'm sure you understand, I must return to my Coven."

"Of course. Thank you for blessing us with your graces." I bowed my head again as Eba did the same, and I carefully slid into the car, with Kisten entering after me. The driver seemed to already know where we were going, pulling away from the airport as soon as the door was closed. I was tempted to glance back at the car Eba was in but fought the urge, instead taking the Alpha's hand in my own.

Kisten returned my grip eagerly, and I looked to see him smiling down at me, although I could see the exhaustion on his face. He had not shifted before coming on the trip, and his animals were already antsy with how much he had been sitting. The plane had a shifting room to accommodate shapeshifters who would need to stretch during a long flight, but it did little for Kisten's needs. He hummed as he saw the worry on my face, pulling me close as he laid a kiss on my forehead.

"I'm okay, really," he whispered and I merely made a soft noise in response, leaning my head against his shoulder as he pulled away. "Eating will help, and I'm sure I'll get to run around while we're here."

"You smelled it, right?" I closed my eyes as I spoke and heard the hum deep in Kisten's chest as he leaned more into the seat.

"They were all drenched in it. Even the Alpha just reeks of fear."

"Why? Is it the Hunter or..." I let the question hang as I squeezed his hand and it took a moment before the Alpha squeezed it back, clearly unsure himself. I sighed heavily as I sat up, finally pulling out my phone as I unlocked it to check the tracker location. My heart pounded as I saw where it was, and the suggested path the app had created for my target. "Hmmm."

"What?"

"He's about four hours south of us," I answered, closing my phone as my sister's voice rose again, although it was clear she was already about to fade again.

'*And heading right to where Eba said we should go.*'

"Mm-hmm," I answered, sighing again as I closed my eyes, leaning into the seat. I felt Kisten as he rested his hand on my lap and I glanced over to see his tired smile. I couldn't help but return it as I reached to stroke his cheek, pulling the Alpha down for a gentle kiss. I felt his grip on my leg tighten as I pulled away, and his eyes swam with his animals as he chuckled.

"Don't rile them up, *Rabe*[1]," he teased, leaning forward to kiss my forehead as I hummed softly, enjoying the gentle gesture. We pulled apart as the car came to a stop and we turned to see Eba's Retainer already waiting for us in front of the hotel. I frowned slightly as we stepped out, but I did my best to hide my confusion as she smiled politely.

"This way." She motioned for us to follow. I noticed that the hotel staff immediately moved to get our luggage for us and I took Kisten's hand again as we stepped inside. The artwork in the lobby caught my eye as we passed through, and I couldn't help but wish we could pause as she led us straight to the elevator. Once there, she handed our room key to Kisten, avoiding eye contact with me as she spoke.

"Your room is on the fourth floor, Room One," she stated, pushing the button to call the elevator for us. "We will meet you here in the morning."

"All right." Kisten nodded and she smiled politely at me as the elevator doors opened. It was clear she was eager to get away as we stepped inside and both Kisten and I shared a look as we were sealed in the box. "I'm gonna say a lot of that fear is directed at you."

"Great," I moaned, but Kisten quickly stopped me, playing with the key in his hand.

"Not of you, per se. It's a hesitant fear and awe," he corrected, his smile twitching as we reached our floor. Somehow, our bags were already waiting outside our room. The Alpha shrugged as he opened the door, allowing me to walk in first as he moved our bags inside. The room was simple, containing a table and couch where one could sit and work in addition to the expected bed and dresser. A small door on the opposite side presumably led to the bathroom and it took all I had not to collapse onto the bed as I sat on the soft material. Kisten finished moving our bags inside before closing the door, pausing as he stopped to look at me. "It's more like they're scared of what you mean, rather than who you actually are."

"What I mean?" I repeated, stroking my cross as I considered what he was saying. "Like what me coming back means for them?"

"Something like that." Kisten shrugged as he collapsed face-first into the bed, and I couldn't help my soft chuckle. The Alpha groaned at me as I pushed against him lightly and he barely moved as I tried to adjust him on the bed. "I'm tired."

"I thought you were antsy."

"I'm both," he pouted, finally adjusting himself on the sheets as he kicked off his shoes, looking up at me as I slid off my own. I moved to join him on the bed and he immediately threw his arm around my waist, closing his eyes. "I just wanna sleep, eat and then run around for a bit."

"I think we can accommodate those wants." I smiled, giving into my own exhaustion as I lay down beside the shifter, gently running my hand through his hair. Kisten purred in response and I closed my eyes, still holding my locket in my hand. I was finally in the place I could get answers and I did my best to relax as I drifted off to sleep next to my fiancé.

8

"We're close." I leaned out of the car as Kisten turned onto the dirt road, my heart pounding as we drove in the plains. As soon as we had woken up, Eba's Retainer and Alpha were waiting for us as promised and sat with us while we ate breakfast. After determining where we planned on going, they handled getting us the car rental and clearance we needed to travel around freely. Even though Eba was the local Overseer, they also oversaw many of the neighboring countries and often had to navigate their way through the various human governments in place. Luckily, the Prime Minister was willing to work with us in my mission and I took a moment to sit back down as I sighed deeply.

"You almost sound like it's a bad thing," Kisten offered and I didn't answer him, looking down to my phone again. The tracker was showing as straight ahead of us and, unsurprisingly, was sitting right outside the Yangudi Rassa region Eba had suggested my necklace came from. The coincidences were starting to seem more and more like design, and I gripped my cross tightly. Despite not being able to talk, I could feel my sister's worry as well and I closed my eyes as Kisten spoke again. "*Is* it a bad thing?"

"We're going regardless," I insisted, tucking my phone away as the jeep jostled again and I glanced out over the plains. None of the landmarks seemed to be jogging my memory and I hummed softly to myself, still stroking the wood. In a lot of ways it made sense; I had been taken to Vitae's court more than three thousand years ago and it was impossible for the land to have remained the same. Between natural erosion and human interference, it was a given that the plains I remembered would be different from how the plains would look now. The fact that my sister had been able to recognize the direction we were taking when Vitae took us was surprising in itself and I slowly dropped my hand away from the locket.

"Hey, Rai." I looked over to Kisten as the Alpha spoke, but he kept his eyes on the road, gripping the wheel tightly. I frowned as I noticed the tension in his body, and carefully reached over to touch him.

"What is it?"

"It's... I want to help you find the answers you need and deal with this new Hunter, but I'm also... worried."

"About?" I pressed, gently rubbing my hand along his lap as I waited for his answer. The shifter took a deep breath as the car bumped again on the dirt path and I could see he was struggling to find the right words. His lips were pouted as he hummed, adjusting his hands as he released the wheel to weave his fingers with mine.

"I mean, aren't you? You've thought things were one way for, what, thousands of years at this point, and suddenly, you're learning that it wasn't what you thought." I felt my chest constrict with his words. "And worst of all, it's about you and what you are. It's not like you're just discovering a new power; your natural power simply isn't what you were told it was. What if..."

The Alpha's voice faded away and I squeezed his fingers tighter as I tried to hide my own concern. Kisten glanced away from the road for a moment to see my face and I took a deep breath, leaning back in my seat as I stared out onto the grass that stretched out on either side of the road.

"You're right, it's... a lot and it is scary," I agreed, sighing softly as I began to stroke his hand. "I thought I knew what I was and I am starting to think that maybe I never did. I don't know what this power is or what it means, but regardless, I need to control it, and find out what the truth is."

"Right," Kisten agreed, but I could still see the worry in his face as he followed the curve of the road, releasing my hand. I opened my mouth to say more but stopped, the right words not coming to mind. I glanced up as the jeep came to a stop and Kisten turned the engine off, looking at me softly. "Road ends here."

I looked over the dash, seeing the barrier that kept us from moving forward with the car. I had almost expected a fence, but it was simply a rope, with totems of hope and forgiveness hanging from it. I frowned as I stepped out of the car, walking up to the barrier as Kisten stepped out behind me. The tracker was showing about a few miles ahead of us and I gently tested the air above the barrier, receiving no magic response as I waved my fingers.

"It's not magic, just respect," I murmured, turning back to see Kisten watching me carefully. His expression still held all his uncertainty and I did my best to smile as I reached out to him. "Well, Sidon's not gonna come to us."

"You would think he would, considering he lured us this far," the Alpha joked, and I allowed myself a slight chuckle as I took his hand in mine. We carefully stepped over the rope, continuing on foot down the dirt road. As we walked, I found my eyes drawn to a large tree that seemed to be further down the path in front of us. There were scattered groups of trees about the plains, but this one stood out for its mere size. It had to be close to eighty feet in height and as we grew closer, I noticed it had a large hole in its trunk, as if something had been carved out of the gargantuan plant.

A sound to my right tore my attention away from the tree and I stopped walking, confused by what I heard. It sounded like laughter, but no human laughter I had ever heard and I peered closely into the bushes next to the path. Kisten seemed surprised by my sudden stop, turning back to look at me as I released his hand.

"What is it?"

"You don't hear that?" I whispered and I glanced at Kisten as he closed his eyes, clearly trying to listen for whatever I was hearing. Kisten growled as he reopened his eyes, moving in front of me as the sound grew closer. "Kisten?"

"Wild shifters," he hissed, and I finally noticed as the grass beyond the bushes moved and the laughter increased. "Shifters who refuse to listen to the Alpha and act like animals. They must have run away to avoid being killed."

"Should...?"

"As long as they keep to themselves, I won't bother them. I'm not their Alpha," Kisten growled and I watched as he started down the path again. The laughter started to die down as he walked away and I slowly started after him, jogging to catch up to the shifter. "But if they attack us, I won't hesitate. They have already forsaken their humanity."

I hummed softly to myself as I heard the laughter move through the grass and I knew the shifters were following us. It was unlikely that too many visitors came out this way and I was starting to wonder if they were the reason why no one came to this area anymore. I had never heard of wild shifters, and I imagined if we hadn't encountered them, I still wouldn't have. The anger in Kisten's walk was similar to the anger he had carried about his father and I reached for his hand as we walked closer to the tree. The Alpha barely paused in his steps, but he took my hand eagerly, squeezing me tightly as I pulled out my phone.

"Hmm." I stopped walking again and Kisten paused with me, the laughter still carrying in the grass beside us. I frowned at the device, tapping my screen to make sure the location hadn't froze on the app.

"What is it?"

"The app says it's right beside us," I growled, glancing into the grass as one of the shifters finally stood, giving us a wide grin. Kisten growled in response, once again stepping in front of me as the woman laughed.

"He-he-he, I suppose this is what you're looking for," she chuckled, waving the small tracker in her hands before tossing it at me. I barely flinched as my power rose and the dark tendrils caught it before it reached Kisten. I slowly brought it to my hand and as I recognized it as the one I had placed on Sidon, my anger starting to rise. "So many visitors lately, none of which belong here."

"So you killed him?" I asked calmly, and Kisten growled once again in front of me as more of the shifters came to stand beside the woman. She giggled again, the sound distorted and harsh as she looked at her companions.

"He was already dead. We merely helped ourselves and found your little toy. Almost choked on it."

"So why are you following us?" Kisten barked and she turned her attention to him, her laughter once again causing her shoulders to shake. Her eyes were piercing when the laughter finally stopped and I could see the saliva dripping from her lips as her canine teeth peeked out.

"Because he wasn't enough, and your little mate smells enticing. Don't want to fight an Alpha, but we outnumber you," she admitted and I started to laugh, unable to help myself as I crushed the tracker in my hand. I watched her assurance change to confusion as the ground started to shake and the black tendrils swam across my skin as my laughter grew. The shifters yelped with fear as they struggled to pull their paws out of the ground, dancing in the grass as they tried to avoid sinking into it. I hummed as my laughter died, solidifying the dirt again as I faced the leader.

"If you believe me the easier catch," I offered, meeting her eyes evenly as some of her fellows backed off, clearly concerned by my show of power – Kisten moved back to my side, and I could see the spots that appeared faintly on his skin, although he hadn't started shifting yet, "then come get me."

She merely growled as she shifted, baring her teeth at me as she leapt for my throat. I didn't even flinch as I heard Kisten move beside me, fully shifting into his leopard form as he intercepted her. She quickly recovered, standing to her feet as Kisten circled her, making it clear he would not let her touch me. I watched as some of the other hyenas shifted in the grass and I knew they would likely make a move for me. The wild shifter knew she stood no chance against

Kisten in a head-on fight, but she was counting on him to try and protect me. I started to laugh again as the tendrils on my body shot out across the ground and I quickly found the other shifters.

Some yelped as they managed to avoid the dark tendrils and I grinned as the two I caught were dragged into the dirt, choking and desperate to escape as I buried them. One even tried to shift back to human to escape, but I focused my power on them more, dragging them down further until no sign remained of them in the grass. The others in the pack snarled and snapped at me, encircling me as I heard Kisten lunge at the leader again. I glanced to see him going in for a killing bite but she managed to avoid him, another of the pack joining her fight against him.

I frowned and narrowed my eyes at the leader of the wild shifters, watching as her paws started to sink into the ground. She quickly yelped as she leapt back into the grass, her companion fleeing with her as Kisten leapt at one of the hyenas near me, killing them in a single move. I flung my hand out when the pack leader attacked me, quickly catching her in my tendrils as she struggled off the ground. I slowly turned to look at her, the black marks swarming through her fur as her eyes met mine, full of fear.

"You should have enjoyed your free meal and left," I growled, barely recognizing my voice as I spoke. I heard her bones start to snap and break as the tendrils dug more into her body. A feeling of joy swirled with my annoyance and I could feel her fear of death as it danced through me. I barely reacted as Kisten killed another of the pack that leapt at me, my attention fully on the shifter in my grasp. "Now you'll be theirs."

"Raiven." I paused as I heard my name, turning away as I looked for the source of the voice. A being I had never seen before was standing further up the road, their golden eyes watching me softly. Their soft white hair seemed to flow around their face and I slowly released the shifter, ignoring her whine of pain as she tried to limp away from me. I didn't recognize their face, but that voice... it couldn't be. "That's enough."

"You," I whispered, stepping in their direction as they smiled softly, closing their eyes as they drew in a deep breath. Their cream-colored robe rustled in the unknown wind, causing the gold trim to twinkle in the sunlight as it revealed the matching tunic beneath. "It can't be you. Vitae..."

"I'm sure Vitae fed you another lie, as she has for so long," they interrupted, still watching me softly as I approached them, unable to help my suspicion. Their golden eyes were patient, just like their voice, and my heart pounded in my chest. A voice that was kind and loving, just as it had been when it whispered to me through a wall, comforting me while we were both captive at Vitae's court. "I assure you, I am as alive as you are."

"*Vogel*[1]." I heard Kisten's voice as he shifted behind me, the rest of the pack turning their attention to their leader. I could vaguely hear her snapping at them as they began to inspect the corpses of their dead companions. Their fear of death still seemed to wash over me, but I ignored it as some of them shifted back to their human form. They quickly picked up the bodies and disappeared back into the grass, hoping to escape us in my distraction. "Who... who is that?"

The being smiled softly as I stopped, searching the eyes of the person in front me as I tried to determine if they were real. When I finally spoke, my voice was barely above a whisper.

"The Seraph."

9

The silence between us dragged on for a moment after I said their name, and the Seraph merely smiled sadly as their eyes met mine. I withdrew my power as I watched them, my heart still pounding as Kisten finally stood next to me. The uncertainty and disbelief sat heavy in my chest, but my eyes and ears argued that it *had* to be them.

"I will apologize again for all of this, Raiven," the Seraph finally offered, looking away from my gaze as they spoke. Their wings fluffed behind them as they shifted their stance, the regret obvious in their voice. "However, finding you was necessary."

"How did you create the Dusters?" I whispered, ignoring their apology as I repeated the question I had asked at the Division headquarters. The Seraph frowned at my question, taking a moment to look away from me before looking up to meet my gaze again.

"As much as I would rather forget my imprisonment by Vitae, I did learn that my blood carries power." The Seraph visibly grimaced as they mentioned their time with Vitae and I felt my chest twist in response. "I seeded tiny amounts of my blood on the wind, and any who breathed in enough would fall under my control. I only had one goal for them: to find you, although I suppose I should have been more specific. I... had not anticipated they would simply start killing."

"You..." I started, unable to help the disbelief in my voice as I maintained my distance from the being in front of me. Despite the voice being muffled in my memories, I couldn't deny they sounded exactly like the Seraph. I had never seen them while I was Vitae's prisoner but their appearance tugged in my memories, as if I had seen it before. I also had never seen or heard their execution directly, but all of us had heard of it; even the First spoke of how bloody Vitae had been when she finished killing them herself.

"I am unfortunately responsible for all the death at the hands of the ones you call 'Dusters'," the Seraph admitted, once again meeting my gaze softly. "I will admit, I don't know how Vitae does it."

"Does what?" Kisten finally spoke, stepping in front of me again as the wind picked up slightly around us. The Seraph's golden eyes flashed as they turned to look at him, their expression changing slightly.

"Use others to meet her needs. I find it... uncomfortable."

"Then why do it?" I demanded, unable to help the slight anger in my voice as I spoke. The Seraph turned to look at me again, a pained expression on their face. I noticed that they swallowed uncomfortably, holding themselves as they answered.

"I did not know how else to find you. My wings can only carry me so far and I had no idea where you had gone to," they answered softly, raising their gaze to me. "This world... it is so foreign from the one I remember, and even if I had understood death would draw you out, it is not something I can do."

"What, kill?" I insisted, my anger only growing as I thought of Sidon. "So you'd rather let others do it for you than get your own hands dirty?"

"You misunderstand. I cannot kill even if I wanted to," the Seraph corrected and I knew my face held my disbelief as they sighed. "Neither can Vitae. We... we were not meant to kill."

"I've seen her kill plenty."

"Only through others can she make that death permanent. No

death caused by her hand or mine will last." Their wings fluffed again as they corrected me, their eyes almost pleading as they met mine. "Only you have that power."

"*Me?*"

"Yes, you... you need to remember, Raiven. Remember what you are." The Seraph fully met my gaze again, turning as they pointed to the tree. I realized that the dirt path we were on ended at the tree and I glanced down to see the Seraph looking at me again. "I was asleep, hiding from Vitae until you started to awaken. When you used your power, it called to me and I knew it was time. Vitae wants nothing more than to keep you in the dark, but I want to help you to remember."

"Why do I need to remember?" I insisted, finally taking a step towards them, as the Seraph brought their hand down, still meeting my gaze evenly. "Why do you care?"

"Oh, Raiven..." Their voice held a myriad of emotions as they said my name, but I picked up on pain and sorrow the most. Their eyes began to glisten as the wind started up again and once their hair settled around their face, tears were pouring down their cheeks. "I care more than I can ever say."

"Wait!" I couldn't help myself as I ran after the Seraph, their form growing transparent as they floated along the path and I heard Kisten as he ran after me. My heart pounded as I considered what the Seraph meant with their words; what did they mean, Vitae couldn't kill by her own hands? Is that why she had created the Hunters? Why they always seemed to be the ones to punish others for her? Had she tried to kill the Seraph but they survived because she couldn't kill?

'*Too many questions!*' my sister yelled in my mind and I paused as I finally stood in front of the tree, my heart pounding as I saw what was at its base. Kisten came up behind me, but I paid the Alpha no attention as I swallowed hard, gripping my cross tightly. When my sister spoke again, her tone was soft and just as conflicted as my thoughts. '*That's...*'

"Your grave," I finished, my eyes locked on the mound of dirt as memories flooded my mind. I had never been able to remember where I buried my sister, but now the memory came back to me as if it had only happened yesterday. "I... had asked for permission to bury you here. Vitae was annoyed, but agreed in the end. But..."

The logic in my brain screamed that it had to be a trick, but I still felt no magic in the air as I stared at the dirt. No grass grew on the mound, and it was exactly as I remembered it after I finished burying my sister. "This was a forest once, and this... this was always the tallest tree. We would travel across the plains, come here once a year to..."

"Raiven?" Kisten called out to me softly, but I kept my back to him as I lifted the locket from over my head, still gripping the wood tightly. The grave seemed mostly undisturbed, save for the other tokens of hope and forgiveness that surrounded the marked earth. It made no sense: a grave this old should not have been recognizable anymore and yet it seemed as if it had been frozen in time, just like the tree that stood over it.

'*Do it*,' my sister whispered softly as I stepped closer to the grave and I took a deep breath as I knelt next on the warm earth. Even without raising my power, I could feel that my sister's body lay beneath the dirt and I slowly pressed the locket into the loose earth. The sounds around me seemed to fade as my power rose on its own, the tendrils snaking slowly around my skin as I closed my eyes. I could feel as they reached for her body in the earth and as soon as I touched her bones, a new sound rose to replace the ones that had faded.

"*Remember and Heal, Two shall become one. Remember and Heal, Two shall become one.*" I opened my eyes as I heard the chant, but I was no longer kneeling on the warm dirt. I was standing in front of the tree, and I looked down as I felt a hand in mine. My heart pounded as they squeezed my fingers and I looked up to see my sister glancing down at me. Her smile was soft and hopeful and she nodded towards the tree as we both looked at the looming giant. The hole in the trunk somehow seemed larger and I nodded as we stepped closer. The rest of our tribesmen continued chanting behind us as we climbed over the roots, helping each other to reach the chasm. *"Remember and Heal, Two shall become One."*

"Azyam, wait!" I collapsed into the hole as my sister finished pulling me up and I took a deep breath as I stood. The hole seemed infinitely bigger as we stood inside it and I looked up to the dark ceiling. The rest of the tree simply disappeared into the black void and I shook my head as I looked back down.

"You okay, Awetash?" My sister's concern was obvious as I brushed myself off, and I did my best to smile as I met her gaze. Her deep brown eyes met my green ones and I chuckled softly as I walked to catch up to her.

"I'm fine," I answered, reaching to take her hand again as we stood in front of the darkness. My sister didn't often show her fear, but this ritual always got to both of us. It was a yearly rite, performed every year on our birthday and every year had the same result. So much felt like it was riding on us succeeding soon, and I gently stroked her fingers as I spoke. "You ready?"

"Always." My sister smiled as she took the lead, walking us further into the tree and the chanting of our tribesman faded in the darkness. We couldn't see anything around us as we walked, the faint fires doing little to light our path. Somehow, we still knew exactly where we were going, and we paused as we reached the divet. The slight incline where... we had been found as infants, crying and wailing deep within the tree.

"Alright." Azyam knelt on her side of the hole and I did the same on my side, holding her hands tightly in mine as we touched our foreheads together. "Do you think this will be it? The year we finally bring her up?"

"Who knows?" I offered, pulling up my power as she did the same, the darkness swirling across our skin as we closed our eyes, focusing on the presence that was deep within the tree. We tightened our hold on each other as we tried to pull the presence up, but it was as stubborn as ever, refusing to budge. We gripped each other tighter as we struggled against it, trying to raise the stubborn spirit that resided in the tree. For a moment, it felt like we might succeed, as I felt it tire and we pulled it closer to us. It quickly regained its strength, however, and we both gasped as we released the power, relaxing our hold on each other as we panted. I shook my head first, unable to help the disappointment in my chest. "I guess not."

"Hey, she released us for a reason." My sister tried to comfort me, gently pulling me up as she stood, holding my hand in the darkness. "It's... just not time yet."

"Yeah..." I agreed as we walked back through the dark hole and I opened my eyes in the present day, my power withdrawing from the ground as I gasped loudly. I felt Kisten's hands on my shoulders as he shook me, the relief plain in his voice.

"Raiven! Rai, are you alright?" I failed to find the words to answer him as I looked to the tree still looming over me. The hole definitely seemed smaller than it had been in my memory. I carefully stood and walked over to it, the Alpha releasing me reluctantly as I continued to ignore his questions. Gripping the locket tightly, I pressed it against the tree, closing my eyes as I felt my sister's presence in my hand.

"Together, Azyam," I whispered and I sent my power deep into the behemoth, searching for the presence that had always been buried in the tree. I opened my eyes with surprise as I felt the presence resonate from the wooden cross in my hand, and I carefully pulled it away, my sister's surprise joining with my own for a moment before changing to understanding.

'*That... makes sense, I guess,*' she scoffed, the laugh in her voice echoed in the sound I made. Her calmness seemed to overtake me, even as my chest ached. '*We never really understood what we had to do.*'

"I didn't survive Whistleblower's attack all those years ago," I whispered, Kisten coming up behind me again as I finally turned to face him. His face held all his confusion and worry and I looked away from his eyes as my chest swirled with all my emotions. "I just... awakened a part of myself, finally pulled it from the tree. That's how I was able to save my sister, place them both in the locket, but I wasn't able to fully awaken her. We weren't both supposed to die."

"Both?" Kisten asked cautiously, and I looked down to the locket in my hand.

"Azyam, my sister. She... she wasn't the only one to come back. When I pulled her soul into the locket, I pulled the rest of the presence from the tree as well. Because I died, I wasn't able to pull her into me," I explained, gripping the wood tighter as tears started in my eyes. "We... we weren't born, we were found in this tree. But we left something behind, something we could never pull out before. I guess I was finally able to pull it up, but still..."

"What? Raiven, I don—"

"I didn't survive that night, we both died. For some reason I came back and I was compelled to save my sister's half, because we never finished the ritual. We never fulfilled our purpose," I whispered, my chest twisting as I tried to come to terms with the memories now flooding my mind. My sister's calm acceptance still sat in my chest and I gripped the locket tighter. "I'm... we're..."

"Raiven?" Kisten asked again, gently touching me as the tears started to flow down my face and I looked up to his gaze, unable to help my wistful smile. "You're what?"

"I'm the Goddess of Death, Vitae's equal and opposite," I answered, unable to help the pain in my chest as I spoke. "I'm... Mortem."

10

"Okay, so let me get this right. You're... a Goddess?"

"Yes."

"And so is Vitae?"

"Yes."

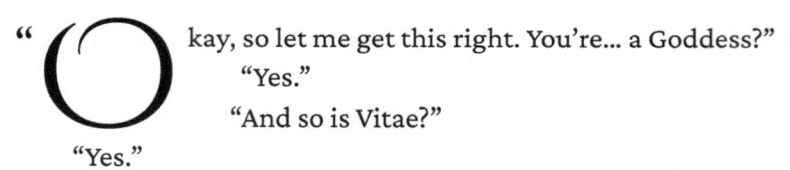

"So she's trying to kill you before you fully reawaken as a Goddess?" Kisten repeated and I nodded, still holding my locket tightly as I sat on the bed. We had returned to our hotel after sunset, and where everyone had been trying to hide their fear and awe of me before, they were obvious about it when we returned. I wasn't sure if it was because they understood something about me had changed or only feared it had, but I was too preoccupied with my own thoughts. My sister sat on the edge of my mind, her presence feeling as consistent as it had when I first had sealed her in the locket.

"So, do..." I looked up as Kisten's voice trailed off and saw how he ran his hand through his hair, clearly trying to process all that I was telling him. Even with the memories, it felt unbelievable to me, and yet I knew and understood it was true. "What about your sister?"

"*I will continue to fade, as I was always going to.*" Kisten jumped as he heard Azyam's voice come from the locket and I felt her slight annoyance as she continued. *"Because we both died, Mortem remains split between us, although it seems since Raiven died second and was able to keep her body, she had already started to awaken as the goddess. I am being pulled into her and until we are whole, Mortem can not reawaken."*

"So why haven't you two... combined?"

"I... we don't know," Azyam admitted, and I squeezed the wood again as her uncertainty filled me. *"Alex... he said I would not disappear, merely live on as part of my sister. She has been slowly absorbing me over the centuries and he was waiting for the day we became one."*

"Which is why your presence has grown fainter over the years," Kisten reasoned and my sister hummed her agreement, her usual admiration for Kisten showing through. The Alpha sighed heavily again as he sat down, carefully placing his hand on mine again. It was clear there were a million worries going through his mind and I was starting to wish I could understand his thoughts as well as I understood my sister's. "So what role does the Seraph play in all this?"

"I don't know," I finally added, glancing up to look at him. "I never really knew the Seraph when we were both Vitae's prisoners, but they must be a deity as well, just like me and Vitae. From the way they spoke about both of us, it was clear they see us as their equals."

"Can't rule out revenge as a motive, either. They did admit that only we have the power to kill permanently," Azyam said and I nodded as I looked away from the shifter again. *"They were also Vitae's prisoner for who knows how long before we were brought there."*

"What happened to Mortem, though? If she, Vitae and the Seraph were all deities, how did the world just forget about them? Did Vitae... erase all of them from history so no one would know about the other two and what she did?" Kisten offered and I frowned as I considered his question. "Is Vitae the reason Mortem disappeared in the first place?"

"It's... possible, and likely how she learned she couldn't actually kill and why she merely imprisoned the Seraph instead of trying to kill them," my sister offered. *"She could have created Hunters originally for the sole*

purpose of killing Mortem once she was reborn. Remember we rose from the tree that held Mortem's power; it's likely that we're just vessels for her soul."

"Then what about Raiven? Once you two join and Mortem is reborn, will she... cease to exist?"

"*We... don't know,*" Azyam whispered and I felt the shifter's grip on me tighten. "*But the process can't be stopped. It's been happening slowly anyway, and if Mortem doesn't reawaken soon, her power will continue to take over Raiven. The power is pushing more and more for her to kill with it again and once she does, it will fully take over...*"

"... and kill everything," I concluded, sighing heavily as I spoke. Kisten squeezed my fingers painfully with my words and I tried to swallow my own worries and concerns. "We have to learn why we haven't combined into Mortem, why we couldn't do it before. Part of it was that one of us needed to die, but—"

"Vitae killing both of you messed that up," Kisten finished, repeating what I had told him earlier. I released the wooden cross to take his hand in mine. "Don't know if I should be furious or relieved that she did."

"I think both are okay," I whispered and the Alpha pulled me against him as I wrapped my arms around him. "We'll figure this out."

"And here you were worried that you would lose me first," he scoffed and I hugged him tighter as my chest ached.

"You might not lose me."

"Hard to be hopeful on a 'might', *Vogel*[1]," Kisten whispered, planting a kiss into my hair as he squeezed me tighter. I didn't answer as I let him hold me, my own heart pounding as I considered what to do. The truth was we didn't have much of an option: Mortem's power was awakening in me and if the past few months were any indication, I had no chance to control it as I was. There was something keeping my sister and me from combining to reawaken the goddess and she was the only one who could stop what was otherwise certain death for the living.

"Is there a chance Vitae knows? That you've been here?" Kisten asked softly and I felt Azyam's concern as I slowly pulled away from him. "Maybe she knows what's needed to revive Mortem."

"*I doubt it. She definitely seemed to think killing both of us would solve her problem, and the whole 'turning into a vampire' was probably the best lie she could think of to fool Raiven, whose memories were corrupted when she died,*" my sister scoffed, her disdain obvious in her tone. "*Forcing her blood on us was probably also damage control, hoping in our semi-awakened state it would allow her some control.*"

"It did, for a while," I added, leaning back into the shifter as I frowned. "I had no memory to argue with what she said and I was compelled to listen at first, but the compulsion faded with time and, I guess, as I absorbed more and more of Azyam."

"Azyam, right," Kisten repeated, sighing heavily once again, his hand drifting to the locket. "And I shouldn't say your name, right?"

"Not unless you want to call up Mortem's power." I closed my eyes as I carefully slid the locket over my head. My sister's presence flickered as I did so, but still felt consistent as I leaned back on the bed. "While it's nice to remember our true names, I now need to make sure no one says mine."

"Well luckily, my father's dead and probably would have refused to use it anyway," Kisten scoffed and I looked up just as the shifter turned away. I leaned forward on the bed again as I watched him, my chest constricting again as I considered his own feelings. Kisten must've felt me watching him, because he slowly turned his soft gaze to me. "What?"

"I love you," I whispered softly, unable to help the tears that started in my eyes. I lifted my hand up to his face and he leaned into the touch, purring gently into my skin. I closed my eyes as I lost the battle with my emotions and the tears rolled down my cheek. "This... I don't want to lose you."

"I'm not going anywhere, Raiven," Kisten insisted, and I felt him pull me close to him again, carefully stroking my hair as he kept purring. I buried my face into his chest as I cried, overcome with worry. "I'm here for you, no matter what we need to do."

"Kisten—"

"I'm not leaving you to face this alone, even if it means losing you," the Alpha insisted, tightening his arms around me as I moved into his lap, wrapping my arms around him. I felt him slide his hand under my chin and raise my gaze to his, smiling at me softly as he cried his silent tears. I twisted in his lap as I leaned up to kiss his soft lips, my chest aching with his pain.

Kisten seemed content to leave the kiss gentle, but I pressed more force onto him, gripping his shirt tightly. The shifter hummed in response as he parted his lips to let me in and I immediately slid my tongue against his, desperate to feel him. His grip on me changed as he hummed into the kiss, unable to help his own desire as he answered me. I moaned softly into our deepening kiss and dug my hands in more as Kisten's hands drifted lower.

"Raiven," he moaned softly against my lips and I mimicked his sound, reaching to remove his shirt as he did the same to mine. I quickly wrapped my arms around him again as our skin touched, aware of my growing desperation to feel my lover. Being wrapped in his arms made me feel safe, loved and the tingling sensation as it danced across my skin only made my chest ache more. "Rai, I..."

"Me too," I echoed, one of my hands snaking its way to his hair as I started pressing kisses into his neck, his hands dancing across my back as he pulled me further into his lap. A soft sound escaped me as I felt how much he wanted me and I moaned into his skin, wrapping my legs around his waist. His hands finally went to my bra and he unsnapped the offensive clothing, forcing me to release him as he pushed it off my arms.

Once it was tossed with our shirts, he merely pressed me into his skin again, moaning softly as he held me tightly. I couldn't help but try to touch every inch of him as I hummed into his skin, watching as his spots started to faintly appear. There was no hint of claws as his hands similarly explored me and I moaned as he leaned down to steal another kiss from my lips.

"As tempting as sex sounds..." he whispered, pulling away from me again to see my face, and my chest constricted as I met his colorful gaze. His eyes swam with all his animals, and yet held so much fear and pain. When we thought we had centuries left together, the idea of being separate was easier to push off. Being faced with the uncertainty of losing me any day, Kisten was feeling the ache that ran through my own chest as I gripped his face with my hands. "... there's something I'd rather have more."

"What's that?"

"Every inch of your skin pressed against mine," he whispered softly, closing his eyes as I pulled him down for another desperate kiss, moaning as I felt him throb against me. "Just... just let me feel you."

"Always," I breathed, carefully sliding from his lap, our hands lingering on each other. I focused on undressing as quickly as I could, sliding back into my mate's arms as he finished kicking away his pants. There were no obstructions between us now as I sat in his lap again, laying my head on his chest as he sighed happily. His hands explored me as if it was the first time he was touching me and I didn't resist as he laid me down on the bed, leaning over me as he maintained the contact. He buried his face into my hair and neck as his hands continued to dance over me, eventually locking one of his hands with mine.

A soft sound flowed from him as I began to stroke his skin the way he had touched mine and he openly moaned and gasped into my neck as I explored him, our legs entangled as we lay side by side on the bed. His member throbbed against me as I pulled him closer to me, but neither of us made an effort to push things further. We rarely took the time to simply enjoy intimacy and I could feel the tears as they started to well in my eyes again.

"I love you," I whispered again, and Kisten finally lifted his head, looking into my eyes with his colorful gaze.

"I love you," he whispered back, gently kissing me as he squeezed my hand in his and I squeezed our legs together in response. The shifter sighed as he pulled from the kiss, lying down beside me again as he continued to meet my gaze. "We'll get through this."

"No matter what," I promised, despite the tears that poured down my face as I tried to smile. Kisten's lips twitched into his own soft expression as he released my hand, gently touching my face.

"No matter what."

II

I groaned softly as I woke up, turning my face away from the bright sunlight as it streamed in through the window. I could already hear Kisten in the bathroom and I stretched noisily, doing my best to shake the sleep from my body.

'*Raiven.*' I heard my sister's voice in my mind and I grabbed the wooden cross as it grew warm against my skin. Since interacting with her grave, it seemed I no longer had to feed the locket my power for her to speak with me, and while she could still withdraw, I could always feel her. Her presence felt weak, but more consistent than before, and I hummed softly before I answered her.

"Yeah?"

'*Been thinking. About everything.*'

"What about it?" I grumbled, forcing myself to sit up as I turned away from the sun, annoyed that it seemed to flood every inch of the bed. I heard the water stop in the bathroom and yawned again as the door opened. Kisten walked out, his hair still wet and shiny from the shower, and I couldn't help my slight smile as I stood.

"Wanna clean up and then we'll figure things out?" the Alpha offered and I nodded happily as I leaned up to kiss him. He echoed my sound as he gently tangled his hand in my hair and I pulled away reluctantly.

"Sounds good," I agreed, slipping into the bathroom as we traded places. It seemed he had already pulled a towel down for me but I ignored it as I turned to the mirror. As expected, I could still see the message he had left for me and my chest warmed at the sight of his *I love you* written in the steam.

'*I have... an idea, I guess?*' My sister finally spoke again as I stepped into my shower, doing my best to let the warm water finish waking me up.

"Okay, what's the idea?"

'*The Siblings... don't you think it's odd how Vitae seemed to want them dead first? She sent her strongest Hunters after the three of them and you,*' Azyam offered and I grunted at the thought. '*And Alex said his memories were the most important thing left in the world. That's why he was willing to die to protect them.*'

"Do you think the Siblings remember Mortem?"

'*I think they remember the truth, whatever that is,*' Azyam corrected, and I couldn't help my acknowledgement as I finished cleaning myself, finally feeling refreshed as I tried to dry my hair. It seemed to have stopped growing now that it reached most of the way down my back, and I hummed with annoyance as I fought with it. '*LeAlexende said he, Alrune and Basina are different from other vampires, but he never said how.*'

"Likely they remember Vitae before she became Mater Vitae, and once they left, she worried they could undo her lies," I continued, finally giving up as I started to simply twist my hair into two long braids. "But Alrune and Basina are dead, and we have no idea where Alex went. He said he was going home, but we don't know–"

'*Where that is,*' she finished and I nodded, still fighting with my hair as I sat in the bathroom. What Azyam was saying made sense, but it didn't give us much of a goal to work towards. '*Lucius has those memories now.*'

"He does, but is going back now the right thing to do?" I answered, standing as I finished with my hair and wrapped myself with the towel. "After all, I still haven't finished my mission with the Dusters and their creator."

'*You think the Seraph will make more? They said the Dusters were created to find you for them.*'

"Yeah, but something is still... off," I admitted, stepping out of the humid bathroom into the dryer warm air. I saw the bag with our clothes sitting on the bed and the shifter nowhere in sight. I went straight for the suitcase, digging out clean clothes to wear. "I don't know what it is, but there's more to what they're saying."

'*Hmm,*' was all Azyam offered and I sighed as I finished dressing. Deciding to wait for Kisten, I moved to the window, glancing out into the city below. The streets weren't very busy, but there were already people moving about, tourists planning out their day and workers trying their best to get to work. My eyes drifted across the crowd, trying to decide what we should do. I stood up straighter as I noticed a single person standing in the crowd, their golden eyes meeting mine.

I started for the door just as Kisten returned. The shifter seemed surprised by my urgency, but he didn't question as he followed me back to the elevator. The box seemed to move too slowly as I insistently pressed the button for the first floor and I nearly flew through the lobby to get outside. Kisten ran to catch me as I glanced around for the Seraph, and I saw them standing in the same spot I had seen from my window.

"Hello, Raiven," they spoke softly as I approached them, their wings still folded as they waited patiently for me. As I drew closer, I noticed that no one else seemed to see or notice them, but all were somehow avoiding the place where they stood. The Seraph noticed my confusion, watching as a tourist walked by them. "This is an illusion, meant only for you. I have noticed... most don't react well to my presence."

"Why is that?" I spat, not trying to hide my distrust as they sighed.

"I wish I understood. I can only guess... it's because they know, and yet do not know, what I am," the Seraph said, wringing their hands together as they looked away from my gaze. "It was easier when everyone knew."

"And what *are* you?" I insisted, crossing my arms as I stood in front of the mirage. Kisten stood beside me, taking my hand in his as I squeezed it tightly. The Seraph returned their gaze to me, a sad look in their golden eyes.

"The Beginning. The Source of Life as we know it to be. All life carries some part of me in them, even you," they answered, and I couldn't help the shiver that ran through me. My heart started to pound as I considered their words, but I couldn't look away from their face as they continued. "Vitae... used me, my blood, to create her... experiments."

"She didn't stop creating because she wanted to. She stopped because she had no choice," I realized and the Seraph nodded, the sadness still obvious in their expression.

"Once I escaped, she had very little of my blood left and she worked through it too quickly." They shifted their weight as they stood and I noticed the illusion shimmered for a moment, as if interference had interrupted their magic. We stood in silence as the Seraph moved awkwardly, as if unsure what else to say. It was clear there was still a lot of trauma for them about their imprisonment by Vitae and I felt my heart ache for them.

Vitae had only kept me locked away for the most part, her torture of me limited to occasional entertainment for others and always mild, if not still terrifying at the time. Considering how often Vitae had created life, however, their torture of the Seraph must have been near constant, and explained why our conversations were so infrequent. They must have spoken to me every chance they had, their brief respite from the hell they were going through under her.

"How... did you escape?" I asked cautiously, watching as the Seraph flinched at my question. They started to hold themselves again, closing their eyes as they shook involuntarily. "Did she kill you and you came back, or...?"

"I had help. A few remembered the truth, and they chose to help me," the Seraph breathed, still keeping their eyes closed as they shivered again. "They... helped me to replace myself with a replica, so it took Vitae a while to realize I was gone. It gave her something to destroy, and few would argue if they were the ones who insisted Vitae killed me."

"The Siblings," I whispered and I felt as Kisten's grip on my hand tightened. He had been doing his best to ignore my conversation, but I could almost feel his concern as I continued. "They are the ones who saved you."

"Others among the vampires helped as well, but they are the only ones who know what Vitae truly is. We weren't sure if you were... her, but we hoped you would be," the Seraph admitted, finally looking at me again as they tried to smile. "I told them to help you escape as well, as I feared Vitae would kill you once she discovered I had left."

"The fear of her doing so is why I left," I admitted, releasing Kisten's hand as I crossed my arms. The Alpha shifted so that he stood with his back to me, shielding me from the gaze of others. "So you set up her lie for her, knowing she would want to hide losing you."

"It was Basina's plan, not mine, but I fear Vitae intends to reclaim her lost prize." The Seraph finally released their arms as they spoke and I felt my heart stop in my chest with their words. They seemed to understand my worry and fear, frowning as our gazes met. "The Lady is coming to find us."

"Lady Night," I hissed, and I felt my sister's concern and anger rise with my own. With Whistleblower dead, Lady Night was the only one of Vitae's original Hunters who remained, and I clenched my fists as I continued. "How did she find you?"

"I told you I went to sleep after I escaped, but it was because I had no choice. I had tried to merely hide, but she always found me. I began to suspect that using my power allowed her to feel me and so I was forced to hibernate," the Seraph admitted, playing with their hands as they spoke. "Since you have not fully awoken yet, I don't think she can feel you in the same way. She does not know you are here, but she fears that you may be."

"So Lady Night is coming to find you—"

"And kill you, if she finds proof that you have been here," the Seraph finished, their eyes pleading with me as I finally looked away. At the moment, I knew we were safe, as Lady Night's powers rendered her basically human during the day. It was once night came that everyone would be in danger and I sighed heavily as I considered what I needed to do.

"I'll warn Eba, and see if they can get a warning out in time. Maybe emergency shelters can be set up, just in case," I muttered, playing with one of my braids as I mused. "If I meet her before she gets to the city, maybe I can—"

"Wait!" I paused as I heard Kisten speak, the shifter still keeping his back to me. The worry and concern was obvious in his voice and I felt my heart pound as he continued. "Are you thinking of facing a Hunter alone?"

"I can't let her reach the city. Lady Night is on a par with your father as far as power is concerned and she doesn't have a crutch like the Grimm," I whispered, trying to keep others from hearing me. I let Kisten take my hand as he reached for it. "I have to intercept her, keep her from coming here."

"Then let me—"

"No. She'll know you are my partner, and Lady Night has an advantage against multiple opponents," I interrupted, squeezing Kisten's hand tightly as I heard him sigh. I knew no words would stop him from worrying about me, but I needed to make him understand. "She chased me during my first few years away from Vitae; trust me when I say I can handle her alone."

"I'll try," the Alpha conceded, and I turned my attention back to the Seraph. They had their eyes on Kisten behind me, but looked down to meet my gaze once they noticed I was looking at them again. Their eyes held all their worry and concern and I did my best to seem confident as I spoke.

"I'll take care of Lady, but that doesn't help with awakening Mortem," I whispered, searching for any answers in their expression. "I don't know why my sister and I haven't merged and Mortem's power is beginning to grow beyond my control. Why were we separated in the first place? Why didn't Mortem reincarnate as one person?"

"I don't know," the Seraph admitted, closing their eyes as they adjusted their stance. I opened my mouth to dispute them, but they managed to speak before I could. "I can only guess it is because of Mortem's own feelings as she died."

"Mortem's—"

"I... wasn't there, I only felt her absence when it was far too late to stop it," the Seraph admitted and I could see the tears and pain from the memory. My heart twisted as I heard the emotion in their voice, having to fight my own tears. "Mortem had never feared death before that moment, she had no reason to. To be hurt and betrayed by one she loved... I can only imagine her anger and sorrow."

'So her conflicted emotions split her into two,' my sister finally spoke and I saw the Seraph's eyes drift to my locket. *'One part carrying her anger and determination, and another—'*

"Her fear and concern," I answered, clutching the wood tightly as the being in front of me nodded. My sister hummed with thought as she considered the idea and I closed my eyes as I spoke again.

"That still doesn't help with merging us into one."

"You need to know the truth."

"Well, how do I find that truth? Why can't you just tell me?" I insisted, releasing Kisten's hand as I stepped toward the illusion. Once again, the image wavered, but the Seraph's face bore the same calm, sad expression they had worn for most of our conversation. I saw their wings move, and for the first time, noticed the many eyes they were hiding by keeping them folded. They seemed to realize I had caught a glimpse, as they carefully pet their own feathers, closing their wings more.

"Would you trust me, or your own memories more?" they finally asked and I was forced to sigh, conceding to their point. I couldn't help my suspicion that the Seraph was up to their own game, and even their warning about Lady Night could be completely selfish in not wanting to be recaptured. I put my hand on my hip as I grabbed my sister's cross, shaking my head as I tried to settle my conflicted emotions. "I wish you would trust me, but I understand why you do not. I will guide you toward the truth, so that you can trust yourself."

"Fine." I finally waved them off and turned to face Kisten as the illusion faded. I gently touched his back as I turned him toward me, and I could still see the argument on his face. "Let's... let's find Eba's Retainer and Alpha. If we're going to protect this city, we have to work fast."

"We do," he replied curtly and I sighed as he walked away from me, heading back to the hotel. I felt my sister rise as I started to feel frustrated and I could sense her concern.

'*You could try to alleviate his fear.*'

"He'll worry anyway," I replied with a shrug, slowly following behind my fiancé as I watched him disappear in the lobby. "He doesn't like being out of control. It's both the best thing about him and—"

'*The worst,*' my sister agreed, and I felt my heart twist as I stood outside the hotel. I could see Kisten inside talking to the front desk, and I took a deep breath as I stepped inside, doing my best to push aside my own frustrations and concerns.

12

I sat heavily on the bed as Kisten and I returned to our room, holding my head as I groaned. The afternoon heat had started to creep into the air and I allowed myself to collapse backwards, already worn out. Eba's Retainer was just as worried as us once I explained to them what was happening, and I could already hear as citizens were hurriedly making preparations for the night. I had warned Eba and the Prime Minister what Lady Night's powers were and they had encouraged all citizens to head to the shelters that were being set up to keep them safe.

"Hours…" I whispered, gripping my cross tightly as I looked to the sunlight that still streamed in through the window to our room. For now, everyone was still safe, but as soon as darkness came, we would be playing by her rules, and Lady Night never played fair. My heart constricted as I considered my own preparations for facing her and I played with the wood in my hand. My sister's thoughts barely felt separate from my own at this point and I hummed thoughtfully as I kept my eyes on the window.

"So are we going to talk or…?" Kisten finally spoke softly and I sighed heavily, closing my eyes as I remained lying down on the bed.

I heard as he noisily sat on the sofa, making his displeasure obvious as he continued. "I'm talking to you, Raiven."

"And I hear you, Kisten."

"Then are we—"

"Talk about what? How much you don't trust me or how much you hate feeling out of control?" I interrupted the Alpha, finally opening my eyes to look at him. Kisten was giving me an annoyed look and I shrugged as I finally sat up. "We both know that's what this is."

"What a novel idea that it could be about how much I'm worried about you," Kisten spat back and I forced myself to take a deep breath as I fought to keep my own emotions under control. I could feel my sister's annoyance starting to join with my own and I hummed angrily as he dropped his head into his hands. "This isn't about me, Raiven. I'm just... worried and I don't understand why you insist on doing this alone."

"Because I know Lady, and just like you knew Whistleblower, I know the best way to face her. Trust me, alone is not how I *want* to do this, I just know it's the *best* way." I sighed, releasing the cross as I turned away from the shifter. I could feel his eyes on me as I stared at the wall, but I refused to meet his gaze as I spoke. "Like I said, she was the Hunter Vitae sent after me when I first ran away. She's practically useless during the day, but she has a huge advantage at night."

"Wha—"

"Her powers give her abilities similar to a Wraith but amplified to a whole other level. She can manipulate shadows, teleport through darkness as well as being stronger and faster at night. The more shadows she has to work with, the deadlier she is," I explained, humming as I remembered my first encounter with the Hunter. It had been terrifying to fight her that night, and I took a deep breath again as I tried to shake off the memory. "That's why fighting her alone is best. If the only shadows she has to work with are mine and the terrain, she's a lot easier to handle. That's also why—"

"You don't want to let her get to the city, so she can't use the buildings," Kisten finished, and I chanced a glance at him as I heard him lean back on the seat. The Alpha seemed exhausted as he closed his eyes, and I fully turned to face him as I waited for him to continue speaking. "I don't like it, but it makes sense."

"And...?"

"And, I don't like it and I'm still gonna worry about you," Kisten repeated, opening his eyes to look at me. I wanted to frown at his answer but settled for humming as our eyes met, still not liking his attitude. The shifter seemed to sense my displeasure as he leaned more into the seat, closing his eyes again. "Look, you didn't like my plan against my father, either, but you went with it because it made sense and was the best plan we had. I can go along with yours without liking it."

I opened my mouth to argue but stopped myself, growling softly as I realized he had a point. I merely clutched my cross as I turned away, no longer knowing what to say. I heard Kisten stand up and I felt the bed shift as he sat on it beside me. The air seemed to brush against me as he reached to touch me but the touch never came and I turned to see him facing away from me, drawing his feet onto the bed.

"Look, Rai. I won't lie, I really kind of hate all of this," he admitted, looking at his nails as he flexed his fingers and I watched as his spots appeared faintly on his skin. "I know it's not your fault and all of it was inevitable anyway, but... I hate it. I don't want to lose you and I hate that all I have to hope for is a 'maybe' with no evidence behind it."

"Kisten—"

"No, I have literally spent the last year fighting for you. Hell, I finally faced my father just so that he couldn't separate us. But now... we're here and I... I hate that there's nothing I can do, I hate..." The Alpha turned away from me, balling his hand into a fist as his voice faded. I felt my chest constrict as I considered his words and I had to swallow the emotion building in my throat. I wanted to say something, but the words wouldn't come as I watched him sigh, releasing the fist. "You're right, I hate that I have no control. That there's nothing I can do to turn the situation to my advantage, to protect you."

"Kisten," I whispered softly, finally forcing myself to reach out as he turned away from me more on the bed. I took a deep breath as I moved closer, wrapping my arms around him as I leaned my head on his back. I could hear his heartbeat in his chest as I closed my eyes, doing my best to focus on the gentle rhythm of his breathing. "You know I don't want to lose you."

"That doesn–"

"I hate all the reminders that I'm going to outlive you," I continued, ignoring him as I wrapped my arms around him tighter. I felt his breath catch as I spoke and I could almost see his expression in my mind as I continued. "I know it's different to you, because you're so much younger than me. To you, we have hundreds of years left, and that seems like plenty of time. But centuries go by so quickly when you're thousands of years old. It feels like no time at all."

"So you're saying what I'm feeling right now, my fear that I'll lose you any day, is the same as what you have felt about losing me?" Kisten hummed and I could hear in his voice he didn't see the comparison. I sighed heavily again, burying my face more into his back.

"Similar, not the same," I corrected, finally opening my eyes as I saw our shadows, cast on the bed by the sunlight. Unbroken by gaps or interruptions, just a unified shape of darkness and I hummed softly as I continued speaking. "I have lost so many, Kisten. So many lives I cherished, gone simply because their lives had a limit and mine does not. I don't... I don't want to watch you go anymore than you wish to watch me leave."

"Raiven?" I barely heard Kisten's voice as I continued staring at our shadows, my mind lost in my memories. I felt his hand as he finally touched my arms around him, and I squeezed him tighter in my daze, unable to help the emotion in my chest. My sister's presence felt both close and distant, and I sighed softly as I closed my eyes again.

"I want there to be a way for us to go together," I whispered quietly, feeling the tears as they began to build behind my eyelids. "I want to go with you, and not be left behind to live without you."

"I simply want to have a life with you, and not be denied that chance," Kisten murmured softly, and I could hear the tears in his voice. "I just wish... I wish there was something I could do."

"You can do what you always have."

"What's that?" I couldn't help my gentle smile as I released the shifter, sliding on the bed until I could see his face. Kisten was giving me a warm look, his colorful eyes showing how much his emotions were affecting his animals. Whereas Kisten used to suppress his emotions to keep them from manifesting, he now freely showed me how he was feeling and I gently stroked his cheek, refusing to look away.

"Love me," I whispered softly and Kisten shook his head, closing his eyes as he leaned into my hand. Despite the look on his face, I could see my simple answer had struck a chord with him, and his lips twitched as he tried to keep from smiling.

"I already do that."

"Then don't stop," I chuckled, altering my position on the bed as I kept my hand on his face. Kisten slowly opened his eyes to meet mine again, and I took a deep breath as I tried to swallow my own feelings. His gaze was so lost and full of pain, as if I had already been taken away from him. "I'm right here, right now. Instead of being upset about what might happen tonight, or tomorrow, or a hundred years from now, shouldn't we... try to enjoy this moment? Simply enjoy the time we have?"

"Are you really trying to get philosophical about our feelings?" Kisten laughed, the soft sound causing my smile to grow as I mimicked his sounds. I gently held his face with both my hands, sighing happily as I met his gaze.

"I'm saying we have two choices: we can sit here and be mad and argue over something rather pointless..." I whispered, pulling his forehead down to mine as he gently laid his hands over mine. I closed my eyes as I felt him squeeze my fingers tightly, and I took another breath as I spoke. "... or we can try our best to accept that there's nothing we can do about that and focus on what we can control."

"Sound advice coming from someone who has never been married," Kisten scoffed and I couldn't help my chuckle as he lifted my face to kiss me. It was barely more than our lips brushing, but it was enough. My heart pounded in my chest as he pulled away, a stupid grin glued to my face.

"Maybe I learned a thing or two from watching others." I shrugged, opening my eyes to meet his again. His expression had softened into reluctant acceptance and I adjusted our hands until our fingers were laced together. "After all, it would be kinda sad if I hadn't figured anything out in my long life."

"Well, I guess you'll just have to teach this youngster the ropes," Kisten joked and I couldn't help my laugh as I leaned away from him.

"Gods, don't say it like that."

"What can I say? I like a woman with experience," Kisten continued, and I pulled away from the Alpha, my laughter growing as he started to laugh as well, chasing after me. I let him climb on top of me, playfully pinning me to the bed as he leaned down to kiss me again. He kept the kiss soft and tender, and our laughter died as he leaned up from me. "You are my goddess already."

"Well, you are a crappy devotee to have," I teased, loving the playfulness I saw enter his gaze as he shifted his weight on top of me. I linked my hands around his neck, giving him a challenging smile as I lay beneath the Alpha. "No wonder you need a woman with experience. Someone has to teach you what to do."

"Well then, your Worship, how should I show my admiration and loyalty?" he purred, burying his face into my neck as he started to leave his usual kisses and licks. I sighed with pleasure as my hand drifted to his hair, not trying to hide how much I enjoyed his attention. "How can I prove my fealty to you and you alone?"

"You're off to a good start," I moaned softly, pulling him closer against me as he continued, once again glancing toward the light that streamed in through the window. We only had a few more hours before night would fall and all our worries would return, but I closed my eyes as I tightened my hand in his hair. Those worries would have their time and, while I could, I just wanted to enjoy being with the man I loved.

13

I took a deep breath as I sat in the grass, the sun setting in the distance behind me. I had Kisten drive me an hour from the city, knowing that Lady Night would detour once she sensed me and I wanted to give her no reason to be anywhere near it. The Alpha had been reluctant to leave, but I sent him off with a kiss, promising I would be fine. I inhaled deeply as I plucked at the still grass, the nervousness in my chest not matching my brave words. The plains were unnaturally quiet, as if nature herself was holding her breath to see what our fight would be like.

The sunset was pretty, bathing the grass around me in gorgeous pinks and oranges and I closed my eyes as the sunlight graced me with the last of its warmth. It was strange how peaceful everything felt and seemed, despite the feeling of dread that followed the disappearing sun. My sister said nothing as we waited, although I could still feel her presence like an annoying hum in the back of my mind. I sighed as I rocked my head, keeping my eyes closed as I plucked at the edge of my shirt. Despite the heat during the day, it got chilly at night, and I had opted to wear long sleeves and pants, grateful for my own foresight in the variety of clothes I packed.

"She's coming," I whispered as I slowly stood, the last of the sunlight dipping below the horizon as the wind began to pick up. My skin started to swarm with my power as I closed my eyes and I felt the ground shake as I stepped forward. It seemed that since being touched by the Seraph's power, my own powers were no longer segregated and I could freely use both abilities at the same time. As soon as the darkness started to creep across the soft brown and green grass, the plains seemed to come alive with noise and I closed my eyes as I walked.

"Well, well, the lost little lamb comes to offer herself to the wolf." I paused as I heard her voice, not bothering to open my eyes as the wind whirled around me. I flexed my fingers as I felt the tendrils dance on my skin, the earth still moving under my feet. "Although it seems the lamb has found herself some new claws."

"That's not all she's found," I offered, and I struggled not to react as I felt her hand glide through my hair, lifting my braids as she laughed. I knew her goal was to try and throw me off balance, and I balled my hands into fists as I fought my instincts. I rolled my shoulders, adjusting the holster as I resisted the urge to draw my gun.

"Oh, I'm aware. Mother has told me all about your 'awakening', how willing you are to undo all she did to keep you docile." Lady Night's laughter drifted away from me and I finally opened my eyes, still failing to see the Hunter. The only shadows she had to work with were my own and the shade of a few nearby trees and I took a deep breath as I heard her voice carry on the wind. "I liked you more when you were a scared little girl, lost without her sister."

"I was never without her," I hummed angrily, lifting my hand as the ground shifted, the nearby trees collapsing as I forced their roots from the dirt. My sister's presence radiated through my chest and I closed my eyes again as I waited for Lady to reveal herself. "Just took me a while to wake up from my nightmare."

"Then you should have stayed asleep!" I quickly turned as the Hunter rose from my own shadow, barely catching her hands as she laughed at me. The silver claws on her fingers clinked as she leapt away from me, standing gracefully as her laughter started to die down. Like Whistleblower and Mother, Lady looked as if she had stepped out of a memory; ginger, oily hair pulled back to reveal a bony, charming face and slitted gray eyes that were watching me carefully. Her short red dress flapped in the wind, only held closed by the black belt she wore around her waist and despite her bare feet, she seemed completely composed in the encroaching night.

"Sorry to disappoint, M'lady," I scoffed, crossing my legs as I bowed, unable to help my snarky expression. Her smile had openly turned to a scowl as I looked up, and I knew she was disappointed her words had not rattled me. She knew I had taken away one of her main advantages by forcing her to face me in the open and I beamed my own smile as I stood up straighter. "But I have no intention of sleeping again."

She said nothing as she moved for me, and I was forced to dodge her attack, drawing my gun as I moved. Even as I turned to fire, I shot my free hand out and I felt as she quickly moved back, avoiding the tendrils as they flew through the air to grab her. Just like Whistleblower, it was obvious she wanted to avoid touching my power and I couldn't help my smirk as I fired, my bullet blowing through her hair as she moved. I stood up straight as I felt her continue to move around me, refusing to give me a clear chance to aim.

"Round and round, she goes..." I whispered softly to myself, barely surprised as I watched her red shape move towards the fallen trees, disappearing into their shadows. Knowing we were evenly matched had her playing it safe, trying to figure out how to get close to me without being in range of either my gun or my power. Using my power to kill her would make the fight easy, but I knew I had to resist the desire, tightening my hold on my gun.

I slowly spread the tendrils across the ground, my focused emotions giving me greater control as I walked toward the fallen tree. The ground shook as the grass shriveled and died while my power slithered through it, and I felt my annoyance building as I slowly touched the tree's trunk, the black marks digging into the bark.

"I would prefer not to be out here all night, Lady," I hummed, snapping the trunk in half as I tried to break up the shadow, forcing her out of it. "I *do* have other things to do rather than dance with you."

"Then let's dance, monster!" she laughed, launching herself at me as I snapped the trunk again. I barely had enough time to bring my hands to my face to toss her away, the tendrils quickly releasing the tree as they rushed back to me. Lady Night took advantage of my imbalance, quickly leaping for me again as I haphazardly shot at her, missing as she dodged. I was forced to knock her away again as my power finally returned, swimming across my skin as I growled.

The whole ground heaved as I lifted my hands, flinging the Hunter into the air as I aimed at her, but she managed to dodge even as I curved the bullet after her. She wasted no time in leaping at me again, managing to scratch my left arm as she slipped by, her laughter dancing past me. My anger grew as I felt the pain, and I knew that her claws were also poisoned as the wound burned, the fire radiating through my arm. Lady Night seemed determined to keep me off balance, reaching to scratch my face as I leaned back from her attack.

"Everything was so nice while you were sleeping!" Lady Night called out as she disappeared into the darkness again, and I sighed with my annoyance, frowning as I realized the moon had disappeared behind some clouds. I had no doubt she was riding in its shadow, and I growled as I sunk my power into the ground again, determined to not let her catch me off guard. "Life thrived as Mother guided it, just as she always has."

"Controlled it, you mean," I scoffed, turning in the patch of dead grass as I waited for the cloud to pass, adjusting my gun in my hand. "Vitae stopped guiding when she decided it was her role to create life and then keep it on her tight leash."

"She was only doing as she was intended, but what would you know?" I hummed angrily as I felt her reach out of the shadow, but I was too late to grab her as she quickly sank back into it. "You don't have any of Mortem's memories. You are just an empty shell carrying her power."

"I'm more than that," I hissed as the cloud passed, but Lady

Night failed to expose herself as the dark tendrils on the ground searched for her. I was barely surprised when I felt hands wrap around my neck and I was pulled to my knees as my own shadow tried to strangle me. The Hunter rose from the ground in front of me, laughing as she pressed her foot onto my chest.

"I think not, Raiven," Lady gloated and I glared as I fought to throw off my shadow, but I quickly found my hands grabbed and pulled into the ground as the Shadow increased its grip on me. I was slammed into the dirt as my power returned to my skin, but unlike how I had done with Whistleblower, I found I couldn't force the tendrils onto Lady's skin and she chuckled above me. "Whistleblower was not prepared to face your evil power, but I was sure to have Mother bless me before I came to see you and the Seraph."

"Bless you?"

"You cannot force your power onto me, Raiven, no matter how hard you try." Lady removed her foot as she leaned over me, fake pity in her eyes as my shadow dug into my skin. I fought to bring my gun back out of the ground as I glared, but I could do little more than twitch as she continued. "I will be sure to kill you permanently for Mother, and return the Seraph to her. After all, the Goddess of Life can't continue her mission without them."

"You..." I struggled to speak, the hands around my throat tightening as I closed my eyes, trying to force the ground to release me. It seemed whatever she had done was negating my powers, and my arm burned more as I finally stopped moving, my shadow seemingly dragging me deeper into it.

'*Azyam!*' I screamed for my sister, to have her help me as she had so many times, but even though I could feel her presence, no answer came to my cry. It was as if she no longer had a voice, but I felt her emotions as if they were my own, her anger and fear sitting in my chest as more of my body disappeared into the shadow. A new idea started to emerge in my frantic thoughts, and I frowned as it took shape in my mind, her confusion joining mine.

"I would say it's a shame, but I think you are too old for such sweet lies," Lady gloated. She leaned down to stroke my face as most of my body disappeared into the shadow and I growled, the new idea still sitting insistently in my mind. I felt Azyam as she pushed me to try it and I closed my eyes as I surrendered. "Goodnight, little Raiven."

I focused my energy on my locket as I felt Azyam's presence fade and it was replaced by the presence that had once resided within the tree. It seemed to grow and swell, and I stopped struggling as the dark tendrils faded from my skin. I could almost sense the Hunter's confusion as she stepped away from me and I allowed myself to be swallowed by the dirt. It felt as if my body disintegrated and for a moment, I could feel everything; each blade of grass, every insect and creature as they crawled and slithered through the ground. In that moment, I was one with the earth, and I struggled to bring my focus back, imagining myself standing behind Lady Night.

"What–" Lady Night barely got the word out before I rose from the ground behind her, wrapping my arm around the Hunter's neck. She twisted and squirmed in my grasp, but I only chuckled, pointing my gun to her head. The dirt fell from my skin as I grinned, the wound in my arm healing as I cocked my gun. She grew still in my grip and I could feel her fear as she gasped wordlessly.

"Goodbye, Lady Night," I whispered as I fired, barely flinching as her blood splattered on my face. I dropped her body as I fired a second time, making sure to shoot her heart as she lay in the dead grass. I took a deep breath as I holstered my gun, crossing my arms as I waited. I was barely surprised as I watched the blood swell from her body and I took a step back as Vitae formed from the liquid, her sour expression evident on her face.

"Once again, you've killed my Retainer."

"Maybe stop sending them after me and I wouldn't have to," I spat back, refusing to look away from her gaze as I spoke. "Seems like you want me to kill them at this point."

"Do you really think reawakening your powers, reclaiming what you once were, will make you happy?" Vitae scoffed and I did my best to hide my conflicted emotions, adjusting my stance as my chest ached. The illusion laughed at my bravado, crossing her arms to match me. "You were happy once you were reborn, once you were allowed to live. Going back to being the Goddess of Death will only make you miserable again."

"I'm sure you've only had the best of intentions with all the lies you've told over the centuries," I shot back, watching as her smile faded. "Were you also helping the Seraph while you tortured them for their blood, all so you could keep up with your little experiments?"

"You're one to talk; after all, it was *you* who showed all the wonderful things I could do with our blood," she shrugged and I frowned as I uncrossed my arms. I wanted to argue her statement, but something in me told me I couldn't. "If you had just stayed in your lane, hadn't tried to overstep your role, the Trinity never would have been ruined."

"Just like you to blame anyone but yourself," I sighed, glancing to the dead body as the illusion started to fade. Vitae's eyes lingered on me as she disappeared, her voice barely more than a whisper.

"Trust me, girl. You will regret becoming Mortem." With that, the illusion ended and I was alone in the plains, staring at the remains of Lady Night's body. I glared at the ground as it opened up to swallow her, leaving no trace of the Hunter on the surface as the tremor ended. I sighed heavily as I finally reached for my phone, glancing to see the time. It was still early in the night and I carefully scrolled to pull up Kisten's number.

"Dammit!" I cursed, gripping the device tightly in my hand as I hesitated calling the Alpha. Despite how much I wanted to ignore Vitae's taunt, she had spoken to the fear that was deep in my heart; that awakening Mortem would go against everything I wanted. My hand shook as I stared at the screen, unable to help the pain and frustration in my chest. "Dammit!"

I glanced up as I saw a light in the distance, and I was surprised when I saw it had wings, zipping up to me across the plains. It circled me before hovering in front of my face and I knew immediately from the golden glow that it was connected to the Seraph. Unlike all the other powers they had shown, I could feel the magic radiating off the light as it hovered in front of me, circling me again as I watched.

"What?" I finally spat and I watched as it flew a short distance away, hovering again as it waited for me to follow. "You...want to show me something?"

The light merely twirled in the air and I crossed my arms again, unable to help my annoyance as I watched it.

"Why? How do I know you're any better than Vitae?" I insisted, and I watched as the light flew back to me, this time hovering near my hand. I slowly held my hand out as it dropped into my palm and I was able to hear the Seraph's voice as it breezed through my mind.

'*You don't and there is little I can do to prove it,*' they sighed and I scoffed, fighting the urge to crush the light in my hand. At least they were honest, and not trying to win me over with assurances that they were somehow doing "the right thing" compared to Vitae. '*However, I am only offering help. You do not have to take it if this is not what you truly desire.*'

"It's not much of a choice when it's either let myself become Mortem now or later."

'*The choice is simply how much control you have,*' the Seraph corrected, and I turned away from the light. '*It is true her power is manifesting within you whether you want it to or not, but you can never become her unless you choose to.*'

"And if I choose not to?" I spat, turning to look as the light's glow faltered in my hand and I could feel the Seraph's doubt as they hesitated to answer me.

'*I... won't tell you what to do.*'

"That doesn't answer the question."

'*You know the answer. Mortem's power will simply do what it is meant to do.*' I closed my eyes as I released the light, uncrossing my arms as I drew a deep breath. I could finally feel Azyam's presence again but I also felt the third presence as I rested on my hand on my chest. It seemed to waver between merging with Azyam and being separate from her and I opened my eyes to see the light waiting patiently on my answer.

"That's not much of a choice," I whispered, and I watched as the light merely flew away from me again, still waiting for me to follow. I glanced up to the moon as I took a deep breath, doing my best to swallow the emotion in my chest. I glanced at my phone again as I saw Kisten's name and I carefully called the shifter.

"Raiven! You–"

"I'm following the Seraph," I interrupted, not giving him a chance to talk as I started after the light, keeping my gaze locked on it. Kisten seemed to understand what I meant and I heard him start the car he was in.

"I'll do my best to catch up. Be careful." I hummed my agreement as I hung up the call, sliding the phone into my pocket as I followed my guide deeper into the dark night.

14

My feet ached as I followed the light deeper into the African plains, the moon still high in the sky above me. I paused for breaks every once in a while but the Seraph seemed insistent on leading me to whatever they wanted to show me. I placed my hand on my chest as I fought to catch my breath, forcing myself to keep walking. I knew Kisten was following me, as I had activated my phone's location for him to follow, but I had no idea how easy it would be for him to catch up with me.

"This better be worth it," I panted, as the light paused again for me to catch up and I growled softly as I approached it. Unlike before, it remained hovering as I stood next to it and I glared as it fluffed its wings. "What now?"

The light circled me again before flying away and I saw a cave in the distance, almost invisible in the night. I groaned as the light hovered at its entrance, waiting for me to catch up as I stumbled through the grass. I fought the urge to collapse once I reached the light again, carefully leaning against the dirt as I removed my shoes. The magic seemed interested in my aching feet, gently touching my hand as I sighed.

'Will you allow me to ease your pain?'

"I'm not really in a position to say no," I spat back, watching as the light grew brighter for a second and the pain in my feet and legs began to fade. I sighed with relief as I slipped my shoes back on, the light fading back to its usual soft glow. "Thanks."

The light merely flew away from me, going deeper into the cave and I sighed wearily as I stood to follow it. The wind on the plains started to pick up behind me and a new sound seemed to be coming toward me as I turned to look into the darkness. Something was definitely moving through the grass and I frowned as my heart pounded, summoning my power to my fingertips.

"Rai." I relaxed as I heard Kisten's voice, the shifter standing from the grass as he finished running toward me. I eagerly returned his embrace, Kisten immediately pressing relieved kisses into my hair. "You're okay."

"Told you I could handle her," I whispered, noticing as the light came back to where I stood with Kisten. I pulled away slightly as it circled us. "But it seems we need to keep moving."

"Let's go," Kisten agreed, taking my hand again as we started following the light deeper into the cave. I noticed that we seemed to be descending deeper into the ground, feeling the drop in temperature as we walked. The Alpha seemed to notice it too, tightening his grip on my hand as he helped me down a ledge. "What could possibly be down here?"

"No idea," I whispered back, watching as the light disappeared from view. It seemed to have reached a larger chasm and I was careful to watch my step in the sudden darkness. Kisten helped me to navigate the incline, lifting me to step over a large boulder as we entered the new space. Once we rejoined the light, I carefully looked around for it, and my eyes widened as I spotted where it waited. "By the Gods, it's..."

"It's cave paintings." Kisten's voice was full of awe as he released my hand, stepping closer to the wall as the light hovered. "This must've been closer to the surface thousands of years ago, and was buried by time as the ground shifted."

"Kisten, look!" I pointed as the light circled the first image in the painting, the wings and features unmistakable as I touched the stone. "It's... the Seraph."

"Yeah, it shows them rising from the sea, the birth of a god... or *the* God, I suppose." Kisten nodded, narrating what he saw as the light continued across the wall. "It seems the Seraph helped to guide early humans, teaching them about tools and fire, until..."

"... they decided it was too much for one being," I whispered, dragging my hand along the wall as I followed, my voice soft as I spoke. The light was hovering by the next painting and I swallowed hard as I forced myself to look at it. The images brought back long dormant memories, and my chest tightened as my hand hovered next to the ancient painting. "So, they created two goddesses. From the heart of the mighty Baobab tree, they created the Goddess of Death. And from the frigid mountains to the north, they created the Goddess of Life."

"Mortem and Vitae."

"Those aren't our names," I corrected, gently touching the painting of my tormentor as I looked at her depiction. It was both her and not her somehow, and I knew the ancient artist had tried to capture her original form. "Vitae was a title that humans gave to her and I guess was one of her favorites. Mortem was my matching title in Latin and I guess it just... stuck. I never cared much about what I was called."

"Then what was your name?" Kisten asked, looking at me as he waited for me to finish explaining. I could hear the uncertainty in his voice as I hesitated, my gaze drifting to the image of the second goddess.

"None of us had names, we simply... were. The humans gave us titles because that's what humans do. Give names to the nameless," I answered, walking after the light to the next painting. "Together, we were a Trinity, simply meant to serve life. The Seraph to Create, Vitae to Guide, and I...to ensure its End. For a Beginning to Matter, it must have an End."

The words spoken to me in a dream seemed to echo in my mind and a feeling of bitterness entered my chest as I stared. The memories flooded my mind as they had when I touched my sister's grave, my voice soft as I continued. "But I... was lonely and miserable. I was respected as a Goddess and one of the Trinity, but not loved. No one loves a reminder of Death, that life eventually must end. But then... I found them."

"Found who?" Kisten carefully walked up to me where I stood with the light and I couldn't help the tears that came to my eyes. Such simple depictions of a past long gone brought a plethora of memories back to my mind, and my heart twisted as I accepted the pain. The shifter gasped as he saw the painting I was standing in front of, and picked up from where I had stopped narrating.

"The Siblings. Vitae didn't make the first vampires. You... you did."

"They were merely babies when they died. It... wasn't uncommon back then, but finding their bodies had been the last straw for me," I whispered, coughing slightly as the tears ran down my face. "I wanted to allow them a chance, a chance to have a life. That was my heinous crime, the act that Vitae decided to kill me for."

"Wait, wha—"

"I shared my blood with the Siblings, rather than just raising them as I could with other dead. It allowed them to have an unnatural life, but it was a life," I continued, sliding to the floor as my legs gave out beneath me. The third presence in my chest seemed to ache with my pain and even Azyam was remorseful as we remembered. "They were never supposed to live forever, but they did seem to have a longer life than the living. For once, I was not alone and I... was loved."

"But Vitae didn't like that?" Kisten let his question hang as he knelt beside me on the ground and we both looked up as the light hovered close to my face. I watched as it flew further into the cave and Kisten slowly stood from me to follow it. "She found out, and wanted to punish you for overstepping. You were Death, but had decided to create a new kind of life. Life beyond her control. She—"

"Killed me for it," I sobbed, the pain in my chest almost too great as I remembered that moment. The moment of betrayal, when the one I had considered a sister killed me for not wanting to be alone. For showing kindness to lives she had abandoned. "She killed me for it, but knew that it would not last. She had no idea how long it would take for me to re-emerge, but she knew I would."

"So she forced her blood on the Siblings, forcing them to come under her command, and destroy your body. Then, by collecting and using your blood, created ten more vampires from the living. Along with the Siblings, they became the First," Kisten continued and I did my best to calm down, taking a deep breath as I wiped the tears from my face. "The Seraph found out what she had done and went to stop her... but they couldn't."

"What did she do to them?" I whispered, cradling my hands against my chest as I waited for him to respond. When the Alpha remained silent, I turned to look at him, noticing the horrified expression on his face as he failed to answer me. The light also seemed to dim as it hovered around the image and I forced myself to stand. I slowly walked over to where they waited for me and once I saw, I couldn't help my desperate whine.

The wall depicted the Seraph with their wings outstretched, the many eyes pierced by spears as golden blood ran down the white feathers. They were surrounded by the Thirteen, with the Siblings being forced to hold the Creator's arms and legs as they cried. The other vampires were the ones driving the spears home as Vitae laughed, her appearance finally changed to the one I knew.

"She had learned about the power of our blood, and she used it to her advantage," I whispered, taking a deep breath as I touched the old paint. My anger grew as I dug my hand into the wall and both the light and Kisten moved away from me as the stone began to crack. I ripped my hand through it as I destroyed the painting, no longer wanting to look at the image of pain and betrayal. "And she wants to say it was my fault."

"Raiven–"

"I. Was. *Dead* when she decided to torture our creator!" I fumed, ripping my hand through the rock again as the tendrils extended from my fingertips, lacerating the stone as I destroyed another section of the wall. I began to destroy the cave in my anger, unable to help the powerlessness that filled my chest. *I had failed my children, I had failed my creator, I had...* "That was you, *Uyar*! You betrayed those children when you let death take them too early. You betrayed *me* when you decided it was your role to control *me!*

"None of this is *my fault!*" I screamed, the whole cave trembling as the ground shook, my tendrils dancing across the stone as I destroyed the paintings. I didn't want to stare at the reminder of my failure, of a story where I had failed in my duty as a Goddess. I ignored Kisten's worried cry as stones from the ceiling started to fall, crashing to the shaking ground as I tried to erase the cave.

"Raiven!" I was forced to pause as Kisten grabbed my arm and I whipped around to face the Alpha, glaring as the tendrils wrapped around his body. He whined with pain as he was forced to his knees, the black marks digging into his skin. I felt the rage from the other two presences in my chest and I barely noticed as blood started to run down Kisten's skin as my power squeezed him. The light quickly returned to my side, resting against my arm as the Seraph's panicked voice ran through my mind.

'*Mortem! Stop, please stop!*' I blinked as I heard their concern and it was as if I woke up from a trance, quickly releasing Kisten as I stepped back. The shifter moaned softly with the pain as I watched him, horrified by what I had almost done. I felt the Seraph's relief as they spoke again, the light still touching my skin. '*It's alright now.*'

"I... failed you," I whispered softly, my eyes locked on Kisten as he sat up, carefully touching his lacerations as he tried to determine how much I had hurt him. "I... failed everyone."

'*You failed no one, Mortem. If anyone has failed, it was I, when I failed to protect you from Vitae,*' the Seraph sighed, and I could hear the tears and remorse in their voice. '*I failed to see what she was becoming, and I failed to stop her.*'

"You..." I started, but the words wouldn't come as I looked to my hands with fear, still hearing as Kisten struggled to stand. I looked up as the light left me, encircling the shifter and I watched as the Seraph healed his wounds as they had done with me. Kisten sighed with relief as he finally stood up straight, giving me a concerned look. I took a step away from him as he began toward me, my fear still heavy in my chest. "No... stay away! I–"

The shifter ignored me as he threw his arms around me, hugging me tightly into his chest as he sighed. He carefully placed kisses into my hair as he always did, petting my curls as he breathed deeply against me. I felt the tears start in my eyes again as the anger in my chest faded, both Azyam and Mortem feeling regret for the pain we had caused him. Kisten hummed softly as he tilted my chin to his face, watching me softly.

"It wasn't your fault, Mortem," Kisten whispered, and I felt as she reacted in my chest to his words. "Vitae would have found out anyway, without you. It's obvious she saw herself as superior to you and eventually even to the one who created her. It was only a matter of time before she would have tried the same thing."

"I–"

"But you are not responsible for what she did," Kisten continued, pressing my face into his chest again as he sighed, leaning his head against me. "And I'm sorry you were alone for so long. I'm sorry no one saw how much you were suffering."

I began to sob again at his words, the pain and ache in my chest too much as I clung to the Alpha. I felt as Azyam's and Mortem's presences faded, but I knew they weren't gone. We were merely united in our anguish and in that moment, we were one person.

15

"What now?" Kisten sighed as we sat on the dirt floor, in the remains of the cave. My outburst had collapsed the entrance to the cave and the Seraph's light was flying though all the tunnels, trying to see if they could find one that led back above ground. "I mean, you have Mortem's memories, but..."

"We're still separate," I agreed, gently touching my cross as I hummed with thought. Both Azyam and Mortem were quiet and it was obvious they were just as confused as me. I sighed as I stroked the wood, trying to work through our emotions. "Something is still missing."

"But what could it be?" Kisten mused, playing with his hands as the light reappeared only to disappear down another tunnel. For a brief moment we were illuminated, only to be plunged back into darkness. "You remember everything. That should be enough, right?"

"Hmmm," was my only response and I sunk back into my thoughts, drawing my knees to my chest. Thousands of years of memories now swirled through my head, and I was struggling to recall anything recent as I searched for an answer. Even the Seraph seemed not to know why I still hadn't been able to reawaken as Mortem and I opened my eyes to look at the dark ground.

Kisten moved closer to me and I carefully reached for him, letting him take my hand as he fumbled for it in the dark. Although Kisten had better dark vision than me, even his eyes could only do so much in the absolute darkness we sat in and I leaned against him as I sighed, still staring into the black nothingness. The shifter laced our fingers together, playing with the ring as he hummed.

"Wish you could've seen my suit," he finally whispered, and I squeezed his hand tighter as I heard the regret in his voice. "They were worse than fussy housewives, but Crispin and Arkrian did a good job."

"I thought we said no teasing?"

"I don't think it's teasing at this point. This is basically a waiting game now." Kisten sighed and I reached up to find his face in the darkness, leaning up to look where I thought he was. I could barely make out the form of his head as I dragged my fingers to his lips, moving to kiss him in the darkness. He hummed softly at the gesture, his hand fumbling to find my face as we kissed.

The kiss grew in desperation as I pushed myself onto him and the shifter let me, moving his hands as he tried not to lose me in the darkness. A gentle glow bathed his face again as the light returned and for a moment, I could see the painful smile on his face before we were plunged into darkness again. I couldn't help the sound that escaped me as I buried my face into his chest, holding him tightly as he stroked my hair.

"I was going to ask you to move in with me before the wedding, you know," Kisten continued, his voice full of his tears as he spoke about the future he wanted to have. A future that he felt had been stolen from us. "I know you have your cats and they don't like me too much, but I wanted to live together."

"Lira and Xris don't hate you," I whispered, unable to help my soft laugh as I spoke into his chest. "They just want to exert dominance over your leopard."

"Still don't appreciate waking up to my clothes smelling like piss!" Kisten shot back and I allowed myself to laugh fully, feeling his chest shake as he did the same. Our laughter died down again, and I rubbed my face against him. "I also really wanted to get married outside."

"Then why did you choose the hotel?" I asked, confused by his admission as I sat up slightly. The shifter carefully slid his hand to find my face, kissing me gently as he hesitated to answer. "You know I wouldn't mind an outside wedding."

"Getting married in the winter time kinda limits our options. You hate snow."

"We could've waited until summer."

"I should have married you last year," Kisten admitted and I felt my heart twist with his words as he stroked my face again. "Fuck all that 'doing things the right way' crap. I should have married you the moment you said you would be mine."

"Kis—"

"I should have had Lucius release me from the Oath that day, let me enjoy the time I had with you," Kisten lamented, and I carefully reached to cradle his face in the darkness. My heart broke as I felt the tears on his face and I carefully touched our foreheads together, unsure what to say. I felt Kisten wrap his arms around me tightly, sobbing as he cried for all the time he wouldn't get with me. He held me like a child refusing to let go of their favorite stuffed toy, his desperation obvious in his body. I felt Mortem's confusion in my chest as I held back my own tears, struggling to find something to say to comfort my lover.

"Kisten," I whispered, wiping away his tears as I spoke, unable to help the soft sound that escaped me as I closed my eyes. "Every moment with you has been amazing."

"But—"

"It may not have been what you or I wanted, but I got to meet and love someone as amazing as you," I continued, finally losing the battle with my own tears. Mortem's interest grew as I cried, rubbing my forehead against his. "I was always happy to have lovers, but I had given up on the idea of having a partner. You gave that to me, even when you avoided me to protect me. Even when you tried to hide how much you cared about me, you proved how much you loved me."

"Raiven," Kisten moaned as I kissed him again, our lips salty from our combined tears as we fumbled in the darkness. My recent memories were finally brought to mind as I thought of the past four years with Kisten, and my heart ached as I broke the kiss. Kisten's voice was still full of his pain and regret as he whispered, wiping my tears from my face. "Raiven, I love you."

"And I love you, Kisten," I whispered back as I leaned down for another kiss. Then I saw the glow of the light as the Seraph returned to where we lay on the ground. I reluctantly sat up from the Alpha as it fluffed its wings again, hovering in front of my face. "Did you find a way out?"

The light flew toward one of the tunnels, hovering as it waited for me and Kisten. I took a deep breath as I stood off the Alpha, helping him to his feet. I took a moment to finish wiping away his tears as he gathered himself, turning his face to mine now that I could see him again. His eyes were red and puffy, but he gave a slight smile as he leaned down to me, kissing my forehead gently.

We walked quietly after the light, the only sounds around us being the scurrying of creatures as they struggled to get out of our way. Kisten and I walked hand in hand, and my mind raced as I still tried to understand why we were still separate. It was clear that Mortem had finally developed as a sort of third presence along with me and my sister, but for some reason, we all were separate entities. None of us could control the power growing stronger in me, and I hummed softly as my thoughts raced.

Maybe... we do need to go back. I thought, as my head started to ache from straining to see in the darkness. *Lucius has Alex's memories and maybe the answer lies there. And it's already been a few days since my thirst...*

I paused in my walk as I remembered my thirst and I watched as Kisten and the light paused ahead of me. I carefully grabbed my locket as my thoughts raced, unable to help my confusion.

"Raiven?"

"Kisten, my thirst," I whispered, looking up as the light flew past him closer to me, hovering in front of my face again. "I haven't felt thirsty at all."

"Shouldn't your thirst have increased?" Kisten seemed equally confused as the light gently touched my hand, allowing me to hear the Seraph's voice again.

'*What thirst?*'

"Ever since I partially awoke as Mortem, I have had a craving for undead blood," I explained, looking down to the light. "I would go on a rampage if denied for too long, and it had been getting worse since I first started using Mortem's power three months ago."

'*There is no reason for you to have a need for blood, undead or otherwise.*' The Seraph was clearly confused and I watched as the light wavered. '*The vampire need for blood was because of Vitae forcing her blood on them, giving them a desire for the blood of the living. You should not crave it.*'

"What if... it's not life I'm looking for?" I mused, glancing away as the new thought entered my mind. I squeezed my locket tighter as I looked down to the light, watching as its wings flapped to maintain its flight. "Vampires, the first undead. They were all originally created from my blood, right?"

'*Yes.*'

"And only those vampires, the First Thirteen, can create more, right?" I pressed, feeling the Seraph's confusion at my questions.

'*Yes, but–*'

"I'm looking for my blood," I reasoned, looking up to see Kisten's expression as he watched me. His confusion was just as obvious as the Seraph, but I watched as he slowly came to the same conclusion as me.

"Recovering the Goddess requires you to recover her blood, the source of her power," Kisten whispered, and I nodded, releasing the cross as the light flew away from me. "You craved it because what you were really craving was your own power."

"Drinking Vitae's blood and not using Mortem's power kept me suppressed, but it couldn't suppress the subconscious desire to recover what I had lost," I reasoned, looking back to the light as it flickered. "That's why I was never allowed to drink from the Siblings. Vitae feared their blood could awaken Mortem sooner."

"Since they were originally created from your blood alone, Vitae's taint in them would be less," Kisten reasoned, sighing heavily as he crossed his arms. "Also explains why she wanted to kill the First, even once she gave up regaining control. Although the Siblings are the best source, they all carry the purest form of your blood."

"And why Alex shared his memories with Lucius," I added, looking up to see the Alpha's face. "If he died, he needed someone to remember who Mortem and the Seraph were and know that I would need the blood of a First to fully awaken."

"But you've been drinking from Lucius for years, and it never did anything to awaken Mortem," Kisten reasoned and I hummed, not having an answer to his counterpoint. "Is there something else that needs to happen, not just drinking the blood?"

"It's possible I needed her memories as well for it to work, something I was missing before," I admitted, walking up to the shifter again as I took his hand. "But only Alex or Lucius would know for certain."

"So I guess we'd—"

"I know where he is." I turned around as I heard the Seraph's voice, seeing them standing in the tunnel behind us. The small light faded from view as they looked at it, turning their golden gaze to me. "I know where the Last Sibling is."

"You—"

"He wished to be left alone when I found him, saying that he wanted to have a chance to see the Goddess again and he was much too weak to be of any use to anyone," the Seraph whispered, looking away again as they spoke. "He knew staying with me would be dangerous, so he returned home."

"But where's home?" Kisten asked and my eyes widened as I began to remember where I found the Siblings.

"Egypt," I whispered, looking up to meet Kisten's gaze as he looked at me. "I found the Siblings in Egypt and that's where the home I made for them was. I doubt the house is still there, but I have no doubt that's where he went."

"Wouldn't Vitae know to—"

"No, she attacked us closer to here," I interrupted, squeezing his hand tightly in mine. "The triplets were with me as I was wandering that night, so she has no idea where they came from. He would be safe there, as long as the local Overseer does not give him away."

"They have not. Although they do not remember the truth, my presence resonated with them," the Seraph spoke, walking closer to us as we turned to face them again. I watched as they gently pulled their wings closed and my heart ached as I remembered the cave painting. I slowly released Kisten as I walked up to them and they watched me with confusion as I stopped in front of them. Taking a deep breath, I gently wrapped my arms around them, hugging them as tightly as I could. I could feel their shock as they hesitated, but slowly I felt them return the gesture.

"You did not deserve that torture," I whispered and I felt their breath catch in their chest, the sound forced as they spoke.

"Deserved or not, it happened. My only wish," the Seraph insisted, gently releasing me as I leaned back, their face holding a gentle expression as they looked down at me, "is to see you happy, Mortem. I thought you were before, but I was merely blind to your misery."

"I..." My voice faded as I felt Azyam and Mortem's presence and both were telling me to hold my words. I swallowed my retort as I released the Seraph, once again turning to face Kisten. The Alpha was watching us patiently, but I could still see the reluctant acceptance in his eyes as I walked back to him. I took his hand in mine as I glanced back at the Seraph, nodding gently in their direction.

"Let's go find LeAlexende."

16

It was late in the afternoon when we finally arrived in Egypt, and I pulled my jacket tighter as Kisten began to drive from the city. It was slightly colder next to the Nile, and I found my heart pounding as I kept my eyes peeled for anything familiar. It had been a struggle to find a new flight to Egypt at such short notice but, true to the Seraph's word, the Overseer seemed to understand that something greater than they knew about was going on. She was able to easily convince the President to allow us clearance and her Retainer had a car waiting for us at the airport.

"Anything striking a chord?" Kisten asked as I leaned further out of the window, letting the cold wind blow against my face and hair. The Seraph had vanished again after seeing us back to the city in Ethiopia, saying they would do their best to keep Vitae distracted. They insisted that until Mortem fully manifested, she would be unable to sense me the way she could the Seraph and until I managed to discover what was holding me back, they would keep her focused on them.

Despite my former suspicion, I now understood the Seraph on a deeper level with Mortem's memories, and my heart ached as I remembered their determination. Whatever guilt I felt at not knowing what the Seraph had suffered at Vitae's hand, they felt infinitely worse for not being able to stop her. While it was possible they wanted Mortem back so they could get revenge on Vitae, Mortem herself seemed to dismiss the idea. It seemed clear that the Seraph's issue was how much they cared about both of the Goddesses they had created and despite Vitae's betrayal, they could not bring themselves to truly hate her for what she had done.

"Not yet," I told him, settling back into my seat as I grabbed the cross around my neck. Azyam and Mortem no longer radiated from the locket but from my own body, but it felt odd to be without it. "I didn't have them too close to the city, just to be safe if anyone discovered they were different."

"How different are they? From the living, I mean," Kisten offered and I sighed as I felt Mortem's pain, playing with the wood in my hand.

"I'm not sure how much Vitae's blood may have changed them, but beyond their longer life, they are alive in every way," I answered softly, closing the window as I shielded my eyes from the sun. "They sleep, they eat, they breathe; the powers were a side effect of giving them my blood, but in all ways they were meant to be alive. The sun sensitivity must be a side effect from Vitae, as the Siblings never had an issue before."

"Hmm," Kisten answered and I glanced at the shifter as he adjusted his stance on the wheel, driving one-handed as he leaned back. He briefly glanced at me and I frowned as I noticed his black eyes. The Alpha hummed as he looked away again, shifting again in his seat. "Spider is feeling antsy."

"Any... any particular reason?"

"Something is off, and I can't tell what. Pardon the pun, but my spider is pretty jumpy and reacts when I'm uneasy, even if I'm not sure why." Kisten sighed, placing both of his hands back in the wheel as he rolled his shoulders. "Shifting into him won't really help, but I wish I knew what was setting him off."

"It's okay," I assured him, glancing back into the bright afternoon. The sun was still up but I understood perfectly what my partner was feeling. Something felt out of place, like sitting in the eye of a hurricane, and the others in my chest agreed. "We feel it, too."

"You and Azyam?"

"And Mortem," I added, still stroking the wood as Mortem began to take an interest in what I was seeing. Unlike with Azyam, whom I could visualize in my mind based on my memories of her, Mortem was mostly a concept to me and I struggled to even equate her to the painting I had seen. It was inadequate for me to truly understand what she was, and I watched my eyes change color in the window as the tendrils started to crawl on my skin. "Stop the car."

"See something?" Kisten carefully pulled into the shoulder as I opened the door, not waiting for him to fully stop the car. Despite the fact that the vehicle was still moving, I stepped out as if it had been stopped, hearing Kisten's panic as he quickly halted the vehicle and scrambled after me. My eyes were focused on the river as I walked, although none of us were sure where I was going. "Raiven!"

"Follow." My voice carried echoes of the other two and I heard Kisten running after me as I walked closer to the lapping shore. The black marks slowly spread out from me as I walked, the long reeds dying as I walked through them. I could hear Kisten as he tried to avoid touching the tendrils, but my eyes were focused on the water as I stopped just short of stepping in. The surface seemed unusually still and calm, just like the disquiet that sat on the air around us. "Move."

With that single word, the water started to bubble and I heard Kisten's gasp as the water parted in front of me, a small path forming on the river bed. To anyone passing by, it would merely look like I was wading through a shallow section of the river and I slowly made my way across, the tendrils spreading out like spider webs as I walked. The Alpha behind me carefully followed, making sure to keep his distance as I stepped on the bank on the opposite side.

"Fucking... bitch!"

I hummed softly as I heard the voice call out and all the tendrils quickly detoured for them as I flung my hand toward it. Kisten finally stood next to me as I lifted the man out of the dying reeds, crushing his bracelet to release the glamor. I narrowed my gaze, watching as he flexed his hands.

"May you—"

"None of that," I whispered, the tendrils swarming his face to cover his mouth, preventing the warlock from speaking his spell. He whimpered as I squeezed his body tighter, forcing him into an uncomfortable position as I held him off the ground. I could almost feel his fear of death as I flexed my fingers, considering how I wanted to kill him. "You have been trailing us."

"So that's what was setting us off," Kisten growled and I glanced to see that his eyes were still as black as mine. I could tell that his spider was sitting ahead of his other animals, but it was no longer fear that had it roused up. The killing intent that poured off my mate was almost as intoxicating as the fear from the man in my grasp and I hummed softly as I turned to Kisten. Mortem seemed intrigued and surprised as I fought from killing the man in my grasp, and I chuckled softly as I watched the Alpha.

"Would you like to kill him?"

"Wh-what?"

"Do you want to kill him? I can feel that you do," I repeated, our black eyes making contact as I looked up to meet his gaze. Even without touching him, I could feel that his spider liked the idea. "He's yours if you want him."

"I—"

"If I do it, I won't be able to stop." I spoke plainly, leaning up into Kisten's face. The feeling of his killing intent was arousing and I could tell from Mortem's interest that her power had not felt like this in the past. Feeling the desire to end life seemed to be unique to me and my use of it, and my lips twitched into a sadistic smile as I curled my fingers toward my prey, enjoying the man's cry of pain. Kisten only looked away from me for a moment, seemingly drawn into my gaze as I continued. "Every time I use this power, it's harder to calm down and it becomes even more difficult to stop myself from killing with it.

So I'll ask again," I whispered, leaning close into Kisten's face as I felt him losing the battle with his animal. I spoke gently against his lips, not hiding the desire in my voice. "Do you want to kill him?"

Kisten didn't answer as he turned away from me, shifting into his spider as he scurried toward the warlock. I could hear the man's panicked sounds as the Alpha drew closer and chuckled as I withdrew the tendrils, Kisten's leaping into the air at the same moment. The man's cry was cut short as Kisten buried his fangs into him, and I hummed with delight as the black marks danced on my skin again.

The feelings in my chest were conflicted as I fought to dismiss the power. Azyam was seemingly disagreeing with the pleasure I felt from feeling the man's death and Mortem merely curious. It was obvious that she had never considered her ability to feel death a good thing and even I had to admit it was strange. I usually didn't enjoy taking a life, unless I truly felt my target was a being without remorse and one that the world would be better without. Even though the man was a servant of Vitae's, for me to relish in death was new and I frowned with my sister's emotion as the power finally faded.

"Rai?" I looked up as Kisten walked back to me, and I could still see the corpse as it lay in the grass. The Alpha shook his head as he approached me and I saw that his eyes were back to normal, the killing intent gone from his body. "You okay?"

"For now," I admitted, humming quietly as I looked to the river. The water was still slightly turbulent from where I had walked across it, but I knew it would soon settle back to its usual calm stillness. "I don't think I'll give you a choice next time."

"Neither do I," Kisten agreed, and I frowned as I looked back to see his concern. "That wasn't like you."

"I'm not sure how much of that was me, or Mortem's power adjusting its tactic to get me to use it," I admitted, feeling both Azyam's and Mortem's concern with my words. "Before, it used my anger, blinding me to what I was doing as I just lashed out to destroy. This time…"

"It made you want it, too." Kisten and I looked up as we heard a new voice and I felt my heart swell. LeAlexende was standing on the dirt path a short way up from us, smiling at me gently as our eyes met. His eyes were still the same soft purple I had grown used to, and he carefully brushed his white hair from his face. "Hello again, Raiven, Kisten."

"Alex—"

"It wasn't all that hard to figure out. The Overseer here hardly ever moves around so much and your power is hard to mistake when it calls to me so powerfully," LeAlexende interrupted, motioning for us to join him as his shoulders shook with suppressed laughter. We carefully climbed up the bank next to him and the vampire met my gaze evenly. His smile changed as he watched me, and I could tell that he was overflowing with happiness. "You have her memories now."

"I do," I admitted, grabbing my necklace as I nodded, refusing to look away from his gaze. My own chest was filled with joy, Mortem ecstatic to see one of her children again and, despite her confusion about the change, I could feel her longing to touch him. "But something is keeping us separate."

"A lot is keeping you three separate, and her blood is also part of that," Alex chuckled. He turned and started walking away.

I stumbled after the Sibling, the three of us unified in our confusion.

"Wait a second, how did you—"

"I spent five hundred years around Mortem before Vitae destroyed our lives," Alex interrupted, not turning to answer me as Kisten grabbed my hand, matching my stride. "I can tell that you are not her, but neither are you like your sister. It stands to reason that both your sister and Mortem still exist separately from you."

"So why haven't they merged?" Kisten asked, squeezing my hand tightly as we walked behind the vampire. Alex didn't answer right away, merely continuing down the dirt path as we followed. I gently stroked Kisten's hand, my heart pounding as we waited for our answer.

"You all have to want it," Alex said finally. He stopped in front of a small house and I frowned as I saw it. The building was nothing like the one from my memories and I looked down to see the former

Overseer watching me. "I'm sure the Seraph told you that you can't become Mortem unless you choose to."

"That—"

"You all have to agree to become of one mind, otherwise, sharing my blood with you will do nothing." Despite his serious tone, LeAlexende was smiling at me wistfully, dragging his eyes to Kisten. "We can stay here until nightfall, then we can go to the appropriate locale. You have been wavering in your conviction, but you have until tonight to truly make up your mind."

"Alex..." My voice faded as I tried to think of something to say and I watched as the vampire sighed softly. LeAlexende walked back to me and I felt Mortem's pride for who he had become as he stood in front of me.

"I'm not telling you what to do, Raiven. As much as I want to see Mortem again, I like you as you are. You and Kisten are good friends to me and I owe my life to both of you." The former Overseer smiled, gently touching my shoulder. His touch made the warmth and ache in my chest swell and I couldn't help the happy sound that escaped me. His eyes were bright with his own happiness and he kept his gaze locked with mine as he continued: "You deserve to have the freedom to choose what you want, and I'll accept whatever decision you make."

With that, the vampire released me and disappeared inside, and my chest tightened as I considered his words, still clutching my wooden locket. Kisten seemed to sense my hesitation, gently pulling me into a hug. The shifter squeezed me tightly, leaning down to whisper in my ear.

"Take your time. I'm here for you," he murmured, gently releasing me as he turned to follow after LeAlexende. I was left standing alone on the dirt path, my heart and chest a mix of emotions as he disappeared into the dark abode.

17

"You know we don't have a choice," I grunted as Azyam repeated herself, leaning back in my chair as I sighed deeply. My real body was sitting outside LeAlexende's house, meditating in the afternoon light while Kisten and Alex rested inside. I had focused on putting myself into a trance-like state, hoping it would allow me to talk to Azyam and Mortem. Talking to my sister was easy, but since I still lacked a visual way to acknowledge Mortem, she hovered like a vague presence between us. She still communicated with feelings and ideas rather than words, and I barely looked up to see my twin's stern gaze. "We have to merge into Mortem."

"Of course that's easy for you to say," I muttered, not trying to hide my snide remark as I felt her annoyance. Despite us having separate bodies in the mindscape I created, I could still feel her emotions as if they were my own and they only annoyed me more. "*You* don't have anything to lose."

"Look, I'm not saying it doesn't suck, but–"

Stop! Mortem's insistence interrupted Azyam's words and we both looked away from each other as the space between us rippled. The Goddess' exhaustion was obvious. *Getting nowhere.*

"Of course we're getting fucking nowhere!" Azyam threw her hands up and I glared at her as she continued. "She *knows* we don't have a choice but she still wants to think that somehow, she can have her cake and eat it, too."

"Well, I'm *sorry* that I actually have something I care about and don't want to lose it," I spat back, fully sitting up in my seat as I resisted the urge to stand. "Sorry that I'm not eager to just jump into the fire and sacrifice myself for the greater good."

"But you *know* we have no choice but to jump, Awetash!"

"Do we?" I finally stood up, balling my hands as Azyam did the same. Her brown eyes matched my green as we glared at each other and I could feel Mortem's growing annoyance with our fighting. Time was hard to judge in this state, so I had no idea how long we had been arguing back and forth but it already felt like an eternity. "It's *my* body, and *I* don't have to do anything I don't want to!"

"So your choice is just to kill Kisten?" Azyam insisted and I squeezed my hand tighter, resisting the desire to punch my twin. "You love him so much that you don't want to merge into Mortem and your decision is to just wait until her power kills him anyway?"

"That–"

"You already almost killed him, or did you conveniently forget that?" Azyam continued, not giving me the chance to speak as she took a step closer. Her braids waved as she moved and I watched as Mortem pushed her back, my sister scoffing as she shook off the presence. "Or are you choosing to ignore that so you can delude yourself into thinking there is a way for you to–"

"I'm not deluding ANYONE!" I yelled, the force of my voice blowing Azyam back into her seat and I felt Mortem's shock as I panted heavily. I grabbed the fabric of my shirt as I looked away, trying my best to control my breathing. "I KNOW that not merging into Mortem won't allow me to keep Kisten."

"Then–"

"SHUT UP!" I insisted, once again waving my hand through the air as the wind blew my sister's braids back. She was watching me angrily, gripping the armrests of her chair tightly as I spoke through gritted teeth. "For once, just shut the fuck up and stop trying to lecture me."

Azyam remained quiet as she glared and I felt Mortem's concern as she settled in between us again. I could still feel my body shaking with my anger and annoyance but I forced myself to close my eyes. I tried to focus on my breathing as I slowly looked back to my twin, watching my own face stare back at me. Everything about her, from her expression to her stance, told me that she thought she was right and I ground my teeth as I finally spoke.

"I'm not stupid, Azyam. I know that not merging with Mortem is just delaying the inevitable," I released my fists as I put my hands together, cupping them as I looked down, "but I can't just rationalize away my fear. I... love him. I don't want to lose him any more than he wants to lose me. Kisten has lost everyone he's ever loved, and he finally took a chance on a future with me, a future he may no longer have."

I closed my eyes as my voice cracked, unable to help my groan of pain as I felt Mortem's pain join my own. I felt a presence touch my face, but when I looked up, I still didn't see anyone between me and my sister. Azyam was looking away from me, but I could tell that her anger had lessened a bit with my words.

"I can't just reason away how I feel... logic away my fear," I whispered, collapsing back into my chair, still keeping my hands together as I looked at the floor. "I can accept all day that it's what we have to do, but I can't change my heart."

"But you haven't accepted it," Azyam said with a sigh and I glanced up as she kept looking away from me. "You keep hoping to find another way out of this."

"Wouldn't you? Not only am I losing myself, not only am I losing the person I love, I'm also being asked to lose my sister. The only one I've had throughout everything," I choked and I glanced up to see my twin looking at me, surprised. I shook my head, my annoyance coming back slightly. "I know... I know that I was going to lose you anyway, but losing everything... you would hope for a way out, too. A way to save at least *something* that you care about."

Azyam said nothing to this and we sat in silence, still no closer to a unified answer than we had been when I entered the trance. I closed my eyes as I leaned back in my seat, my head starting to hurt as my chest ached. I knew in my head what my answer had to be, but it didn't make choosing any easier. I felt Mortem's presence move again, and when I opened my eyes, I couldn't help but be surprised by what I saw.

Sitting on the ground between me and my twin was Mortem, but she was no longer a vague, unseen presence. Her four arms were folded in her lap as she sat, her silver horn shining in the dark sea that was her hair. The stars danced on her dark clothing as she moved, slowly turning to look at me. She seemed to be trying to emulate the form from the cave painting, giving herself a voice in our discussion.

'You both seem to think that the only way is to merge into me.' Although her voice still had no quality or sound to it, I could understand her words and I frowned as I tried to understand what was happening. It was like the words simply appeared in my mind and I knew that they were hers. *'Why can we not simply merge into you?'*

"What do you mean?"

'Alex merely said we needed to agree to become one. Until now, I simply have not cared what happens, so my apathy has been as much of a problem as Raiven's indecision,' Mortem repeated, turning to look at Azyam as she continued. My twin was sitting up, watching the Goddess with an interested look. *'You two have both assumed it means you must join into me, since I am presumably the original. Why can we not simply agree to join into her and allow her to become the new Goddess?'*

"But what difference would that make, if any?" Azyam pressed and Mortem carefully shook her head, the illusion disrupting slightly as she did so.

'I don't know.'

"Then—"

'But there is a chance that, rather than bringing me back, a new person will be created, one that is more like Raiven and will retain her personality. All of our memories should survive, so the new consciousness

will still have the knowledge they need. Reviving me will lose all of Raven's memories, time and experiences that will be lost forever,' Mortem admitted, casting a soft gaze to her lap that made my chest hurt again with her pain. *'And I truly do not wish to return. I did not have the strength to stand up to Vitae, and returning as I am, I still would not be able to do anything against her. Only Raiven has that strength.'*

"But I–"

"And as much as I feel Raiven fumbles it, she has grown over the centuries to stand more on her own," Azyam admitted and I lifted my gaze to her as she refused to look at me. She had her legs crossed as she stared into the darkness, tapping her foot in the air as she spoke. "I have long since accepted that I have no future and I wouldn't know what to do with one."

"So...?"

'We agree that you should be the one to inherit Mortem's powers, to create a new future rather than sacrifice to bring back the past.' Mortem turned to face me and for a moment, I was lost in her black eyes. Even though I knew her appearance was not a perfect replica of what the Goddess had once been, it was somehow fitting to what her presence was now: a shadow, an echo of a once ancient being. *'You have endured Vitae, both mentally and physically, and inherited the memories and will of the Goddess of Death. All you need is control.'*

"But there is no guarantee that I won't simply be pulled into you, regardless of our intentions," I sighed and I heard Azyam scoff, finally looking at me. Her lips were pursed into an annoyed expression, her arms crossed as our eyes met.

"But that's better than five minutes ago, isn't it? Even if what survives is not the same you, if we are the ones who dissolve, what is left will be more you than us," she insisted, standing up as Mortem did the same. I looked between the two of them as my twin moved to stand next to the illusion. "Out of the three of us, you're the only one who has a desire for a future and we're choosing to support that. Intentions matter, and we want yours to survive."

"But–"

"You're right; there was a time when I wanted it and you didn't.

There was a time when I would have said you *owed* this chance to me. But that... that was a long time ago." Azyam sighed, once again closing her eyes as she spoke. When she reopened them, only acceptance remained in her gaze. "I've said it before, I have no future, and I'm not vindictive enough to try and take yours away."

'And I have no desire to return. I am too weak... and maybe I always was,' Mortem admitted, taking a deep breath as the illusion distorted again. 'I was the Goddess of Death but I was afraid to be active in my role. Perhaps if I had been, I would not have been defeated so easily.'

I said nothing to their words, my heart still in turmoil as I closed my eyes. I could feel the cold that was creeping into the evening air with the fading light and I slowly stood, walking toward the pair. I carefully raised my hands to both of them, unable to help the tears shining in my eyes.

"I can't promise I won't fuck it up."

'No one is asking for perfection.'

"Just do the best you can," my sister insisted, raising her hand to meet mine as Mortem did the same, and we all closed our eyes. I could almost feel their hands on me as they both faded from the mindscape I had created and I slowly opened my eyes, pulling myself out of my trance. I was still sitting in the dirt behind LeAlexende's house and I raised my head to the red and purple sky above me. I brought my hand to my chest as I stood, able to feel Azyam and Mortem's presence as they swirled inside me. A breeze seemed to have picked up in the evening air and I hummed softly as I watched the clouds.

"Rai?" I turned to see Kisten waiting in the doorway, watching me patiently as he leaned against the frame. His emotions were hidden behind his calm expression and I turned away again to look at the darkening sky. I could hear as LeAlexende moved around in the house behind him and I closed my eyes to the breeze as I squeezed my locket, our combined determination filling me.

"I'm ready."

18

I shivered as I pulled my jacket closer, following behind LeAlexende as we climbed the narrow cliff face. Kisten followed behind me and I resisted the desire to look back at him as we walked. As soon as the sun had fully set, LeAlexende insisted we set out, telling Kisten where to drive as we headed back up the Nile. About halfway back to the city, Alex had him stop, saying that where we needed to go would require a short hike.

"Here," Alex said finally, glancing back as he stood in front of a narrow entrance into the rock face. "It's through here."

"What is?" I breathed, noticing the cryptic yet kind smile on the vampire's face. It was still unusual to see LeAlexende with his blue eyes, even though I knew that was the color his eyes had always been. He had removed the necklace maintaining his glamor before we set out, saying it would have been destroyed anyway by the rite he needed to perform.

"You'll see," was the only reply he offered as he disappeared into the orange rocks and I drew a deep breath as I felt Kisten stand behind me. Steeling myself, I walked after the former Overseer, noticing that, unlike the cave we had found the paintings in, this was clearly a man-made entrance. The walls and floor were too smooth for it to have been a natural occurrence and I gently ran my hand along the surface as we walked deeper into the cave. My heart paused as I heard a fire being lit further in, and I could see the shadows flickering on the wall as Alex disappeared into the cavern.

When I stepped in, I almost tripped over my feet on the stairs that led down into the space. Inside the rock was carved a large room, with four or five rows that stepped deeper into the cavern. At the base of the final step was a large pool of water and I saw LeAlexende walking around, lighting all the ancient braziers. The ceiling seemed to stretch on forever into the darkness, although I could make out the faintest markings in the stone. The cavern almost seemed too big to have been carved by human hands, but considering the narrow entrance, anyone else would have been hard pressed to enter.

"Amazing..." Kisten said in awe as he stepped in behind me, but I found my gaze was drawn to another part of the room, where a simple seating area seemed to be carved into the wall. I couldn't help but notice the two shapes that seemed to be hiding in the darkness and I started to step toward them when Alex's voice stopped me.

"It's Alrune and Basina," he whispered, and I turned to see the sad smile on his face as he lit the final brazier. I turned back to notice the shapes were lying prone, hands across their chests, in the flickering shadows. "It was our wish to be brought here if we died, so that even if we weren't alive, we could be present when you came back. It was not easy, but I was able to recover both of their bodies."

"Hmm," I hummed softly as my power came to my hands and the dark tendrils slithered across the steps toward the dead vampires. I heard LeAlexende's slight gasp as my power touched them, and I could feel the faintest desire to raise them. I focused on that small impulse, allowing the tendrils to lift the bodies from the stone floor as I groaned from the effort. It seemed to be taking more energy to revive the vampires than any other being I had tried to raise and my head pounded as I gasped for air. I was soon forced to release my concentration as I started to collapse, the tendrils sliding back to my skin. I never reached the floor, however, as I found myself being held up by three pairs of hands.

"You..." I looked up as I heard a feminine voice and felt like I was staring at Nisaba again as I met her blue eyes. The main difference was her expression was sterner and I carefully leaned away as they stood me back up.

Alex was standing next to me and his voice came out choked.

"A... Alrune? Basina?" His voice carried his tears and I looked at the two sisters as Basina smiled. She slouched in her all-black outfit, crossing her ankles as she glanced at Alrune and tossed her braid over her shoulder. The eldest sister was still wearing a 15th century dress, although her white hair flowed behind her back as she stared at me. "Are—"

"Seems the Seraph was right about her, although you should know this is only a temp thing," Basina interrupted, turning her deeper blue eyes to me. "After all, we can't be double undead. I'd say we have a day, maybe two before we die again."

"This is the one who would become Mother?" Alrune finally spoke, looking me up and down with a stern expression. I met her gaze even as the tendrils danced on my skin, the power still not fully calming down as her lips twitched. "I doth admit, she carries herself well."

"Oof, Alrune, maybe don't talk too much while you're alive again," Basina chuckled, shaking her head as Alrune turned her stern expression to her younger sister.

"And just what might be wrong with my speech?"

"It's about six centuries outdated," Alex said with a smile, clearly thrilled to see the two of them again as he stepped forward. The trio openly embraced and I gently rested my hand on Kisten's as he touched my shoulder. The tendrils started to move toward him but I hummed with annoyance, my head pounding more fiercely as I fought to keep them off the shifter. LeAlexende turned to look at me. "But more importantly, since she brought you back, you can help me."

"Of course," the women answered and I looked at their hands as

Alrune and Alex reached for me. Basina was already wading into the pool. I carefully released Kisten as I took their hands and the pair began to lead me to the water.

"Raiven!" I glanced back as Kisten called for me and for a moment, he let me see the pain on his face. I did my best to smile as I saw the tears welling in his worried expression and I closed my eyes as I turned away from him. I could feel Azyam's and Mortem's reassurance in my chest as the Siblings released me, LeAlexende standing in front while Alrune and Basina surrounded me. Even though the section we all stood on only had the water up to our waists, I could tell the pool went much deeper, and I began to wonder if it was as deep as the ceiling was tall.

We stood perfectly still as the water settled around us and I groaned softly as I struggled to maintain my grip on Mortem's power. The tendrils seemed intent on seeking out something to destroy and I finally let out a soft groan as I balled my hands in the water. I heard Kisten's whine about his inability to help, but I forced myself not to look at him as I waited for the vampires, silently praying that whatever they were gonna do, they would do it soon.

"Goddess of Death, Herald of the Night," Alrune whispered. I felt the power start to settle down and I noticed her voice sounded much louder than it should have. It was as if she was whispering into a loudspeaker and I was tempted to turn, but Alex gently shook his head as Basina spoke next.

"Carrier of the Stars, Mother of the End..." Basina's light and playful tone was replaced by a serious one and I felt as the power in me seemed to turn inward, the black marks disappearing as it felt like they had started to squeeze my own bones. I couldn't prevent my cry of pain as I started to fall forward, but once again Alrune and Basina caught me. I felt one of them grab my hair, pulling my head back as I looked up to LeAlexende.

The vampire was smiling at me softly as he brought his wrist to his mouth, his eyes almost the same black color they had been when he shared his memories with Lucius. I watched as his fangs broke the skin and in that moment, the thirst hit me like a speeding train. I struggled against the hold his sisters had on me as I leaned for his blood, no longer able to even focus on the pain Mortem's power was causing throughout my whole body.

"*Saadhaal, MT, Kifo, Mortem,*" Alex finally whispered, moving his wrist so it hovered over my mouth and I couldn't help as I stuck my tongue out, desperate to taste his sweet blood. Azyam and Mortem's wills had joined with my own and I barely noticed that their Sibling closed his eyes as he continued. "Walk among us once more."

As soon as the blood ran down my throat, it felt as if time around me came to halt and I was the only one who could still move. I swallowed the blood as I stood, gently freeing myself from Alrune and Basina as I took a deep breath. I looked up to see Azyam and Mortem facing me in the pool, but Mortem was no longer a vague memory or presence. She was as solid as my twin and I, smiling softly with her black gaze as she closed her eyes.

"Here we are at last, Azyam, Raiven," she breathed, her voice soothing my soul and I felt the warmth in my chest. I slowly stepped away from the trio as she continued speaking in that soft, flowing voice. "You both have carried me for so long, and I know I can entrust the future to you."

"Like I said, no promises," I joked, unable to help my smile at the mirth that entered her expression. Her hair moved as if it was floating underwater and the bark wriggled on her arms as she lifted them from the pool, reaching out to me.

"None are needed, Raiven." I reached for her as she neared me, and where our fingers should have touched, she vanished, a soft smile on her face. I took a deep breath as she disappeared into me, dropping my arms as I faced Azyam, whose smile was more melancholic. We stood in silence for a while, neither of us knowing what to say. It was a moment we had always known was inevitable, but neither of us could have imagined this was how we would be saying our goodbyes.

"So, this is it!" She laughed, releasing a deep breath as our eyes met. "After all these years, you're finally gonna let me go."

"You know I can't do that," I answered, raising my arms to

embrace her as I sighed, refusing to look away from her. "You're gonna be with me always, just like you always have been."

I could see my words took her by surprise and my chest ached as I saw her tears. Taking a moment to brush them away, I watched as she reached to embrace me, slowly walking toward me in the water. My hands wavered slightly as the pain in my chest grew, but I forced myself to keep my arms outstretched, watching as her body began to disappear just as Mortem's had.

"I know I was always harsh to you and I know I never said it enough, but... I love you, sis," Azyam whispered and I closed my eyes, unable to help the tears that finally flowed down my cheeks. "I have always loved you."

"I know," I whispered quietly, feeling her presence merge into me as she finished disappearing and I fell to my knees in the water, unable to control my grief at finally losing her. My heart felt as if it was made of lead as I fell deeper into the pool, the water barely splashing as I collapsed below the surface. As I sank into the dark water, I felt disconnected from my body, closing my eyes as the sensation grew.

So, this is it, I thought, my sense of self beginning to fade as I finally hit the bottom of the pool, although the sensation was numb. I could barely hold onto my thoughts and I made a soft noise as I thought of the group waiting for me above the water. The Siblings would be pleased with whoever rose from the water, but Kisten...

Kisten. I felt my faraway heart twist as I thought of the shifter and I moaned softly in my thoughts as the darkness finished taking over my mind. *'I'm sorry, Kisten.'*

19

I carefully opened my eyes as time started again. I felt the water splashing all around me as I slowly sat up from the bottom of the pool. I heard the Siblings gasp as they struggled to move out of the way, and I opened my eyes to the gently lit cave. I lifted my head toward the ceiling to balance out the weight I felt on my forehead from the horn, and I gently moved my hands in the water, my hair feeling weightless as I sat.

Raiven... I thought, the name of one of my predecessors flashing through my mind as I stared into the rock ceiling above me. The others, Azyam and Mortem, had chosen her will to be passed on and I hummed with the happiness in my chest. Their sacrifice had not been in vain, and I shivered with my overwhelming joy.

I turned to look down at LeAlexende far below me, standing in the pool next to Alrune and Basina. All three vampires were crying as they looked up at me and I smiled at them gently, lifting one of my lower hands through the water to them. All three of them gripped my giant fingers, and were openly sobbing now as I smiled at them.

"There is no reason to cry," I assured them, my voice flowing like a night breeze as I spoke. They responded by gripping me tighter, all clearly emotional at finally seeing me and hearing my voice again.

"Mother, we missed you—"

"Forgive us for—"

"Shhh." I interrupted their cries of forgiveness and sorrow, meeting their gaze as the triplets looked up to me. "There is no need for such words. Let us be happy with the outcome, shall we?"

"Yes, Mother, always." They nodded in unison, once again pressing their faces into my hand as they gripped my fingers. I raised my gaze to see Kisten, who was looking at me with shock and awe. The shifter was standing with his hands clasped together tightly, and even from my enormous height, towering above him, I could see the pain and confusion in his stance. I carefully reached one of my upper arms to him and I watched as he looked at my giant palm with confusion.

"Hello, Kisten." My heart ached in my chest as I smiled at the shifter, and it pounded as I waited for his reaction. All the memories of our relationship swam in my thoughts and I only hoped he would still accept me, despite the change I had undergone.

"... Raiven?" he questioned, seeming almost reluctant to touch me as he looked back to meet my gaze. My smile grew brighter as I encouraged him to take my hand, the stars twinkling on my clothing as I moved. I gently pulled my hand from the vampires, folding both of my lower hands in my lap as I did my best to think of a way to respond.

"Do you trust me?" I finally asked calmly, watching as he looked back to my giant hand. I took a deep breath as I waited for his answer, his uncertainty starting to infect me as the shifter grappled with his emotions.

"I... I don't know what to think," he answered, and I couldn't help my slight chuckle at his honesty. He chanced a glance at LeAlexende still in the pool, who seemed to be doing his best to encourage him and I smiled as the Alpha raised his gaze to me. I understood his hesitance and confusion, but I also knew no words would be able to convince him. He needed to touch me, feel me, and understand what I had become.

"Trust me," I insisted, and I watched as he looked at my hand again, carefully reaching out to touch me. As soon as his skin met mine, I moved toward the shifter, shrinking in size and forsaking my second pair of arms as I did so. I continued to shrink until I was looking up at him, our fingers laced together as I smiled at Kisten. The awe and shock seemed to increase as he stared into my eyes, and I gently brought his hand to my face. "I'm not quite the same Raiven anymore."

"Your eyes..." he started, and I nodded, hearing as the triplets finally began their slow ascent out of the pool. I could hear LeAlexende's hushed whispering as he ushered the girls toward the entrance and I couldn't help my soft laugh.

"Like I said, I'm not the same, as I now carry traits from all three of them."

"You mean, Azyam and Mortem, right? They are... a part of you?" Kisten offered cautiously and I nodded, doing my best to maintain my smile. He was searching my mismatched eyes, looking for any semblance of the old Raiven that remained. "So, you're not really Raiven anymore."

"It's... a bit more complicated than that. I can say that I mostly still *feel* like Raiven," I admitted, humming softly as I leaned more into his touch. "I still... have the same love for you, Kisten, that hasn't changed. I would... still like to be with you and marry you, if you will have me."

"*Have* you?" I felt him pull his hand away, unable to help the ache in my chest as I frowned. I was quickly surprised as I felt his arms wrap around me and he carefully lifted me into the air, spinning me as my hair floated around me. When he set me back down, I felt him grab my face, the tears pouring down his cheeks as he smiled at me. "I will *always* have you."

"Kisten." Tears of relief poured down my face in response to his and he carefully stroked away the streaks left in their wake. "You–"

"You remember me, and you still love me," Kisten interrupted, beaming brightly at me as he spoke. So much love and relief shone in his chartreuse eyes and I couldn't hold back the tears that continued to well in mine. "That is so much more than I ever dared to hope for.

If I could, I would kiss both Azyam and Mortem to thank them for letting me keep you."

"Or you could just kiss me," I replied smartly and I loved the exasperated look that entered his expression. The tightness of his smile was balanced by the love that filled his face and I hummed softly as Kisten adjusted his arms to hold me.

The Alpha leaned down to kiss me, careful to avoid my horn as he did so, and I found myself clinging to him as he indulged in me. His touch and kiss were gentle and desperate at the same time, as if he needed to make sure I hadn't disappeared. When he finally pulled back from me, he brought his hands back to my face, releasing a broken laugh.

"The eyes are gonna take some getting used to," he admitted, searching my soft gaze as I smiled up at him. "Gonna guess that was one of them?"

"Azyam's eyes were always brown, Raiven's green. She was the root to my leaves, I guess in reverence to the tree that we all came from." I sighed, closing my eyes again as I gently touched his hands with my own. I allowed my horn to fade as my hair fell, the weight almost enough to pull my head back from his touch. "I had to keep us together somehow, we loved each other so much."

"Hmm," the Alpha hummed, touching our foreheads together as he took a deep breath, still trying to process what had happened. "So, you're... mostly Raiven, with echoes of the other two? What does that really mean?"

"I have all of their memories and pieces of their personalities, but Azyam and Mortem chose to surrender to me, deciding Raiven's will and personality should live on," I whispered, humming with happiness. "For the most part, it worked, but you can hardly merge the lives and experiences of three people and not expect someone new to emerge. I still feel like Raiven and yet, I know I am not the same."

"Someone new..." Kisten whispered, his voice deep with his thoughts as he considered my explanation. I merely squeezed his hands under mine, waiting patiently for him to speak. "Then it feels wrong to keep calling you Raiven."

"I still like the name," I insisted and Kisten laughed, gripping me tighter. "And I still believe in the reason I chose it. Honestly, all things considered, perhaps it was always meant to be my name."

"Reason?"

"I carry death in my wake, whether it is my intention or not. It follows me as a friend, for better or for worse." I opened my eyes as he pulled back, taking a deep breath as he searched my eyes with his again. I suppose he liked whatever he found, because he merely shook his head.

"Raiven it is," he conceded, gently taking my hands in his as he glanced around the room. "You probably need to claim it again then, make sure your power won't be affected by any other name."

"What do you mean?"

"You are a new person now, but if you don't claim a name, it's possible you could still be affected by all of the old ones. Azyam, Awetash, Mortem." Kisten spoke calmly, and even as he said them, I could feel the tiniest jump of my power as it reacted to the old chains. "Carrying all three binds you to all the old names, unless you override it by giving yourself one you want."

"Like when I was nameless..." I conceded, glancing up to see his gaze. "You seem to know a lot about this for someone who has never changed his name."

"Not that I've ever dealt with it, but I've seen my share over the centuries. I do know how dangerous it can be," he said, with a shrug. I made a soft noise as he spoke, gently stepping away from him as he smiled patiently. I closed my eyes as I held my hands to my chest, taking in a deep breath. Before I even began to speak, I felt my power starting to react, anticipating the bind.

"I... am... Raiven," I stated calmly, my power radiating out from me as the stone shook beneath our feet. I was certain the Siblings felt the tremor as well, if they were still just outside the cave, and I slowly opened my eyes as the tremor died away. Kisten was still smiling with the same expression and I couldn't help but match it as I stepped back towards him. I buried my face into his chest as soon as I reached him, the joy only growing in my heart. "Now and forever."

"Forever," Kisten repeated, squeezing me into him as he laid gentle kisses in my hair. I felt him pause, rubbing his face against the dark strands as he spoke again. "Seems like we have a moment alone."

"It does," I purred, gently pulling away from the embrace as I guided him along the steps. Kisten frowned softly at me, until comprehension filled his face as I moved toward the seating area and he chuckled as he shook his head.

"Really, Rai?"

I shrugged as he laughed, stepping up onto the cleared space as the shifter followed me, wasting no time as he pushed me onto my back. I wrapped my arms around the Alpha as he breathed in my scent, humming softly against my skin. I moaned quietly as my body shivered, my voice barely above a whisper as I spoke.

"Why not?"

20

Kisten kept his face buried in my neck, his hands sliding across my bare shoulders. I didn't try to hide my soft hum as I enjoyed his touch, tempted to allow my outfit to fade away as he sat up slightly, his finger gently touching the silver accents on my skin. His face held his confusion as he traced their shape.

"Are they...?"

"They are a part of me, but I don't have to keep them if you don't like them," I answered, closing my eyes as he stroked them, unable to help the soft moan that escaped me. "They are only permanent in my goddess form."

"Hmm," the shifter answered, and I opened my eyes to see his conflicted gaze. I carefully sat up, reaching to stroke his face as I lifted his face to mine.

"What's wrong?"

"I'm... it's still a little weird," Kisten admitted, leaning into my hand as he closed his eyes, purring softly. "I mean, you smell like Raiven, and I know you are still her in some ways, but knowing you're different, actually understanding that you're a goddess now..."

"It's intimidating? Scary, not really knowing how much I've

changed?" I offered and the Alpha nodded his agreement, still keeping his eyes closed as he turned to kiss my hand. I frowned slightly as I watched his expression, and I gently pushed him back, the shifter allowing me to slide into his lap. I carefully reached to adjust my skirt, smiling softly as I leaned my head against his. "Then let's start over."

"Start over?"

"I'm not Mortem, not the Goddess of Death. I may have her powers, her title and her memories, but I'm not a goddess at heart," I whispered, cupping Kisten's face in my hands as I kissed his forehead, gently working my way down to his lips. The shifter eagerly let me in and I felt his grip on me tighten as he did his best to avoid the silver ribs on my exposed mid-section. I pulled back from the kiss, whispering my next words against his lips. "I'm just a regular Supe who got a power boost and who wants to be loved by her fiancé."

"I can work with that," Kisten chuckled, leaning up to kiss me again as his hands moved higher, gently stroking the silver spine that graced my skin. A moan escaped me as I tightened my hold on his face and the alpha repeated his action, leaving me panting when he broke the kiss again. "Sensitive, huh?"

"I guess so," I answered shakily and Kisten laughed as he touched the purple fabric on my chest, watching it as the stars twinkled. I carefully grabbed his wrist and slid his hand underneath, shaking slightly as I felt his hand against my breast. He wasted no time in touching me, burying his face back into my neck as I moved my hands to his hair.

Kisten took his time as he explored the changes to my body, dragging his kisses from my neck to my collar bone as he continued to play with my chest. I couldn't help the soft moans and sounds that escaped from me and I yelped softly as I was picked up, the shifter placing me on the table. He leaned over me as he gently laid me back, taking a moment to steal another kiss from my lips.

"Kisten...?" I gave him a questioning look as he slid back down my body, sliding my skirt up higher as he knelt on the ground. I understood his intention as he gently spread my legs and, instead of my usual embarrassment, I only felt trepid excitement as the shifter moaned softly, pressing a gentle kiss into my soft skin.

"I have to," he whispered, his voice thick with desire as he buried his face in me, and my legs immediately wrapped around his shoulders as I felt his tongue against me. I did little to hide my moans as the Alpha indulged in my taste, his own sounds only serving to excite me more. Something about the sensations felt new and intense, even though I knew Kisten often enjoyed my body this way.

Is it because it's my first time experiencing it? I thought, my hands finally finding their way to his hair as the shifter growled softly, adjusting his grip as I moaned loudly. Even though Raiven's body and memories allowed me to remember the feeling, there was a difference between remembering a feeling and experiencing it with my new mind. I could feel my orgasm building and I pushed Kisten back, panting heavily as I heard him gasp.

"Something the matter?"

"Yes," I managed, loosening my legs as I encouraged him to lean over me, kissing him deeply to enjoy my taste on his lips. Kisten moaned openly into my kiss and I could feel his member as he throbbed against me, only causing my need to increase. I pushed him up from me again as I gasped, meeting his chartreuse eyes with my mismatched pair. "I need you inside me."

"So impatient," Kisten teased, moving against me as I moaned, wrapping my legs around his waist. Despite his words, I knew he was as eager to love me as I was to have him, and I couldn't help my smirk as I met his gaze.

"Can you blame me?" I chuckled, sliding my hands under his shirt as I lifted it over his head, the shifter standing up slightly as I tossed it to the floor. I chased after the Alpha, not willing to let him get away from me as I stroked his chest. "It feels like it's been forever."

"Does it now?" Kisten purred, rubbing his skin against mine as he ran his hands along my silver spine, causing my back to arch more as I moaned loudly. The shifter chuckled into my skin as he continued stroking me, clearly enjoying this new aspect to my body. "I don't know, Raiven, it seems there's so much more to learn about you now."

"Kisten, if you—" I started to protest but I was interrupted as he moved his hips into me and I could only gasp as I felt his member throb through his jeans. The Alpha knew exactly the effect he was having on me as he continued to grind himself against me, stroking the silver bones on my skin as I squirmed and moaned against him. Every part of me longed to have him inside me, but I was completely at his mercy as the shifter moved his hand to my hair, pulling my head back.

"Look at you, just a simmering puddle in my hands," he cooed, dragging his tongue along my neck as I shivered, still a panting and moaning mess in his hands. The deep, throaty chuckle only made me moan again and he gently kissed my cheeks before whispering in my ear. "Why don't you get rid of this clothing for me?"

I didn't answer as I closed my eyes, removing the purple cloth from my body as I concentrated, although I felt my head grow heavy again as my horn reappeared. I heard Kisten's chuckle as he noticed and I felt as he released my hair to stroke it. A pleasurable sensation shot through my whole body and I wrapped my legs tighter around him, unable to help my body's reaction.

"These silver bones really are sensitive, aren't they?" Kisten laughed and I merely nodded wordlessly against him as I moaned into his bare chest. The shifter pushed me back as he smiled down at me, gently cupping my face with his free hand. "I think I've teased you enough."

"Yes..." I managed, barely meeting his gaze through my half-closed eyes as he placed his hands on the table. He was no longer holding me up, so I quickly placed my own hands on the table, keeping myself from falling back as he smiled down at me.

"Well, if you want it, then do it yourself, dear Goddess," he commanded and I wasted no time in pushing him up, reaching for his jeans. Kisten merely chuckled as I freed him from the pants, stroking his member as I slid myself on the table. I gently guided him to my slick opening, tightening my legs around him as I slid him inside. The shifter released a sound of his own as his hips moved, thrusting himself deeper into me. I wrapped my arms around him as he moved his hands to my waist, thrusting his hips until he was completely buried inside me.

I shivered as I rubbed my face against him, doing my best to avoid poking the shifter with my horn. My whole body felt on fire as he throbbed inside me, but it wasn't painful like the Oath's fire had been. Rather, the flame that burned on my skin was a fire of passion and I moaned into his skin as Kisten paused, one of his hands moving back to the silver on my skin. I gasped loudly as I clung to him more, my legs shaking as the Alpha chuckled in my ear again.

"Happy now, Goddess?"

"No," I managed to moan, shivering again as he continued stroking my silver spine and he tightened the hand on my waist. He thrust his hips into me again, and I dug my fingers into his back, moaning loudly with the friction. "Please, Kisten."

"Then say it, *Rabe*[1]," Kisten whispered and I chuckled softly as I closed my eyes, pulling the shifter down as I whispered into his ear.

"Love me senseless, *Mein Alpha*." Hearing me speak his native tongue seemed to unhinge something in the shifter, and Kisten began to pound himself into me, gripping me tightly as he moved. I didn't even try to quiet my sounds, clinging to the Alpha as he loved me, his hands moving to the table as he dug his nails into the wood. I could only moan in response, my mind still lost in the haze of this carnal activity, this need to be filled. I soon felt my orgasm building again and I rubbed myself against Kisten more, desperate to feel him.

"*Vogel*[2]..." He panted heavily above me as he moaned, his hands returning to my skin as he began to move quicker, stroking every inch of my sacred flesh. As his fingers found their way to the silver bones, my release hit me and I cried out loudly as I clung to my lover. Kisten paused as I shivered against him, rubbing my horn against his face as I panted with my orgasm. The Alpha leaned up from me as I loosened my grip, my eyes still hazy from the pleasure.

"Kis... Kisten..."

"I'm not done with you, *Meine Göttin*[3]," Kisten purred, carefully pulling out as he picked me up from the table. I soon found myself pressed into it again as the shifter flipped me, teasing my slick opening with his hand again. "You came before me."

"Your fault," I managed, touching my horn to the table as the shifter pressed his fingers further into me, and I shook as I waited for him to fill me again. Kisten merely chuckled in response as he leaned over me and I moaned loudly as I felt his member press into my opening. The shifter slid his hand to my neck as he thrust himself into me and I closed my eyes as I felt him fill me. "Fuck, Kisten."

"As you wish," he growled into my back, and I couldn't help the sound I let out as he began to pound himself into me. I felt the pleasure grow with each thrust, my breath catching every time Kisten buried his full length inside me again. I could feel my orgasm building again, every thrust sending me closer and closer to that sweet ecstasy. I was unable to help my transformation as my second set of arms appeared again, gripping the table tightly as I moaned in time with his movements.

I felt Kisten's fangs as the shifter brushed his lips against my skin and I gently reached up to touch his face, cradling him against me as he sought his release. I could tell he was fighting the desire to bite me, to hold me in place and claim me as his. The Alpha growled into my skin and my voice flowed like the night wind when I finally spoke.

"*Mark me,*" I whispered, and as soon as the words left me, I felt the shifter's fangs dig into my neck. The simple pleasure of having his fangs so deep inside me, moving as every thrust rocked my body... it was overwhelming, it was *pleasure*. I could feel my body tightening around his member and Kisten growled as he felt my orgasm wash over me again. The shifter moved over me desperately as he sought his own and he withdrew his fangs as he growled loudly, finally filling me with his warm seed as I moaned.

I panted as Kisten pulled himself out and I was left leaning on the table, still trying to recover my breath. I felt as he gently touched my shoulder and I forced myself up, turning to see his face. He was looking at my bleeding neck with concern, and I gently touched the black blood.

"Don't... worry," I panted, running my hand along the wound as I healed it. I watched the surprised expression flit across his face before it disappeared, Kisten shaking his head as he laughed.

"Honestly, I'm not that surprised." The Alpha glanced back to the pool, holding his hand out to me as he smiled. "Kinda convenient to have a bath right here, huh?"

"Mm-hmm," I agreed, taking his hand as he guided me into the water, careful to lead me down the steps. He gently sat on the last step and I collapsed into his lap, earning myself a grunt as I leaned against him. I sighed happily as I felt the warm water on my skin, closing my eyes as I dragged all four of my hands across the surface. "I'm glad the arms didn't freak you out."

"Rai, about an hour ago you were the size of the room," Kisten scoffed and I opened my eyes as he tilted my head back. He leaned to the side to avoid my horn, still smiling down at me as he shook his head. "If you being like fifty feet tall didn't scare me away, four arms isn't going to."

"I'm not fifty feet tall," I pouted, and the Alpha shook his head as he leaned down to kiss me. I gently returned the gesture, although I was still pouting when he pulled away. "I'm closer to forty."

"Point stands," he sighed, releasing my face as he wrapped his arms around me, sighing happily in the water. "It may still take a while to get used to, but I'm right here, Raiven. Right where I wanna be."

I didn't answer as I took a deep breath, closing my eyes as I leaned into the shifter. I hummed softly as I concentrated, once again dismissing my second set of arms and my horn as I grunted. I looked up to see Kisten still watching me, his gaze soft and full of love as our eyes met. I turned around in the pool, throwing my arms around his neck as I leaned up for another kiss. As he held me close, returning my gesture eagerly, I thanked Azyam and Mortem for their decision. My heart swelled as I indulged in the man in my arms, knowing our love was safe.

21

By the time the Siblings returned, Kisten and I were sitting at the table, merely enjoying the soft sounds of the water as it flowed. I remembered that the water flowed from an underground offshoot from the Nile, and by stimulating the ground slightly, I could keep the pool clean and fresh. I smiled softly as the vampires returned, leaning up from the Alpha as I greeted them.

"Welcome back."

"Hi..." I frowned softly as Basina's voice faded and I stood up and walked over to them. All three seemed to be in a pensive mood and I gently touched LeAlexende's shoulder as I stood in front of them.

"Did something happen?"

"No, we..." Alex's voice faded as he turned to look at his sister, but both of the girls were also avoiding my gaze. "We wanted to say we're sorry."

"*Sorry?*" My frown only grew as I released the former Overseer and I saw the three exchange a glance as I stepped back. I heard Kisten finally stand from the table and I leaned into the shifter as I waited for the Siblings to explain. "Sorry for what?"

"When Vitae... when she killed you..." Basina started but she sighed heavily, her voice catching again as she spoke. I watched as

Alrune gently touched her sister's shoulder, stepping in front of her younger siblings as she finally met my gaze.

"We wanted to apologize for not protecting you, Mother," Alrune declared, speaking clearly and matter-of-factly as she forced herself to meet my eyes. I could see the tears she was refusing to let fall and I hummed softly as she continued. "We failed as your children and your First, and we never got to express our regret."

"*Filii*[1]," I started, leaning away from Kisten as I opened my arms to the vampires. All three looked at me, shocked, but I could see fearful hope in Alex's and Basina's eyes. "I have never and would never blame you for what happened. It was an oversight for me and the Seraph to not realize the path Vitae had started down, but no one is responsible for what she did other than her."

"But..."

"You were children, Alrune, and taught by me to respect Vitae's role just as I had," I interrupted, my heart aching for the three in front of me. For millennia, they had carried guilt over what Vitae had done, for not being able to protect me, for not standing up to her as she forced them to do her will and tears welled in my own eyes as I smiled at them. "You did your best, and that's all I could ever ask for."

"Mo... Mother..." LeAlexende's voice cracked as he lost the fight with his tears, and I motioned my hands to the trio, inviting them to hug me. All three collapsed into my arms and I stroked their backs as I hushed them, the vampires sobbing into my skin. I gently kissed each of their heads, squeezing them tightly before I stepped back, gently wiping away their tears as I summoned my second set of arms. I allowed each of the vampires to take a hand, casting my gaze between them.

"For me, it is enough that I had one last chance to see all three of you, and allow you to meet my mate." I turned to look at Kisten, who was watching us with a gentle expression. A blush slowly spread across his cheeks, and I couldn't help my chuckle as he looked away nervously. Kisten didn't blush very often, but it was always adorable to me when I could bring that red color to his cheeks. "Alex knows him well enough and, though you don't have long, I'm happy Alrune and Basina get to meet him as well."

"I know about Kisten, but never had a chance to meet him in person. He saved Alex and Lucius from his father, right?" Basina shrugged, releasing my hand as she walked up to the Alpha. Kisten did his best to stay calm, but I could see his nervousness increasing as she looked up at him. "Thank you for that."

"Actually, I killed my father a while ago," the shifter mentioned, smiling awkwardly as Alrune also approached him. "He came to America to find Alex and I decided I would stop running from him."

"Hmmm, I suppose he is fine," Alrune huffed, circling the shifter as both Alex and I struggled to hide our laughter. It was clear Kisten was uncomfortable being scrutinized by the two sisters, but the vampires continued their investigation of him. Basina was the first to lean away from him, seemingly pleased with whatever she found.

"Well, if Mother likes him, it's good enough for me and I can add another thanks for killing that bastard. Just sorry I let him get me the way he did," she said with a sigh, crossing her arms again as she glanced back at me. "In the end, as long as she's happy, I'm happy."

"I suppose I feel the same. After all, it is enough to get this night," Alrune agreed, leaning away from Kisten as the shifter sighed with relief. I sighed happily as the sister turned back to face me and I folded all my hands behind my back. "Thank you, Mother."

"You can just call me Raiven." I smiled, seeing the confliction on their faces as I chuckled. "I'm not really Mortem anymore, although I do have her memories and love for you three as her children. There's no need to keep calling me that."

"But–"

"It does no good to argue, Alrune!" LeAlexende laughed, finally relaxing as he wiped away the last of his tears. I shook my head as he sat on the steps, looking at his sisters as Alrune frowned at him. "Just call her what she wants."

"But..." Alrune seemed ready to push her point, but soon we were all distracted as we heard a noise outside the room. I felt a tingle run across my skin and I quickly started toward the entrance as I recognized the feeling. As I finally stepped back into the night air, I found the Seraph sitting, looking up into the night sky with their beautiful wings folded behind them. I hummed softly to myself as I approached them, joining them on the edge of the cliff.

We sat in silence for a while, although I could tell the other four were watching us from inside. The moonlight on the Nile was nostalgic, and I found my thoughts drifting to a time long gone, before Vitae's betrayal.

"I see you made your choice," the Seraph said finally and I shrugged as I leaned back on my lower arms. The night was surprisingly calm, and I noticed that the Seraph still had their wings closed as we looked out over the river. My mind returned to the cave painting depicting their torture and I frowned at the thought. My memories told me that the Seraph was once proud of their wings and to see them purposefully hide them made my heart ache. "Welcome back."

"Yeah, it's something," I agreed, looking up to the bright moon. "Thank you, for helping me."

"Are you... happy?" they asked quietly and I turned to look at them as they folded their hands in their lap. I sat up as I gently touched their hands, noticing their flinch as I did so.

"I mean, I'm glad my power isn't going to run amok anymore," I joked, gently taking their hand in mine as they finally turned that golden gaze to me. I did my best to smile as I met their sad expression, my heart aching for them as much as it had for the Siblings. "I was never unhappy before."

"But neither were you happy."

"It was... complicated," I admitted, shrugging as I gazed out to the river again. "I was content, but I guess I felt like I was missing the love you and Vitae had. I was okay with the way things were, but I guess Vitae didn't feel the same way."

"I suppose... not," they agreed, squeezing my hand as they also looked out toward the water. We sat in silence again for a moment, the Seraph sighing as they spoke again. "I should have–"

"Don't you start, either," I interrupted, turning their attention to me as I frowned. The Seraph was looking at me with surprise, and I rolled my eyes as I continued. "We are not responsible for what Vitae chose to do."

"But—"

"No. We are not guilty for loving and respecting her, and assuming she felt the same," I insisted, slowly pulling them to their feet as I faced them. The Seraph watched me curiously as they stood, tears in the corner of their eyes. "Her choices are her own."

The Seraph remained silent as they watched me with surprise and I huffed as I released them. I chuckled as my regular clothes returned to my body and I shook my long hair, gently parting it as I got ready to braid it. I was barely surprised as I felt three pairs of hands take my hair instead and I sighed happily as the Siblings began to style my hair. They had often loved to do it in their youth so I was hardly surprised that they jumped at the chance to do it now.

"You... have changed." The Seraph smiled at last, a tear finally rolling down their face as they closed their golden eyes. I scoffed at their words, but they raised their hands to interrupt me before I could speak. "I know you are not Mortem, but all the same, you have changed."

"Well, you can hardly mesh three separate experiences together and expect me not to," I smirked, shaking my head as I felt the vampires finish with their braids. "Maybe it's time for a change. Maybe this world has no more need for Gods."

"Perhaps it doesn't," the Seraph agreed, glancing over to Kisten where the Alpha still stood in the entryway. I turned to see my lover and he smiled awkwardly under our gaze, another blush coming to his cheeks. "Perhaps, it is our turn to live."

"Took the words ri—" I was interrupted as a cold shiver ran through my whole body, almost causing me to double over in pain. From the way the Seraph reacted, I could tell they felt it, too and I struggled to recover my breath as I fought to stand.

"Raiven!" Alex's voice was full of concern as the Siblings gently helped me to stand back up and I met the Seraph's concerned expression. Somehow, without words, I knew exactly what I had felt and the pain in my chest was no longer from the sudden cold snap, but from fear. The Seraph's eyes searched mine with desperation, as if they hoped they were wrong, hoping with all their being that it *couldn't be her.*

Before I could speak, Kisten's phone began to echo in the night air and I watched as the Alpha frowned, scrambling for the device. It was an alarm I had never heard before and from the fear that immediately spread across the shifter's face, I knew what it was for.

"Rai, it's—"

"*Vitae,*" I breathed, finally standing up straight as I did my best to work through my fear. "She's in Decver. Feeling me awaken has caused her to panic, so she's hoping to destroy what I care about. She's hoping to draw me out."

"Then—"

"I'm going," I insisted, cutting off Alrune as I turned to her. The eldest's concern was plain on her face and it was clear that Basina and LeAlexende shared her fear and worry. "I will *not* allow her to do as she pleases this time."

"She has Evalyn on her side, that fucking bitch," Kisten breathed, his breath shaky as he leaned against the wall, clearly growing weak. It was obvious that Lucius was using the Oath to draw power from the Alpha, although I had no doubt it was more of an effort to weaken Eve. "Lucius is doing his best, but he needs help. The Oath of Power won't subdue her for long."

"He's getting it." I turned to the Seraph, their eyes holding their confliction. On one hand, I could see that they wanted to stop Vitae as much as I did, but their expression held the same conflict that it had thousands of years ago; could they bring themselves to turn on their own creation? Were they willing to shoulder the burden of that choice? I took a deep breath as I met their gaze evenly, unwavering in my determination. "We're coming."

"... Yes," The Seraph finally agreed and I took their hand as I walked over to the shifter. Kisten nearly collapsed against me and I did my best to support my partner as I felt the Siblings reach out to me. They seemed to understand what I intended to do, and they each grabbed a piece of my clothing, indicating their desire to help. I closed my eyes as I tried to prepare myself, the Seraph squeezing my hand. "Can you do it with this many?"

"As long as no one lets go, it should be fine," I insisted, carefully pressing a kiss on Kisten's forehead as he whined from the fatigue. "Keep your eyes closed, and don't let go, no matter what. Trust me."

The Alpha merely nodded into my shoulder and I carefully released my breath, holding a perfect image of the Coven in my mind. As we slowly sank into the ground and my consciousness spread into the earth around us, I kept that single image in my mind, determined to stop Vitae.

22

The chaos was noticeable the moment we arrived, the living space already in disarray as we materialized. Despite being underground, I could feel the intense magic in the area, and the cold shiver that I had felt in Africa seemed intensified this close to the source. Kisten moaned and I released the Seraph as I carefully set the Alpha on the ground. His skin was starting to pale from the fatigue and, while I knew Lucius would not allow the Oath to kill him, my chest twisted at the sight.

"Stay here," I commanded, gently brushing his hair from his face as he slowly opened his eyes to look at me. Despite his weakness, I could see the argument in his eyes and I shook my head. "Until you recover, you'll just be in danger. I doubt Vitae has forgotten what you mean to me, and she'll do her best to use you against me."

"Rai..."

"Trust me, *Mein Liebling*[1]. I won't try to stop you from helping," I assured him, cradling his face in my hands. He sighed heavily as he closed his eyes and I gently kissed his forehead. "This has been your home longer than mine, and you deserve to help protect it. But please, for me, let yourself recover."

"Raiven." I released my lover as I heard Alex's voice behind me.

He stood in between his sisters, with the Seraph standing slightly behind them. It seemed they all believed me to be in charge of our little group and I tried to swallow my pounding heart as I moved away from Kisten.

"LeAlexende," I turned to the Siblings as I took a deep breath, the three vampires patiently waiting for me to speak, "help Lucius. He has been practicing with your power, but he could use your help. Alrune, Basina, help with the other Hunters."

"Other Hu–"

"There's no way Vitae came alone and she will be depending on Evalyn to draw me out," I interrupted, and I watched as they slowly nodded, accepting my logic. "She'll have brought every Hunter she has left and while our Coven is powerful, it'll take multiple members to handle each one. Find those who are struggling and help them."

"Yes, Raiven," Alrune answered solemnly and I took a deep breath as I pulled all three of them in for a hug. I squeezed them all tightly, taking in their individual scents as I spoke into their hair.

"If it gets too dangerous, flee and save those you can," I commanded, pulling back to meet each set of blue eyes. All three nodded slowly and I smiled softly to lessen their fears. "I still want to have lunch later today with my daughters and new son."

Alex laughed quietly as I released them, watching as the Siblings quickly moved above ground. As soon as they vanished out the open door, I turned to the Seraph, my expression once again serious. Their expression still held their confliction and I cleared my throat to get their attention. They flinched slightly as they met my eyes, playing with their hands as they spoke.

"You want me with you?"

"I do. I know that you can't really hurt her, but I'm not expecting you to," I agreed, turning back to glance at the shifter on the floor. Kisten still had his eyes closed, seemingly resting as he tried to do as I asked. I took a deep breath as I looked back to my Creator, determination in my eyes. "I need to ask you something."

"Ask."

"What... what would happen if Vitae drank my blood?" I

breathed and I saw the Seraph stiffen at the thought. They looked away from me and it was obvious my question had distressed them. "Seraph?"

"It... would undo the effects of *my* blood," they finally whispered, still refusing to meet my gaze. "She would lose her godhood and no longer be the Goddess of Life."

"Her gem?" I offered and the Seraph nodded, chancing a glance at me as I continued. "What about me? Could I create the same effect if I removed my horn?"

"Wha-what?" the Seraph gave me a horrified look as I waited for their answer, refusing to turn away. "Raiven, that would... you would..."

"Would removing my horn take away my godhood?" I repeated, not reacting to their obvious distress at my question. As they realized my determination, they slowly nodded, pain and worry still in their eyes as I finally looked away toward the hallway.

"I can't kill her. I can't risk what that might mean for all those that carry her blood," I admitted, starting into the darkness as the Seraph followed me. I noticed for the first time that they glowed, their soft light showing the panic as everyone had fled the Coven. Evalyn must've started at the Landing and alerted everyone right away, causing most to run above ground without worrying about closing doors. I saw that the barrier to the space was still in place as I hummed, grateful for Yoreile's dedication. "Relieving us of godhood is the next best idea for stopping her and saving everyone."

"I trust you... Raiven," the Seraph agreed and the heat accosted us as soon as we stepped through the barrier. The ash on the wind made us turn away from it and my heart pounded as I saw the rising flames. The anger in my chest grew as I considered the Ala's betrayal and a part of me wished I could be the one to kill Evalyn. However, I knew Lucius had earned his right to end her life and I took a deep breath as I pulled out my phone.

"Raiven!" the Director's voice was panicked as he answered, but I didn't give him a chance to continue speaking as I interrupted him.

"Where is Vitae?"

"Uh... last anyone reported, she was on the west side of the city. Her Hunters are everywhere; the south side of the city is basically destroyed," he panted and I glanced up as I felt the flames creep closer to me and the Seraph. "Raiven, where are—"

"Evacuate anyone left on the south side. Make it a priority for all S-men agents to get everyone out of there," I instructed, starting toward the edge of the building as the Seraph followed. "I'll draw Vitae there, so let me know as soon as they have everyone moved to safety."

"Rai—"

"Trust me," I insisted, turning away from the fire as we turned the corner. The Seraph was quick to wave the flames away, and in a moment, the fire was put out, leaving only smoldering ruins behind. Most of the shops were little more than hollowed-out piles of ashes, and my heart pounded as I saw movement in the rubble. I was forced to drop my phone as I extended my power, the tendrils grabbing a beam as it started to collapse onto a survivor.

"Go! It's not safe here, head to the northside!" I watched as they struggled to free themselves, quickly moving to help someone with them. As soon as they were clear, I allowed the beam to fall, turning back to meet the Seraph's horrified gaze. "We'll head for the south side of the city, saving and helping who we can until I get an all-clear."

"Yes," the Seraph breathed, and I picked my phone up from the ground, shaking the broken glass from the screen.

"Raiven! Raiven, are you—"

"I'll help where I can, but focus on getting me that arena to face her," I insisted, as the Seraph and I began moving through the smoldering buildings. "My phone is busted, so a magic signal would be best."

"Will do. Be careful, Raiven." I grunted as I hung up the call, tossing the device into the ruins as I leapt over a broken wall. I heard as the Seraph landed beside me and I began to run through the streets, being sure to keep my dark tendrils on my skin as I headed for the south side of the city. I knew Vitae would follow the flow of our power, and the Seraph seemed to understand my intention, finally opening their wings as they flew beside me.

Turning a corner, I was forced to stop as I caught a body flying toward me, and I was surprised by the cocky laugh that came from the being in my arms. I pushed him away slightly as his golden hair blew in my face and I couldn't help my annoyed smile.

"Wondered if you were gonna show!" Crispin quickly stood up from me and caught the streetlight that was thrown at us, showing off his inhuman strength as he tossed it to the side. His shirt was torn in several places and his right arm was already bleeding from a massive gash as the vampire smiled at me. "Where's the Alpha?"

"Recovering at the Coven, since Lucius was draining him," I answered, watching as the Seraph intercepted the car thrown at us, their wings blowing the vehicle back to the Hunter. I didn't recognize them, but from the way the metal car was crumpled by their gaze, I could only guess their powers were metal-based. Aselis, Eleventh in the Coven, tried to land a hit in their distraction, but the Hunter was quick to dodge, sending the cyclops flying into another building. I saw two other bodies in the rubble and I couldn't help the way my heart twisted.

"Where's Justina?"

"Helping the Division and quite mad about it. She wants to help fight, but I told her someone needs to protect Noelle." Crispin laughed, turning away as he leaned down, launching another car at the Hunter. I watched as the vehicle was suddenly covered in flames, and we both glanced up to see Basina walk through the alley. The flames seemed to disrupt the Hunter's ability as they dodged to avoid the hit. Crispin let out another hearty laugh as the vampire looked at us, smiling brightly. "Oh, so *that's* how it works."

"Shall we?" Basina offered and Cripsin grinned, rushing toward his adversary again with his fellow vampire at his side. Aselis also freed himself from the rubble and I noticed a slight glimmer as blond hair moved behind the Hunter. They managed to dodge Kisca as the pixie attempted to stab them, but failed to completely avoid Basina's flames.

"Let's go!" I insisted, forcing myself to turn away from the fight. As much as I wanted to make sure we didn't lose any more members of the Coven, I knew the best way for me to help them was to stop Vitae, and the Seraph and I once again took off through the darkened streets. The sounds of the various fights seemed to echo through the streets and we were forced to pause again as a wave of fire passed in front of us.

"RAIVEN!" I growled as I looked up, unsurprised to see Evalyn standing on the roof of a building. Her skin was bright red from her flames, and her tail twitched behind her as she glared down at me. "Here was me thinking I would miss my chance to kill you myself!"

"Good luck, bitch!" I smirked, not hesitating as I raised a wall of earth to block her fire. I lowered the earth to see her scowl and I couldn't help my grin. "Where's Lucius? Run away because you realized he's not as weak as you thought?"

"I–" The ala was interrupted as a blast of wind knocked her off the roof and I shielded my face as the fire around us was blown out. I looked back to see Alex and Lucius appear on another roof, LeAlexende finally showing off his white wings as he helped Lucius. The Overseer's face held relief at seeing me, but another flash of fire stopped him from saying anything.

"Keep moving! We can handle her!" Alex chirped, smiling brightly as Lucius waved his hand, dispelling the fire once again as Evalyn growled from the ground. For a moment, she seemed intent on stopping me, but the Overseer was faster, using some combination of wind and electricity to place himself between Eve and I.

"Go," was his quiet command and, despite no longer being bound by the Oath, I obeyed, leaving the ala to him as we continued to the south side. As we neared that part of the city, I saw more and more destroyed buildings, and I couldn't help but wonder what had happened to cause the damage. Soon, we stood at ground zero, and I covered my mouth at the sight and smell, the Seraph also gasping behind me.

The whole block was leveled, not a single beam or object left standing straight and the scene was painted in splotches of red. I could make out the bodies of more Coven members among the various corpses trapped in the wreckage, Emelia among them as I caught sight of her dirty blonde hair. My body started to shake with my anger and the tendrils swam across my skin as I saw movement beneath the rubble.

"*You!*" I snarled, the black marks quickly ensnaring the Hunter, pulling them from their haven as they struggled to free themselves. The anger in my chest seemed to consume me as I squeezed them in my grasp, and I turned to face the Hunter as they spat at me.

"Monster! You would—"

"I'm not the one that just destroyed *hundreds* of lives in the name of the so-called 'Goddess of Life'," I sneered, squeezing my hand until I heard their bones start to snap and they screamed with pain as the tendrils wrapped around them tighter. Their own blood began to drip onto the scene of their crime and I scoffed with disgust as I dropped the corpse. "Just shut up and die."

"Raiven..." I heard the concern in the Seraph's voice as I refused to turn to them, instead looking to the night sky. A column of bright yellow light seemed to illuminate the darkness from another part of the city and I nodded as I recognized it as Sherry's magic. I closed my eyes as I readied myself, and the Seraph's voice was panicked as they spoke again.

"Raiven, you—"

"We're playing by her rules this time. I won't let fear stop me from beating her!" I yelled back, spreading my arms out as my form began to grow and change. I could hear the yells of confusion and fear as I started to tower over the buildings and I shook my head as my horn materialized. I opened my eyes to the night sky as my transformation finished, taking a deep breath as I readied myself to face Vitae.

"Hmmm, so I see you've gotten over your fear at last." I turned as I heard her voice, watching as she also rose from the ground, finally taking a form she had abandoned for millenia. Her blonde hair began to brighten to vivid yellow, the butterfly flapping its wings as it graced her head once more. Her dress twisted and swayed as it changed forms, the white fur around her neck perfectly mimicking the snowy mountain top she had been born from. The bright red jewel at the base of her neck reflected perfectly as she opened her rainbow-colored eyes, glaring at me as she smirked. The gloves on her arms gleamed like ice as she flung her arm out, sending icicles shooting past me. I did my best to ignore them as I faced her, the bark dancing on my legs and arms.

"Nice to see you, too."

23

I barely turned as the Seraph began to rise from the ground next to me, the power washing over me like a gentle touch. Rather than having a humanoid form like me or Vitae, they became merely a shining orb of light, their one pair of wings multiplying into five, all of the golden eyes focusing on Vitae as she stood across from us.

"I'm sure you were hoping to never see me again," I hummed, crossing my arms as I stood across from my fellow goddess. Vitae scoffed at my statement, mirroring my stance.

"If I had been smart, I would have killed you for certain that second time instead of keeping you around," Vitae spat, her cold voice forcing my body to shiver as I folded my second set of arms. Catching movement to my left, I glanced round and noticed Lucius fighting Evalyn, while Alex was doing his best to help the Overseer with the control of his wind. I looked up on the city as I noticed other battlefields, the Coven doing their best to battle the Hunters Vitae had brought with her. I was relieved to see that she had fewer than I had feared; it seemed she only had Evalyn and two others beyond the one I had killed, giving a chance to those who were daring to fight back. "I thought keeping you in a semi-sealed state was better than waiting for you to revive again, but you outplayed me."

"You were wrong to think that merely imprisoning me would keep me naive," I shot back, waving my arm over the space between us as the bark climbed up my arm and pavements cracked as stone rose through the ground to block us from the rest of the city. Vitae frowned as she saw the wall, turning her glare to me once again. "Instead, you gave me the confidence I needed to face you."

"Then let's see how you do!" She quickly flung her arm out, ice shooting along the ground as I was forced to dodge. The black tendrils appeared across my body as they shot out along the ground toward the Goddess, but Vitae growled as she shielded herself with more ice. I chuckled softly as I ran toward her, enjoying the surprise I saw in her face as she tried to move. I was faster and I forced the goddess to lock hands with me as I reached her. My tendrils started toward her body, but were stopped by her own red marks, the gem in her chest glowing softly.

"Seems I'm not the only one who's learned some new things," I smirked, releasing Vitae as I shoved her into the stone and she barely managed to stop herself from colliding as a giant rose sprouted behind her. I quickly killed the plant with my tendrils, earning myself another sound of displeasure from Vitae.

"You were the one who taught me, opened my eyes," she jabbed, more giant thorns tearing through the rubble as they made their way toward me. I hummed with annoyance as I shifted the ground, pulling her roses back into the earth before they could reach me. I sent an attack of my own, two spears of stone breaking the concrete to impale her, but Vitae managed to dodge, carelessly destroying more of the abandoned block we stood in. "You taught me new ways to use my power."

"Don't blame me for your choice," I seethed, my mind racing as I considered what to do next. Being in our true forms meant we couldn't move as fast, and I knew I needed to get close to her again. My only chance of getting her to swallow my blood was to try and restrain her somehow, but I knew she would do her best to keep me away.

Just as I thought this, I saw two spears of light shoot past me and Vitae hissed as one grazed her exposed shoulder. We both turned to see the Seraph floating in the air behind me, their wings flapping slowly as they did their best to hover. A few of their eyes were bleeding and the anger in my chest grew as I realized Vitae's torture had lasting effects on them. I growled as I turned back to face my fellow goddess, the bark on my upper set of arms climbing to my shoulders. I raised my hands to the dark sky, roots shooting along the ground as more spears of light flew past me.

Vitae growled as she dodged the spears, freezing the roots as she stepped on them and shattered the wood with her heel. She glanced up as I erected another wall of stone to our left, locking us into a 'v' shaped arena. The goddess glared at me as she realized the only way out was to come closer to me and the Seraph, before a pitiful smile replaced her annoyance.

"You forget who I am, Mortem!" she laughed, ice rising beneath her feet as she tried to rise over my barriers. I created another giant root as I started to chase after her, both of us rising into the air as she tried to escape me. The tendrils from my body slithered along the stone before encasing the ice, shattering the base. This staggered her for a moment, but she quickly adapted as she reshaped her pillar. "Death cannot destroy life!"

"Not trying to," I whispered under my breath, running along the root as we rose higher in the air, already way above my stone barrier. I knew she was trying to bring me to a higher altitude, where I would struggle to breathe and she could gain an advantage over me. I stopped climbing as she stood above me, smiling down her nose at me.

"Had enough?"

"We're just starting to have fun," I chuckled, watching the confusion on her face as her pillar started to sway. I saw her quickly glance to the ground, growling as she noticed what I had done. My roots were fully intertwined with her ice, and they squeezed her tower, slowly destroying the base again. "It seems *you* are the one who forgot what my powers were."

"You... you bitch!" Vitae jumped from her tower as the ice started to crack and shatter, landing on the root behind me as I turned. She slashed at me with her clawed hand, sending her red tendrils toward me. I ducked underneath them, sending my own at her feet as she jumped away, summoning another pillar of ice to catch her. "You–"

She was interrupted as golden light began to wrap around her mouth and I watched as it quickly engulfed her, pinning her arms to her side. I wasted no time as I slid down my root, leaping onto her ice pillar as it cracked beneath us. Her eyes grew wide with fear as I managed to wrap her in my tendrils as well, the black and gold weaving to hold her in place. I groaned with pain as my body was pierced by ice spears, but I refused to let go.

"Life is done with you, Vitae," I panted, bringing my free hand to my mouth as my fangs grew. I saw the horror in her eyes increase as I bit into my own wrist and she desperately tried to struggle against me and the Seraph. I saw the golden light flicker and I lifted my eyes to see the Seraph as they hovered near the ground. Most of the eyes in their wings were nothing more than bleeding holes, and I knew I had to enact my plan now. I hovered my bleeding hand over her, letting the black blood drip onto her face. "They don't need us anymore."

"No! I–" As soon as the golden light left her body, I forced my wrist to her mouth, my whole body racked with pain as the ice from her spears tried to freeze me in place. I saw her rainbow eyes dim as she was forced to swallow my blood, and various cries of pain and confusion came out from the city below us. The ice beneath us started to crack as I released her, and we both fell to the ground.

The rubble exploded as we collided with it and I was forced to cough up more blood as I lay in the concrete. I did my best to melt her ice with my flames and I willed my body to sit up, wanting to see if my plan had worked or not. Vitae still lay on the ground, her red tendrils swimming across her body as she coughed and hacked. Realizing I only had a moment to act, I reached up to my own forehead, grabbing the horn firmly with my hands.

Please let this work, I prayed in my mind as I pulled, screaming in time with my fellow goddess as I started to remove it from my body. Through my pain and tears, I could see her hands at her throat, desperately trying to keep her jewel in her skin. All the red tendrils slowly made their way back to their source and Vitae finally sat up as I finished pulling the horn from my skin, a thin line of blood running down my forehead.

In that moment, I felt the power leave my body and a new fire ran through my veins as I screamed again. Vitae seemed to be feeling the same pain, her scream piercing the night with my own. I wanted to claw at my skin to let the blood out, anything to get rid of the burning sensation that had infected every inch of my veins. As suddenly as it had started, it faded and I panted, feeling like I had just been ground into a pulp.

"What... what have you done!" Vitae screamed at me, but we both began to shrink in our craters, each cradling the symbol of our godhood. The horn in my hand shrank with me as the pain seemed to increase, and I felt as if I would throw up as I finally returned to a normal size. I barely had a moment to recover as Vitae grabbed my chest covering, lifting me from the ground. She firmly held her gem in her other hand, her rainbow eyes wild and angry. "What did you do to me?"

"We... are no longer goddesses, Vitae. Just Immortals," I breathed, unable to help my slight smile as she dropped me in surprise. I gave a loud groan as I bounced on the hard concrete, my body still hurting. I was surprised by how quickly she had managed to get up but I guessed that her outrage was numbing her to the pain that still rampaged through my body. "Our blood... no longer has power to create or control. We're normal."

"You selfish, conniving–"

"Life doesn't need either of us anymore," I continued, forcing myself to stand as I saw the Seraph's light approaching us, growing smaller as they gave up their true form. I clutched my head as it pounded, the black blood still running down my face from where I had removed my horn. I noticed a similar line of blood running down Vitae's chest, a small gash remaining from where her jewel had been. "It hasn't for a long time. All it needed was to lose your controlling hand, so it can mature on its own."

"Look what she did!" Vitae screamed, turning to the Seraph as they approached us and I couldn't help scoffing at her childish behavior. Like a teenager mad at being punished for something they did, she held her gem out to the Seraph, anger and desperation in her eyes. "Fix—Fix it! Fix me!"

"There... is nothing to fix," the Seraph stated plainly, and I could see the realization sinking in her eyes as she stared at them. Their golden eyes were full of their usual sadness, but there was a firmness to their voice they had lacked before. I nodded as they continued, my heart aching for them. "You stopped performing the role I created you for when you chose to kill her and imprison me. You stopped fulfilling your duty when you began to use others to kill for you."

"But she—"

"There has not been a Goddess of Life for a long time," the Seraph stated firmly, meeting her gaze evenly as they spoke. I noticed for the first time that their eyes were more than simply gold, but contained all the colors of a rich sunset in the dark night. They gently flapped their wings before folding them, giving Vitae a stern gaze. "You should have been removed a long time ago."

"But... but..." she stammered, falling to her knees as she clutched her lost mark and her shoulders started to shake as she cried. I grunted as I looked to the lip of the crater we stood in, noticing both Alrune and Basina as they looked down at us. I frowned at seeing them, and I noticed as Lucius and Alex slowly appeared as well, the Overseer helping the Sibling to walk. My attention was pulled back to Vitae as she hiccuped through her tears, her voice coming out hoarse and choked. "But she... she overstepped first! She created undead life!"

"Life *you* corrupted and turned against its purpose!" I spat back, clutching my horn as I tried to manage my anger. "My role was to ensure life never grew out of control and that no end happened unjustly. Reviving the Siblings was simply to serve that purpose."

"But... they lived—"

"Yes, they lived longer than I thought they would, but if *you* had not given them *your* blood, they would have *died*," I breathed, my anger obvious in my words as she looked at me with bewilderment. "I am Death; any life I create cannot last forever, just as no one you killed could stay dead forever. We were never supposed to be able to take each other's roles, *that was the whole point!*"

"You—"

"You were the one who decided it was *your right* to take our roles from us!" I yelled, grabbing the fur lining to her dress, unable to help my anger and heartache. I saw fear flash through her eyes and I knew she thought I was going to kill her. "I loved you as my sister! Yes, I was jealous at times, yes, at times I disliked you, but I never wanted to hurt you over it. I *never* wanted to kill you the way you killed me."

I dropped the former goddess, scoffing as I heard her thud to the ground, doing little to break her own fall. "You blame me for breaking the Trinity, but the one who destroyed us was *you*."

"I—" Her voice faded as her tears continued down her cheeks, her rainbow eyes fading back to an icy blue as she completely released her true appearance. All signs of our fight disappeared from her skin as I sighed, shaking my head as I released my form. I brushed my hand across my stomach as I realized I could no longer hide my silver bones as they sat under my shirt, flinching slightly with the touch. Vitae still stared at me blankly and I hated it as the ache in my chest grew.

"You are not powerless; you just can't control Supernaturals anymore," I said sadly, turning away from her gaze as I spoke. I fought the tears as they welled in my eyes; despite all that she had done, just like the Seraph, I couldn't help that I still cared. "You can also die whenever you want, if that's what you want to do."

"D... die?"

"If you return to your mountain, you'll become a part of it again, ending your existence," the Seraph explained, causing me to look at them. Their gold eyes held a hint of sadness, but I mostly noticed relief. "Raiven may do the same."

"I will, but I intend to stay alive just a little longer," I breathed, looking back up to the crater's lip to notice more beings looking down at us, catching Kisten as he seemed to be addressing a wound LeAlexende had received. My heart swelled at the sight of him and I couldn't help the smile in my voice as I continued, "And actually enjoy life for a bit."

"You..." Vitae's voice was soft and I looked back at the woman as she sat on the ground. She was no longer looking at me. Instead, her eyes were locked on the dull jewel in her hand. It seemed the pain had finally caught up with her and I hummed softly as I continued speaking.

"You can do whatever you want, Vitae. I have no intention of doing anything more to you." I lifted my horn as I looked at it, the bone now a dull gray as I held it. A part of my own chest twinged with pain as I considered what I had done to both of us, but I shook it off as I spoke. "But if you come after me or those I care about again, I will put you in that mountain myself."

Vitae still said nothing as she continued crying and I turned away from her, debating how to climb to the top of the hole. I grunted softly as I tried to summon my power, and another root rose from the ground, slowly lifting me to the crater's edge. I gently stepped onto the pavement as everyone turned to look at me, and I couldn't help my slight smile.

"Hey."

24

"Raiven!" I was immediately accosted by the two sisters, both hugging me tightly as I did my best to catch them. I gently pushed them off me, unable to hide my grimace of pain. As soon as they noticed my discomfort they released me, both embarrassed by their excitement. Alrune was the first to recover, quickly returning to her authoritative persona as she did her best to smooth her torn dress. "You seem to be... alright."

"I'll live," I huffed, glancing at the horn I still held in my hand. It glowed in the sparse light despite its dull color and I sighed as I looked back up to the vampire. "For now, at least."

"What... what does this mean?" LeAlexende's voice came from behind his sisters and as he sat on the ground, I noticed that he was missing an arm. It seemed that Kisten had wrapped the wound as best he could, but I frowned as I noticed that he wasn't regenerating the limb at all. He seemed to notice my confusion, humming as he shrugged, his wings fluffing. "Seems I can't heal big wounds anymore. Healing from Aurel's attempt on my life made my already weak state worse."

"I... see," I nodded, gripping my horn tightly as I debated how to answer his question. "Well, for starters, Vitae can't control you all.

Her blood carries no power over Supernaturals anymore, so you are free. Other than that, time will show what the other effects will be."

"The Hunters died right after whatever you did." I turned as I heard Yoreile's voice, the warlock being supported by Grace and Quinn as he tried to stand. It was obvious he had also taken a bad wound to his side and he hissed with pain as he tried to keep speaking. "They... they all..."

"Let me take this one, *Rakkaani*[1]." Quinn smiled, adjusting the man in his arms as he winced himself from a wound in his leg. Glancing behind the trio, I could see other members of the Coven, including Kisca and Crispin. It seemed only seven members had managed to survive the fight and my heart twisted as I considered all those we lost. "As soon as you forced your blood on her, they all began to scream in pain and just... disintegrated."

"It was like they were little more than extensions of her," Lucius added, looking away from me as he stared at the ground. I noticed the strange look on his face, frowning as he didn't turn to face me. "Vessels to do her will alone."

"What about Evalyn?"

"She had enough of Vitae's blood to be affected, but not enough to die like the others," Lucius whispered, adjusting his stance as he continued looking at the broken rubble we stood on. I finally saw the tears in the corner of his eyes and my confusion only grew. I carefully walked up to the Overseer, gently placing my hand on his shoulder.

"Lucius..." I spoke his name softly and the vampire only sighed as he closed his eyes, still refusing to face me. "What happened?"

"I lost my arm killing her," LeAlexende called out nonchalantly, and I looked back to the Sibling with surprise as he finally stood with Kisten's help. "She was trying to appeal to Lucius to save her, and I didn't give her the chance to try and take him with her. She managed to claim my arm, but I can't say it wasn't satisfying."

"Alex," I scoffed and the vampire merely shrugged with his usual dismissing smile.

"To be fair, I *really* hated this one," LeAlexende admitted and I frowned at his words as he pulled away from Kisten. He carefully made his way to the Overseer and I released Lucius as Alex reached to take my place, using his wings to help balance his body. "You need to stop choosing Retainers that piss me off."

"I'll keep that in mind," Lucius whispered, still not looking at the Sibling, but Alex seemed to have little patience for his mopey mood. He limped in front of the vampire, using his remaining hand to force Lucius to look at him. "Wha—"

We all gasped as LeAlexende kissed Lucius, wrapping his arm around the Overseer's neck to support his weight. The Sibling pulled away after a moment, another gentle smile on his face as he glanced over to all of us watching. Alex chuckled as he turned back to Lucius, enjoying the look of surprise on the vampire's face.

"Can't tell you how long I've wanted to do that without worrying," Alex said with a grin and I could only shake my head as Lucius finally reacted, wrapping his arm around the man in his arms as he kissed him again. I cleared my throat as I turned away from the pair, noticing the look of disapproval on Alrune's face and the amusement on Basina's.

"I can't understand why he still chooses him, after all this time," Alrune scoffed, causing Basina to chuckle as she looked at her sister.

"Well, he didn't need your approval then, and he certainly doesn't need it now," the vampire shot back, meeting my gaze as I waited for her to explain. "Alex has had a thing for Lucius ever since he was turned. Lucius was the first vampire Vitae created from a living person, so he's been around almost as long as us."

"I see," I hummed, hearing as Lucius and Alex separated, walking back to join us as the Seraph finally rose from the crater. They seemed to be in pain as they landed on the concrete next to me and I noticed the golden blood still running down their feathers as they quickly closed their wings.

"She... is gone," they breathed and I merely hummed in response as I frowned. They noticed my expression, their lips twitching into a half-hearted smile. "I do not know what she will do or where she will go, but to say she is devastated is to put it mildly."

"Good. If 'devastated' is the worse she gets, it's still not nearly what she deserves," I scoffed, squeezing the horn tighter in my hand. "She ended thousands of lives on a whim, tortured her creator and killed me just because she felt like it was her right. Fuck her."

"I wish... I could share your sentiment, Raiven." I felt my anger lessen slightly with their soft tone, and I watched the Seraph as they took a deep breath, closing their eyes. "I, however, still love her, despite what she has done. I created her after all, and it is hard for me not to love my only two creations."

I said nothing to this, merely sighing as I finally looked at Kisten. He was looking at the horn in my hand, although he finally raised his eyes to mine when he felt me looking. The Alpha gently cleared his throat, picking up his kit as he moved over to Yoreile, motioning Grace and Quinn to set the warlock down. They followed his command, and I frowned as he began to tear Yoreile's shirt and dress his wound.

"So... what happens to you now?" LeAlexende finally asked again, and I took a deep breath as I lifted the horn.

"Well, I also gave up my abilities as a Goddess, so I'm little more than just a really powerful Supernatural." I shrugged, turning the object in my hand as it glittered. "I'm not quite sure what I can and can't do yet, but I know that I can no longer create undead."

"So you can't raise zombies?"

"No, I'm sure I can do that just fine." I shook my head, smiling slightly at Basina's question. "My blood doesn't carry much power anymore, so I can't create undead the way I created you three. I'm not even sure if I can manipulate undead anymore."

"What about your..." Lucius's voice faded as I turned to face him, glancing down as I noticed Kisten's flinch. I hummed with understanding as I smiled, meeting the Overseer's blue gaze. "Is your life... shorter now?"

"I will die, eventually, but it'll take so long for me to die naturally that I'm still essentially Immortal," I chuckled, seeing the relief in the Alpha's body as he continued working. "I can die whenever I want by returning to my tree, but I still got some things I wanna do."

"More like *someone*," Crispin quipped, wincing as the pixie next to him jabbed him in his bleeding arm. I shook my head as I laughed, everyone else joining in as we stood in the destroyed block. My laughter paused as I felt another presence approaching us and I looked across the craters to see the Director and Brandon step into view. Both looked exhausted and I gently waved to them as they looked up to us.

"It's going to be a busy day," Lucius breathed and I noticed the sky was beginning to brighten. I turned to Alrune and Basina, both examining their bodies for signs of decay and they smiled as they looked at me.

"Looks like you can still get that lunch," Basina joked and I couldn't help the sound that escaped me as I shook my head. I heard as Kisten stood up again, this time walking toward me with a soft look. He gently wrapped his arms around me, burying his face into my neck as he squeezed me tightly in his arms. I eagerly returned his gesture, taking a moment to breathe him in.

"You're alright?"

"Of course," the Alpha whispered, rubbing his face against my skin as he gently placed a kiss on my neck. "I ran into Liel and Quinn trying to protect Yoreile and Grace, and I tried to help but... Liel... she was too badly injured."

I couldn't help the tears that welled in my eyes at his implied meaning and I glanced among the surviving Coven members, realizing that the banshee was indeed absent. My chest ached as my anger returned, and I felt a burning desire to track down Vitae and force her to pay for all the lives she had taken from me. I was pulled from my thoughts as Kisten began to speak again, seemingly unaware of my growing rage.

"Once we saw you, we came toward this side of the city."

"Wait, you–" I started, but Kisten quickly silenced me by squeezing me in his arms.

"Once again, you were huge and you guys were climbing toward the sky." The shifter laughed, humming softly. "I'm pretty sure the whole world saw you, if I know the way the news likes to capture everything."

"Right." I frowned, forgetting about the possibility of our fight being captured on video. I didn't particularly like the idea that the whole world now knew that Gods and Goddess had existed, but I merely shrugged as I released the shifter, Kisten still smiling down at me.

"I need to get to the hospital, no doubt they need me," he breathed and I chuckled, reaching up to run my fingers through his hair.

"I'm not going to see you for days."

"You could always come and help," the Alpha shot back, leaning down to kiss my forehead where the horn had once been. In the early light of dawn, I could see the blood and weariness on his face, but I knew he would still go to work and push himself to the point of exhaustion to help with the wounded. I turned to the Seraph, seeing their neutral expression as they watched us.

"Will you stay and help?" I asked, as the Director and Brandon finally reached us, both looking to the Seraph with awe and surprise. "I know that reasonably, you can't heal everyone, but–"

"I will offer aid where I can. I would like to 'live' as well, if you don't mind." I watched as the Seraph shifted their form again, groaning painfully as they finally dismissed their bleeding wings and looked more normal in their dark pants and dress shirt. I smiled as I released the shifter in my arms, finally facing both of the humans as they stared in wonder at the horn in my hand. The Director was the first to recover, shaking his head as he adjusted his glasses. Despite being human, it was clear both he and Brandon had participated in the fighting to a certain degree, as their clothing was ripped and covered in blood as well.

"You never fail to surprise, Raiven," the Director said and I couldn't help the smile that crept across my face. "I'm sure the debrief for this one will be far past unbelievable."

"You know me, I like to impress." I shrugged, earning myself a soft chuckle from both men as Kisten pressed another kiss into my hair. I turned back to the rising sun as Lucius moved to talk to the Director and the Seraph began to follow Kisten as the Alpha did his best to pick up LeAlexende to take him to the hospital. I could hear the other Coven members trying to determine who else needed to go to the hospital and who could recover on their own and I breathed in the fresh morning air.

I reached for the wooden cross that still sat against my chest, gripping it tightly in my hand. The wood would be forever silent, but the thought didn't pain me as it had before. For the first time in a long while, I had no reason to be afraid, and my heart swelled as the first strip of color found its way into the brightening sky.

EPILOGUE

I quietly slipped out into the hallway, sighing with relief that no one had been paying attention as I stood in the silent corridor. My wedding reception was happening in the room behind me, and I pushed myself off the door as I walked toward the giant glass window in front of me. The hotel's garden looked magical in the winter night air, and I couldn't resist the allure as I stepped out.

"Hmmm," I sighed, as I walked through the icy garden, my thoughts drifting to my wedding earlier in the afternoon and the party I had left. I was still wearing the same dress, the purple fabric flowing as I made my way through the green foliage. The ceremony had been perfect, with Shannon, Vanessa and Justina looking just as magical in their dresses. Lucius' words had been poignant and heartfelt and I felt my chest swell as I remembered them.

"Love that stretches beyond the reach of time..." I quoted, still moving through the chilly night as I recalled my Overseer's words. Lucius had been uncertain about taking me back into the Coven, unsure if I could be bound by the Oath now that I had recovered my former blood. I insisted we try anyway and, to the surprise of both of us, it worked better than before. While I could still resist his commands slightly, the pain was near unbearable compared to the slight annoyance it had been before and Lucius allowed me to reclaim my position as Second.

Despite spring being around the corner, the last few threads of winter still clung in the air and I shivered slightly, rubbing my bare shoulders. I summoned a gentle fire to my hands as I warmed myself, dismissing the flame once I no longer felt a chill in my body. My stomach growled softly with my use of power and I frowned as I touched it, surprised by my hunger.

Despite the small wedding, it had been quite a hassle to increase the food for the reception and I couldn't help my chuckle as I remembered Kisten's frantic phone calls. We discovered that one side effect of taking away Vitae's power was that all vampires reverted to be more like the Siblings, and lost their need for blood. They suddenly found they needed to eat and drink like the living and while they no longer craved blood, taking the blood of the living allowed them to heal faster and increased their power. We still weren't sure if this meant they would eventually lose their sun sensitivity, or die, but at least both Lucius and LeAlexende seemed fine with the idea that their long lives might finally end.

"Those two..." I shook my head as I looked at my reflection in the icy pond, gently pulling on my shorter curls. After seeing Alrune and Basina back to the secret bath for death to reclaim them, Alex returned with me to the Capital, officially becoming Lucius' partner. With the threat of Vitae and Hunters officially gone, it seemed the pair were willing to give their forbidden romance a chance, and they were eager to make up for millennia of lost opportunity.

"Look who ran away from her own wedding!" I looked up from the ice as I heard Kisten's voice, and I turned to see the shifter leaning against one of the lamps along the path, smiling as he watched me. His dark gray suit shimmered in the soft light, and I could just see the purple vest as he stood up straight. The silver tie flashed as he took off the jacket, sliding it around my bare shoulders as he kissed my cheek. "It's cold, *Meine Göttin*[1]."

"I told you, I'm not a goddess anymore. You don't have to call me that." I shook my head as I scoffed, but the Alpha merely laughed as he pressed another kiss in my hair, squeezing his jacket as he ran his hands down my arms. "And I didn't run away, I just... needed a moment."

"I also believe I told you before that you are and always will be a goddess to me, one I was lucky enough to marry," Kisten whispered and I merely shook my head as I leaned back into his embrace. He wrapped his arms around me tightly and we stood in silence in the still garden, enjoying the moment away from the chaos. When he spoke again, I could barely hear his voice. "I understand. It still feels so... surreal."

"Definitely not how we thought it would be," I agreed, closing my eyes as a slight wind finally started to pick up through the plants. I hummed softly as I leaned more into the shifter, Kisten squeezing me in his grip. "It's taken a lot to get here."

"And most of it in the past few months," Kisten agreed and I remained silent as he continued. "Makes you wonder how different things would have been, if I hadn't pushed you away for a year."

"I'm pretty sure all that would have changed is we would have been married sooner and your proposal would have been less dramatic," I scoffed and the Alpha merely laughed behind me as he laid a gentle kiss on my shoulder. "Whistleblower would have been a lot madder if I had been your wife already."

"As far as that bastard knew, you were. He has no idea how 'courting' works," Kisten growled and I gently stroked his arm to calm him down. The Alpha took a deep breath, pressing his face into my hair. "Would have made the whole Mortem thing less stressful."

"Less stressful?" I laughed, shaking my head at the thought. "I think it would have made it worse."

"At least I would've been able to say you were my wife if I'd lost you," the shifter whispered and I squeezed his arm in my grip as I heard the pain in his voice. "But we should stop dwelling on the past. As Alex likes to remind us–"

"– we deserve to be happy," I finished, sighing as he loosened his grip, spinning me in his arms so I faced him. He slid his hands under the jacket as I held it around my shoulders, his hands squeezing my waist as he hummed. There was so much love in the Alpha's chartreuse eyes as his gaze met my mismatched pair and I felt like my heart would explode. "Although I'm sure the worst is behind us."

"And I'm sure we have more trials waiting to test us," he laughed, and I leaned my head against his chest as I closed my eyes. "Like taxes."

"Or moving in together."

"Or children." I felt Kisten's heart pound as he spoke and I quickly leaned away from him to meet his excited gaze.

"No time soon."

"You are no fun," the shifter chuckled, and I could do little more than smile as he leaned down to kiss me, his hand sliding against my cheek. I leaned up more to indulge my husband and shivered against him as he slid his other hand down my silver spine. I barely managed a glare as he pulled away, smiling mischievously. "Can't say I'm not excited to try."

"Still don't know if it's possible, Kisten. Still technically half dead."

"Well, it doesn't hurt to try as much as possible and hope I get lucky. After all, it worked for Crispin and Justina," the Alpha purred, and I shook my head, chucking softly as another gust of wind blew through the garden. Kisten's grip on me tightened again, and he leaned down to me, whispering seductively in my ear. "We've already left, nothing stopping us from going upstairs to get started."

"Now who's trying to run away from his own wedding?" I teased, gently pushing his face up from me as I tapped his nose, earning myself a soft laugh. I laid my head against his chest again as he returned to gently holding me, rocking me as we stood. I took a deep breath as I sighed, enjoying the scent of his cologne as I spoke. "We should head back soon. Everyone will think it's Lucius' and Alex's wedding if we don't."

"Please, at least you weren't the one who had to try and keep all his retainers away every time Alex came to visit. And don't get me started about trying to distract *Evalyn*," Kisten groaned, releasing me as he took my hand and we began our walk back inside. "Just trying to keep her off him long enough for those two to sneak in a kiss made me want to let her find them. LeAlexende could've killed her then, saved himself an arm and saved us all the trouble."

"Well, hindsight's 20/20," I shrugged, removing the Alpha's jacket as he held the door open for me. Kisten took a moment to shake the cold from his body before accepting his jacket back from me but instead of putting it back on, he just slung it over his shoulder. "Like you taking my bet over the flowers."

"I still call foul on that," Kisten complained, groaning as he threw his head back and I laughed as his anguish. "You talked her into saying yes."

"I did no such thing. I just know Justina and yes, she was a bitch about it, but I knew she wanted it," I hummed, taking a deep breath as we stood outside the ballroom. As much as I loved everyone Kisten had invited, I simply found it exhausting to be around so many people at once. As I tried to prepare myself to reenter the party, I felt as the Alpha lifted my hand, gently kissing my fingers as he played with my wedding ring. The rainbow-colored stone glittered under the hotel lights and I hummed as I pulled my hand to my chest.

My wedding ring was the Arcus Pluvius, recut and reset into a new band to be a suitable wedding gift from my creator. I had tried to return the ring, but the Seraph had insisted I keep it, offering it as an apology that they would miss the wedding. They said they wanted to travel the world, to learn and see all the changes that had happened while they were sleeping, but they promised to return to the Capital when they were done. I was slightly sad they had missed the wedding, but I knew the Seraph was always keeping an eye on me, as sometimes I caught glimpses of one of their little lights.

"Hmmm..." I hummed again as I considered all the others I wished could have been at my wedding. So many friends that I had made over my long life would have loved to see me finally get married, and of course there was Azyam, Alrune and Basina. Despite the day I got to spend with the sisters, my heart ached that they had not been able to share in this day as Alex could, and my chest tightened slightly as I considered their undeserved deaths.

"Azyam..." I whispered quietly, gripping my ring hand tighter. Even though I knew she wasn't completely gone, I couldn't help but wish she could have seen me to this point. I chuckled softly as I considered how she would berate me if she could hear my thoughts, unable to help my soft smile. Kisten often teased me for sounding like her sometimes, and I gently ran a hand over my chest as I closed my eyes.

"Ready?" Kisten's voice pulled me out of my thoughts again, and I released my ring as I nodded, watching as he placed his hand on the door. I glanced up to see his encouraging smile, and I felt the pain in my heart turn to joy once again. As the door opened back to our friends and chosen family, I knew that my future, despite all the ones I had lost, was bright and full of love.

And that was more than I could have ever dreamed.

As Raiven's story ends...
A new one begins.
In Their Eyes
Dark Secrets Book 1

About the Author

Kirro Burrows grew up on the sandy beaches of Florida, so they know a thing or two about having their head in the clouds. Creating new worlds and exploring character dynamics is the air they breathe and crafting thrilling, realistic stories are their bread and butter. When not traveling for inspiration, Kirro can be found decorating beautiful cakes in their kitchen while caring for their blooming family or sneaking some work on their illustrations and comics. There's always something new going on with them, and that's the way they like it.

To learn more about Kirro Burrows and discover more Next Chapter authors, visit our website at www.nextchapter.pub.

NOTES

CHAPTER 1

1. Latin "Thank You"

CHAPTER 2

1. Russian "Geez" or "Oh my"

CHAPTER 3

1. Irish "my Love"

CHAPTER 8

1. German "The pup"

CHAPTER 10

1. Russian "Sister"

CHAPTER 16

1. German "Bird"

CHAPTER 18

1. German "my love"

CHAPTER 20

1. Russian "Sister"
2. Russian "Raven"

CHAPTER 1

1. German "Raven"
2. German "The Pup"

CHAPTER 2

1. Russian "Yes"

CHAPTER 4

1. German "Bird"

CHAPTER 6

1. German "Gift"
2. German "Son"
3. German "Pitiful"
4. German "Boy"

CHAPTER 9

1. German "Bird"

CHAPTER 10

1. German "Son"
2. German "the boy"

CHAPTER 11

1. German "Bitch"

CHAPTER 13

1. German "Bird"

CHAPTER 15

1. German "Raven"

CHAPTER 16

1. German "Bitch"

CHAPTER 20

1. German "my love"

CHAPTER 22

1. German "Little Boy"
2. German "Monster"

CHAPTER 24

1. German "The Monstrous one"
2. German "Dear son of mine"

CHAPTER 1

1. Russian "sister"
2. Russian "chicken"
3. Russian "my dear"
4. German "bird"
5. Italian "my sir" or "my lord" (noting respect)
6. Sumerian "mother"

CHAPTER 3

1. German "Bird"

CHAPTER 6

1. Latin "You must stop."
2. Latin "No."
3. Latin "Why?"

CHAPTER 7

1. German "Raven"

CHAPTER 8

1. German "Bird"

CHAPTER 10

1. German "Bird"

CHAPTER 20

1. German "Raven"
2. German "Bird"
3. German "My Goddess"

CHAPTER 21

1. Latin "Children"

CHAPTER 22

1. German "My Love"

CHAPTER 24

1. Finnish "my love"

EPILOGUE

1. German "my Goddess"

Sealed Blood
ISBN: 978-4-82418-029-2
Paperback Edition

Published by
Next Chapter
2-5-6 SANNO
SANNO BRIDGE
143-0023 Ota-Ku, Tokyo
+818035793528

26th May 2023